JACK KEROUAC

JACK KEROUAC

ROAD NOVELS 1957–1960
On the Road
The Dharma Bums
The Subterraneans
Tristessa
Lonesome Traveler
From the Journals 1949–1954

Douglas Brinkley, *editor*

THE LIBRARY OF AMERICA

———

Contents

ON THE ROAD

Part One

I

I FIRST met Dean not long after my wife and I split up. I had just gotten over a serious illness that I won't bother to talk about, except that it had something to do with the miserably weary split-up and my feeling that everything was dead. With the coming of Dean Moriarty began the part of my life you could call my life on the road. Before that I'd often dreamed of going West to see the country, always vaguely planning and never taking off. Dean is the perfect guy for the road because he actually was born on the road, when his parents were passing through Salt Lake City in 1926, in a jalopy, on their way to Los Angeles. First reports of him came to me through Chad King, who'd shown me a few letters from him written in a New Mexico reform school. I was tremendously interested in the letters because they so naïvely and sweetly asked Chad to teach him all about Nietzsche and all the wonderful intellectual things that Chad knew. At one point Carlo and I talked about the letters and wondered if we would ever meet the strange Dean Moriarty. This is all far back, when Dean was not the way he is today, when he was a young jailkid shrouded in mystery. Then news came that Dean was out of reform school and was coming to New York for the first time; also there was talk that he had just married a girl called Marylou.

One day I was hanging around the campus and Chad and Tim Gray told me Dean was staying in a cold-water pad in East Harlem, the Spanish Harlem. Dean had arrived the night before, the first time in New York, with his beautiful little sharp chick Marylou; they got off the Greyhound bus at 50th Street and cut around the corner looking for a place to eat and went right in Hector's, and since then Hector's cafeteria has always been a big symbol of New York for Dean. They spent money on beautiful big glazed cakes and creampuffs.

All this time Dean was telling Marylou things like this: "Now, darling, here we are in New York and although I haven't quite

3

told you everything that I was thinking about when we crossed Missouri and especially at the point when we passed the Booneville reformatory which reminded me of my jail problem, it is absolutely necessary now to postpone all those leftover things concerning our personal lovethings and at once begin thinking of specific worklife plans . . ." and so on in the way that he had in those early days.

I went to the cold-water flat with the boys, and Dean came to the door in his shorts. Marylou was jumping off the couch; Dean had dispatched the occupant of the apartment to the kitchen, probably to make coffee, while he proceeded with his loveproblems, for to him sex was the one and only holy and important thing in life, although he had to sweat and curse to make a living and so on. You saw that in the way he stood bobbing his head, always looking down, nodding, like a young boxer to instructions, to make you think he was listening to every word, throwing in a thousand "Yeses" and "That's rights." My first impression of Dean was of a young Gene Autry—trim, thin-hipped, blue-eyed, with a real Oklahoma accent—a sideburned hero of the snowy West. In fact he'd just been working on a ranch, Ed Wall's in Colorado, before marrying Marylou and coming East. Marylou was a pretty blonde with immense ringlets of hair like a sea of golden tresses; she sat there on the edge of the couch with her hands hanging in her lap and her smoky blue country eyes fixed in a wide stare because she was in an evil gray New York pad that she'd heard about back West, and waiting like a longbodied emaciated Modigliani surrealist woman in a serious room. But, outside of being a sweet little girl, she was awfully dumb and capable of doing horrible things. That night we all drank beer and pulled wrists and talked till dawn, and in the morning, while we sat around dumbly smoking butts from ashtrays in the gray light of a gloomy day, Dean got up nervously, paced around, thinking, and decided the thing to do was to have Marylou make breakfast and sweep the floor. "In other words we've got to get on the ball, darling, what I'm saying, otherwise it'll be fluctuating and lack of true knowledge or crystallization of our plans." Then I went away.

During the following week he confided in Chad King that he absolutely had to learn how to write from him; Chad said I was a writer and he should come to me for advice. Meanwhile Dean had gotten a job in a parking lot, had a fight with Marylou in their Hoboken apartment—God knows why they went there—and she was so mad and so down deep vindictive that she reported to the police some false trumped-up hysterical crazy charge, and Dean had to lam from Hoboken. So he had no place to live. He came right out to Paterson, New Jersey, where I was living with my aunt, and one night while I was studying there was a knock on the door, and there was Dean, bowing, shuffling obsequiously in the dark of the hall, and saying, "Hel-lo, you remember me—Dean Moriarty? I've come to ask you to show me how to write."

"And where's Marylou?" I asked, and Dean said she'd apparently whored a few dollars together and gone back to Denver—"the whore!" So we went out to have a few beers because we couldn't talk like we wanted to talk in front of my aunt, who sat in the living room reading her paper. She took one look at Dean and decided that he was a madman.

In the bar I told Dean, "Hell, man, I know very well you didn't come to me only to want to become a writer, and after all what do I really know about it except you've got to stick to it with the energy of a benny addict." And he said, "Yes, of course, I know exactly what you mean and in fact all those problems have occurred to me, but the thing that I want is the realization of those factors that should one depend on Schopenhauer's dichotomy for any inwardly realized . . ." and so on in that way, things I understood not a bit and he himself didn't. In those days he really didn't know what he was talking about; that is to say, he was a young jailkid all hung-up on the wonderful possibilities of becoming a real intellectual, and he liked to talk in the tone and using the words, but in a jumbled way, that he had heard from "real intellectuals"—although, mind you, he wasn't so naïve as that in all other things, and it took him just a few months with Carlo Marx to become completely *in there* with all the terms and jargon. Nonetheless we understood each other on other levels of madness, and I agreed that he could stay at my house till he found a job and furthermore we agreed to go out West sometime. That was the winter of 1947.

One night when Dean ate supper at my house—he already

had the parking-lot job in New York—he leaned over my shoulder as I typed rapidly away and said, "Come on man, those girls won't wait, make it fast."

I said, "Hold on just a minute, I'll be right with you soon as I finish this chapter," and it was one of the best chapters in the book. Then I dressed and off we flew to New York to meet some girls. As we rode in the bus in the weird phosphorescent void of the Lincoln Tunnel we leaned on each other with fingers waving and yelled and talked excitedly, and I was beginning to get the bug like Dean. He was simply a youth tremendously excited with life, and though he was a con-man, he was only conning because he wanted so much to live and to get involved with people who would otherwise pay no attention to him. He was conning me and I knew it (for room and board and "how-to-write," etc.), and he knew I knew (this has been the basis of our relationship), but I didn't care and we got along fine—no pestering, no catering; we tiptoed around each other like heartbreaking new friends. I began to learn from him as much as he probably learned from me. As far as my work was concerned he said, "Go ahead, everything you do is great." He watched over my shoulder as I wrote stories, yelling, "Yes! That's right! Wow! Man!" and "Phew!" and wiped his face with his handkerchief. "Man, wow, there's so many things to do, so many things to write! How to even *begin* to get it all down and without modified restraints and all hung-up on like literary inhibitions and grammatical fears . . ."

"That's right, man, now you're talking." And a kind of holy lightning I saw flashing from his excitement and his visions, which he described so torrentially that people in buses looked around to see the "overexcited nut." In the West he'd spent a third of his time in the poolhall, a third in jail, and a third in the public library. They'd seen him rushing eagerly down the winter streets, bareheaded, carrying books to the poolhall, or climbing trees to get into the attics of buddies where he spent days reading or hiding from the law.

We went to New York—I forget what the situation was, two colored girls—there were no girls there; they were supposed to meet him in a diner and didn't show up. We went to his parking lot where he had a few things to do—change his clothes in the shack in back and spruce up a bit in front of a cracked mirror and so on, and then we took off. And that was the night Dean met Carlo Marx. A tremendous thing happened when Dean met Carlo Marx. Two keen minds that they are, they took to each other at the drop of a hat. Two piercing eyes glanced into two piercing eyes—the holy con-man with the shining mind, and the sorrowful poetic con-man with the dark mind that is Carlo Marx. From that moment on I saw very little of Dean, and I was a little sorry too. Their energies met head-on, I was a lout compared, I couldn't keep up with them. The whole mad swirl of everything that was to come began then; it would mix up all my friends and all I had left of my family in a big dust cloud over the American Night. Carlo told him of Old Bull Lee, Elmer Hassel, Jane: Lee in Texas growing weed, Hassel on Riker's Island, Jane wandering on Times Square in a benzedrine hallucination, with her baby girl in her arms and ending up in Bellevue. And Dean told Carlo of unknown people in the West like Tommy Snark, the clubfooted poolhall rotation shark and cardplayer and queer saint. He told him of Roy Johnson, Big Ed Dunkel, his boyhood buddies, his street buddies, his innumerable girls and sex-parties and pornographic pictures, his heroes, heroines, adventures. They rushed down the street together, digging everything in the early way they had, which later became so much sadder and perceptive and blank. But then they danced down the streets like dingledodies, and I shambled after as I've been doing all my life after people who interest me, because the only people for me are the mad ones, the ones who are mad to live, mad to talk, mad to be saved, desirous of everything at the same time, the ones who never yawn or say a commonplace thing, but burn, burn, burn like fabulous yellow roman candles exploding like spiders across the stars and in the middle you see the blue centerlight pop and everybody goes "Awww!" What did they call such young people in Goethe's Germany? Wanting dearly to learn how to write like Carlo, the first thing you know, Dean was attacking him with a great amorous soul such as only a con-man can have. "Now, Carlo, let *me* speak—here's what *I'm* saying . . ." I didn't see them for about two weeks, during which time they cemented their relationship to fiendish allday-allnight-talk proportions.

Then came spring, the great time of traveling, and everybody in the scattered gang was getting ready to take one trip or another. I was busily at work on my novel and when I came to the halfway mark, after a trip down South with my aunt to visit my brother Rocco, I got ready to travel West for the very first time.

Dean had already left. Carlo and I saw him off at the 34th Street Greyhound station. Upstairs they had a place where you could make pictures for a quarter. Carlo took off his glasses and looked sinister. Dean made a profile shot and looked coyly around. I took a straight picture that made me look like a thirty-year-old Italian who'd kill anybody who said anything against his mother. This picture Carlo and Dean neatly cut down the middle with a razor and saved a half each in their wallets. Dean was wearing a real Western business suit for his big trip back to Denver; he'd finished his first fling in New York. I say fling, but he only worked like a dog in parking lots. The most fantastic parking-lot attendant in the world, he can back a car forty miles an hour into a tight squeeze and stop at the wall, jump out, race among fenders, leap into another car, circle it fifty miles an hour in a narrow space, back swiftly into tight spot, *hump*, snap the car with the emergency so that you see it bounce as he flies out; then clear to the ticket shack, sprinting like a track star, hand a ticket, leap into a newly arrived car before the owner's half out, leap literally under him as he steps out, start the car with the door flapping, and roar off to the next available spot, arc, pop in, brake, out, run; working like that without pause eight hours a night, evening rush hours and after-theater rush hours, in greasy wino pants with a frayed fur-lined jacket and beat shoes that flap. Now he'd bought a new suit to go back in; blue with pencil stripes, vest and all— eleven dollars on Third Avenue, with a watch and watch chain, and a portable typewriter with which he was going to start writing in a Denver rooming house as soon as he got a job there. We had a farewell meal of franks and beans in a Seventh Avenue Riker's, and then Dean got on the bus that said Chicago and roared off into the night. There went our wrangler. I promised myself to go the same way when spring really bloomed and opened up the land.

And this was really the way that my whole road experience

began, and the things that were to come are too fantastic not to tell.

Yes, and it wasn't only because I was a writer and needed new experiences that I wanted to know Dean more, and because my life hanging around the campus had reached the completion of its cycle and was stultified, but because, somehow, in spite of our difference in character, he reminded me of some long-lost brother; the sight of his suffering bony face with the long sideburns and his straining muscular sweating neck made me remember my boyhood in those dye-dumps and swim-holes and riversides of Paterson and the Passaic. His dirty workclothes clung to him so gracefully, as though you couldn't buy a better fit from a custom tailor but only earn it from the Natural Tailor of Natural Joy, as Dean had, in his stresses. And in his excited way of speaking I heard again the voices of old companions and brothers under the bridge, among the motorcycles, along the wash-lined neighborhood and drowsy doorsteps of afternoon where boys played guitars while their older brothers worked in the mills. All my other current friends were "intellectuals"—Chad the Nietzschean anthropologist, Carlo Marx and his nutty surrealist low-voiced serious staring talk, Old Bull Lee and his critical anti-everything drawl—or else they were slinking criminals like Elmer Hassel, with that hip sneer; Jane Lee the same, sprawled on the Oriental cover of her couch, sniffing at the *New Yorker*. But Dean's intelligence was every bit as formal and shining and complete, without the tedious intellectualness. And his "criminality" was not something that sulked and sneered; it was a wild yea-saying overburst of American joy; it was Western, the west wind, an ode from the Plains, something new, long prophesied, long a-coming (he only stole cars for joy rides). Besides, all my New York friends were in the negative, nightmare position of putting down society and giving their tired bookish or political or psychoanalytical reasons, but Dean just raced in society, eager for bread and love; he didn't care one way or the other, "so long's I can get that lil ole gal with that lil sumpin down there tween her legs, boy," and "so long's we can *eat*, son, y'ear me? I'm *hungry*, I'm *starving*, let's *eat right now!*"—and off we'd rush to *eat*, whereof, as saith Ecclesiastes, "It is your portion under the sun."

A western kinsman of the sun, Dean. Although my aunt warned me that he would get me in trouble, I could hear a new call and see a new horizon, and believe it at my young age; and a little bit of trouble or even Dean's eventual rejection of me as a buddy, putting me down, as he would later, on starving sidewalks and sickbeds—what did it matter? I was a young writer and I wanted to take off.

Somewhere along the line I knew there'd be girls, visions, everything; somewhere along the line the pearl would be handed to me.

2

In the month of July 1947, having saved about fifty dollars from old veteran benefits, I was ready to go to the West Coast. My friend Remi Boncœur had written me a letter from San Francisco, saying I should come and ship out with him on an around-the-world liner. He swore he could get me into the engine room. I wrote back and said I'd be satisfied with any old freighter so long as I could take a few long Pacific trips and come back with enough money to support myself in my aunt's house while I finished my book. He said he had a shack in Mill City and I would have all the time in the world to write there while we went through the rigmarole of getting the ship. He was living with a girl called Lee Ann; he said she was a marvelous cook and everything would jump. Remi was an old prep-school friend, a Frenchman brought up in Paris and a really mad guy—I didn't know how mad at this time. So he expected me to arrive in ten days. My aunt was all in accord with my trip to the West; she said it would do me good, I'd been working so hard all winter and staying in too much; she even didn't complain when I told her I'd have to hitchhike some. All she wanted was for me to come back in one piece. So, leaving my big half-manuscript sitting on top of my desk, and folding back my comfortable home sheets for the last time one morning, I left with my canvas bag in which a few fundamental things were packed and took off for the Pacific Ocean with the fifty dollars in my pocket.

I'd been poring over maps of the United States in Paterson for months, even reading books about the pioneers and savoring names like Platte and Cimarron and so on, and on the road-map was one long red line called Route 6 that led from the tip of Cape Cod clear to Ely, Nevada, and there dipped down to Los Angeles. I'll just stay on 6 all the way to Ely, I said to myself and confidently started. To get to 6 I had to go up to Bear Mountain. Filled with dreams of what I'd do in Chicago, in Denver, and then finally in San Fran, I took the Seventh Avenue subway to the end of the line at 242nd Street, and there took a trolley into Yonkers; in downtown Yonkers I transferred to an outgoing trolley and went to the city limits on the east bank of the Hudson River. If you drop a rose in the Hudson River at its mysterious source in the Adirondacks, think of all the places it journeys by as it goes out to sea forever —think of that wonderful Hudson Valley. I started hitching up the thing. Five scattered rides took me to the desired Bear Mountain Bridge, where Route 6 arched in from New England. It began to rain in torrents when I was let off there. It was mountainous. Route 6 came over the river, wound around a traffic circle, and disappeared into the wilderness. Not only was there no traffic but the rain came down in buckets and I had no shelter. I had to run under some pines to take cover; this did no good; I began crying and swearing and socking myself on the head for being such a damn fool. I was forty miles north of New York; all the way up I'd been worried about the fact that on this, my big opening day, I was only moving north instead of the so-longed-for west. Now I was stuck on my northernmost hangup. I ran a quarter-mile to an abandoned cute English-style filling station and stood under the dripping eaves. High up over my head the great hairy Bear Mountain sent down thunderclaps that put the fear of God in me. All I could see were smoky trees and dismal wilderness rising to the skies. "What the hell am I doing up here?" I cursed, I cried for Chicago. "Even now they're all having a big time, they're doing this, I'm not there, when will I get there!"—and so on. Finally a car stopped at the empty filling station; the man and the two women in it wanted to study a map. I stepped right up and gestured in the rain; they consulted; I looked like a maniac, of course, with my hair all wet, my shoes sopping. My shoes, damn fool that I am, were Mexican huaraches, plantlike sieves not fit for the rainy night of America and the raw road night. But the people let me in and rode me *back* to Newburgh, which I accepted as a better alternative than being trapped in the Bear Mountain wilderness all night. "Besides," said the man, "there's no traffic passes through 6. If you want to go to Chicago you'd do better going across the Holland Tunnel in New York and head for Pittsburgh," and I knew he was right. It was my dream that screwed up, the stupid hearthside idea that it would be wonderful to follow one great red line across America instead of trying various roads and routes.

In Newburgh it had stopped raining. I walked down to the river, and I had to ride back to New York in a bus with a delegation of schoolteachers coming back from a weekend in the mountains—chatter-chatter blah-blah, and me swearing for all the time and the money I'd wasted, and telling myself, I wanted to go west and here I've been all day and into the night going up and down, north and south, like something that can't get started. And I swore I'd be in Chicago tomorrow, and made sure of that, taking a bus to Chicago, spending most of my money, and didn't give a damn, just as long as I'd be in Chicago tomorrow.

3

It was an ordinary bus trip with crying babies and hot sun, and countryfolk getting on at one Penn town after another, till we got on the plain of Ohio and really rolled, up by Ashtabula and straight across Indiana in the night. I arrived in Chi quite early in the morning, got a room in the Y, and went to bed with a very few dollars in my pocket. I dug Chicago after a good day's sleep.

The wind from Lake Michigan, bop at the Loop, long walks around South Halsted and North Clark, and one long walk after midnight into the jungles, where a cruising car followed me as a suspicious character. At this time, 1947, bop was going like mad all over America. The fellows at the Loop blew, but with a tired air, because bop was somewhere between its Charlie Parker Ornithology period and another period that began with Miles Davis. And as I sat there listening to that sound of the night which bop has come to represent for all of us, I thought of all my friends from one end of the country to the other and how they were really all in the same vast backyard doing something so frantic and rushing-about. And for the first time in my life, the following afternoon, I went into the West. It was a warm and beautiful day for hitchhiking. To get out of the impossible complexities of Chicago traffic I took a bus to Joliet, Illinois, went by the Joliet pen, stationed myself just outside town after a walk through its leafy rickety streets behind, and pointed my way. All the way from New York to Joliet by bus, and I had spent more than half my money.

My first ride was a dynamite truck with a red flag, about thirty miles into great green Illinois, the truckdriver pointing out the place where Route 6, which we were on, intersects Route 66 before they both shoot west for incredible distances. Along about three in the afternoon, after an apple pie and ice cream in a roadside stand, a woman stopped for me in a little coupe. I had a twinge of hard joy as I ran after the car. But she was a middle-aged woman, actually the mother of sons my age, and wanted somebody to help her drive to Iowa. I was all for it. Iowa! Not so far from Denver, and once I got to Denver I could relax. She drove the first few hours, at one point insisted on visiting an old church somewhere, as if we were tourists, and then I took over the wheel and, though I'm not much of a driver, drove clear through the rest of Illinois to Davenport, Iowa, via Rock Island. And here for the first time in my life I saw my beloved Mississippi River, dry in the summer haze, low water, with its big rank smell that smells like the raw body of America itself because it washes it up. Rock Island—railroad tracks, shacks, small downtown section; and over the bridge to Davenport, same kind of town, all smelling of sawdust in the warm midwest sun. Here the lady had to go on to her Iowa hometown by another route, and I got out.

The sun was going down. I walked, after a few cold beers, to the edge of town, and it was a long walk. All the men were driving home from work, wearing railroad hats, baseball hats, all kinds of hats, just like after work in any town anywhere. One of them gave me a ride up the hill and left me at a lonely crossroads on the edge of the prairie. It was beautiful there. The only cars that came by were farmer-cars; they gave me suspicious looks, they clanked along, the cows were coming home. Not a truck. A few cars zipped by. A hotrod kid came by with his scarf flying. The sun went all the way down and I was standing in the purple darkness. Now I was scared. There weren't even any lights in the Iowa countryside; in a minute nobody would be able to see me. Luckily a man going back to Davenport gave me a lift downtown. But I was right where I started from.

I went to sit in the bus station and think this over. I ate another apple pie and ice cream; that's practically all I ate all the way across the country, I knew it was nutritious and it was delicious, of course. I decided to gamble. I took a bus in downtown Davenport, after spending a half-hour watching a waitress in the bus-station café, and rode to the city limits, but this time near the gas stations. Here the big trucks roared, wham, and inside two minutes one of them cranked to a stop for me. I ran for it with my soul whoopeeing. And what a driver—a great big tough truckdriver with popping eyes and a hoarse raspy voice who just slammed and kicked at everything and got his rig under way and paid hardly any attention to me. So I could rest my tired soul a little, for one of the biggest troubles hitchhiking is having to talk to innumerable people, make them feel that they didn't make a mistake picking you up, even entertain them almost, all of which is a great strain when you're going all the way and don't plan to sleep in hotels. The guy just yelled above the roar, and all I had to do was yell back, and we relaxed. And he balled that thing clear to Iowa City and yelled me the funniest stories about how he got around the law in every town that had an unfair speed limit, saying over and over again, "Them goddam cops can't put no flies on *my* ass!" Just as we rolled into Iowa City he saw another truck coming behind us, and because he had to turn off at Iowa City he blinked his tail lights at the other guy and slowed down for me to jump out, which I did with my bag, and the other truck, acknowledging this exchange, stopped for me, and once again,

in the twink of nothing, I was in another big high cab, all set
to go hundreds of miles across the night, and was I happy!
And the new truckdriver was as crazy as the other and yelled
just as much, and all I had to do was lean back and roll on. Now
I could see Denver looming ahead of me like the Promised
Land, way out there beneath the stars, across the prairie of
Iowa and the plains of Nebraska, and I could see the greater
vision of San Francisco beyond, like jewels in the night. He
balled the jack and told stories for a couple of hours, then, at a
town in Iowa where years later Dean and I were stopped on
suspicion in what looked like a stolen Cadillac, he slept a few
hours in the seat. I slept too, and took one little walk along the
lonely brick walls illuminated by one lamp, with the prairie
brooding at the end of each little street and the smell of the
corn like dew in the night.

   He woke up with a start at dawn. Off we roared, and an hour
later the smoke of Des Moines appeared ahead over the green
cornfields. He had to eat his breakfast now and wanted to take
it easy, so I went right on into Des Moines, about four miles,
hitching a ride with two boys from the University of Iowa; and
it was strange sitting in their brand-new comfortable car and
hearing them talk of exams as we zoomed smoothly into town.
Now I wanted to sleep a whole day. So I went to the Y to get
a room; they didn't have any, and by instinct I wandered down
to the railroad tracks—and there're a lot of them in Des Moines
—and wound up in a gloomy old Plains inn of a hotel by the
locomotive roundhouse, and spent a long day sleeping on a
big clean hard white bed with dirty remarks carved in the wall
beside my pillow and the beat yellow windowshades pulled
over the smoky scene of the railyards. I woke up as the sun was
reddening; and that was the one distinct time in my life, the
strangest moment of all, when I didn't know who I was—I was
far away from home, haunted and tired with travel, in a cheap
hotel room I'd never seen, hearing the hiss of steam outside,
and the creak of the old wood of the hotel, and footsteps upstairs, and all the sad sounds, and I looked at the cracked high
ceiling and really didn't know who I was for about fifteen
strange seconds. I wasn't scared; I was just somebody else,
some stranger, and my whole life was a haunted life, the life of
a ghost. I was halfway across America, at the dividing line

between the East of my youth and the West of my future, and maybe that's why it happened right there and then, that strange red afternoon.

But I had to get going and stop moaning, so I picked up my bag, said so long to the old hotelkeeper sitting by his spittoon, and went to eat. I ate apple pie and ice cream—it was getting better as I got deeper into Iowa, the pie bigger, the ice cream richer. There were the most beautiful bevies of girls everywhere I looked in Des Moines that afternoon—they were coming home from high school—but I had no time now for thoughts like that and promised myself a ball in Denver. Carlo Marx was already in Denver; Dean was there; Chad King and Tim Gray were there, it was their hometown; Marylou was there; and there was mention of a mighty gang including Ray Rawlins and his beautiful blond sister Babe Rawlins; two waitresses Dean knew, the Bettencourt sisters; and even Roland Major, my old college writing buddy, was there. I looked forward to all of them with joy and anticipation. So I rushed past the pretty girls, and the prettiest girls in the world live in Des Moines.

A guy with a kind of toolshack on wheels, a truck full of tools that he drove standing up like a modern milkman, gave me a ride up the long hill, where I immediately got a ride from a farmer and his son heading out for Adel in Iowa. In this town, under a big elm tree near a gas station, I made the acquaintance of another hitchhiker, a typical New Yorker, an Irishman who'd been driving a truck for the post office most of his work years and was now headed for a girl in Denver and a new life. I think he was running away from something in New York, the law most likely. He was a real red-nose young drunk of thirty and would have bored me ordinarily, except that my senses were sharp for any kind of human friendship. He wore a beat sweater and baggy pants and had nothing with him in the way of a bag—just a toothbrush and handkerchiefs. He said we ought to hitch together. I should have said no, because he looked pretty awful on the road. But we stuck together and got a ride with a taciturn man to Stuart, Iowa, a town in which we were really stranded. We stood in front of the railroad-ticket shack in Stuart, waiting for the westbound traffic till the sun went down, a good five hours, dawdling away the time, at first telling about ourselves, then he told dirty stories, then we just kicked pebbles and made goofy noises of one kind and another. We got bored. I decided to spend a buck on beer; we went to an old saloon in Stuart and had a few. There he got as drunk as he ever did in his Ninth Avenue night back home, and yelled joyously in my ear all the sordid dreams of his life. I kind of liked him; not because he was a good sort, as he later proved to be, but because he was enthusiastic about things. We got back on the road in the darkness, and of course nobody stopped and nobody came by much. That went on till three o'clock in the morning. We spent some time trying to sleep on the bench at the railroad ticket office, but the telegraph clicked all night and we couldn't sleep, and big freights were slamming around outside. We didn't know how to hop a proper chain gang; we'd never done it before; we didn't know whether they were going east or west or how to find out or what boxcars and flats and de-iced reefers to pick, and so on. So when the Omaha bus came through just before dawn we hopped on it and joined the sleeping passengers—I paid for his fare as well as mine. His name was Eddie. He reminded me of my cousin-in-law from the Bronx. That was why I stuck with him. It was like having an old friend along, a smiling good-natured sort to goof along with.

We arrived at Council Bluffs at dawn; I looked out. All winter I'd been reading of the great wagon parties that held council there before hitting the Oregon and Santa Fe trails; and of course now it was only cute suburban cottages of one damn kind and another, all laid out in the dismal gray dawn. Then Omaha, and, by God, the first cowboy I saw, walking along the bleak walls of the wholesale meat warehouses in a ten-gallon hat and Texas boots, looked like any beat character of the brickwall dawns of the East except for the getup. We got off the bus and walked clear up the hill, the long hill formed over the millenniums by the mighty Missouri, alongside of which Omaha is built, and got out to the country and stuck our thumbs out. We got a brief ride from a wealthy rancher in a ten-gallon hat, who said the valley of the Platte was as great as the Nile Valley of Egypt, and as he said so I saw the great trees in the distance that snaked with the riverbed and the great verdant fields around it, and almost agreed with him.

Then as we were standing at another crossroads and it was starting to get cloudy another cowboy, this one six feet tall in a modest half-gallon hat, called us over and wanted to know if either one of us could drive. Of course Eddie could drive, and he had a license and I didn't. Cowboy had two cars with him that he was driving back to Montana. His wife was at Grand Island, and he wanted us to drive one of the cars there, where she'd take over. At that point he was going north, and that would be the limit of our ride with him. But it was a good hundred miles into Nebraska, and of course we jumped for it. Eddie drove alone, the cowboy and myself following, and no sooner were we out of town than Eddie started to ball that jack ninety miles an hour out of sheer exuberance. "Damn me, what's that boy doing!" the cowboy shouted, and took off after him. It began to be like a race. For a minute I thought Eddie was trying to get away with the car—and for all I know that's what he meant to do. But the cowboy stuck to him and caught up with him and tooted the horn. Eddie slowed down. The cowboy tooted to stop. "Damn, boy, you're liable to get a flat going that speed. Can't you drive a little slower?"

"Well, I'll be damned, was I really going ninety?" said Eddie. "I didn't realize it on this smooth road."

"Just take it a little easy and we'll all get to Grand Island in one piece."

"Sure thing." And we resumed our journey. Eddie had calmed down and probably even got sleepy. So we drove a hundred miles across Nebraska, following the winding Platte with its verdant fields.

"During the depression," said the cowboy to me, "I used to hop freights at least once a month. In those days you'd see hundreds of men riding a flatcar or in a boxcar, and they weren't just bums, they were all kinds of men out of work and going from one place to another and some of them just wandering. It was like that all over the West. Brakemen never bothered you in those days. I don't know about today. Nebraska I ain't got no use for. Why in the middle nineteen thirties this place wasn't nothing but a big dustcloud as far as the eye could see. You couldn't breathe. The ground was black. I was here in those days. They can give Nebraska back to the Indians far as I'm concerned. I hate this damn place more than any place in the world. Montana's my home now—Missoula. You come up there sometime and see God's country." Later in the afternoon I slept when he got tired talking—he was an interesting talker.

We stopped along the road for a bite to eat. The cowboy went off to have a spare tire patched, and Eddie and I sat down in a kind of homemade diner. I heard a great laugh, the greatest laugh in the world, and here came this rawhide old-timer Nebraska farmer with a bunch of other boys into the diner; you could hear his raspy cries clear across the plains, across the whole gray world of them that day. Everybody else laughed with him. He didn't have a care in the world and had the hugest regard for everybody. I said to myself, Wham, listen to that man laugh. That's the West, here I am in the West. He came booming into the diner, calling Maw's name, and she made the sweetest cherry pie in Nebraska, and I had some with a mountainous scoop of ice cream on top. "Maw, rustle me up some grub afore I have to start eatin myself raw or some damn silly idee like that." And he threw himself on a stool and went hyaw hyaw hyaw hyaw. "And thow some beans in it." It was the spirit of the West sitting right next to me. I wished I knew his whole raw life and what the hell he'd been doing all these years besides laughing and yelling like that. Whooee, I told my soul, and the cowboy came back and off we went to Grand Island.

We got there in no time flat. He went to fetch his wife and off to whatever fate awaited him, and Eddie and I resumed on the road. We got a ride from a couple of young fellows— wranglers, teenagers, country boys in a put-together jalopy— and were left off somewhere up the line in a thin drizzle of rain. Then an old man who said nothing—and God knows why he picked us up—took us to Shelton. Here Eddie stood forlornly in the road in front of a staring bunch of short, squat Omaha Indians who had nowhere to go and nothing to do. Across the road was the railroad track and the watertank saying SHELTON. "Damn me," said Eddie with amazement, "I've been in this town before. It was years ago, during the war, at night, late at night when everybody was sleeping. I went out on the platform to smoke, and there we was in the middle of nowhere and black as hell, and I look up and see that name Shelton written on the watertank. Bound for the Pacific, everybody snoring, every damn dumb sucker, and we only stayed a few minutes, stoking up or something, and off we went. Damn me, this Shelton! I hated this place ever since!" And we were stuck in Shelton. As in Davenport, Iowa, somehow all the cars were farmer-cars, and once in a while a tourist car, which is worse, with old men driving and their wives pointing out the sights or poring over maps, and sitting back looking at everything with suspicious faces.

The drizzle increased and Eddie got cold; he had very little clothing. I fished a wool plaid shirt from my canvas bag and he put it on. He felt a little better. I had a cold. I bought cough drops in a rickety Indian store of some kind. I went to the little two-by-four post office and wrote my aunt a penny postcard. We went back to the gray road. There she was in front of us, Shelton, written on the watertank. The Rock Island balled by. We saw the faces of Pullman passengers go by in a blur. The train howled off across the plains in the direction of our desires. It started to rain harder.

A tall, lanky fellow in a gallon hat stopped his car on the wrong side of the road and came over to us; he looked like a sheriff. We prepared our stories secretly. He took his time coming over. "You boys going to get somewhere, or just going?" We didn't understand his question, and it was a damned good question.

"Why?" we said.

"Well, I own a little carnival that's pitched a few mile down the road and I'm looking for some old boys willing to work and make a buck for themselves. I've got a roulette concession and a wooden-ring concession, you know, the kind you throw around dolls and take your luck. You boys want to work for me, you can get thirty per cent of the take."

"Room and board?"

"You can get a bed but no food. You'll have to eat in town. We travel some." We thought it over. "It's a good opportunity," he said, and waited patiently for us to make up our minds. We felt silly and didn't know what to say, and I for one didn't want to get hung-up with a carnival. I was in such a bloody hurry to get to the gang in Denver.

I said, "I don't know, I'm going as fast as I can and I don't think I have the time." Eddie said the same thing, and the old man waved his hand and casually sauntered back to his car and drove off. And that was that. We laughed about it awhile and speculated about what it would have been like. I had visions of a dark and dusty night on the plains, and the faces of Nebraska families wandering by, with their rosy children looking at everything with awe, and I know I would have felt like the devil himself rooking them with all those cheap carnival tricks. And the Ferris wheel revolving in the flatlands darkness, and, Godalmighty, the sad music of the merry-go-round and me wanting to get on to my goal—and sleeping in some gilt wagon on a bed of burlap.

Eddie turned out to be a pretty absent-minded pal of the road. A funny old contraption rolled by, driven by an old man; it was made of some kind of aluminum, square as a box—a trailer, no doubt, but a weird, crazy Nebraska homemade trailer. He was going very slow and stopped. We rushed up; he said he could only take one; without a word Eddie jumped in and slowly rattled from my sight, and wearing my wool plaid shirt. Well, alackaday, I kissed the shirt good-by; it had only sentimental value in any case. I waited in our personal god-awful Shelton for a long, long time, several hours, and I kept thinking it was getting night; actually it was only early afternoon, but dark. Denver, Denver, how would I ever get to Denver? I was just about giving up and planning to sit over coffee when a fairly new car stopped, driven by a young guy. I ran like mad.

"Where you going?"

"Denver."

"Well, I can take you a hundred miles up the line."

"Grand, grand, you saved my life."

"I used to hitchhike myself, that's why I always pick up a fellow."

"I would too if I had a car." And so we talked, and he told me about his life, which wasn't very interesting, and I started to sleep some and woke up right outside the town of Gothenburg, where he let me off.

4

The greatest ride in my life was about to come up, a truck, with a flatboard at the back, with about six or seven boys sprawled out on it, and the drivers, two young blond farmers from Minnesota, were picking up every single soul they found on that road—the most smiling, cheerful couple of handsome bumpkins you could ever wish to see, both wearing cotton shirts and overalls, nothing else; both thick-wristed and earnest, with broad howareyou smiles for anybody and anything that came across their path. I ran up, said "Is there room?" They said, "Sure, hop on, 'sroom for everybody."

I wasn't on the flatboard before the truck roared off; I lurched, a rider grabbed me, and I sat down. Somebody passed a bottle of rotgut, the bottom of it. I took a big swig in the wild, lyrical, drizzling air of Nebraska. "Whooee, here we go!" yelled a kid in a baseball cap, and they gunned up the truck to seventy and passed everybody on the road. "We been riding this sonofabitch since Des Moines. These guys never stop. Every now and then you have to yell for pisscall, otherwise you have to piss off the air, and hang on, brother, hang on."

I looked at the company. There were two young farmer boys from North Dakota in red baseball caps, which is the standard North Dakota farmer-boy hat, and they were headed for the harvests; their old men had given them leave to hit the road for a summer. There were two young city boys from Columbus, Ohio, high-school football players, chewing gum, winking, singing in the breeze, and they said they were hitchhiking around the United States for the summer. "We're going to LA!" they yelled.

"What are you going to do there?"

"Hell, we don't know. Who cares?"

Then there was a tall slim fellow who had a sneaky look. "Where you from?" I asked. I was lying next to him on the platform; you couldn't sit without bouncing off, it had no rails. And he turned slowly to me, opened his mouth, and said, "Mon-ta-na."

Finally there were Mississippi Gene and his charge. Mississippi Gene was a little dark guy who rode freight trains around the country, a thirty-year-old hobo but with a youthful look so you couldn't tell exactly what age he was. And he sat on the boards crosslegged, looking out over the fields without saying anything for hundreds of miles, and finally at one point he turned to me and said, "Where *you* headed?"

I said Denver.

"I got a sister there but I ain't seed her for several couple years." His language was melodious and slow. He was patient. His charge was a sixteen-year-old tall blond kid, also in hobo rags; that is to say, they wore old clothes that had been turned black by the soot of railroads and the dirt of boxcars and sleeping on the ground. The blond kid was also quiet and he seemed to be running away from something, and it figured to be the law the way he looked straight ahead and wet his lips in worried thought. Montana Slim spoke to them occasionally with a sardonic and insinuating smile. They paid no attention to him. Slim was all insinuation. I was afraid of his long goofy grin that he opened up straight in your face and held there half-moronically.

"You got any money?" he said to me.

"Hell no, maybe enough for a pint of whisky till I get to Denver. What about you?"

"I know where I can get some."

"Where?"

"Anywhere. You can always folly a man down an alley, can't you?"

"Yeah, I guess you can."

"I ain't beyond doing it when I really need some dough. Headed up to Montana to see my father. I'll have to get off this rig at Cheyenne and move up some other way. These crazy boys are going to Los Angeles."

"Straight?"

"All the way—if you want to go to LA you got a ride."

I mulled this over; the thought of zooming all night across Nebraska, Wyoming, and the Utah desert in the morning, and then most likely the Nevada desert in the afternoon, and actually arriving in Los Angeles within a foreseeable space of time almost made me change my plans. But I had to go to Denver. I'd have to get off at Cheyenne too, and hitch south ninety miles to Denver.

I was glad when the two Minnesota farmboys who owned the truck decided to stop in North Platte and eat; I wanted to have a look at them. They came out of the cab and smiled at all of us. "Pisscall!" said one. "Time to eat!" said the other. But they were the only ones in the party who had money to buy food. We all shambled after them to a restaurant run by a bunch of women, and sat around over hamburgers and coffee while they wrapped away enormous meals just as if they were back in their mother's kitchen. They were brothers; they were transporting farm machinery from Los Angeles to Minnesota and making good money at it. So on their trip to the Coast empty they picked up everybody on the road. They'd done this about five times now; they were having a hell of a time. They liked everything. They never stopped smiling. I tried to talk to them —a kind of dumb attempt on my part to befriend the captains of our ship—and the only responses I got were two sunny smiles and large white cornfed teeth.

Everybody had joined them in the restaurant except the two hobo kids, Gene and his boy. When we all got back they were still sitting in the truck, forlorn and disconsolate. Now the darkness was falling. The drivers had a smoke; I jumped at the chance to go buy a bottle of whisky to keep warm in the rushing cold air of night. They smiled when I told them. "Go ahead, hurry up."

"You can have a couple shots!" I reassured them.

"Oh no, we never drink, go ahead."

Montana Slim and the two high-school boys wandered the streets of North Platte with me till I found a whisky store. They chipped in some, and Slim some, and I bought a fifth. Tall, sullen men watched us go by from false-front buildings; the main street was lined with square box-houses. There were immense vistas of the plains beyond every sad street. I felt something different in the air in North Platte, I didn't know what it was. In five minutes I did. We got back on the truck and roared off. It got dark quickly. We all had a shot, and suddenly I looked, and the verdant farmfields of the Platte began to disappear and in their stead, so far you couldn't see to the end, appeared long flat wastelands of sand and sagebrush. I was astounded.

"What in the hell is this?" I cried out to Slim.

"This is the beginning of the rangelands, boy. Hand me another drink."

"Whoopee!" yelled the high-school boys. "Columbus, so long! What would Sparkie and the boys say if they was here. Yow!"

The drivers had switched up front; the fresh brother was gunning the truck to the limit. The road changed too: humpy in the middle, with soft shoulders and a ditch on both sides about four feet deep, so that the truck bounced and teetered from one side of the road to the other—miraculously only when there were no cars coming the opposite way—and I thought we'd all take a somersault. But they were tremendous drivers. How that truck disposed of the Nebraska nub—the nub that sticks out over Colorado! And soon I realized I was actually at last over Colorado, though not officially in it, but looking southwest toward Denver itself a few hundred miles away. I yelled for joy. We passed the bottle. The great blazing stars came out, the far-receding sand hills got dim. I felt like an arrow that could shoot out all the way.

And suddenly Mississippi Gene turned to me from his cross-legged, patient reverie, and opened his mouth, and leaned close, and said, "These plains put me in the mind of Texas."

"Are you from Texas?"

"No sir, I'm from Green-vell Muzz-sippy." And that was the way he said it.

"Where's that kid from?"

"He got into some kind of trouble back in Mississippi, so I offered to help him out. Boy's never been out on his own. I take care of him best as I can, he's only a child." Although Gene was white there was something of the wise and tired old Negro in him, and something very much like Elmer Hassel, the New York dope addict, in him, but a railroad Hassel, a traveling epic Hassel, crossing and recrossing the country every year, south in the winter and north in the summer, and only because he had no place he could stay in without getting tired of it and because there was nowhere to go but everywhere, keep rolling under the stars, generally the Western stars.

"I been to Og-den a couple times. If you want to ride on to Og-den I got some friends there we could hole up with."

"I'm going to Denver from Cheyenne."

"Hell, go right straight thu, you don't get a ride like this every day."

This too was a tempting offer. What was in Ogden? "What's Ogden?" I said.

"It's the place where most of the boys pass thu and always meet there; you're liable to see anybody there."

In my earlier days I'd been to sea with a tall rawboned fellow from Louisiana called Big Slim Hazard, William Holmes Hazard, who was hobo by choice. As a little boy he'd seen a hobo come up to ask his mother for a piece of pie, and she had given it to him, and when the hobo went off down the road the little boy had said, "Ma, what is that fellow?" "Why, that's a ho-bo." "Ma, I want to be a ho-bo someday." "Shet your mouth, that's not for the like of the Hazards." But he never forgot that day, and when he grew up, after a short spell playing football at LSU, he did become a hobo. Big Slim and I spent many nights telling stories and spitting tobacco juice in paper containers. There was something so indubitably reminiscent of Big Slim Hazard in Mississippi Gene's demeanor that I said, "Do you happen to have met a fellow called Big Slim Hazard somewhere?"

And he said, "You mean the tall fellow with the big laugh?"

"Well, that sounds like him. He came from Ruston, Louisiana."

"That's right. Louisiana Slim he's sometimes called. Yessir, I shore have met Big Slim."

"And he used to work in the East Texas oil fields?"

"East Texas is right. And now he's punching cows."

And that was exactly right; and still I couldn't believe Gene could have really known Slim, whom I'd been looking for, more or less, for years. "And he used to work in tugboats in New York?"

"Well now, I don't know about that."

"I guess you only knew him in the West."

"I reckon. I ain't never been to New York."

"Well, damn me, I'm amazed you know him. This is a big country. Yet I knew you must have known him."

"Yessir, I know Big Slim pretty well. Always generous with his money when he's got some. Mean, tough fellow, too; I seen him flatten a policeman in the yards at Cheyenne, one punch." That sounded like Big Slim; he was always practicing that one punch in the air; he looked like Jack Dempsey, but a young Jack Dempsey who drank.

"Damn!" I yelled into the wind, and I had another shot, and by now I was feeling pretty good. Every shot was wiped away by the rushing wind of the open truck, wiped away of its bad effects, and the good effect sank in my stomach. "Cheyenne, here I come!" I sang. "Denver, look out for your boy."

Montana Slim turned to me, pointed at my shoes, and commented, "You reckon if you put them things in the ground something'll grow up?"—without cracking a smile, of course, and the other boys heard him and laughed. And they were the silliest shoes in America; I brought them along specifically because I didn't want my feet to sweat in the hot road, and except for the rain in Bear Mountain they proved to be the best possible shoes for my journey. So I laughed with them. And the shoes were pretty ragged by now, the bits of colored leather sticking up like pieces of a fresh pineapple and my toes showing through. Well, we had another shot and laughed. As in a dream we zoomed through small crossroads towns smack out of the darkness, and passed long lines of lounging harvest hands and cowboys in the night. They watched us pass in one motion of the head, and we saw them slap their thighs from the continuing dark the other side of town—we were a funny-looking crew.

A lot of men were in this country at that time of the year; it was harvest time. The Dakota boys were fidgeting. "I think we'll get off at the next pisscall; seems like there's a lot of work around here."

"All you got to do is move north when it's over here," counseled Montana Slim, "and jes follow the harvest till you get to Canada." The boys nodded vaguely; they didn't take much stock in his advice.

Meanwhile the blond young fugitive sat the same way; every now and then Gene leaned out of his Buddhistic trance over the rushing dark plains and said something tenderly in the boy's ear. The boy nodded. Gene was taking care of him, of his moods and his fears. I wondered where the hell they would go and what they would do. They had no cigarettes. I squandered my pack on them, I loved them so. They were grateful and gracious. They never asked, I kept offering. Montana Slim had his own but never passed the pack. We zoomed through another crossroads town, passed another line of tall lanky men in jeans clustered in the dim light like moths on the desert, and returned to the tremendous darkness, and the stars overhead were pure and bright because of the increasingly thin air as we mounted the high hill of the western plateau, about a foot a mile, so they say, and no trees obstructing any low-leveled stars anywhere. And once I saw a moody whitefaced cow in the sage by the road as we flitted by. It was like riding a railroad train, just as steady and just as straight.

By and by we came to a town, slowed down, and Montana Slim said, "Ah, pisscall," but the Minnesotans didn't stop and went right on through. "Damn, I gotta go," said Slim.

"Go over the side," said somebody.

"Well, I *will*," he said, and slowly, as we all watched, he inched to the back of the platform on his haunch, holding on as best he could, till his legs dangled over. Somebody knocked on the window of the cab to bring this to the attention of the brothers. Their great smiles broke as they turned. And just as Slim was ready to proceed, precarious as it was already, they began zigzagging the truck at seventy miles an hour. He fell back a moment; we saw a whale's spout in the air; he struggled back to a sitting position. They swung the truck. Wham, over he went on his side, watering all over himself. In the roar we could hear him faintly cursing, like the whine of a man far across the hills. "Damn . . . damn . . ." He never knew we were doing this deliberately; he just struggled, as grim as Job. When he was finished, as such, he was wringing wet, and now he had to edge and shimmy his way back, and with a most woebegone look, and everybody laughing, except the sad blond boy, and the Minnesotans roaring in the cab. I handed him the bottle to make up for it.

"What the hail," he said, "was they doing that on purpose?"

"They sure were."

"Well, damn me, I didn't know that. I know I tried it back in Nebraska and didn't have half so much trouble."

We came suddenly into the town of Ogallala, and here the fellows in the cab called out, "*Pisscall!*" and with great good delight. Slim stood sullenly by the truck, ruing a lost opportunity. The two Dakota boys said good-by to everybody and figured they'd start harvesting here. We watched them disappear in the night toward the shacks at the end of town where lights were burning, where a watcher of the night in jeans said the employment men would be. I had to buy more cigarettes. Gene and the blond boy followed me to stretch their legs. I walked into the least likely place in the world, a kind of lonely Plains soda fountain for the local teenage girls and boys. They were dancing, a few of them, to the music on the jukebox. There was a lull when we came in. Gene and Blondey just stood there, looking at nobody; all they wanted was cigarettes. There were some pretty girls, too. And one of them made eyes at Blondey and he never saw it, and if he had he wouldn't have cared, he was so sad and gone.

I bought a pack each for them; they thanked me. The truck was ready to go. It was getting on midnight now, and cold. Gene, who'd been around the country more times than he could count on his fingers and toes, said the best thing to do now was for all of us to bundle up under the big tarpaulin or we'd freeze. In this manner, and with the rest of the bottle, we kept warm as the air grew ice-cold and pinged our ears. The stars seemed to get brighter the more we climbed the High Plains. We were in Wyoming now. Flat on my back, I stared straight up at the magnificent firmament, glorying in the time I was making, in how far I had come from sad Bear Mountain after all, and tingling with kicks at the thought of what lay ahead of me in Denver—whatever, whatever it would be. And Mississippi Gene began to sing a song. He sang it in a melodious, quiet voice, with a river accent, and it was simple, just "I got a purty little girl, she's sweet six-teen, she's the purti-est thing you ever seen," repeating it with other lines thrown in, all concerning how far he'd been and how he wished he could go back to her but he done lost her.

I said, "Gene, that's the prettiest song."

"It's the sweetest I know," he said with a smile.

"I hope you get where you're going, and be happy when you do."

"I always make out and move along one way or the other."

Montana Slim was asleep. He woke up and said to me, "Hey, Blackie, how about you and me investigatin' Cheyenne together tonight before you go to Denver?"

"Sure thing." I was drunk enough to go for anything.

As the truck reached the outskirts of Cheyenne, we saw the high red lights of the local radio station, and suddenly we were bucking through a great crowd of people that poured along both sidewalks. "Hell's bells, it's Wild West Week," said Slim. Big crowds of businessmen, fat businessmen in boots and ten-gallon hats, with their hefty wives in cowgirl attire, bustled and whoopeed on the wooden sidewalks of old Cheyenne; farther down were the long stringy boulevard lights of new down-town Cheyenne, but the celebration was focusing on Old-town. Blank guns went off. The saloons were crowded to the sidewalk. I was amazed, and at the same time I felt it was ridiculous: in my first shot at the West I was seeing to what absurd devices it had fallen to keep its proud tradition. We had to jump off the truck and say good-by; the Minnesotans weren't interested in hanging around. It was sad to see them go, and I realized that I would never see any of them again, but that's the way it was. "You'll freeze your ass tonight," I warned. "Then you'll burn 'em in the desert tomorrow afternoon."

"That's all right with me long's as we get out of this cold night," said Gene. And the truck left, threading its way through the crowds, and nobody paying attention to the strangeness of the kids inside the tarpaulin, staring at the town like babes from a coverlet. I watched it disappear into the night.

5

I was with Montana Slim and we started hitting the bars. I had about seven dollars, five of which I foolishly squandered that night. First we milled with all the cowboy-dudded tourists and oilmen and ranchers, at bars, in doorways, on the sidewalk; then for a while I shook Slim, who was wandering a little slap-happy in the street from all the whisky and beer: he was that kind of drinker; his eyes got glazed, and in a minute he'd be telling an absolute stranger about things. I went into a chili joint and the waitress was Mexican and beautiful. I ate, and then I wrote her a little love note on the back of the bill. The chili joint was deserted; everybody was somewhere else, drinking. I told her to turn the bill over. She read it and laughed. It was a little poem about how I wanted her to come and see the night with me.

"I'd love to, Chiquito, but I have a date with my boy friend."

"Can't you shake him?"

"No, no, I don't," she said sadly, and I loved the way she said it.

"Some other time I'll come by here," I said, and she said, "Any time, kid." Still I hung around, just to look at her, and had another cup of coffee. Her boy friend came in sullenly and wanted to know when she was off. She bustled around to close the place quick. I had to get out. I gave her a smile when I left. Things were going on as wild as ever outside, except that the fat burpers were getting drunker and whooping up louder. It was funny. There were Indian chiefs wandering around in big headdresses and really solemn among the flushed drunken faces. I saw Slim tottering along and joined him.

He said, "I just wrote a postcard to my Paw in Montana. You reckon you can find a mailbox and put it in?" It was a strange request; he gave me the postcard and tottered through the swinging doors of a saloon. I took the card, went to the box, and took a quick look at it. "Dear Paw, I'll be home Wednesday. Everything's all right with me and I hope the same is with you. Richard." It gave me a different idea of him; how tenderly polite he was with his father. I went in the bar and joined him. We picked up two girls, a pretty young blonde and a fat brunette. They were dumb and sullen, but we wanted to make them. We took them to a rickety nightclub that was already closing, and there I spent all but two dollars on Scotches for them and beer for us. I was getting drunk and didn't care; everything was fine. My whole being and purpose was pointed at the little blonde. I wanted to go in there with all my strength. I hugged her and wanted to tell her. The nightclub closed and we all wandered out in the rickety dusty streets. I looked up at the sky; the pure, wonderful stars were still there, burning. The girls wanted to go to the bus station, so we all went, but they apparently wanted to meet some sailor who was there waiting for them, a cousin of the fat girl's, and the sailor had friends with him. I said to the blonde, "What's up?" She said she wanted to go home, in Colorado just over the line south of Cheyenne. "I'll take you in a bus," I said.

"No, the bus stops on the highway and I have to walk across that damn prairie all by myself. I spend all afternoon looking at the damn thing and I don't aim to walk over it tonight."

"Ah, listen, we'll take a nice walk in the prairie flowers."

"There ain't no flowers there," she said. "I want to go to New York. I'm sick and tired of this. Ain't no place to go but Cheyenne and ain't nothin in Cheyenne."

"Ain't nothin in New York."

"Hell there ain't," she said with a curl of her lips.

The bus station was crowded to the doors. All kinds of people were waiting for buses or just standing around; there were a lot of Indians, who watched everything with their stony eyes. The girl disengaged herself from my talk and joined the sailor and the others. Slim was dozing on a bench. I sat down. The floors of bus stations are the same all over the country, always covered with butts and spit and they give a feeling of sadness that only bus stations have. For a moment it was no different from being in Newark, except for the great hugeness outside that I loved so much. I rued the way I had broken up the purity of my entire trip, not saving every dime, and dawdling and not really making time, fooling around with this sullen girl and spending all my money. It made me sick. I hadn't slept in so long I got too tired to curse and fuss and went off to sleep; I curled up on the seat with my canvas bag for a pillow, and slept till eight o'clock in the morning among the dreamy murmurs and noises of the station and of hundreds of people passing.

I woke up with a big headache. Slim was gone—to Montana, I guess. I went outside. And there in the blue air I saw for the first time, far off, the great snowy tops of the Rocky Mountains. I took a deep breath. I had to get to Denver at once. First I ate a breakfast, a modest one of toast and coffee and one egg, and then I cut out of town to the highway. The Wild West festival was still going on; there was a rodeo, and the whooping and jumping were about to start all over again. I left it behind me. I wanted to see my gang in Denver. I crossed a railroad overpass and reached a bunch of shacks where two highways forked off, both for Denver. I took the one nearest the mountains so I could look at them, and pointed myself that way. I got a ride right off from a young fellow from Connecticut who was driving around the country in his jalopy, painting; he was the son of an editor in the East. He talked and talked; I was sick from drinking and from the altitude. At one point I almost had to stick my head out the window. But by the time he let me off at Longmont, Colorado, I was feeling normal again and had even started telling him about the state of my own travels. He wished me luck.

It was beautiful in Longmont. Under a tremendous old tree was a bed of green lawn-grass belonging to a gas station. I asked the attendant if I could sleep there, and he said sure; so I stretched out a wool shirt, laid my face flat on it, with an elbow out, and with one eye cocked at the snowy Rockies in the hot sun for just a moment. I fell asleep for two delicious hours, the only discomfort being an occasional Colorado ant. And here I am in Colorado! I kept thinking gleefully. Damn! damn! damn! I'm making it! And after a refreshing sleep filled with cobwebby dreams of my past life in the East I got up, washed in the station men's room, and strode off, fit and slick as a fiddle, and got me a rich thick milkshake at the roadhouse to put some freeze in my hot, tormented stomach.

Incidentally, a very beautiful Colorado gal shook me that cream; she was all smiles too; I was grateful, it made up for last night. I said to myself, Wow! What'll *Denver* be like! I got on that hot road, and off I went in a brand-new car driven by a Denver businessman of about thirty-five. He went seventy. I tingled all over; I counted minutes and subtracted miles. Just ahead, over the rolling wheatfields all golden beneath the distant snows of Estes, I'd be seeing old Denver at last. I pictured myself in a Denver bar that night, with all the gang, and in their eyes I would be strange and ragged and like the Prophet who has walked across the land to bring the dark Word, and the only Word I had was "Wow!" The man and I had a long, warm conversation about our respective schemes in life, and before I knew it we were going over the wholesale fruitmarkets outside Denver; there were smokestacks, smoke, railyards, red-brick buildings, and the distant downtown gray-stone buildings, and here I was in Denver. He let me off at Larimer Street. I stumbled along with the most wicked grin of joy in the world, among the old bums and beat cowboys of Larimer Street.

6

In those days I didn't know Dean as well as I do now, and the first thing I wanted to do was look up Chad King, which I did. I called up his house, talked to his mother—she said, "Why, Sal, what are you doing in Denver?" Chad is a slim blond boy with a strange witch-doctor face that goes with his interest in anthropology and prehistory Indians. His nose beaks softly and almost creamily under a golden flare of hair; he has the beauty and grace of a Western hotshot who's danced in road-houses and played a little football. A quavering twang comes out when he speaks. "The thing I always liked, Sal, about the Plains Indians was the way they always got s'danged embarrassed after they boasted the number of scalps they got. In Ruxton's *Life in the Far West* there's an Indian who gets red all over blushing because he got so many scalps and he runs like hell into the plains, to glory over his deeds in hiding. Damn, that tickled *me*!"

Chad's mother located him, in the drowsy Denver afternoon, working over his Indian basket-making at the local museum. I called him there; he came and picked me up in his old Ford coupe that he used to take trips in the mountains, to dig for Indian objects. He came into the bus station wearing jeans and a big smile. I was sitting on my bag on the floor talking to the very same sailor who'd been in the Cheyenne bus station with me, asking him what happened to the blonde. He was so bored he didn't answer. Chad and I got in his little coupe and the first thing he had to do was get maps at the State building. Then he had to see an old schoolteacher, and so on, and all I wanted to do was drink beer. And in the back of my mind was the wild thought, Where is Dean and what is he doing right now? Chad had decided not to be Dean's friend any more, for some odd reason, and he didn't even know where he lived.

"Is Carlo Marx in town?"

"Yes." But he wasn't talking to him any more either. This was the beginning of Chad King's withdrawal from our general gang. I was to take a nap in his house that afternoon. The word was that Tim Gray had an apartment waiting for me up Colfax Avenue, that Roland Major was already living in it and was waiting for me to join him. I sensed some kind of conspiracy in the air, and this conspiracy lined up two groups in the gang: it was Chad King and Tim Gray and Roland Major, together with the Rawlinses, generally agreeing to ignore Dean Moriarty and Carlo Marx. I was smack in the middle of this interesting war.

It was a war with social overtones. Dean was the son of a wino, one of the most tottering bums of Larimer Street, and Dean had in fact been brought up generally on Larimer Street and thereabouts. He used to plead in court at the age of six to have his father set free. He used to beg in front of Larimer alleys and sneak the money back to his father, who waited among the broken bottles with an old buddy. Then when Dean grew up he began hanging around the Glenarm poolhalls; he set a Denver record for stealing cars and went to the reformatory. From the age of eleven to seventeen he was usually in reform school. His specialty was stealing cars, gunning for girls coming out of high school in the afternoon, driving them out to the mountains, making them, and coming back to sleep in any available hotel bathtub in town. His father, once a respectable and hardworking tinsmith, had become a wine alcoholic, which is worse than a whisky alcoholic, and was reduced to riding freights to Texas in the winter and back to Denver in the summer. Dean had brothers on his dead mother's side—she died when he was small—but they disliked him. Dean's only buddies were the poolhall boys. Dean, who had the tremendous energy of a new kind of American saint, and Carlo were the underground monsters of that season in Denver, together with the poolhall gang, and, symbolizing this most beautifully, Carlo had a basement apartment on Grant Street and we all met there many a night that went to dawn—Carlo, Dean, myself, Tom Snark, Ed Dunkel, and Roy Johnson. More of these others later.

My first afternoon in Denver I slept in Chad King's room while his mother went on with her housework downstairs and Chad worked at the library. It was a hot high-plains afternoon in July. I would not have slept if it hadn't been for Chad King's father's invention. Chad King's father, a fine kind man, was in his seventies, old and feeble, thin and drawn-out, and telling stories with a slow, slow relish; good stories, too, about his boyhood on the North Dakota plains in the eighties, when for diversion he rode ponies bareback and chased after coyotes with a club. Later he became a country schoolteacher in the Oklahoma panhandle, and finally a businessman of many devices in Denver. He still had his old office over a garage down the street—the rolltop desk was still there, together with countless dusty papers of past excitement and moneymaking. He had invented a special air-conditioner. He put an ordinary fan in a window frame and somehow conducted cool water through coils in front of the whirring blades. The result was perfect—within four feet of the fan—and then the water apparently turned into steam in the hot day and the downstairs part of the house was just as hot as usual. But I was sleeping right under the fan on Chad's bed, with a big bust of Goethe staring at me, and I comfortably went to sleep, only to wake up in twenty minutes freezing to death. I put a blanket on and still I was cold. Finally it was so cold I couldn't sleep, and I went downstairs. The old man asked me how his invention worked. I said it worked damned good, and I meant it within bounds. I liked the man. He was lean with memories. "I once made a spot remover that has since been copied by big firms in the East. I've been trying to collect on that for some years now. If I only had enough money to raise a decent lawyer . . ." But it was too late to raise a decent lawyer; and he sat in his house dejectedly. In the evening we had a wonderful dinner his mother cooked, venison steak that Chad's uncle had shot in the mountains. But where was Dean?

7

The following ten days were, as W. C. Fields said, "fraught with eminent peril"—and mad. I moved in with Roland Major in the really swank apartment that belonged to Tim Gray's folks. We each had a bedroom, and there was a kitchenette with food in the icebox, and a huge living room where Major sat in his silk dressing gown composing his latest Hemingwayan short story—a choleric, red-faced, pudgy hater of everything, who could turn on the warmest and most charming smile in the world when real life confronted him sweetly in the night. He sat like that at his desk, and I jumped around over the thick soft rug, wearing only my chino pants. He'd just written a story about a guy who comes to Denver for the first time. His name is Phil. His traveling companion is a mysterious and quiet fellow called Sam. Phil goes out to dig Denver and gets hung-up with arty types. He comes back to the hotel room. Lugubriously he says, "Sam, they're here too." And Sam is just looking out the window sadly. "Yes," says Sam, "I know." And the point was that Sam didn't have to go and look to know this. The arty types were all over America, sucking up its blood. Major and I were great pals; he thought I was the farthest thing from an arty type. Major liked good wines, just like Hemingway. He reminisced about his recent trip to France. "Ah, Sal, if you could sit with me high in the Basque country with a cool bottle of Poignon Dix-neuf, then you'd know there are other things besides boxcars."

"I know that. It's just that I love boxcars and I love to read the names on them like Missouri Pacific, Great Northern, Rock Island Line. By Gad, Major, if I could tell you everything that happened to me hitching here."

The Rawlinses lived a few blocks away. This was a delightful family—a youngish mother, part owner of a decrepit, ghost-town hotel, with five sons and two daughters. The wild son was Ray Rawlins, Tim Gray's boyhood buddy. Ray came roaring in to get me and we took to each other right away. We went off and drank in the Colfax bars. One of Ray's sisters was a beautiful blonde called Babe—a tennis-playing, surf-riding doll of the West. She was Tim Gray's girl. And Major, who was only passing through Denver and doing so in real style in the apartment, was going out with Tim Gray's sister Betty. I was the only guy without a girl. I asked everybody, "Where's Dean?" They made smiling negative answers.

Then finally it happened. The phone rang, and it was Carlo Marx. He gave me the address of his basement apartment. I said, "What are you doing in Denver? I mean what are you *doing*? What's going on?"

"Oh, wait till I tell you."

I rushed over to meet him. He was working in May's department store nights; crazy Ray Rawlins called him up there from a bar, getting janitors to run after Carlo with a story that somebody had died. Carlo immediately thought it was me who had died. And Rawlins said over the phone, "Sal's in Denver," and gave him my address and phone.

"And where is Dean?"

"Dean is in Denver. Let me tell you." And he told me that Dean was making love to two girls at the same time, they being Marylou, his first wife, who waited for him in a hotel room, and Camille, a new girl, who waited for him in a hotel room. "Between the two of them he rushes to me for our own unfinished business."

"And what business is that??"

"Dean and I are embarked on a tremendous season together. We're trying to communicate with absolute honesty and absolute completeness everything on our minds. We've had to take benzedrine. We sit on the bed, crosslegged, facing each other. I have finally taught Dean that he can do anything he wants, become mayor of Denver, marry a millionairess, or become the greatest poet since Rimbaud. But he keeps rushing out to see the midget auto races. I go with him. He jumps and yells, excited. You know, Sal, Dean is really hung-up on things like that." Marx said "Hmm" in his soul and thought about this.

"What's the schedule?" I said. There was always a schedule in Dean's life.

"The schedule is this: I came off work a half-hour ago. In that time Dean is balling Marylou at the hotel and gives me time to change and dress. At one sharp he rushes from Marylou to Camille—of course neither one of them knows what's going on—and bangs her once, giving me time to arrive at one-thirty. Then he comes out with me—first he has to beg with Camille, who's already started hating me—and we come here to talk till six in the morning. We usually spend more time than that, but it's getting awfully complicated and he's pressed for time. Then at six he goes back to Marylou—and he's going to spend all day tomorrow running around to get the necessary papers for their divorce. Marylou's all for it, but she insists on banging in the interim. She says she loves him—so does Camille."

Then he told me how Dean had met Camille. Roy Johnson, the poolhall boy, had found her in a bar and took her to a hotel; pride taking over his sense, he invited the whole gang to come up and see her. Everybody sat around talking with Camille. Dean did nothing but look out the window. Then when everybody left, Dean merely looked at Camille, pointed at his wrist, made the sign "four" (meaning he'd be back at four), and went out. At three the door was locked to Roy Johnson. At four it was opened to Dean. I wanted to go right out and see the madman. Also he had promised to fix me up; he knew all the girls in Denver.

Carlo and I went through rickety streets in the Denver night. The air was soft, the stars so fine, the promise of every cobbled alley so great, that I thought I was in a dream. We came to the rooming house where Dean haggled with Camille. It was an old red-brick building surrounded by wooden garages and old trees that stuck up from behind fences. We went up carpeted stairs. Carlo knocked; then he darted to the back to hide; he didn't want Camille to see him. I stood in the door. Dean opened it stark naked. I saw a brunette on the bed, one beautiful creamy thigh covered with black lace, look up with mild wonder.

"Why, Sa-a-al!" said Dean. "Well now—ah—ahem—yes, of course, you've arrived—you old sonumbitch you finally got on that old road. Well, now, look here—we must—yes, yes, at once—we must, we really must! Now Camille—" And he swirled on her. "Sal is here, this is my old buddy from New Yor-r-k, this is his first night in Denver and it's absolutely necessary for me to take him out and fix him up with a girl."

"But what time will you be back?"

"It is now" (looking at his watch) "exactly one-fourteen. I shall be back at exactly *three*-fourteen, for our hour of reverie together, real sweet reverie, darling, and then, as you know, as I told you and as we agreed, I have to go and see the one-legged lawyer about those papers—in the middle of the night, strange as it seems and as I tho-ro-ly explained." (This was a coverup for his rendezvous with Carlo, who was still hiding.) "So now in this exact minute I must dress, put on my pants, go back to life, that is to outside life, streets and what not, as we agreed, it is now one-*fifteen* and time's running, running—"

"Well, all right, Dean, but please be sure and be back at three."

"Just as I said, darling, and remember not three but three-fourteen. Are we straight in the deepest and most wonderful depths of our souls, dear darling?" And he went over and kissed her several times. On the wall was a nude drawing of Dean, enormous dangle and all, done by Camille. I was amazed. Everything was so crazy.

Off we rushed into the night; Carlo joined us in an alley. And we proceeded down the narrowest, strangest, and most crooked little city street I've ever seen, deep in the heart of Denver Mexican-town. We talked in loud voices in the sleeping stillness. "Sal," said Dean, "I have just the girl waiting for you at this very minute—if she's off duty" (looking at his watch). "A waitress, Rita Bettencourt, fine chick, slightly hung-up on a few sexual difficulties which I've tried to straighten up and I think you can manage, you fine gone daddy you. So we'll go there at once—we must bring beer, no, they have some themselves, and damn!" he said socking his palm. "I've just got to get into her sister Mary tonight."

"What?" said Carlo. "I thought we were going to talk."

"Yes, yes, after."

"Oh, these Denver doldrums!" yelled Carlo to the sky.

"Isn't he the finest sweetest fel-low in the world?" said Dean, punching me in the ribs. "Look at him. *Look* at him!" And Carlo began his monkey dance in the streets of life as I'd seen him do so many times everywhere in New York.

And all I could say was, "Well, what the hell are we doing in Denver?"

"Tomorrow, Sal, I know where I can find you a job," said

Dean, reverting to businesslike tones. "So I'll call on you, soon as I have an hour off from Marylou, and cut right into that apartment of yours, say hello to Major, and take you on a trolley (damn, I've no car) to the Camargo markets, where you can begin working at once and collect a paycheck come Friday. We're really all of us bottomly broke. I haven't had time to work in weeks. Friday night beyond all doubt the three of us—the old threesome of Carlo, Dean, and Sal—must go to the midget auto races, and for that I can get us a ride from a guy downtown I know. . . ." And on and on into the night.

We got to the house where the waitress sisters lived. The one for me was still working; the sister that Dean wanted was in. We sat down on her couch. I was scheduled at this time to call Ray Rawlins. I did. He came over at once. Coming into the door, he took off his shirt and undershirt and began hugging the absolute stranger, Mary Bettencourt. Bottles rolled on the floor. Three o'clock came. Dean rushed off for his hour of reverie with Camille. He was back on time. The other sister showed up. We all needed a car now, and we were making too much noise. Ray Rawlins called up a buddy with a car. He came. We all piled in; Carlo was trying to conduct his scheduled talk with Dean in the back seat, but there was too much confusion. "Let's all go to my apartment!" I shouted. We did; the moment the car stopped there I jumped out and stood on my head in the grass. All my keys fell out; I never found them. We ran, shouting, into the building. Roland Major stood barring our way in his silk dressing gown.

"I'll have no goings-on like this in Tim Gray's apartment!"

"What?" we all shouted. There was confusion. Rawlins was rolling in the grass with one of the waitresses. Major wouldn't let us in. We swore to call Tim Gray and confirm the party and also invite him. Instead we all rushed back to the Denver downtown hangouts. I suddenly found myself alone in the street with no money. My last dollar was gone.

I walked five miles up Colfax to my comfortable bed in the apartment. Major had to let me in. I wondered if Dean and Carlo were having their heart-to-heart. I would find out later. The nights in Denver are cool, and I slept like a log.

8

Then everybody began planning a tremendous trek to the mountains. This started in the morning, together with a phone call that complicated matters—my old road friend Eddie, who took a blind chance and called; he remembered some of the names I had mentioned. Now I had the opportunity to get my shirt back. Eddie was with his girl in a house off Colfax. He wanted to know if I knew where to find work, and I told him to come over, figuring Dean would know. Dean arrived, hurrying, while Major and I were having a hasty breakfast. Dean wouldn't even sit down. "I have a thousand things to do, in fact hardly any time to take you down Camargo, but let's go, man."

"Wait for my road buddy Eddie."

Major found our hurrying troubles amusing. He'd come to Denver to write leisurely. He treated Dean with extreme deference. Dean paid no attention. Major talked to Dean like this: "Moriarty, what's this I hear about you sleeping with three girls at the same time?" And Dean shuffled on the rug and said, "Oh yes, oh yes, that's the way it goes," and looked at his watch, and Major snuffed down his nose. I felt sheepish rushing off with Dean—Major insisted he was a moron and a fool. Of course he wasn't, and I wanted to prove it to everybody somehow.

We met Eddie. Dean paid no attention to him either, and off we went in a trolley across the hot Denver noon to find the jobs. I hated the thought of it. Eddie talked and talked the way he always did. We found a man in the markets who agreed to hire both of us; work started at four o'clock in the morning and went till six P.M. The man said, "I like boys who like to work."

"You've got your man," said Eddie, but I wasn't so sure about myself. "I just won't sleep," I decided. There were so many other interesting things to do.

Eddie showed up the next morning; I didn't. I had a bed, and Major bought food for the icebox, and in exchange for that I cooked and washed the dishes. Meantime I got all involved in everything. A big party took place at the Rawlinses' one night. The Rawlins mother was gone on a trip. Ray Rawlins called everybody he knew and told them to bring whisky; then he went through his address book for girls. He made me do most of the talking. A whole bunch of girls showed up. I phoned Carlo to find out what Dean was doing now. Dean was coming to Carlo's at three in the morning. I went there after the party.

Carlo's basement apartment was on Grant Street in an old red-brick rooming house near a church. You went down an alley, down some stone steps, opened an old raw door, and went through a kind of cellar till you came to his board door. It was like the room of a Russian saint: one bed, a candle burning, stone walls that oozed moisture, and a crazy makeshift ikon of some kind that he had made. He read me his poetry. It was called "Denver Doldrums." Carlo woke up in the morning and heard the "vulgar pigeons" yakking in the street outside his cell; he saw the "sad nightingales" nodding on the branches and they reminded him of his mother. A gray shroud fell over the city. The mountains, the magnificent Rockies that you can see to the west from any part of town, were "papier-mâché." The whole universe was crazy and cockeyed and extremely strange. He wrote of Dean as a "child of the rainbow" who bore his torment in his agonized priapus. He referred to him as "Oedipus Eddie" who had to "scrape bubble gum off windowpanes." He brooded in his basement over a huge journal in which he was keeping track of everything that happened every day—everything Dean did and said.

Dean came on schedule. "Everything's straight," he announced. "I'm going to divorce Marylou and marry Camille and go live with her in San Francisco. But this is only after you and I, dear Carlo, go to Texas, dig Old Bull Lee, that gone cat I've never met and both of you've told me so much about, and then I'll go to San Fran."

Then they got down to business. They sat on the bed cross-legged and looked straight at each other. I slouched in a nearby chair and saw all of it. They began with an abstract thought, discussed it; reminded each other of another abstract point forgotten in the rush of events; Dean apologized but promised he could get back to it and manage it fine, bringing up illustrations.

Carlo said, "And just as we were crossing Wazee I wanted to tell you about how I felt of your frenzy with the midgets and it was just then, remember, you pointed out that old bum with the baggy pants and said he looked just like your father?"

"Yes, yes, of course I remember; and not only that, but it started a train of my own, something real wild that I had to tell you, I'd forgotten it, now you just reminded me of it . . ." and two new points were born. They hashed these over. Then Carlo asked Dean if he was honest and specifically if he was being honest with *him* in the bottom of his soul.

"Why do you bring that up again?"

"There's one last thing I want to know——"

"But, dear Sal, you're listening, you're sitting there, we'll ask Sal. What would he say?"

And I said, "That last thing is what you can't get, Carlo. Nobody can get to that last thing. We keep on living in hopes of catching it once for all."

"No, no, no, you're talking absolute bullshit and Wolfean romantic posh!" said Carlo.

And Dean said, "I didn't mean that at all, but we'll let Sal have his own mind, and in fact, don't you think, Carlo, there's a kind of a dignity in the way he's sitting there and digging us, crazy cat came all the way across the country—old Sal won't tell, old Sal won't tell."

"It isn't that I won't tell," I protested. "I just don't know what you're both driving at or trying to get at. I know it's too much for anybody."

"Everything you say is negative."

"Then what is it you're trying to do?"

"Tell him."

"No, you tell him."

"There's nothing to tell," I said and laughed. I had on Carlo's hat. I pulled it down over my eyes. "I want to sleep," I said.

"Poor Sal always wants to sleep." I kept quiet. They started in again. "When you borrowed that nickel to make up the check for the chicken-fried steaks——"

"No, man, the chili! Remember, the Texas Star?"

"I was mixing it with Tuesday. When you borrowed that nickel you said, now listen, you said, 'Carlo, this is the last time

I'll impose on you,' as if, and really, you meant that I had agreed with you about no more imposing."

"No, no, no, I didn't mean that—you harken back now if you will, my dear fellow, to the night Marylou was crying in the room, and when, turning to you and indicating by my extra added sincerity of tone which we both knew was contrived but had its intention, that is, by my play-acting I showed that— But wait, that isn't it."

"Of course that isn't it! Because you forget that— But I'll stop accusing you. Yes is what I said . . ." And on, on into the night they talked like this. At dawn I looked up. They were tying up the last of the morning's matters. "When I said to you that I had to sleep *because* of Marylou, that is, seeing her this morning at ten, I didn't bring my peremptory tone to bear in regard to what you'd just said about the unnecessariness of sleep but only, *only*, mind you, because of the fact that I absolutely, simply, purely and without any whatevers have to sleep now, I mean, man, my eyes are closing, they're redhot, sore, tired, beat . . ."

"Ah, child," said Carlo.

"We'll just have to sleep now. Let's stop the machine."

"You can't stop the machine!" yelled Carlo at the top of his voice. The first birds sang.

"Now, when I raise my hand," said Dean, "we'll stop talking, we'll both understand purely and without any hassle that we are simply stopping talking, and we'll just sleep."

"You can't stop the machine like that."

"Stop the machine," I said. They looked at me.

"He's been awake all this time, listening. What were you thinking, Sal?" I told them that I was thinking they were very amazing maniacs and that I had spent the whole night listening to them like a man watching the mechanism of a watch that reached clear to the top of Berthoud Pass and yet was made with the smallest works of the most delicate watch in the world. They smiled. I pointed my finger at them and said, "If you keep this up you'll both go crazy, but let me know what happens as you go along."

I walked out and took a trolley to my apartment, and Carlo Marx's papier-mâché mountains grew red as the great sun rose from the eastward plains.

9

In the evening I was involved in that trek to the mountains and didn't see Dean or Carlo for five days. Babe Rawlins had the use of her employer's car for the weekend. We brought suits and hung them on the car windows and took off for Central City, Ray Rawlins driving, Tim Gray lounging in the back, and Babe up front. It was my first view of the interior of the Rockies. Central City is an old mining town that was once called the Richest Square Mile in the World, where a veritable shelf of silver had been found by the old buzzards who roamed the hills. They grew wealthy overnight and had a beautiful little opera house built in the midst of their shacks on the steep slope. Lillian Russell had come there, and opera stars from Europe. Then Central City became a ghost town, till the energetic Chamber of Commerce types of the new West decided to revive the place. They polished up the opera house, and every summer stars from the Metropolitan came out and performed. It was a big vacation for everybody. Tourists came from everywhere, even Hollywood stars. We drove up the mountain and found the narrow streets chock full of chichi tourists. I thought of Major's Sam, and Major was right. Major himself was there, turning on his big social smile to everybody and ooh-ing and aah-ing most sincerely over everything. "Sal," he cried, clutching my arm, "just look at this old town. Think how it was a hundred—what the hell, only eighty, sixty years ago; they had opera!"

"Yeah," I said, imitating one of his characters, "but *they're* here."

"The bastards," he cursed. But he went off to enjoy himself, Betty Gray on his arm.

Babe Rawlins was an enterprising blonde. She knew of an old miner's house at the edge of town where we boys could sleep for the weekend; all we had to do was clean it out. We could also throw vast parties there. It was an old shack of a thing covered with an inch of dust inside; it had a porch and a well in back. Tim Gray and Ray Rawlins rolled up their sleeves and started in cleaning it, a major job that took them all afternoon and part of the night. But they had a bucket of beer-bottles and everything was fine.

As for me, I was scheduled to be a guest at the opera that afternoon, escorting Babe on my arm. I wore a suit of Tim's. Only a few days ago I'd come into Denver like a bum; now I was all racked up sharp in a suit, with a beautiful well-dressed blonde on my arm, bowing to dignitaries and chatting in the lobby under chandeliers. I wondered what Mississippi Gene would say if he could see me.

The opera was *Fidelio*. "What gloom!" cried the baritone, rising out of the dungeon under a groaning stone. I cried for it. That's how I see life too. I was so interested in the opera that for a while I forgot the circumstances of my crazy life and got lost in the great mournful sounds of Beethoven and the rich Rembrandt tones of his story.

"Well, Sal, how did you like the production for this year?" asked Denver D. Doll proudly in the street outside. He was connected with the opera association.

"What gloom, what gloom," I said. "It's absolutely great."

"The next thing you'll have to do is meet the members of the cast," he went on in his official tones, but luckily he forgot this in the rush of other things, and vanished.

Babe and I went back to the miner's shack. I took off my duds and joined the boys in the cleaning. It was an enormous job. Roland Major sat in the middle of the front room that had already been cleaned and refused to help. On a little table in front of him he had his bottle of beer and his glass. As we rushed around with buckets of water and brooms he reminisced. "Ah, if you could just come with me sometime and drink Cinzano and hear the musicians of Bandol, then you'd be living. Then there's Normandy in the summers, the sabots, the fine old Calvados. Come on, Sam," he said to his invisible pal. "Take the wine out of the water and let's see if it got cold enough while we fished." Straight out of Hemingway, it was.

We called out to girls who went by in the street. "Come on help us clean up the joint. Everybody's invited to our party tonight." They joined us. We had a huge crew working for us. Finally the singers in the opera chorus, mostly young kids, came over and pitched in. The sun went down.

Our day's work over, Tim, Rawlins, and I decided to sharp up for the big night. We went across town to the rooming house where the opera stars were living. Across the night we heard the beginning of the evening performance. "Just right," said Rawlins. "Latch on to some of these razors and towels and we'll spruce up a bit." We also took hairbrushes, colognes, shaving lotions, and went laden into the bathroom. We all took baths and sang. "Isn't this great?" Tim Gray kept saying. "Using the opera stars' bathroom and towels and shaving lotion and electric razors."

It was a wonderful night. Central City is two miles high; at first you get drunk on the altitude, then you get tired, and there's a fever in your soul. We approached the lights around the opera house down the narrow dark street; then we took a sharp right and hit some old saloons with swinging doors. Most of the tourists were in the opera. We started off with a few extra-size beers. There was a player piano. Beyond the back door was a view of mountainsides in the moonlight. I let out a yahoo. The night was on.

We hurried back to our miner's shack. Everything was in preparation for the big party. The girls, Babe and Betty, cooked up a snack of beans and franks, and then we danced and started on the beer for fair. The opera over, great crowds of young girls came piling into our place. Rawlins and Tim and I licked our lips. We grabbed them and danced. There was no music, just dancing. The place filled up. People began to bring bottles. We rushed out to hit the bars and rushed back. The night was getting more and more frantic. I wished Dean and Carlo were there—then I realized they'd be out of place and unhappy. They were like the man with the dungeon stone and the gloom, rising from the underground, the sordid hipsters of America, a new beat generation that I was slowly joining.

The boys from the chorus showed up. They began singing "Sweet Adeline." They also sang phrases such as "Pass me the beer" and "What are you doing with your face hanging out?" and great long baritone howls of "Fi-de-lio!" "Ah me, what gloom!" I sang. The girls were terrific. They went out in the backyard and necked with us. There were beds in the other rooms, the uncleaned dusty ones, and I had a girl sitting on one and was talking with her when suddenly there was a great in-rush of young ushers from the opera, who just grabbed girls and kissed them without proper come-ons. Teenagers, drunk, disheveled, excited—they ruined our party. Inside of five minutes every single girl was gone and a great big fraternity-type party got under way with banging of beerbottles and roars.

Ray and Tim and I decided to hit the bars. Major was gone, Babe and Betty were gone. We tottered into the night. The opera crowd was jamming the bars from bar to wall. Major was shouting above heads. The eager, bespectacled Denver D. Doll was shaking hands with everybody and saying, "Good afternoon, how are you?" and when midnight came he was saying, "Good afternoon, how are *you*?" At one point I saw him going off somewhere with a dignitary. Then he came back with a middle-aged woman; next minute he was talking to a couple of young ushers in the street. The next minute he was shaking my hand without recognizing me and saying, "Happy New Year, m'boy." He wasn't drunk on liquor, just drunk on what he liked—crowds of people milling. Everybody knew him. "Happy New Year," he called, and sometimes "Merry Christmas." He said this all the time. At Christmas he said Happy Halloween.

There was a tenor in the bar who was highly respected by everyone; Denver Doll had insisted that I meet him and I was trying to avoid it; his name was D'Annunzio or some such thing. His wife was with him. They sat sourly at a table. There was also some kind of Argentinian tourist at the bar. Rawlins gave him a shove to make room; he turned and snarled. Rawlins handed me his glass and knocked him down on the brass rail with one punch. The man was momentarily out. There were screams; Tim and I scooted Rawlins out. There was so much confusion the sheriff couldn't even thread his way through the crowd to find the victim. Nobody could identify Rawlins. We went to other bars. Major staggered up a dark street. "What the hell's the matter? Any fights? Just call on me." Great laughter rang from all sides. I wondered what the Spirit of the Mountain was thinking, and looked up and saw jackpines in the moon, and saw ghosts of old miners, and wondered about it. In the whole eastern dark wall of the Divide this night there was silence and the whisper of the wind, except in the ravine where we roared; and on the other side of the Divide was the great Western Slope, and the big plateau that went to Steamboat Springs, and dropped, and led you to the Eastern Colorado desert and the Utah desert; all in darkness now as we fumed and screamed in our mountain nook, mad drunken Americans in the mighty land. We were on the roof of America and all we could do was yell, I guess—across the night, eastward over the Plains, where somewhere an old man with white hair was probably walking toward us with the Word, and would arrive any minute and make us silent.

Rawlins insisted on going back to the bar where he'd fought. Tim and I didn't like it but stuck to him. He went up to D'Annunzio, the tenor, and threw a highball in his face. We dragged him out. A baritone singer from the chorus joined us and we went to a regular Central City bar. Here Ray called the waitress a whore. A group of sullen men were ranged along the bar; they hated tourists. One of them said, "You boys better be out of here by the count of ten." We were. We staggered back to the shack and went to sleep.

In the morning I woke up and turned over; a big cloud of dust rose from the mattress. I yanked at the window; it was nailed. Tim Gray was in the bed too. We coughed and sneezed. Our breakfast consisted of stale beer. Babe came back from her hotel and we got our things together to leave.

Everything seemed to be collapsing. As we were going out to the car Babe slipped and fell flat on her face. Poor girl was overwrought. Her brother and Tim and I helped her up. We got in the car; Major and Betty joined us. The sad ride back to Denver began.

Suddenly we came down from the mountain and overlooked the great sea-plain of Denver; heat rose as from an oven. We began to sing songs. I was itching to get on to San Francisco.

10

That night I found Carlo and to my amazement he told me he'd been in Central City with Dean.

"What did you do?"

"Oh, we ran around the bars and then Dean stole a car and we drove back down the mountain curves ninety miles an hour."

"I didn't see you."

"We didn't know you were there."

"Well, man, I'm going to San Francisco."

"Dean has Rita lined up for you tonight."

"Well, then, I'll put it off." I had no money. I sent my aunt an airmail letter asking her for fifty dollars and said it would be the last money I'd ask; after that she would be getting money back from me, as soon as I got that ship.

Then I went to meet Rita Bettencourt and took her back to the apartment. I got her in my bedroom after a long talk in the dark of the front room. She was a nice little girl, simple and true, and tremendously frightened of sex. I told her it was beautiful. I wanted to prove this to her. She let me prove it, but I was too impatient and proved nothing. She sighed in the dark. "What do you want out of life?" I asked, and I used to ask that all the time of girls.

"I don't know," she said. "Just wait on tables and try to get along." She yawned. I put my hand over her mouth and told her not to yawn. I tried to tell her how excited I was about life and the things we could do together; saying that, and planning to leave Denver in two days. She turned away wearily. We lay on our backs, looking at the ceiling and wondering what God had wrought when He made life so sad. We made vague plans to meet in Frisco.

My moments in Denver were coming to an end, I could feel it when I walked her home, on the way back I stretched out on the grass of an old church with a bunch of hobos, and their talk made me want to get back on that road. Every now and then one would get up and hit a passer-by for a dime. They talked of harvests moving north. It was warm and soft. I wanted to go and get Rita again and tell her a lot more things, and really make love to her this time, and calm her fears about men. Boys and girls in America have such a sad time together; sophistication demands that they submit to sex immediately without proper preliminary talk. Not courting talk—real straight talk about souls, for life is holy and every moment is precious. I heard the Denver and Rio Grande locomotive howling off to the mountains. I wanted to pursue my star further.

Major and I sat sadly talking in the midnight hours. "Have you ever read *Green Hills of Africa*? It's Hemingway's best."

We wished each other luck. We would meet in Frisco. I saw
Rawlins under a dark tree in the street. "Good-by, Ray. When
do we meet again?" I went to look for Carlo and Dean—
nowhere to be found. Tim Gray shot his hand up in the air and
said, "So you're leaving, Yo." We called each other Yo. "Yep,"
I said. The next few days I wandered around Denver. It
seemed to me every bum on Larimer Street maybe was Dean
Moriarty's father; Old Dean Moriarty they called him, the
Tinsmith. I went in the Windsor Hotel, where father and son
had lived and where one night Dean was frightfully waked up
by the legless man on the rollerboard who shared the room
with them; he came thundering across the floor on his terrible
wheels to touch the boy. I saw the little midget newspaper-
selling woman with the short legs, on the corner of Curtis and
15th. I walked around the sad honkytonks of Curtis Street;
young kids in jeans and red shirts; peanut shells, movie marquees, shooting parlors. Beyond the glittering street was darkness, and beyond the darkness the West. I had to go.

At dawn I found Carlo. I read some of his enormous journal, slept there, and in the morning, drizzly and gray, tall, six-
foot Ed Dunkel came in with Roy Johnson, a handsome kid,
and Tom Snark, the clubfooted poolshark. They sat around
and listened with abashed smiles as Carlo Marx read them his
apocalyptic, mad poetry. I slumped in my chair, finished. "Oh
ye Denver birds!" cried Carlo. We all filed out and went up
a typical cobbled Denver alley between incinerators smoking
slowly. "I used to roll my hoop up this alley," Chad King had
told me. I wanted to see him do it; I wanted to see Denver ten
years ago when they were all children, and in the sunny cherry
blossom morning of springtime in the Rockies rolling their
hoops up the joyous alleys full of promise—the whole gang.
And Dean, ragged and dirty, prowling by himself in his preoccupied frenzy.

Roy Johnson and I walked in the drizzle; I went to Eddie's
girl's house to get back my wool plaid shirt, the shirt of Shelton, Nebraska. It was there, all tied up, the whole enormous
sadness of a shirt. Roy Johnson said he'd meet me in Frisco.
Everybody was going to Frisco. I went and found my money
had arrived. The sun came out, and Tim Gray rode a trolley
with me to the bus station. I bought my ticket to San Fran,

spending half of the fifty, and got on at two o'clock in the afternoon. Tim Gray waved good-by. The bus rolled out of the storied, eager Denver streets. "By God, I gotta come back and see what else will happen!" I promised. In a last-minute phone call Dean said he and Carlo might join me on the Coast; I pondered this, and realized I hadn't talked to Dean for more than five minutes in the whole time.

II

I was two weeks late meeting Remi Boncœur. The bus trip from Denver to Frisco was uneventful except that my whole soul leaped to it the nearer we got to Frisco. Cheyenne again, in the afternoon this time, and then west over the range; crossing the Divide at midnight at Creston, arriving at Salt Lake City at dawn—a city of sprinklers, the least likely place for Dean to have been born; then out to Nevada in the hot sun, Reno by night-fall, its twinkling Chinese streets; then up the Sierra Nevada, pines, stars, mountain lodges signifying Frisco romances—a little girl in the back seat, crying to her mother, "Mama when do we get home to Truckee?" And Truckee itself, homey Truckee, and then down the hill to the flats of Sacramento. I suddenly realized I was in California. Warm, palmy air—air you can kiss—and palms. Along the storied Sacramento River on a superhighway; into the hills again; up, down; and suddenly the vast expanse of bay (it was just before dawn) with the sleepy lights of Frisco festooned across. Over the Oakland Bay Bridge I slept soundly for the first time since Denver; so that I was rudely jolted in the bus station at Market and Fourth into the memory of the fact that I was three thousand two hundred miles from my aunt's house in Paterson, New Jersey. I wandered out like a haggard ghost, and there she was, Frisco—long, bleak streets with trolley wires all shrouded in fog and whiteness. I stumbled around a few blocks. Weird bums (Mission and Third) asked me for dimes in the dawn. I heard music somewhere. "Boy, am I going to dig all this later! But now I've got to find Remi Boncœur."

Mill City, where Remi lived, was a collection of shacks in a valley, housing-project shacks built for Navy Yard workers during the war; it was in a canyon, and a deep one, treed profusedly on all slopes. There were special stores and barber shops and tailor shops for the people of the project. It was, so they say, the only community in America where whites and Negroes lived together voluntarily; and that was so, and so wild and joyous a place I've never seen since. On the door of Remi's shack was the note he had pinned up there three weeks ago.

Sal Paradise! [in huge letters, printed] If nobody's home climb in through the window.

> Signed,
> Remi Boncoeur.

The note was weatherbeaten and gray by now.

I climbed in and there he was, sleeping with his girl, Lee Ann—on a bed he stole from a merchant ship, as he told me later; imagine the deck engineer of a merchant ship sneaking over the side in the middle of the night with a bed, and heaving and straining at the oars to shore. This barely explains Remi Boncœur.

The reason I'm going into everything that happened in San Fran is because it ties up with everything else all the way down the line. Remi Boncœur and I met at prep school years ago; but the thing that really linked us together was my former wife. Remi found her first. He came into my dorm room one night and said, "Paradise, get up, the old maestro has come to see you." I got up and dropped some pennies on the floor when I put my pants on. It was four in the afternoon; I used to sleep all the time in college. "All right, all right, don't drop your gold all over the place. I have found the gonest little girl in the world and I am going straight to the Lion's Den with her tonight." And he dragged me to meet her. A week later she was going with me. Remi was a tall, dark, handsome Frenchman (he looked like a kind of Marseille black-marketeer of twenty); because he was French he had to talk in jazz American; his English was perfect, his French was perfect. He liked to dress sharp, slightly on the collegiate side, and go out with fancy blondes and spend a lot of money. It's not that he ever blamed me for taking off with his girl; it was only a point that always tied us together; that guy was loyal to me and had real affection for me, and God knows why.

When I found him in Mill City that morning he had fallen on the beat and evil days that come to young guys in their middle twenties. He was hanging around waiting for a ship, and to earn his living he had a job as a special guard in the barracks across the canyon. His girl Lee Ann had a bad tongue and gave him a calldown every day. They spent all week saving pennies and went out Saturdays to spend fifty bucks in three hours. Remi wore shorts around the shack, with a crazy Army cap on his head. Lee Ann went around with her hair up in pincurls. Thus attired, they yelled at each other all week. I never saw so many snarls in all my born days. But on Saturday night, smiling graciously at each other, they took off like a pair of successful Hollywood characters and went on the town.

Remi woke up and saw me come in the window. His great laugh, one of the greatest laughs in the world, dinned in my ear. "Aaaaah Paradise, he comes in through the window, he follows instructions to a T. Where have you been, you're two weeks late!" He slapped me on the back, he punched Lee Ann in the ribs, he leaned on the wall and laughed and cried, he pounded the table so you could hear it everywhere in Mill City, and that great long "Aaaaah" resounded around the canyon. "Paradise!" he screamed. "The one and only indispensable Paradise."

I had just come through the little fishing village of Sausalito, and the first thing I said was, "There must be a lot of Italians in Sausalito."

"There must be a lot of Italians in Sausalito!" he shouted at the top of his lungs. "Aaaaah!" He pounded himself, he fell on the bed, he almost rolled on the floor. "Did you hear what Paradise said? There must be a lot of Italians in Sausalito? Aaaahhaaa! Hoo! Wow! Whee!" He got red as a beet, laughing. "Oh, you slay me, Paradise, you're the funniest man in the world, and here you are, you finally got here, he came in through the window, you saw him, Lee Ann, he followed instructions and came in through the window. Aaah! Hooo!"

The strange thing was that next door to Remi lived a Negro called Mr. Snow whose laugh, I swear on the Bible, was positively and finally the one greatest laugh in all this world. This

Mr. Snow began his laugh from the supper table when his old wife said something casual; he got up, apparently choking, leaned on the wall, looked up to heaven, and started; he staggered through the door, leaning on neighbors' walls; he was drunk with it, he reeled throughout Mill City in the shadows, raising his whooping triumphant call to the demon god that must have prodded him to do it. I don't know if he ever finished supper. There's a possibility that Remi, without knowing it, was picking up from this amazing man, Mr. Snow. And though Remi was having worklife problems and bad lovelife with a sharp-tongued woman, he at least had learned to laugh almost better than anyone in the world, and I saw all the fun we were going to have in Frisco.

The pitch was this: Remi slept with Lee Ann in the bed across the room, and I slept in the cot by the window. I was not to touch Lee Ann. Remi at once made a speech concerning this. "I don't want to find you two playing around when you think I'm not looking. You can't teach the old maestro a new tune. This is an original saying of mine." I looked at Lee Ann. She was a fetching hunk, a honey-colored creature, but there was hate in her eyes for both of us. Her ambition was to marry a rich man. She came from a small town in Oregon. She rued the day she ever took up with Remi. On one of his big showoff weekends he spent a hundred dollars on her and she thought she'd found an heir. Instead she was hung-up in this shack, and for lack of anything else she had to stay there. She had a job in Frisco; she had to take the Greyhound bus at the crossroads and go in every day. She never forgave Remi for it.

I was to stay in the shack and write a shining original story for a Hollywood studio. Remi was going to fly down in a stratosphere liner with this harp under his arm and make us all rich; Lee Ann was to go with him; he was going to introduce her to his buddy's father, who was a famous director and an intimate of W. C. Fields. So the first week I stayed in the shack in Mill City, writing furiously at some gloomy tale about New York that I thought would satisfy a Hollywood director, and the trouble with it was that it was too sad. Remi could barely read it, and so he just carried it down to Hollywood a few weeks later. Lee Ann was too bored and hated us too much to bother reading it. I spent countless rainy hours drinking coffee and scribbling. Finally I told Remi it wouldn't do; I wanted a job; I had to depend on them for cigarettes. A shadow of disappointment crossed Remi's brow—he was always being disappointed about the funniest things. He had a heart of gold.

He arranged to get me the same kind of job he had, as a guard in the barracks. I went through the necessary routine, and to my surprise the bastards hired me. I was sworn in by the local police chief, given a badge, a club, and now I was a special policeman. I wondered what Dean and Carlo and Old Bull Lee would say about this. I had to have navy-blue trousers to go with my black jacket and cop cap; for the first two weeks I had to wear Remi's trousers; since he was so tall, and had a potbelly from eating voracious meals out of boredom, I went flapping around like Charlie Chaplin to my first night of work. Remi gave me a flashlight and his .32 automatic.

"Where'd you get this gun?" I asked.

"On my way to the Coast last summer I jumped off the train at North Platte, Nebraska, to stretch my legs, and what did I see in the window but this unique little gun, which I promptly bought and barely made the train."

And I tried to tell him what North Platte meant to me, buying the whisky with the boys, and he slapped me on the back and said I was the funniest man in the world.

With the flashlight to illuminate my way, I climbed the steep walls of the south canyon, got up on the highway streaming with cars Frisco-bound in the night, scrambled down the other side, almost falling, and came to the bottom of a ravine where a little farmhouse stood near a creek and where every blessed night the same dog barked at me. Then it was a fast walk along a silvery, dusty road beneath inky trees of California—a road like in *The Mark of Zorro* and a road like all the roads you see in Western B movies. I used to take out my gun and play cowboys in the dark. Then I climbed another hill and there were the barracks. These barracks were for the temporary quartering of overseas construction workers. The men who came through stayed there, waiting for their ship. Most of them were bound for Okinawa. Most of them were running away from something—usually the law. There were tough groups from Alabama, shifty men from New York, all kinds from all over. And, knowing full well how horrible it would be to work a full year in Okinawa, they drank. The job of the special guards was to see that they didn't tear the barracks down. We had our headquarters in the main building, just a wooden contraption with panel-walled offices. Here at a rolltop desk we sat around, shifting our guns off our hips and yawning, and the old cops told stories.

It was a horrible crew of men, men with cop-souls, all except Remi and myself. Remi was only trying to make a living, and so was I, but these men wanted to make arrests and get compliments from the chief of police in town. They even said that if you didn't make at least one a month you'd be fired. I gulped at the prospect of making an arrest. What actually happened was that I was as drunk as anybody in the barracks the night all hell broke loose.

This was a night when the schedule was so arranged that I was all alone for six hours—the only cop on the grounds; and everybody in the barracks seemed to have gotten drunk that night. It was because their ship was leaving in the morning. They drank like seamen the night before the anchor goes up. I sat in the office with my feet on the desk, reading *Blue Book* adventures about Oregon and the north country, when suddenly I realized there was a great hum of activity in the usually quiet night. I went out. Lights were burning in practically every damned shack on the grounds. Men were shouting, bottles were breaking. It was do or die for me. I took my flashlight and went to the noisiest door and knocked. Someone opened it about six inches.

"What do *you* want?"

I said, "I'm guarding these barracks tonight and you boys are supposed to keep quiet as much as you can"—or some such silly remark. They slammed the door in my face. I stood looking at the wood of it against my nose. It was like a Western movie; the time had come for me to assert myself. I knocked again. They opened up wide this time. "Listen," I said, "I don't want to come around bothering you fellows, but I'll lose my job if you make too much noise."

"Who are you?"

"I'm a guard here."

"Never seen you before."

"Well, here's my badge."

"What are you doing with that pistolcracker on your ass?"

"It isn't mine," I apologized. "I borrowed it."

"Have a drink, fer krissakes." I didn't mind if I did. I took two.

I said, "Okay, boys? You'll keep quiet, boys? I'll get hell, you know."

"It's all right, kid," they said. "Go make your rounds. Come back for another drink if you want one."

And I went to all the doors in this manner, and pretty soon I was as drunk as anybody else. Come dawn, it was my duty to put up the American flag on a sixty-foot pole, and this morning I put it up upside down and went home to bed. When I came back in the evening the regular cops were sitting around grimly in the office.

"Say, bo, what was all the noise around here last night? We've had complaints from people who live in those houses across the canyon."

"I don't know," I said. "It sounds pretty quiet right now."

"The whole contingent's gone. You was supposed to keep order around here last night—the chief is yelling at you. And another thing—do you know you can go to jail for putting the American flag upside down on a government pole?"

"Upside down?" I was horrified; of course I hadn't realized it. I did it every morning mechanically.

"Yessir," said a fat cop who'd spent twenty-two years as a guard in Alcatraz. "You could go to jail for doing something like that." The others nodded grimly. They were always sitting around on their asses; they were proud of their jobs. They handled their guns and talked about them. They were itching to shoot somebody. Remi and me.

The cop who had been an Alcatraz guard was potbellied and about sixty, retired but unable to keep away from the atmospheres that had nourished his dry soul all his life. Every night he drove to work in his '35 Ford, punched the clock exactly on time, and sat down at the rolltop desk. He labored painfully over the simple form we all had to fill out every night— rounds, time, what happened, and so on. Then he leaned back and told stories. "You should have been here about two months ago when me and Sledge" (that was another cop, a youngster who wanted to be a Texas Ranger and had to be satisfied with his present lot) "arrested a drunk in Barrack G. Boy, you should have seen the blood fly. I'll take you over there tonight and show you the stains on the wall. We had him bouncing from one wall to another. First Sledge hit him, and then me, and then he subsided and went quietly. That fellow swore to kill us when he got out of jail—got thirty days. Here it is *sixty* days, and he ain't showed up." And this was the big point of the story. They'd put such a fear in him that he was too yellow to come back and try to kill them.

The old cop went on, sweetly reminiscing about the horrors of Alcatraz. "We used to march 'em like an Army platoon to breakfast. Wasn't one man out of step. Everything went like clockwork. You should have seen it. I was a guard there for twenty-two years. Never had any trouble. Those boys knew we meant business. A lot of fellows get soft guarding prisoners, and they're the ones that usually get in trouble. Now you take you—from what I've been observing about you, you seem to me a little bit too *leenent* with the men." He raised his pipe and looked at me sharp. "They take advantage of that, you know."

I knew that. I told him I wasn't cut out to be a cop.

"Yes, but that's the job that you *applied for.* Now you got to make up your mind one way or the other, or you'll never get anywhere. It's your duty. You're sworn in. You can't compromise with things like this. Law and order's got to be kept."

I didn't know what to say; he was right; but all I wanted to do was sneak out into the night and disappear somewhere, and go and find out what everybody was doing all over the country.

The other cop, Sledge, was tall, muscular, with a black-haired crew-cut and a nervous twitch in his neck—like a boxer who's always punching one fist into another. He rigged himself out like a Texas Ranger of old. He wore a revolver down low, with ammunition belt, and carried a small quirt of some kind, and pieces of leather hanging everywhere, like a walking torture chamber: shiny shoes, low-hanging jacket, cocky hat, everything but boots. He was always showing me holds—reaching down under my crotch and lifting me up nimbly. In point of strength I could have thrown him clear to the ceiling with the same hold, and I knew it well; but I never let him know for fear he'd want a wrestling match. A wrestling match with a guy like that would end up in shooting. I'm sure he was a better shot; I'd never had a gun in my life. It scared me even to load one. He desperately wanted to make arrests. One night we were alone on duty and he came back red-faced mad.

"I told some boys in there to keep quiet and they're still making noise. I told them twice. I always give a man two chances. Not three. You come with me and I'm going back there and arrest them."

"Well, let *me* give them a third chance," I said. "I'll talk to them."

"No, sir, I never gave a man more than two chances." I sighed. Here we go. We went to the offending room, and Sledge opened the door and told everybody to file out. It was embarrassing. Every single one of us was blushing. This is the story of America. Everybody's doing what they think they're supposed to do. So what if a bunch of men talk in loud voices and drink the night? But Sledge wanted to prove something. He made sure to bring me along in case they jumped him. They might have. They were all brothers, all from Alabama. We strolled back to the station, Sledge in front and me in back.

One of the boys said to me, "Tell that crotch-eared mean-ass to take it easy on us. We might get fired for this and never get to Okinawa."

"I'll talk to him."

In the station I told Sledge to forget it. He said, for everybody to hear, and blushing, "I don't give anybody no more than two chances."

"What the hail," said the Alabaman, "what difference does it make? We might lose our jobs." Sledge said nothing and filled out the arrest forms. He arrested only one of them; he called the prowl car in town. They came and took him away. The other brothers walked off sullenly. "What's Ma going to say?" they said. One of them came back to me. "You tell that Texass sonofabitch if my brother ain't out of jail tomorrow night he's going to get his ass fixed." I told Sledge, in a neutral way, and he said nothing. The brother was let off easy and nothing happened. The contingent shipped out; a new wild bunch came in. If it hadn't been for Remi Boncœur I wouldn't have stayed at this job two hours.

But Remi Boncœur and I were on duty alone many a night, and that's when everything jumped. We made our first round of the evening in a leisurely way, Remi trying all the doors to see if they were locked and hoping to find one unlocked. He'd say, "For years I've an idea to develop a dog into a superthief who'd go into these guys' rooms and take dollars out of their pockets. I'd train him to take nothing but green money; I'd make him smell it all day long. If there was any humanly possible way, I'd train him to take only twenties." Remi was full of mad schemes; he talked about that dog for weeks. Only once he found an unlocked door. I didn't like the idea, so I sauntered on down the hall. Remi stealthily opened it up. He came face to face with the barracks supervisor. Remi hated that man's face. He asked me, "What's the name of that Russian author you're always talking about—the one who put the newspapers in his shoe and walked around in a stovepipe hat he found in a garbage pail?" This was an exaggeration of what I'd told Remi of Dostoevski. "Ah, that's it—that's *it*—Dostioffski. A man with a face like that supervisor can only have one name—it's Dostioffski." The only unlocked door he ever found belonged to Dostioffski. D. was asleep when he heard someone fiddling with his doorknob. He got up in his pajamas. He came to the door looking twice as ugly as usual. When Remi opened it he saw a haggard face suppurated with hatred and dull fury.

"What is the meaning of this?"

"I was only trying this door. I thought this was the—ah—mop room. I was looking for a mop."

"What do you *mean* you were looking for a mop?"

"Well—ah."

And I stepped up and said, "One of the men puked in the hall upstairs. We have to mop it up."

"This is *not* the mop room. This is *my* room. Another incident like this and I'll have you fellows investigated and thrown out! Do you understand me clearly?"

"A fellow puked upstairs," I said again.

"The mop room is down the hall. Down there." And he pointed, and waited for us to go and get a mop, which we did, and foolishly carried it upstairs.

I said, "Goddammit, Remi, you're always getting us into trouble. Why don't you lay off? Why do you have to steal all the time?"

"The world owes me a few things, that's all. You can't teach the old maestro a new tune. You go on talking like that and I'm going to start calling you Dostioffski."

Remi was just like a little boy. Somewhere in his past, in his lonely schooldays in France, they'd taken everything from him; his stepparents just stuck him in schools and left him there; he was browbeaten and thrown out of one school after another; he walked the French roads at night devising curses out of his innocent stock of words. He was out to get back everything he'd lost; there was no end to his loss; this thing would drag on forever.

The barracks cafeteria was our meat. We looked around to make sure nobody was watching, and especially to see if any of our cop friends were lurking about to check on us; then I squatted down, and Remi put a foot on each shoulder and up he went. He opened the window, which was never locked since he saw to it in the evenings, scrambled through, and came down on the flour table. I was a little more agile and just jumped and crawled in. Then we went to the soda fountain. Here, realizing a dream of mine from infancy, I took the cover off the chocolate ice cream and stuck my hand in wrist-deep and hauled me up a skewer of ice cream and licked at it. Then we got ice-cream boxes and stuffed them, poured chocolate syrup over and sometimes strawberries too, then walked around in the kitchens, opened iceboxes, to see what we could take home in our pockets. I often tore off a piece of roast beef and wrapped it in a napkin. "You know what President Truman said," Remi would say. "We must cut down on the cost of living."

One night I waited a long time as he filled a huge box full of groceries. Then we couldn't get it through the window. Remi had to unpack everything and put it back. Later in the night, when he went off duty and I was all alone on the base, a strange thing happened. I was taking a walk along the old canyon trail, hoping to meet a deer (Remi had seen deer around, that country being wild even in 1947), when I heard a frightening noise in the dark. It was a huffing and puffing. I thought it was a rhinoceros coming for me in the dark. I grabbed my gun. A tall figure appeared in the canyon gloom; it had an enormous head. Suddenly I realized it was Remi with a huge box of groceries on his shoulder. He was moaning and groaning from the enormous weight of it. He'd found the key to the cafeteria somewhere and had got his groceries out the front door. I said, "Remi, I thought you were home; what the hell are you doing?"

And he said, "Paradise, I have told you several times what President Truman said, *we must cut down on the cost of living.*" And I heard him huff and puff into the darkness. I've already described that awful trail back to our shack, up hill and down dale. He hid the groceries in the tall grass and came back to me. "Sal, I just can't make it alone. I'm going to divide it into two boxes and you're going to help me."

"But I'm on duty."

"I'll watch the place while you're gone. Things are getting rough all around. We've just got to make it the best way we can, and that's all there is to it." He wiped his face. "Whoo! I've told you time and time again, Sal, that we're buddies, and we're in this thing together. There's just no two ways about it. The Dostioffskis, the cops, the Lee Anns, all the evil skulls of this world, are out for our skin. It's up to us to see that nobody pulls any schemes on us. They've got a lot more up their sleeves besides a dirty arm. Remember that. You can't teach the old maestro a new tune."

I finally asked, "Whatever are we going to do about shipping out?" We'd been doing these things for ten weeks. I was making fifty-five bucks a week and sending my aunt an average of forty. I'd spent only one evening in San Francisco in all that time. My life was wrapped in the shack, in Remi's battles with Lee Ann, and in the middle of the night at the barracks.

Remi was gone off in the dark to get another box. I struggled with him on that old Zorro road. We piled up the groceries a mile high on Lee Ann's kitchen table. She woke up and rubbed her eyes.

"You know what President Truman said?" She was delighted. I suddenly began to realize that everybody in America is a natural-born thief. I was getting the bug myself. I even began to try to see if doors were locked. The other cops were getting suspicious of us; they saw it in our eyes; they understood with unfailing instinct what was on our minds. Years of experience had taught them the likes of Remi and me.

In the daytime Remi and I went out with the gun and tried

to shoot quail in the hills. Remi sneaked up to within three feet of the clucking birds and let go a blast of the .32. He missed. His tremendous laugh roared over the California woods and over America. "The time has come for you and me to go and see the Banana King."

It was Saturday; we got all spruced up and went down to the bus station on the crossroads. We rode into San Francisco and strolled through the streets. Remi's huge laugh resounded everywhere we went. "You must write a story about the Banana King," he warned me. "Don't pull any tricks on the old maestro and write about something else. The Banana King is your meat. There stands the Banana King." The Banana King was an old man selling bananas on the corner. I was completely bored. But Remi kept punching me in the ribs and even dragging me along by the collar. "When you write about the Banana King you write about the human-interest things of life." I told him I didn't give a damn about the Banana King. "Until you learn to realize the importance of the Banana King you will know absolutely nothing about the human-interest things of the world," said Remi emphatically.

There was an old rusty freighter out in the bay that was used as a buoy. Remi was all for rowing out to it, so one afternoon Lee Ann packed a lunch and we hired a boat and went out there. Remi brought some tools. Lee Ann took all her clothes off and lay down to sun herself on the flying bridge. I watched her from the poop. Remi went clear down to the boiler rooms below, where rats scurried around, and began hammering and banging away for copper lining that wasn't there. I sat in the dilapidated officer's mess. It was an old, old ship and had been beautifully appointed, with scrollwork in the wood, and built-in seachests. This was the ghost of the San Francisco of Jack London. I dreamed at the sunny messboard. Rats ran in the pantry. Once upon a time there'd been a blue-eyed sea captain dining in here.

I joined Remi in the bowels below. He yanked at everything loose. "Not a thing. I thought there'd be copper, I thought there'd be at least an old wrench or two. This ship's been stripped by a bunch of thieves." It had been standing in the bay for years. The copper had been stolen by a hand that was a hand no more.

I said to Remi, "I'd love to sleep in this old ship some night when the fog comes in and the thing creaks and you hear the big B-O of the buoys."

Remi was astounded; his admiration for me doubled. "Sal, I'll pay you five dollars if you have the nerve to do that. Don't you realize this thing may be haunted by the ghosts of old sea captains? I'll not only pay you five, I'll row you out and pack you a lunch and lend you blankets and candle."

"Agreed!" I said. Remi ran to tell Lee Ann. I wanted to jump down from a mast and land right in her, but I kept my promise to Remi. I averted my eyes from her.

Meanwhile I began going to Frisco more often; I tried everything in the books to make a girl. I even spent a whole night with a girl on a park bench, till dawn, without success. She was a blonde from Minnesota. There were plenty of queers. Several times I went to San Fran with my gun and when a queer approached me in a bar john I took out the gun and said, "Eh? Eh? What's that you say?" He bolted. I've never understood why I did that; I knew queers all over the country. It was just the loneliness of San Francisco and the fact that I had a gun. I had to show it to someone. I walked by a jewelry store and had the sudden impulse to shoot up the window, take out the finest rings and bracelets, and run to give them to Lee Ann. Then we could flee to Nevada together. The time was coming for me to leave Frisco or I'd go crazy.

I wrote long letters to Dean and Carlo, who were now at Old Bull's shack in the Texas bayou. They said they were ready to come join me in San Fran as soon as this-and-that was ready. Meanwhile everything began to collapse with Remi and Lee Ann and me. The September rains came, and with them harangues. Remi had flown down to Hollywood with her, taking my sad silly movie original, and nothing had happened. The famous director was drunk and paid no attention to them; they hung around his Malibu Beach cottage; they started fighting in front of other guests; and they flew back.

The final topper was the racetrack. Remi saved all his money, about a hundred dollars, spruced me up in some of his clothes, put Lee Ann on his arm, and off we went to Golden Gate racetrack near Richmond across the bay. To show you what a heart that guy had, he put half of our stolen groceries in a tremendous brown paper bag and took them to a poor widow he knew in Richmond in a housing project much like our own, wash flapping in the California sun. We went with him. There were sad ragged children. The woman thanked Remi. She was the sister of some seaman he vaguely knew. "Think nothing of it, Mrs. Carter," said Remi in his most elegant and polite tones. "There's plenty more where that came from."

We proceeded to the racetrack. He made incredible twenty-dollar bets to win, and before the seventh race he was broke. With our last two food dollars he placed still another bet and lost. We had to hitchhike back to San Francisco. I was on the road again. A gentleman gave us a ride in his snazzy car. I sat up front with him. Remi was trying to put a story down that he'd lost his wallet in back of the grandstand at the track. "The truth is," I said, "we lost all our money on the races, and to forestall any more hitching from racetracks, from now on we go to a bookie, hey, Remi?" Remi blushed all over. The man finally admitted he was an official of the Golden Gate track. He let us off at the elegant Palace Hotel; we watched him disappear among the chandeliers, his pockets full of money, his head held high.

"Wagh! Whoo!" howled Remi in the evening streets of Frisco. "Paradise rides with the man who runs the racetrack and *swears* he's switching to bookies. Lee Ann, Lee Ann!" He punched and mauled her. "Positively the funniest man in the world! There must be a lot of Italians in Sausalito. Aaah-how!" He wrapped himself around a pole to laugh.

That night it started raining as Lee Ann gave dirty looks to both of us. Not a cent left in the house. The rain drummed on the roof. "It's going to last for a week," said Remi. He had taken off his beautiful suit; he was back in his miserable shorts and Army cap and T-shirt. His great brown sad eyes stared at the planks of the floor. The gun lay on the table. We could hear Mr. Snow laughing his head off across the rainy night somewhere.

"I get so sick and tired of that sonofabitch," snapped Lee Ann. She was on the go to start trouble. She began needling Remi. He was busy going through his little black book, in which were names of people, mostly seamen, who owed him money. Beside their names he wrote curses in red ink. I dreaded the day I'd ever find my way into that book. Lately I'd been sending so much money to my aunt that I only bought four or five dollars' worth of groceries a week. In keeping with what President Truman said, I added a few more dollars' worth. But Remi felt it wasn't my proper share; so he'd taken to hanging the grocery slips, the long ribbon slips with itemized prices, on the wall of the bathroom for me to see and understand. Lee Ann was convinced Remi was hiding money from her, and that I was too, for that matter. She threatened to leave him.

Remi curled his lip. "Where do you think you'll go?"

"Jimmy."

"*Jimmy?* A cashier at the racetrack? Do you hear that, Sal, Lee Ann is going to go and put the latch on a cashier at the racetrack. Be sure and bring your broom, dear, the horses are going to eat a lot of oats this week with my hundred-dollar bill."

Things grew to worse proportions; the rain roared. Lee Ann originally lived in the place first, so she told Remi to pack up and get out. He started packing. I pictured myself all alone in this rainy shack with that untamed shrew. I tried to intervene. Remi pushed Lee Ann. She made a jump for the gun. Remi gave me the gun and told me to hide it; there was a clip of eight shells in it. Lee Ann began screaming, and finally she put on her raincoat and went out in the mud to find a cop, and what a cop—if it wasn't our old friend Alcatraz. Luckily he wasn't home. She came back all wet. I hid in my corner with my head between my knees. Gad, what was I doing three thousand miles from home? Why had I come here? Where was my slow boat to China?

"And another thing, you dirty man," yelled Lee Ann. "Tonight was the last time I'll ever make you your filthy brains and eggs, and your filthy lamb curry, so you can fill your filthy belly and get fat and sassy right before my eyes."

"It's all right," Remi just said quietly. "It's perfectly all right. When I took up with you I didn't expect roses and moonshine and I'm not surprised this day. I tried to do a few things for you—I tried my best for both of you; you've both let me down. I'm terribly, terribly disappointed in both of you," he continued in absolute sincerity. "I thought something would come of us together, something fine and lasting, I tried, I flew to Hollywood, I got Sal a job, I bought you beautiful dresses, I tried to introduce you to the finest people in San Francisco. You refused, you both refused to follow the slightest wish I had. I asked for nothing in return. Now I ask for one last favor and then I'll never ask a favor again. My stepfather is coming to San Francisco next Saturday night. All I ask is that you come with me and try to look as though everything is the way I've written him. In other words, you, Lee Ann, you are my girl, and you, Sal, you are my friend. I've arranged to borrow a hundred dollars for Saturday night. I'm going to see that my father has a good time and can go away without any reason in the world to worry about me."

This surprised me. Remi's stepfather was a distinguished doctor who had practiced in Vienna, Paris, and London. I said, "You mean to tell me you're going to spend a hundred dollars on your stepfather? He's got more money than you'll ever have! You'll be in debt, man!"

"That's all right," said Remi quietly and with defeat in his voice. "I ask only one last thing of you—that you *try* at least to make things look all right and *try* to make a good impression. I love my stepfather and I respect him. He's coming with his young wife. We must show him every courtesy." There were times when Remi was really the most gentlemanly person in the world. Lee Ann was impressed, and looked forward to meeting his stepfather; she thought he might be a catch, if his son wasn't.

Saturday night rolled around. I had already quit my job with the cops, just before being fired for not making enough arrests, and this was going to be my last Saturday night. Remi and Lee Ann went to meet his stepfather at the hotel room first; I had traveling money and got crocked in the bar downstairs. Then I went up to join them all, late as hell. His father opened the door, a distinguished tall man in pince-nez. "Ah," I said on seeing him. "Monsieur Boncœur, how are you? *Je suis haut!*" I cried, which was intended to mean in French, "I am high, I have been drinking," but means absolutely nothing in French. The doctor was perplexed. I had already screwed up Remi. He blushed at me.

We all went to a swank restaurant to eat—Alfred's, in North Beach, where poor Remi spent a good fifty dollars for the five of us, drinks and all. And now came the worst thing. Who

should be sitting at the bar in Alfred's but my old friend
Roland Major! He had just arrived from Denver and got a job
on a San Francisco paper. He was crocked. He wasn't even
shaved. He rushed over and slapped me on the back as I lifted
a highball to my lips. He threw himself down on the booth
beside Dr. Boncœur and leaned over the man's soup to talk to
me. Remi was red as a beet.

"Won't you introduce your friend, Sal?" he said with a weak
smile.

"Roland Major of the San Francisco *Argus*," I tried to say
with a straight face. Lee Ann was furious at me.

Major began chatting in the monsieur's ear. "How do you
like teaching high-school French?" he yelled.

"Pardon me, but I don't teach high-school French."

"Oh, I thought you taught high-school French." He was
being deliberately rude. I remembered the night he wouldn't
let us have our party in Denver; but I forgave him.

I forgave everybody, I gave up, I got drunk. I began talking
moonshine and roses to the doctor's young wife. I drank so
much I had to go to the men's room every two minutes, and
to do so I had to hop over Dr. Boncœur's lap. Everything was
falling apart. My stay in San Francisco was coming to an end.
Remi would never talk to me again. It was horrible because I
really loved Remi and I was one of the very few people in the
world who knew what a genuine and grand fellow he was. It
would take years for him to get over it. How disastrous all this
was compared to what I'd written him from Paterson, planning my red line Route 6 across America. Here I was at the
end of America—no more land—and now there was nowhere
to go but back. I determined at least to make my trip a circular
one: I decided then and there to go to Hollywood and back
through Texas to see my bayou gang; then the rest be damned.

Major was thrown out of Alfred's. Dinner was over anyway,
so I joined him; that is to say, Remi suggested it, and I went
off with Major to drink. We sat at a table in the Iron Pot and
Major said, "Sam, I don't like that fairy at the bar," in a loud
voice.

"Yeah, Jake?" I said.

"Sam," he said, "I think I'll get up and conk him."

"No, Jake," I said, carrying on with the Hemingway imitation. "Just aim from here and see what happens." We ended up swaying on a street corner.

In the morning, as Remi and Lee Ann slept, and as I looked with some sadness at the big pile of wash Remi and I were scheduled to do in the Bendix machine in the shack in the back (which had always been such a joyous sunny operation among the colored women and with Mr. Snow laughing his head off), I decided to leave. I went out on the porch. "No, dammit," I said to myself, "I promised I wouldn't leave till I climbed that mountain." That was the big side of the canyon that led mysteriously to the Pacific Ocean.

So I stayed another day. It was Sunday. A great heat wave descended; it was a beautiful day, the sun turned red at three. I started up the mountain and got to the top at four. All those lovely California cottonwoods and eucalypti brooded on all sides. Near the peak there were no more trees, just rocks and grass. Cattle were grazing on the top of the coast. There was the Pacific, a few more foothills away, blue and vast and with a great wall of white advancing from the legendary potato patch where Frisco fogs are born. Another hour and it would come streaming through the Golden Gate to shroud the romantic city in white, and a young man would hold his girl by the hand and climb slowly up a long white sidewalk with a bottle of Tokay in his pocket. That was Frisco; and beautiful women standing in white doorways, waiting for their men; and Coit Tower, and the Embarcadero, and Market Street, and the eleven teeming hills.

I spun around till I was dizzy; I thought I'd fall down as in a dream, clear off the precipice. Oh where is the girl I love? I thought, and looked everywhere, as I had looked everywhere in the little world below. And before me was the great raw bulge and bulk of my American continent; somewhere far across, gloomy, crazy New York was throwing up its cloud of dust and brown steam. There is something brown and holy about the East; and California is white like washlines and emptyheaded—at least that's what I thought then.

12

In the morning Remi and Lee Ann were asleep as I quietly packed and slipped out the window the same way I'd come in, and left Mill City with my canvas bag. And I never spent that night on the old ghost ship—the *Admiral Freebee*, it was called —and Remi and I were lost to each other.

In Oakland I had a beer among the bums of a saloon with a wagon wheel in front of it, and I was on the road again. I walked clear across Oakland to get on the Fresno road. Two rides took me to Bakersfield, four hundred miles south. The first was the mad one, with a burly blond kid in a souped-up rod. "See that toe?" he said as he gunned the heap to eighty and passed everybody on the road. "Look at it." It was swathed in bandages. "I just had it amputated this morning. The bastards wanted me to stay in the hospital. I packed my bag and left. What's a toe?" Yes, indeed, I said to myself, look out now, and I hung on. You never saw a driving fool like that. He made Tracy in no time. Tracy is a railroad town; brakemen eat surly meals in diners by the tracks. Trains howl away across the valley. The sun goes down long and red. All the magic names of the valley unrolled—Manteca, Madera, all the rest. Soon it got dusk, a grapy dusk, a purple dusk over tangerine groves and long melon fields; the sun the color of pressed grapes, slashed with burgundy red, the fields the color of love and Spanish mysteries. I stuck my head out the window and took deep breaths of the fragrant air. It was the most beautiful of all moments. The madman was a brakeman with the Southern Pacific and he lived in Fresno; his father was also a brakeman. He lost his toe in the Oakland yards, switching, I didn't quite understand how. He drove me into buzzing Fresno and let me off by the south side of town. I went for a quick Coke in a little grocery by the tracks, and here came a melancholy Armenian youth along the red boxcars, and just at that moment a locomotive howled, and I said to myself, Yes, yes, Saroyan's town.

I had to go south; I got on the road. A man in a brand-new pickup truck picked me up. He was from Lubbock, Texas, and was in the trailer business. "You want to buy a trailer?" he asked me. "Any time, look me up." He told stories about his father in Lubbock. "One night my old man left the day's receipts settin on top of the safe, plumb forgot. What happened —a thief came in the night, acetylene torch and all, broke open the safe, riffled up the papers, kicked over a few chairs, and left. And that thousand dollars was settin right there on top of the safe, what do you know about that?"

He let me off south of Bakersfield, and then my adventure began. It grew cold. I put on the flimsy Army raincoat I'd bought in Oakland for three dollars and shuddered in the road. I was standing in front of an ornate Spanish-style motel that was lit like a jewel. The cars rushed by, LA-bound. I gestured frantically. It was too cold. I stood there till midnight, two hours straight, and cursed and cursed. It was just like Stuart, Iowa, again. There was nothing to do but spend a little over two dollars for a bus the remaining miles to Los Angeles. I walked back along the highway to Bakersfield and into the station, and sat down on a bench.

I had bought my ticket and was waiting for the LA bus when all of a sudden I saw the cutest little Mexican girl in slacks come cutting across my sight. She was in one of the buses that had just pulled in with a big sigh of airbrakes; it was discharging passengers for a rest stop. Her breasts stuck out straight and true; her little flanks looked delicious; her hair was long and lustrous black; and her eyes were great big blue things with timidities inside. I wished I was on her bus. A pain stabbed my heart, as it did every time I saw a girl I loved who was going the opposite direction in this too-big world. The announcer called the LA bus. I picked up my bag and got on, and who should be sitting there alone but the Mexican girl. I dropped right opposite her and began scheming right off. I was so lonely, so sad, so tired, so quivering, so broken, so beat, that I got up my courage, the courage necessary to approach a strange girl, and acted. Even then I spent five minutes beating my thighs in the dark as the bus rolled down the road.

You gotta, you gotta or you'll die! Damn fool, talk to her! What's wrong with you? Aren't you tired enough of yourself by now? And before I knew what I was doing I leaned across the aisle to her (she was trying to sleep on the seat) and said, "Miss, would you like to use my raincoat for a pillow?"

She looked up with a smile and said, "No, thank you very much."

I sat back, trembling; I lit a butt. I waited till she looked at me, with a sad little sidelook of love, and I got right up and leaned over her. "May I sit with you, miss?"

"If you wish."

And this I did. "Where going?"

"LA." I loved the way she said "LA"; I love the way everybody says "LA" on the Coast; it's their one and only golden town when all is said and done.

"That's where I'm going too!" I cried. "I'm very glad you let me sit with you, I was very lonely and I've been traveling a hell of a lot." And we settled down to telling our stories. Her story was this: She had a husband and child. The husband beat her, so she left him, back at Sabinal, south of Fresno, and was going to LA to live with her sister awhile. She left her little son with her family, who were grape-pickers and lived in a shack in the vineyards. She had nothing to do but brood and get mad. I felt like putting my arms around her right away. We talked and talked. She said she loved to talk with me. Pretty soon she was saying she wished she could go to New York too. "Maybe we could!" I laughed. The bus groaned up Grapevine Pass and then we were coming down into the great sprawls of light. Without coming to any particular agreement we began holding hands, and in the same way it was mutely and beautifully and purely decided that when I got my hotel room in LA she would be beside me. I ached all over for her; I leaned my head in her beautiful hair. Her little shoulders drove me mad; I hugged her and hugged her. And she loved it.

"I love love," she said, closing her eyes. I promised her beautiful love. I gloated over her. Our stories were told; we subsided into silence and sweet anticipatory thoughts. It was as simple as that. You could have all your Peaches and Bettys and Marylous and Ritas and Camilles and Inezes in this world; this was my girl and my kind of girlsoul, and I told her that. She confessed she saw me watching her in the bus station. "I thought you was a nice college boy."

"Oh, I'm a college boy!" I assured her. The bus arrived in Hollywood. In the gray, dirty dawn, like the dawn when Joel McCrea met Veronica Lake in a diner, in the picture *Sullivan's Travels*, she slept in my lap. I looked greedily out the window: stucco houses and palms and drive-ins, the whole mad thing, the ragged promised land, the fantastic end of America. We got off the bus at Main Street, which was no different from where you get off a bus in Kansas City or Chicago or Boston— red brick, dirty, characters drifting by, trolleys grating in the hopeless dawn, the whorey smell of a big city.

And here my mind went haywire, I don't know why. I began getting the foolish paranoiac visions that Teresa, or Terry—her name—was a common little hustler who worked the buses for a guy's bucks by making appointments like ours in LA where she brought the sucker first to a breakfast place, where her pimp waited, and then to a certain hotel to which he had access with his gun or his whatever. I never confessed this to her. We ate breakfast and a pimp kept watching us; I fancied Terry was making secret eyes at him. I was tired and felt strange and lost in a faraway, disgusting place. The goof of terror took over my thoughts and made me act petty and cheap. "Do you know that guy?" I said.

"What guy you mean, ho-ney?" I let it drop. She was slow and hung-up about everything she did; it took her a long time to eat; she chewed slowly and stared into space, and smoked a cigarette, and kept talking, and I was like a haggard ghost, suspicioning every move she made, thinking she was stalling for time. This was all a fit of sickness. I was sweating as we went down the street hand in hand. The first hotel we hit had a room, and before I knew it I was locking the door behind me and she was sitting on the bed taking off her shoes. I kissed her meekly. Better she'd never know. To relax our nerves I knew we needed whisky, especially me. I ran out and fiddled all over twelve blocks, hurrying till I found a pint of whisky for sale at a newsstand. I ran back, all energy. Terry was in the bathroom, fixing her face. I poured one big drink in a water glass, and we had slugs. Oh, it was sweet and delicious and worth my whole lugubrious voyage. I stood behind her at the mirror, and we danced in the bathroom that way. I began talking about my friends back east.

I said, "You ought to meet a great girl I know called Dorie. She's a six-foot redhead. If you came to New York she'd show you where to get work."

"Who is this six-foot redhead?" she demanded suspiciously. "Why do you tell me about her?" In her simple soul she

couldn't fathom my kind of glad, nervous talk. I let it drop.
She began to get drunk in the bathroom.

"Come on to bed!" I kept saying.

"Six-foot redhead, hey? And I thought you was a nice college boy, I saw you in your lovely sweater and I said to myself,
Hmm, ain't he nice? No! And no! And no! You have to be a
goddam pimp like all of them!"

"What on earth are you talking about?"

"Don't stand there and tell me that six-foot redhead ain't a
madame, 'cause I know a madame when I hear about one, and
you, you're just a pimp like all the rest I meet, everybody's a
pimp."

"Listen, Terry, I am not a pimp. I swear to you on the Bible I
am not a pimp. Why should I be a pimp? My only interest is
you."

"All the time I thought I met a nice boy. I was so glad, I
hugged myself and said, Hmm, a real nice boy instead of a
pimp."

"Terry," I pleaded with all my soul. "Please listen to me and
understand, I'm not a pimp." An hour ago I'd thought *she* was
a hustler. How sad it was. Our minds, with their store of madness, had diverged. O gruesome life, how I moaned and
pleaded, and then I got mad and realized I was pleading with
a dumb little Mexican wench and I told her so; and before I
knew it I picked up her red pumps and hurled them at the
bathroom door and told her to get out. "Go on, beat it!" I'd
sleep and forget it; I had my own life, my own sad and ragged
life forever. There was a dead silence in the bathroom. I took
my clothes off and went to bed.

Terry came out with tears of sorriness in her eyes. In her
simple and funny little mind had been decided the fact that a
pimp does not throw a woman's shoes against the door and
does not tell her to get out. In reverent and sweet little silence
she took all her clothes off and slipped her tiny body into the
sheets with me. It was brown as grapes. I saw her poor belly
where there was a Caesarian scar; her hips were so narrow she
couldn't bear a child without getting gashed open. Her legs
were like little sticks. She was only four foot ten. I made love
to her in the sweetness of the weary morning. Then, two tired
angels of some kind, hung-up forlornly in an LA shelf, having

found the closest and most delicious thing in life together, we fell asleep and slept till late afternoon.

13

For the next fifteen days we were together for better or for worse. When we woke up we decided to hitchhike to New York together; she was going to be my girl in town. I envisioned wild complexities with Dean and Marylou and everybody—a season, a new season. First we had to work to earn enough money for the trip. Terry was all for starting at once with the twenty dollars I had left. I didn't like it. And, like a damn fool, I considered the problem for two days, as we read the want ads of wild LA papers I'd never seen before in my life, in cafeterias and bars, until my twenty dwindled to just over ten. We were very happy in our little hotel room. In the middle of the night I got up because I couldn't sleep, pulled the cover over baby's bare brown shoulder, and examined the LA night. What brutal, hot, siren-whining nights they are! Right across the street there was trouble. An old rickety rundown rooming house was the scene of some kind of tragedy. The cruiser was pulled up below and the cops were questioning an old man with gray hair. Sobbings came from within. I could hear everything, together with the hum of my hotel neon. I never felt sadder in my life. LA is the loneliest and most brutal of American cities; New York gets god-awful cold in the winter but there's a feeling of wacky comradeship somewhere in some streets. LA is a jungle.

South Main Street, where Terry and I took strolls with hot dogs, was a fantastic carnival of lights and wildness. Booted cops frisked people on practically every corner. The beatest characters in the country swarmed on the sidewalks—all of it under those soft Southern California stars that are lost in the brown halo of the huge desert encampment LA really is. You could smell tea, weed, I mean marijuana, floating in the air, together with the chili beans and beer. That grand wild sound of bop floated from beer parlors; it mixed medleys with every kind of cowboy and boogie-woogie in the American night.

Everybody looked like Hassel. Wild Negroes with bop caps
and goatees came laughing by; then long-haired brokendown
hipsters straight off Route 66 from New York; then old desert
rats, carrying packs and heading for a park bench at the Plaza;
then Methodist ministers with raveled sleeves, and an occasional Nature Boy saint in beard and sandals. I wanted to meet
them all, talk to everybody, but Terry and I were too busy
trying to get a buck together.

We went to Hollywood to try to work in the drugstore at
Sunset and Vine. Now there was a corner! Great families off
jalopies from the hinterlands stood around the sidewalk gaping
for sight of some movie star, and the movie star never showed
up. When a limousine passed they rushed eagerly to the curb
and ducked to look: some character in dark glasses sat inside
with a bejeweled blonde. "Don Ameche! Don Ameche!" "No,
George Murphy! George Murphy!" They milled around,
looking at one another. Handsome queer boys who had come
to Hollywood to be cowboys walked around, wetting their
eyebrows with hincty fingertip. The most beautiful little gone
gals in the world cut by in slacks; they came to be starlets; they
ended up in drive-ins. Terry and I tried to find work at the
drive-ins. It was no soap anywhere. Hollywood Boulevard was
a great, screaming frenzy of cars; there were minor accidents at
least once a minute; everybody was rushing off toward the farthest palm—and beyond that was the desert and nothingness.
Hollywood Sams stood in front of swank restaurants, arguing
exactly the same way Broadway Sams argue at Jacob's Beach,
New York, only here they wore light-weight suits and their talk
was cornier. Tall, cadaverous preachers shuddered by. Fat
screaming women ran across the boulevard to get in line for
the quiz shows. I saw Jerry Colonna buying a car at Buick Motors; he was inside the vast plate-glass window, fingering his
mustachio. Terry and I ate in a cafeteria downtown which was
decorated to look like a grotto, with metal tits spurting everywhere and great impersonal stone buttockses belonging to
deities and soapy Neptune. People ate lugubrious meals around
the waterfalls, their faces green with marine sorrow. All the
cops in LA looked like handsome gigolos; obviously they'd
come to LA to make the movies. Everybody had come to make
the movies, even me. Terry and I were finally reduced to trying

to get jobs on South Main Street among the beat countermen and dishgirls who made no bones about their beatness, and even there it was no go. We still had ten dollars.

"Man, I'm going to get my clothes from Sis and we'll hitch-hike to New York," said Terry. "Come on, man. Let's do it. 'If you can't boogie I know I'll show you how.'" That last part was a song of hers she kept singing. We hurried to her sister's house in the sliverous Mexican shacks somewhere beyond Alameda Avenue. I waited in a dark alley behind Mexican kitchens because her sister wasn't supposed to see me. Dogs ran by. There were little lamps illuminating the little rat alleys. I could hear Terry and her sister arguing in the soft, warm night. I was ready for anything.

Terry came out and led me by the hand to Central Avenue, which is the colored main drag of LA. And what a wild place it is, with chickenshacks barely big enough to house a jukebox, and the jukebox blowing nothing but blues, bop, and jump. We went up dirty tenement stairs and came to the room of Terry's friend Margarina, who owed Terry a skirt and a pair of shoes. Margarina was a lovely mulatto; her husband was black as spades and kindly. He went right out and bought a pint of whisky to host me proper. I tried to pay part of it, but he said no. They had two little children. The kids bounced on the bed; it was their play-place. They put their arms around me and looked at me with wonder. The wild humming night of Central Avenue—the night of Hamp's "Central Avenue Breakdown"—howled and boomed along outside. They were singing in the halls, singing from their windows, just hell be damned and look out. Terry got her clothes and we said good-by. We went down to a chickenshack and played records on the jukebox. A couple of Negro characters whispered in my ear about tea. One buck. I said okay, bring it. The connection came in and motioned me to the cellar toilet, where I stood around dumbly as he said, "Pick up, man, pick up."

"Pick up what?" I said.

He had my dollar already. He was afraid to point at the floor. It was no floor, just basement. There lay something that looked like a little brown turd. He was absurdly cautious. "Got to look out for myself, things ain't cool this past week." I picked up the turd, which was a brown-paper cigarette, and went back to Terry, and off we went to the hotel room to get high. Nothing happened. It was Bull Durham tobacco. I wished I was wiser with my money.

Terry and I had to decide absolutely and once and for all what to do. We decided to hitch to New York with our remaining money. She picked up five dollars from her sister that night. We had about thirteen or less. So before the daily room rent was due again we packed up and took off on a red car to Arcadia, California, where Santa Anita racetrack is located under snow-capped mountains. It was night. We were pointed toward the American continent. Holding hands, we walked several miles down the road to get out of the populated district. It was a Saturday night. We stood under a roadlamp, thumbing, when suddenly cars full of young kids roared by with streamers flying. "Yaah! Yaah! we won! we won!" they all shouted. Then they yoohooed us and got great glee out of seeing a guy and a girl on the road. Dozens of such cars passed, full of young faces and "throaty young voices," as the saying goes. I hated every one of them. Who did they think they were, yaahing at somebody on the road just because they were little high-school punks and their parents carved the roast beef on Sunday afternoons? Who did they think they were, making fun of a girl reduced to poor circumstances with a man who wanted to belove? We were minding our own business. And we didn't get a blessed ride. We had to walk back to town, and worst of all we needed coffee and had the misfortune of going into the only place open, which was a high-school soda fountain, and all the kids were there and remembered us. Now they saw that Terry was Mexican, a Pachuco wildcat; and that her boy was worse than that.

With her pretty nose in the air she cut out of there and we wandered together in the dark up along the ditches of the highways. I carried the bags. We were breathing fogs in the cold night air. I finally decided to hide from the world one more night with her, and the morning be damned. We went into a motel court and bought a comfortable little suite for about four dollars—shower, bathtowels, wall radio, and all. We held each other tight. We had long, serious talks and took baths and discussed things with the light on and then with the light out. Something was being proved, I was convincing her of something, which she accepted, and we concluded the pact in the dark, breathless, then pleased, like little lambs.

In the morning we boldly struck out on our new plan. We were going to take a bus to Bakersfield and work picking grapes. After a few weeks of that we were headed for New York in the proper way, by bus. It was a wonderful afternoon, riding up to Bakersfield with Terry: we sat back, relaxed, talked, saw the countryside roll by, and didn't worry about a thing. We arrived in Bakersfield in late afternoon. The plan was to hit every fruit wholesaler in town. Terry said we could live in tents on the job. The thought of living in a tent and picking grapes in the cool California mornings hit me right. But there were no jobs to be had, and much confusion, with everybody giving us innumerable tips, and no job materialized. Nevertheless we ate a Chinese dinner and set out with reinforced bodies. We went across the SP tracks to Mexican town. Terry jabbered with her brethren, asking for jobs. It was night now, and the little Mextown street was one blazing bulb of lights: movie marquees, fruit stands, penny arcades, five-and-tens, and hundreds of rickety trucks and mud-spattered jalopies, parked. Whole Mexican fruit-picking families wandered around eating popcorn. Terry talked to everybody. I was beginning to despair. What I needed —what Terry needed, too—was a drink, so we bought a quart of California port for thirty-five cents and went to the railroad yards to drink. We found a place where hobos had drawn up crates to sit over fires. We sat there and drank the wine. On our left were the freight cars, sad and sooty red beneath the moon; straight ahead the lights and airport pokers of Bakersfield proper; to our right a tremendous aluminum Quonset warehouse. Ah, it was a fine night, a warm night, a wine-drinking night, a moony night, and a night to hug your girl and talk and spit and be heavengoing. This we did. She was a drinking little fool and kept up with me and passed me and went right on talking till midnight. We never budged from those crates. Occasionally bums passed, Mexican mothers passed with children, and the prowl car came by and the cop got out to leak, but most of the time we were alone and mixing up our souls ever more and ever more till it would be terribly hard to say goodby. At midnight we got up and goofed toward the highway.

Terry had a new idea. We would hitchhike to Sabinal, her

hometown, and live in her brother's garage. Anything was all right with me. On the road I made Terry sit down on my bag to make her look like a woman in distress, and right off a truck stopped and we ran for it, all glee-giggles. The man was a good man; his truck was poor. He roared and crawled on up the valley. We got to Sabinal in the wee hours before dawn. I had finished the wine while Terry slept, and I was proper stoned. We got out and roamed the quiet leafy square of the little California town—a whistle stop on the SP. We went to find her brother's buddy, who would tell us where he was. Nobody home. As dawn began to break I lay flat on my back in the lawn of the town square and kept saying over and over again, "You won't tell what he done up in Weed, will you? What'd he do up in Weed? You won't tell will you? What'd he do up in Weed?" This was from the picture *Of Mice and Men*, with Burgess Meredith talking to the foreman of the ranch. Terry giggled. Anything I did was all right with her. I could lie there and go on doing that till the ladies came out for church and she wouldn't care. But finally I decided we'd be all set soon because of her brother, and I took her to an old hotel by the tracks and we went to bed comfortably.

In the bright, sunny morning Terry got up early and went to find her brother. I slept till noon; when I looked out the window I suddenly saw an SP freight going by with hundreds of hobos reclining on the flatcars and rolling merrily along with packs for pillows and funny papers before their noses, and some munching on good California grapes picked up by the siding. "Damn!" I yelled. "Hooee! It *is* the promised land." They were all coming from Frisco; in a week they'd all be going back in the same grand style.

Terry arrived with her brother, his buddy, and her child. Her brother was a wild-buck Mexican hotcat with a hunger for booze, a great good kid. His buddy was a big flabby Mexican who spoke English without much accent and was loud and overanxious to please. I could see he had eyes for Terry. Her little boy was Johnny, seven years old, dark-eyed and sweet. Well, there we were, and another wild day began.

Her brother's name was Rickey. He had a '38 Chevy. We piled into that and took off for parts unknown. "Where we going?" I asked. The buddy did the explaining—his name was

Ponzo, that's what everybody called him. He stank. I found out why. His business was selling manure to farmers; he had a truck. Rickey always had three or four dollars in his pocket and was happy-go-lucky about things. He always said, "That's right, man, there you go—dah you go, dah you go!" And he went. He drove seventy miles an hour in the old heap, and we went to Madera beyond Fresno to see some farmers about manure.

Rickey had a bottle. "Today we drink, tomorrow we work. Dah you go, man—take a shot!" Terry sat in back with her baby; I looked back at her and saw the flush of homecoming joy on her face. The beautiful green countryside of October in California reeled by madly. I was guts and juice again and ready to go.

"Where do we go now, man?"

"We go find a farmer with some manure laying around. Tomorrow we drive back in the truck and pick it up. Man, we'll make a lot of money. Don't worry about nothing."

"We're all in this together!" yelled Ponzo. I saw that was so—everywhere I went, everybody was in it together. We raced through the crazy streets of Fresno and on up the valley to some farmers in back roads. Ponzo got out of the car and conducted confused conversations with old Mexican farmers; nothing, of course, came of it.

"What we need is a drink!" yelled Rickey, and off we went to a crossroads saloon. Americans are always drinking in crossroads saloons on Sunday afternoon; they bring their kids; they gabble and brawl over brews; everything's fine. Come night-fall the kids start crying and the parents are drunk. They go weaving back to the house. Everywhere in America I've been in crossroads saloons drinking with whole families. The kids eat popcorn and chips and play in back. This we did. Rickey and I and Ponzo and Terry sat drinking and shouting with the music; little baby Johnny goofed with other children around the jukebox. The sun began to get red. Nothing had been accomplished. What was there to accomplish? "*Mañana*," said Rickey. "*Mañana*, man, we make it; have another beer, man, dah you go, *dah you go!*"

We staggered out and got in the car; off we went to a highway bar. Ponzo was a big, loud, vociferous type who knew everybody in San Joaquin Valley. From the highway bar I went with him alone in the car to find a farmer; instead we wound up in Madera Mextown, digging the girls and trying to pick up a few for him and Rickey. And then, as purple dusk descended over the grape country, I found myself sitting dumbly in the car as he argued with some old Mexican at the kitchen door about the price of a watermelon the old man grew in the back yard. We got the watermelon; we ate it on the spot and threw the rinds on the old man's dirt sidewalk. All kinds of pretty little girls were cutting down the darkening street. I said, "Where in the hell are we?"

"Don't worry, man," said big Ponzo. "Tomorrow we make a lot of money; tonight we don't worry." We went back and picked up Terry and her brother and the kid and drove to Fresno in the highway lights of night. We were all raving hungry. We bounced over the railroad tracks in Fresno and hit the wild streets of Fresno Mextown. Strange Chinese hung out of windows, digging the Sunday night streets; groups of Mex chicks swaggered around in slacks; mambo blasted from jukeboxes; the lights were festooned around like Halloween. We went into a Mexican restaurant and had tacos and mashed pinto beans rolled in tortillas; it was delicious. I whipped out my last shining five-dollar bill which stood between me and the New Jersey shore and paid for Terry and me. Now I had four bucks. Terry and I looked at each other.

"Where we going to sleep tonight, baby?"

"I don't know."

Rickey was drunk; now all he was saying was, "Dah you go, man—dah you go, man," in a tender and tired voice. It had been a long day. None of us knew what was going on, or what the Good Lord appointed. Poor little Johnny fell asleep on my arm. We drove back to Sabinal. On the way we pulled up sharp at a roadhouse on Highway 99. Rickey wanted one last beer. In back of the roadhouse were trailers and tents and a few rickety motel-style rooms. I inquired about the price and it was two bucks. I asked Terry how about it, and she said fine because we had the kid on our hands now and had to make him comfortable. So after a few beers in the saloon, where sullen Okies reeled to the music of a cowboy band, Terry and I and Johnny went into a motel room and got ready to hit the sack. Ponzo kept hanging around; he had no place to sleep. Rickey slept at his father's house in the vineyard shack.

"Where do you live, Ponzo?" I asked.

"Nowhere, man. I'm supposed to live with Big Rosey but she threw me out last night. I'm gonna get my truck and sleep in it tonight."

Guitars tinkled. Terry and I gazed at the stars together and kissed. "*Mañana*," she said. "Everything'll be all right tomorrow, don't you think, Sal-honey, man?"

"Sure, baby, *mañana*." It was always *mañana*. For the next week that was all I heard—*mañana*, a lovely word and one that probably means heaven.

Little Johnny jumped in bed, clothes and all, and went to sleep; sand spilled out of his shoes, Madera sand. Terry and I got up in the middle of the night and brushed the sand off the sheets. In the morning I got up, washed, and took a walk around the place. We were five miles out of Sabinal in the cotton fields and grape vineyards. I asked the big fat woman who owned the camp if any of the tents were vacant. The cheapest one, a dollar a day, was vacant. I fished up a dollar and moved into it. There were a bed, a stove, and a cracked mirror hanging from a pole; it was delightful. I had to stoop to get in, and when I did there was my baby and my baby boy. We waited for Rickey and Ponzo to arrive with the truck. They arrived with beer bottles and started to get drunk in the tent.

"How about the manure?"

"Too late today. Tomorrow, man, we make a lot of money; today we have a few beers. What do you say, beer?" I didn't have to be prodded. "Dah you go—*dah you go!*" yelled Rickey. I began to see that our plans for making money with the manure truck would never materialize. The truck was parked outside the tent. It smelled like Ponzo.

That night Terry and I went to bed in the sweet night air beneath our dewy tent. I was just getting ready to go to sleep when she said, "You want to love me now?"

I said, "What about Johnny?"

"He don't mind. He's asleep." But Johnny wasn't asleep and he said nothing.

The boys came back the next day with the manure truck and drove off to find whisky; they came back and had a big time in the tent. That night Ponzo said it was too cold and slept on the ground in our tent, wrapped in a big tarpaulin smelling of cowflaps. Terry hated him; she said he hung around with her brother in order to get close to her.

Nothing was going to happen except starvation for Terry and me, so in the morning I walked around the countryside asking for cotton-picking work. Everybody told me to go to the farm across the highway from the camp. I went, and the farmer was in the kitchen with his women. He came out, listened to my story, and warned me he was paying only three dollars per hundred pounds of picked cotton. I pictured myself picking at least three hundred pounds a day and took the job. He fished out some long canvas bags from the barn and told me the picking started at dawn. I rushed back to Terry, all glee. On the way a grape truck went over a bump in the road and threw off great bunches of grapes on the hot tar. I picked them up and took them home. Terry was glad. "Johnny and me'll come with you and help."

"Pshaw!" I said. "No such thing!"

"You see, you see, it's very hard picking cotton. I show you how."

We ate the grapes, and in the evening Rickey showed up with a loaf of bread and a pound of hamburg and we had a picnic. In a larger tent next to ours lived a whole family of Okie cotton-pickers; the grandfather sat in a chair all day long, he was too old to work; the son and daughter, and their children, filed every dawn across the highway to my farmer's field and went to work. At dawn the next day I went with them. They said the cotton was heavier at dawn because of the dew and you could make more money than in the afternoon. Nevertheless they worked all day from dawn to sundown. The grandfather had come from Nebraska during the great plague of the thirties—that selfsame dustcloud my Montana cowboy had told me about—with the entire family in a jalopy truck. They had been in California ever since. They loved to work. In the ten years the old man's son had increased his children to the number of four, some of whom were old enough now to pick cotton. And in that time they had progressed from ragged poverty in Simon Legree fields to a kind of smiling respectability in better tents, and that was all. They were extremely proud of their tent.

"Ever going back to Nebraska?"

"Pshaw, there's nothing back there. What we want to do is buy a trailer."

We bent down and began picking cotton. It was beautiful. Across the field were the tents, and beyond them the sere brown cottonfields that stretched out of sight to the brown arroyo foothills and then the snow-capped Sierras in the blue morning air. This was so much better than washing dishes on South Main Street. But I knew nothing about picking cotton. I spent too much time disengaging the white ball from its crackly bed; the others did it in one flick. Moreover, my fingertips began to bleed; I needed gloves, or more experience. There was an old Negro couple in the field with us. They picked cotton with the same God-blessed patience their grandfathers had practiced in ante-bellum Alabama; they moved right along their rows, bent and blue, and their bags increased. My back began to ache. But it was beautiful kneeling and hiding in that earth. If I felt like resting I did, with my face on the pillow of brown moist earth. Birds sang an accompaniment. I thought I had found my life's work. Johnny and Terry came waving at me across the field in the hot lullal noon and pitched in with me. Be damned if little Johnny wasn't faster than I was!—and of course Terry was twice as fast. They worked ahead of me and left me piles of clean cotton to add to my bag—Terry workmanlike piles, Johnny little childly piles. I stuck them in with sorrow. What kind of old man was I that couldn't support his own ass, let alone theirs? They spent all afternoon with me. When the sun got red we trudged back together. At the end of the field I unloaded my burden on a scale; it weighed fifty pounds, and I got a buck fifty. Then I borrowed a bicycle from one of the Okie boys and rode down 99 to a crossroads grocery store where I bought cans of cooked spaghetti and meatballs, bread, butter, coffee, and cake, and came back with the bag on the handlebars. LA-bound traffic zoomed by; Frisco-bound harassed my tail. I swore and swore. I looked up at the dark sky and prayed to God for a better break in life and a better chance to do something for the little people I loved.

Nobody was paying any attention to me up there. I should have known better. It was Terry who brought my soul back; on the tent stove she warmed up the food, and it was one of the greatest meals of my life, I was so hungry and tired. Sighing like an old Negro cotton-picker, I reclined on the bed and smoked a cigarette. Dogs barked in the cool night. Rickey and Ponzo had given up calling in the evenings. I was satisfied with that. Terry curled up beside me, Johnny sat on my chest, and they drew pictures of animals in my notebook. The light of our tent burned on the frightful plain. The cowboy music twanged in the roadhouse and carried across the fields, all sadness. It was all right with me. I kissed my baby and we put out the lights.

In the morning the dew made the tent sag; I got up with my towel and toothbrush and went to the general motel toilet to wash; then I came back, put on my pants, which were all torn from kneeling in the earth and had been sewed by Terry in the evening, put on my ragged straw hat, which had originally served as Johnny's toy hat, and went across the highway with my canvas cotton-bag.

Every day I earned approximately a dollar and a half. It was just enough to buy groceries in the evening on the bicycle. The days rolled by. I forgot all about the East and all about Dean and Carlo and the bloody road. Johnny and I played all the time; he liked me to throw him up in the air and down in the bed. Terry sat mending clothes. I was a man of the earth, precisely as I had dreamed I would be, in Paterson. There was talk that Terry's husband was back in Sabinal and out for me; I was ready for him. One night the Okies went mad in the roadhouse and tied a man to a tree and beat him to a pulp with sticks. I was asleep at the time and only heard about it. From then on I carried a big stick with me in the tent in case they got the idea we Mexicans were fouling up their trailer camp. They thought I was a Mexican, of course; and in a way I am.

But now it was October and getting much colder in the nights. The Okie family had a woodstove and planned to stay for the winter. We had nothing, and besides the rent for the tent was due. Terry and I bitterly decided we'd have to leave. "Go back to your family," I said. "For God's sake, you can't be batting around tents with a baby like Johnny; the poor little tyke is cold." Terry cried because I was criticizing her motherly instincts; I meant no such thing. When Ponzo came in the truck one gray afternoon we decided to see her family about the situation. But I mustn't be seen and would have to hide in the vineyard. We started for Sabinal; the truck broke down, and simultaneously it started to rain wildly. We sat in the old truck, cursing. Ponzo got out and toiled in the rain. He was a good old guy after all. We promised each other one more big bat. Off we went to a rickety bar in Sabinal Mextown and spent an hour sopping up the brew. I was through with my chores in the cottonfield. I could feel the pull of my own life calling me back. I shot my aunt a penny postcard across the land and asked for another fifty.

We drove to Terry's family's shack. It was situated on the old road that ran between the vineyards. It was dark when we got there. They left me off a quarter-mile away and drove to the door. Light poured out of the door; Terry's six other brothers were playing their guitars and singing. The old man was drinking wine. I heard shouts and arguments above the singing. They called her a whore because she'd left her no-good husband and gone to LA and left Johnny with them. The old man was yelling. But the sad, fat brown mother prevailed, as she always does among the great fellahin peoples of the world, and Terry was allowed to come back home. The brothers began to sing gay songs, fast. I huddled in the cold, rainy wind and watched everything across the sad vineyards of October in the valley. My mind was filled with that great song "Lover Man" as Billie Holiday sings it; I had my own concert in the bushes. "Someday we'll meet, and you'll dry all my tears, and whisper sweet, little things in my ear, hugging and a-kissing, oh what we've been missing, Lover Man, oh where can you be . . ." It's not the words so much as the great harmonic tune and the way Billie sings it, like a woman stroking her man's hair in soft lamplight. The winds howled. I got cold.

Terry and Ponzo came back and we rattled off in the old truck to meet Rickey. Rickey was now living with Ponzo's woman, Big Rosey; we tooted the horn for him in rickety alleys. Big Rosey threw him out. Everything was collapsing. That night we slept in the truck. Terry held me tight, of course, and told me not to leave. She said she'd work picking grapes and make enough money for both of us; meanwhile I could live in Farmer Heffelfinger's barn down the road from her family. I'd have nothing to do but sit in the grass all day and eat grapes. "You like that?"

In the morning her cousins came to get us in another truck. I suddenly realized thousands of Mexicans all over the countryside knew about Terry and me and that it must have been a juicy, romantic topic for them. The cousins were very polite and in fact charming. I stood on the truck, smiling pleasantries, talking about where we were in the war and what the pitch was. There were five cousins in all, and every one of them was nice. They seemed to belong to the side of Terry's family that didn't fuss off like her brother. But I loved that wild Rickey. He swore he was coming to New York to join me. I pictured him in New York, putting off everything till *mañana*. He was drunk in a field someplace that day.

I got off the truck at the crossroads, and the cousins drove Terry home. They gave me the high sign from the front of the house; the father and mother weren't home, they were off picking grapes. So I had the run of the house for the afternoon. It was a four-room shack; I couldn't imagine how the whole family managed to live in there. Flies flew over the sink. There were no screens, just like in the song, "The window she is broken and the rain she is coming in." Terry was at home now and puttering around pots. Her two sisters giggled at me. The little children screamed in the road.

When the sun came out red through the clouds of my last valley afternoon, Terry led me to Farmer Heffelfinger's barn. Farmer Heffelfinger had a prosperous farm up the road. We put crates together, she brought blankets from the house, and I was all set except for a great hairy tarantula that lurked at the pinpoint top of the barn roof. Terry said it wouldn't harm me if I didn't bother it. I lay on my back and stared at it. I went out to the cemetery and climbed a tree. In the tree I sang "Blue Skies." Terry and Johnny sat in the grass; we had grapes. In California you chew the juice out of grapes and spit the skin away, a real luxury. Nightfall came. Terry went home for supper and came to the barn at nine o'clock with delicious tortillas and mashed beans. I lit a woodfire on the cement floor of the barn to make light. We made love on the crates. Terry got up and cut right back to the shack. Her father was yelling at her; I could hear him from the barn. She'd left me a cape to keep warm; I threw it over my shoulder and skulked through the moonlit vineyard to see what was going on. I crept to the end of a row and knelt in the warm dirt. Her five brothers were singing melodious songs in Spanish. The stars bent over the little roof; smoke poked from the stovepipe chimney. I smelled mashed beans and chili. The old man growled. The brothers kept right on yodeling. The mother was silent. Johnny and the kids were giggling in the bedroom. A California home; I hid in the grapevines, digging it all. I felt like a million dollars; I was adventuring in the crazy American night.

Terry came out, slamming the door behind her. I accosted her on the dark road. "What's the matter?"

"Oh, we fight all the time. He wants me to go to work tomorrow. He says he don't want me foolin around. Sallie, I want to go to New York with you."

"But how?"

"I don't know, honey. I'll miss you. I love you."

"But I have to leave."

"Yes, yes. We lay down one more time, then you leave." We went back to the barn; I made love to her under the tarantula. What was the tarantula doing? We slept awhile on the crates as the fire died. She went back at midnight; her father was drunk; I could hear him roaring; then there was silence as he fell asleep. The stars folded over the sleeping countryside.

In the morning Farmer Heffelfinger stuck his head through the horse gate and said, "How you doing, young fella?"

"Fine. I hope it's all right my staying here."

"Sure thing. You going with that little Mexican floozy?"

"She's a very nice girl."

"Very pretty too. I think the bull jumped the fence. She's got blue eyes." We talked about his farm.

Terry brought my breakfast. I had my canvas bag all packed and ready to go to New York, as soon as I picked up my money in Sabinal. I knew it was waiting there for me by now. I told Terry I was leaving. She had been thinking about it all night and was resigned to it. Emotionlessly she kissed me in the vineyard and walked off down the row. We turned at a dozen paces, for love is a duel, and looked at each other for the last time.

"See you in New York, Terry," I said. She was supposed to

drive to New York in a month with her brother. But we both knew she wouldn't make it. At a hundred feet I turned to look at her. She just walked on back to the shack, carrying my breakfast plate in one hand. I bowed my head and watched her. Well, lackadaddy, I was on the road again.

I walked down the highway to Sabinal, eating black walnuts from the walnut tree. I went on the SP tracks and balanced along the rail. I passed a watertower and a factory. This was the end of something. I went to the telegraph office of the railroad for my money order from New York. It was closed. I swore and sat on the steps to wait. The ticket master got back and invited me in. The money was in; my aunt had saved my lazy butt again. "Who's going to win the World Series next year?" said the gaunt old ticket master. I suddenly realized it was fall and that I was going back to New York.

I walked along the tracks in the long sad October light of the valley, hoping for an SP freight to come along so I could join the grape-eating hobos and read the funnies with them. It didn't come. I got out on the highway and hitched a ride at once. It was the fastest, whoopingest ride of my life. The driver was a fiddler for a California cowboy band. He had a brand-new car and drove eighty miles an hour. "I don't drink when I drive," he said and handed me a pint. I took a drink and offered him one. "What the hail," he said and drank. We made Sabinal to LA in the amazing time of four hours flat about 250 miles. He dropped me off right in front of Columbia Pictures in Hollywood; I was just in time to run in and pick up my rejected original. Then I bought my bus ticket to Pittsburgh. I didn't have enough money to go all the way to New York. I figured to worry about that when I got to Pittsburgh.

With the bus leaving at ten, I had four hours to dig Hollywood alone. First I bought a loaf of bread and salami and made myself ten sandwiches to cross the country on. I had a dollar left. I sat on the low cement wall in back of a Hollywood parking lot and made the sandwiches. As I labored at this absurd task, great Kleig lights of a Hollywood première stabbed in the sky, that humming West Coast sky. All around me were the noises of the crazy gold-coast city. And this was my Hollywood career—this was my last night in Hollywood, and I was spreading mustard on my lap in back of a parking-lot john.

14

At dawn my bus was zooming across the Arizona desert—
Indio, Blythe, Salome (where she danced); the great dry
stretches leading to Mexican mountains in the south. Then we
swung north to the Arizona mountains, Flagstaff, clifftowns. I
had a book with me I stole from a Hollywood stall, "*Le Grand
Meaulnes*" by Alain-Fournier, but I preferred reading the
American landscape as we went along. Every bump, rise, and
stretch in it mystified my longing. In inky night we crossed
New Mexico; at gray dawn it was Dalhart, Texas; in the bleak
Sunday afternoon we rode through one Oklahoma flat-town
after another; at nightfall it was Kansas. The bus roared on. I
was going home in October. Everybody goes home in October.

We arrived in St. Louis at noon. I took a walk down by the
Mississippi River and watched the logs that came floating from
Montana in the north—grand Odyssean logs of our continen-
tal dream. Old steamboats with their scrollwork more scrolled
and withered by weathers sat in the mud inhabited by rats.
Great clouds of afternoon overtopped the Mississippi Valley.
The bus roared through Indiana cornfields that night; the
moon illuminated the ghostly gathered husks; it was almost
Halloween. I made the acquaintance of a girl and we necked
all the way to Indianapolis. She was nearsighted. When we got
off to eat I had to lead her by the hand to the lunch counter.
She bought my meals; my sandwiches were all gone. In exchange I told her long stories. She was coming from Washington State, where she had spent the summer picking apples.
Her home was on an upstate New York farm. She invited me
to come there. We made a date to meet at a New York hotel
anyway. She got off at Columbus, Ohio, and I slept all the way
to Pittsburgh. I was wearier than I'd been for years and years.
I had three hundred and sixty-five miles yet to hitchhike to
New York, and a dime in my pocket. I walked five miles to get
out of Pittsburgh, and two rides, an apple truck and a big
trailer truck, took me to Harrisburg in the soft Indian-summer
rainy night. I cut right along. I wanted to get home.

It was the night of the Ghost of the Susquehanna. The Ghost
was a shriveled little old man with a paper satchel who claimed

he was headed for "Canady." He walked very fast, com-
manding me to follow, and said there was a bridge up ahead
we could cross. He was about sixty years old; he talked incessantly of the meals he had, how much butter they gave him for
pancakes, how many extra slices of bread, how the old men
had called him from a porch of a charity home in Maryland
and invited him to stay for the weekend, how he took a nice
warm bath before he left; how he found a brand-new hat by
the side of the road in Virginia and that was it on his head;
how he hit every Red Cross in town and showed them his
World War I credentials; how the Harrisburg Red Cross was
not worthy of the name; how he managed in this hard world.
But as far as I could see he was just a semi-respectable walking
hobo of some kind who covered the entire Eastern Wilderness
on foot, hitting Red Cross offices and sometimes bumming on
Main Street corners for a dime. We were bums together. We
walked seven miles along the mournful Susquehanna. It is a
terrifying river. It has bushy cliffs on both sides that lean like
hairy ghosts over the unknown waters. Inky night covers all.
Sometimes from the railyards across the river rises a great red
locomotive flare that illuminates the horrid cliffs. The little
man said he had a fine belt in his satchel and we stopped for
him to fish it out. "I got me a fine belt here somewheres—got
it in Frederick, Maryland. Damn, now did I leave that thing on
the counter at Fredericksburg?"

"You mean Frederick."

"No, no, Fredericksburg, *Virginia!*" He was always talking
about Frederick, Maryland, and Fredericksburg, Virginia. He
walked right in the road in the teeth of advancing traffic and
almost got hit several times. I plodded along in the ditch. Any
minute I expected the poor little madman to go flying in the
night, dead. We never found that bridge. I left him at a railroad underpass and, because I was so sweaty from the hike, I
changed shirts and put on two sweaters; a roadhouse illuminated my sad endeavors. A whole family came walking down
the dark road and wondered what I was doing. Strangest thing
of all, a tenorman was blowing very fine blues in this Pennsylvania hick house; I listened and moaned. It began to rain hard.
A man gave me a ride back to Harrisburg and told me I was on
the wrong road. I suddenly saw the little hobo standing under

a sad streetlamp with his thumb stuck out—poor forlorn man, poor lost sometimeboy, now broken ghost of the penniless wilds. I told my driver the story and he stopped to tell the old man.

"Look here, fella, you're on your way west, not east."

"Heh?" said the little ghost. "Can't tell me I don't know my way around here. Been walkin this country for years. I'm headed for Canady."

"But this ain't the road to Canada, this is the road to Pittsburgh and Chicago." The little man got disgusted with us and walked off. The last I saw of him was his bobbing little white bag dissolving in the darkness of the mournful Alleghenies.

I thought all the wilderness of America was in the West till the Ghost of the Susquehanna showed me different. No, there is a wilderness in the East; it's the same wilderness Ben Franklin plodded in the oxcart days when he was postmaster, the same as it was when George Washington was a wild-buck Indian-fighter, when Daniel Boone told stories by Pennsylvania lamps and promised to find the Gap, when Bradford built his road and men whooped her up in log cabins. There were not great Arizona spaces for the little man, just the bushy wilderness of eastern Pennsylvania, Maryland, and Virginia, the backroads, the black-tar roads that curve among the mournful rivers like Susquehanna, Monongahela, old Potomac and Monocacy.

That night in Harrisburg I had to sleep in the railroad station on a bench; at dawn the station masters threw me out. Isn't it true that you start your life a sweet child believing in everything under your father's roof? Then comes the day of the Laodiceans, when you know you are wretched and miserable and poor and blind and naked, and with the visage of a gruesome grieving ghost you go shuddering through nightmare life. I stumbled haggardly out of the station; I had no more control. All I could see of the morning was a whiteness like the whiteness of the tomb. I was starving to death. All I had left in the form of calories were the last of the cough drops I'd bought in Shelton, Nebraska, months ago; these I sucked for their sugar. I didn't know how to panhandle. I stumbled out of town with barely enough strength to reach the city limits. I knew I'd be arrested if I spent another night in Harrisburg.

Cursed city! The ride I proceeded to get was with a skinny, haggard man who believed in controlled starvation for the sake of health. When I told him I was starving to death as we rolled east he said, "Fine, fine, there's nothing better for you. I myself haven't eaten for three days. I'm going to live to be a hundred and fifty years old." He was a bag of bones, a floppy doll, a broken stick, a maniac. I might have gotten a ride with an affluent fat man who'd say, "Let's stop at this restaurant and have some pork chops and beans." No, I had to get a ride that morning with a maniac who believed in controlled starvation for the sake of health. After a hundred miles he grew lenient and took out bread-and-butter sandwiches from the back of the car. They were hidden among his salesman samples. He was selling plumbing fixtures around Pennsylvania. I devoured the bread and butter. Suddenly I began to laugh. I was all alone in the car, waiting for him as he made business calls in Allentown, and I laughed and laughed. Gad, I was sick and tired of life. But the madman drove me home to New York.

Suddenly I found myself on Times Square. I had traveled eight thousand miles around the American continent and I was back on Times Square; and right in the middle of a rush hour, too, seeing with my innocent road-eyes the absolute madness and fantastic hoorair of New York with its millions and millions hustling forever for a buck among themselves, the mad dream—grabbing, taking, giving, sighing, dying, just so they could be buried in those awful cemetery cities beyond Long Island City. The high towers of the land—the other end of the land, the place where Paper America is born. I stood in a subway doorway, trying to get enough nerve to pick up a beautiful long butt, and every time I stooped great crowds rushed by and obliterated it from my sight, and finally it was crushed. I had no money to go home in the bus. Paterson is quite a few miles from Times Square. Can you picture me walking those last miles through the Lincoln Tunnel or over the Washington Bridge and into New Jersey? It was dusk. Where was Hassel? I dug the square for Hassel; he wasn't there, he was in Riker's Island, behind bars. Where Dean? Where everybody? Where life? I had my home to go to, my place to lay my head down and figure the losses and figure the gain that I knew was in there somewhere too. I had to panhandle two bits for the bus. I finally hit a Greek minister who was standing around the corner. He gave me the quarter with a nervous lookaway. I rushed immediately to the bus.

When I got home I ate everything in the icebox. My aunt got up and looked at me. "Poor little Salvatore," she said in Italian. "You're thin, you're thin. Where have you been all this time?" I had on two shirts and two sweaters; my canvas bag had torn cottonfield pants and the tattered remnants of my huarache shoes in it. My aunt and I decided to buy a new electric refrigerator with the money I had sent her from California; it was to be the first one in the family. She went to bed, and late at night I couldn't sleep and just smoked in bed. My half-finished manuscript was on the desk. It was October, home, and work again. The first cold winds rattled the windowpane, and I had made it just in time. Dean had come to my house, slept several nights there, waiting for me; spent afternoons talking to my aunt as she worked on a great rag rug woven of all the clothes in my family for years, which was now finished and spread on my bedroom floor, as complex and as rich as the passage of time itself; and then he had left, two days before I arrived, crossing my path probably somewhere in Pennsylvania or Ohio, to go to San Francisco. He had his own life there; Camille had just gotten an apartment. It had never occurred to me to look her up while I was in Mill City. Now it was too late and I had also missed Dean.

Part Two

I

IT was over a year before I saw Dean again. I stayed home all
that time, finished my book and began going to school on
the GI Bill of Rights. At Christmas 1948 my aunt and I went
down to visit my brother in Virginia, laden with presents. I had
been writing to Dean and he said he was coming East again;
and I told him if so he would find me in Testament, Virginia,
between Christmas and New Year's. One day when all our
Southern relatives were sitting around the parlor in Testament,
gaunt men and women with the old Southern soil in their
eyes, talking in low, whining voices about the weather, the
crops, and the general weary recapitulation of who had a baby,
who got a new house, and so on, a mud-spattered '49 Hudson
drew up in front of the house on the dirt road. I had no idea
who it was. A weary young fellow, muscular and ragged in a
T-shirt, unshaven, red-eyed, came to the porch and rang the
bell. I opened the door and suddenly realized it was Dean. He
had come all the way from San Francisco to my brother
Rocco's door in Virginia, and in an amazingly short time,
because I had just written my last letter, telling where I was. In
the car I could see two figures sleeping. "I'll be goddamned!
Dean! Who's in the car?"

"Hel-lo, hel-lo, man, it's Marylou. And Ed Dunkel. We
gotta have place to wash up immediately, we're dog-tired."

"But how did you get here so fast?"

"Ah, man, that Hudson goes!"

"Where did you get it?"

"I bought it with my savings. I've been working on the railroad, making four hundred dollars a month."

There was utter confusion in the following hour. My Southern relatives had no idea what was going on, or who or what
Dean, Marylou, and Ed Dunkel were; they dumbly stared. My
aunt and my brother Rocky went in the kitchen to consult.

There were, in all, eleven people in the little Southern house. Not only that, but my brother had just decided to move from that house, and half his furniture was gone; he and his wife and baby were moving closer to the town of Testament. They had bought a new parlor set and their old one was going to my aunt's house in Paterson, though we hadn't yet decided how. When Dean heard this he at once offered his services with the Hudson. He and I would carry the furniture to Paterson in two fast trips and bring my aunt back at the end of the second trip. This was going to save us a lot of money and trouble. It was agreed upon. My sister-in-law made a spread, and the three battered travelers sat down to eat. Marylou had not slept since Denver. I thought she looked older and more beautiful now.

I learned that Dean had lived happily with Camille in San Francisco ever since that fall of 1947; he got a job on the railroad and made a lot of money. He became the father of a cute little girl, Amy Moriarty. Then suddenly he blew his top while walking down the street one day. He saw a '49 Hudson for sale and rushed to the bank for his entire roll. He bought the car on the spot. Ed Dunkel was with him. Now they were broke. Dean calmed Camille's fears and told her he'd be back in a month. "I'm going to New York and bring Sal back." She wasn't too pleased at this prospect.

"But what is the purpose of all this? Why are you doing this to me?"

"It's nothing, it's nothing, darling—ah—hem—Sal has pleaded and begged with me to come and get him, it is absolutely necessary for me to—but we won't go into all these explanations—and I'll tell you why . . . No, listen, I'll tell you why." And he told her why, and of course it made no sense.

Big tall Ed Dunkel also worked on the railroad. He and Dean had just been laid off during a seniority lapse because of a drastic reduction of crews. Ed had met a girl called Galatea who was living in San Francisco on her savings. These two mindless cads decided to bring the girl along to the East and have her foot the bill. Ed cajoled and pleaded; she wouldn't go unless he married her. In a whirlwind few days Ed Dunkel married Galatea, with Dean rushing around to get the necessary papers, and a few days before Christmas they rolled out of

San Francisco at seventy miles per, headed for LA and the snowless southern road. In LA they picked up a sailor in a travel bureau and took him along for fifteen dollars' worth of gas. He was bound for Indiana. They also picked up a woman with her idiot daughter, for four dollars' gas fare to Arizona. Dean sat the idiot girl with him up front and dug her, as he said, "All the *way*, man! such a gone sweet little soul. Oh, we talked, we talled of fires and the desert turning to a paradise and her parrot that swore in Spanish." Dropping off these passengers, they proceeded to Tucson. All along the way Galatea Dunkel, Ed's new wife, kept complaining that she was tired and wanted to sleep in a motel. If this kept up they'd spend all her money long before Virginia. Two nights she forced a stop and blew tens on motels. By the time they got to Tucson she was broke. Dean and Ed gave her the slip in a hotel lobby and resumed the voyage alone, with the sailor, and without a qualm.

Ed Dunkel was a tall, calm, unthinking fellow who was completely ready to do anything Dean asked him; and at this time Dean was too busy for scruples. He was roaring through Las Cruces, New Mexico, when he suddenly had an explosive yen to see his sweet first wife Marylou again. She was up in Denver. He swung the car north, against the feeble protests of the sailor, and zoomed into Denver in the evening. He ran and found Marylou in a hotel. They had ten hours of wild lovemaking. Everything was decided again: they were going to stick. Marylou was the only girl Dean ever really loved. He was sick with regret when he saw her face again, and, as of yore, he pleaded and begged at her knees for the joy of her being. She understood Dean; she stroked his hair; she knew he was mad. To soothe the sailor, Dean fixed him up with a girl in a hotel room over the bar where the old poolhall gang always drank. But the sailor refused the girl and in fact walked off in the night and they never saw him again; he evidently took a bus to Indiana.

Dean, Marylou, and Ed Dunkel roared east along Colfax and out to the Kansas plains. Great snowstorms overtook them. In Missouri, at night, Dean had to drive with his scarf-wrapped head stuck out the window, with snowglasses that made him look like a monk peering into the manuscripts of the snow, because the windshield was covered with an inch of ice. He drove by the birth county of his forebears without a thought. In the morning the car skidded on an icy hill and flapped into a ditch. A farmer offered to help them out. They got hung-up when they picked up a hitchhiker who promised them a dollar if they'd let him ride to Memphis. In Memphis he went into his house, puttered around looking for the dollar, got drunk, and said he couldn't find it. They resumed across Tennessee; the bearings were beat from the accident. Dean had been driving ninety; now he had to stick to a steady seventy or the whole motor would go whirring down the mountainside. They crossed the Great Smoky Mountains in midwinter. When they arrived at my brother's door they had not eaten for thirty hours—except for candy and cheese crackers.

They ate voraciously as Dean, sandwich in hand, stood bowed and jumping before the big phonograph, listening to a wild bop record I had just bought called "The Hunt," with Dexter Gordon and Wardell Gray blowing their tops before a screaming audience that gave the record fantastic frenzied volume. The Southern folk looked at one another and shook their heads in awe. "What kind of friends does Sal have, anyway?" they said to my brother. He was stumped for an answer. Southerners don't like madness the least bit, not Dean's kind. He paid absolutely no attention to them. The madness of Dean had bloomed into a weird flower. I didn't realize this till he and I and Marylou and Dunkel left the house for a brief spin-the-Hudson, when for the first time we were alone and could talk about anything we wanted. Dean grabbed the wheel, shifted to second, mused a minute, rolling, suddenly seemed to decide something and shot the car full-jet down the road in a fury of decision.

"All right now, children," he said, rubbing his nose and bending down to feel the emergency and pulling cigarettes out of the compartment, and swaying back and forth as he did these things and drove. "The time has come for us to decide what we're going to do for the next week. Crucial, crucial. Ahem!" He dodged a mule wagon; in it sat an old Negro plodding along. "Yes!" yelled Dean. "Yes! Dig him! Now consider his soul—stop awhile and consider." And he slowed down the car for all of us to turn and look at the old jazzbo moaning along. "Oh yes, dig him sweet; now there's thoughts in that mind that I would give my last arm to know; to climb in there and find out just what he's poor-ass pondering about this year's turnip greens and ham. Sal, you don't know it but I once lived with a farmer in Arkansas for a whole year, when I was eleven. I had awful chores, I had to skin a dead horse once. Haven't been to Arkansas since Christmas nineteen-forty-three, five years ago, when Ben Gavin and I were chased by a man with a gun who owned the car we were trying to steal; I say all this to show you that of the South I can speak. I have known—I mean, man, I dig the South, I know it in and out—I've dug your letters to me about it. Oh yes, oh yes," he said, trailing off and stopping altogether, and suddenly jumping the car back to seventy and hunching over the wheel. He stared doggedly ahead. Marylou was smiling serenely. This was the new and complete Dean, grown to maturity. I said to myself, My God, he's changed. Fury spat out of his eyes when he told of things he hated; great glows of joy replaced this when he suddenly got happy; every muscle twitched to live and go. "Oh, man, the things I could tell you," he said, poking me, "Oh, man, we must absolutely find the time— What has happened to Carlo? We all get to see Carlo, darlings, first thing tomorrow. Now, Marylou, we're getting some bread and meat to make a lunch for New York. How much money do you have, Sal? We'll put everything in the back seat, Mrs. P's furniture, and all of us will sit up front cuddly and close and tell stories as we zoom to New York. Marylou, honeythighs, you sit next to me, Sal next, then Ed at the window, big Ed to cut off drafts, whereby he comes into using the robe this time. And then we'll all go off to sweet life, 'cause now is the time and *we all know time!*" He rubbed his jaw furiously, he swung the car and passed three trucks, he roared into downtown Testament, looking in every direction and seeing everything in an arc of 180 degrees around his eyeballs without moving his head. Bang, he found a parking space in no time, and we were parked. He leaped out of the car. Furiously he hustled into the railroad station; we followed sheepishly. He bought cigarettes. He had become absolutely mad in his movements; he seemed to be doing everything at the same time. It was a shaking of the head, up and down, sideways; jerky, vigorous hands; quick walking, sitting, crossing the legs, uncrossing, getting up, rubbing the hands, rubbing his fly, hitching his pants, looking up and saying "Am," and sudden slitting of the eyes to see everywhere; and all the time he was grabbing me by the ribs and talking, talking.

It was very cold in Testament; they'd had an unseasonable snow. He stood in the long bleak main street that runs along the railroad, clad in nothing but a T-shirt and low-hanging pants with the belt unbuckled, as though he was about to take them off. He came sticking his head in to talk to Marylou; he backed away, fluttering his hands before her. "Oh yes, I know! I know *you*, I know *you*, darling!" His laugh was maniacal; it started low and ended high, exactly like the laugh of a radio maniac, only faster and more like a titter. Then he kept reverting to businesslike tones. There was no purpose in our coming downtown, but he found purposes. He made us all hustle, Marylou for the lunch groceries, me for a paper to dig the weather report, Ed for cigars. Dean loved to smoke cigars. He smoked one over the paper and talked. "Ah, our holy American slopjaws in Washington are planning fur-ther inconveniences—ah-hem!—aw—hup! hup!" And he leaped off and rushed to see a colored girl that just then passed outside the station. "Dig her," he said, standing with limp finger pointed, fingering himself with a goofy smile, "that little gone black lovely. Ah! Hmm!" We got in the car and flew back to my brother's house.

I had been spending a quiet Christmas in the country, as I realized when we got back into the house and I saw the Christmas tree, the presents, and smelled the roasting turkey and listened to the talk of the relatives, but now the bug was on me again, and the bug's name was Dean Moriarty and I was off on another spurt around the road.

2

We packed my brother's furniture in back of the car and took off at dark, promising to be back in thirty hours—thirty hours for a thousand miles north and south. But that's the way Dean wanted it. It was a tough trip, and none of us noticed it; the heater was not working and consequently the windshield developed fog and ice; Dean kept reaching out while driving seventy to wipe it with a rag and make a hole to see the road. "Ah, holy hole!" In the spacious Hudson we had plenty of room for all four of us to sit up front. A blanket covered our laps. The radio was not working. It was a brand-new car bought five days ago, and already it was broken. There was only one installment paid on it, too. Off we went, north to Washington, on 301, a straight two-lane highway without much traffic. And Dean talked, no one else talked. He gestured furiously, he leaned as far as me sometimes to make a point, sometimes he had no hands on the wheel and yet the car went as straight as an arrow, not for once deviating from the white line in the middle of the road that unwound, kissing our left front tire.

It was a completely meaningless set of circumstances that made Dean come, and similarly I went off with him for no reason. In New York I had been attending school and romancing around with a girl called Lucille, a beautiful Italian honey-haired darling that I actually wanted to marry. All these years I was looking for the woman I wanted to marry. I couldn't meet a girl without saying to myself, What kind of wife would she make? I told Dean and Marylou about Lucille. Marylou wanted to know all about Lucille, she wanted to meet her. We zoomed through Richmond, Washington, Baltimore, and up to Philadelphia on a winding country road and talked. "I want to marry a girl," I told them, "so I can rest my soul with her till we both get old. This can't go on all the time—all this franticness and jumping around. We've got to go someplace, find something."

"Ah now, man," said Dean, "I've been digging you for years about the *home* and marriage and all those fine wonderful things about your soul." It was a sad night; it was also a merry night. In Philadelphia we went into a lunchcart and ate hamburgers with our last food dollar. The counterman—it was three A.M.—heard us talk about money and offered to give us the hamburgers free, plus more coffee, if we all pitched in and washed dishes in the back because his regular man hadn't shown up. We jumped to it. Ed Dunkel said he was an old pearldiver from way back and pitched his long arms into the dishes. Dean stood googing around with a towel, so did Mary-lou. Finally they started necking among the pots and pans; they withdrew to a dark corner in the pantry. The counter-man was satisfied as long as Ed and I did the dishes. We fin-ished them in fifteen minutes. When daybreak came we were zooming through New Jersey with the great cloud of Metro-politan New York rising before us in the snowy distance. Dean had a sweater wrapped around his ears to keep warm. He said we were a band of Arabs coming in to blow up New York. We swished through the Lincoln Tunnel and cut over to Times Square; Marylou wanted to see it.

"Oh damn, I wish I could find Hassel. Everybody look sharp, see if they can find him." We all scoured the sidewalks. "Good old gone Hassel. Oh you should have *seen* him in Texas."

So now Dean had come about four thousand miles from Frisco, via Arizona and up to Denver, inside four days, with in-numerable adventures sandwiched in, and it was only the beginning.

3

We went to my house in Paterson and slept. I was the first to wake up, late in the afternoon. Dean and Marylou were sleeping on my bed, Ed and I on my aunt's bed. Dean's bat-tered unhinged trunk lay sprawled on the floor with socks sticking out. A phone call came for me in the drugstore down-stairs. I ran down; it was from New Orleans. It was Old Bull Lee, who'd moved to New Orleans. Old Bull Lee in his high, whining voice was making a complaint. It seemed a girl called Galatea Dunkel had just arrived at his house for a guy Ed Dunkel; Bull had no idea who these people were. Galatea Dunkel was a tenacious loser. I told Bull to reassure her that Dunkel was with Dean and me and that most likely we'd be picking her up in New Orleans on the way to the Coast. Then the girl herself talked on the phone. She wanted to know how Ed was. She was all concerned about his happiness.

"How did you get from Tucson to New Orleans?" I asked. She said she wired home for money and took a bus. She was determined to catch up with Ed because she loved him. I went upstairs and told Big Ed. He sat in the chair with a worried look, an angel of a man, actually.

"All right, now," said Dean, suddenly waking up and leaping out of bed, "what we must do is eat, at once. Marylou, rustle around the kitchen see what there is. Sal, you and I go downstairs and call Carlo. Ed, you see what you can do straightening out the house." I followed Dean, bustling downstairs.

The guy who ran the drugstore said, "You just got another call—this one from San Francisco—for a guy called Dean Moriarty. I said there wasn't anybody by that name." It was sweetest Camille, calling Dean. The drugstore man, Sam, a tall, calm friend of mine, looked at me and scratched his head. "Geez, what are you running, an international whorehouse?"

Dean tittered maniacally. "I dig you, man!" He leaped into the phone booth and called San Francisco collect. Then we called Carlo at his home in Long Island and told him to come over. Carlo arrived two hours later. Meanwhile Dean and I got ready for our return trip alone to Virginia to pick up the rest of the furniture and bring my aunt back. Carlo Marx came, poetry under his arm, and sat in an easy chair, watching us with beady eyes. For the first half-hour he refused to say anything; at any rate, he refused to commit himself. He had quieted down since the Denver Doldrum days; the Dakar Doldrums had done it. In Dakar, wearing a beard, he had wandered the back streets with little children who led him to a witch-doctor who told him his fortune. He had snapshots of crazy streets with grass huts, the hip back-end of Dakar. He said he almost jumped off the ship like Hart Crane on the way back. Dean sat on the floor with a music box and listened with tremendous amazement at the little song it played, "A Fine Romance"— "Little tinkling whirling doodlebells. Ah! Listen! We'll all bend down together and look into the center of the music box till we learn about the secrets—tinklydoodlebell, whee." Ed Dunkel was also sitting on the floor; he had my drumsticks; he suddenly began beating a tiny beat to go with the music box, that we barely could hear. Everybody held his breath to listen. "Tick . . . tack . . . tick-tick . . . tack-tack." Dean cupped a hand over his ear; his mouth hung open; he said, "Ah! Whee!"

Carlo watched this silly madness with slitted eyes. Finally he slapped his knee and said, "I have an announcement to make."

"Yes? Yes?"

"What is the meaning of this voyage to New York? What kind of sordid business are you on now? I mean, man, whither goest thou? Whither goest thou, America, in thy shiny car in the night?"

"Whither goest thou?" echoed Dean with his mouth open. We sat and didn't know what to say; there was nothing to talk about any more. The only thing to do was go. Dean leaped up and said we were ready to go back to Virginia. He took a shower, I cooked up a big platter of rice with all that was left in the house, Marylou sewed his socks, and we were ready to go. Dean and Carlo and I zoomed into New York. We promised to see Carlo in thirty hours, in time for New Year's Eve. It was night. We left him at Times Square and went back through the expensive tunnel and into New Jersey and on the road. Taking turns at the wheel, Dean and I made Virginia in ten hours.

"Now this is the first time we've been alone and in a position to talk for years," said Dean. And he talked all night. As in a dream, we were zooming back through sleeping Washington and back in the Virginia wilds, crossing the Appomattox River at daybreak, pulling up at my brother's door at eight A.M. And all this time Dean was tremendously excited about everything he saw, everything he talked about, every detail of every moment that passed. He was out of his mind with real belief. "And of course now no one can tell us that there is no God. We've passed through all forms. You remember, Sal, when I first came to New York and I wanted Chad King to teach me about Nietzsche. You see how long ago? Everything is fine, God exists, we know time. Everything since the Greeks has been predicated wrong. You can't make it with geometry and geometrical systems of thinking. It's all *this!*" He wrapped his finger in his fist; the car hugged the line straight and true. "And not only that but we both understand that I couldn't have time to explain why I know and you know God exists." At one point I moaned about life's troubles—how poor my family was, how much I wanted to help Lucille, who was also poor and had a daughter. "Troubles, you see, is the generalization-word for what God exists in. The thing is not to get hung-up. My head rings!" he cried, clasping his head. He rushed out of the car like Groucho Marx to get cigarettes—that furious, ground-hugging walk with the coattails flying, except that he had no coattails. "Since Denver, Sal, a lot of things— Oh, the things —I've thought and thought. I used to be in reform school all the time, I was a young punk, asserting myself—stealing cars a psychological expression of my position, hincty to show. All my jail-problems are pretty straight now. As far as I know I shall never be in jail again. The rest is not my fault." We passed a little kid who was throwing stones at the cars in the road. "Think of it," said Dean. "One day he'll put a stone through a man's windshield and the man will crash and die—all on account of that little kid. You see what I mean? God exists without qualms. As we roll along this way I am positive beyond doubt that everything will be taken care of for us—that even you, as you drive, fearful of the wheel" (I hated to drive and drove carefully)—"the thing will go along of itself and you won't go off the road and I can sleep. Furthermore we know America, we're at home; I can go anywhere in America and get what I want because it's the same in every corner, I know the people, I know what they do. We give and take and go in the incredibly complicated sweetness zigzagging every side." There was nothing clear about the things he said, but what he meant to say was somehow made pure and clear. He used the word "pure" a great deal. I had never dreamed Dean would become a mystic. These were the first days of his mysticism, which would lead to the strange, ragged W. C. Fields saintliness of his later days.

Even my aunt listened to him with a curious half-ear as we roared back north to New York that same night with the furniture in the back. Now that my aunt was in the car, Dean settled down to talking about his worklife in San Francisco. We went over every single detail of what a brakeman has to do, demonstrating every time we passed yards, and at one point he even jumped out of the car to show me how a brakeman gives a highball at a meet at a siding. My aunt retired to the back seat and went to sleep. In Washington at four A.M. Dean again called Camille collect in Frisco. Shortly after this, as we pulled out of Washington, a cruising car overtook us with siren going and we had a speeding ticket in spite of the fact that we were going about thirty. It was the California license plate that did it. "You guys think you can rush through here as fast as you want just because you come from California?" said the cop.

I went with Dean to the sergeant's desk and we tried to explain to the police that we had no money. They said Dean would have to spend the night in jail if we didn't round up the money. Of course my aunt had it, fifteen dollars; she had twenty in all, and it was going to be just fine. And in fact while we were arguing with the cops one of them went out to peek at my aunt, who sat wrapped in the back of the car. She saw him.

"Don't worry, I'm not a gun moll. If you want to come and search the car, go right ahead. I'm going home with my nephew, and this furniture isn't stolen; it's my niece's, she just had a baby and she's moving to her new house." This flabbergasted Sherlock and he went back in the station house. My aunt had to pay the fine for Dean or we'd be stuck in Washington; I had no license. He promised to pay it back, and he actually did, exactly a year and a half later and to my aunt's pleased surprise. My aunt—a respectable woman hung-up in this sad world, and well she knew the world. She told us about the cop. "He was hiding behind the tree, trying to see what I looked like. I told him—I told him to search the car if he wanted. I've nothing to be ashamed of." She knew Dean had something to be ashamed of, and me too, by virtue of my being with Dean, and Dean and I accepted this sadly.

My aunt once said the world would never find peace until men fell at their women's feet and asked for forgiveness. But Dean knew this; he'd mentioned it many times. "I've pleaded and pleaded with Marylou for a peaceful sweet understanding of pure love between us forever with all hassles thrown out—she understands; her mind is bent on something else—she's after me; she won't understand how much I love her, she's knitting my doom."

"The truth of the matter is we don't understand our women; we blame on them and it's all our fault," I said.

"But it isn't as simple as that," warned Dean. "Peace will come suddenly, we won't understand when it does—see, man?" Doggedly, bleakly, he pushed the car through New Jersey; at dawn I drove into Paterson as he slept in the back. We arrived at the house at eight in the morning to find Marylou and Ed Dunkel sitting around smoking butts from the ash-trays; they hadn't eaten since Dean and I left. My aunt bought groceries and cooked up a tremendous breakfast.

4

Now it was time for the Western threesome to find new living quarters in Manhattan proper. Carlo had a pad on York Avenue; they were moving in that evening. We slept all day, Dean and I, and woke up as a great snowstorm ushered in New Year's Eve, 1948. Ed Dunkel was sitting in my easy chair, telling about the previous New Year's. "I was in Chicago. I was broke. I was sitting at the window of my hotel room on North Clark Street and the most delicious smell rose to my nostrils from the bakery downstairs. I didn't have a dime but I went down and talked to the girl. She gave me bread and cof-fee cakes free. I went back to my room and ate them. I stayed in my room all night. In Farmington, Utah, once, where I went to work with Ed Wall—you know Ed Wall, the rancher's son in Denver—I was in my bed and all of a sudden I saw my dead mother standing in the corner with light all around her. I said, 'Mother!' She disappeared. I have visions all the time," said Ed Dunkel, nodding his head.

"What are you going to do about Galatea?"

"Oh, we'll see. When we get to New Orleans. Don't you think so, huh?" He was starting to turn to me as well for ad-vice; one Dean wasn't enough for him. But he was already in love with Galatea, pondering it.

"What are you going to do with yourself, Ed?" I asked.

"I don't know," he said. "I just go along. I dig life." He re-peated it, following Dean's line. He had no direction. He sat reminiscing about that night in Chicago and the hot coffee cakes in the lonely room.

The snow whirled outside. A big party was on hand in New York; we were all going. Dean packed his broken trunk, put it in the car, and we all took off for the big night. My aunt was happy with the thought that my brother would be visiting her the following week; she sat with her paper and waited for the midnight New Year's Eve broadcast from Times Square. We roared into New York, swerving on ice. I was never scared when Dean drove; he could handle a car under any circumstances. The radio had been fixed and now he had wild bop to urge us along the night. I didn't know where all this was leading; I didn't care.

Just about that time a strange thing began to haunt me. It was this: I had forgotten something. There was a decision that I was about to make before Dean showed up, and now it was driven clear out of my mind but still hung on the tip of my mind's tongue. I kept snapping my fingers, trying to remember it. I even mentioned it. And I couldn't even tell if it was a real decision or just a thought I had forgotten. It haunted and flabbergasted me, made me sad. It had to do somewhat with the Shrouded Traveler. Carlo Marx and I once sat down together, knee to knee, in two chairs, facing, and I told him a dream I had about a strange Arabian figure that was pursuing me across the desert; that I tried to avoid; that finally overtook me just before I reached the Protective City. "Who is this?" said Carlo. We pondered it. I proposed it was myself, wearing a shroud. That wasn't it. Something, someone, some spirit was pursuing all of us across the desert of life and was bound to catch us before we reached heaven. Naturally, now that I look back on it, this is only death: death will overtake us before heaven. The one thing that we yearn for in our living days, that makes us sigh and groan and undergo sweet nauseas of all kinds, is the remembrance of some lost bliss that was probably experienced in the womb and can only be reproduced (though we hate to admit it) in death. But who wants to die? In the rush of events I kept thinking about this in the back of my mind. I told it to Dean and he instantly recognized it as the mere simple longing for pure death; and because we're all of us never in life again, he, rightly, would have nothing to do with it, and I agreed with him then.

We went looking for my New York gang of friends. The crazy flowers bloom there too. We went to Tom Saybrook's first. Tom is a sad, handsome fellow, sweet, generous, and amenable; only once in a while he suddenly has fits of depression and rushes off without saying a word to anyone. This night he was overjoyed. "Sal, where did you find these absolutely wonderful people? I've never seen anyone like them."

"I found them in the West."

Dean was having his kicks; he put on a jazz record, grabbed Marylou, held her tight, and bounced against her with the beat of the music. She bounced right back. It was a real love dance. Ian MacArthur came in with a huge gang. The New Year's weekend began, and lasted three days and three nights. Great gangs got in the Hudson and swerved in the snowy New York streets from party to party. I brought Lucille and her sister to the biggest party. When Lucille saw me with Dean and Marylou her face darkened—she sensed the madness they put in me.

"I don't like you when you're with them."

"Ah, it's all right, it's just kicks. We only live once. We're having a good time."

"No, it's sad and I don't like it."

Then Marylou began making love to me; she said Dean was going to stay with Camille and she wanted me to go with her. "Come back to San Francisco with us. We'll live together. I'll be a good girl for you." But I knew Dean loved Marylou, and I also knew Marylou was doing this to make Lucille jealous, and I wanted nothing of it. Still and all, I licked my lips for the luscious blonde. When Lucille saw Marylou pushing me into the corners and giving me the word and forcing kisses on me she accepted Dean's invitation to go out in the car; but they just talked and drank some of the Southern moonshine I left in the compartment. Everything was being mixed up, and all was falling. I knew my affair with Lucille wouldn't last much longer. She wanted me to be *her way*. She was married to a longshoreman who treated her badly. I was willing to marry her and take her baby daughter and all if she divorced the husband; but there wasn't even enough money to get a divorce and the whole thing was hopeless, besides which Lucille would never understand me because I like too many things and get all confused and hung-up running from one falling star to another till I drop. This is the night, what it does to you. I had nothing to offer anybody except my own confusion.

The parties were enormous; there were at least a hundred people at a basement apartment in the West Nineties. People overflowed into the cellar compartments near the furnace. Something was going on in every corner, on every bed and couch—not an orgy but just a New Year's party with frantic screaming and wild radio music. There was even a Chinese girl. Dean ran like Groucho Marx from group to group, digging everybody. Periodically we rushed out to the car to pick up more people. Damion came. Damion is the hero of my New York gang, as Dean is the chief hero of the Western. They immediately took a dislike to each other. Damion's girl suddenly socked Damion on the jaw with a roundhouse right. He stood reeling. She carried him home. Some of our mad newspaper friends came in from the office with bottles. There was a tremendous and wonderful snowstorm going on outside. Ed Dunkel met Lucille's sister and disappeared with her; I forgot to say that Ed Dunkel is a very smooth man with the women. He's six foot four, mild, affable, agreeable, bland, and delightful. He helps women on with their coats. That's the way to do things. At five o'clock in the morning we were all rushing through the backyard of a tenement and climbing in through a window of an apartment where a huge party was going on. At dawn we were back at Tom Saybrook's. People were drawing pictures and drinking stale beer. I slept on a couch with a girl called Mona in my arms. Great groups filed in from the old Columbia Campus bar. Everything in life, all the faces of life, were piling into the same dank room. At Ian MacArthur's the party went on. Ian MacArthur is a wonderful sweet fellow who wears glasses and peers out of them with delight. He began to learn "Yes!" to everything, just like Dean at this time, and hasn't stopped since. To the wild sounds of Dexter Gordon and Wardell Gray blowing "The Hunt," Dean and I played catch with Marylou over the couch; she was no small doll either. Dean went around with no undershirt, just his pants, barefoot, till it was time to hit the car and fetch more people. Everything happened. We found the wild, ecstatic Rollo Greb and spent a night at his house on Long Island. Rollo lives in a nice house with his aunt; when she dies the house is all his. Meanwhile she refuses to comply with any of his wishes and hates his friends. He brought this ragged gang of Dean, Marylou, Ed, and me, and began a roaring party. The woman prowled upstairs; she threatened to call the police. "Oh, shut up, you old bag!"

yelled Greb. I wondered how he could live with her like this.
He had more books than I've ever seen in all my life—two libraries, two rooms loaded from floor to ceiling around all four
walls, and such books as the Apocryphal Something-or-Other
in ten volumes. He played Verdi operas and pantomimed them
in his pajamas with a great rip down the back. He didn't give a
damn about anything. He is a great scholar who goes reeling
down the New York waterfront with original seventeenth-
century musical manuscripts under his arm, shouting. He
crawls like a big spider through the streets. His excitement
blew out of his eyes in stabs of fiendish light. He rolled his
neck in spastic ecstasy. He lisped, he writhed, he flopped, he
moaned, he howled, he fell back in despair. He could hardly
get a word out, he was so excited with life. Dean stood before
him with head bowed, repeating over and over again, "Yes . . .
Yes . . . Yes." He took me into a corner. "That Rollo Greb is
the greatest, most wonderful of all. That's what I was trying to
tell you—that's what I want to be. I want to be like him. He's
never hung-up, he goes every direction, he lets it all out, he
knows time, he has nothing to do but rock back and forth.
Man, he's the end! You see, if you go like him all the time
you'll finally get it."

"Get what?"

"IT! IT! I'll tell you—now no time, we have no time now."
Dean rushed back to watch Rollo Greb some more.

George Shearing, the great jazz pianist, Dean said, was exactly like Rollo Greb. Dean and I went to see Shearing at Birdland in the midst of the long, mad weekend. The place was
deserted, we were the first customers, ten o'clock. Shearing
came out, blind, led by the hand to his keyboard. He was a
distinguished-looking Englishman with a stiff white collar,
slightly beefy, blond, with a delicate English-summer's-night
air about him that came out in the first rippling sweet number
he played as the bass-player leaned to him reverently and
thrummed the beat. The drummer, Denzil Best, sat motionless except for his wrists snapping the brushes. And Shearing
began to rock; a smile broke over his ecstatic face; he began to
rock in the piano seat, back and forth, slowly at first, then the
beat went up, and he began rocking fast, his left foot jumped
up with every beat, his neck began to rock crookedly, he

brought his face down to the keys, he pushed his hair back, his combed hair dissolved, he began to sweat. The music picked up. The bass-player hunched over and socked it in, faster and faster, it seemed faster and faster, that's all. Shearing began to play his chords; they rolled out of the piano in great rich showers, you'd think the man wouldn't have time to line them up. They rolled and rolled like the sea. Folks yelled for him to "Go!" Dean was sweating; the sweat poured down his collar. "There he is! That's him! Old God! Old God Shearing! Yes! Yes! Yes!" And Shearing was conscious of the madman behind him, he could hear every one of Dean's gasps and imprecations, he could sense it though he couldn't see. "That's right!" Dean said. "Yes!" Shearing smiled; he rocked. Shearing rose from the piano, dripping with sweat; these were his great 1949 days before he became cool and commercial. When he was gone Dean pointed to the empty piano seat. "God's empty chair," he said. On the piano a horn sat; its golden shadow made a strange reflection along the desert caravan painted on the wall behind the drums. God was gone; it was the silence of his departure. It was a rainy night. It was the myth of the rainy night. Dean was popeyed with awe. This madness would lead nowhere. I didn't know what was happening to me, and I suddenly realized it was only the tea that we were smoking; Dean had bought some in New York. It made me think that everything was about to arrive—the moment when you know all and everything is decided forever.

5

I left everybody and went home to rest. My aunt said I was wasting my time hanging around with Dean and his gang. I knew that was wrong, too. Life is life, and kind is kind. What I wanted was to take one more magnificent trip to the West Coast and get back in time for the spring semester in school. And what a trip it turned out to be! I only went along for the ride, and to see what else Dean was going to do, and finally, also, knowing Dean would go back to Camille in Frisco, I wanted to have an affair with Marylou. We got ready to cross the groaning continent again. I drew my GI check and gave Dean eighteen dollars to mail to his wife; she was waiting for him to come home and she was broke. What was on Marylou's mind I don't know. Ed Dunkel, as ever, just followed.

There were long, funny days spent in Carlo's apartment before we left. He went around in his bathrobe and made semi-ironical speeches: "Now I'm not trying to take your hincty sweets from you, but it seems to me the time has come to decide what you are and what you're going to do." Carlo was working as typist in an office. "I want to know what all this sitting around the house all day is intended to mean. What all this talk is and what you propose to do. Dean, why did you leave Camille and pick up Marylou?" No answer—giggles. "Marylou, why are you traveling around the country like this and what are your womanly intentions concerning the shroud?" Same answer. "Ed Dunkel, why did you abandon your new wife in Tucson and what are you doing here sitting on your big fat ass? Where's your home? What's your job?" Ed Dunkel bowed his head in genuine befuddlement. "Sal—how comes it you've fallen on such sloppy days and what have you done with Lucille?" He adjusted his bathrobe and sat facing us all. "The days of wrath are yet to come. The balloon won't sustain you much longer. And not only that, but it's an abstract balloon. You'll all go flying to the West Coast and come staggering back in search of your stone."

In these days Carlo had developed a tone of voice which he hoped sounded like what he called The Voice of Rock; the whole idea was to stun people into the realization of the rock. "You pin a dragon to your hats," he warned us; "you're up in the attic with the bats." His mad eyes glittered at us. Since the Dakar Doldrums he had gone through a terrible period which he called the Holy Doldrums, or Harlem Doldrums, when he lived in Harlem in midsummer and at night woke up in his lonely room and heard "the great machine" descending from the sky; and when he walked on 125th Street "under water" with all the other fish. It was a riot of radiant ideas that had come to enlighten his brain. He made Marylou sit on his lap and commanded her to subside. He told Dean, "Why don't you just sit down and relax? Why do you jump around so much?" Dean ran around, putting sugar in his coffee and saying, "Yes!

Yes! Yes!" At night Ed Dunkel slept on the floor on cushions, Dean and Marylou pushed Carlo out of bed, and Carlo sat up in the kitchen over his kidney stew, mumbling the predictions of the rock. I came in days and watched everything.

Ed Dunkel said to me, "Last night I walked clear down to Times Square and just as I arrived I suddenly realized I was a ghost—it was my ghost walking on the sidewalk." He said these things to me without comment, nodding his head emphatically. Ten hours later, in the midst of someone else's conversation, Ed said, "Yep, it was my ghost walking on the sidewalk."

Suddenly Dean leaned to me earnestly and said, "Sal, I have something to ask of you—very important to me—I wonder how you'll take it—we're buddies, aren't we?"

"Sure are, Dean." He almost blushed. Finally he came out with it: he wanted me to work Marylou. I didn't ask him why because I knew he wanted to see what Marylou was like with another man. We were sitting in Ritzy's Bar when he proposed the idea; we'd spent an hour walking Times Square, looking for Hassel. Ritzy's Bar is the hoodlum bar of the streets around Times Square; it changes names every year. You walk in there and you don't see a single girl, even in the booths, just a great mob of young men dressed in all varieties of hoodlum cloth, from red shirts to zoot suits. It is also the hustlers' bar—the boys who make a living among the sad old homos of the Eighth Avenue night. Dean walked in there with his eyes slitted to see every single face. There were wild Negro queers, sullen guys with guns, shiv-packing seamen, thin, noncommittal junkies, and an occasional well-dressed middle-aged detective, posing as a bookie and hanging around half for interest and half for duty. It was the typical place for Dean to put down his request. All kinds of evil plans are hatched in Ritzy's Bar—you can sense it in the air—and all kinds of mad sexual routines are initiated to go with them. The safecracker proposes not only a certain loft on 14th Street to the hoodlum, but that they sleep together. Kinsey spent a lot of time in Ritzy's Bar, interviewing some of the boys; I was there the night his assistant came, in 1945. Hassel and Carlo were interviewed.

Dean and I drove back to the pad and found Marylou in bed. Dunkel was roaming his ghost around New York. Dean told her what we had decided. She said she was pleased. I wasn't so sure myself. I had to prove that I'd go through with it. The bed had been the deathbed of a big man and sagged in the middle. Marylou lay there, with Dean and myself on each side of her, poised on the upjutting mattress-ends, not knowing what to say. I said, "Ah hell, I can't do this."

"Go on, man, you promised!" said Dean.

"What about Marylou?" I said. "Come on, Marylou, what do you think?"

"Go ahead," she said.

She embraced me and I tried to forget old Dean was there. Every time I realized he was there in the dark, listening for every sound, I couldn't do anything but laugh. It was horrible.

"We must all relax," said Dean.

"I'm afraid I can't make it. Why don't you go in the kitchen a minute?"

Dean did so. Marylou was so lovely, but I whispered, "Wait until we be lovers in San Francisco; my heart isn't in it." I was right, she could tell. It was three children of the earth trying to decide something in the night and having all the weight of past centuries ballooning in the dark before them. There was a strange quiet in the apartment. I went and tapped Dean and told him to go to Marylou; and I retired to the couch. I could hear Dean, blissful and blabbering and frantically rocking. Only a guy who's spent five years in jail can go to such maniacal helpless extremes; beseeching at the portals of the soft source, mad with a completely physical realization of the origins of life-bliss; blindly seeking to return the way he came. This is the result of years looking at sexy pictures behind bars; looking at the legs and breasts of women in popular magazines; evaluating the hardness of the steel halls and the softness of the woman who is not there. Prison is where you promise yourself the right to live. Dean had never seen his mother's face. Every new girl, every new wife, every new child was an addition to his bleak impoverishment. Where was his father?—old bum Dean Moriarty the Tinsmith, riding freights, working as a scullion in railroad cookshacks, stumbling, down-crashing in wino alley nights, expiring on coal piles, dropping his yellowed teeth one by one in the gutters of the West. Dean had every right to die the sweet deaths of complete love of his Marylou. I didn't want to interfere, I just wanted to follow.

Carlo came back at dawn and put on his bathrobe. He wasn't sleeping any more those days. "Ech!" he screamed. He was going out of his mind from the confusion of jam on the floor, pants, dresses thrown around, cigarette butts, dirty dishes, open books—it was a great forum we were having. Every day the world groaned to turn and we were making our appalling studies of the night. Marylou was black and blue from a fight with Dean about something; his face was scratched. It was time to go.

We drove to my house, a whole gang of ten, to get my bag and call Old Bull Lee in New Orleans from the phone in the bar where Dean and I had our first talk years ago when he came to my door to learn to write. We heard Bull's whining voice eighteen hundred miles away. "Say, what do you boys expect me to do with this Galatea Dunkel? She's been here two weeks now, hiding in her room and refusing to talk to either Jane or me. Have you got this character Ed Dunkel with you? For krissakes bring him down and get rid of her. She's sleeping in our best bedroom and's run clear out of money. This ain't a hotel." He assured Bull with whoops and cries over the phone —there was Dean, Marylou, Carlo, Dunkel, me, Ian MacArthur, his wife, Tom Saybrook, God knows who else, all yelling and drinking beer over the phone at befuddled Bull, who above all things hated confusion. "Well," he said, "maybe you'll make better sense when you gets down here if you gets down here." I said good-by to my aunt and promised to be back in two weeks and took off for California again.

6

It was drizzling and mysterious at the beginning of our journey. I could see that it was all going to be one big saga of the mist. "Whooee!" yelled Dean. "Here we go!" And he hunched over the wheel and gunned her; he was back in his element, everybody could see that. We were all delighted, we all realized we were leaving confusion and nonsense behind and performing our one and noble function of the time, *move*. And we moved! We flashed past the mysterious white signs in the night somewhere in New Jersey that say SOUTH (with an arrow) and WEST (with an arrow) and took the south one. New Orleans! It burned in our brains. From the dirty snows of "frosty fagtown New York," as Dean called it, all the way to the greeneries and river smells of old New Orleans at the washed-out bottom of America; then west. Ed was in the back seat; Marylou and Dean and I sat in front and had the warmest talk about the goodness and joy of life. Dean suddenly became tender. "Now dammit, look here, all of you, we all must admit that everything is fine and there's no need in the world to worry, and in fact we should realize what it would mean to us to UNDERSTAND that we're not REALLY worried about ANY-THING. Am I right?" We all agreed. "Here we go, we're all to-gether . . . What did we do in New York? Let's forgive." We all had our spats back there. "That's behind us, merely by miles and inclinations. Now we're heading down to New Or-leans to dig Old Bull Lee and ain't that going to be kicks and listen will you to this old tenorman blow his top"—he shot up the radio volume till the car shuddered—"and listen to him tell the story and put down true relaxation and knowledge."

We all jumped to the music and agreed. The purity of the road. The white line in the middle of the highway unrolled and hugged our left front tire as if glued to our groove. Dean hunched his muscular neck, T-shirted in the winter night, and blasted the car along. He insisted I drive through Baltimore for traffic practice; that was all right, except he and Marylou insisted on steering while they kissed and fooled around. It was crazy; the radio was on full blast. Dean beat drums on the dashboard till a great sag developed in it; I did too. The poor Hudson—the slow boat to China—was receiving her beating.

"Oh man, what kicks!" yelled Dean. "Now Marylou, listen really, honey, you know that I'm hotrock capable of everything at the same time and I have unlimited energy—now in San Francisco we must go on living together. I know just the place for you—at the end of the regular chain-gang run—I'll be home just a cut-hair less than every two days and for twelve hours at a stretch, and *man*, you know what we can do in twelve hours, darling. Meanwhile I'll go right on living at Camille's like nothin, see, she won't know. We can work it, we've done it before." It was all right with Marylou, she was really out for Camille's scalp. The understanding had been that Marylou would switch to me in Frisco, but I now began to see they were going to stick and I was going to be left alone on my butt at the other end of the continent. But why think about that when all the golden land's ahead of you and all kinds of unforeseen events wait lurking to surprise you and make you glad you're alive to see?

We arrived in Washington at dawn. It was the day of Harry Truman's inauguration for his second term. Great displays of war might were lined along Pennsylvania Avenue as we rolled by in our battered boat. There were B-29s, PT boats, artillery, all kinds of war material that looked murderous in the snowy grass; the last thing was a regular small ordinary lifeboat that looked pitiful and foolish. Dean slowed down to look at it. He kept shaking his head in awe. "What are these people up to? Harry's sleeping somewhere in this town. . . . Good old Harry. . . . Man from Missouri, as I am. . . . That must be his own boat."

Dean went to sleep in the back seat and Dunkel drove. We gave him specific instructions to take it easy. No sooner were we snoring than he gunned the car up to eighty, bad bearings and all, and not only that but he made a triple pass at a spot where a cop was arguing with a motorist—he was in the fourth lane of a four-lane highway, going the wrong way. Naturally the cop took after us with his siren whining. We were stopped. He told us to follow him to the station house. There was a mean cop in there who took an immediate dislike to Dean; he could smell jail all over him. He sent his cohort outdoors to question Marylou and me privately. They wanted to know how old Marylou was, they were trying to whip up a Mann Act idea. But she had her marriage certificate. Then they took me aside alone and wanted to know who was sleeping with Marylou. "Her husband," I said quite simply. They were curious. Something was fishy. They tried some amateur Sherlocking by asking the same questions twice, expecting us to make a slip. I said, "Those two fellows are going back to work on the railroad in California, this is the short one's wife, and I'm a friend on a two-week vacation from college."

The cop smiled and said, "Yeah? Is this really your own wallet?"

Finally the mean one inside fined Dean twenty-five dollars. We told them we only had forty to go all the way to the Coast; they said that made no difference to them. When Dean protested, the mean cop threatened to take him back to Pennsylvania and slap a special charge on him.

"What charge?"

"Never mind what charge. Don't worry about *that*, wise guy."

We had to give them the twenty-five. But first Ed Dunkel, that culprit, offered to go to jail. Dean considered it. The cop was infuriated; he said, "If you let your partner go to jail I'm taking you back to Pennsylvania right now. You hear that?" All we wanted to do was go. "Another speeding ticket in Virginia and you lose your car," said the mean cop as a parting volley. Dean was red in the face. We drove off silently. It was just like an invitation to steal to take our trip-money away from us. They knew we were broke and had no relatives on the road or to wire to for money. The American police are involved in psychological warfare against those Americans who don't frighten them with imposing papers and threats. It's a Victorian police force; it peers out of musty windows and wants to inquire about everything, and can make crimes if the crimes don't exist to its satisfaction. "Nine lines of crime, one of boredom," said Louis-Ferdinand Céline. Dean was so mad he wanted to come back to Virginia and shoot the cop as soon as he had a gun.

"Pennsylvania!" he scoffed. "I wish I knew what that charge was! Vag, probably; take all my money and charge me vag. Those guys have it so damn easy. They'll out and shoot you if you complain, too." There was nothing to do but get happy with ourselves again and forget about it. When we got through Richmond we began forgetting about it, and soon everything was okay.

Now we had fifteen dollars to go all the way. We'd have to pick up hitchhikers and bum quarters off them for gas. In the Virginia wilderness suddenly we saw a man walking on the road. Dean zoomed to a stop. I looked back and said he was only a bum and probably didn't have a cent.

"We'll just pick him up for kicks!" Dean laughed. The man was a ragged, bespectacled mad type, walking along reading a paperbacked muddy book he'd found in a culvert by the road.

He got in the car and went right on reading; he was incredibly filthy and covered with scabs. He said his name was Hyman Solomon and that he walked all over the USA, knocking and sometimes kicking at Jewish doors and demanding money: "Give me money to eat, I am a Jew."

He said it worked very well and that it was coming to him. We asked him what he was reading. He didn't know. He didn't bother to look at the title page. He was only looking at the words, as though he had found the real Torah where it belonged, in the wilderness.

"See? See? See?" cackled Dean, poking my ribs. "I told you it was kicks. Everybody's kicks, man!" We carried Solomon all the way to Testament. My brother by now was in his new house on the other side of town. Here we were back on the long, bleak street with the railroad track running down the middle and the sad, sullen Southerners loping in front of hardware stores and five-and-tens.

Solomon said, "I see you people need a little money to continue your journey. You wait for me and I'll go hustle up a few dollars at a Jewish home and I'll go along with you as far as Alabama." Dean was all beside himself with happiness; he and I rushed off to buy bread and cheese spread for a lunch in the car. Marylou and Ed waited in the car. We spent two hours in Testament waiting for Hyman Solomon to show up; he was hustling for his bread somewhere in town, but we couldn't see him. The sun began to grow red and late.

Solomon never showed up so we roared out of Testament. "Now you see, Sal, God does exist, because we keep getting hung-up with this town, no matter what we try to do, and you'll notice the strange Biblical name of it, and that strange Biblical character who made us stop here once more, and all things tied together all over like rain connecting everybody the world over by chain touch. . . ." Dean rattled on like this; he was overjoyed and exuberant. He and I suddenly saw the whole country like an oyster for us to open; and the pearl was there, the pearl was there. Off we roared south. We picked up another hitchhiker. This was a sad young kid who said he had an aunt who owned a grocery store in Dunn, North Carolina, right outside Fayetteville. "When we get there can you bum a buck off her? Right! Fine! Let's go!" We were in Dunn in an hour, at dusk. We drove to where the kid said his aunt had the grocery store. It was a sad little street that dead-ended at a factory wall. There was a grocery store but there was no aunt. We wondered what the kid was talking about. We asked him how far he was going; he didn't know. It was a big hoax; once upon a time, in some lost back-alley adventure, he had seen the grocery store in Dunn, and it was the first story that popped into his disordered, feverish mind. We bought him a hot dog, but Dean said we couldn't take him along because we needed room to sleep and room for hitchhikers who could buy a little gas. This was sad but true. We left him in Dunn at nightfall.

I drove through South Carolina and beyond Macon, Georgia, as Dean, Marylou, and Ed slept. All alone in the night I had my own thoughts and held the car to the white line in the holy road. What was I doing? Where was I going? I'd soon find out. I got dog-tired beyond Macon and woke up Dean to resume. We got out of the car for air and suddenly both of us were stoned with joy to realize that in the darkness all around us was fragrant green grass and the smell of fresh manure and warm waters. "We're in the South! We've left the winter!" Faint daybreak illuminated green shoots by the side of the road. I took a deep breath; a locomotive howled across the darkness, Mobile-bound. So were we. I took off my shirt and exulted. Ten miles down the road Dean drove into a filling station with the motor off, noticed that the attendant was fast asleep at the desk, jumped out, quietly filled the gas tank, saw to it the bell didn't ring, and rolled off like an Arab with a five-dollar tankful of gas for our pilgrimage.

I slept and woke up to the crazy exultant sounds of music and Dean and Marylou talking and the great green land rolling by. "Where are we?"

"Just passed the tip of Florida, man—Flomaton, it's called." Florida! We were rolling down to the coastal plain and Mobile; up ahead were great soaring clouds of the Gulf of Mexico. It was only thirty-two hours since we'd said good-by to everybody in the dirty snows of the North. We stopped at a gas station, and there Dean and Marylou played piggyback around the tanks and Dunkel went inside and stole three packs of cigarettes without trying. We were fresh out. Rolling into Mobile over the long tidal highway, we all took our winter clothes off and enjoyed the Southern temperature. This was when Dean started telling his life story and when, beyond Mobile, he came upon an obstruction of wrangling cars at a crossroads and instead of slipping around them just balled right through the driveway of a gas station and went right on without relaxing his steady continental seventy. We left gaping faces behind us. He went right on with his tale. "I tell you it's true, I started at nine, with a girl called Milly Mayfair in back of Rod's garage on Grant Street—same street Carlo lived on in Denver. That's when my father was still working at the smithy's a bit. I remember my aunt yelling out the window, 'What are you doing down there in back of the garage?' Oh honey Marylou, if I'd only known you then! Wow! How sweet you musta been at nine." He tittered maniacally; he stuck his finger in her mouth and licked it; he took her hand and rubbed it over himself. She just sat there, smiling serenely.

Big long Ed Dunkel sat looking out the window, talking to himself. "Yes sir, I thought I was a ghost that night." He was also wondering what Galatea Dunkel would say to him in New Orleans.

Dean went on. "One time I rode a freight from New Mexico clear to LA—I was eleven years old, lost my father at a siding, we were all in a hobo jungle, I was with a man called Big Red, my father was out drunk in a boxcar—it started to roll—Big Red and I missed it—I didn't see my father for months. I rode a long freight all the way to California, really flying, first-class freight, a desert Zipper. All the way I rode over the couplings —you can imagine how dangerous, I was only a kid, I didn't know—clutching a loaf of bread under one arm and the other hooked around the brake bar. This is no story, this is true. When I got to LA I was so starved for milk and cream I got a job in a dairy and the first thing I did I drank two quarts of heavy cream and puked."

"Poor Dean," said Marylou, and she kissed him. He stared ahead proudly. He loved her.

We were suddenly driving along the blue waters of the Gulf, and at the same time a momentous mad thing began on the radio; it was the Chicken Jazz'n Gumbo disk-jockey show from New Orleans, all mad jazz records, colored records, with the disk jockey saying, "Don't worry 'bout *nothing!*" We saw

New Orleans in the night ahead of us with joy. Dean rubbed his hands over the wheel. "Now we're going to get our kicks!" At dusk we were coming into the humming streets of New Orleans. "Oh, smell the people!" yelled Dean with his face out the window, sniffing. "Ah! God! Life!" He swung around a trolley. "Yes!" He darted the car and looked in every direction for girls. "Look at *her!*" The air was so sweet in New Orleans it seemed to come in soft bandannas; and you could smell the river and really smell the people, and mud, and molasses, and every kind of tropical exhalation with your nose suddenly removed from the dry ices of a Northern winter. We bounced in our seats. "And dig her!" yelled Dean, pointing at another woman. "Oh, I love, love, love women! I think women are wonderful! I love women!" He spat out the window; he groaned; he clutched his head. Great beads of sweat fell from his forehead from pure excitement and exhaustion.

We bounced the car up on the Algiers ferry and found ourselves crossing the Mississippi River by boat. "Now we must all get out and dig the river and the people and smell the world," said Dean, bustling with his sunglasses and cigarettes and leaping out of the car like a jack-in-the-box. We followed. On rails we leaned and looked at the great brown father of waters rolling down from mid-America like the torrent of broken souls—bearing Montana logs and Dakota muds and Iowa vales and things that had drowned in Three Forks, where the secret began in ice. Smoky New Orleans receded on one side; old, sleepy Algiers with its warped woodsides bumped us on the other. Negroes were working in the hot afternoon, stoking the ferry furnaces that burned red and made our tires smell. Dean dug them, hopping up and down in the heat. He rushed around the deck and upstairs with his baggy pants hanging halfway down his belly. Suddenly I saw him eagering on the flying bridge. I expected him to take off on wings. I heard his mad laugh all over the boat—"Hee-hee-hee-hee-hee!" Marylou was with him. He covered everything in a jiffy, came back with the full story, jumped in the car just as everybody was tooting to go, and we slipped off, passing two or three cars in a narrow space, and found ourselves darting through Algiers.

"Where? Where?" Dean was yelling.

We decided first to clean up at a gas station and inquire for

Bull's whereabouts. Little children were playing in the drowsy river sunset; girls were going by with bandannas and cotton blouses and bare legs. Dean ran up the street to see everything. He looked around; he nodded; he rubbed his belly. Big Ed sat back in the car with his hat over his eyes, smiling at Dean. I sat on the fender. Marylou was in the women's john. From bushy shores where infinitesimal men fished with sticks, and from delta sleeps that stretched up along the reddening land, the big humpbacked river with its mainstream leaping came coiling around Algiers like a snake, with a nameless rumble. Drowsy, peninsular Algiers with all her bees and shanties was like to be washed away someday. The sun slanted, bugs flipflopped, the awful waters groaned.

We went to Old Bull Lee's house outside town near the river levee. It was on a road that ran across a swampy field. The house was a dilapidated old heap with sagging porches running around and weeping willows in the yard; the grass was a yard high, old fences leaned, old barns collapsed. There was no one in sight. We pulled right into the yard and saw washtubs on the back porch. I got out and went to the screen door. Jane Lee was standing in it with her eyes cupped toward the sun. "Jane," I said. "It's me. It's us."

She knew that. "Yes, I know. Bull isn't here now. Isn't that a fire or something over there?" We both looked toward the sun.

"You mean the sun?"

"Of course I don't mean the sun—I heard sirens that way. Don't you know a peculiar glow?" It was toward New Orleans; the clouds were strange.

"I don't see anything," I said.

Jane snuffed down her nose. "Same old Paradise."

That was the way we greeted each other after four years; Jane used to live with my wife and me in New York. "And is Galatea Dunkel here?" I asked. Jane was still looking for her fire; in those days she ate three tubes of benzedrine paper a day. Her face, once plump and Germanic and pretty, had become stony and red and gaunt. She had caught polio in New Orleans and limped a little. Sheepishly Dean and the gang came out of the car and more or less made themselves at home. Galatea Dunkel came out of her stately retirement in the back of the house to meet her tormentor. Galatea was a serious girl. She was pale and looked like tears all over. Big Ed passed his hand through his hair and said hello. She looked at him steadily.

"Where have you been? Why did you do this to me?" And she gave Dean a dirty look; she knew the score. Dean paid absolutely no attention; what he wanted now was food; he asked Jane if there was anything. The confusion began right there.

Poor Bull came home in his Texas Chevy and found his house invaded by maniacs; but he greeted me with a nice warmth I hadn't seen in him for a long time. He had bought this house in New Orleans with some money he had made growing black-eyed peas in Texas with an old college schoolmate whose father, a mad paretic, had died and left a fortune. Bull himself only got fifty dollars a week from his own family, which wasn't too bad except that he spent almost that much per week on his drug habit—and his wife was also expensive, gobbling up about ten dollars' worth of benny tubes a week. Their food bill was the lowest in the country; they hardly ever ate; nor did the children—they didn't seem to care. They had two wonderful children: Dodie, eight years old; and little Ray, one year. Ray ran around stark naked in the yard, a little blond child of the rainbow. Bull called him "the Little Beast," after W. C. Fields. Bull came driving into the yard and unrolled himself from the car bone by bone, and came over wearily, wearing glasses, felt hat, shabby suit, long, lean, strange, and laconic, saying, "Why, Sal, you finally got here; let's go in the house and have a drink."

It would take all night to tell about Old Bull Lee; let's just say now, he was a teacher, and it may be said that he had every right to teach because he spent all his time learning; and the things he learned were what he considered to be and called "the facts of life," which he learned not only out of necessity but because he wanted to. He dragged his long, thin body around the entire United States and most of Europe and North Africa in his time, only to see what was going on; he married a White Russian countess in Yugoslavia to get her away from the Nazis in the thirties; there are pictures of him with the international cocaine set of the thirties—gangs with wild hair, leaning on one another; there are other pictures of

him in a Panama hat, surveying the streets of Algiers; he never
saw the White Russian countess again. He was an exterminator
in Chicago, a bartender in New York, a summons-server in
Newark. In Paris he sat at café tables, watching the sullen
French faces go by. In Athens he looked up from his *ouzo* at
what he called the ugliest people in the world. In Istanbul he
threaded his way through crowds of opium addicts and rug-
sellers, looking for the facts. In English hotels he read Speng-
ler and the Marquis de Sade. In Chicago he planned to hold
up a Turkish bath, hesitated just for two minutes too long for
a drink, and wound up with two dollars and had to make a run
for it. He did all these things merely for the experience. Now
the final study was the drug habit. He was now in New Orleans, slipping along the streets with shady characters and
haunting connection bars.

    There is a strange story about his college days that illustrates
something else about him: he had friends for cocktails in his
well-appointed rooms one afternoon when suddenly his pet
ferret rushed out and bit an elegant teacup queer on the ankle
and everybody hightailed it out the door, screaming. Old Bull
leaped up and grabbed his shotgun and said, "He smells that
old rat again," and shot a hole in the wall big enough for fifty
rats. On the wall hung a picture of an ugly old Cape Cod
house. His friends said, "Why do you have that ugly thing
hanging there?" and Bull said, "I like it because it's ugly." All
his life was in that line. Once I knocked on his door in the
60th Street slums of New York and he opened it wearing a
derby hat, a vest with nothing underneath, and long striped
sharpster pants; in his hands he had a cookpot, birdseed in the
pot, and was trying to mash the seed to roll in cigarettes. He
also experimented in boiling codeine cough syrup down to a
black mash—that didn't work too well. He spent long hours
with Shakespeare—the "Immortal Bard," he called him—on
his lap. In New Orleans he had begun to spend long hours
with the Mayan Codices on his lap, and, although he went on
talking, the book lay open all the time. I said once, "What's
going to happen to us when we die?" and he said, "When you
die you're just dead, that's all." He had a set of chains in his
room that he said he used with his psychoanalyst; they were

experimenting with narcoanalysis and found that Old Bull had seven separate personalities, each growing worse and worse on the way down, till finally he was a raving idiot and had to be restrained with chains. The top personality was an English lord, the bottom the idiot. Halfway he was an old Negro who stood in line, waiting with everyone else, and said, "Some's bastards, some's ain't, that's the score."

Bull had a sentimental streak about the old days in America, especially 1910, when you could get morphine in a drugstore without prescription and Chinese smoked opium in their evening windows and the country was wild and brawling and free, with abundance and any kind of freedom for everyone. His chief hate was Washington bureaucracy; second to that, liberals; then cops. He spent all his time talking and teaching others. Jane sat at his feet; so did I; so did Dean; and so had Carlo Marx. We'd all learned from him. He was a gray, non-descript-looking fellow you wouldn't notice on the street, unless you looked closer and saw his mad, bony skull with its strange youthfulness—a Kansas minister with exotic, phenomenal fires and mysteries. He had studied medicine in Vienna; had studied anthropology, read everything; and now he was settling to his life's work, which was the study of things themselves in the streets of life and the night. He sat in his chair; Jane brought drinks, martinis. The shades by his chair were always drawn, day and night; it was his corner of the house. On his lap were the Mayan Codices and an air gun which he occasionally raised to pop benzedrine tubes across the room. I kept rushing around, putting up new ones. We all took shots and meanwhile we talked. Bull was curious to know the reason for this trip. He peered at us and snuffed down his nose, *thfump*, like a sound in a dry tank.

"Now, Dean, I want you to sit quiet a minute and tell me what you're doing crossing the country like this."

Dean could only blush and say, "Ah well, you know how it is."

"Sal, what are you going to the Coast for?"

"Only for a few days. I'm coming back to school."

"What's the score with this Ed Dunkel? What kind of character is he?" At that moment Ed was making up to Galatea in the bedroom; it didn't take him long. We didn't know what to tell Bull about Ed Dunkel. Seeing that we didn't know anything about ourselves, he whipped out three sticks of tea and said to go ahead, supper'd be ready soon.

"Ain't nothing better in the world to give you an appetite. I once ate a horrible lunchcart hamburg on tea and it seemed like the most delicious thing in the world. I just got back from Houston last week, went to see Dale about our black-eyed peas. I was sleeping in a motel one morning when all of a sudden I was blasted out of bed. This damn fool had just shot his wife in the room next to mine. Everybody stood around confused, and the guy just got in his car and drove off, left the shotgun on the floor for the sheriff. They finally caught him in Houma, drunk as a lord. Man ain't safe going around this country any more without a gun." He pulled back his coat and showed us his revolver. Then he opened the drawer and showed us the rest of his arsenal. In New York he once had a sub-machine-gun under his bed. "I got something better than that now—a German Scheintoth gas gun; look at this beauty, only got one shell. I could knock out a hundred men with this gun and have plenty of time to make a getaway. Only thing wrong, I only got one shell."

"I hope I'm not around when you try it," said Jane from the kitchen. "How do *you* know it's a gas shell?" Bull snuffed; he never paid any attention to her sallies but he heard them. His relation with his wife was one of the strangest: they talked till late at night; Bull liked to hold the floor, he went right on in his dreary monotonous voice, she tried to break in, she never could; at dawn he got tired and then Jane talked and he listened, snuffing and going *thfump* down his nose. She loved that man madly, but in a delirious way of some kind; there was never any mooching and mincing around, just talk and a very deep companionship that none of us would ever be able to fathom. Something curiously unsympathetic and cold between them was really a form of humor by which they communicated their own set of subtle vibrations. Love is all; Jane was never more than ten feet away from Bull and never missed a word he said, and he spoke in a very low voice, too.

Dean and I were yelling about a big night in New Orleans

and wanted Bull to show us around. He threw a damper on this. "New Orleans is a very dull town. It's against the law to go to the colored section. The bars are insufferably dreary."

I said, "There must be some ideal bars in town."

"The ideal bar doesn't exist in America. An ideal bar is something that's gone beyond our ken. In nineteen ten a bar was a place where men went to meet during or after work, and all there was was a long counter, brass rails, spittoons, player piano for music, a few mirrors, and barrels of whisky at ten cents a shot together with barrels of beer at five cents a mug. Now all you get is chromium, drunken women, fags, hostile bartenders, anxious owners who hover around the door, worried about their leather seats and the law; just a lot of screaming at the wrong time and deadly silence when a stranger walks in."

We argued about bars. "All right," he said, "I'll take you to New Orleans tonight and show you what I mean." And he deliberately took us to the dullest bars. We left Jane with the children; supper was over; she was reading the want ads of the New Orleans *Times-Picayune*. I asked her if she was looking for a job; she only said it was the most interesting part of the paper. Bull rode into town with us and went right on talking. "Take it easy, Dean, we'll get there, I hope; hup, there's the ferry, you don't have to drive us clear into the river." He held on. Dean had gotten worse, he confided in me. "He seems to me to be headed for his ideal fate, which is compulsive psychosis dashed with a jigger of psychopathic irresponsibility and violence." He looked at Dean out of the corner of his eye. "If you go to California with this madman you'll never make it. Why don't you stay in New Orleans with me? We'll play the horses over to Graetna and relax in my yard. I've got a nice set of knives and I'm building a target. Some pretty juicy dolls downtown, too, if that's in your line these days." He snuffed. We were on the ferry and Dean had leaped out to lean over the rail. I followed, but Bull sat on in the car, snuffing, *thfump*. There was a mystic wraith of fog over the brown waters that night, together with dark driftwoods; and across the way New Orleans glowed orange-bright, with a few dark ships at her hem, ghostly fogbound Cereno ships with Spanish balconies and ornamental poops, till you got up close and saw they were just old freighters from Sweden and Panama. The ferry fires glowed in the night; the same Negroes plied the shovel and sang. Old Big Slim Hazard had once worked on the Algiers ferry as a deckhand; this made me think of Mississippi Gene too; and as the river poured down from mid-America by star-light I knew, I knew like mad that everything I had ever known and would ever know was One. Strange to say, too, that night we crossed the ferry with Bull Lee a girl committed suicide off the deck; either just before or just after us; we saw it in the paper the next day.

We hit all the dull bars in the French Quarter with Old Bull and went back home at midnight. That night Marylou took everything in the books; she took tea, goofballs, benny, liquor, and even asked Old Bull for a shot of M, which of course he didn't give her; he did give her a martini. She was so saturated with elements of all kinds that she came to a standstill and stood goofy on the porch with me. It was a wonderful porch Bull had. It ran clear around the house; by moonlight with the willows it looked like an old Southern mansion that had seen better days. In the house Jane sat reading the want ads in the living room; Bull was in the bathroom taking his fix, clutching his old black necktie in his teeth for a tourniquet and jabbing with the needle into his woesome arm with the thousand holes; Ed Dunkel was sprawled out with Galatea in the massive master bed that Old Bull and Jane never used; Dean was rolling tea; and Marylou and I imitated Southern aristocracy.

"Why, Miss Lou, you look lovely and most fetching tonight."

"Why, thank you, Crawford, I sure do appreciate the nice things you do say."

Doors kept opening around the crooked porch, and members of our sad drama in the American night kept popping out to find out where everybody was. Finally I took a walk alone to the levee. I wanted to sit on the muddy bank and dig the Mis-sissippi River; instead of that I had to look at it with my nose against a wire fence. When you start separating the people from their rivers what have you got? "Bureaucracy!" says Old Bull; he sits with Kafka on his lap, the lamp burns above him, he snuffs, *thfump*. His old house creaks. And the Montana log rolls by in the big black river of the night. "'Tain't nothin but bureaucracy. And unions! Especially unions!" But dark laughter would come again.

7

It was there in the morning when I got up bright and early and found Old Bull and Dean in the back yard. Dean was wearing his gas-station coveralls and helping Bull. Bull had found a great big piece of thick rotten wood and was desperately yanking with a hammerhook at little nails imbedded in it. We stared at the nails; there were millions of them; they were like worms.

"When I get all these nails out of this I'm going to build me a shelf that'll last a *thousand years!*" said Bull, every bone shuddering with boyish excitement. "Why, Sal, do you realize the shelves they build these days crack under the weight of knickknacks after six months or generally collapse? Same with houses, same with clothes. These bastards have invented plastics by which they could make houses that last *forever*. And tires. Americans are killing themselves by the millions every year with defective rubber tires that get hot on the road and blow up. They could make tires that never blow up. Same with tooth powder. There's a certain gum they've invented and they won't show it to anybody that if you chew it as a kid you'll never get a cavity for the rest of your born days. Same with clothes. They can make clothes that last forever. They prefer making cheap goods so's everybody'll have to go on working and punching timeclocks and organizing themselves in sullen unions and floundering around while the big grab goes on in Washington and Moscow." He raised his big piece of rotten wood. "Don't you think this'll make a splendid shelf?"

It was early in the morning; his energy was at its peak. The poor fellow took so much junk into his system he could only weather the greater proportion of his day in that chair with the lamp burning at noon, but in the morning he was magnificent. We began throwing knives at the target. He said he'd seen an Arab in Tunis who could stick a man's eye from forty feet. This got him going on his aunt, who went to the Casbah in the thirties. "She was with a party of tourists led by a guide. She had a diamond ring on her little finger. She leaned on a wall to rest a minute and an Ay-rab rushed up and appropriated her ring finger before she could let out a cry, my dear. She suddenly realized she had no little finger. Hi-hi-hi-hi-hi!" When he laughed he compressed his lips together and made it come out from his belly, from far away, and doubled up to lean on his knees. He laughed a long time. "Hey Jane!" he yelled gleefully. "I was just telling Dean and Sal about my aunt in the Casbah!"

"I heard you," she said across the lovely warm Gulf morning from the kitchen door. Great beautiful clouds floated overhead, valley clouds that made you feel the vastness of old tumbledown holy America from mouth to mouth and tip to tip. All pep and juices was Bull. "Say, did I ever tell you about Dale's father? He was the funniest old man you ever saw in your life. He had paresis, which eats away the forepart of your brain and you get so's you're not responsible for anything that comes into your mind. He had a house in Texas and had carpenters working twenty-four hours a day putting on new wings. He'd leap up in the middle of the night and say, 'I don't want that goddam wing; put it over there.' The carpenters had to take everything down and start all over again. Come dawn you'd see them hammering away at the new wing. Then the old man'd get bored with that and say, 'Goddammit, I wanta go to Maine!' And he'd get into his car and drive off a hundred miles an hour—great showers of chicken feathers followed his track for hundreds of miles. He'd stop his car in the middle of a Texas town just to get out and buy some whisky. Traffic would honk all around him and he'd come rushing out of the store, yelling, 'Thet your goddam noith, you bunth of bathats!' He lisped; when you have paresis you lips, I mean you lisps. One night he came to my house in Cincinnati and tooted the horn and said, 'Come on out and let's go to Texas to see Dale.' He was going back from Maine. He claimed he bought a house— oh, we wrote a story about him at college, where you see this horrible shipwreck and people in the water clutching at the sides of the lifeboat, and the old man is there with a machete, hackin at their fingers. 'Get away, ya bunth a bathats, thith my

cottham boath!' Oh, he was horrible. I could tell you stories
about him all day. Say, ain't this a nice day?"

And it sure was. The softest breezes blew in from the levee;
it was worth the whole trip. We went into the house after Bull
to measure the wall for a shelf. He showed us the dining-room
table he built. It was made of wood six inches thick. "This is
a table that'll last a thousand years!" said Bull, leaning his long
thin face at us maniacally. He banged on it.

In the evenings he sat at this table, picking at his food and
throwing the bones to the cats. He had seven cats. "I love cats.
I especially like the ones that squeal when I hold 'em over the
bathtub." He insisted on demonstrating; someone was in the
bathroom. "Well," he said, "we can't do that now. Say, I been
having a fight with the neighbors next door." He told us about
the neighbors; they were a vast crew with sassy children who
threw stones over the rickety fence at Dodie and Ray and
sometimes at Old Bull. He told them to cut it out; the old
man rushed out and yelled something in Portuguese. Bull
went in the house and came back with his shotgun, upon
which he leaned demurely; the incredible simper on his face
beneath the long hatbrim, his whole body writhing coyly and
snakily as he waited, a grotesque, lank, lonely clown beneath
the clouds. The sight of him the Portuguese must have thought
something out of an old evil dream.

We scoured the yard for things to do. There was a tremendous fence Bull had been working on to separate him from the
obnoxious neighbors; it would never be finished, the task was
too much. He rocked it back and forth to show how solid it
was. Suddenly he grew tired and quiet and went in the house
and disappeared in the bathroom for his pre-lunch fix. He came
out glassy-eyed and calm, and sat down under his burning
lamp. The sunlight poked feebly behind the drawn shade.
"Say, why don't you fellows try my orgone accumulator? Put
some juice in your bones. I always rush up and take off ninety
miles an hour for the nearest whorehouse, hor-hor-hor!" This
was his "laugh" laugh—when he wasn't really laughing. The
orgone accumulator is an ordinary box big enough for a man
to sit inside on a chair: a layer of wood, a layer of metal, and
another layer of wood gather in orgones from the atmosphere
and hold them captive long enough for the human body to ab-

sorb more than a usual share. According to Reich, orgones are vibratory atmospheric atoms of the life-principle. People get cancer because they run out of orgones. Old Bull thought his orgone accumulator would be improved if the wood he used was as organic as possible, so he tied bushy bayou leaves and twigs to his mystical outhouse. It stood there in the hot, flat yard, an exfoliate machine clustered and bedecked with maniacal contrivances. Old Bull slipped off his clothes and went in to sit and moon over his navel. "Say, Sal, after lunch let's you and me go play the horses over to the bookie joint in Graetna." He was magnificent. He took a nap after lunch in his chair, the air gun on his lap and little Ray curled around his neck, sleeping. It was a pretty sight, father and son, a father who would certainly never bore his son when it came to finding things to do and talk about. He woke up with a start and stared at me. It took him a minute to recognize who I was. "What are you going to the Coast for, Sal?" he asked, and went back to sleep in a moment.

In the afternoon we went to Graetna, just Bull and me. We drove in his old Chevy. Dean's Hudson was low and sleek; Bull's Chevy was high and rattly. It was just like 1910. The bookie joint was located near the waterfront in a big chromium-leather bar that opened up in the back to a tremendous hall where entries and numbers were posted on the wall. Louisiana characters lounged around with *Racing Forms*. Bull and I had a beer, and casually Bull went over to the slot machine and threw a half-dollar piece in. The counters clicked "Jackpot"—"Jackpot"—"Jackpot"—and the last "Jackpot" hung for just a moment and slipped back to "Cherry." He had lost a hundred dollars or more just by a hair. "Damn!" yelled Bull. "They got these things adjusted. You could see it right then. I had the jackpot and the mechanism clicked it back. Well, what you gonna do." We examined the *Racing Form*. I hadn't played the horses in years and was bemused with all the new names. There was one horse called Big Pop that sent me into a temporary trance thinking of my father, who used to play the horses with me. I was just about to mention it to Old Bull when he said, "Well I think I'll try this Ebony Corsair here."

Then I finally said it. "Big Pop reminds me of my father."

He mused for just a second, his clear blue eyes fixed on mine hypnotically so that I couldn't tell what he was thinking or where he was. Then he went over and bet on Ebony Corsair. Big Pop won and paid fifty to one.

"Damn!" said Bull. "I should have known better, I've had experience with this before. Oh, when will we ever learn?"

"What do you mean?"

"Big Pop is what I mean. You had a vision, boy, a *vision*. Only damn fools pay no attention to visions. How do you know your father, who was an old horseplayer, just didn't momentarily communicate to you that Big Pop was going to win the race? The name brought the feeling up in you, he took advantage of the name to communicate. That's what I was thinking about when you mentioned it. My cousin in Missouri once bet on a horse that had a name that reminded him of his mother, and it won and paid a big price. The same thing happened this afternoon." He shook his head. "Ah, let's go. This is the last time I'll ever play the horses with you around; all these visions drive me to distraction." In the car as we drove back to his old house he said, "Mankind will someday realize that we are actually in contact with the dead and with the other world, whatever it is; right now we could predict, if we only exerted enough mental will, what is going to happen within the next hundred years and be able to take steps to avoid all kinds of catastrophes. When a man dies he undergoes a mutation in his brain that we know nothing about now but which will be very clear someday if scientists get on the ball. The bastards right now are only interested in seeing if they can blow up the world."

We told Jane about it. She sniffed. "It sounds silly to me." She plied the broom around the kitchen. Bull went in the bathroom for his afternoon fix.

Out on the road Dean and Ed Dunkel were playing basketball with Dodie's ball and a bucket nailed on a lamppost. I joined in. Then we turned to feats of athletic prowess. Dean completely amazed me. He had Ed and me hold a bar of iron up to our waists, and just standing there he popped right over it, holding his heels. "Go ahead, raise it." We kept raising it till it was chest-high. Still he jumped over it with ease. Then he tried the running broad jump and did at least twenty feet and more. Then I raced him down the road. I can do the hundred in 10:5. He passed me like the wind. As we ran I had a mad vision of Dean running through all of life just like that—his bony face outthrust to life, his arms pumping, his brow sweating, his legs twinkling like Groucho Marx, yelling, "Yes! Yes, man, you sure can go!" But nobody could go as fast as he could, and that's the truth. Then Bull came out with a couple of knives and started showing us how to disarm a would-be shivver in a dark alley. I for my part showed him a very good trick, which is falling on the ground in front of your adversary and gripping him with your ankles and flipping him over on his hands and grabbing his wrists in full nelson. He said it was pretty good. He demonstrated some jujitsu. Little Dodie called her mother to the porch and said, "Look at the silly men." She was such a cute sassy little thing that Dean couldn't take his eyes off her.

"Wow. Wait till *she* grows up! Can you see *her* cuttin down Canal Street with her cute eyes. Ah! Oh!" He hissed through his teeth.

We spent a mad day in downtown New Orleans walking around with the Dunkels. Dean was out of his mind that day. When he saw the T & NO freight trains in the yard he wanted to show me everything at once. "You'll be brakeman 'fore I'm through with ya!" He and I and Ed Dunkel ran across the tracks and hopped a freight at three individual points; Marylou and Galatea were waiting in the car. We rode the train a half-mile into the piers, waving at switchmen and flagmen. They showed me the proper way to get off a moving car; the back foot first and let the train go away from you and come around and place the other foot down. They showed me the refrigerator cars, the ice compartments, good for a ride on any winter night in a string of empties. "Remember what I told you about New Mexico to LA?" cried Dean. "This was the way I hung on . . ."

We got back to the girls an hour late and of course they were mad. Ed and Galatea had decided to get a room in New Orleans and stay there and work. This was okay with Bull, who was getting sick and tired of the whole mob. The invitation, originally, was for me to come alone. In the front room, where Dean and Marylou slept, there were jam and coffee stains and empty benny tubes all over the floor; what's more it was Bull's workroom and he couldn't get on with his shelves. Poor Jane was driven to distraction by the continual jumping and running around on the part of Dean. We were waiting for my next GI check to come through; my aunt was forwarding it. Then we were off, the three of us—Dean, Marylou, me. When the check came I realized I hated to leave Bull's wonderful house so suddenly, but Dean was all energies and ready to do.

In a sad red dusk we were finally seated in the car and Jane, Dodie, little boy Ray, Bull, Ed, and Galatea stood around in the high grass, smiling. It was good-by. At the last moment Dean and Bull had a misunderstanding over money; Dean had wanted to borrow; Bull said it was out of the question. The feeling reached back to Texas days. Con-man Dean was antagonizing people away from him by degrees. He giggled maniacally and didn't care; he rubbed his fly, stuck his finger in Marylou's dress, slurped up her knee, frothed at the mouth, and said, "Darling, you know and I know that everything is straight between us at last beyond the furthest abstract definition in metaphysical terms or any terms you want to specify or sweetly impose or harken back . . ." and so on, and zoom went the car and we were off again for California.

8

What is that feeling when you're driving away from people and they recede on the plain till you see their specks dispersing?— it's the too-huge world vaulting us, and it's good-by. But we lean forward to the next crazy venture beneath the skies.

We wheeled through the sultry old light of Algiers, back on the ferry, back toward the mud-splashed, crabbed old ships across the river, back on Canal, and out; on a two-lane highway to Baton Rouge in purple darkness; swung west there, crossed the Mississippi at a place called Port Allen. Port Allen —where the river's all rain and roses in a misty pinpoint darkness and where we swung around a circular drive in yellow foglight and suddenly saw the great black body below a bridge and crossed eternity again. What is the Mississippi River?—a washed clod in the rainy night, a soft plopping from drooping Missouri banks, a dissolving, a riding of the tide down the eternal waterbed, a contribution to brown foams, a voyaging past endless vales and trees and levees, down along, down along, by Memphis, Greenville, Eudora, Vicksburg, Natchez, Port Allen, and Port Orleans and Port of the Deltas, by Potash, Venice, and the Night's Great Gulf, and out.

With the radio on to a mystery program, and as I looked out the window and saw a sign that said USE COOPER'S PAINT and I said, "Okay, I will," we rolled across the hoodwink night of the Louisiana plains—Lawtell, Eunice, Kinder, and De Quincy, western rickety towns becoming more bayou-like as we reached the Sabine. In Old Opelousas I went into a grocery store to buy bread and cheese while Dean saw to gas and oil. It was just a shack; I could hear the family eating supper in the back. I waited a minute; they went on talking. I took bread and cheese and slipped out the door. We had barely enough money to make Frisco. Meanwhile Dean took a carton of cigarettes from the gas station and we were stocked for the voyage—gas, oil, cigarettes, and food. Crooks don't know. He pointed the car straight down the road.

Somewhere near Starks we saw a great red glow in the sky ahead; we wondered what it was; in a moment we were passing it. It was a fire beyond the trees; there were many cars parked on the highway. It must have been some kind of fish-fry, and on the other hand it might have been anything. The country turned strange and dark near Deweyville. Suddenly we were in the swamps.

"Man, do you imagine what it would be like if we found a jazzjoint in these swamps, with great big black fellas moanin guitar blues and drinkin snakejuice and makin signs at us?"

"Yes!"

There were mysteries around here. The car was going over a dirt road elevated off the swamps that dropped on both sides and drooped with vines. We passed an apparition; it was a Negro man in a white shirt walking along with his arms upspread to the inky firmament. He must have been praying or calling down a curse. We zoomed right by; I looked out the back window to see his white eyes. "Whoo!" said Dean. "Look out. We better not stop in this here country." At one point we got stuck at a crossroads and stopped the car anyway. Dean turned off the headlamps. We were surrounded by a great forest of viny trees in which we could almost hear the slither of a million copperheads. The only thing we could see was the red ampere button on the Hudson dashboard. Marylou squealed with fright. We began laughing maniac laughs to scare her. We were scared too. We wanted to get out of this mansion of the snake, this mireful drooping dark, and zoom on back to familiar American ground and cowtowns. There was a smell of oil and dead water in the air. This was a manuscript of the night we couldn't read. An owl hooted. We took a chance on one of the dirt roads, and pretty soon we were crossing the evil old Sabine River that is responsible for all these swamps. With amazement we saw great structures of light ahead of us. "Texas! It's Texas! Beaumont oil town!" Huge oil tanks and refineries loomed like cities in the oily fragrant air.

"I'm glad we got out of there," said Marylou. "Let's play some more mystery programs now."

We zoomed through Beaumont, over the Trinity River at Liberty, and straight for Houston. Now Dean got talking about his Houston days in 1947. "Hassel! That mad Hassel! I look for him everywhere I go and I never find him. He used to get us so hung-up in Texas here. We'd drive in with Bull for groceries and Hassel'd disappear. We'd have to go looking for him in every shooting gallery in town." We were entering Houston. "We had to look for him in this spade part of town most of the time. Man, he'd be blasting with every mad cat he could find. One night we lost him and took a hotel room. We were supposed to bring ice back to Jane because her food was rotting. It took us two days to find Hassel. I got hung-up myself—I gunned shopping women in the afternoon, right here, downtown, supermarkets"—we flashed by in the empty night—"and found a real gone dumb girl who was out of her mind and just wandering, trying to steal an orange. She was from Wyoming. Her beautiful body was matched only by her idiot mind. I found her babbling and took her back to the room. Bull was drunk trying to get this young Mexican kid drunk. Carlo was writing poetry on heroin. Hassel didn't show up till midnight at the jeep. We found him sleeping in the back seat. The ice was all melted. Hassel said he took about five sleeping pills. Man, if my memory could only serve me right the way my mind works I could tell you every detail of the things we did. Ah, but we know time. Everything takes care of itself. I could close my eyes and this old car would take care of itself."

In the empty Houston streets of four o'clock in the morning a motorcycle kid suddenly roared through, all bespangled and bedecked with glittering buttons, visor, slick black jacket, a Texas poet of the night, girl gripped on his back like a papoose, hair flying, onward-going, singing, "Houston, Austin, Fort Worth, Dallas—and sometimes Kansas City—and sometimes old Antone, ah-haaaaa!" They pinpointed out of sight. "Wow! Dig that gone gal on his belt! Let's all blow!" Dean tried to catch up with them. "Now wouldn't it be fine if we could all get together and have a real going goofbang together with everybody sweet and fine and agreeable, no hassles, no infant rise of protest or body woes misconceptalized or sumpin? Ah! but we know time." He bent to it and pushed the car.

Beyond Houston his energies, great as they were, gave out and I drove. Rain began to fall just as I took the wheel. Now we were on the great Texas plain and, as Dean said, "You drive and drive and you're still in Texas tomorrow night." The rain lashed down. I drove through a rickety little cowtown with a muddy main street and found myself in a dead end. "Hey, what do I do?" They were both asleep. I turned and crawled back through town. There wasn't a soul in sight and not a single light. Suddenly a horseman in a raincoat appeared in my headlamps. It was the sheriff. He had a ten-gallon hat, drooping in the torrent. "Which way to Austin?" He told me politely and I started off. Outside town I suddenly saw two headlamps flaring directly at me in the lashing rain. Whoops, I thought I was on the wrong side of the road; I eased right and found myself rolling in the mud; I rolled back to the road. Still the headlamps came straight for me. At the last moment I realized the other driver was on the wrong side of the road and didn't know it. I swerved at thirty into the mud; it was flat, no ditch, thank God. The offending car backed up in the downpour. Four sullen fieldworkers, snuck from their chores to brawl in drinking fields, all white shirts and dirty brown arms, sat looking at me dumbly in the night. The driver was as drunk as the lot.

He said, "Which way t'Houston?" I pointed my thumb back. I was thunderstruck in the middle of the thought that they had done this on purpose just to ask directions, as a panhandler advances on you straight up the sidewalk to bar your way. They gazed ruefully at the floor of their car, where empty bottles rolled, and clanked away. I started the car; it was stuck in the mud a foot deep. I sighed in the rainy Texas wilderness.

"Dean," I said, "wake up."

"What?"

"We're stuck in the mud."

"What happened?" I told him. He swore up and down. We put on old shoes and sweaters and barged out of the car into the driving rain. I put my back on the rear fender and lifted and heaved; Dean stuck chains under the swishing wheels. In a minute we were covered with mud. We woke up Marylou to these horrors and made her gun the car while we pushed. The tormented Hudson heaved and heaved. Suddenly it jolted out and went skidding across the road. Marylou pulled it up just in time, and we got in. That was that—the work had taken thirty minutes and we were soaked and miserable.

I fell asleep, all caked with mud; and in the morning when I woke up the mud was solidified and outside there was snow. We were near Fredericksburg, in the high plains. It was one of the worst winters in Texas and Western history, when cattle perished like flies in great blizzards and snow fell on San Francisco and LA. We were all miserable. We wished we were back in New Orleans with Ed Dunkel. Marylou was driving; Dean was sleeping. She drove with one hand on the wheel and the other reaching back to me in the back seat. She cooed promises about San Francisco. I slavered miserably over it. At ten I took the wheel—Dean was out for hours—and drove several hundred dreary miles across the bushy snows and ragged sage hills. Cowboys went by in baseball caps and earmuffs, looking for cows. Comfortable little homes with chimneys smoking appeared along the road at intervals. I wished we could go in for buttermilk and beans in front of the fireplace.

At Sonora I again helped myself to free bread and cheese

while the proprietor chatted with a big rancher on the other side of the store. Dean huzzahed when he heard it; he was hungry. We couldn't spend a cent on food. "Yass, yass," said Dean, watching the ranchers loping up and down Sonora main street, "every one of them is a bloody millionaire, thousand head of cattle, workhands, buildings, money in the bank. If I lived around here I'd go be an idjit in the sagebrush, I'd be jackrabbit, I'd lick up the branches, I'd look for pretty cowgirls—hee-hee-hee-hee! Damn! Bam!" He socked himself. "Yes! Right! Oh me!" We didn't know what he was talking about any more. He took the wheel and flew the rest of the way across the state of Texas, about five hundred miles, clear to El Paso, arriving at dusk and not stopping except once when he took all his clothes off, near Ozona, and ran yipping and leaping naked in the sage. Cars zoomed by and didn't see him. He scurried back to the car and drove on. "Now Sal, now Marylou, I want both of you to do as I'm doing, disemburden yourselves of all that clothes—now what's the sense of clothes? now that's what I'm sayin—and sun your pretty bellies with me. Come on!" We were driving west into the sun; it fell in through the windshield. "Open your belly as we drive into it." Marylou complied; unfuddyduddied, so did I. We sat in the front seat, all three. Marylou took out cold cream and applied it to us for kicks. Every now and then a big truck zoomed by; the driver in high cab caught a glimpse of a golden beauty sitting naked with two naked men: you could see them swerve a moment as they vanished in our rear-view window. Great sage plains, snowless now, rolled on. Soon we were in the orange-rocked Pecos Canyon country. Blue distances opened up in the sky. We got out of the car to examine an old Indian ruin. Dean did so stark naked. Marylou and I put on our overcoats. We wandered among the old stones, hooting and howling. Certain tourists caught sight of Dean naked in the plain but they could not believe their eyes and wobbled on.

Dean and Marylou parked the car near Van Horn and made love while I went to sleep. I woke up just as we were rolling down the tremendous Rio Grande Valley through Clint and Ysleta to El Paso. Marylou jumped to the back seat, I jumped to the front seat, and we rolled along. To our left across the vast Rio Grande spaces were the moorish-red mounts of the

Mexican border, the land of the Tarahumare; soft dusk played on the peaks. Straight ahead lay the distant lights of El Paso and Juárez, sown in a tremendous valley so big that you could see several railroads puffing at the same time in every direction, as though it was the Valley of the World. We descended into it.

"Clint, Texas!" said Dean. He had the radio on to the Clint station. Every fifteen minutes they played a record; the rest of the time it was commercials about a high-school correspondence course. "This program is beamed all over the West," cried Dean excitedly. "Man, I used to listen to it day and night in reform school and prison. All of us used to write in. You get a high-school diploma by mail, facsimile thereof, if you pass the test. All the young wranglers in the West, I don't care who, at one time or another write in for this; it's all they hear; you tune the radio in Sterling, Colorado, Lusk, Wyoming, I don't care where, you get Clint, Texas, Clint, Texas. And the music is always cowboy hillbilly and Mexican, absolutely the worst program in the entire history of the country and nobody can do anything about it. They have a tremendous beam; they've got the whole land hogtied." We saw the high antenna beyond the shacks of Clint. "Oh, man, the things I could tell you!" cried Dean, almost weeping. Eyes bent on Frisco and the Coast, we came into El Paso as it got dark, broke. We absolutely had to get some money for gas or we'd never make it.

We tried everything. We buzzed the travel bureau, but no one was going west that night. The travel bureau is where you go for share-the-gas rides, legal in the West. Shifty characters wait with battered suitcases. We went to the Greyhound bus station to try to persuade somebody to give us the money instead of taking a bus for the Coast. We were too bashful to approach anyone. We wandered around sadly. It was cold outside. A college boy was sweating at the sight of luscious Marylou and trying to look unconcerned. Dean and I consulted but decided we weren't pimps. Suddenly a crazy dumb young kid, fresh out of reform school, attached himself to us, and he and Dean rushed out for a beer. "Come on, man, let's go mash somebody on the head and get his money."

"I dig you, man!" yelled Dean. They dashed off. For a moment I was worried; but Dean only wanted to dig the streets of

El Paso with the kid and get his kicks. Marylou and I waited in the car. She put her arms around me.

I said, "Dammit, Lou, wait till we get to Frisco."

"I don't care. Dean's going to leave me anyway."

"When are you going back to Denver?"

"I don't know. I don't care what I'm doing. Can I go back east with you?"

"We'll have to get some money in Frisco."

"I know where you can get a job in a lunchcart behind the counter, and I'll be a waitress. I know a hotel where we can stay on credit. We'll stick together. Gee, I'm sad."

"What are you sad about, kid?"

"I'm sad about everything. Oh damn, I wish Dean wasn't so crazy now." Dean came twinkling back, giggling, and jumped in the car.

"What a crazy cat that was, whoo! Did I dig him! I used to know thousands of guys like that, they're all the same, their minds work in uniform clockwork, oh, the infinite ramifications, no time, no time . . ." And he shot up the car, hunched over the wheel, and roared out of El Paso. "We'll just have to pick up hitchhikers. I'm positive we'll find some. Hup! hup! here we go. Look out!" he yelled at a motorist, and swung around him, and dodged a truck and bounced over the city limits. Across the river were the jewel lights of Juárez and the sad dry land and the jewel stars of Chihuahua. Marylou was watching Dean as she had watched him clear across the country and back, out of the corner of her eye—with a sullen, sad air, as though she wanted to cut off his head and hide it in her closet, an envious and rueful love of him so amazingly himself, all raging and sniffy and crazy-wayed, a smile of tender dotage but also sinister envy that frightened me about her, a love she knew would never bear fruit because when she looked at his hangjawed bony face with its male self-containment and absentmindedness she knew he was too mad. Dean was convinced Marylou was a whore; he confided in me that she was a pathological liar. But when she watched him like this it was love too; and when Dean noticed he always turned with his big false flirtatious smile, with the eyelashes fluttering and the teeth pearly white, while a moment ago he was only dreaming in his eternity. Then Marylou and I both laughed—and Dean gave no sign of discomfiture, just a goofy glad grin that said to us, Ain't we gettin our kicks *anyway*? And that was it.

Outside El Paso, in the darkness, we saw a small huddled figure with thumb stuck out. It was our promised hitchhiker. We pulled up and backed to his side. "How much money you got, kid?" The kid had no money; he was about seventeen, pale, strange, with one undeveloped crippled hand and no suitcase. "Ain't he *sweet*?" said Dean, turning to me with a serious awe. "Come on in, fella, we'll take you out—" The kid saw his advantage. He said he had an aunt in Tulare, California, who owned a grocery store and as soon as we got there he'd have some money for us. Dean rolled on the floor laughing, it was so much like the kid in North Carolina. "Yes! Yes!" he yelled. "We've *all* got aunts; well, let's go, let's see the aunts and the uncles and the grocery stores all the way ALONG that road!!" And we had a new passenger, and a fine little guy he turned out to be, too. He didn't say a word, he listened to us. After a minute of Dean's talk he was probably convinced he had joined a car of madmen. He said he was hitchhiking from Alabama to Oregon, where his home was. We asked him what he was doing in Alabama.

"I went to visit my uncle; he said he'd have a job for me in a lumber mill. The job fell through, so I'm comin back home."

"Goin home," said Dean, "goin home, yes, I know, we'll take you home, far as Frisco anyhow." But we didn't have any money. Then it occurred to me I could borrow five dollars from my old friend Hal Hingham in Tucson, Arizona. Immediately Dean said it was all settled and we were going to Tucson. And we did.

We passed Las Cruces, New Mexico, in the night and arrived in Arizona at dawn. I woke up from a deep sleep to find everybody sleeping like lambs and the car parked God knows where, because I couldn't see out the steamy windows. I got out of the car. We were in the mountains: there was a heaven of sunrise, cool purple airs, red mountainsides, emerald pastures in valleys, dew, and transmuting clouds of gold; on the ground gopher holes, cactus, mesquite. It was time for me to drive on. I pushed Dean and the kid over and went down the mountain with the clutch in and the motor off to save gas. In this manner I rolled into Benson, Arizona. It occurred to me that I had a pocket watch Rocco had just given me for a birthday present, a four-dollar watch. At the gas station I asked the man if he knew a pawnshop in Benson. It was right next door to the station. I knocked, someone got up out of bed, and in a minute I had a dollar for the watch. It went into the tank. Now we had enough gas for Tucson. But suddenly a big pistol-packing trooper appeared, just as I was ready to pull out, and asked to see my driver's license. "The fella in the back seat has the license," I said. Dean and Marylou were sleeping together under the blanket. The cop told Dean to come out. Suddenly he whipped out his gun and yelled, "Keep your hands up!"

"Offisah," I heard Dean say in the most unctious and ridiculous tones, "offisah, I was only buttoning my flah." Even the cop almost smiled. Dean came out, muddy, ragged, T-shirted, rubbing his belly, cursing, looking everywhere for his license and his car papers. The cop rummaged through our back trunk. All the papers were straight.

"Only checking up," he said with a broad smile. "You can go on now. Benson ain't a bad town actually; you might enjoy it if you had breakfast here."

"Yes yes yes," said Dean, paying absolutely no attention to him, and drove off. We all sighed with relief. The police are suspicious when gangs of youngsters come by in new cars without a cent in their pockets and have to pawn watches. "Oh, they're always interfering," said Dean, "but he was a much better cop than that rat in Virginia. They try to make headline arrests; they think every car going by is some big Chicago gang. They ain't got nothin else to do." We drove on to Tucson.

Tucson is situated in beautiful mesquite riverbed country, overlooked by the snowy Catalina range. The city was one big construction job; the people transient, wild, ambitious, busy, gay; washlines, trailers; bustling downtown streets with banners; altogether very Californian. Fort Lowell Road, out where Hingham lived, wound along lovely riverbed trees in the flat desert. We saw Hingham himself brooding in the yard. He was a writer; he had come to Arizona to work on his book in peace. He was a tall, gangly, shy satirist who mumbled to you with his head turned away and always said funny things. His wife and baby were with him in the dobe house, a small one that his

Indian stepfather had built. His mother lived across the yard in her own house. She was an excited American woman who loved pottery, beads, and books. Hingham had heard of Dean through letters from New York. We came down on him like a cloud, every one of us hungry, even Alfred, the crippled hitchhiker. Hingham was wearing an old sweater and smoking a pipe in the keen desert air. His mother came out and invited us into her kitchen to eat. We cooked noodles in a great pot.

Then we all drove to a crossroads liquor store, where Hingham cashed a check for five dollars and handed me the money.

There was a brief good-by. "It certainly was pleasant," said Hingham, looking away. Beyond some trees, across the sand, a great neon sign of a roadhouse glowed red. Hingham always went there for a beer when he was tired of writing. He was very lonely, he wanted to get back to New York. It was sad to see his tall figure receding in the dark as we drove away, just like the other figures in New York and New Orleans: they stand uncertainly underneath immense skies, and everything about them is drowned. Where go? what do? what for?—sleep. But this foolish gang was bending onward.

9

Outside Tucson we saw another hitchhiker in the dark road. This was an Okie from Bakersfield, California, who put down his story. "*Hot* damn, I left Bakersfield with the travel-bureau car and left my gui-tar in the trunk of another one and they never showed up—gui-tar and cowboy duds; you see, I'm a moo-sician, I was headed for Arizona to play with Johnny Mackaw's Sagebrush Boys. Well, hell, here I am in Arizona, broke, and m'gui-tar's been stoled. You boys drive me back to Bakersfield and I'll get the money from my brother. How much you want?" We wanted just enough gas to make Frisco from Bakersfield, about three dollars. Now we were five in the car. "Evenin, ma'am," he said, tipping his hat to Marylou, and we were off.

In the middle of the night we overtopped the lights of Palm Springs from a mountain road. At dawn, in snowy passes, we

labored toward the town of Mojave, which was the entryway
to the great Tehachapi Pass. The Okie woke up and told funny
stories; sweet little Alfred sat smiling. Okie told us he knew a
man who forgave his wife for shooting him and got her out of
prison, only to be shot a second time. We were passing the
women's prison when he told it. Up ahead we saw Tehachapi
Pass starting up. Dean took the wheel and carried us clear to
the top of the world. We passed a great shroudy cement factory in the canyon. Then we started down. Dean cut off the
gas, threw in the clutch, and negotiated every hairpin turn and
passed cars and did everything in the books without the bene-
fit of accelerator. I held on tight. Sometimes the road went up
again briefly; he merely passed cars without a sound, on pure
momentum. He knew every rhythm and every kick of a firstclass pass. When it was time to U-turn left around a low stone
wall that overlooked the bottom of the world, he just leaned
far over to his left, hands on the wheel, stiff-armed, and carried
it that way; and when the turn snaked to the right again, this
time with a cliff on our left, he leaned far to the right, making
Marylou and me lean with him. In this way we floated and
flapped down to the San Joaquin Valley. It lay spread a mile
below, virtually the floor of California, green and wondrous
from our aerial shelf. We made thirty miles without using gas.

Suddenly we were all excited. Dean wanted to tell me everything he knew about Bakersfield as we reached the city limits.
He showed me rooming houses where he stayed, railroad
hotels, poolhalls, diners, sidings where he jumped off the
engine for grapes, Chinese restaurants where he ate, park
benches where he met girls, and certain places where he'd
done nothing but sit and wait around. Dean's California—
wild, sweaty, important, the land of lonely and exiled and eccentric lovers come to forgather like birds, and the land where
everybody somehow looked like broken-down, handsome,
decadent movie actors. "Man, I spent hours on that very chair
in front of that drugstore!" He remembered all—every
pinochle game, every woman, every sad night. And suddenly
we were passing the place in the railyards where Terry and I
had sat under the moon, drinking wine, on those bum crates,
in October 1947, and I tried to tell him. But he was too excited.
"This is where Dunkel and I spent a whole morning drinking

beer, trying to make a real gone little waitress from
Watsonville—no, Tracy, yes, Tracy—and her name was
Esmeralda—oh, man, something like that." Marylou was
planning what to do the moment she arrived in Frisco. Alfred
said his aunt would give him plenty of money up in Tulare.
The Okie directed us to his brother in the flats outside town.

We pulled up at noon in front of a little rose-covered shack,
and the Okie went in and talked with some women. We waited
fifteen minutes. "I'm beginning to think this guy has no more
money than I have," said Dean. "We get more hung-up!
There's probably nobody in the family that'll give him a cent
after that fool escapade." The Okie came out sheepishly and
directed us to town.

"*Hot* damn, I wisht I could find my brother." He made inquiries. He probably felt he was our prisoner. Finally we went
to a big bread bakery, and the Okie came out with his brother,
who was wearing coveralls and was apparently the truck mechanic inside. He talked with his brother a few minutes. We
waited in the car. Okie was telling all his relatives his adventures and about the loss of his guitar. But he got the money,
and he gave it to us, and we were all set for Frisco. We thanked
him and took off.

Next stop was Tulare. Up the valley we roared. I lay in the
back seat, exhausted, giving up completely, and sometime in
the afternoon, while I dozed, the muddy Hudson zoomed by
the tents outside Sabinal where I had lived and loved and
worked in the spectral past. Dean was bent rigidly over the
wheel, pounding the rods. I was sleeping when we finally arrived in Tulare; I woke up to hear the insane details. "Sal, wake
up! Alfred found his aunt's grocery store, but do you know
what happened? His aunt shot her husband and went to jail.
The store's closed down. We didn't get a cent. Think of it! The
things that happen; the Okie told us the same likewise story,
the trou-bles on all sides, the complications of events—whee,
damn!" Alfred was biting his fingernails. We were turning off
the Oregon road at Madera, and there we made our farewell
with little Alfred. We wished him luck and Godspeed to Oregon. He said it was the best ride he ever had.

It seemed like a matter of minutes when we began rolling in
the foothills before Oakland and suddenly reached a height

and saw stretched out ahead of us the fabulous white city of San Francisco on her eleven mystic hills with the blue Pacific and its advancing wall of potato-patch fog beyond, and smoke and goldenness in the late afternoon of time. "There she blows!" yelled Dean. "Wow! Made it! Just enough gas! Give me water! No more land! We can't go any further 'cause there ain't no more land! Now Marylou, darling, you and Sal go immediately to a hotel and wait for me to contact you in the morning as soon as I have definite arrangements made with Camille and call up Frenchman about my railroad watch and you and Sal buy the first thing hit town a paper for the want ads and work-plans." And he drove into the Oakland Bay Bridge and it carried us in. The downtown office buildings were just sparkling on their lights; it made you think of Sam Spade. When we staggered out of the car on O'Farrell Street and sniffed and stretched, it was like getting on shore after a long voyage at sea; the slopy street reeled under our feet; secret chop sueys from Frisco Chinatown floated in the air. We took all our things out of the car and piled them on the sidewalk.

Suddenly Dean was saying good-by. He was bursting to see Camille and find out what had happened. Marylou and I stood dumbly in the street and watched him drive away. "You see what a bastard he is?" said Marylou. "Dean will leave you out in the cold any time it's in his interest."

"I know," I said, and I looked back east and sighed. We had no money. Dean hadn't mentioned money. "Where are we going to stay?" We wandered around, carrying our bundles of rags in the narrow romantic streets. Everybody looked like a broken-down movie extra, a withered starlet; disenchanted stunt-men, midget auto-racers, poignant California characters with their end-of-the-continent sadness, handsome, decadent, Casanova-ish men, puffy-eyed motel blondes, hustlers, pimps, whores, masseurs, bellhops—a lemon lot, and how's a man going to make a living with a gang like that?

10

Nevertheless Marylou had been around these people—not far from the Tenderloin—and a gray-faced hotel clerk let us have a room on credit. That was the first step. Then we had to eat, and didn't do so till midnight, when we found a nightclub singer in her hotel room who turned an iron upside down on a coathanger in the wastebasket and warmed up a can of pork and beans. I looked out the window at the winking neons and said to myself, Where is Dean and why isn't he concerned about our welfare? I lost faith in him that year. I stayed in San Francisco a week and had the beatest time of my life. Marylou and I walked around for miles, looking for food-money. We even visited some drunken seamen in a flophouse on Mission Street that she knew; they offered us whisky.

In the hotel we lived together two days. I realized that, now Dean was out of the picture, Marylou had no real interest in me; she was trying to reach Dean through me, his buddy. We had arguments in the room. We also spent entire nights in bed and I told her my dreams. I told her about the big snake of the world that was coiled in the earth like a worm in an apple and would someday nudge up a hill to be thereafter known as Snake Hill and fold out upon the plain, a hundred miles long and devouring as it went along. I told her this snake was Satan. "What's going to happen?" she squealed; meanwhile she held me tight.

"A saint called Doctor Sax will destroy it with secret herbs which he is at this very moment cooking up in his underground shack somewhere in America. It may also be disclosed that the snake is just a husk of doves; when the snake dies great clouds of seminal-gray doves will flutter out and bring tidings of peace around the world." I was out of my mind with hunger and bitterness.

One night Marylou disappeared with a nightclub owner. I was waiting for her by appointment in a doorway across the street, at Larkin and Geary, hungry, when she suddenly stepped out of the foyer of the fancy apartment house with her girl friend, the nightclub owner, and a greasy old man with a roll. Originally she'd just gone in to see her girl friend. I saw what a whore she was. She was afraid to give me the sign, though she saw me in that doorway. She walked on little feet and got in the Cadillac and off they went. Now I had nobody, nothing.

I walked around, picking butts from the street. I passed a fish-'n-chips joint on Market Street, and suddenly the woman in there gave me a terrified look as I passed; she was the proprietress, she apparently thought I was coming in there with a gun to hold up the joint. I walked on a few feet. It suddenly occurred to me this was my mother of about two hundred years ago in England, and that I was her footpad son, returning from gaol to haunt her honest labors in the hashery. I stopped, frozen with ecstasy on the sidewalk. I looked down Market Street. I didn't know whether it was that or Canal Street in New Orleans: it led to water, ambiguous, universal water, just as 42nd Street, New York, leads to water, and you never know where you are. I thought of Ed Dunkel's ghost on Times Square. I was delirious. I wanted to go back and leer at my strange Dickensian mother in the hash joint. I tingled all over from head to foot. It seemed I had a whole host of memories leading back to 1750 in England and that I was in San Francisco now only in another life and in another body. "No," that woman seemed to say with that terrified glance, "don't come back and plague your honest, hard-working mother. You are no longer like a son to me—and like your father, my first husband. 'Ere this kindly Greek took pity on me." (The proprietor was a Greek with hairy arms.) "You are no good, inclined to drunkenness and routs and final disgraceful robbery of the fruits of my 'umble labors in the hashery. O son! did you not ever go on your knees and pray for deliverance for all your sins and scoundrel's acts? Lost boy! Depart! Do not haunt my soul; I have done well forgetting you. Reopen no old wounds, be as if you had never returned and looked in to me—to see my laboring humilities, my few scrubbed pennies—hungry to grab, quick to deprive, sullen, unloved, mean-minded son of my flesh. Son! Son!" It made me think of the Big Pop vision in Graetna with Old Bull. And for just a moment I had reached the point of ecstasy that I always wanted to reach, which was the complete step across chronological time into timeless shadows, and wonderment in the bleakness of the mortal realm, and the sensation of death kicking at my heels to move on, with a phantom dogging its own heels, and myself hurrying to a plank where all the angels dove off and flew into the holy void of uncreated emptiness, the potent and inconceivable radiancies shining in bright Mind Essence, innumerable lotus-lands falling open in the magic mothswarm of heaven. I could hear an indescribable seething roar which wasn't in my ear but everywhere and had nothing to do with sounds. I realized that I had died and been reborn numberless times but just didn't remember especially because the transitions from life to death and back to life are so ghostly easy, a magical action for naught, like falling asleep and waking up again a million times, the utter casualness and deep ignorance of it. I realized it was only because of the stability of the intrinsic Mind that these ripples of birth and death took place, like the action of wind on a sheet of pure, serene, mirror-like water. I felt sweet, swinging bliss, like a big shot of heroin in the mainline vein; like a gulp of wine late in the afternoon and it makes you shudder; my feet tingled. I thought I was going to die the very next moment. But I didn't die, and walked four miles and picked up ten long butts and took them back to Marylou's hotel room and poured their tobacco in my old pipe and lit up. I was too young to know what had happened. In the window I smelled all the food of San Francisco. There were seafood places out there where the buns were hot, and the baskets were good enough to eat too; where the menus themselves were soft with foody esculence as though dipped in hot broths and roasted dry and good enough to eat too. Just show me the bluefish spangle on a seafood menu and I'd eat it; let me smell the drawn butter and lobster claws. There were places where they specialized in thick red roast beef *au jus*, or roast chicken basted in wine. There were places where hamburgs sizzled on grills and the coffee was only a nickel. And oh, that pan-fried chow mein flavored air that blew into my room from Chinatown, vying with the spaghetti sauces of North Beach, the soft-shell crab of Fisherman's Wharf—nay, the ribs of Fillmore turning on spits! Throw in the Market Street chili beans, red-hot, and frenchfried potatoes of the Embarcadero wino night, and steamed clams from Sausalito across the bay, and that's my ah-dream of San Francisco. Add fog, hunger-making raw fog, and the throb of neons in the soft night, the clack of high-heeled beauties, white doves in a Chinese grocery window . . .

II

That was the way Dean found me when he finally decided I was worth saving. He took me home to Camille's house. "Where's Marylou, man?"

"The whore ran off." Camille was a relief after Marylou; a well-bred, polite young woman, and she was aware of the fact that the eighteen dollars Dean had sent her was mine. But O where went thou, sweet Marylou? I relaxed a few days in Camille's house. From her living-room window in the wooden tenement on Liberty Street you could see all of San Francisco burning green and red in the rainy night. Dean did the most ridiculous thing of his career the few days I was there. He got a job demonstrating a new kind of pressure cooker in the kitchens of homes. The salesman gave him piles of samples and pamphlets. The first day Dean was a hurricane of energy. I drove all over town with him as he made appointments. The idea was to get invited socially to a dinner party and then leap up and start demonstrating the pressure cooker. "Man," cried Dean excitedly, "this is even crazier than the time I worked for Sinah. Sinah sold encyclopedias in Oakland. Nobody could turn him down. He made long speeches, he jumped up and down, he laughed, he cried. One time we broke into an Okie house where everybody was getting ready to go to a funeral. Sinah got down on his knees and prayed for the deliverance of the deceased soul. All the Okies started crying. He sold a complete set of encyclopedias. He was the maddest guy in the world. I wonder where he is. We used to get next to pretty young daughters and feel them up in the kitchen. This afternoon I had the gonest housewife in her little kitchen—arm around her, demonstrating. Ah! Hmm! Wow!"

"Keep it up, Dean," I said. "Maybe someday you'll be mayor of San Francisco." He had the whole cookpot spiel worked out; he practiced on Camille and me in the evenings.

One morning he stood naked, looking at all San Francisco

out the window as the sun came up. He looked like someday he'd be the pagan mayor of San Francisco. But his energies ran out. One rainy afternoon the salesman came around to find out what Dean was doing. Dean was sprawled on the couch. "Have you been trying to sell these?"

"No," said Dean, "I have another job coming up."

"Well, what are you going to do about all these samples?"

"I don't know." In a dead silence the salesman gathered up his sad pots and left. I was sick and tired of everything and so was Dean.

But one night we suddenly went mad together again; we went to see Slim Gaillard in a little Frisco nightclub. Slim Gaillard is a tall, thin Negro with big sad eyes who's always saying, "Right-orooni" and "How 'bout a little bourbon-orooni." In Frisco great eager crowds of young semi-intellectuals sat at his feet and listened to him on the piano, guitar, and bongo drums. When he gets warmed up he takes off his shirt and undershirt and really goes. He does and says anything that comes into his head. He'll sing "Cement Mixer, Put-ti Put-ti" and suddenly slow down the beat and brood over his bongos with fingertips barely tapping the skin as everybody leans forward breathlessly to hear; you think he'll do this for a minute or so, but he goes right on, for as long as an hour, making an imperceptible little noise with the tips of his fingernails, smaller and smaller all the time till you can't hear it any more and sounds of traffic come in the open door. Then he slowly gets up and takes the mike and says, very slowly, "Great-orooni . . . fine-ovauti . . . hello-orooni . . . bourbon-orooni . . . all-orooni . . . how are the boys in the front row making out with their girls-orooni . . . orooni . . . vauti . . . oroonirooni . . ." He keeps this up for fifteen minutes, his voice getting softer and softer till you can't hear. His great sad eyes scan the audience.

Dean stands in the back, saying, "God! Yes!"—and clasping his hands in prayer and sweating. "Sal, Slim knows time, he knows time." Slim sits down at the piano and hits two notes, two Cs, then two more, then one, then two, and suddenly the big burly bass-player wakes up from a reverie and realizes Slim is playing "C-Jam Blues" and he slugs in his big forefinger on the string and the big booming beat begins and everybody starts rocking and Slim looks just as sad as ever, and they blow jazz for half an hour, and then Slim goes mad and grabs the bongos and plays tremendous rapid Cubana beats and yells crazy things in Spanish, in Arabic, in Peruvian dialect, in Egyptian, in every language he knows, and he knows innumerable languages. Finally the set is over; each set takes two hours. Slim Gaillard goes and stands against a post, looking sadly over everybody's head as people come to talk to him. A bourbon is slipped into his hand. "Bourbon-orooni—thank-you-ovauti . . ." Nobody knows where Slim Gaillard is. Dean once had a dream that he was having a baby and his belly was all bloated up blue as he lay on the grass of a California hospital. Under a tree, with a group of colored men, sat Slim Gaillard. Dean turned despairing eyes of a mother to him. Slim said, "There you go-orooni." Now Dean approached him, he approached his God; he thought Slim was God; he shuffled and bowed in front of him and asked him to join us. "Right-orooni," says Slim; he'll join anybody but he won't guarantee to be there with you in spirit. Dean got a table, bought drinks, and sat stiffly in front of Slim. Slim dreamed over his head. Every time Slim said, "Orooni," Dean said, "Yes!" I sat there with these two madmen. Nothing happened. To Slim Gaillard the whole world was just one big orooni.

That same night I dug Lampshade on Fillmore and Geary. Lampshade is a big colored guy who comes into musical Frisco saloons with coat, hat, and scarf and jumps on the bandstand and starts singing; the veins pop in his forehead; he heaves back and blows a big foghorn blues out of every muscle in his soul. He yells at people while he's singing: "*Don't die to go to heaven, start in on Doctor Pepper and end up on whisky!*" His voice booms over everything. He grimaces, he writhes, he does everything. He came over to our table and leaned over to us and said, "Yes!" And then he staggered out to the street to hit another saloon. Then there's Connie Jordan, a madman who sings and flips his arms and ends up splashing sweat on everybody and kicking over the mike and screaming like a woman; and you see him late at night, exhausted, listening to wild jazz sessions at Jamson's Nook with big round eyes and limp shoulders, a big gooky stare into space, and a drink in front of him. I never saw such crazy musicians. Everybody in Frisco blew. It was the end of the continent; they didn't give a damn. Dean and I goofed around San Francisco in this manner until I got my next GI check and got ready to go back home.

What I accomplished by coming to Frisco I don't know. Camille wanted me to leave; Dean didn't care one way or the other. I bought a loaf of bread and meats and made myself ten sandwiches to cross the country with again; they were all going to go rotten on me by the time I got to Dakota. The last night Dean went mad and found Marylou somewhere down-town and we got in the car and drove all over Richmond across the bay, hitting Negro jazz shacks in the oil flats. Marylou went to sit down and a colored guy pulled the chair out from under her. The gals approached her in the john with propositions. I was approached too. Dean was sweating around. It was the end; I wanted to get out.

At dawn I got my New York bus and said good-by to Dean and Marylou. They wanted some of my sandwiches. I told them no. It was a sullen moment. We were all thinking we'd never see one another again and we didn't care.

Part Three

I

IN the spring of 1949 I had a few dollars saved from my GI education checks and I went to Denver, thinking of settling down there. I saw myself in Middle America, a patriarch. I was lonesome. Nobody was there—no Babe Rawlins, Ray Rawlins, Tim Gray, Betty Gray, Roland Major, Dean Moriarty, Carlo Marx, Ed Dunkel, Roy Johnson, Tommy Snark, nobody. I wandered around Curtis Street and Larimer Street, worked awhile in the wholesale fruit market where I almost got hired in 1947—the hardest job of my life; at one point the Japanese kids and I had to move a whole boxcar a hundred feet down the rail by hand with a jack-gadget that made it move a quarter-inch with each yank. I lugged watermelon crates over the ice floor of reefers into the blazing sun, sneezing. In God's name and under the stars, what for?

At dusk I walked. I felt like a speck on the surface of the sad red earth. I passed the Windsor Hotel, where Dean Moriarty had lived with his father in the depression thirties, and as of yore I looked everywhere for the sad and fabled tinsmith of my mind. Either you find someone who looks like your father in places like Montana or you look for a friend's father where he is no more.

At lilac evening I walked with every muscle aching among the lights of 27th and Welton in the Denver colored section, wishing I were a Negro, feeling that the best the white world had offered was not enough ecstasy for me, not enough life, joy, kicks, darkness, music, not enough night. I stopped at a little shack where a man sold hot red chili in paper containers; I bought some and ate it, strolling in the dark mysterious streets. I wished I were a Denver Mexican, or even a poor overworked Jap, anything but what I was so drearily, a "white man" disillusioned. All my life I'd had white ambitions; that was why I'd abandoned a good woman like Terry in the San Joaquin Valley. I passed the dark porches of Mexican and

Negro homes; soft voices were there, occasionally the dusky knee of some mysterious sensual gal; and dark faces of the men behind rose arbors. Little children sat like sages in ancient rocking chairs. A gang of colored women came by, and one of the young ones detached herself from motherlike elders and came to me fast—"Hello Joe!"—and suddenly saw it wasn't Joe, and ran back, blushing. I wished I were Joe. I was only myself, Sal Paradise, sad, strolling in this violet dark, this unbearably sweet night, wishing I could exchange worlds with the happy, true-hearted, ecstatic Negroes of America. The raggedy neighborhoods reminded me of Dean and Marylou, who knew these streets so well from childhood. How I wished I could find them.

Down at 23rd and Welton a softball game was going on under floodlights which also illuminated the gas tank. A great eager crowd roared at every play. The strange young heroes of all kinds, white, colored, Mexican, pure Indian, were on the field, performing with heart-breaking seriousness. Just sandlot kids in uniform. Never in my life as an athlete had I ever permitted myself to perform like this in front of families and girl friends and kids of the neighborhood, at night, under lights; always it had been college, big-time, sober-faced; no boyish, human joy like this. Now it was too late. Near me sat an old Negro who apparently watched the games every night. Next to him was an old white bum; then a Mexican family, then some girls, some boys—all humanity, the lot. Oh, the sadness of the lights that night! The young pitcher looked just like Dean. A pretty blonde in the seats looked just like Marylou. It was the Denver Night; all I did was die.

> Down in Denver, down in Denver
> All I did was die

Across the street Negro families sat on their front steps, talking and looking up at the starry night through the trees and just relaxing in the softness and sometimes watching the game. Many cars passed in the street meanwhile, and stopped at the corner when the light turned red. There was excitement and the air was filled with the vibration of really joyous life that knows nothing of disappointment and "white sorrows" and all that. The old Negro man had a can of beer in his coat pocket, which he proceeded to open; and the old white man enviously eyed the can and groped in his pocket to see if *he* could buy a can too. How I died! I walked away from there.

I went to see a rich girl I knew. In the morning she pulled a hundred-dollar bill out of her silk stocking and said, "You've been talking of a trip to Frisco; that being the case, take this and go and have your fun." So all my problems were solved and I got a travel-bureau car for eleven dollars' gas-fare to Frisco and zoomed over the land.

Two fellows were driving this car; they said they were pimps. Two other fellows were passengers with me. We sat tight and bent our minds to the goal. We went over Berthoud Pass, down to the great plateau, Tabernash, Troublesome, Kremmling; down Rabbit Ears Pass to Steamboat Springs, and out; fifty miles of dusty detour; then Craig and the Great American Desert. As we crossed the Colorado-Utah border I saw God in the sky in the form of huge gold sunburning clouds above the desert that seemed to point a finger at me and say, "Pass here and go on, you're on the road to heaven." Ah well, alackaday, I was more interested in some old rotted covered wagons and pool tables sitting in the Nevada desert near a Coca-Cola stand and where there were huts with the weatherbeaten signs still flapping in the haunted shrouded desert wind, saying, "Rattle-snake Bill lived here" or "Broken-mouth Annie holed up here for years." Yes, zoom! In Salt Lake City the pimps checked on their girls and we drove on. Before I knew it, once again I was seeing the fabled city of San Francisco stretched on the bay in the middle of the night. I ran immediately to Dean. He had a little house now. I was burning to know what was on his mind and what would happen now, for there was nothing behind me any more, all my bridges were gone and I didn't give a damn about anything at all. I knocked on his door at two o'clock in the morning.

2

He came to the door stark naked and it might have been the President knocking for all he cared. He received the world in the raw. "Sal!" he said with genuine awe. "I didn't think you'd actually do it. You've finally come to *me*."

"Yep," I said. "Everything fell apart in me. How are things with you?"

"Not so good, not so good. But we've got a million things to talk about. Sal, the time has *fi-nally* come for us to talk and get with it." We agreed it was about time and went in. My arrival was somewhat like the coming of the strange most evil angel in the home of the snow-white fleece, as Dean and I began talking excitedly in the kitchen downstairs, which brought forth sobs from upstairs. Everything I said to Dean was answered with a wild, whispering, shuddering "*Yes!*" Camille knew what was going to happen. Apparently Dean had been quiet for a few months; now the angel had arrived and he was going mad again. "What's the matter with her?" I whispered.

He said, "She's getting worse and worse, man, she cries and makes tantrums, won't let me out to see Slim Gaillard, gets mad every time I'm late, then when I stay home she won't talk to me and says I'm an utter beast." He ran upstairs to soothe her. I heard Camille yell, "*You're a liar, you're a liar, you're a liar!*" I took the opportunity to examine the very wonderful house they had. It was a two-story crooked, rickety wooden cottage in the middle of tenements, right on top of Russian Hill with a view of the bay; it had four rooms, three upstairs and one immense sort of basement kitchen downstairs. The kitchen door opened onto a grassy court where washlines were. In back of the kitchen was a storage room where Dean's old shoes still were caked an inch thick with Texas mud from the night the Hudson got stuck on the Brazos River. Of course the Hudson was gone; Dean hadn't been able to make further payments on it. He had no car at all now. Their second baby was accidentally coming. It was horrible to hear Camille sobbing so. We couldn't stand it and went out to buy beer and brought it back to the kitchen. Camille finally went to sleep or spent the night staring blankly at the dark. I had no idea what was really wrong, except perhaps Dean had driven her mad after all.

After my last leaving of Frisco he had gone crazy over Marylou again and spent months haunting her apartment on Divisadero, where every night she had a different sailor in and he peeked down through her mail-slot and could see her bed. There he saw Marylou sprawled in the mornings with a boy. He trailed her around town. He wanted absolute proof that she was a whore. He loved her, he sweated over her. Finally he got hold of some bad green, as it's called in the trade—green, uncured marijuana—quite by mistake, and smoked too much of it.

"The first day," he said, "I lay rigid as a board in bed and couldn't move or say a word; I just looked straight up with my eyes open wide. I could hear buzzing in my head and saw all kinds of wonderful technicolor visions and felt wonderful. The second day everything came to me, EVERYTHING I'd ever done or known or read or heard of or conjectured came back to me and rearranged itself in my mind in a brand-new logical way and because I could think of nothing else in the interior concerns of holding and catering to the amazement and gratitude I felt, I kept saying, 'Yes, yes, yes, yes.' Not loud. Just 'Yes,' real quiet, and these green tea visions lasted until the third day. I had understood everything by then, my whole life was decided, I knew I loved Marylou, I knew I had to find my father wherever he is and save him, I knew you were my buddy et cetera, I knew how great Carlo is. I knew a thousand things about everybody everywhere. Then the third day I began having a terrible series of waking nightmares, and they were so absolutely horrible and grisly and green that I just lay there doubled up with my hands around my knees, saying, 'Oh, oh, oh, ah, oh . . .' The neighbors heard me and sent for a doctor. Camille was away with the baby, visiting her folks. The whole neighborhood was concerned. They came in and found me lying on the bed with my arms stretched out forever. Sal, I ran to Marylou with some of that tea. And do you know that the same thing happened to that dumb little box?—the same visions, the same logic, the same final decision about everything, the view of all truths in one painful lump leading to nightmares and pain—ack! Then I knew I loved her so much I wanted to kill her. I ran home and beat my head on the wall. I ran to Ed Dunkel; he's back in Frisco with Galatea; I asked him about a guy we know has a gun, I went to the guy, I got the gun, I ran to Marylou, I looked down the mail-slot, she was sleeping with a guy, had to retreat and hesitate, came back in an hour, I barged in, she was alone—and I gave her the gun and told her to kill me. She held the gun in her hand the longest time. I asked her for a sweet dead pact. She didn't want. I said one of us had to die. She said no. I beat my head on the wall. Man, I was out of my mind. She'll tell you, she talked me out of it."

"Then what happened?"

"That was months ago—after you left. She finally married a used-car dealer, dumb bastit has promised to kill me if he finds me, if necessary I shall have to defend myself and kill him and I'll go to San Quentin, 'cause, Sal, one more rap of *any* kind and I go to San Quentin for life—that's the end of me. Bad hand and all." He showed me his hand. I hadn't noticed in the excitement that he had suffered a terrible accident to his hand. "I hit Marylou on the brow on February twenty-sixth at six o'clock in the evening—in fact six-ten, because I remember I had to make my hotshot freight in an hour and twenty minutes —the last time we met and the last time we decided everything, and now listen to this: my thumb only deflected off her brow and she didn't even have a bruise and in fact laughed, but my thumb broke above the wrist and a horrible doctor made a setting of the bones that was difficult and took three separate castings, twenty-three combined hours of sitting on hard benches waiting, et cetera, and the final cast had a traction pin stuck through the tip of my thumb, so in April when they took off the cast the pin infected my bone and I developed osteomyelitis which has become chronic, and after an operation which failed and a month in a cast the result was the amputation of a wee bare piece off the tip-ass end."

He unwrapped the bandages and showed me. The flesh, about half an inch, was missing under the nail.

"It got from worse to worse. I had to support Camille and Amy and had to work as fast as I could at Firestone as mold man, curing recapped tires and later hauling big hunnerd-fifty-pound tires from the floor to the top of the cars—could only use my good hand and kept banging the bad—broke it again, had it reset again, and it's getting all infected and swoled again. So now I take care of baby while Camille works. You see? Heeby-jeebies, I'm classification three-A, jazz-hounded

Moriarty has a sore butt, his wife gives him daily injections of penicillin for his thumb, which produces hives, for he's allergic. He must take sixty thousand units of Fleming's juice within a month. He must take one tablet every four hours for this month to combat allergy produced from his juice. He must take codeine aspirin to relieve the pain in his thumb. He must have surgery on his leg for an inflamed cyst. He must rise next Monday at six A.M. to get his teeth cleaned. He must see a foot doctor twice a week for treatment. He must take cough syrup each night. He must blow and snort constantly to clear his nose, which has collapsed just under the bridge where an operation some years ago weakened it. He lost his thumb on his throwing arm. Greatest seventy-yard passer in the history of New Mexico State Reformatory. And yet—and yet, I've never felt better and finer and happier with the world and to see little lovely children playing in the sun and I am so glad to see you, my fine gone wonderful Sal, and I know, I *know* everything will be all right. You'll see her tomorrow, my terrific darling beautiful daughter can now stand alone for thirty seconds at a time, she weighs twenty-two pounds, is twenty-nine inches long. I've just figured out she is thirty-one-and-a-quarter-per-cent English, twenty-seven-and-a-half-per-cent Irish, twenty-five-per-cent German, eight-and-three-quarters per-cent Dutch, seven-and-a-half-per-cent Scotch, one-hundred-per-cent wonderful." He fondly congratulated me for the book I had finished, which was now accepted by the publishers. "We know life, Sal, we're growing older, each of us, little by little, and are coming to know things. What you tell me about your life I understand well, I've always dug your feelings, and now in fact you're ready to hook up with a real great girl if you can only find her and cultivate her and make her mind your soul as I have tried so hard with these damned women of mine. Shit! shit! shit!" he yelled.

And in the morning Camille threw both of us out, baggage and all. It began when we called Roy Johnson, old Denver Roy, and had him come over for beer, while Dean minded the baby and did the dishes and the wash in the backyard but did a sloppy job of it in his excitement. Johnson agreed to drive us to Mill City to look for Remi Boncœur. Camille came in from work at the doctor's office and gave us all the sad look of a harassed woman's life. I tried to show this haunted woman that I had no mean intentions concerning her home life by saying hello to her and talking as warmly as I could, but she knew it was a con and maybe one I'd learned from Dean, and only gave a brief smile. In the morning there was a terrible scene: she lay on the bed sobbing, and in the midst of this I suddenly had the need to go to the bathroom, and the only way I could get there was through her room. "Dean, Dean," I cried, "where's the nearest bar?"

"Bar?" he said, surprised; he was washing his hands in the kitchen sink downstairs. He thought I wanted to get drunk. I told him my dilemma and he said, "Go right ahead, she does that all the time." No, I couldn't do that. I rushed out to look for a bar; I walked uphill and downhill in a vicinity of four blocks on Russian Hill and found nothing but laundromats, cleaners, soda fountains, beauty parlors. I came back to the crooked little house. They were yelling at each other as I slipped through with a feeble smile and locked myself in the bathroom. A few moments later Camille was throwing Dean's things on the living-room floor and telling him to pack. To my amazement I saw a full-length oil painting of Galatea Dunkel over the sofa. I suddenly realized that all these women were spending months of loneliness and womanliness together, chatting about the madness of the men. I heard Dean's maniacal giggle across the house, together with the wails of his baby. The next thing I knew he was gliding around the house like Groucho Marx, with his broken thumb wrapped in a huge white bandage sticking up like a beacon that stands motionless above the frenzy of the waves. Once again I saw his pitiful huge battered trunk with socks and dirty underwear sticking out; he bent over it, throwing in everything he could find. Then he got his suitcase, the beatest suitcase in the USA. It was made of paper with designs on it to make it look like leather, and hinges of some kind pasted on. A great rip ran down the top; Dean lashed on a rope. Then he grabbed his seabag and threw things into that. I got my bag, stuffed it, and as Camille lay in bed saying, "Liar! Liar! Liar!" we leaped out of the house and struggled down the street to the nearest cable car—a mass of men and suitcases with that enormous bandaged thumb sticking up in the air.

That thumb became the symbol of Dean's final development. He no longer cared about anything (as before) but now
he also *cared about everything in principle*; that is to say, it was
all the same to him and he belonged to the world and there was
nothing he could do about it. He stopped me in the middle of
the street.

"Now, man, I know you're probably real bugged; you just
got to town and we get thrown out the first day and you're
wondering what I've done to deserve this and so on—together
with all horrible appurtenances—hee-hee-hee!—but look at
me. Please, Sal, look at me."

I looked at him. He was wearing a T-shirt, torn pants
hanging down his belly, tattered shoes; he had not shaved, his
hair was wild and bushy, his eyes bloodshot, and that tremendous bandaged thumb stood supported in midair at heart-level
(he had to hold it up that way), and on his face was the goofi-
est grin I ever saw. He stumbled around in a circle and looked
everywhere.

"What do my eyeballs see? Ah—the blue sky. Long-fellow!"
He swayed and blinked. He rubbed his eyes. "Together with
windows—have you ever dug windows? Now let's talk about
windows. I have seen some really crazy windows that made
faces at me, and some of them had shades drawn and so they
winked." Out of his seabag he fished a copy of Eugene Sue's
Mysteries of Paris and, adjusting the front of his T-shirt, began
reading on the street corner with a pedantic air. "Now really,
Sal, let's dig everything as we go along . . ." He forgot about
that in an instant and looked around blankly. I was glad I had
come, he needed me now.

"Why did Camille throw you out? What are you going to
do?"

"Eh?" he said. "Eh? Eh?" We racked our brains for where to
go and what to do. I realized it was up to me. Poor, poor Dean
—the devil himself had never fallen farther; in idiocy, with infected thumb, surrounded by the battered suitcases of his
motherless feverish life across America and back numberless
times, an undone bird. "Let's walk to New York," he said,
"and as we do so let's take stock of everything along the way
—yass." I took out my money and counted it; I showed it to
him.

"I have here," I said, "the sum of eighty-three dollars and change, and if you come with me let's go to New York—and after that let's go to Italy."

"Italy?" he said. His eyes lit up. "Italy, yass—how shall we get there, dear Sal?"

I pondered this. "I'll make some money, I'll get a thousand dollars from the publishers. We'll go dig all the crazy women in Rome, Paris, all those places; we'll sit at sidewalk cafés; we'll live in whorehouses. Why not go to Italy?"

"Why yass," said Dean, and then realized I was serious and looked at me out of the corner of his eye for the first time, for I'd never committed myself before with regard to his burdensome existence, and that look was the look of a man weighing his chances at the last moment before the bet. There were triumph and insolence in his eyes, a devilish look, and he never took his eyes off mine for a long time. I looked back at him and blushed.

I said, "What's the matter?" I felt wretched when I asked it. He made no answer but continued looking at me with the same wary insolent side-eye.

I tried to remember everything he'd done in his life and if there wasn't something back there to make him suspicious of something now. Resolutely and firmly I repeated what I said —"Come to New York with me; I've got the money." I looked at him; my eyes were watering with embarrassment and tears. Still he stared at me. Now his eyes were blank and looking through me. It was probably the pivotal point of our friendship when he realized I had actually spent some hours thinking about him and his troubles, and he was trying to place that in his tremendously involved and tormented mental categories. Something clicked in both of us. In me it was suddenly concern for a man who was years younger than I, five years, and whose fate was wound with mine across the passage of the recent years; in him it was a matter that I can ascertain only from what he did afterward. He became extremely joyful and said everything was settled. "What was that look?" I asked. He was pained to hear me say that. He frowned. It was rarely that Dean frowned. We both felt perplexed and uncertain of something. We were standing on top of a hill on a beautiful sunny day in San Francisco; our shadows fell across the sidewalk. Out of the tenement next to Camille's house filed eleven Greek men and women who instantly lined themselves up on the sunny pavement while another backed up across the narrow street and smiled at them over a camera. We gaped at these ancient people who were having a wedding party for one of their daughters, probably the thousandth in an unbroken dark generation of smiling in the sun. They were well dressed, and they were strange. Dean and I might have been in Cyprus for all of that. Gulls flew overhead in the sparkling air.

"Well," said Dean in a very shy and sweet voice, "shall we go?"

"Yes," I said, "let's go to Italy." And so we picked up our bags, he the trunk with his one good arm and I the rest, and staggered to the cable-car stop; in a moment rolled down the hill with our legs dangling to the sidewalk from the jiggling shelf, two broken-down heroes of the Western night.

3

First thing, we went to a bar down on Market Street and decided everything—that we would stick together and be buddies till we died. Dean was very quiet and preoccupied, looking at the old bums in the saloon that reminded him of his father. "I think he's in Denver—this time we must absolutely find him, he may be in County Jail, he may be around Larimer Street again, but he's to be found. Agreed?"

Yes, it was agreed; we were going to do everything we'd never done and had been too silly to do in the past. Then we promised ourselves two days of kicks in San Francisco before starting off, and of course the agreement was to go by travel bureau in share-the-gas cars and save as much money as possible. Dean claimed he no longer needed Marylou though he still loved her. We both agreed he would make out in New York.

Dean put on his pin-stripe suit with a sports shirt, we stashed our gear in a Greyhound bus locker for ten cents, and we took off to meet Roy Johnson who was going to be our chauffeur for two-day Frisco kicks. Roy agreed over the phone to do so.

He arrived at the corner of Market and Third shortly thereafter and picked us up. Roy was now living in Frisco, working
as a clerk and married to a pretty little blonde called Dorothy.
Dean confided that her nose was too long—this was his big
point of contention about her, for some strange reason—but
her nose wasn't too long at all. Roy Johnson is a thin, dark,
handsome kid with a pin-sharp face and combed hair that he
keeps shoving back from the sides of his head. He had an extremely earnest approach and a big smile. Evidently his wife,
Dorothy, had wrangled with him over the chauffeuring idea—
and, determined to make a stand as the man of the house (they
lived in a little room), he nevertheless stuck by his promise to
us, but with consequences; his mental dilemma resolved itself
in a bitter silence. He drove Dean and me all over Frisco at all
hours of day and night and never said a word; all he did was go
through red lights and make sharp turns on two wheels, and
this was telling us the shifts to which we'd put him. He was
midway between the challenge of his new wife and the challenge of his old Denver poolhall gang leader. Dean was pleased,
and of course unperturbed by the driving. We paid absolutely
no attention to Roy and sat in the back and yakked.

The next thing was to go to Mill City to see if we could find
Remi Boncœur. I noticed with some wonder that the old ship
Admiral Freebee was no longer in the bay; and then of course
Remi was no longer in the second-to-last compartment of the
shack in the canyon. A beautiful colored girl opened the door
instead; Dean and I talked to her a great deal. Roy Johnson
waited in the car, reading Eugene Sue's *Mysteries of Paris.* I
took one last look at Mill City and knew there was no sense
trying to dig up the involved past; instead we decided to go
see Galatea Dunkel about sleeping accommodations. Ed had
left her again, was in Denver, and damned if she still didn't
plot to get him back. We found her sitting crosslegged on the
Oriental-type rug of her four-room tenement flat on upper
Mission with a deck of fortune cards. Good girl. I saw sad
signs that Ed Dunkel had lived here awhile and then left out of
stupors and disinclinations only.

"He'll come back," said Galatea. "That guy can't take care
of himself without me." She gave a furious look at Dean and
Roy Johnson. "It was Tommy Snark who did it this time. All

the time before he came Ed was perfectly happy and worked and we went out and had wonderful times. Dean, you know that. Then they'd sit in the bathroom for hours, Ed in the bathtub and Snarky on the seat, and talk and talk and talk—such silly things."

Dean laughed. For years he had been chief prophet of that gang and now they were learning his technique. Tommy Snark had grown a beard and his big sorrowful blue eyes had come looking for Ed Dunkel in Frisco; what happened (actually and no lie), Tommy had his small finger amputated in a Denver mishap and collected a good sum of money. For no reason under the sun they decided to give Galatea the slip and go to Portland, Maine, where apparently Snark had an aunt. So they were now either in Denver, going through, or already in Portland.

"When Tom's money runs out Ed'll be back," said Galatea, looking at her cards. "Damn fool—he doesn't know anything and never did. All he has to do is know that I love him."

Galatea looked like the daughter of the Greeks with the sunny camera as she sat there on the rug, her long hair streaming to the floor, plying the fortune-telling cards. I got to like her. We even decided to go out that night and hear jazz, and Dean would take a six-foot blonde who lived down the street, Marie.

That night Galatea, Dean, and I went to get Marie. This girl had a basement apartment, a little daughter, and an old car that barely ran and which Dean and I had to push down the street as the girls jammed at the starter. We went to Galatea's, and there everybody sat around—Marie, her daughter, Galatea, Roy Johnson, Dorothy his wife—all sullen in the overstuffed furniture as I stood in a corner, neutral in Frisco problems, and Dean stood in the middle of the room with his balloon-thumb in the air breast-high, giggling. "Gawd damn," he said, "we're all losing our fingers—hawr-hawr-hawr."

"Dean, why do you act so foolish?" said Galatea. "Camille called and said you left her. Don't you realize you have a daughter?"

"He didn't leave her, she kicked him out!" I said, breaking my neutrality. They all gave me dirty looks; Dean grinned. "And with that thumb, what do you expect the poor guy to

do?" I added. They all looked at me; particularly Dorothy
Johnson lowered a mean gaze on me. It wasn't anything but
a sewing circle, and the center of it was the culprit, Dean—
responsible, perhaps, for everything that was wrong. I looked
out the window at the buzzing night-street of Mission; I
wanted to get going and hear the great jazz of Frisco—and remember, this was only my second night in town.

"I think Marylou was very, very wise leaving you, Dean,"
said Galatea. "For years now you haven't had any sense of responsibility for anyone. You've done so many awful things I
don't know what to say to you."

And in fact that was the point, and they all sat around
looking at Dean with lowered and hating eyes, and he stood on
the carpet in the middle of them and giggled—he just giggled.
He made a little dance. His bandage was getting dirtier all the
time; it began to flop and unroll. I suddenly realized that Dean,
by virtue of his enormous series of sins, was becoming the
Idiot, the Imbecile, the Saint of the lot.

"You have absolutely no regard for anybody but yourself
and your damned kicks. All you think about is what's hanging
between your legs and how much money or fun you can get
out of people and then you just throw them aside. Not only
that but you're silly about it. It never occurs to you that life is
serious and there are people trying to make something decent
out of it instead of just goofing all the time."

That's what Dean was, the HOLY GOOF.

"Camille is crying her heart out tonight, but don't think for
a minute she wants you back, she said she never wanted to see
you again and she said it was to be final this time. Yet you stand
here and make silly faces, and I don't think there's a care in your
heart."

This was not true; I knew better and I could have told them
all. I didn't see any sense in trying it. I longed to go and put
my arm around Dean and say, Now look here, all of you, remember just one thing: this guy has his troubles too, and another thing, he never complains and he's given all of you a
damned good time just being himself, and if that isn't enough
for you then send him to the firing squad, that's apparently
what you're itching to do anyway . . .

Nevertheless Galatea Dunkel was the only one in the gang

who wasn't afraid of Dean and could sit there calmly, with her face hanging out, telling him off in front of everybody. There were earlier days in Denver when Dean had everybody sit in the dark with the girls and just talked, and talked, and talked, with a voice that was once hypnotic and strange and was said to make the girls come across by sheer force of persuasion and the content of what he said. This was when he was fifteen, sixteen. Now his disciples were married and the wives of his disciples had him on the carpet for the sexuality and the life he had helped bring into being. I listened further.

"Now you're going East with Sal," Galatea said, "and what do you think you're going to accomplish by that? Camille has to stay home and mind the baby now you're gone—how can she keep her job?—and she never wants to see you again and I don't blame her. If you see Ed along the road you tell him to come back to me or I'll kill him."

Just as flat as that. It was the saddest night. I felt as if I was with strange brothers and sisters in a pitiful dream. Then a complete silence fell over everybody; where once Dean would have talked his way out, he now fell silent himself, but standing in front of everybody, ragged and broken and idiotic, right under the lightbulbs, his bony mad face covered with sweat and throbbing veins, saying, "Yes, yes, yes," as though tremendous revelations were pouring into him all the time now, and I am convinced they were, and the others suspected as much and were frightened. He was BEAT—the root, the soul of Beatific. What was he knowing? He tried all in his power to tell me what he was knowing, and they envied that about me, my position at his side, defending him and drinking him in as they once tried to do. Then they looked at me. What was I, a stranger, doing on the West Coast this fair night? I recoiled from the thought.

"We're going to Italy," I said, I washed my hands of the whole matter. Then, too, there was a strange sense of maternal satisfaction in the air, for the girls were really looking at Dean the way a mother looks at the dearest and most errant child, and he with his sad thumb and all his revelations knew it well, and that was why he was able, in tick-tocking silence, to walk out of the apartment without a word, to wait for us downstairs as soon as we'd made up our minds about *time*. This was what we sensed about the ghost on the sidewalk. I looked out the window. He was alone in the doorway, digging the street. Bitterness, recriminations, advice, morality, sadness—everything was behind him, and ahead of him was the ragged and ecstatic joy of pure being.

"Come on, Galatea, Marie, let's go hit the jazz joints and forget it. Dean will be dead someday. Then what can you say to him?"

"The sooner he's dead the better," said Galatea, and she spoke officially for almost everyone in the room.

"Very well, then," I said, "but now he's alive and I'll bet you want to know what he does next and that's because he's got the secret that we're all busting to find and it's splitting his head wide open and if he goes mad don't worry, it won't be your fault but the fault of God."

They objected to this; they said I really didn't know Dean; they said he was the worst scoundrel that ever lived and I'd find out someday to my regret. I was amused to hear them protest so much. Roy Johnson rose to the defense of the ladies and said he knew Dean better than anybody, and all Dean was, was just a very interesting and even amusing con-man. I went out to find Dean and we had a brief talk about it.

"Ah, man, don't worry, everything is perfect and fine." He was rubbing his belly and licking his lips.

4

The girls came down and we started out on our big night, once more pushing the car down the street. "Wheeoo! let's go!" cried Dean, and we jumped in the back seat and clanked to the little Harlem on Folsom Street.

Out we jumped in the warm, mad night, hearing a wild tenorman bawling horn across the way, going "EE-YAH! EE-YAH! EE-YAH!" and hands clapping to the beat and folks yelling, "Go, go, go!" Dean was already racing across the street with his thumb in the air, yelling, "Blow, man, blow!" A bunch of colored men in Saturday-night suits were whooping it up in front. It was a sawdust saloon with a small bandstand on which the fellows huddled with their hats on, blowing over people's heads, a crazy place; crazy floppy women wandered around sometimes in their bathrobes, bottles clanked in alleys. In back of the joint in a dark corridor beyond the splattered toilets scores of men and women stood against the wall drinking wine-spodiodi and spitting at the stars—wine and whisky. The behatted tenorman was blowing at the peak of a wonderfully satisfactory free idea, a rising and falling riff that went from "EE-yah!" to a crazier "EE-de-lee-yah!" and blasted along to the rolling crash of butt-scarred drums hammered by a big brutal Negro with a bullneck who didn't give a damn about anything but punishing his busted tubs, crash, rattle-ti-boom, crash. Uproars of music and the tenorman *had it* and everybody knew he had it. Dean was clutching his head in the crowd, and it was a mad crowd. They were all urging that tenorman to hold it and keep it with cries and wild eyes, and he was raising himself from a crouch and going down again with his horn, looping it up in a clear cry above the furor. A six-foot skinny Negro woman was rolling her bones at the man's hornbell, and he just jabbed it at her, "Ee! ee! ee!"

Everybody was rocking and roaring. Galatea and Marie with beer in their hands were standing on their chairs, shaking and jumping. Groups of colored guys stumbled in from the street, falling over one another to get there. "Stay with it, man!" roared a man with a foghorn voice, and let out a big groan that must have been heard clear out in Sacramento, ah-haa! "Whoo!" said Dean. He was rubbing his chest, his belly; the sweat splashed from his face. Boom, kick, that drummer was kicking his drums down the cellar and rolling the beat upstairs with his murderous sticks, rattlety-boom! A big fat man was jumping on the platform, making it sag and creak. "Yoo!" The pianist was only pounding the keys with spreadeagled fingers, chords, at intervals when the great tenorman was drawing breath for another blast—Chinese chords, shuddering the piano in every timber, chink, and wire, boing! The tenorman jumped down from the platform and stood in the crowd, blowing around; his hat was over his eyes; somebody pushed it back for him. He just hauled back and stamped his foot and blew down a hoarse, baughing blast, and drew breath, and raised the horn and blew high, wide, and screaming in the air.

Dean was directly in front of him with his face lowered to the
bell of the horn, clapping his hands, pouring sweat on the
man's keys, and the man noticed and laughed in his horn a
long quivering crazy laugh, and everybody else laughed and
they rocked and rocked; and finally the tenorman decided to
blow his top and crouched down and held a note in high C for
a long time as everything else crashed along and the cries increased and I thought the cops would come swarming from
the nearest precinct. Dean was in a trance. The tenorman's
eyes were fixed straight on him; he had a madman who not
only understood but cared and wanted to understand more
and much more than there was, and they began dueling for
this; everything came out of the horn, no more phrases, just
cries, cries, "Baugh" and down to "Beep!" and up to "*EEEEE!*"
and down to clinkers and over to sideways-echoing horn-
sounds. He tried everything, up, down, sideways, upside down,
horizontal, thirty degrees, forty degrees, and finally he fell
back in somebody's arms and gave up and everybody pushed
around and yelled, "Yes! Yes! He blowed that one!" Dean
wiped himself with his handkerchief.

   Then up stepped the tenorman on the bandstand and asked
for a slow beat and looked sadly out the open door over
people's heads and began singing "Close Your Eyes." Things
quieted down a minute. The tenorman wore a tattered suede
jacket, a purple shirt, cracked shoes, and zoot pants without
press; he didn't care. He looked like a Negro Hassel. His big
brown eyes were concerned with sadness, and the singing of
songs slowly and with long, thoughtful pauses. But in the second chorus he got excited and grabbed the mike and jumped
down from the bandstand and bent to it. To sing a note he had
to touch his shoetops and pull it all up to blow, and he blew so
much he staggered from the effect, and only recovered himself
in time for the next long slow note. "Mu-u-u-usic pla-a-a-a-
a-ay!" He leaned back with his face to the ceiling, mike held
below. He shook, he swayed. Then he leaned in, almost falling
with his face against the mike. "Ma-a-a-ake it dream-y for dancing"—and he looked at the street outside with his lips curled
in scorn, Billie Holiday's hip sneer—"while we go roman-n-n-
cing"—he staggered sideways—"Lo-o-o-ove's holida-a-ay"—
he shook his head with disgust and weariness at the whole

world—"Will make it seem"—what would it make it seem? everybody waited; he mourned—"O-kay." The piano hit a chord. "So baby come on just clo-o-o-ose your pretty little ey-y-y-y-yes"—his mouth quivered, he looked at us, Dean and me, with an expression that seemed to say, Hey now, what's this thing we're all doing in this sad brown world?—and then he came to the end of his song, and for this there had to be elaborate preparations, during which time you could send all the messages to Garcia around the world twelve times and what difference did it make to anybody? because here we were dealing with the pit and prunejuice of poor beat life itself in the god-awful streets of man, so he said it and sang it, "Close —your—" and blew it way up to the ceiling and through to the stars and on out—"Ey-y-y-y-y-es"—and staggered off the platform to brood. He sat in the corner with a bunch of boys and paid no attention to them. He looked down and wept. He was the greatest.

Dean and I went over to talk to him. We invited him out to the car. In the car he suddenly yelled, "Yes! ain't nothin I like better than good kicks! Where do we go?" Dean jumped up and down in the seat, giggling maniacally. "Later! later!" said the tenorman. "I'll get my boy to drive us down to Jamson's Nook, I got to sing. Man, I *live* to sing. Been singin 'Close Your Eyes' for two weeks—I don't want to sing nothin else. What are you boys up to?" We told him we were going to New York in two days. "Lord, I ain't never been there and they tell me it's a real jumpin town but I ain't got no cause complainin where I am. I'm married, you know."

"Oh yes?" said Dean, lighting up. "And where is the darling tonight?"

"What do you *mean*?" said the tenorman, looking at him out of the corner of his eye. "I tole you I was *married* to her, didn't I?"

"Oh yes, oh yes," said Dean. "I was just asking. Maybe she has friends? or sisters? A ball, you know, I'm just looking for a ball."

"Yah, what good's a ball, life's too sad to be ballin all the time," said the tenorman, lowering his eye to the street. "Shheee-it!" he said. "I ain't got no money and I don't care tonight."

We went back in for more. The girls were so disgusted with
Dean and me for gunning off and jumping around that they
had left and gone to Jamson's Nook on foot; the car wouldn't
run anyway. We saw a horrible sight in the bar: a white hipster
fairy had come in wearing a Hawaiian shirt and was asking the
big drummer if he could sit in. The musicians looked at him
suspiciously. "Do you blow?" He said he did, mincing. They
looked at one another and said, "Yeah, yeah, that's what the
man does, shhh-ee-it!" So the fairy sat down at the tubs and
they started the beat of a jump number and he began stroking
the snares with soft goofy bop brushes, swaying his neck
with that complacent Reichianalyzed ecstasy that doesn't
mean anything except too much tea and soft foods and goofy
kicks on the cool order. But he didn't care. He smiled joyously
into space and kept the beat, though softly, with bop sub-
tleties, a giggling, rippling background for big solid foghorn
blues the boys were blowing, unaware of him. The big Negro
bullneck drummer sat waiting for his turn. "What that man
doing?" he said. "Play the music!" he said. "What in hell!" he
said. "Shh-ee-eet!" and looked away, disgusted.

The tenorman's boy showed up; he was a little taut Negro
with a great big Cadillac. We all jumped in. He hunched over
the wheel and blew the car clear across Frisco without stopping once, seventy miles an hour, right through traffic and nobody even noticed him, he was so good. Dean was in ecstasies.
"Dig this guy, man! dig the way he sits there and don't move a
bone and just balls that jack and can talk all night while he's
doing it, only thing is he doesn't bother with talking, ah, man,
the things, the things I could—I wish—oh, yes. Let's go, let's
not stop—go now! Yes!" And the boy wound around a corner
and bowled us right in front of Jamson's Nook and was
parked. A cab pulled up; out of it jumped a skinny, withered
little Negro preacherman who threw a dollar at the cabby and
yelled, "Blow!" and ran into the club and dashed right
through the downstairs bar, yelling, "Blowblowblow!" and
stumbled upstairs, almost falling on his face, and blew the
door open and fell into the jazz-session room with his hands
out to support him against anything he might fall on, and he
fell right on Lampshade, who was working as a waiter in Jamson's Nook that season, and the music was there blasting and

blasting and he stood transfixed in the open door, screaming, "Blow for me, man, blow!" And the man was a little short Negro with an alto horn that Dean said obviously lived with his grandmother just like Tom Snark, slept all day and blew all night, and blew a hundred choruses before he was ready to jump for fair, and that's what he was doing.

"It's Carlo Marx!" screamed Dean above the fury.

And it was. This little grandmother's boy with the taped-up alto had beady, glittering eyes; small, crooked feet; spindly legs; and he hopped and flopped with his horn and threw his feet around and kept his eyes fixed on the audience (which was just people laughing at a dozen tables, the room thirty by thirty feet and low ceiling), and he never stopped. He was very simple in his ideas. What he liked was the surprise of a new simple variation of a chorus. He'd go from "ta-tup-tader-rara . . . ta-tup-tader-rara," repeating and hopping to it and kissing and smiling into his horn, to "ta-tup-EE-da-de-dera-RUP! ta-tup-EE-da-de-dera-RUP!" and it was all great moments of laughter and understanding for him and everyone else who heard. His tone was clear as a bell, high, pure, and blew straight in our faces from two feet away. Dean stood in front of him, oblivious to everything else in the world, with his head bowed, his hands socking in together, his whole body jumping on his heels and the sweat, always the sweat, pouring and splashing down his tormented collar to lie actually in a pool at his feet. Galatea and Marie were there, and it took us five minutes to realize it. Whoo, Frisco nights, the end of the continent and the end of doubt, all dull doubt and tomfoolery, good-by. Lampshade was roaring around with his trays of beer; everything he did was in rhythm; he yelled at the waitress with the beat; "Hey now, babybaby, make a way, make a way, it's Lampshade comin your way," and he hurled by her with the beers in the air and roared through the swinging doors into the kitchen and danced with the cooks and came sweating back. The hornman sat absolutely motionless at a corner table with an untouched drink in front of him, staring gook-eyed into space, his hands hanging at his sides till they almost touched the floor, his feet outspread like lolling tongues, his body shriveled into absolute weariness and entranced sorrow and what-all was on his mind: a man who knocked himself out every evening and let the others put the quietus to him in the night. Everything swirled around him like a cloud. And that little grandmother's alto, that little Carlo Marx, hopped and monkeydanced with his magic horn and blew two hundred choruses of blues, each one more frantic than the other, and no signs of failing energy or willingness to call anything a day. The whole room shivered.

On the corner of Fourth and Folsom an hour later I stood with Ed Fournier, a San Francisco alto man who waited with me while Dean made a phone call in a saloon to have Roy Johnson pick us up. It wasn't anything much, we were just talking, except that suddenly we saw a very strange and insane sight. It was Dean. He wanted to give Roy Johnson the address of the bar, so he told him to hold the phone a minute and ran out to see, and to do this he had to rush pellmell through a long bar of brawling drinkers in white shirtsleeves, go to the middle of the street, and look at the post signs. He did this, crouched low to the ground like Groucho Marx, his feet carrying him with amazing swiftness out of the bar, like an apparition, with his balloon thumb stuck up in the night, and came to a whirling stop in the middle of the road, looking everywhere above him for the signs. They were hard to see in the dark, and he spun a dozen times in the road, thumb upheld, in a wild, anxious silence, a wild-haired person with a ballooning thumb held up like a great goose of the sky, spinning and spinning in the dark, the other hand distractedly inside his pants. Ed Fournier was saying, "I blow a sweet tone wherever I go and if people don't like it ain't nothin I can do about it. Say, man, that buddy of yours is a crazy cat, looka him over there"—and we looked. There was a big silence everywhere as Dean saw the signs and rushed back in the bar, practically going under someone's legs as they came out and gliding so fast through the bar that everybody had to do a double take to see him. A moment later Roy Johnson showed up, and with the same amazing swiftness. Dean glided across the street and into the car, without a sound. We were off again.

"Now, Roy, I know you're all hung-up with your wife about this thing but we absolutely must make Forty-sixth and Geary in the incredible time of three minutes or everything is lost. Ahem! Yes! (Cough-cough.) In the morning Sal and I are leaving for New York and this is absolutely our last night of kicks and I know you won't mind."

No, Roy Johnson didn't mind; he only drove through every red light he could find and hurried us along in our foolishness. At dawn he went home to bed. Dean and I had ended up with a colored guy called Walter who ordered drinks at the bar and had them lined up and said, "Wine-spodiodi!" which was a shot of port wine, a shot of whisky, and a shot of port wine. "Nice sweet jacket for all that bad whisky!" he yelled.

He invited us to his home for a bottle of beer. He lived in the tenements in back of Howard. His wife was asleep when we came in. The only light in the apartment was the bulb over her bed. We had to get up on a chair and unscrew the bulb as she lay smiling there; Dean did it, fluttering his lashes. She was about fifteen years older than Walter and the sweetest woman in the world. Then we had to plug in the extension over her bed, and she smiled and smiled. She never asked Walter where he'd been, what time it was, nothing. Finally we were set in the kitchen with the extension and sat down around the humble table to drink the beer and tell the stories. Dawn. It was time to leave and move the extension back to the bedroom and screw back the bulb. Walter's wife smiled and smiled as we repeated the insane thing all over again. She never said a word.

Out on the dawn street Dean said, "Now you see, man, there's *real* woman for you. Never a harsh word, never a complaint, or modified; her old man can come in any hour of the night with anybody and have talks in the kitchen and drink the beer and leave any old time. This is a man, and that's his castle." He pointed up at the tenement. We stumbled off. The big night was over. A cruising car followed us suspiciously for a few blocks. We bought fresh doughnuts in a bakery on Third Street and ate them in the gray, ragged street. A tall, bespectacled, well-dressed fellow came stumbling down the street with a Negro in a truck-driving cap. They were a strange pair. A big truck rolled by and the Negro pointed at it excitedly and tried to express his feeling. The tall white man furtively looked over his shoulder and counted his money. "It's Old Bull Lee!" giggled Dean. "Counting his money and worried about everything, and all that other boy wants to do is talk about trucks and things he knows." We followed them awhile.

Holy flowers floating in the air, were all these tired faces in the dawn of Jazz America.

We had to sleep; Galatea Dunkel's was out of the question. Dean knew a railroad brakeman called Ernest Burke who lived with his father in a hotel room on Third Street. Originally he'd been on good terms with them, but lately not so, and the idea was for me to try persuading them to let us sleep on their floor. It was horrible. I had to call from a morning diner. The old man answered the phone suspiciously. He remembered me from what his son had told him. To our surprise he came down to the lobby and let us in. It was just a sad old brown Frisco hotel. We went upstairs and the old man was kind enough to give us the entire bed. "I have to get up anyway," he said and retired to the little kitchenette to brew coffee. He began telling stories about his railroading days. He reminded me of my father. I stayed up and listened to the stories. Dean, not listening, was washing his teeth and bustling around and saying, "Yes, that's right," to everything he said. Finally we slept; and in the morning Ernest came back from a Western Division run and took the bed as Dean and I got up. Now old Mr. Burke dolled himself up for a date with his middle-aged sweetheart. He put on a green tweed suit, a cloth cap, also green tweed, and stuck a flower in his lapel.

"These romantic old broken-down Frisco brakemen live sad but eager lives of their own," I told Dean in the toilet. "It was very kind of him to let us sleep here."

"Yass, yass," said Dean, not listening. He rushed out to get a travel-bureau car. My job was to hurry to Galatea Dunkel's for our bags. She was sitting on the floor with her fortune-telling cards.

"Well, good-by, Galatea, and I hope everything works out fine."

"When Ed gets back I'm going to take him to Jamson's Nook every night and let him get his fill of madness. Do you think that'll work, Sal? I don't know what to do."

"What do the cards say?"

"The ace of spades is far away from him. The heart cards always surround him—the queen of hearts is never far. See this jack of spades? That's Dean, he's always around."

"Well, we're leaving for New York in an hour."

"Someday Dean's going to go on one of these trips and never come back."

She let me take a shower and shave, and then I said good-by and took the bags downstairs and hailed a Frisco taxi-jitney, which was an ordinary taxi that ran a regular route and you could hail it from any corner and ride to any corner you want for about fifteen cents, cramped in with other passengers like on a bus, but talking and telling jokes like in a private car. Mission Street that last day in Frisco was a great riot of construction work, children playing, whooping Negroes coming home from work, dust, excitement, the great buzzing and vibrating hum of what is really America's most excited city—and overhead the pure blue sky and the joy of the foggy sea that always rolls in at night to make everybody hungry for food and further excitement. I hated to leave; my stay had lasted sixty-odd hours. With frantic Dean I was rushing through the world without a chance to see it. In the afternoon we were buzzing toward Sacramento and eastward again.

5

The car belonged to a tall, thin fag who was on his way home to Kansas and wore dark glasses and drove with extreme care; the car was what Dean called a "fag Plymouth"; it had no pickup and no real power. "Effeminate car!" whispered Dean in my ear. There were two other passengers, a couple, typical halfway tourists who wanted to stop and sleep everywhere. The first stop would have to be Sacramento, which wasn't even the faintest beginning of the trip to Denver. Dean and I sat alone in the back seat and left it up to them and talked. "Now, man, that alto man last night had IT—he held it once he found it; I've never seen a guy who could hold so long." I wanted to know what "IT" meant. "Ah well"—Dean laughed—"now you're asking me impon-de-rables—ahem! Here's a guy and everybody's there, right? Up to him to put down what's on everybody's mind. He starts the first chorus, then lines up his ideas, people, yeah, yeah, but get it, and then he rises to his fate and has to blow equal to it. All of a sudden somewhere in the middle of the chorus he *gets it*—everybody looks up and knows; they listen; he picks it up and carries. Time stops. He's filling empty space with the substance of our lives, confessions of his bellybottom strain, remembrance of ideas, rehashes of old blowing. He has to blow across bridges and come back and do it with such infinite feeling soul-exploratory for the tune of the moment that everybody knows it's not the tune that counts but IT—" Dean could go no further; he was sweating telling about it.

Then I began talking; I never talked so much in all my life. I told Dean that when I was a kid and rode in cars I used to imagine I held a big scythe in my hand and cut down all the trees and posts and even sliced every hill that zoomed past the window. "Yes! Yes!" yelled Dean. "I used to do it too only different scythe—tell you why. Driving across the West with the long stretches my scythe had to be immeasurably longer and it had to curve over distant mountains, slicing off their tops, and reach another level to get at further mountains and at the same time clip off every post along the road, regular throbbing poles. For this reason—O man, I have to tell you, NOW, I have IT— I have to tell you the time my father and I and a pisspoor bum from Larimer Street took a trip to Nebraska in the middle of the depression to sell flyswatters. And how we made them, we bought pieces of ordinary regular old screen and pieces of wire that we twisted double and little pieces of blue and red cloth to sew around the edges and all of it for a matter of cents in a five-and-ten and made thousands of flyswatters and got in the old bum's jalopy and went clear around Nebraska to every farmhouse and sold them for a nickel apiece—mostly for charity the nickels were given us, two bums and a boy, apple pies in the sky, and my old man in those days was always singing 'Hallelujah, I'm a bum, bum again.' And man, now listen to this, after two whole weeks of incredible hardship and bouncing around and hustling in the heat to sell these awful makeshift flyswatters they started to argue about the division of the proceeds and had a big fight on the side of the road and then made up and bought wine and began drinking wine and didn't stop for five days and five nights while I huddled and cried in the background, and when they were finished every last cent was spent and we were right back where we started from,

Larimer Street. And my old man was arrested and I had to plead at court to the judge to let him go cause he was my pa and I had no mother. Sal, I made great mature speeches at the age of eight in front of interested lawyers . . ." We were hot; we were going east; we were excited.

"Let me tell you more," I said, "and only as a parenthesis within what you're saying and to conclude my last thought. As a child lying back in my father's car in the back seat I also had a vision of myself on a white horse riding alongside over every possible obstacle that presented itself: this included dodging posts, hurling around houses, sometimes jumping over when I looked too late, running over hills, across sudden squares with traffic that I had to dodge through incredibly—"

"Yes! Yes! Yes!" breathed Dean ecstatically. "Only difference with me was, I myself ran, I had no horse. You were a Eastern kid and dreamed of horses; of course we won't assume such things as we both know they are really dross and literary ideas, but merely that I in my perhaps wilder schizophrenia actually *ran* on foot along the car and at incredible speeds sometimes ninety, making it over every bush and fence and farmhouse and sometimes taking quick dashes to the hills and back without losing a moment's ground . . ."

We were telling these things and both sweating. We had completely forgotten the people up front who had begun to wonder what was going on in the back seat. At one point the driver said, "For God's sakes, you're rocking the boat back there." Actually we were; the car was swaying as Dean and I both swayed to the rhythm and the IT of our final excited joy in talking and living to the blank tranced end of all innumerable riotous angelic particulars that had been lurking in our souls all our lives.

"Oh, man! man! man!" moaned Dean. "And it's not even the beginning of it—and now here we are at last going east together, we've never gone east together, Sal, think of it, we'll dig Denver together and see what everybody's doing although that matters little to us, the point being that we know what IT is and we know TIME and we know that everything is really FINE." Then he whispered, clutching my sleeve, sweating, "Now you just dig them in front. They have worries, they're counting the miles, they're thinking about where to sleep tonight, how much money for gas, the weather, how they'll get there—and all the time they'll get there anyway, you see. But they need to worry and betray time with urgencies false and otherwise, purely anxious and whiny, their souls really won't be at peace unless they can latch on to an established and proven worry and having once found it they assume facial expressions to fit and go with it, which is, you see, unhappiness, and all the time it all flies by them and they know it and that *too* worries them no end. Listen! Listen! 'Well now,'" he mimicked, "'I don't know—maybe we shouldn't get gas in that station. I read recently in *National Petroffious Petroleum News* that this kind of gas has a great deal of O-Octane *gook* in it and someone once told me it even had semi-official high-frequency *cock* in it, and I don't know, well I just don't feel like it anyway . . .' Man, you dig all this." He was poking me furiously in the ribs to understand. I tried my wildest best. Bing, bang, it was all Yes! Yes! Yes! in the back seat and the people up front were mopping their brows with fright and wishing they'd never picked us up at the travel bureau. It was only the beginning, too.

In Sacramento the fag slyly bought a room in a hotel and invited Dean and me to come up for a drink, while the couple went to sleep at relatives', and in the hotel room Dean tried everything in the book to get money from the fag. It was insane. The fag began by saying he was very glad we had come along because he liked young men like us, and would we believe it, but he really didn't like girls and had recently concluded an affair with a man in Frisco in which he had taken the male role and the man the female role. Dean plied him with businesslike questions and nodded eagerly. The fag said he would like nothing better than to know what Dean thought about all this. Warning him first that he had once been a hustler in his youth, Dean asked him how much money he had. I was in the bathroom. The fag became extremely sullen and I think suspicious of Dean's final motives, turned over no money, and made vague promises for Denver. He kept counting his money and checking on his wallet. Dean threw up his hands and gave up. "You see, man, it's better not to bother. Offer them what they secretly want and they of course immediately become panic-stricken." But he had sufficiently conquered the owner of the Plymouth to take over the wheel without remonstrance, and now we really traveled.

We left Sacramento at dawn and were crossing the Nevada desert by noon, after a hurling passage of the Sierras that made the fag and the tourists cling to each other in the back seat. We were in front, we took over. Dean was happy again. All he needed was a wheel in his hand and four on the road. He talked about how bad a driver Old Bull Lee was and to demonstrate —"Whenever a huge big truck like that one coming loomed into sight it would take Bull infinite time to spot it, 'cause he couldn't *see*, man, he can't *see*." He rubbed his eyes furiously to show. "And I'd say, 'Whoop, look out, Bull, a truck,' and he'd say, 'Eh? what's that you say, Dean?' 'Truck! truck!' and at the *very* last *moment* he would go right up to the truck like this—" And Dean hurled the Plymouth head-on at the truck roaring our way, wobbled and hovered in front of it a moment, the truckdriver's face growing gray before our eyes, the people in the back seat subsiding in gasps of horror, and swung away at the last moment. "Like that, you see, exactly like that, how bad he was." I wasn't scared at all; I knew Dean. The people in the back seat were speechless. In fact they were afraid to complain: God knew what Dean would do, they thought, if they should ever complain. He balled right across the desert in this manner, demonstrating various ways of how not to drive, how his father used to drive jalopies, how great drivers made curves, how bad drivers hove over too far in the beginning and had to scramble at the curve's end, and so on. It was a hot, sunny afternoon. Reno, Battle Mountain, Elko, all the towns along the Nevada road shot by one after another, and at dusk we were in the Salt Lake flats with the lights of Salt Lake City infinitesimally glimmering almost a hundred miles across the mirage of the flats, twice showing, above and below the curve of the earth, one clear, one dim. I told Dean that the thing that bound us all together in this world was invisible, and to prove it pointed to long lines of telephone poles that curved off out of sight over the bend of a hundred miles of salt. His floppy bandage, all dirty now, shuddered in the air, his face was a light. "Oh yes, man, dear God, yes, yes!" Suddenly he stopped the car and collapsed. I turned and saw him huddled in the corner of the seat, sleeping. His face was down on his good hand, and the bandaged hand automatically and dutifully remained in the air.

The people in the back seat sighed with relief. I heard them whispering mutiny. "We can't let him drive any more, he's absolutely crazy, they must have let him out of an asylum or something."

I rose to Dean's defense and leaned back to talk to them. "He's not crazy, he'll be all right, and don't worry about his driving, he's the best in the world."

"I just can't stand it," said the girl in a suppressed, hysterical whisper. I sat back and enjoyed nightfall on the desert and waited for poorchild Angel Dean to wake up again. We were on a hill overlooking Salt Lake City's neat patterns of light and he opened his eyes to the place in this spectral world where he was born, unnamed and bedraggled, years ago.

"Sal, Sal, look, this is where I was born, think of it! People change, they eat meals year after year and change with every meal. *EE!* Look!" He was so excited it made me cry. Where would it all lead? The tourists insisted on driving the car the rest of the way to Denver. Okay, we didn't care. We sat in the back and talked. But they got too tired in the morning and Dean took the wheel in the eastern Colorado desert at Craig. We had spent almost the entire night crawling cautiously over Strawberry Pass in Utah and lost a lot of time. They went to sleep. Dean headed pellmell for the mighty wall of Berthoud Pass that stood a hundred miles ahead on the roof of the world, a tremendous Gibraltarian door shrouded in clouds. He took Berthoud Pass like a June bug—same as at Tehachapi, cutting off the motor and floating it, passing everybody and never halting the rhythmic advance that the mountains themselves intended, till we overlooked the great hot plain of Denver again —and Dean was home.

It was with a great deal of silly relief that these people let us off the car at the corner of 27th and Federal. Our battered suitcases were piled on the sidewalk again; we had longer ways to go. But no matter, the road is life.

6

Now we had a number of circumstances to deal with in Denver, and they were of an entirely different order from those of 1947. We could either get another travel-bureau car at once or stay a few days for kicks and look for his father.

We were both exhausted and dirty. In the john of a restaurant I was at a urinal blocking Dean's way to the sink and I stepped out before I was finished and resumed at another urinal, and said to Dean, "Dig this trick."

"Yes, man," he said, washing his hands at the sink, "it's a very good trick but awful on your kidneys and because you're getting a little older now every time you do this eventually years of misery in your old age, awful kidney miseries for the days when you sit in parks."

It made me mad. "Who's old? I'm not much older than you are!"

"I wasn't saying that, man!"

"Ah," I said, "you're always making cracks about my age. I'm no old fag like that fag, you don't have to warn me about *my* kidneys." We went back to the booth and just as the waitress set down the hot-roast-beef sandwiches—and ordinarily Dean would have leaped to wolf the food at once—I said to cap my anger, "And I don't want to hear any more of it." And suddenly Dean's eyes grew tearful and he got up and left his food steaming there and walked out of the restaurant. I wondered if he was just wandering off forever. I didn't care, I was so mad—I had flipped momentarily and turned it down on Dean. But the sight of his uneaten food made me sadder than anything in years. I shouldn't have said that . . . he likes to eat so much . . . He's never left his food like this . . . What the hell. That's showing him, anyway.

Dean stood outside the restaurant for exactly five minutes and then came back and sat down. "Well," I said, "what were you doing out there, knotting up your fists? Cursing me, thinking up new gags about my kidneys?"

Dean mutely shook his head. "No, man, no, man, you're all completely wrong. If you want to know, well—"

"Go ahead, tell me." I said all this and never looked up from my food. I felt like a beast.

"I was crying," said Dean.

"Ah hell, you never cry."

"You say that? Why do you think I don't cry?"

"You don't die enough to cry." Every one of these things I said was a knife at myself. Everything I had ever secretly held against my brother was coming out: how ugly I was and what filth I was discovering in the depths of my own impure psychologies.

Dean was shaking his head. "No, man, I was crying."

"Go on, I bet you were so mad you had to leave."

"Believe me, Sal, really do believe me if you've ever believed anything about me." I knew he was telling the truth and yet I didn't want to bother with the truth and when I looked up at him I think I was cockeyed from cracked intestinal twistings in my awful belly. Then I knew I was wrong.

"Ah, man, Dean, I'm sorry, I never acted this way before with you. Well, now you know me. You know I don't have close relationships with anybody any more—I don't know what to do with these things. I hold things in my hand like pieces of crap and don't know where to put it down. Let's forget it." The holy con-man began to eat. "It's not my fault! it's not my fault!" I told him. "Nothing in this lousy world is my fault, don't you see that? I don't want it to be and it can't be and it *won't* be."

"Yes, man, yes, man. But please harken back and believe me."

"I do believe you, I do." This was the sad story of that afternoon. All kinds of tremendous complications arose that night when Dean and I went to stay with the Okie family.

These had been neighbors of mine in my Denver solitude of two weeks before. The mother was a wonderful woman in jeans who drove coal trucks in winter mountains to support her kids, four in all, her husband having left her years before when they were traveling around the country in a trailer. They had rolled all the way from Indiana to LA in that trailer. After many a good time and a big Sunday-afternoon drunk in crossroads bars and laughter and guitar-playing in the night, the big lout had suddenly walked off across the dark field and never returned. Her children were wonderful. The eldest was a boy,

who wasn't around that summer but in a camp in the mountains; next was a lovely thirteen-year-old daughter who wrote
poetry and picked flowers in the fields and wanted to grow up
and be an actress in Hollywood, Janet by name; then came the
little ones, little Jimmy who sat around the campfire at night
and cried for his "pee-tater" before it was half roasted, and
little Lucy who made pets of worms, horny toads, beetles, and
anything that crawled, and gave them names and places to live.
They had four dogs. They lived their ragged and joyous lives
on the little new-settlement street and were the butt of the
neighbors' semi-respectable sense of propriety only because
the poor woman's husband had left her and because they littered up the yard. At night all the lights of Denver lay like a
great wheel on the plain below, for the house was in that part
of the West where the mountains roll down foothilling to the
plain and where in primeval times soft waves must have washed
from sea-like Mississippi to make such round and perfect stools
for the island-peaks like Evans and Pike and Longs. Dean went
there and of course he was all sweats and joy at the sight of
them, especially Janet, but I warned him not to touch her, and
probably didn't have to. The woman was a great man's woman
and took to Dean right away but she was bashful and he was
bashful. She said Dean reminded her of the husband gone.
"Just like him—oh, he was a crazy one, I tell ya!"

The result was uproarious beer-drinking in the littered living
room, shouting suppers, and booming Lone Ranger radio.
The complications rose like clouds of butterflies: the woman—
Frankie, everyone called her—was finally about to buy a jalopy
as she had been threatening to do for years, and had recently
come into a few bucks toward one. Dean immediately took
over the responsibility of selecting and naming the price of the
car, because of course he wanted to use it himself so as of yore
he could pick up girls coming out of high school in the afternoons and drive them up to the mountains. Poor innocent
Frankie was always agreeable to anything. But she was afraid to
part with her money when they got to the car lot and stood
before the salesman. Dean sat right down in the dust of
Alameda Boulevard and beat his fists on his head. "For a hunnerd you *can't* get anything better!" He swore he'd never talk
to her again, he cursed till his face was purple, he was about to

jump in the car and drive it away anyway. "Oh these dumb dumb dumb Okies, they'll never change, how com-pletely and how unbelievably dumb, the moment it comes time to act, this paralysis, scared, hysterical, nothing frightens em more than what they *want*—it's *my father my father my father* all over again!"

Dean was very excited that night because his cousin Sam Brady was meeting us at a bar. He was wearing a clean T-shirt and beaming all over. "Now listen, Sal, I must tell you about Sam—he's my cousin."

"By the way, have you looked for your father?"

"This afternoon, man, I went down to Jiggs' Buffet where he used to pour draft beer in tender befuddlement and get hell from the boss and go staggering out—no—and I went to the old barbershop next to the Windsor—no, not there—old fella told me he thought he was—imagine!—working in a railroad gandy-dancing cookshack or sumpin for the *Boston and Maine* in New England! But I don't believe him, they make up frac-tious stories for a dime. Now listen to hear. In my childhood Sam Brady my close cousin was my absolute hero. He used to bootleg whisky from the mountains and one time he had a tremendous fist fight with his brother that lasted two hours in the yard and had the women screaming and terrified. We used to sleep together. The one man in the family who took tender concern for me. And tonight I'm going to see him again for the first time in seven years, he just got back from Missouri."

"And what's the pitch?"

"No pitch, man, I only want to know what's been happening in the family—I have a family, remember—and most particu-larly, Sal, I want him to tell me things that I've forgotten in my childhood. I want to remember, remember, I do!" I never saw Dean so glad and excited. While we waited for his cousin in the bar he talked to a lot of younger downtown hipsters and hustlers and checked on new gangs and goings-on. Then he made inquiries after Marylou, since she'd been in Denver re-cently. "Sal, in my young days when I used to come to this corner to steal change off the newsstand for bowery beef stew, that rough-looking cat you see out there standing had nothing but murder in his heart, got into one horrible fight after an-other, I remember his scars even, till now years and y-e-a-r-s of standing on the corner have finally softened him and chastened him ragely, here completely he's become sweet and willing and patient with everybody, he's become a *fixture* on the corner, you see how things happen?"

Then Sam arrived, a wiry, curly-haired man of thirty-five with work-gnarled hands. Dean stood in awe before him. "No," said Sam Brady, "I don't drink any more."

"See? See?" whispered Dean in my ear. "He doesn't drink any more and he used to be the biggest whiskyleg in town; he's got religion now, he told me over the phone, dig him, dig the change in a man—my hero has become so strange." Sam Brady was suspicious of his young cousin. He took us out for a spin in his old rattly coupe and immediately he made his position clear in regard to Dean.

"Now look, Dean, I don't believe you any more or anything you're going to try to tell me. I came to see you tonight because there's a paper I want you to sign for the family. Your father is no longer mentioned among us and we want absolutely nothing to do with him, and, I'm sorry to say, with you either, any more." I looked at Dean. His face dropped and darkened.

"Yass, yass," he said. The cousin continued to drive us around and even bought us ice-cream pops. Nevertheless Dean plied him with innumerable questions about the past and the cousin supplied the answers and for a moment Dean almost began to sweat again with excitement. Oh, where was his raggedy father that night? The cousin dropped us off at the sad lights of a carnival on Alameda Boulevard at Federal. He made an appointment with Dean for the paper-signing next afternoon and left. I told Dean I was sorry he had nobody in the world to believe in him.

"Remember that I believe in you. I'm infinitely sorry for the foolish grievance I held against you yesterday afternoon."

"All right, man, it's agreed," said Dean. We dug the carnival together. There were merry-go-rounds, Ferris wheels, popcorn, roulette wheels, sawdust, and hundreds of young Denver kids in jeans wandering around. Dust rose to the stars together with every sad music on earth. Dean was wearing washed-out tight levis and a T-shirt and looked suddenly like a real Denver character again. There were motorcycle kids with visors and mustaches and beaded jackets hanging around the shrouds in back of the tents with pretty girls in levis and rose shirts. There were a lot of Mexican girls too, and one amazing little girl about three feet high, a midget, with the most beautiful and tender face in the world, who turned to her companion and said, "Man, let's call up Gomez and cut out." Dean stopped dead in his tracks at the sight of her. A great knife stabbed him from the darkness of the night. "Man, I love her, oh, *love* her . . ." We had to follow her around for a long time. She finally went across the highway to make a phone call in a motel booth and Dean pretended to be looking through the pages of the directory but was really all wound tight watching her. I tried to open up a conversation with the lovey-doll's friends but they paid no attention to us. Gomez arrived in a rattly truck and took the girls off. Dean stood in the road, clutching his breast. "Oh, man, I almost died. . . ."

"Why the hell didn't you talk to her?"

"I can't, I couldn't . . ." We decided to buy some beer and go up to Okie Frankie's and play records. We hitched on the road with a bag of beer cans. Little Janet, Frankie's thirteen-year-old daughter, was the prettiest girl in the world and was about to grow up into a gone woman. Best of all were her long, tapering, sensitive fingers that she used to talk with, like a Cleopatra Nile dance. Dean sat in the farthest corner of the room, watching her with slitted eyes and saying, "Yes, yes, yes." Janet was already aware of him; she turned to me for protection. Previous months of that summer I had spent a lot of time with her, talking about books and little things she was interested in.

7

Nothing happened that night; we went to sleep. Everything happened the next day. In the afternoon Dean and I went to downtown Denver for our various chores and to see the travel bureau for a car to New York. On the way home in the late afternoon we started out for Okie Frankie's, up Broadway, where Dean suddenly sauntered into a sports-goods store, calmly picked up a softball on the counter, and came out, popping it up and down in his palm. Nobody noticed; nobody ever notices such things. It was a drowsy, hot afternoon. We played catch as we went along. "We'll get a travel-bureau car for sure tomorrow."

A woman friend had given me a big quart of Old Granddad bourbon. We started drinking it at Frankie's house. Across the cornfield in back lived a beautiful young chick that Dean had been trying to make ever since he arrived. Trouble was brewing. He threw too many pebbles in her window and frightened her. As we drank the bourbon in the littered living room with all its dogs and scattered toys and sad talk, Dean kept running out the back kitchen door and crossing the cornfield to throw pebbles and whistle. Once in a while Janet went out to peek. Suddenly Dean came back pale. "Trouble, m'boy. That gal's mother is after me with a shotgun and she got a gang of high-school kids to beat me up from down the road."

"What's this? Where are they?"

"Across the cornfield, m'boy." Dean was drunk and didn't care. We went out together and crossed the cornfield in the moonlight. I saw groups of people on the dark dirt road.

"Here they come!" I heard.

"Wait a minute," I said. "What's the matter, please?"

The mother lurked in the background with a big shotgun across her arm. "That damn friend of yours been annoying us long enough. I'm not the kind to call the law. If he comes back here once more I'm gonna shoot and shoot to kill." The high-school boys were clustered with their fists knotted. I was so drunk I didn't care either, but I soothed everybody some.

I said, "He won't do it again. I'll watch him; he's my brother and listens to me. Please put your gun away and don't bother about anything."

"Just one more time!" she said firmly and grimly across the dark. "When my husband gets home I'm sending him after you."

"You don't have to do that; he won't bother you any more, understand. Now be calm and it's okay." Behind me Dean was cursing under his breath. The girl was peeking from her bedroom window. I knew these people from before and they trusted me enough to quiet down a bit. I took Dean by the arm and back we went over the moony cornrows.

"Woo-hee!" he yelled. "I'm gonna git drunk tonight." We went back to Frankie and the kids. Suddenly Dean got mad at a record little Janet was playing and broke it over his knee: it was a hillbilly record. There was an early Dizzy Gillespie there that he valued—"Congo Blues," with Max West on drums. I'd given it to Janet before, and I told her as she wept to take it and break it over Dean's head. She went over and did so. Dean gaped dumbly, sensing everything. We all laughed. Everything was all right. Then Frankie-Maw wanted to go out and drink beer in the roadhouse saloons. "Lessgo!" yelled Dean. "Now dammit, if you'd bought that car I showed you Tuesday we wouldn't have to walk."

"I didn't like that damn car!" yelled Frankie. Yang, yang, the kids started to cry. Dense, mothlike eternity brooded in the crazy brown parlor with the sad wallpaper, the pink lamp, the excited faces. Little Jimmy was frightened; I put him to sleep on the couch and trussed the dog on him. Frankie drunkenly called a cab and suddenly while we were waiting for it a phone call came for me from my woman friend. She had a middle-aged cousin who hated my guts, and that earlier afternoon I had written a letter to Old Bull Lee, who was now in Mexico City, relating the adventures of Dean and myself and under what circumstances we were staying in Denver. I wrote: "I have a woman friend who gives me whisky and money and big suppers."

I foolishly gave this letter to her middle-aged cousin to mail, right after a fried-chicken supper. He opened it, read it, and took it at once to her to prove to her that I was a con-man. Now she was calling me tearfully and saying she never wanted to see me again. Then the triumphant cousin got on the phone and began calling me a bastard. As the cab honked outside and the kids cried and the dogs barked and Dean danced with Frankie I yelled every conceivable curse I could think over that phone and added all kinds of new ones, and in my drunken frenzy I told everybody over the phone to go to hell and slammed it down and went out to get drunk.

We stumbled over one another to get out of the cab at the

roadhouse, a hillbilly roadhouse near the hills, and went in and ordered beers. Everything was collapsing, and to make things inconceivably more frantic there was an ecstatic spastic fellow in the bar who threw his arms around Dean and moaned in his face, and Dean went mad again with sweats and insanity, and to add still more to the unbearable confusion Dean rushed out the next moment and stole a car right from the driveway and took a dash to downtown Denver and came back with a newer, better one. Suddenly in the bar I looked up and saw cops and people were milling around the driveway in the headlights of cruisers, talking about the stolen car. "Somebody's been stealing cars left and right here!" the cop was saying. Dean stood right in back of him, listening and saying, "Ah yass, ah yass." The cops went off to check. Dean came in the bar and rocked back and forth with the poor spastic kid who had just gotten married that day and was having a tremendous drunk while his bride waited somewhere. "Oh, man, this guy is the greatest in the world!" yelled Dean. "Sal, Frankie, I'm going out and get a real good car this time and we'll all go and with Tony too" (the spastic saint) "and have a big drive in the mountains." And he rushed out. Simultaneously a cop rushed in and said a car stolen from downtown Denver was parked in the driveway. People discussed it in knots. From the window I saw Dean jump into the nearest car and roar off, and not a soul noticed him. A few minutes later he was back in an entirely different car, a brand-new convertible. "This one is a beaut!" he whispered in my ear. "The other one coughed too much—I left it at the crossroads, saw that lovely parked in front of a farmhouse. Took a spin in Denver. Come on, man, let's *all* go riding." All the bitterness and madness of his entire Denver life was blasting out of his system like daggers. His face was red and sweaty and mean.

"No, I ain't gonna have nothing to do with stolen cars."

"Aw, come on, man! Tony'll come with me, won't you, amazing darling Tony?" And Tony—a thin, dark-haired, holy-eyed moaning foaming lost soul—leaned on Dean and groaned and groaned, for he was sick suddenly and then for some odd intuitive reason he became terrified of Dean and threw up his hands and drew away with terror writhing in his face. Dean bowed his head and sweated. He ran out and drove away.

Frankie and I found a cab in the driveway and decided to go home. As the cabby drove us up the infinitely dark Alameda Boulevard along which I had walked many and many a lost night the previous months of the summer, singing and moaning and eating the stars and dropping the juices of my heart drop by drop on the hot tar, Dean suddenly hove up behind us in the stolen convertible and began tooting and tooting and crowding us over and screaming. The cabby's face grew white.

"Just a friend of mine," I said. Dean got disgusted with us and suddenly shot ahead at ninety miles an hour, throwing spectral dust across the exhaust. Then he turned in at Frankie's road and pulled up in front of the house; just as suddenly he took off again, U-turned, and went back toward town as we got out of the cab and paid the fare. A few moments later as we waited anxiously in the dark yard, he returned with still another car, a battered coupe, stopped it in a cloud of dust in front of the house, and just staggered out and went straight into the bedroom and flopped dead drunk on the bed. And there we were with a stolen car right on our doorstep.

I had to wake him up; I couldn't get the car started to dump it somewhere far off. He stumbled out of bed, wearing just his jockey shorts, and we got in the car together, while the kids giggled from the windows, and went bouncing and flying straight over the hard alfalfa-rows at the end of the road whomp-ti-whomp till finally the car couldn't take any more and stopped dead under an old cottonwood near the old mill. "Can't go any farther," said Dean simply and got out and started walking back over the cornfield, about half a mile, in his shorts in the moonlight. We got back to the house and he went to sleep. Everything was in a horrible mess, all of Denver, my woman friend, cars, children, poor Frankie, the living room splattered with beer and cans, and I tried to sleep. A cricket kept me awake for some time. At night in this part of the West the stars, as I had seen them in Wyoming, are big as roman candles and as lonely as the Prince of the Dharma who's lost his ancestral grove and journeys across the spaces between points in the handle of the Big Dipper, trying to find it again. So they slowly wheeled the night, and then long before actual sunrise the great red light appeared far over the dun bleak land toward West Kansas and the birds took up their trill above Denver.

8

Horrible nauseas possessed us in the morning. First thing Dean did was go out across the cornfield to see if the car would carry us East. I told him no, but he went anyway. He came back pale. "Man, that's a detective's car and every precinct in town knows my fingerprints from the year that I stole five hundred cars. You see what I do with them, I just wanta ride, man! I gotta go! Listen, we're going to wind up in jail if we don't get out of here this very instant."

"You're damned right," I said, and we began packing as fast as our hands could go. Dangling neckties and shirttails, we said quick good-bys to our sweet little family and stumbled off toward the protective road where nobody would know us. Little Janet was crying to see us, or me, or whatever it was, go —and Frankie was courteous, and I kissed her and apologized.

"He sure is a crazy one," she said. "Sure reminds me of my husband that run away. Just exactly the same guy. I sure hope my Mickey don't grow up that way, they all do now."

And I said good-by to little Lucy, who had her pet beetle in her hand, and little Jimmy was asleep. All this in the space of seconds, in a lovely Sunday morning dawn, as we stumbled off with our wretched baggage. We hurried. Every minute we expected a cruising car to appear from around a country bend and come sloping for us.

"If that woman with the shotgun ever finds out, we're cooked," said Dean. "We *must* get a cab. Then we're safe." We were about to wake up a farm family to use their phone, but the dog drove us away. Every minute things became more dangerous; the coupe would be found wrecked in the cornfield by an early-rising country man. One lovely old lady let us use her phone finally, and we called a downtown Denver cab, but he didn't come. We stumbled on down the road. Early-morning traffic began, every car looking like a cruiser. Then we suddenly saw the cruiser coming and I knew it was the end of my life as I had known it and that it was entering a new and horrible stage of jails and iron sorrows. But the cruiser was our taxi, and from that moment on we flew east.

At the travel bureau there was a tremendous offer for some-one to drive a '47 Cadillac limousine to Chicago. The owner had been driving up from Mexico with his family and got tired and put them all on a train. All he wanted was identification and for the car to get there. My papers assured him everything would come off right. I told him not to worry. I told Dean, "And don't scrounge with this car." Dean was jumping up and down with excitement to see it. We had to wait an hour. We lay on the grass near the church where in 1947 I had passed some time with panhandling hobos after seeing Rita Betten-court home, and there I fell asleep from sheer horror exhaus-tion with my face to the afternoon birds. In fact they were playing organ music somewhere. But Dean hustled around town. He talked up an acquaintance with a waitress in a lun-cheonette, made a date to take her driving in his Cadillac that afternoon, and came back to wake me with the news. Now I felt better. I rose to the new complications.

When the Cadillac arrived, Dean instantly drove off with it "to get gas," and the travel-bureau man looked at me and said, "When's he coming back? The passengers are all ready to go." He showed me two Irish boys from an Eastern Jesuit school waiting with their suitcases on the benches.

"He just went for gas. He'll be right back." I cut down to the corner and watched Dean as he kept the motor running for the waitress, who had been changing in her hotel room; in fact I could see her from where I stood, in front of her mirror, primping and fixing her silk stockings, and I wished I could go along with them. She came running out and jumped in the Cadillac. I wandered back to reassure the travel-bureau boss and the passengers. From where I stood in the door I saw a faint flash of the Cadillac crossing Cleveland Place with Dean, T-shirted and joyous, fluttering his hands and talking to the girl and hunching over the wheel to go as she sat sadly and proudly beside him. They went to a parking lot in broad day-light, parked near the brick wall at the back (a lot Dean had worked in once), and there, he claims, he made it with her, in nothing flat; not only that but persuaded her to follow us east as soon as she had her pay on Friday, come by bus, and meet us at Ian MacArthur's pad on Lexington Avenue in New York. She agreed to come; her name was Beverly. Thirty minutes and Dean roared back, deposited the girl at her hotel, with kisses, farewells, promises, and zoomed right up to the travel bureau to pick up the crew.

"Well, it's about time!" said the Broadway Sam travel-bureau boss. "I thought you'd gone off with that Cadillac."

"It's my responsibility," I said, "don't worry"—and said that because Dean was in such obvious frenzy everybody could guess his madness. Dean became businesslike and assisted the Jesuit boys with their baggage. They were hardly seated, and I had hardly waved good-by to Denver, before he was off, the big motor thrumming with immense birdlike power. Not two miles out of Denver the speedometer broke because Dean was pushing well over 110 miles an hour.

"Well, no speedometer, I won't know how fast I'm going. I'll just ball that jack to Chicago and tell by time." It didn't seem we were even going seventy but all the cars fell from us like dead flies on the straightaway highway leading up to Greeley. "Reason why we're going northeast is because, Sal, we must absolutely visit Ed Wall's ranch in Sterling, you've got to meet him and see his ranch and this boat cuts so fast we can make it without any time trouble and get to Chicago long before that man's train." Okay, I was for it. It began to rain but Dean never slackened. It was a beautiful big car, the last of the old-style limousines, black, with a big elongated body and whitewall tires and probably bulletproof windows. The Jesuit boys—St. Bonaventura—sat in the back, gleeful and glad to be underway, and they had no idea how fast we were going. They tried to talk but Dean said nothing and took off his T-shirt and drove barechested. "Oh, that Beverly is a sweet gone little gal —she's going to join me in New York—we're going to get married as soon as I can get divorce papers from Camille— everything's jumping, Sal, and we're off. Yes!" The faster we left Denver the better I felt, and we were doing it *fast*. It grew dark when we turned off the highway at Junction and hit a dirt road that took us across dismal East Colorado plains to Ed Wall's ranch in the middle of Coyote Nowhere. But it was still raining and the mud was slippery and Dean slowed to seventy, but I told him to slow even more or we'd slide, and he said, "Don't worry, man, you know me."

"Not this time," I said. "You're really going much too fast." And he was flying along there on that slippery mud and just as I said that we hit a complete left turn in the highway and Dean socked the wheel over to make it but the big car skidded in the grease and wobbled hugely.

"Look out!" yelled Dean, who didn't give a damn and wrestled with his Angel a moment, and we ended up backass in the ditch with the front out on the road. A great stillness fell over everything. We heard the whining wind. We were in the middle of the wild prairie. There was a farmhouse a quarter-mile up the road. I couldn't stop swearing, I was so mad and disgusted with Dean. He said nothing and went off to the farmhouse in the rain, with a coat, to look for help.

"Is he your brother?" the boys asked in the back seat. "He's a devil with a car, isn't he?—and according to his story he must be with the women."

"He's mad," I said, "and yes, he's my brother." I saw Dean coming back with the farmer in his tractor. They hooked chains on and the farmer hauled us out of the ditch. The car was muddy brown, a whole fender was crushed. The farmer charged us five dollars. His daughters watched in the rain. The prettiest, shyest one hid far back in the field to watch and she had good reason because she was absolutely and finally the most beautiful girl Dean and I ever saw in all our lives. She was about sixteen, and had Plains complexion like wild roses, and the bluest eyes, the most lovely hair, and the modesty and quickness of a wild antelope. At every look from us she flinched. She stood there with the immense winds that blew clear down from Saskatchewan knocking her hair about her lovely head like shrouds, living curls of them. She blushed and blushed.

We finished our business with the farmer, took one last look at the prairie angel, and drove off, slower now, till dark came and Dean said Ed Wall's ranch was dead ahead. "Oh, a girl like that scares me," I said. "I'd give up everything and throw myself on her mercy and if she didn't want me I'd just as simply go and throw myself off the edge of the world." The Jesuit boys giggled. They were full of corny quips and Eastern college talk and had nothing on their bird-beans except a lot of ill-understood Aquinas for stuffing for their pepper. Dean and I paid absolutely no attention to them. As we crossed the muddy plains he told stories about his cowboy days, he showed us the stretch of road where he spent an entire morning riding; and where he'd done fence-mending as soon as we hit Wall's property, which was immense; and where old Wall, Ed's father, used to come clattering on the rangeland grass chasing a heifer and howling, "Git im, git im, goddammit!" "He had to have a new car every six months," said Dean. "He just couldn't care. When a stray got away from us he'd drive right after it as far as the nearest waterhole and then get out and run after it on foot. Counted every cent he ever made and put it in a pot. A mad old rancher. I'll show you some of his old wrecks near the bunkhouse. This is where I came on probation after my last hitch in a joint. This is where I lived when I wrote those letters you saw to Chad King." We turned off the road and wound across a path through the winter pasture. A mournful group of whitefaced cows suddenly milled across our headlights. "There they are! Wall's cows! We'll never be able to get through them. We'll have to get out and whoop em up! Hee-hee-hee!!" But we didn't have to do that and only inched along through them, sometimes gently bumping as they milled and mooed like a sea around the car doors. Beyond we saw the light of Ed Wall's ranch house. Around this lonely light stretched hundreds of miles of plains.

The kind of utter darkness that falls on a prairie like that is inconceivable to an Easterner. There were no stars, no moon, no light whatever except the light of Mrs. Wall's kitchen. What lay beyond the shadows of the yard was an endless view of the world that you wouldn't be able to see till dawn. After knocking on the door and calling out in the dark for Ed Wall, who was milking cows in the barn, I took a short careful walk into that darkness, about twenty feet and no more. I thought I heard coyotes. Wall said it was probably one of his father's wild horses whinnying in the distance. Ed Wall was about our age, tall, rangy, spike-toothed, laconic. He and Dean used to stand around on Curtis Street corners and whistle at girls. Now he took us graciously into his gloomy, brown, unused parlor and fished around till he found dull lamps and lit them and said to Dean, "What in the hell happened to yore thumb?"

"I socked Marylou and it got infected so much they had to amputate the end of it."

"What in the hell did you go and do that for?" I could see he used to be Dean's older brother. He shook his head; the milk pail was still at his feet. "You always been a crackbrained son-ofabitch anyhow."

Meanwhile his young wife prepared a magnificent spread in the big ranch kitchen. She apologized for the peach ice cream: "It ain't nothin but cream and peaches froze up together." Of course it was the only real ice cream I ever had in my whole life. She started sparsely and ended up abundantly; as we ate, new things appeared on the table. She was a well-built blonde but like all women who live in the wide spaces she complained a little of the boredom. She enumerated the radio programs she usually listened to at this time of night. Ed Wall sat just staring at his hands. Dean ate voraciously. He wanted me to go along with him in the fiction that I owned the Cadillac, that I was a very rich man and that he was my friend and chauffeur. It made no impression on Ed Wall. Every time the stock made sounds in the barn he raised his head to listen.

"Well, I hope you boys make it to New York." Far from believing that tale about my owning the Cadillac, he was convinced Dean had stolen it. We stayed at the ranch about an hour. Ed Wall had lost faith in Dean just like Sam Brady—he looked at him warily when he looked. There were riotous days in the past when they had stumbled around the streets of Laramie, Wyoming, arm-in-arm when the haying was over, but all this was dead and gone.

Dean hopped in his chair convulsively. "Well yes, well yes, and now I think we'd better be cutting along because we gotta be in Chicago by tomorrow night and we've already wasted several hours." The college boys thanked Wall graciously and we were off again. I turned to watch the kitchen light recede in the sea of night. Then I leaned ahead.

9

In no time at all we were back on the main highway and that night I saw the entire state of Nebraska unroll before my eyes. A hundred and ten miles an hour straight through, an arrow road, sleeping towns, no traffic, and the Union Pacific streamliner falling behind us in the moonlight. I wasn't frightened at all that night; it was perfectly legitimate to go 110 and talk and have all the Nebraska towns—Ogallala, Gothenburg, Kearney, Grand Island, Columbus—unreel with dreamlike rapidity as we roared ahead and talked. It was a magnificent car; it could hold the road like a boat holds on water. Gradual curves were its singing ease. "Ah, man, what a dreamboat," sighed Dean. "Think if you and I had a car like this what we could do. Do you know there's a road that goes down Mexico and all the way to Panama?—and maybe all the way to the bottom of South America where the Indians are seven feet tall and eat cocaine on the mountainside? Yes! You and I, Sal, we'd dig the whole world with a car like this because, man, the road must eventually lead to the whole world. Ain't nowhere else it can go—right? Oh, and are we going to cut around old Chi with this thing! Think of it, Sal, I've never been to Chicago in all my life, never stopped."

"We'll come in there like gangsters in this Cadillac!"

"Yes! And girls! We can pick up girls, in fact, Sal, I've decided to make extra-special fast time so we can have an entire evening to cut around in this thing. Now you just relax and I'll ball the jack all the way."

"Well, how fast are you going now?"

"A steady one-ten I figure—you wouldn't notice it. We've still got all Iowa in the daytime and then I'll make that old Illinois in nothing flat." The boys fell asleep and we talked and talked all night.

It was remarkable how Dean could go mad and then suddenly continue with his soul—which I think is wrapped up in a fast car, a coast to reach, and a woman at the end of the road—calmly and sanely as though nothing had happened. "I get like that every time in Denver now—I can't make that town any more. Gookly, gooky, Dean's a spooky. Zoom!" I told him I had been over this Nebraska road before in '47. He had too. "Sal, when I was working for the New Era Laundry in Los Angeles, nineteen forty-four, falsifying my age, I made a trip to Indianapolis Speedway for the express purpose of seeing the Memorial Day classic, hitchhiking by day and stealing cars by night to make time. Also I had a twenty-dollar Buick back in LA, my first car, it couldn't pass the brake and light inspection so I decided I needed an out-of-state license to operate the car without arrest so went through here to get the license. As I was hitchhiking through one of these very towns, with the plates concealed under my coat, a nosy sheriff who thought I was pretty young to be hitchhiking accosted me on the main drag. He found the plates and threw me in the two-cell jail with a county delinquent who should have been in the home for the old since he couldn't feed himself (the sheriff's wife fed him) and sat through the day drooling and slobbering. After investigation, which included corny things like a fatherly quiz, then an abrupt turnabout to frighten me with threats, a comparison of my handwriting, et cetera, and after I made the most magnificent speech of my life to get out of it, concluding with the confession that I was lying about my car-stealing past and was only looking for my paw who was a farmhand hereabouts, he let me go. Of course I missed the races. The following fall I did the same thing again to see the Notre Dame–California game in South Bend, Indiana—trouble none this time and, Sal, I had just the money for the ticket and not an extra cent and didn't eat anything all up and back except for what I could panhandle from all kinds of crazy cats I met on the road and at the same time gun gals. Only guy in the United States of America that ever went to so much trouble to see a ballgame."

I asked him the circumstances of his being in LA in 1944. "I was arrested in Arizona, the joint absolutely the worst joint I've ever been in. I had to escape and pulled the greatest escape in my life, speaking of escapes, you see, in a general way. In the woods, you know, and crawling, and swamps—up around that mountain country. Rubber hoses and the works and accidental so-called death facing me I had to cut out of those woods along the ridge so as to keep away from trails and paths and roads. Had to get rid of my joint clothes and sneaked the neatest theft of a shirt and pants from a gas station outside Flagstaff, arriving LA two days later clad as gas attendant and walked to the first station I saw and got hired and got myself a room and changed name (Lee Buliay) and spent an exciting year in LA, including a whole gang of new friends and some really great girls, that season ending when we were all driving on Hollywood Boulevard one night and I told my buddy to steer the car while I kissed my girl—I was at the wheel, see—and *he didn't hear me* and we ran smack into a post but only going twenty and I broke my nose. You've seen before my nose—the crooked Grecian curve up here. After that I went to Denver and met Marylou in a soda fountain that spring. Oh, man, she was only fifteen and wearing jeans and just waiting for someone to pick her up. Three days three nights of talk in the Ace Hotel, third floor, southeast corner room, holy memento room and sacred scene of my days—she was so sweet then, so *young*, hmm, ahh! But hey, look down there in the night thar, hup, hup, a buncha old bums by a fire by the rail, damn me." He almost slowed down. "You see, I never know whether my father's there or not." There were some figures by the tracks, reeling in front of a woodfire. "I never know whether to ask. He might be anywhere." We drove on. Somewhere behind us or in front of us in the huge night his father lay drunk under a bush, and no doubt about it—spittle on his chin, water on his pants, molasses in his ears, scabs on his nose, maybe blood in his hair and the moon shining down on him.

I took Dean's arm. "Ah, man, we're sure going home now." New York was going to be his permanent home for the first time. He jiggled all over; he couldn't wait.

"And think, Sal, when we get to Pennsy we'll start hearing that gone Eastern bop on the disk jockeys. Geeyah, roll, old boat, roll!" The magnificent car made the wind roar; it made the plains unfold like a roll of paper; it cast hot tar from itself with deference—an imperial boat. I opened my eyes to a fanning dawn; we were hurling up to it. Dean's rocky dogged face as ever bent over the dashlight with a bony purpose of its own.

"What are you thinking, Pops?"

"Ah-ha, ah-ha, same old thing, y'know—gurls gurls gurls."

I went to sleep and woke up to the dry, hot atmosphere of

July Sunday morning in Iowa, and still Dean was driving and
driving and had not slackened his speed; he took the curvy
corndales of Iowa at a minimum of eighty and the straightaway 110 as usual, unless both-ways traffic forced him to fall in
line at a crawling and miserable sixty. When there was a chance
he shot ahead and passed cars by the half-dozen and left them
behind in a cloud of dust. A mad guy in a brand-new Buick saw
all this on the road and decided to race us. When Dean was
just about to pass a passel the guy shot by us without warning
and howled and tooted his horn and flashed the tail lights for
challenge. We took off after him like a big bird. "Now wait,"
laughed Dean, "I'm going to tease that sonofabitch for a
dozen miles or so. Watch." He let the Buick go way ahead and
then accelerated and caught up with it most impolitely. Mad
Buick went out of his mind; he gunned up to a hundred. We
had a chance to see who he was. He seemed to be some kind
of Chicago hipster traveling with a woman old enough to be—
and probably actually was—his mother. God knows if she was
complaining, but he raced. His hair was dark and wild, an Italian from old Chi; he wore a sports shirt. Maybe there was an
idea in his mind that we were a new gang from LA invading
Chicago, maybe some of Mickey Cohen's men, because the
limousine looked every bit the part and the license plates were
California. Mainly it was just road kicks. He took terrible
chances to stay ahead of us; he passed cars on curves and barely
got back in line as a truck wobbled into view and loomed up
huge. Eighty miles of Iowa we unreeled in this fashion, and
the race was so interesting that I had no opportunity to be
frightened. Then the mad guy gave up, pulled up at a gas station, probably on orders from the old lady, and as we roared
by he waved gleefully. On we sped, Dean barechested, I with
my feet on the dashboard, and the college boys sleeping in the
back. We stopped to eat breakfast at a diner run by a white-
haired lady who gave us extra-large portions of potatoes as
church-bells rang in the nearby town. Then off again.

"Dean, don't drive so fast in the daytime."

"Don't worry, man, I know what I'm doing." I began to
flinch. Dean came up on lines of cars like the Angel of Terror.
He almost rammed them along as he looked for an opening.
He teased their bumpers, he eased and pushed and craned

around to see the curve, then the huge car leaped to his touch and passed, and always by a hair we made it back to our side as other lines filed by in the opposite direction and I shuddered. I couldn't take it any more. It is only seldom that you find a long Nebraskan straightaway in Iowa, and when we finally hit one Dean made his usual 110 and I saw flashing by outside several scenes that I remembered from 1947—a long stretch where Eddie and I had been stranded two hours. All that old road of the past unreeling dizzily as if the cup of life had been overturned and everything gone mad. My eyes ached in nightmare day.

"Ah hell, Dean, I'm going in the back seat, I can't stand it any more, I can't look."

"Hee-hee-hee!" tittered Dean and he passed a car on a narrow bridge and swerved in dust and roared on. I jumped in the back seat and curled up to sleep. One of the boys jumped in front for the fun. Great horrors that we were going to crash this very morning took hold of me and I got down on the floor and closed my eyes and tried to go to sleep. As a seaman I used to think of the waves rushing beneath the shell of the ship and the bottomless deeps thereunder—now I could feel the road some twenty inches beneath me, unfurling and flying and hissing at incredible speeds across the groaning continent with that mad Ahab at the wheel. When I closed my eyes all I could see was the road unwinding into me. When I opened them I saw flashing shadows of trees vibrating on the floor of the car. There was no escaping it. I resigned myself to all. And still Dean drove, he had no thought of sleeping till we got to Chicago. In the afternoon we crossed old Des Moines again. Here of course we got snarled in traffic and had to go slow and I got back in the front seat. A strange pathetic accident took place. A fat colored man was driving with his entire family in a sedan in front of us; on the rear bumper hung one of those canvas desert waterbags they sell tourists in the desert. He pulled up sharp, Dean was talking to the boys in the back and didn't notice, and we rammed him at five miles an hour smack on the waterbag, which burst like a boil and squirted water in the air. No other damage except a bent bumper. Dean and I got out to talk to him. The upshot of it was an exchange of addresses and some talk, and Dean not taking his eyes off the

man's wife whose beautiful brown breasts were barely concealed inside a floppy cotton blouse. "Yass, yass." We gave him
the address of our Chicago baron and went on.

The other side of Des Moines a cruising car came after us
with the siren growling, with orders to pull over. "Now what?"

The cop came out. "Were you in an accident coming in?"

"Accident? We broke a guy's waterbag at the junction."

"He says he was hit and run by a bunch in a stolen car." This
was one of the few instances Dean and I knew of a Negro's
acting like a suspicious old fool. It so surprised us we laughed.
We had to follow the patrolman to the station and there spent
an hour waiting in the grass while they telephoned Chicago to
get the owner of the Cadillac and verify our position as hired
drivers. Mr. Baron said, according to the cop, "Yes, that is my
car but I can't vouch for anything else those boys might have
done."

"They were in a minor accident here in Des Moines."

"Yes, you've already told me that—what I meant was, I can't
vouch for anything they might have done in the past."

Everything was straightened out and we roared on. Newton, Iowa, it was, where I'd taken that dawn walk in 1947. In
the afternoon we crossed drowsy old Davenport again and the
low-lying Mississippi in her sawdust bed; then Rock Island, a
few minutes of traffic, the sun reddening, and sudden sights of
lovely little tributary rivers flowing softly among the magic trees
and greeneries of mid-American Illinois. It was beginning to
look like the soft sweet East again; the great dry West was accomplished and done. The state of Illinois unfolded before my
eyes in one vast movement that lasted a matter of hours as
Dean balled straight across at the same speed. In his tiredness
he was taking greater chances than ever. At a narrow bridge
that crossed one of these lovely little rivers he shot precipi-
tately into an almost impossible situation. Two slow cars ahead
of us were bumping over the bridge; coming the other way
was a huge truck-trailer with a driver who was making a close
estimate of how long it would take the slow cars to negotiate
the bridge, and his estimate was that by the time he got there
they'd be over. There was absolutely no room on the bridge for
the truck and any cars going the other direction. Behind the
truck cars pulled out and peeked for a chance to get by it.

In front of the slow cars other slow cars were pushing along. The road was crowded and everyone exploding to pass. Dean came down on all this at 110 miles an hour and never hesitated. He passed the slow cars, swerved, and almost hit the left rail of the bridge, went head-on into the shadow of the unslowing truck, cut right sharply, just missed the truck's left front wheel, almost hit the first slow car, pulled out to pass, and then had to cut back in line when another car came out from behind the truck to look, all in a matter of two seconds, flashing by and leaving nothing more than a cloud of dust instead of a horrible five-way crash with cars lurching in every direction and the great truck humping its back in the fatal red afternoon of Illinois with its dreaming fields. I couldn't get it out of my mind, also, that a famous bop clarinetist had died in an Illinois car-crash recently, probably on a day like this. I went to the back seat again.

The boys stayed in the back too now. Dean was bent on Chicago before nightfall. At a road-rail junction we picked up two hobos who rounded up a half-buck between them for gas. A moment before sitting around piles of railroad ties, polishing off the last of some wine, now they found themselves in a muddy but unbowed and splendid Cadillac limousine headed for Chicago in precipitous haste. In fact the old boy up front who sat next to Dean never took his eyes off the road and prayed his poor bum prayers, I tell you. "Well," they said, "we never knew we'd get to Chicaga sa fast." As we passed drowsy Illinois towns where the people are so conscious of Chicago gangs that pass like this in limousines every day, we were a strange sight: all of us unshaven, the driver barechested, two bums, myself in the back seat, holding on to a strap and my head leaned back on the cushion looking at the countryside with an imperious eye—just like a new California gang come to contest the spoils of Chicago, a band of desperados escaped from the prisons of the Utah moon. When we stopped for Cokes and gas at a small-town station people came out to stare at us but they never said a word and I think made mental notes of our descriptions and heights in case of future need. To transact business with the girl who ran the gas-pump Dean merely threw on his T-shirt like a scarf and was curt and abrupt as usual and got back in the car and off we roared again. Pretty soon the redness turned purple, the last of the enchanted rivers flashed by, and we saw distant smokes of Chicago beyond the drive. We had come from Denver to Chicago via Ed Wall's ranch, 1180 miles, in exactly seventeen hours, not counting the two hours in the ditch and three at the ranch and two with the police in Newton, Iowa, for a mean average of seventy miles per hour across the land, with one driver. Which is a kind of crazy record.

10

Great Chicago glowed red before our eyes. We were suddenly on Madison Street among hordes of hobos, some of them sprawled out on the street with their feet on the curb, hundreds of others milling in the doorways of saloons and alleys. "Wup! wup! look sharp for old Dean Moriarty there, he may be in Chicago by accident this year." We let out the hobos on this street and proceeded to downtown Chicago. Screeching trolleys, newsboys, gals cutting by, the smell of fried food and beer in the air, neons winking—"We're in the big town, Sal! Whooee!" First thing to do was park the Cadillac in a good dark spot and wash up and dress for the night. Across the street from the YMCA we found a red-brick alley between buildings, where we stashed the Cadillac with her snout pointed to the street and ready to go, then followed the college boys up to the Y, where they got a room and allowed us to use their facilities for an hour. Dean and I shaved and showered, I dropped my wallet in the hall, Dean found it and was about to sneak it in his shirt when he realized it was ours and was right disappointed. Then we said good-by to those boys, who were glad they'd made it in one piece, and took off to eat in a cafeteria. Old brown Chicago with the strange semi-Eastern, semi-Western types going to work and spitting. Dean stood in the cafeteria rubbing his belly and taking it all in. He wanted to talk to a strange middle-aged colored woman who had come into the cafeteria with a story about how she had no money but she had buns with her and would they give her butter. She came in flapping her hips, was turned down, and went out flipping her butt. "Whoo!" said Dean. "Let's follow her down the street, let's take her to the ole Cadillac in the alley. We'll have a ball." But we forgot that and headed straight for North Clark Street, after a spin in the Loop, to see the hootchy-kootchy joints and hear the bop. And what a night it was. "Oh, man," said Dean to me as we stood in front of a bar, "dig the street of life, the Chinamen that cut by in Chicago. What a weird town —wow, and that woman in that window up there, just looking down with her big breasts hanging from her nightgown, big wide eyes. Whee. Sal, we gotta go and never stop going till we get there."

"Where we going, man?"

"I don't know but we gotta go." Then here came a gang of young bop musicians carrying their instruments out of cars. They piled right into a saloon and we followed them. They set themselves up and started blowing. There we were! The leader was a slender, drooping, curly-haired, pursy-mouthed tenorman, thin of shoulder, draped loose in a sports shirt, cool in the warm night, self-indulgence written in his eyes, who picked up his horn and frowned in it and blew cool and complex and was dainty stamping his foot to catch ideas, and ducked to miss others—and said, "Blow," very quietly when the other boys took solos. Then there was Prez, a husky, handsome blond like a freckled boxer, meticulously wrapped inside his sharkskin plaid suit with the long drape and the collar falling back and the tie undone for exact sharpness and casualness, sweating and hitching up his horn and writhing into it, and a tone just like Lester Young himself. "You see, man, Prez has the technical anxieties of a money-making musician, he's the only one who's well dressed, see him grow worried when he blows a clinker, but the leader, that cool cat, tells him not to worry and just blow and blow—the mere sound and serious exuberance of the music is all *he* cares about. He's an artist. He's teaching young Prez the boxer. Now the others dig!!" The third sax was an alto, eighteen-year-old cool, contemplative young Charlie-Parker-type Negro from high school, with a broadgash mouth, taller than the rest, grave. He raised his horn and blew into it quietly and thoughtfully and elicited birdlike phrases and architectural Miles Davis logics. These were the children of the great bop innovators.

Once there was Louis Armstrong blowing his beautiful top in the muds of New Orleans; before him the mad musicians who had paraded on official days and broke up their Sousa marches into ragtime. Then there was swing, and Roy Eldridge, vigorous and virile, blasting the horn for everything it had in waves of power and logic and subtlety—leaning to it with glittering eyes and a lovely smile and sending it out broadcast to rock the jazz world. Then had come Charlie Parker, a kid in his mother's woodshed in Kansas City, blowing his taped-up alto among the logs, practicing on rainy days, coming out to watch the old swinging Basie and Benny Moten band that had Hot Lips Page and the rest—Charlie Parker leaving home and coming to Harlem, and meeting mad Thelonius Monk and madder Gillespie—Charlie Parker in his early days when he was flipped and walked around in a circle while playing. Somewhat younger than Lester Young, also from KC, that gloomy, saintly goof in whom the history of jazz was wrapped; for when he held his horn high and horizontal from his mouth he blew the greatest; and as his hair grew longer and he got lazier and stretched-out, his horn came down halfway; till it finally fell all the way and today as he wears his thick-soled shoes so that he can't feel the sidewalks of life his horn is held weakly against his chest, and he blows cool and easy getout phrases. Here were the children of the American bop night.

Stranger flowers yet—for as the Negro alto mused over everyone's head with dignity, the young, tall, slender, blond kid from Curtis Street, Denver, jeans and studded belt, sucked on his mouthpiece while waiting for the others to finish; and when they did he started, and you had to look around to see where the solo was coming from, for it came from angelical smiling lips upon the mouthpiece and it was a soft, sweet, fairy-tale solo on an alto. Lonely as America, a throatpierced sound in the night.

What of the others and all the soundmaking? There was the bass-player, wiry redhead with wild eyes, jabbing his hips at the fiddle with every driving slap, at hot moments his mouth hanging open trancelike. "Man, there's a cat who can really *bend* his girl!" The sad drummer, like our white hipster in Frisco Folsom Street, completely goofed, staring into space, chewing gum, wide-eyed, rocking the neck with Reich kick and complacent ecstasy. The piano—a big husky Italian truck-driving kid with meaty hands, a burly and thoughtful joy. They played an hour. Nobody was listening. Old North Clark bums lolled at the bar, whores screeched in anger. Secret Chinamen went by. Noises of hootchy-kootchy interfered. They went right on. Out on the sidewalk came an apparition—a sixteen-year-old kid with a goatee and a trombone case. Thin as rickets, mad-faced, he wanted to join this group and blow with them. They knew him and didn't want to bother with him. He crept into the bar and surreptitiously undid his trombone and raised it to his lips. No opening. Nobody looked at him. They finished, packed up, and left for another bar. He wanted to jump, skinny Chicago kid. He slapped on his dark glasses, raised the trombone to his lips alone in the bar, and went "Baugh!" Then he rushed out after them. They wouldn't let him play with them, just like the sandlot football team in back of the gas tank. "All these guys live with their grandmothers just like Tom Snark and our Carlo Marx alto," said Dean. We rushed after the whole gang. They went into Anita O'Day's club and there unpacked and played till nine o'clock in the morning. Dean and I were there with beers.

At intermissions we rushed out in the Cadillac and tried to pick up girls all up and down Chicago. They were frightened of our big, scarred, prophetic car. In his mad frenzy Dean backed up smack on hydrants and tittered maniacally. By nine o'clock the car was an utter wreck; the brakes weren't working any more; the fenders were stove in; the rods were rattling. Dean couldn't stop it at red lights, it kept kicking convulsively over the roadway. It had paid the price of the night. It was a muddy boot and no longer a shiny limousine. "Whee!" The boys were still blowing at Neets'.

Suddenly Dean stared into the darkness of a corner beyond the bandstand and said, "Sal, God has arrived."

I looked. *George Shearing.* And as always he leaned his blind head on his pale hand, all ears opened like the ears of an elephant, listening to the American sounds and mastering them for his own English summer's-night use. Then they urged him to get up and play. He did. He played innumerable choruses with amazing chords that mounted higher and higher till the sweat splashed all over the piano and everybody listened in awe and fright. They led him off the stand after an hour. He went back to his dark corner, old God Shearing, and the boys said, "There ain't nothin left after that."

But the slender leader frowned. "Let's blow anyway."

Something would come of it yet. There's always more, a little further—it never ends. They sought to find new phrases after Shearing's explorations; they tried hard. They writhed and twisted and blew. Every now and then a clear harmonic cry gave new suggestions of a tune that would someday be the only tune in the world and would raise men's souls to joy. They found it, they lost, they wrestled for it, they found it again, they laughed, they moaned—and Dean sweated at the table and told them to go, go, go. At nine o'clock in the morning everybody—musicians, girls in slacks, bartenders, and the one little skinny, unhappy trombonist—staggered out of the club into the great roar of Chicago day to sleep until the wild bop night again.

Dean and I shuddered in the raggedness. It was now time to return the Cadillac to the owner, who lived out on Lake Shore Drive in a swank apartment with an enormous garage underneath managed by oil-scarred Negroes. We drove out there and swung the muddy heap into its berth. The mechanic did not recognize the Cadillac. We handed the papers over. He scratched his head at the sight of it. We had to get out fast. We did. We took a bus back to downtown Chicago and that was that. And we never heard a word from our Chicago baron about the condition of his car, in spite of the fact that he had our addresses and could have complained.

II

It was time for us to move on. We took a bus to Detroit. Our money was now running quite low. We lugged our wretched baggage through the station. By now Dean's thumb bandage was almost as black as coal and all unrolled. We were both as miserable-looking as anybody could be after all the things we'd done. Exhausted, Dean fell asleep in the bus that roared across the state of Michigan. I took up a conversation with a gorgeous country girl wearing a low-cut cotton blouse that displayed the beautiful sun-tan on her breast tops. She was dull. She spoke of evenings in the country making popcorn on the porch. Once this would have gladdened my heart but because her heart was not glad when she said it I knew there was nothing in it but the idea of what one should do. "And what else do you do for fun?" I tried to bring up boy friends and sex. Her great dark eyes surveyed me with emptiness and a kind of chagrin that reached back generations and generations in her blood from not having done what was crying to be done —whatever it was, and everybody knows what it was. "What do you want out of life?" I wanted to take her and wring it out of her. She didn't have the slightest idea what she wanted. She mumbled of jobs, movies, going to her grandmother's for the summer, wishing she could go to New York and visit the Roxy, what kind of outfit she would wear—something like the one she wore last Easter, white bonnet, roses, rose pumps, and lavender gabardine coat. "What do you do on Sunday afternoons?" I asked. She sat on her porch. The boys went by on bicycles and stopped to chat. She read the funny papers, she reclined on the hammock. "What do you do on a warm summer's night?" She sat on the porch, she watched the cars in the road. She and her mother made popcorn. "What does your father do on a summer's night?" He works, he has an all-night shift at the boiler factory, he's spent his whole life supporting a woman and her outpoppings and no credit or adoration. "What does your brother do on a summer's night?" He rides around on his bicycle, he hangs out in front of the soda fountain. "What is he aching to do? What are we all aching to do? What do we want?" She didn't know. She yawned. She was sleepy. It was too much. Nobody could tell. Nobody would ever tell. It was all over. She was eighteen and most lovely, and lost.

And Dean and I, ragged and dirty as if we had lived off locust, stumbled out of the bus in Detroit. We decided to stay up in all-night movies on Skid Row. It was too cold for parks. Hassel had been here on Detroit Skid Row, he had dug every shooting gallery and all-night movie and every brawling bar with his dark eyes many a time. His ghost haunted us. We'd never find him on Times Square again. We thought maybe by accident Old Dean Moriarty was here too—but he was not. For thirty-five cents each we went into the beat-up old movie and sat down in the balcony till morning, when we were shooed downstairs. The people who were in that all-night movie were the end. Beat Negroes who'd come up from Alabama to work in car factories on a rumor; old white bums; young longhaired hipsters who'd reached the end of the road and were drinking wine; whores, ordinary couples, and housewives with nothing to do, nowhere to go, nobody to believe in. If you sifted all Detroit in a wire basket the beater solid core of dregs couldn't be better gathered. The picture was Singing Cowboy Eddie Dean and his gallant white horse Bloop, that was number one; number two double-feature film was George Raft, Sidney Greenstreet, and Peter Lorre in a picture about Istanbul. We saw both of these things six times each during the night. We saw them waking, we heard them sleeping, we sensed them dreaming, we were permeated completely with the strange Gray Myth of the West and the weird dark Myth of the East when morning came. All my actions since then have been dictated automatically to my subconscious by this horrible osmotic experience. I heard big Greenstreet sneer a hundred times; I heard Peter Lorre make his sinister come-on; I was with George Raft in his paranoiac fears; I rode and sang with Eddie Dean and shot up the rustlers innumerable times. People slugged out of bottles and turned around and looked everywhere in the dark theater for something to do, somebody to talk to. In the head everybody was guiltily quiet, nobody talked. In the gray dawn that puffed ghostlike about the windows of the theater and hugged its eaves I was sleeping with my head on the wooden arm of a seat as six attendants of the theater converged with their night's total of swept-up rubbish and created a huge dusty pile that reached to my nose as I snored head down—till they almost swept me away too. This was reported to me by Dean, who was watching from ten seats behind. All the cigarette butts, the bottles, the matchbooks, the come and the gone were swept up in this pile. Had they taken me with it, Dean would never have seen me again. He would have had to roam the entire United States and look in every garbage pail from coast to coast before he found me embryonically convoluted among the rubbishes of my life, his life, and the life of everybody concerned and not concerned. What would I have said to him from my rubbish womb? "Don't bother me, man, I'm happy where I am. You lost me one night in Detroit in August nineteen forty-nine. What right have you to come and disturb my reverie in this pukish can?" In 1942 I was the star in one of the filthiest dramas of all time. I was a seaman, and went to the Imperial Café on Scollay Square in Boston to drink; I drank sixty glasses of beer and retired to the toilet, where I wrapped myself around the toilet bowl and went to sleep. During the night at least a hundred seamen and assorted civilians came in and cast their sentient debouchments on me till I was unrecognizably caked. What difference does it make after all?—anonymity in the world of men is better than fame in heaven, for what's heaven? what's earth? All in the mind.

Gibberishly Dean and I stumbled out of this horror-hole at dawn and went to find our travel-bureau car. After spending a good part of the morning in Negro bars and chasing gals and listening to jazz records on jukeboxes, we struggled five miles in local buses with all our crazy gear and got to the home of a man who was going to charge us four dollars apiece for the ride to New York. He was a middle-aged blond fellow with glasses, with a wife and kid and a good home. We waited in the yard while he got ready. His lovely wife in cotton kitchen dress offered us coffee but we were too busy talking. By this time Dean was so exhausted and out of his mind that everything he saw delighted him. He was reaching another pious frenzy. He sweated and sweated. The moment we were in the new Chrysler and off to New York the poor man realized he had contracted a ride with two maniacs, but he made the best of it and in fact got used to us just as we passed Briggs Stadium and talked about next year's Detroit Tigers.

In the misty night we crossed Toledo and went onward across old Ohio. I realized I was beginning to cross and recross towns in America as though I were a traveling salesman —raggedy travelings, bad stock, rotten beans in the bottom of my bag of tricks, nobody buying. The man got tired near

Pennsylvania and Dean took the wheel and drove clear the rest of the way to New York, and we began to hear the Symphony Sid show on the radio with all the latest bop, and now we were entering the great and final city of America. We got there in early morning. Times Square was being torn up, for New York never rests. We looked for Hassel automatically as we passed.

In an hour Dean and I were out at my aunt's new flat in Long Island, and she herself was busily engaged with painters who were friends of the family, and arguing with them about the price as we stumbled up the stairs from San Francisco. "Sal," said my aunt, "Dean can stay here a few days and after that he has to get out, do you understand me?" The trip was over. Dean and I took a walk that night among the gas tanks and railroad bridges and fog lamps of Long Island. I remember him standing under a streetlamp.

"Just as we passed that other lamp I was going to tell you a further thing, Sal, but now I am parenthetically continuing with a new thought and by the time we reach the next I'll return to the original subject, agreed?" I certainly agreed. We were so used to traveling we had to walk all over Long Island, but there was no more land, just the Atlantic Ocean, and we could only go so far. We clasped hands and agreed to be friends forever.

Not five nights later we went to a party in New York and I saw a girl called Inez and told her I had a friend with me that she ought to meet sometime. I was drunk and told her he was a cowboy. "Oh, I've always wanted to meet a cowboy."

"Dean?" I yelled across the party—which included Angel Luz García, the poet; Walter Evans; Victor Villanueva, the Venezuelan poet; Jinny Jones, a former love of mine; Carlo Marx; Gene Dexter; and innumerable others—"Come over here, man." Dean came bashfully over. An hour later, in the drunkenness and chichiness of the party ("It's in honor of the end of the summer, of course"), he was kneeling on the floor with his chin on her belly and telling her and promising her everything and sweating. She was a big, sexy brunette—as García said, "Something straight out of Degas," and generally like a beautiful Parisian coquette. In a matter of days they were dickering with Camille in San Francisco by long-distance telephone for the necessary divorce papers so they could get married. Not only that, but a few months later Camille gave birth to Dean's second baby, the result of a few nights' rapport early in the year. And another matter of months and Inez had a baby. With one illegitimate child in the West somewhere, Dean then had four little ones and not a cent, and was all troubles and ecstasy and speed as ever. So we didn't go to Italy.

Part Four

I

I CAME into some money from selling my book. I straightened out my aunt with rent for the rest of the year. Whenever spring comes to New York I can't stand the suggestions of the land that come blowing over the river from New Jersey and I've got to go. So I went. For the first time in our lives I said good-by to Dean in New York and left him there. He worked in a parking lot on Madison and 40th. As ever he rushed around in his ragged shoes and T-shirt and belly-hanging pants all by himself, straightening out immense noon-time rushes of cars.

When usually I came to visit him at dusk there was nothing to do. He stood in the shack, counting tickets and rubbing his belly. The radio was always on. "Man, have you dug that mad Marty Glickman announcing basketball games—up-to-midcourt-bounce-fake-set-shot, swish, two points. Absolutely the greatest announcer I ever heard." He was reduced to simple pleasures like these. He lived with Inez in a coldwater flat in the East Eighties. When he came home at night he took off all his clothes and put on a hip-length Chinese silk jacket and sat in his easy chair to smoke a waterpipe loaded with tea. These were his coming-home pleasures, together with a deck of dirty cards. "Lately I've been concentrating on this deuce of diamonds. Have you noticed where her other hand is? I'll bet you can't tell. Look long and try to see." He wanted to lend me the deuce of diamonds, which depicted a tall, mournful fellow and a lascivious, sad whore on a bed trying a position. "Go ahead, man, I've used it many times!" Inez cooked in the kitchen and looked in with a wry smile. Everything was all right with her. "Dig her? Dig her, man? That's Inez. See, that's all she does, she pokes her head in the door and smiles. Oh, I've talked with her and we've got everything straightened out most beautifully. We're going to go and live on a farm in Pennsylvania this summer—station wagon for me to cut back to New York for kicks, nice big house, and have a lot of kids in the next few years. Ahem! Harrumph! Egad!" He leaped out of the chair and put on a Willie Jackson record, "Gator Tail." He stood before it, socking his palms and rocking and pumping his knees to the beat. "Whoo! That sonumbitch! First time I heard him I thought he'd die the next night, but he's still alive."

This was exactly what he had been doing with Camille in Frisco on the other side of the continent. The same battered trunk stuck out from under the bed, ready to fly. Inez called up Camille on the phone repeatedly and had long talks with her; they even talked about his joint, or so Dean claimed. They exchanged letters about Dean's eccentricities. Of course he had to send Camille part of his pay every month for support or he'd wind up in the workhouse for six months. To make up lost money he pulled tricks in the lot, a change artist of the first order. I saw him wish a well-to-do man Merry Christmas so volubly a five-spot in change for twenty was never missed. We went out and spent it in Birdland, the bop joint. Lester Young was on the stand, eternity on his huge eyelids.

One night we talked on the corner of 47th Street and Madison at three in the morning. "Well, Sal, damn, I wish you weren't going, I really do, it'll be my first time in New York without my old buddy." And he said, "New York, I stop over in it, Frisco's my hometown. All the time I've been here I haven't had any girl but Inez—this only happens to me in New York! Damn! But the mere thought of crossing that awful continent again— Sal, we haven't talked straight in a long time." In New York we were always jumping around frantically with crowds of friends at drunken parties. It somehow didn't seem to fit Dean. He looked more like himself huddling in the cold, misty spray of the rain on empty Madison Avenue at night. "Inez loves me; she's told me and promised me I can do anything I want and there'll be a minimum of trouble. You see, man, you get older and troubles pile up. Someday you and me'll be coming down an alley together at sundown and looking in the cans to see."

"You mean we'll end up old bums?"

"Why not, man? Of course we will if we want to, and all that. There's no harm ending that way. You spend a whole life of non-interference with the wishes of others, including politicians and the rich, and nobody bothers you and you cut along and make it your own way." I agreed with him. He was reaching his Tao decisions in the simplest direct way. "What's your road, man?—holyboy road, madman road, rainbow road, guppy road, any road. It's an anywhere road for anybody anyhow. Where body how?" We nodded in the rain. "Sheeit, and you've got to look out for your boy. He ain't a man 'less he's a jumpin man—do what the doctor say. I'll tell you, Sal, straight, no matter where I live, my trunk's always sticking out from under the bed, I'm ready to leave or get thrown out. I've decided to leave everything out of my hands. *You've* seen me try and break my ass to make it and *you* know that it doesn't matter and we know time—how to slow it up and walk and dig and just old-fashioned spade kicks, what other kicks are there? *We* know." We sighed in the rain. It was falling all up and down the Hudson Valley that night. The great world piers of the sea-wide river were drenched in it, old steamboat landings at Poughkeepsie were drenched in it, old Split Rock Pond of sources was drenched in it, Vanderwhacker Mount was drenched in it.

"So," said Dean, "I'm cutting along in my life as it leads me. You know I recently wrote my old man in jail in Seattle—I got the first letter in years from him the other day."

"Did you?"

"Yass, yass. He said he wants to see the 'babby' spelt with two b's when he can get to Frisco. I found a thirteen-a-month coldwater pad on East Fortieth; if I can send him the money he'll come and live in New York—if he gets here. I never told you much about my sister but you know I have a sweet little kid sister; I'd like to get her to come and live with me too."

"Where is she?"

"Well, that's just it, I don't know—he's going to try to find her, the old man, but *you* know what he'll really do."

"So he went to Seattle?"

"And straight to messy jail."

"Where was he?"

"Texas, Texas—so you see, man, my soul, the state of things, my position—you notice I get quieter."

"Yes, that's true." Dean had grown quiet in New York. He

wanted to talk. We were freezing to death in the cold rain. We made a date to meet at my aunt's house before I left.

He came the following Sunday afternoon. I had a television set. We played one ballgame on the TV, another on the radio, and kept switching to a third and kept track of all that was happening every moment. "Remember, Sal, Hodges is on second in Brooklyn so while the relief pitcher is coming in for the Phillies we'll switch to Giants-Boston and at the same time notice there DiMaggio has three balls count and the pitcher is fiddling with the resin bag, so we quickly find out what happened to Bobby Thomson when we left him thirty seconds ago with a man on third. Yes!"

Later in the afternoon we went out and played baseball with the kids in the sooty field by the Long Island railyard. We also played basketball so frantically the younger boys said, "Take it easy, you don't have to kill yourself." They bounced smoothly all around us and beat us with ease. Dean and I were sweating. At one point Dean fell flat on his face on the concrete court. We huffed and puffed to get the ball away from the boys; they turned and flipped it away. Others darted in and smoothly shot over our heads. We jumped at the basket like maniacs, and the younger boys just reached up and grabbed the ball from our sweating hands and dribbled away. We were like hotrock blackbelly tenorman *Mad* of American back-alley go-music trying to play basketball against Stan Getz and Cool Charlie. They thought we were crazy. Dean and I went back home playing catch from each sidewalk of the street. We tried extra-special catches, diving over bushes and barely missing posts. When a car came by I ran alongside and flipped the ball to Dean just barely behind the vanishing bumper. He darted and caught it and rolled in the grass, and flipped it back for me to catch on the other side of a parked bread truck. I just made it with my meat hand and threw it back so Dean had to whirl and back up and fall on his back across the hedges. Back in the house Dean took his wallet, harrumphed, and handed my aunt the fifteen dollars he owed her from the time we got a speeding ticket in Washington. She was completely surprised and pleased. We had a big supper. "Well, Dean," said my aunt, "I hope you'll be able to take care of your new baby that's coming and stay married this time."

"Yes, yass, yes."

"You can't go all over the country having babies like that. Those poor little things'll grow up helpless. You've got to offer them a chance to live." He looked at his feet and nodded. In the raw red dusk we said good-by, on a bridge over a superhighway.

"I hope you'll be in New York when I get back," I told him. "All I hope, Dean, is someday we'll be able to live on the same street with our families and get to be a couple of oldtimers together."

"That's right, man—you know that I pray for it completely mindful of the troubles we both had and the troubles coming, as your aunt knows and reminds me. I didn't want the new baby, Inez insisted, and we had a fight. Did you know Marylou got married to a used-car dealer in Frisco and she's having a baby?"

"Yes. We're all getting in there now." Ripples in the upside-down lake of the void, is what I should have said. The bottom of the world is gold and the world is upside down. He took out a snapshot of Camille in Frisco with the new baby girl. The shadow of a man crossed the child on the sunny pavement, two long trouser legs in the sadness. "Who's that?"

"That's only Ed Dunkel. He came back to Galatea, they're gone to Denver now. They spent a day taking pictures."

Ed Dunkel, his compassion unnoticed like the compassion of saints. Dean took out other pictures. I realized these were all the snapshots which our children would look at someday with wonder, thinking their parents had lived smooth, well-ordered, stabilized-within-the-photo lives and got up in the morning to walk proudly on the sidewalks of life, never dreaming the raggedy madness and riot of our actual lives, our actual night, the hell of it, the senseless nightmare road. All of it inside endless and beginningless emptiness. Pitiful forms of ignorance. "Good-by, good-by." Dean walked off in the long red dusk. Locomotives smoked and reeled above him. His shadow followed him, it aped his walk and thoughts and very being. He turned and waved coyly, bashfully. He gave me the boomer's highball, he jumped up and down, he yelled something I didn't catch. He ran around in a circle. All the time he came closer to the concrete corner of the railroad overpass. He made one last signal. I waved back. Suddenly he bent to his life and walked quickly out of sight. I gaped into the bleakness of my own days. I had an awful long way to go too.

2

The following midnight, singing this little song,

> Home in Missoula,
> Home in Truckee,
> Home in Opelousas,
> Ain't no home for me.
> Home in old Medora,
> Home in Wounded Knee,
> Home in Ogallala,
> Home I'll never be,

I took the Washington bus; wasted some time there wandering around; went out of my way to see the Blue Ridge, heard the bird of Shenandoah and visited Stonewall Jackson's grave; at dusk stood expectorating in the Kanawha River and walked the hillbilly night of Charleston, West Virginia; at midnight Ashland, Kentucky, and a lonely girl under the marquee of a closed-up show. The dark and mysterious Ohio, and Cincinnati at dawn. Then Indiana fields again, and St. Louis as ever in its great valley clouds of afternoon. The muddy cobbles and the Montana logs, the broken steamboats, the ancient signs, the grass and the ropes by the river. The endless poem. By night Missouri, Kansas fields, Kansas night-cows in the secret wides, crackerbox towns with a sea for the end of every street; dawn in Abilene. East Kansas grasses become West Kansas range-lands that climb up to the hill of the Western night.

Henry Glass was riding the bus with me. He had got on at Terre Haute, Indiana, and now he said to me, "I've told you why I hate this suit I'm wearing, it's lousy—but ain't all." He showed me papers. He had just been released from Terre Haute federal pen; the rap was for stealing and selling cars in Cincinnati. A young, curly-haired kid of twenty. "Soon's I get to Denver I'm selling this suit in a pawnshop and getting me jeans. Do you know what they did to me in that prison? Solitary confinement with a Bible; I used it to sit on the stone floor; when they seed I was doing that they took the Bible away and brought back a leetle pocket-size one so big. Couldn't sit on it so I read the whole Bible and Testament. Hey-hey—" he poked me, munching his candy, he was always eating candy because his stomach had been ruined in the pen and couldn't stand anything else—"you know they's some real hot things in that Bi-ble." He told me what it was to "signify." "Anybody that's leaving jail soon and starts talking about his release date is 'signifying' to the other fellas that have to stay. We take him by the neck and say, 'Don't signify with *me*!' Bad thing, to signify—y'hear me?"

"I won't signify, Henry."

"Anybody signify with me, my nose opens up, I get mad enough to kill. You know why I been in jail all my life? Because I lost my temper when I was thirteen years old. I was in a movie with a boy and he made a crack about my mother—you know that dirty word—and I took out my jackknife and cut up his throat and woulda killed him if they hadn't drug me off. Judge said, 'Did you know what you were doing when you attacked your friend?' 'Yessir, Your Honor, I did, I wanted to kill the sonofabitch and still do.' So I didn't get no parole and went straight to reform school. I got piles too from sitting in solitary. Don't ever go to a federal pen, they're worstest. Sheet, I could talk all night it's ben so long since I talked to somebody. You don't know how *good* I feel coming out. You just sitting in that bus when I got on—riding through Terre Haute—what was you thinking?"

"I was just sitting there riding."

"Me, I was singing. I sat down next to you 'cause I was afraid to set down next to any gals for fear I go crazy and reach under their dress. I gotta wait awhile."

"Another hitch in prison and you'll be put away for life. You better take it easy from now."

"That's what I intend to do, only trouble is m'nose opens up and I can't tell what I'm doing."

He was on his way to live with his brother and sister-in-law; they had a job for him in Colorado. His ticket was bought by the feds, his destination the parole. Here was a young kid like

Dean had been; his blood boiled too much for him to bear; his nose opened up; but no native strange saintliness to save him from the iron fate.

"Be a buddy and watch m'nose don't open up in Denver, will you, Sal? Mebbe I can get to my brother's safe."

When we arrived in Denver I took him by the arm to Larimer Street to pawn the penitentiary suit. The old Jew immediately sensed what it was before it was half unwrapped. "I don't want that damn thing here; I get them every day from the Canyon City boys."

All of Larimer Street was overrun with ex-cons trying to sell their prison-spun suits. Henry ended up with the thing under his arm in a paper bag and walked around in brand-new jeans and sports shirt. We went to Dean's old Glenarm bar—on the way Henry threw the suit in an ashcan—and called up Tim Gray. It was evening now.

"You?" chuckled Tim Gray. "Be right over."

In ten minutes he came loping into the bar with Stan Shephard. They'd both had a trip to France and were tremendously disappointed with their Denver lives. They loved Henry and bought him beers. He began spending all his penitentiary money left and right. Again I was back in the soft, dark Denver night with its holy alleys and crazy houses. We started hitting all the bars in town, roadhouses out on West Colfax, Five Points Negro bars, the works.

Stan Shephard had been waiting to meet me for years and now for the first time we were suspended together in front of a venture. "Sal, ever since I came back from France I ain't had any idea what to do with myself. Is it true you're going to Mexico? Hot damn, I could go with you? I can get a hundred bucks and once I get there sign up for GI Bill in Mexico City College."

Okay, it was agreed, Stan was coming with me. He was a rangy, bashful, shock-haired Denver boy with a big con-man smile and slow, easy-going Gary Cooper movements. "Hot damn!" he said and stuck his thumbs on his belt and ambled down the street, swaying from side to side but slowly. His grandfather was having it out with him. He had been opposed to France and now he was opposed to the idea of going to Mexico. Stan was wandering around Denver like a bum because of his fight with his grandfather. That night after we'd done all our drinking and restrained Henry from getting his nose opened up in the Hot Shoppe on Colfax, Stan scraggled off to sleep in Henry's hotel room on Glenarm. "I can't even come home late—my grandfather starts fighting with me, then he turns on my mother. I tell you, Sal, I got to get out of Denver quick or I'll go crazy."

Well, I stayed at Tim Gray's and then later Babe Rawlins fixed up a neat little basement room for me and we all ended up there with parties every night for a week. Henry vanished off to his brother's and we never saw him again and never will know if anybody's signified with him since and if they've put him away in an iron hall or if he busts his gaskets in the night free.

Tim Gray, Stan, Babe, and I spent an entire week of afternoons in lovely Denver bars where the waitresses wear slacks and cut around with bashful, loving eyes, not hardened waitresses but waitresses that fall in love with the clientele and have explosive affairs and huff and sweat and suffer from one bar to another; and we spent the same week in nights at Five Points listening to jazz, drinking booze in crazy Negro saloons and gabbing till five o'clock in the morn in my basement. Noon usually found us reclined in Babe's back yard among the little Denver kids who played cowboys and Indians and dropped on us from cherry trees in bloom. I was having a wonderful time and the whole world opened up before me because I had no dreams. Stan and I plotted to make Tim Gray come with us, but Tim was stuck to his Denver life.

I was getting ready to go to Mexico when suddenly Denver Doll called me one night and said, "Well, Sal, guess who's coming to Denver?" I had no idea. "He's on his way already, I got this news from my grapevine. Dean bought a car and is coming out to join you." Suddenly I had a vision of Dean, a burning shuddering frightful Angel, palpitating toward me across the road, approaching like a cloud, with enormous speed, pursuing me like the Shrouded Traveler on the plain, bearing down on me. I saw his huge face over the plains with the mad, bony purpose and the gleaming eyes; I saw his wings; I saw his old jalopy chariot with thousands of sparking flames shooting out from it; I saw the path it burned over the road; it even made its own road and went over the corn, through cities, destroying bridges, drying rivers. It came like wrath to the West. I knew Dean had gone mad again. There was no chance to send money to either wife if he took all his savings out of the bank and bought a car. Everything was up, the jig and all. Behind him charred ruins smoked. He rushed westward over the groaning and awful continent again, and soon he would arrive. We made hasty preparations for Dean. News was that he was going to drive me to Mexico.

"Do you think he'll let me come along?" asked Stan in awe.

"I'll talk to him," I said grimly. We didn't know what to expect. "Where will he sleep? What's he going to eat? Are there any girls for him?" It was like the imminent arrival of Gargantua; preparations had to be made to widen the gutters of Denver and foreshorten certain laws to fit his suffering bulk and bursting ecstasies.

3

It was like an old-fashioned movie when Dean arrived. I was in Babe's house in a golden afternoon. A word about the house. Her mother was away in Europe. The chaperon aunt was called Charity; she was seventy-five years old and spry as a chicken. In the Rawlins family, which stretched all over the West, she was continually shuttling from one house to another and making herself generally useful. At one time she'd had dozens of sons. They were all gone; they'd all abandoned her. She was old but she was interested in everything we did and said. She shook her head sadly when we took slugs of whisky in the living room. "Now you might go out in the yard for that, young man." Upstairs—it was a kind of boarding house that summer—lived a guy called Tom who was hopelessly in love with Babe. He came from Vermont, from a rich family, they said, and had a career waiting for him there and everything, but he preferred being where Babe was. In the evenings he sat in the living room with his face burning behind a newspaper and every time one of us said anything he heard but made no sign. He particularly burned when Babe said something. When we forced him to put down the paper he looked at us with incalculable boredom and suffering. "Eh? Oh yes, I suppose so." He usually said just that.

Charity sat in her corner, knitting, watching us all with her birdy eyes. It was her job to chaperon, it was up to her to see nobody swore. Babe sat giggling on the couch. Tim Gray, Stan Shephard, and I sprawled around in chairs. Poor Tom suffered the tortures. He got up, yawned, and said, "Well, another day another dollar, good night," and disappeared upstairs. Babe had no use whatever for him as a lover. She was in love with Tim Gray; he wriggled like an eel out of her grasp. We were sitting around like this on a sunny afternoon toward suppertime when Dean pulled up in front in his jalopy and jumped out in a tweed suit with vest and watch chain.

"Hup! hup!" I heard out on the street. He was with Roy Johnson, who'd just returned from Frisco with his wife Dorothy and was living in Denver again. So were Dunkel and Galatea Dunkel, and Tom Snark. Everybody was in Denver again. I went out on the porch. "Well, m'boy," said Dean, sticking out his big hand, "I see everything is all right on this end of the stick. Hello hello hello," he said to everybody. "Oh yes, Tim Gray, Stan Shephard, howd'y'do!" We introduced him to Charity. "Oh yass, howd'y'do. This is m'friend Roy Johnson here, was so kind as to accompany me, harrumph! egad! kaff! kaff! Major Hoople, sir," he said, sticking out his hand to Tom, who stared at him. "Yass, yass. Well, Sal old man, what's the story, when do we take off for Mexico? Tomorrow afternoon? Fine, fine. Ahem! And now, Sal, I have exactly sixteen minutes to make it to Ed Dunkel's house, where I am about to recover my old railroad watch which I can pawn on Larimer Street before closing time, meanwhile buzzing very quickly and as thoroughly as time allows to see if my old man by chance may be in Jiggs' Buffet or some of the other bars and then I have an appointment with the barber Doll always told me to patronize and I have not myself changed over the years and continue with that policy—kaff! kaff! At six o'clock *sharp!*—sharp, hear me?—I want you to be right here where I'll come buzzing by to get you for one quick run to Roy Johnson's house, play Gillespie and assorted bop records, an hour of relaxation prior to any kind of further evening you

and Tim and Stan and Babe may have planned for tonight irrespective of my arrival which incidentally was exactly forty-five minutes ago in my old thirty-seven Ford which you see parked out there, I made it together with a long pause in Kansas City seeing my cousin, not Sam Brady but the younger one . . ."
And saying all these things, he was busily changing from his suitcoat to T-shirt in the living-room alcove just out of sight of everyone and transferring his watch to another pair of pants that he got out of the same old battered trunk.

"And Inez?" I said. "What happened in New York?"

"Officially, Sal, this trip is to get a Mexican divorce, cheaper and quicker than any kind. I've Camille's agreement at last and everything is straight, everything is fine, everything is lovely and we know that we are now not worried about a single thing, don't we, Sal?"

Well, okay, I'm always ready to follow Dean, so we all bustled to the new set of plans and arranged a big night, and it was an unforgettable night. There was a party at Ed Dunkel's brother's house. Two of his other brothers are bus-drivers. They sat there in awe of everything that went on. There was a lovely spread on the table, cake and drinks. Ed Dunkel looked happy and prosperous. "Well, are you all set with Galatea now?"

"Yessir," said Ed, "I sure am. I'm about to go to Denver U, you know, me and Roy."

"What are you going to take up?"

"Oh, sociology and all that field, you know. Say, Dean gets crazier every year, don't he?"

"He sure does."

Galatea Dunkel was there. She was trying to talk to somebody, but Dean held the whole floor. He stood and performed before Shephard, Tim, Babe, and myself, who all sat side by side in kitchen chairs along the wall. Ed Dunkel hovered nervously behind him. His poor brother was thrust into the background. "Hup! hup!" Dean was saying, tugging at his shirt, rubbing his belly, jumping up and down. "Yass, well—we're all together now and the years have rolled severally behind us and yet you see none of us have really changed, that's what so amazing, the dura—the dura—bility—in fact to prove that I have here a deck of cards with which I can tell very accurate fortunes of all sorts." It was the dirty deck. Dorothy Johnson and Roy Johnson sat stiffly in a corner. It was a mournful party. Then Dean suddenly grew quiet and sat in a kitchen chair between Stan and me and stared straight ahead with rocky doglike wonder and paid no attention to anybody. He simply disappeared for a moment to gather up more energy. If you touched him he would sway like a boulder suspended on a pebble on the precipice of a cliff. He might come crashing down or just sway rocklike. Then the boulder exploded into a flower and his face lit up with a lovely smile and he looked around like a man waking up and said, "Ah, look at all the nice people that are sitting here with me. Isn't it nice! Sal, why, like I was tellin Min just t'other day, why, urp, ah, yes!" He got up and went across the room, hand outstretched to one of the bus-drivers in the party. "Howd'y'do. My name is Dean Moriarty. Yes, I remember you well. Is everything all right? Well, well. Look at the lovely cake. Oh, can I have some? Just me? Miserable me?" Ed's sister said yes. "Oh, how wonderful. People are so nice. Cakes and pretty things set out on a table and all for the sake of wonderful little joys and delights. Hmm, ah, yes, excellent, splendid, harrumph, egad!" And he stood swaying in the middle of the room, eating his cake and looking at everyone with awe. He turned and looked around behind him. Everything amazed him, everything he saw. People talked in groups all around the room, and he said, "Yes! That's right!" A picture on the wall made him stiffen to attention. He went up and looked closer, he backed up, he stooped, he jumped up, he wanted to see from all possible levels and angles, he tore at his T-shirt in exclamation, "Damn!" He had no idea of the impression he was making and cared less. People were now beginning to look at Dean with maternal and paternal affection glowing in their faces. He was finally an Angel, as I always knew he would become; but like any Angel he still had rages and furies, and that night when we all left the party and repaired to the Windsor bar in one vast brawling gang, Dean became frantically and demoniacally and seraphically drunk.

Remember that the Windsor, once Denver's great Gold Rush hotel and in many respects a point of interest—in the big saloon downstairs bullet holes are still in the walls—had once been Dean's home. He'd lived here with his father in one of the rooms upstairs. He was no tourist. He drank in this saloon like the ghost of his father; he slopped down wine, beer, and whisky like water. His face got red and sweaty and he bellowed and hollered at the bar and staggered across the dance-floor where honkytonkers of the West danced with girls and tried to play the piano, and he threw his arms around ex-cons and shouted with them in the uproar. Meanwhile everybody in our party sat around two immense tables stuck together. There were Denver D. Doll, Dorothy and Roy Johnson, a girl from Buffalo, Wyoming, who was Dorothy's friend, Stan, Tim Gray, Babe, me, Ed Dunkel, Tom Snark, and several others, thirteen in all. Doll was having a great time: he took a peanut machine and set it on the table before him and poured pennies in it and ate peanuts. He suggested we all write something on a penny postcard and mail it to Carlo Marx in New York. We wrote crazy things. The fiddle music whanged in the Larimer Street night. "Isn't it fun?" yelled Doll. In the men's room Dean and I punched the door and tried to break it but it was an inch thick. I cracked a bone in my middle finger and didn't even realize it till the next day. We were fumingly drunk. Fifty glasses of beer sat on our tables at one time. All you had to do was rush around and sip from each one. Canyon City ex-cons reeled and gabbled with us. In the foyer outside the saloon old former prospectors sat dreaming over their canes under the tocking old clock. This fury had been known by them in greater days. Everything swirled. There were scattered parties everywhere. There was even a party in a castle to which we all drove—except Dean, who ran off elsewhere—and in this castle we sat at a great table in the hall and shouted. There were a swimming pool and grottoes outside. I had finally found the castle where the great snake of the world was about to rise up.

Then in the late night it was just Dean and I and Stan Shephard and Tim Gray and Ed Dunkel and Tommy Snark in one car and everything ahead of us. We went to Mexican town, we went to Five Points, we reeled around. Stan Shephard was out of his mind with joy. He kept yelling, "Sonofa*bitch*! Hot *damn*!" in a high squealing voice and slapping his knees. Dean was mad about him. He repeated everything Stan said and phewed and wiped the sweat off his face. "Are we gonna get our kicks, Sal, travelin down to Mexico with this cat Stan!

Yes!" It was our last night in holy Denver, we made it big and wild. It all ended up with wine in the basement by candlelight, and Charity creeping around upstairs in her nightgown with a flashlight. We had a colored guy with us now, called himself Gomez. He floated around Five Points and didn't give a damn. When we saw him, Tommy Snark called out, "Hey, is your name Johnny?"

Gomez just backed up and passed us once more and said, "Now will you repeat what you said?"

"I said are you the guy they call Johnny?"

Gomez floated back and tried again. "Does this look a little more like him? Because I'm tryin my best to be Johnny but I just can't find the way."

"Well, *man*, come on with us!" cried Dean, and Gomez jumped in and we were off. We whispered frantically in the basement so as not to create disturbance with the neighbors. At nine o'clock in the morning everybody had left except Dean and Shephard, who were still yakking like maniacs. People got up to make breakfast and heard strange subterranean voices saying, "Yes! Yes!" Babe cooked a big breakfast. The time was coming to scat off to Mexico.

Dean took the car to the nearest station and had everything shipshape. It was a '37 Ford sedan with the right-side door unhinged and tied on the frame. The right-side front seat was also broken, and you sat there leaning back with your face to the tattered roof. "Just like Min 'n' Bill," said Dean. "We'll go coughing and bouncing down to Mexico; it'll take us days and days." I looked over the map: a total of over a thousand miles, mostly Texas, to the border at Laredo, and then another 767 miles through all Mexico to the great city near the cracked Isthmus and Oaxacan heights. I couldn't imagine this trip. It was the most fabulous of all. It was no longer east-west, but magic *south*. We saw a vision of the entire Western Hemisphere rockribbing clear down to Tierra del Fuego and us flying down the curve of the world into other tropics and other worlds. "Man, this will finally take us to IT!" said Dean with definite faith. He tapped my arm. "Just wait and see. Hoo! Whee!"

I went with Shephard to conclude the last of his Denver business, and met his poor grandfather, who stood in the door of the house, saying, "Stan—Stan—Stan."

"What is it, Granpaw?"

"Don't go."

"Oh, it's settled, I *have* to go now; why do you have to do that?" The old man had gray hair and large almond eyes and a tense, mad neck.

"Stan," he simply said, "don't go. Don't make your old grandfather cry. Don't leave me alone again." It broke my heart to see all this.

"Dean," said the old man, addressing me, "don't take my Stan away from me. I used to take him to the park when he was a little boy and explain the swans to him. Then his little sister drowned in the same pond. I don't want you to take my boy away."

"No," said Stan, "we're leaving now. Good-by." He struggled with his grips.

His grandfather took him by the arm. "Stan, Stan, Stan, don't go, don't go, don't go."

We fled with our heads bowed, and the old man still stood in the doorway of his Denver side-street cottage with the beads hanging in the doors and the overstuffed furniture in the parlor. He was as white as a sheet. He was still calling Stan. There was something paralyzed about his movements, and he did nothing about leaving the doorway, but just stood in it, muttering, "Stan," and "Don't go," and looking after us anxiously as we rounded the corner.

"God, Shep, I don't know what to say."

"Never mind!" Stan moaned. "He's always been like that."

We met Stan's mother at the bank, where she was drawing money for him. She was a lovely white-haired woman, still very young in appearance. She and her son stood on the marble floor of the bank, whispering. Stan was wearing a levi outfit, jacket and all, and looked like a man going to Mexico sure enough. This was his tender existence in Denver, and he was going off with the flaming tyro Dean. Dean came popping around the corner and met us just on time. Mrs. Shephard insisted on buying us all a cup of coffee.

"Take care of my Stan," she said. "No telling what things might happen in that country."

"We'll all watch over each other," I said. Stan and his mother strolled on ahead, and I walked in back with crazy

Dean; he was telling me about the inscriptions carved on toilet walls in the East and in the West.

"They're entirely different; in the East they make cracks and corny jokes and obvious references, scatological bits of data and drawings; in the West they just write their names, Red O'Hara, Blufftown Montana, came by here, date, real solemn, like, say, Ed Dunkel, the reason being the enormous loneliness that differs just a shade and cut hair as you move across the Mississippi." Well, there was a lonely guy in front of us, for Shephard's mother was a lovely mother and she hated to see her son go but knew he had to go. I saw he was fleeing his grandfather. Here were the three of us—Dean looking for his father, mine dead, Stan fleeing his old one, and going off into the night together. He kissed his mother in the rushing crowds of 17th and she got in a cab and waved at us. Good-by, good-by.

We got in the car at Babe's and said good-by to her. Tim was riding with us to his house outside town. Babe was beautiful that day; her hair was long and blond and Swedish, her freckles showed in the sun. She looked exactly like the little girl she had been. There was a mist in her eyes. She might join us later with Tim—but she didn't. Good-by, good-by.

We roared off. We left Tim in his yard on the Plains outside town and I looked back to watch Tim Gray recede on the plain. That strange guy stood there for a full two minutes watching us go away and thinking God knows what sorrowful thoughts. He grew smaller and smaller, and still he stood motionless with one hand on a washline, like a captain, and I was twisted around to see more of Tim Gray till there was nothing but a growing absence in space, and the space was the eastward view toward Kansas that led all the way back to my home in Atlantis.

Now we pointed our rattly snout south and headed for Castle Rock, Colorado, as the sun turned red and the rock of the mountains to the west looked like a Brooklyn brewery in November dusks. Far up in the purple shades of the rock there was someone walking, walking, but we could not see; maybe that old man with the white hair I had sensed years ago up in the peaks. Zacatecan Jack. But he was coming closer to me, if only ever just behind. And Denver receded back of us like the city of salt, her smokes breaking up in the air and dissolving to our sight.

4

It was May. And how can homely afternoons in Colorado with its farms and irrigation ditches and shady dells—the places where little boys go swimming—produce a bug like the bug that bit Stan Shephard? He had his arm draped over the broken door and was riding along and talking happily when suddenly a bug flew into his arm and embedded a long stinger in it that made him howl. It had come out of an American afternoon. He yanked and slapped at his arm and dug out the stinger, and in a few minutes his arm had begun to swell and hurt. Dean and I couldn't figure what it was. The thing was to wait and see if the swelling went down. Here we were, heading for unknown southern lands, and barely three miles out of hometown, poor old hometown of childhood, a strange feverish exotic bug rose from secret corruptions and sent fear into our hearts. "What is it?"

"I've never known of a bug around here that can make a swelling like that."

"Damn!" It made the trip seem sinister and doomed. We drove on. Stan's arm got worse. We'd stop at the first hospital and have him get a shot of penicillin. We passed Castle Rock, came to Colorado Springs at dark. The great shadow of Pike's Peak loomed to our right. We bowled down the Pueblo highway. "I've hitched thousands and thousands of times on this road," said Dean. "I hid behind that exact wire fence there one night when I suddenly took fright for no reason whatever."

We all decided to tell our stories, but one by one, and Stan was first. "We've got a long way to go," preambled Dean, "and so you must take every indulgence and deal with every single detail you can bring to mind—and still it won't all be told. Easy, easy," he cautioned Stan, who began telling his story, "you've got to relax too." Stan swung into his life story as we shot across the dark. He started with his experiences in France but to round out ever-growing difficulties he came back and

started at the beginning with his boyhood in Denver. He and
Dean compared times they'd seen each other zooming around
on bicycles. "One time you've forgotten, I know—Arapahoe
Garage? Recall? I bounced a ball at you on the corner and you
knocked it back to me with your fist and it went in the sewer.
Grammar days. Now recall?" Stan was nervous and feverish.
He wanted to tell Dean everything. Dean was now arbiter, old
man, judge, listener, approver, nodder. "Yes, yes, go on please."
We passed Walsenburg; suddenly we passed Trinidad, where
Chad King was somewhere off the road in front of a campfire
with perhaps a handful of anthropologists and as of yore he too
was telling his life story and never dreamed we were passing
at that exact moment on the highway, headed for Mexico,
telling our own stories. O sad American night! Then we were
in New Mexico and passed the rounded rocks of Raton and
stopped at a diner, ravingly hungry for hamburgers, some of
which we wrapped in a napkin to eat over the border below.
"The whole vertical state of Texas lies before us, Sal," said
Dean. "Before we made it horizontal. Every bit as long. We'll
be in Texas in a few minutes and won't be out till tomorrow
this time and won't stop driving. Think of it."

We drove on. Across the immense plain of night lay the first
Texas town, Dalhart, which I'd crossed in 1947. It lay glimmering on the dark floor of the earth, fifty miles away. The
land by moonlight was all mesquite and wastes. On the horizon was the moon. She fattened, she grew huge and rusty, she
mellowed and rolled, till the morning star contended and dews
began to blow in our windows—and still we rolled. After
Dalhart—empty crackerbox town—we bowled for Amarillo,
and reached it in the morning among windy panhandle grasses
that only a few years ago waved around a collection of buffalo
tents. Now there were gas stations and new 1950 jukeboxes
with immense ornate snouts and ten-cent slots and awful songs.
All the way from Amarillo to Childress, Dean and I pounded
plot after plot of books we'd read into Stan, who asked for it
because he wanted to know. At Childress in the hot sun we
turned directly south on a lesser road and highballed across
abysmal wastes to Paducah, Guthrie, and Abilene, Texas. Now
Dean had to sleep, and Stan and I sat in the front seat and

drove. The old car burned and bopped and struggled on. Great clouds of gritty wind blew at us from shimmering spaces. Stan rolled right along with stories about Monte Carlo and Cagnes-sur-Mer and the blue places near Menton where dark-faced people wandered among white walls.

Texas is undeniable: we burned slowly into Abilene and all woke up to look at it. "Imagine living in this town a thousand miles from cities. Whoop, whoop, over there by the tracks, old town Abilene where they shipped the cows and shot it up for gumshoes and drank red-eye. Look out there!" yelled Dean out the window with his mouth contorted like W. C. Fields. He didn't care about Texas or any place. Red-faced Texans paid him no mind and hurried along the burning sidewalks. We stopped to eat on the highway south of town. Nightfall seemed like a million miles away as we resumed for Coleman and Brady—the heart of Texas, only, wildernesses of brush with an occasional house near a thirsty creek and a fifty-mile dirt road detour and endless heat. "Old dobe Mexico's a long way away," said Dean sleepily from the back seat, "so keep her rolling, boys, and we'll be kissing señoritas b'dawn 'cause this old Ford can roll if y'know how to talk to her and ease her along—except the back end's about to fall but don't worry about it till we get there." And he went to sleep.

I took the wheel and drove to Fredericksburg, and here again I was crisscrossing the old map again, same place Mary-lou and I had held hands on a snowy morning in 1949, and where was Marylou now? "Blow!" yelled Dean in a dream and I guess he was dreaming of Frisco jazz and maybe Mexican mambo to come. Stan talked and talked; Dean had wound him up the night before and now he was never going to stop. He was in England by now, relating adventures hitchhiking on the English road, London to Liverpool, with his hair long and his pants ragged, and strange British truck-drivers giving him lifts in glooms of the Europe void. We were all red-eyed from the continual mistral-winds of old Tex-ass. There was a rock in each of our bellies and we knew we were getting there, if slowly. The car pushed forty with shuddering effort. From Fredericksburg we descended the great western high plains. Moths began smashing our windshield. "Getting down into the hot country now, boys, the desert rats and the tequila. And this is my first time this far south in Texas," added Dean with wonder. "Gawd-damn! this is where my old man comes in the wintertime, sly old bum."

Suddenly we were in absolutely tropical heat at the bottom of a five-mile-long hill, and up ahead we saw the lights of old San Antonio. You had the feeling all this used to be Mexican territory indeed. Houses by the side of the road were different, gas stations beater, fewer lamps. Dean delightedly took the wheel to roll us into San Antonio. We entered town in a wilderness of Mexican rickety southern shacks without cellars and with old rocking chairs on the porch. We stopped at a mad gas station to get a grease job. Mexicans were standing around in the hot light of the overhead bulbs that were blackened by valley summerbugs, reaching down into a soft-drink box and pulling out beer bottles and throwing the money to the attendant. Whole families lingered around doing this. All around there were shacks and drooping trees and a wild cinnamon smell in the air. Frantic teenage Mexican girls came by with boys. "Hoo!" yelled Dean. "*Si! Mañana!*" Music was coming from all sides, and all kinds of music. Stan and I drank several bottles of beer and got high. We were already almost out of America and yet definitely in it and in the middle of where it's maddest. Hotrods blew by. San Antonio, ah-haa!

"Now, men, listen to me—we might as well goof a coupla hours in San Antone and so we will go and find a hospital clinic for Stan's arm and you and I, Sal, will cut around and get these streets dug—look at those houses across the street, you can see right into the front room and all the purty daughters layin around with *True Love* magazines, whee! Come, let's go!"

We drove around aimlessly awhile and asked people for the nearest hospital clinic. It was near downtown, where things looked more sleek and American, several semi-skyscrapers and many neons and chain drugstores, yet with cars crashing through from the dark around town as if there were no traffic laws. We parked the car in the hospital driveway and I went with Stan to see an intern while Dean stayed in the car and changed. The hall of the hospital was full of poor Mexican women, some of them pregnant, some of them sick or bringing their little sick kiddies. It was sad. I thought of poor Terry and

wondered what she was doing now. Stan had to wait an entire
hour till an intern came along and looked at his swollen arm.
There was a name for the infection he had, but none of us
bothered to pronounce it. They gave him a shot of penicillin.

Meanwhile Dean and I went out to dig the streets of Mexican San Antonio. It was fragrant and soft—the softest air I'd
ever known—and dark, and mysterious, and buzzing. Sudden
figures of girls in white bandannas appeared in the humming
dark. Dean crept along and said not a word. "Oh, this is too
wonderful to do anything!" he whispered. "Let's just creep
along and see everything. Look! Look! A crazy San Antonio
pool shack." We went in. A dozen boys were shooting pool at
three tables, all Mexicans. Dean and I bought Cokes and
shoved nickels in the jukebox and played Wynonie Blues Harris and Lionel Hampton and Lucky Millinder and jumped.
Meanwhile Dean warned me to watch.

"Dig, now, out of the corner of your eye and as we listen to
Wynonie blow about his baby's pudding and as we also smell
the soft air as you say—dig the kid, the crippled kid shooting
pool at table one, the butt of the joint's jokes, y'see, he's been
the butt all his life. The other fellows are merciless but they
love him."

The crippled kid was some kind of malformed midget with a
great big beautiful face, much too large, in which enormous
brown eyes moistly gleamed. "Don't you see, Sal, a San Antonio Mex Tom Snark, the same story the world over. See, they
hit him on the ass with a cue? Ha-ha-ha! hear them laugh. You
see, he wants to win the game, he's bet four bits. Watch!
Watch!" We watched as the angelic young midget aimed for a
bank shot. He missed. The other fellows roared. "Ah, man,"
said Dean, "and now watch." They had the little boy by the
scruff of the neck and were mauling him around, playful. He
squealed. He stalked out in the night but not without a backward bashful, sweet glance. "Ah, man, I'd love to know that
gone little cat and what he thinks and what kind of girls he
has—oh, man, I'm high on this air!" We wandered out and negotiated several dark, mysterious blocks. Innumerable houses
hid behind verdant, almost jungle-like yards; we saw glimpses
of girls in front rooms, girls on porches, girls in the bushes
with boys. "I never knew this mad San Antonio! Think what

Mexico'll be like! Lessgo! Lessgo!" We rushed back to the hospital. Stan was ready and said he felt much better. We put our arms around him and told him everything we'd done.

And now we were ready for the last hundred and fifty miles to the magic border. We leaped into the car and off. I was so exhausted by now I slept all the way through Dilley and Encinal to Laredo and didn't wake up till they were parking the car in front of a lunchroom at two o'clock in the morning. "Ah," sighed Dean, "the end of Texas, the end of America, we don't know no more." It was tremendously hot: we were all sweating buckets. There was no night dew, not a breath of air, nothing except billions of moths smashing at bulbs everywhere and the low, rank smell of a hot river in the night nearby —the Rio Grande, that begins in cool Rocky Mountain dales and ends up fashioning world-valleys to mingle its heats with the Mississippi muds in the great Gulf.

Laredo was a sinister town that morning. All kinds of cabdrivers and border rats wandered around, looking for opportunities. There weren't many; it was too late. It was the bottom and dregs of America where all the heavy villains sink, where disoriented people have to go to be near a specific elsewhere they can slip into unnoticed. Contraband brooded in the heavy syrup air. Cops were red-faced and sullen and sweaty, no swagger. Waitresses were dirty and disgusted. Just beyond, you could feel the enormous presence of whole great Mexico and almost smell the billion tortillas frying and smoking in the night. We had no idea what Mexico would really be like. We were at sea level again, and when we tried to eat a snack we could hardly swallow it. I wrapped it up in napkins for the trip anyway. We felt awful and sad. But everything changed when we crossed the mysterious bridge over the river and our wheels rolled on official Mexican soil, though it wasn't anything but carway for border inspection. Just across the street Mexico began. We looked with wonder. To our amazement, it looked exactly like Mexico. It was three in the morning, and fellows in straw hats and white pants were lounging by the dozen against battered pocky storefronts.

"Look—at—those—cats!" whispered Dean, "Oo," he breathed softly, "wait, wait." The Mexican officials came out, grinning, and asked please if we would take out our baggage.

We did. We couldn't take our eyes from across the street. We were longing to rush right up there and get lost in those mysterious Spanish streets. It was only Nuevo Laredo but it looked like Holy Lhasa to us. "Man, those guys are up all night," whispered Dean. We hurried to get our papers straightened. We were warned not to drink tapwater now we were over the border. The Mexicans looked at our baggage in a desultory way. They weren't like officials at all. They were lazy and tender. Dean couldn't stop staring at them. He turned to me. "See how the *cops* are in this country. I can't believe it!" He rubbed his eyes. "I'm dreaming." Then it was time to change our money. We saw great stacks of pesos on a table and learned that eight of them made an American buck, or thereabouts. We changed most of our money and stuffed the big rolls in our pockets with delight.

5

Then we turned our faces to Mexico with bashfulness and wonder as those dozens of Mexican cats watched us from under their secret hatbrims in the night. Beyond were music and all-night restaurants with smoke pouring out of the door. "Whee," whispered Dean very softly.

"Thassall!" A Mexican official grinned. "You boys all set. Go ahead. Welcome Mehico. Have good time. Watch you money. Watch you driving. I say this to you personal, I'm Red, everybody call me Red. Ask for Red. Eat good. Don't worry. Everything fine. Is not hard enjoin yourself in Mehico."

"*Yes!*" shuddered Dean and off we went across the street into Mexico on soft feet. We left the car parked, and all three of us abreast went down the Spanish street into the middle of the dull brown lights. Old men sat on chairs in the night and looked like Oriental junkies and oracles. No one was actually looking at us, yet everybody was aware of everything we did. We turned sharp left into the smoky lunchroom and went in to music of campo guitars on an American 'thirties jukebox. Shirt-sleeved Mexican cabdrivers and straw-hatted Mexican hipsters sat at stools, devouring shapeless messes of tortillas,

beans, tacos, whatnot. We bought three bottles of cold beer—
cerveza was the name of beer—for about thirty Mexican cents
or ten American cents each. We bought packs of Mexican cigarettes for six cents each. We gazed and gazed at our wonderful Mexican money that went so far, and played with it and
looked around and smiled at everyone. Behind us lay the
whole of America and everything Dean and I had previously
known about life, and life on the road. We had finally found
the magic land at the end of the road and we never dreamed the
extent of the magic. "*Think* of these cats staying up all hours
of the night," whispered Dean. "And think of this big continent ahead of us with those enormous Sierra Madre mountains we saw in the movies, and the jungles all the way down
and a whole desert plateau as big as ours and reaching clear
down to Guatemala and God knows where, whoo! What'll we
do? What'll we do? Let's move!" We got out and went back to
the car. One last glimpse of America across the hot lights of
the Rio Grande bridge, and we turned our back and fender to
it and roared off.

Instantly we were out in the desert and there wasn't a light
or a car for fifty miles across the flats. And just then dawn was
coming over the Gulf of Mexico and we began to see the
ghostly shapes of yucca cactus and organpipe on all sides.
"What a wild country!" I yelped. Dean and I were completely
awake. In Laredo we'd been half dead. Stan, who'd been to
foreign countries before, just calmly slept in the back seat.
Dean and I had the whole of Mexico before us.

"Now, Sal, we're leaving everything behind us and entering
a new and unknown phase of things. All the years and troubles
and kicks—and now *this!* so that we can safely think of nothing
else and just go on ahead with our faces stuck out like this, you
see, and *understand* the world as, really and genuinely speaking,
other Americans haven't done before us—they were here,
weren't they? The Mexican war. Cutting across here with
cannon."

"This road," I told him, "is also the route of old American
outlaws who used to skip over the border and go down to old
Monterrey, so if you'll look out on that graying desert and picture the ghost of an old Tombstone hellcat making his lonely
exile gallop into the unknown, you'll see further . . ."

"It's the world," said Dean. "My God!" he cried, slapping the wheel. "It's the world! We can go right on to South America if the road goes. Think of it! Son-of-a-*bitch*! Gawd-*damn*!" We rushed on. The dawn spread immediately and we began to see the white sand of the desert and occasional huts in the distance off the road. Dean slowed down to peer at them. "Real beat huts, man, the kind you only find in Death Valley and much worse. These people don't *bother* with appearances." The first town ahead that had any consequence on the map was called Sabinas Hidalgo. We looked forward to it eagerly. "And the road don't look any different than the American road," cried Dean, "except one mad thing and if you'll notice, right here, the mileposts are written in kilometers and they click off the distance to Mexico City. See, it's the only city in the entire land, everything points to it." There were only 767 more miles to that metropolis; in kilometers the figure was over a thousand. "Damn! I gotta go!" cried Dean. For a while I closed my eyes in utter exhaustion and kept hearing Dean pound the wheel with his fists and say, "Damn," and "What kicks!" and "Oh, what a land!" and "Yes!" We arrived at Sabinas Hidalgo, across the desert, at about seven o'clock in the morning. We slowed down completely to see this. We woke up Stan in the back seat. We sat up straight to dig. The main street was muddy and full of holes. On each side were dirty broken-down adobe fronts. Burros walked in the street with packs. Barefoot women watched us from dark doorways. The street was completely crowded with people on foot beginning a new day in the Mexican countryside. Old men with handlebar mustaches stared at us. The sight of three bearded, bedraggled American youths instead of the usual well-dressed tourists was of unusual interest to them. We bounced along over Main Street at ten miles an hour, taking everything in. A group of girls walked directly in front of us. As we bounced by, one of them said, "Where you going, man?"

I turned to Dean, amazed. "Did you hear what she said?"

Dean was so astounded he kept on driving slowly and saying, "Yes, I heard what she said, I certainly damn well did, oh me, oh my, I don't know what to do I'm so excited and sweetened in this morning world. We've finally got to heaven. It couldn't be cooler, it couldn't be grander, it couldn't be any*thing*."

"Well, let's go back and pick em up!" I said.

"Yes," said Dean and drove right on at five miles an hour. He was knocked out, he didn't have to do the usual things he would have done in America. "There's millions of them all along the road!" he said. Nevertheless he U-turned and came by the girls again. They were headed for work in the fields; they smiled at us. Dean stared at them with rocky eyes. "Damn," he said under his breath. "*Oh!* This is too great to be true. Gurls, gurls. And particularly right now in my stage and condition, Sal, I am digging the interiors of these homes as we pass them—these gone doorways and you look inside and see beds of straw and little brown kids sleeping and stirring to wake, their thoughts congealing from the empty mind of sleep, their selves rising, and the mothers cooking up breakfast in iron pots, and dig them shutters they have for windows and the old men, the *old men* are so cool and grand and not bothered by anything. There's no *suspicion* here, nothing like that. Everybody's cool, everybody looks at you with such straight brown eyes and they don't say anything, just *look*, and in that look all of the human qualities are soft and subdued and still there. Dig all the foolish stories you read about Mexico and the sleeping gringo and all that crap—and crap about greasers and so on—and all it is, people here are straight and kind and don't put down any bull. I'm so amazed by this." Schooled in the raw road night, Dean was come into the world to see it. He bent over the wheel and looked both ways and rolled along slowly. We stopped for gas the other side of Sabinas Hidalgo. Here a congregation of local straw-hatted ranchers with handlebar mustaches growled and joked in front of antique gas-pumps. Across the fields an old man plodded with a burro in front of his switch stick. The sun rose pure on pure and ancient activities of human life.

Now we resumed the road to Monterrey. The great mountains rose snow-capped before us; we bowled right for them. A gap widened and wound up a pass and we went with it. In a matter of minutes we were out of the mesquite desert and climbing among cool airs in a road with a stone wall along the precipice side and great whitewashed names of presidents on the cliffsides—ALEMAN! We met nobody on this high road. It wound among the clouds and took us to the great plateau on top. Across this plateau the big manufacturing town of Monterrey sent smoke to the blue skies with their enormous Gulf clouds written across the bowl of day like fleece. Entering Monterrey was like entering Detroit, among great long walls of factories, except for the burros that sunned in the grass before them and the sight of thick city adobe neighborhoods with thousands of shifty hipsters hanging around doorways and whores looking out of windows and strange shops that might have sold anything and narrow sidewalks crowded with Hongkong-like humanity. "Yow!" yelled Dean. "And all in that sun. Have you dug this Mexican sun, Sal? It makes you high. Whoo! I want to get on and on—this road drives *me!!*" We mentioned stopping in the excitements of Monterrey, but Dean wanted to make extra-special time to get to Mexico City, and besides he knew the road would get more interesting, especially ahead, always ahead. He drove like a fiend and never rested. Stan and I were completely bushed and gave it up and had to sleep. I looked up outside Monterrey and saw enormous weird twin peaks beyond Old Monterrey, beyond where the outlaws went.

Montemorelos was ahead, a descent again to hotter altitudes. It grew exceedingly hot and strange. Dean absolutely had to wake me up to see this. "Look, Sal, you *must* not miss." I looked. We were going through swamps and alongside the road at ragged intervals strange Mexicans in tattered rags walked along with machetes hanging from their rope belts, and some of them cut at the bushes. They all stopped to watch us without expression. Through the tangled bush we occasionally saw thatched huts with African-like bamboo walls, just stick huts. Strange young girls, dark as the moon, stared from mysterious verdant doorways. "Oh, man, I want to stop and twiddle thumbs with the little darlings," cried Dean, "but notice the old lady or the old man is always somewhere around— in the back usually, sometimes a hundred yards, gathering twigs and wood or tending animals. They're never alone. Nobody's ever alone in this country. While you've been sleeping I've been digging this road and this country, and if I could only tell you all the thoughts I've had, man!" He was sweating. His eyes were red-streaked and mad and also subdued and tender—he had found people like himself. We bowled right

through the endless swamp country at a steady forty-five. "Sal,
I think the country won't change for a long time. If you'll
drive, I'll sleep now."

I took the wheel and drove among reveries of my own,
through Linares, through hot, flat swamp country, across the
steaming Rio Soto la Marina near Hidalgo, and on. A great
verdant jungle valley with long fields of green crops opened
before me. Groups of men watched us pass from a narrow old-
fashioned bridge. The hot river flowed. Then we rose in altitude till a kind of desert country began reappearing. The city
of Gregoria was ahead. The boys were sleeping, and I was
alone in my eternity at the wheel, and the road ran straight as
an arrow. Not like driving across Carolina, or Texas, or Arizona, or Illinois; but like driving across the world and into the
places where we would finally learn ourselves among the
Fellahin Indians of the world, the essential strain of the basic
primitive, wailing humanity that stretches in a belt around the
equatorial belly of the world from Malaya (the long fingernail
of China) to India the great subcontinent to Arabia to Morocco to the selfsame deserts and jungles of Mexico and over
the waves to Polynesia to mystic Siam of the Yellow Robe and
on around, on around, so that you hear the same mournful
wail by the rotted walls of Cádiz, Spain, that you hear 12,000
miles around in the depths of Benares the Capital of the
World. These people were unmistakably Indians and were not
at all like the Pedros and Panchos of silly civilized American
lore—they had high cheekbones, and slanted eyes, and soft
ways; they were not fools, they were not clowns; they were
great, grave Indians and they were the source of mankind and
the fathers of it. The waves are Chinese, but the earth is an
Indian thing. As essential as rocks in the desert are they in the
desert of "history." And they knew this when we passed, ostensibly self-important moneybag Americans on a lark in their
land; they knew who was the father and who was the son of
antique life on earth, and made no comment. For when de-
struction comes to the world of "history" and the Apocalypse
of the Fellahin returns once more as so many times before,
people will still stare with the same eyes from the caves of
Mexico as well as from the caves of Bali, where it all began and
where Adam was suckled and taught to know. These were my

growing thoughts as I drove the car into the hot, sunbaked town of Gregoria.

Earlier, back at San Antonio, I had promised Dean, as a joke, that I would get him a girl. It was a bet and a challenge. As I pulled up the car at the gas station near sunny Gregoria a kid came across the road on tattered feet, carrying an enormous windshield-shade, and wanted to know if I'd buy. "You like? Sixty peso. *Habla Español? Sesenta peso*. My name Victor."

"Nah," I said jokingly, "buy señorita."

"Sure, sure!" he cried excitedly. "I get you gurls, onnytime. Too hot now," he added with distaste. "No good gurls when hot day. Wait tonight. You like shade?"

I didn't want the shade but I wanted the girls. I woke up Dean. "Hey, man, I told you in Texas I'd get you a girl—all right, stretch your bones and wake up, boy; we've got girls waiting for us."

"What? what?" he cried, leaping up, haggard. "Where? where?"

"This boy Victor's going to show us where."

"Well, lessgo, lessgo!" Dean leaped out of the car and clasped Victor's hand. There was a group of other boys hanging around the station and grinning, half of them barefoot, all wearing floppy straw hats. "Man," said Dean to me, "ain't this a nice way to spend an afternoon. It's so much *cooler* than Denver poolhalls. Victor, you got gurls? Where? *A donde?*" he cried in Spanish. "Dig that, Sal, I'm speaking Spanish."

"Ask him if we can get any tea. Hey kid, you got ma-ree-wa-na?"

The kid nodded gravely. "Sho, onnytime, mon. Come with me."

"Hee! Whee! Hoo!" yelled Dean. He was wide awake and jumping up and down in that drowsy Mexican street. "Let's all go!" I was passing Lucky Strikes to the other boys. They were getting great pleasure out of us and especially Dean. They turned to one another with cupped hands and rattled off comments about the mad American cat. "Dig them, Sal, talking about us and digging. Oh my goodness, what a world!" Victor got in the car with us, and we lurched off. Stan Shephard had been sleeping soundly and woke up to this madness.

We drove way out to the desert the other side of town and

turned on a rutty dirt road that made the car bounce as never before. Up ahead was Victor's house. It sat on the edge of cactus flats overtopped by a few trees, just an adobe crackerbox, with a few men lounging around in the yard. "Who that?" cried Dean, all excited.

"Those my brothers. My mother there too. My sistair too. That my family. I married, I live downtown."

"What about your mother?" Dean flinched. "What she say about marijuana."

"Oh, she get it for me." And as we waited in the car Victor got out and loped over to the house and said a few words to an old lady, who promptly turned and went to the garden in back and began gathering dry fronds of marijuana that had been pulled off the plants and left to dry in the desert sun. Meanwhile Victor's brothers grinned from under a tree. They were coming over to meet us but it would take a while for them to get up and walk over. Victor came back, grinning sweetly.

"Man," said Dean, "that Victor is the sweetest, gonest, franticest little bangtail cat I've ever in all my life met. Just look at him, look at his cool slow walk. There's no need to hurry around here." A steady, insistent desert breeze blew into the car. It was very hot.

"You see how hot?" said Victor, sitting down with Dean in the front seat and pointing up at the burning roof of the Ford. "You have ma-ree-gwana and it no hot no more. You wait."

"Yes," said Dean, adjusting his dark glasses, "I wait. For sure, Victor m'boy."

Presently Victor's tall brother came ambling along with some weed piled on a page of newspaper. He dumped it on Victor's lap and leaned casually on the door of the car to nod and smile at us and say, "Hallo." Dean nodded and smiled pleasantly at *him*. Nobody talked; it was fine. Victor proceeded to roll the biggest bomber anybody ever saw. He rolled (using brown bag paper) what amounted to a tremendous Corona cigar of tea. It was huge. Dean stared at it, popeyed. Victor casually lit it and passed it around. To drag on this thing was like leaning over a chimney and inhaling. It blew into your throat in one great blast of heat. We held our breaths and all let out just about simultaneously. Instantly we were all high. The sweat froze on our foreheads and it was suddenly like the beach at Acapulco. I looked out the back window of the car, and another and the strangest of Victor's brothers—a tall Peruvian of an Indian with a sash over his shoulder—leaned grinning on a post, too bashful to come up and shake hands. It seemed the car was surrounded by brothers, for another one appeared on Dean's side. Then the strangest thing happened. Everybody became so high that usual formalities were dispensed with and the things of immediate interest were concentrated on, and now it was the strangeness of Americans and Mexicans blasting together on the desert and, more than that, the strangeness of seeing in close proximity the faces and pores of skins and calluses of fingers and general abashed cheekbones of another world. So the Indian brothers began talking about us in low voices and commenting; you saw them look, and size, and compare mutualities of impression, or correct and modify, "Yeh, yeh"; while Dean and Stan and I commented on them in English.

"Will you d-i-g that weird brother in the back that hasn't moved from that post and hasn't by one cut hair diminished the intensity of the glad *funny* bashfulness of his smile? And the one to my left here, older, more sure of himself but sad, like hung-up, like a bum even maybe, in town, while Victor is respectably married—he's like a gawddam Egyptian king, that you see. These guys are real *cats*. Ain't never seen anything like it. And they're talking and wondering about us, like see? Just like we are but with a difference of their own, their interest probably resolving around how we're dressed—same as ours, really—but the strangeness of the things we have in the car and the strange ways that we laugh so different from them, and maybe even the way we smell compared to them. Nevertheless I'd give my eye-teeth to know what they're saying about us." And Dean tried. "Hey Victor, man—what you brother say just then?"

Victor turned mournful high brown eyes on Dean. "Yeah, yeah."

"No, you didn't understand my question. What you boys talking about?"

"Oh," said Victor with great perturbation, "you no like this mar-gwana?"

"Oh, yeah, yes fine! What you *talk* about?"

"Talk? Yes, we talk. How you like Mexico?" It was hard to come around without a common language. And everybody grew quiet and cool and high again and just enjoyed the breeze from the desert and mused separate national and racial and personal high-eternity thoughts.

It was time for the girls. The brothers eased back to their station under the tree, the mother watched from her sunny doorway, and we slowly bounced back to town.

But now the bouncing was no longer unpleasant; it was the most pleasant and graceful billowy trip in the world, as over a blue sea, and Dean's face was suffused with an unnatural glow that was like gold as he told us to understand the springs of the car now for the first time and dig the ride. Up and down we bounced, and even Victor understood and laughed. Then he pointed left to show which way to go for the girls, and Dean, looking left with indescribable delight and leaning that way, pulled the wheel around and rolled us smoothly and surely to the goal, meanwhile listening to Victor's attempt to speak and saying grandly and magniloquently "Yes, of course! There's not a doubt in my mind! Decidedly, man! Oh, indeed! Why, pish, posh, you say the dearest things to me! Of course! Yes! Please go on!" To this Victor talked gravely and with magnificent Spanish eloquence. For a mad moment I thought Dean was understanding everything he said by sheer wild insight and sudden revelatory genius inconceivably inspired by his glowing happiness. In that moment, too, he looked so exactly like Franklin Delano Roosevelt—some delusion in my flaming eyes and floating brain—that I drew up in my seat and gasped with amazement. In myriad pricklings of heavenly radiation I had to struggle to see Dean's figure, and he looked like God. I was so high I had to lean my head back on the seat; the bouncing of the car sent shivers of ecstasy through me. The mere thought of looking out the window at Mexico—which was now something else in my mind—was like recoiling from some gloriously riddled glittering treasure-box that you're afraid to look at because of your eyes, they bend inward, the riches and the treasures are too much to take all at once. I gulped. I saw streams of gold pouring through the sky and right across the tattered roof of the poor old car, right across my eyeballs and indeed right inside them; it was everywhere. I looked out the window at the hot, sunny streets and saw a woman in a doorway and I thought she was listening to every word we said and nodding to herself—routine paranoiac visions due to tea. But the stream of gold continued. For a long time I lost consciousness in my lower mind of what we were doing and only came around sometime later when I looked up from fire and silence like waking from sleep to the world, or waking from void to a dream, and they told me we were parked outside Victor's house and he was already at the door of the car with his little baby son in his arms, showing him to us.

"You see my baby? Hees name Pérez, he six month age."

"Why," said Dean, his face still transfigured into a shower of supreme pleasure and even bliss, "he is the prettiest child I have ever seen. Look at those eyes. Now, Sal and Stan," he said, turning to us with a serious and tender air, "I want you par-ti-cu-lar-ly to see the eyes of this little Mexican boy who is the son of our wonderful friend Victor, and notice how he will come to manhood with his own particular soul bespeaking itself through the windows which are his eyes, and such lovely eyes surely do prophesy and indicate the loveliest of souls." It was a beautiful speech. And it was a beautiful baby. Victor mournfully looked down at his angel. We all wished we had a little son like that. So great was our intensity over the child's soul that he sensed something and began a grimace which led to bitter tears and some unknown sorrow that we had no means to soothe because it reached too far back into innumerable mysteries and time. We tried everything; Victor smothered him in his neck and rocked, Dean cooed, I reached over and stroked the baby's little arms. His bawls grew louder. "Ah," said Dean, "I'm awfully sorry, Victor, that we've made him sad."

"He is not sad, baby cry." In the doorway in back of Victor, too bashful to come out, was his little barefoot wife, with anxious tenderness waiting for the babe to be put back in her arms so brown and soft. Victor, having shown us his child, climbed back into the car and proudly pointed to the right.

"Yes," said Dean, and swung the car over and directed it through narrow Algerian streets with faces on all sides watching us with gentle wonder. We came to the whorehouse. It was a magnificent establishment of stucco in the golden sun. In the street, and leaning on the windowsills that opened into the whorehouse, were two cops, saggy-trousered, drowsy, bored, who gave us brief interested looks as we walked in, and stayed there the entire three hours that we cavorted under their noses, until we came out at dusk and at Victor's bidding gave them the equivalent of twenty-four cents each, just for the sake of form.

And in there we found the girls. Some of them were reclining on couches across the dance floor, some of them were boozing at the long bar to the right. In the center an arch led into small cubicle shacks that looked like the places where you put on your bathing suit at public municipal beaches. These shacks were in the sun of the court. Behind the bar was the proprietor, a young fellow who instantly ran out when we told him we wanted to hear mambo music and came back with a stack of records, mostly by Pérez Prado, and put them on over the loudspeaker. In an instant all the city of Gregoria could hear the good times going on at the Sala de Baile. In the hall itself the din of the music—for this is the real way to play a jukebox and what it was originally for—was so tremendous that it shattered Dean and Stan and me for a moment in the realization that we had never dared to play music as loud as we wanted, and this was how loud we wanted. It blew and shuddered directly at us. In a few minutes half that portion of town was at the windows, watching the *Americanos* dance with the gals. They all stood, side by side with the cops, on the dirt sidewalk, leaning in with indifference and casualness. "More Mambo Jambo," "Chattanooga de Mambo," "Mambo Numero Ocho"—all these tremendous numbers resounded and flared in the golden, mysterious afternoon like the sounds you expect to hear on the last day of the world and the Second Coming. The trumpets seemed so loud I thought they could hear them clear out in the desert, where the trumpets had originated anyway. The drums were mad. The mambo beat is the conga beat from Congo, the river of Africa and the world; it's really the world beat. Oom-*ta*, ta-poo-*poom*—oom-*ta*, ta-poo-*poom*. The piano montunos showered down on us from the speaker. The cries of the leader were like great gasps in the air. The final trumpet choruses that came with drum climaxes on conga and bongo drums, on the great mad Chattanooga record, froze Dean in his tracks for a moment till he shuddered and sweated; then when the trumpets bit the drowsy air with their quivering echoes, like a cavern's or a cave's, his eyes grew large and round as though seeing the devil, and he closed them tight. I myself was shaken like a puppet by it; I heard the trumpets flail the light I had seen and trembled in my boots.

On the fast "Mambo Jambo" we danced frantically with the girls. Through our deliriums we began to discern their varying personalities. They were great girls. Strangely the wildest one was half Indian, half white, and came from Venezuela, and only eighteen. She looked as if she came from a good family. What she was doing whoring in Mexico at that age and with that tender cheek and fair aspect, God knows. Some awful grief had driven her to it. She drank beyond all bounds. She threw down drinks when it seemed she was about to chuck up the last. She overturned glasses continually, the idea also being to make us spend as much money as possible. Wearing her flimsy housecoat in broad afternoon, she frantically danced with Dean and clung about his neck and begged and begged for everything. Dean was so stoned he didn't know what to start with, girls or mambo. They ran off to the lockers. I was set upon by a fat and uninteresting girl with a puppy dog, who got sore at me when I took a dislike to the dog because it kept trying to bite me. She compromised by putting it away in the back, but by the time she returned I had been hooked by another girl, better looking but not the best, who clung to my neck like a leech. I was trying to break loose to get at a sixteen-year-old colored girl who sat gloomily inspecting her navel through an opening in her short shirty dress across the hall. I couldn't do it. Stan had a fifteen-year-old girl with an almond-colored skin and a dress that was buttoned halfway down and halfway up. It was mad. A good twenty men leaned in that window, watching.

At one point the mother of the little colored girl—not colored, but dark—came in to hold a brief and mournful convocation with her daughter. When I saw that, I was too ashamed to try for the one I really wanted. I let the leech take me off to the back, where, as in a dream, to the din and roar of more loudspeakers inside, we made the bed bounce a half-hour. It was just a square room with wooden slats and no ceiling, ikon

in a corner, a washbasin in another. All up and down the dark
hall the girls were calling, "*Agua, agua caliente!*" which means
"hot water." Stan and Dean were also out of sight. My girl
charged thirty pesos, or about three dollars and a half, and
begged for an extra ten pesos and gave a long story about
something. I didn't know the value of Mexican money; for all
I knew I had a million pesos. I threw money at her. We rushed
back to dance. A greater crowd was gathered in the street. The
cops looked as bored as usual. Dean's pretty Venezuelan
dragged me through a door and into another strange bar that
apparently belonged to the whorehouse. Here a young bartender was talking and wiping glasses and an old man with
handlebar mustache sat discussing something earnestly. And
here too the mambo roared over another loudspeaker. It
seemed the whole world was turned on. Venezuela clung about
my neck and begged for drinks. The bartender wouldn't give
her one. She begged and begged, and when he gave it to her
she spilled it and this time not on purpose, for I saw the chagrin in her poor sunken lost eyes. "Take it easy, baby," I told
her. I had to support her on the stool; she kept slipping off.
I've never seen a drunker woman, and only eighteen. I bought
her another drink; she was tugging at my pants for mercy. She
gulped it up. I didn't have the heart to try her. My own girl was
about thirty and took care of herself better. With Venezuela
writhing and suffering in my arms, I had a longing to take her
in the back and undress her and only talk to her—this I told
myself. I was delirious with want of her and the other little
dark girl.

Poor Victor, all this time he stood on the brass rail of the bar
with his back to the counter and jumped up and down gladly
to see his three American friends cavort. We bought him drinks.
His eyes gleamed for a woman but he wouldn't accept any,
being faithful to his wife. Dean thrust money at him. In this
welter of madness I had an opportunity to see what Dean was
up to. He was so out of his mind he didn't know who I was
when I peered at his face. "Yeah, yeah!" is all he said. It seemed
it would never end. It was like a long, spectral Arabian dream
in the afternoon in another life—Ali Baba and the alleys and
the courtesans. Again I rushed off with my girl to her room;
Dean and Stan switched the girls they'd had before; and we

were out of sight a moment, and the spectators had to wait for the show to go on. The afternoon grew long and cool.

Soon it would be mysterious night in old gone Gregoria. The mambo never let up for a moment, it frenzied on like an endless journey in the jungle. I couldn't take my eyes off the little dark girl and the way, like a queen, she walked around and was even reduced by the sullen bartender to menial tasks such as bringing us drinks and sweeping the back. Of all the girls in there she needed the money most; maybe her mother had come to get money from her for her little infant sisters and brothers. Mexicans are poor. It never, never occurred to me just to approach her and give her some money. I have a feeling she would have taken it with a degree of scorn, and scorn from the likes of her made me flinch. In my madness I was actually in love with her for the few hours it all lasted; it was the same unmistakable ache and stab across the mind, the same sighs, the same pain, and above all the same reluctance and fear to approach. Strange that Dean and Stan also failed to approach her; her unimpeachable dignity was the thing that made her poor in a wild old whorehouse, and think of that. At one point I saw Dean leaning like a statue toward her, ready to fly, and befuddlement cross his face as she glanced coolly and imperiously his way and he stopped rubbing his belly and gaped and finally bowed his head. For she was the queen.

Now Victor suddenly clutched at our arms in the furor and made frantic signs.

"What's the matter?" He tried everything to make us understand. Then he ran to the bar and grabbed the check from the bartender, who scowled at him, and took it to us to see. The bill was over three hundred pesos, or thirty-six American dollars, which is a lot of money in any whorehouse. Still we couldn't sober up and didn't want to leave, and though we were all run out we still wanted to hang around with our lovely girls in this strange Arabian paradise we had finally found at the end of the hard, hard road. But night was coming and we had to get on to the end; and Dean saw that, and began frowning and thinking and trying to straighten himself out, and finally I broached the idea of leaving once and for all. "So much ahead of us, man, it won't make any difference."

"That's right!" cried Dean, glassy-eyed, and turned to his

Venezuelan. She had finally passed out and lay on a wooden bench with her white legs protruding from the silk. The gallery in the window took advantage of the show; behind them red shadows were beginning to creep, and somewhere I heard a baby wail in a sudden lull, remembering I was in Mexico after all and not in a pornographic hasheesh daydream in heaven.

We staggered out; we had forgotten Stan; we ran back in to get him and found him charmingly bowing to the new evening whores, who had just come in for night shift. He wanted to start all over again. When he is drunk he lumbers like a man ten feet tall and when he is drunk he can't be dragged away from women. Moreover women cling to him like ivy. He insisted on staying and trying some of the newer, stranger, more proficient señoritas. Dean and I pounded him on the back and dragged him out. He waved profuse good-bys to everybody— the girls, the cops, the crowds, the children in the street outside; he blew kisses in all directions to ovations of Gregoria and staggered proudly among the gangs and tried to speak to them and communicate his joy and love of everything this fine afternoon of life. Everybody laughed; some slapped him on the back. Dean rushed over and paid the policemen the four pesos and shook hands and grinned and bowed with them. Then he jumped in the car, and the girls we had known, even Venezuela, who was wakened for the farewell, gathered around the car, huddling in their flimsy duds, and chattered good-bys and kissed us, and Venezuela even began to weep—though not for us, we knew, not altogether for us, yet enough and good enough. My dusky darling love had disappeared in the shadows inside. It was all over. We pulled out and left joys and celebrations over hundreds of pesos behind us, and it didn't seem like a bad day's work. The haunting mambo followed us a few blocks. It was all over. "Good-by, Gregoria!" cried Dean, blowing it a kiss.

Victor was proud of us and proud of himself. "Now you like bath?" he asked. Yes, we all wanted wonderful bath.

And he directed us to the strangest thing in the world: it was an ordinary American-type bathhouse one mile out of town on the highway, full of kids splashing in a pool and showers inside a stone building for a few centavos a crack, with soap and towel from the attendant. Besides this, it was also a sad kiddy park with swings and a broken-down merry-go-round, and in the fading red sun it seemed so strange and so beautiful. Stan and I got towels and jumped right into ice-cold showers inside and came out refreshed and new. Dean didn't bother with a shower, and we saw him far across the sad park, strolling arm in arm with good Victor and chatting volubly and pleasantly and even leaning excitedly toward him to make a point, and pounding his fist. Then they resumed the arm-in-arm position and strolled. The time was coming to say good-by to Victor, so Dean was taking the opportunity to have moments alone with him and to inspect the park and get his views on things in general and in all dig him as only Dean could do.

Victor was very sad now that we had to go. "You come back Gregoria, see me?"

"Sure, man!" said Dean. He even promised to take Victor back to the States if he so wished it. Victor said he would have to mull this over.

"I got wife and kid—ain't got a money—I see." His sweet polite smile glowed in the redness as we waved to him from the car. Behind him were the sad park and the children.

6

Immediately outside Gregoria the road began to drop, great trees arose on each side, and in the trees as it grew dark we heard the great roar of billions of insects that sounded like one continuous high-screeching cry. "Whoo!" said Dean, and he turned on his headlights and they weren't working. "What! what! damn now what?" And he punched and fumed at his dashboard. "Oh, my, we'll have to drive through the jungle without lights, think of the horror of that, the only time I'll see is when another car comes by and there just *aren't* any cars! And of course no lights? Oh, what'll we do, dammit?"

"Let's just drive. Maybe we ought to go back, though?"

"No, never-never! Let's go on. I can barely see the road. We'll make it." And now we shot in inky darkness through the scream of insects, and the great, rank, almost rotten smell descended, and we remembered and realized that the map

indicated just after Gregoria the beginning of the Tropic of
Cancer. "We're in a new tropic! No wonder the smell! Smell
it!" I stuck my head out the window; bugs smashed at my face;
a great screech rose the moment I cocked my ear to the wind.
Suddenly our lights were working again and they poked ahead,
illuminating the lonely road that ran between solid walls of
drooping, snaky trees as high as a hundred feet.

"Son-of-a-*bitch*!" yelled Stan in the back. "Hot *damn*!" He
was still so high. We suddenly realized he was still high and the
jungle and troubles made no difference to his happy soul. We
began laughing, all of us.

"To hell with it! We'll just throw ourselves on the gawd-
damn jungle, we'll sleep in it tonight, let's go!" yelled Dean.
"Ole Stan is right. Ole Stan don't care! He's so high on those
women and that tea and that crazy out-of-this-world impossi-
ble-to-absorb mambo blasting so loud that my eardrums still
beat to it—whee! he's so high he knows what he's doing!" We
took off our T-shirts and roared through the jungle, barechested. No towns, nothing, lost jungle, miles and miles, and
down-going, getting hotter, the insects screaming louder, the
vegetation growing higher, the smell ranker and hotter until
we began to get used to it and like it. "I'd just like to get
naked and roll and roll in that jungle," said Dean. "No, hell,
man, that's what I'm going to do soon's I find a good spot."
And suddenly Limón appeared before us, a jungle town, a few
brown lights, dark shadows, enormous skies overhead, and a
cluster of men in front of a jumble of woodshacks—a tropical
crossroads.

We stopped in the unimaginable softness. It was as hot as the
inside of a baker's oven on a June night in New Orleans. All up
and down the street whole families were sitting around in the
dark, chatting; occasional girls came by, but extremely young
and only curious to see what we looked like. They were barefoot and dirty. We leaned on the wooden porch of a broken-
down general store with sacks of flour and fresh pineapple
rotting with flies on the counter. There was one oil lamp in
here, and outside a few more brown lights, and the rest all
black, black, black. Now of course we were so tired we had to
sleep at once and moved the car a few yards down a dirt road
to the backside of town. It was so incredibly hot it was impos-

sible to sleep. So Dean took a blanket and laid it out on the soft, hot sand in the road and flopped out. Stan was stretched on the front seat of the Ford with both doors open for a draft, but there wasn't even the faintest puff of a wind. I, in the back seat, suffered in a pool of sweat. I got out of the car and stood swaying in the blackness. The whole town had instantly gone to bed; the only noise now was barking dogs. How could I ever sleep? Thousands of mosquitoes had already bitten all of us on chest and arms and ankles. Then a bright idea came to me: I jumped up on the steel roof of the car and stretched out flat on my back. Still there was no breeze, but the steel had an element of coolness in it and dried my back of sweat, clotting up thousands of dead bugs into cakes on my skin, and I realized the jungle takes you over and you become it. Lying on the top of the car with my face to the black sky was like lying in a closed trunk on a summer night. For the first time in my life the weather was not something that touched me, that caressed me, froze or sweated me, but became me. The atmosphere and I became the same. Soft infinitesimal showers of microscopic bugs fanned down on my face as I slept, and they were extremely pleasant and soothing. The sky was starless, utterly unseen and heavy. I could lie there all night long with my face exposed to the heavens, and it would do me no more harm than a velvet drape drawn over me. The dead bugs mingled with my blood; the live mosquitoes exchanged further portions; I began to tingle all over and to smell of the rank, hot, and rotten jungle, all over from hair and face to feet and toes. Of course I was barefoot. To minimize the sweat I put on my bug-smeared T-shirt and lay back again. A huddle of darkness on the blacker road showed where Dean was sleeping. I could hear him snoring. Stan was snoring too.

Occasionally a dim light flashed in town, and this was the sheriff making his rounds with a weak flashlight and mumbling to himself in the jungle night. Then I saw his light jiggling toward us and heard his footfalls coming soft on the mats of sand and vegetation. He stopped and flashed the car. I sat up and looked at him. In a quivering, almost querulous, and extremely tender voice he said, "*Dormiendo?*" indicating Dean in the road. I knew this meant "sleep."

"*Si, dormiendo.*"

"*Bueno, bueno,*" he said to himself and with reluctance and sadness turned away and went back to his lonely rounds. Such lovely policemen God hath never wrought in America. No suspicions, no fuss, no bother: he was the guardian of the sleeping town, period.

I went back to my bed of steel and stretched out with my arms spread. I didn't even know if branches or open sky were directly above me, and it made no difference. I opened my mouth to it and drew deep breaths of jungle atmosphere. It was not air, never air, but the palpable and living emanation of trees and swamp. I stayed awake. Roosters began to crow the dawn across the brakes somewhere. Still no air, no breeze, no dew, but the same Tropic of Cancer heaviness held us all pinned to earth, where we belonged and tingled. There was no sign of dawn in the skies. Suddenly I heard the dogs barking furiously across the dark, and then I heard the faint clip-clop of a horse's hooves. It came closer and closer. What kind of mad rider in the night would this be? Then I saw an apparition: a wild horse, white as a ghost, came trotting down the road directly toward Dean. Behind him the dogs yammered and contended. I couldn't see them, they were dirty old jungle dogs, but the horse was white as snow and immense and almost phosphorescent and easy to see. I felt no panic for Dean. The horse saw him and trotted right by his head, passed the car like a ship, whinnied softly, and continued on through town, bedeviled by the dogs, and clip-clopped back to the jungle on the other side, and all I heard was the faint hoofbeat fading away in the woods. The dogs subsided and sat to lick themselves. What was this horse? What myth and ghost, what spirit? I told Dean about it when he woke up. He thought I'd been dreaming. Then he recalled faintly dreaming of a white horse, and I told him it had been no dream. Stan Shephard slowly woke up. The faintest movements, and we were sweating profusely again. It was still pitch dark. "Let's start the car and blow some air!" I cried. "I'm dying of heat."

"Right!" We roared out of town and continued along the mad highway with our hair flying. Dawn came rapidly in a gray haze, revealing dense swamps sunk on both sides, with tall, forlorn, viny trees leaning and bowing over tangled bottoms. We bowled right along the railroad tracks for a while. The strange radio-station antenna of Ciudad Mante appeared ahead, as if we were in Nebraska. We found a gas station and loaded the tank just as the last of the jungle-night bugs hurled themselves in a black mass against the bulbs and fell fluttering at our feet in huge wriggly groups, some of them with wings a good four inches long, others frightful dragonflies big enough to eat a bird, and thousands of immense yangling mosquitoes and unnamable spidery insects of all sorts. I hopped up and down on the pavement for fear of them; I finally ended up in the car with my feet in my hands, looking fearfully at the ground where they swarmed around our wheels. "Lessgo!" I yelled. Dean and Stan weren't perturbed at all by the bugs; they calmly drank a couple of bottles of Mission Orange and kicked them away from the water cooler. Their shirts and pants, like mine, were soaked in the blood and black of thousands of dead bugs. We smelled our clothes deeply.

"You know, I'm beginning to like this smell," said Stan. "I can't smell myself any more."

"It's a strange, good smell," said Dean. "I'm not going to change my shirt till Mexico City, I want to take it all in and remember it." So off we roared again, creating air for our hot, caked faces.

Then the mountains loomed ahead, all green. After this climb we would be on the great central plateau again and ready to roll ahead to Mexico City. In no time at all we soared to an elevation of five thousand feet among misty passes that overlooked steaming yellow rivers a mile below. It was the great River Moctezuma. The Indians along the road began to be extremely weird. They were a nation in themselves, mountain Indians, shut off from everything else but the Pan-American Highway. They were short and squat and dark, with bad teeth; they carried immense loads on their backs. Across enormous vegetated ravines we saw patchworks of agriculture on steep slopes. They walked up and down those slopes and worked the crops. Dean drove the car five miles an hour to see. "Whooee, this I never thought existed!" High on the highest peak, as great as any Rocky Mountain peak, we saw bananas growing. Dean got out of the car to point, to stand around rubbing his belly. We were on a ledge where a little thatched hut suspended itself over the precipice of the world. The sun created golden hazes that obscured the Moctezuma, now more than a mile below.

In the yard in front of the hut a little three-year-old Indian girl stood with her finger in her mouth, watching us with big brown eyes. "She's probably never seen anybody parked here before in her entire life!" breathed Dean. "Hel-lo, little girl. How are you? Do you like us?" The little girl looked away bashfully and pouted. We began to talk and she again examined us with finger in mouth. "Gee, I wish there was something I could give her! *Think of it*, being born and living on this ledge—this ledge representing all you know of life. Her father is probably groping down the ravine with a rope and getting his pineapples out of a cave and hacking wood at an eighty-degree angle with all the bottom below. She'll never, never leave here and know anything about the outside world. It's a nation. Think of the wild chief they must have! They probably, off the road, over that bluff, miles back, must be even wilder and stranger, yeah, because the Pan-American Highway partially civilizes this nation on this road. Notice the beads of sweat on her brow," Dean pointed out with a grimace of pain. "It's not the kind of sweat we have, it's oily and it's *always there* because it's *always* hot the year round and she knows nothing of non-sweat, she was born with sweat and dies with sweat." The sweat on her little brow was heavy, sluggish; it didn't run; it just stood there and gleamed like a fine olive oil. "What that must do to their souls! How different they must be in their private concerns and evaluations and wishes!" Dean drove on with his mouth hanging in awe, ten miles an hour, desirous to see every possible human being on the road. We climbed and climbed.

As we climbed, the air grew cooler and the Indian girls on the road wore shawls over their heads and shoulders. They hailed us desperately; we stopped to see. They wanted to sell us little pieces of rock crystal. Their great brown, innocent eyes looked into ours with such soulful intensity that not one of us had the slightest sexual thought about them; moreover they were very young, some of them eleven and looking almost thirty. "Look at those eyes!" breathed Dean. They were like the eyes of the Virgin Mother when she was a child. We saw in them the tender and forgiving gaze of Jesus. And they stared unflinching into ours. We rubbed our nervous blue eyes and looked again. Still they penetrated us with sorrowful and hypnotic gleam. When they talked they suddenly became frantic and almost silly. In their silence they were themselves. "They've only *recently* learned to sell these crystals, since the highway was built about ten years back—up until that time this entire nation must have been *silent*!"

The girls yammered around the car. One particularly soulful child gripped at Dean's sweaty arm. She yammered in Indian. "Ah yes, ah yes, dear one," said Dean tenderly and almost sadly. He got out of the car and went fishing around in the battered trunk in the back—the same old tortured American trunk— and pulled out a wristwatch. He showed it to the child. She whimpered with glee. The others crowded around with amazement. Then Dean poked in the little girl's hand for "the sweetest and purest and smallest crystal she has personally picked from the mountain for me." He found one no bigger than a berry. And he handed her the wristwatch dangling. Their mouths rounded like the mouths of chorister children. The lucky little girl squeezed it to her ragged breaststrobes. They stroked Dean and thanked him. He stood among them with his ragged face to the sky, looking for the next and highest and final pass, and seemed like the Prophet that had come to them. He got back in the car. They hated to see us go. For the longest time, as we mounted a straight pass, they waved and ran after us. We made a turn and never saw them again, and they were still running after us. "Ah, this breaks my heart!" cried Dean, punching his chest. "How far do they carry out these loyalties and wonders! What's going to happen to them? Would they try to follow the car all the way to Mexico City if we drove slow enough?"

"Yes," I said, for I knew.

We came into the dizzying heights of the Sierra Madre Oriental. The banana trees gleamed golden in the haze. Great fogs yawned beyond stone walls along the precipice. Below, the Moctezuma was a thin golden thread in a green jungle mat. Strange crossroad towns on top of the world rolled by, with shawled Indians watching us from under hatbrims and *rebozos*. Life was dense, dark, ancient. They watched Dean, serious and insane at his raving wheel, with eyes of hawks. All had their hands outstretched. They had come down from the back mountains and higher places to hold forth their hands for something they thought civilization could offer, and they never dreamed the sadness and the poor broken delusion of it. They didn't know that a bomb had come that could crack all our bridges and roads and reduce them to jumbles, and we would be as poor as they someday, and stretching out our hands in the same, same way. Our broken Ford, old thirties upgoing America Ford, rattled through them and vanished in dust.

We had reached the approaches of the last plateau. Now the sun was golden, the air keen blue, and the desert with its occasional rivers a riot of sandy, hot space and sudden Biblical tree shade. Now Dean was sleeping and Stan driving. The shepherds appeared, dressed as in first times, in long flowing robes, the women carrying golden bundles of flax, the men staves. Under great trees on the shimmering desert the shepherds sat and convened, and the sheep moiled in the sun and raised dust beyond. "Man, man," I yelled to Dean, "wake up and see the shepherds, wake up and see the golden world that Jesus came from, with your own eyes you can tell!"

He shot his head up from the seat, saw one glimpse of it all in the fading red sun, and dropped back to sleep. When he woke up he described it to me in detail and said, "Yes, man, I'm glad you told me to look. Oh, Lord, what shall I do? Where will I go?" He rubbed his belly, he looked to heaven with red eyes, he almost wept.

The end of our journey impended. Great fields stretched on both sides of us; a noble wind blew across the occasional immense tree groves and over old missions turning salmon pink in the late sun. The clouds were close and huge and rose. "Mexico City by dusk!" We'd made it, a total of nineteen hundred miles from the afternoon yards of Denver to these vast and Biblical areas of the world, and now we were about to reach the end of the road.

"Shall we change our insect T-shirts?"

"Naw, let's wear them into town, hell's bells." And we drove into Mexico City.

A brief mountain pass took us suddenly to a height from which we saw all of Mexico City stretched out in its volcanic crater below and spewing city smokes and early dusklights.

Down to it we zoomed, down Insurgentes Boulevard, straight toward the heart of town at Reforma. Kids played soccer in enormous sad fields and threw up dust. Taxi-drivers overtook us and wanted to know if we wanted girls. No, we didn't want girls now. Long, ragged adobe slums stretched out on the plain; we saw lonely figures in the dimming alleys. Soon night would come. Then the city roared in and suddenly we were passing crowded cafés and theaters and many lights. Newsboys yelled at us. Mechanics slouched by, barefoot, with wrenches and rags. Mad barefoot Indian drivers cut across us and surrounded us and tooted and made frantic traffic. The noise was incredible. No mufflers are used on Mexican cars. Horns are batted with glee continual. "Whee!" yelled Dean. "Look out!" He staggered the car through the traffic and played with everybody. He drove like an Indian. He got on a circular glorietta drive on Reforma Boulevard and rolled around it with its eight spokes shooting cars at us from all directions, left, right, *izquierda*, dead ahead, and yelled and jumped with joy. "This is traffic I've always dreamed of! Everybody *goes!*" An ambulance came balling through. American ambulances dart and weave through traffic with siren blowing; the great world-wide Fellahin Indian ambulances merely come through at eighty miles an hour in the city streets, and everybody just has to get out of the way and they don't pause for anybody or any circumstances and fly straight through. We saw it reeling out of sight on skittering wheels in the breaking-up moil of dense downtown traffic. The drivers were Indians. People, even old ladies, ran for buses that never stopped. Young Mexico City businessmen made bets and ran by squads for buses and athletically jumped them. The bus-drivers were barefoot, sneering and insane, and sat low and squat in T-shirts at the low, enormous wheels. Ikons burned over them. The lights in the buses were brown and greenish, and dark faces were lined on wooden benches.

In downtown Mexico City thousands of hipsters in floppy straw hats and long-lapeled jackets over bare chests padded along the main drag, some of them selling crucifixes and weed in the alleys, some of them kneeling in beat chapels next to Mexican burlesque shows in sheds. Some alleys were rubble, with open sewers, and little doors led to closet-size bars stuck in adobe walls. You had to jump over a ditch to get your drink, and in the bottom of the ditch was the ancient lake of the Aztec. You came out of the bar with your back to the wall and edged back to the street. They served coffee mixed with rum and nutmeg. Mambo blared from everywhere. Hundreds of whores lined themselves along the dark and narrow streets and their sorrowful eyes gleamed at us in the night. We wandered in a frenzy and a dream. We ate beautiful steaks for forty-eight cents in a strange tiled Mexican cafeteria with generations of marimba musicians standing at one immense marimba—also wandering singing guitarists, and old men on corners blowing trumpets. You went by the sour stink of pulque saloons; they gave you a water glass of cactus juice in there, two cents. Nothing stopped; the streets were alive all night. Beggars slept wrapped in advertising posters torn off fences. Whole families of them sat on the sidewalk, playing little flutes and chuckling in the night. Their bare feet stuck out, their dim candles burned, all Mexico was one vast Bohemian camp. On corners old women cut up the boiled heads of cows and wrapped morsels in tortillas and served them with hot sauce on newspaper napkins. This was the great and final wild uninhibited Fellahin-childlike city that we knew we would find at the end of the road. Dean walked through with his arms hanging zombie-like at his sides, his mouth open, his eyes gleaming, and conducted a ragged and holy tour that lasted till dawn in a field with a boy in a straw hat who laughed and chatted with us and wanted to play catch, for nothing ever ended.

Then I got fever and became delirious and unconscious. Dysentery. I looked up out of the dark swirl of my mind and I knew I was on a bed eight thousand feet above sea level, on a roof of the world, and I knew that I had lived a whole life and many others in the poor atomistic husk of my flesh, and I had all the dreams. And I saw Dean bending over the kitchen table. It was several nights later and he was leaving Mexico City already. "What you doin, man?" I moaned.

"Poor Sal, poor Sal, got sick. Stan'll take care of you. Now listen to hear if you can in your sickness: I got my divorce from Camille down here and I'm driving back to Inez in New York tonight if the car holds out."

"All that again?" I cried.

"All that again, good buddy. Gotta get back to my life. Wish I could stay with you. Pray I can come back." I grabbed the cramps in my belly and groaned. When I looked up again bold noble Dean was standing with his old broken trunk and looking down at me. I didn't know who he was any more, and he knew this, and sympathized, and pulled the blanket over my shoulders. "Yes, yes, yes, I've got to go now. Old fever Sal, good-by." And he was gone. Twelve hours later in my sorrowful fever I finally came to understand that he was gone. By that time he was driving back alone through those banana mountains, this time at night.

When I got better I realized what a rat he was, but then I had to understand the impossible complexity of his life, how he had to leave me there, sick, to get on with his wives and woes. "Okay, old Dean, I'll say nothing."

Part Five

DEAN drove from Mexico City and saw Victor again in Gregoria and pushed that old car all the way to Lake Charles, Louisiana, before the rear end finally dropped on the road as he had always known it would. So he wired Inez for airplane fare and flew the rest of the way. When he arrived in New York with the divorce papers in his hands, he and Inez immediately went to Newark and got married; and that night, telling her everything was all right and not to worry, and making logics where there was nothing but inestimable sorrowful sweats, he jumped on a bus and roared off again across the awful continent to San Francisco to rejoin Camille and the two baby girls. So now he was three times married, twice divorced, and living with his second wife.

In the fall I myself started back home from Mexico City and one night just over Laredo border in Dilley, Texas, I was standing on the hot road underneath an arc-lamp with the summer moths smashing into it when I heard the sound of footsteps from the darkness beyond, and lo, a tall old man with flowing white hair came clomping by with a pack on his back, and when he saw me as he passed, he said, "*Go moan for man,*" and clomped on back to his dark. Did this mean that I should at last go on my pilgrimage on foot on the dark roads around America? I struggled and hurried to New York, and one night I was standing in a dark street in Manhattan and called up to the window of a loft where I thought my friends were having a party. But a pretty girl stuck her head out the window and said, "Yes? Who is it?"

"Sal Paradise," I said, and heard my name resound in the sad and empty street.

"Come on up," she called. "I'm making hot chocolate." So I went up and there she was, the girl with the pure and innocent dear eyes that I had always searched for and for so long. We agreed to love each other madly. In the winter we planned to migrate to San Francisco, bringing all our beat furniture and broken belongings with us in a jalopy panel truck. I wrote

274

to Dean and told him. He wrote back a huge letter eighteen thousand words long, all about his young years in Denver, and said he was coming to get me and personally select the old truck himself and drive us home. We had six weeks to save up the money for the truck and began working and counting every cent. And suddenly Dean arrived anyway, five and a half weeks in advance, and nobody had any money to go through with the plan.

I was taking a walk in the middle of the night and came back to my girl to tell her what I thought about during my walk. She stood in the dark little pad with a strange smile. I told her a number of things and suddenly I noticed the hush in the room and looked around and saw a battered book on the radio. I knew it was Dean's high-eternity-in-the-afternoon Proust. As in a dream I saw him tiptoe in from the dark hall in his stocking feet. He couldn't talk any more. He hopped and laughed, he stuttered and fluttered his hands and said, "Ah—ah—you must listen to hear." We listened, all ears. But he forgot what he wanted to say. "Really listen—ahem. Look, dear Sal—sweet Laura—I've come—I'm gone—but wait—ah yes." And he stared with rocky sorrow into his hands. "Can't talk no more—do you understand that it is—or might be— But listen!" We all listened. He was listening to sounds in the night. "Yes!" he whispered with awe. "But you see—no need to talk any more—and further."

"But why did you come so soon, Dean?"

"Ah," he said, looking at me as if for the first time, "so soon, yes. We—we'll know—that is, I don't know. I came on the railroad pass—cabooses—old hard-bench coaches—Texas—played flute and wooden sweet potato all the way." He took out his new wooden flute. He played a few squeaky notes on it and jumped up and down in his stocking feet. "See?" he said. "But of course, Sal, I can talk as soon as ever and have many things to say to you in fact with my own little bangtail mind I've been reading and reading this gone Proust all the way across the country and digging a great number of things I'll never have TIME to tell you about and we STILL haven't talked of Mexico and our parting there in fever—but no need to talk. Absolutely, now, yes?"

"All right, we won't talk." And he started telling the story of what he did in LA on the way over in every possible detail, how he visited a family, had dinner, talked to the father, the sons, the sisters—what they looked like, what they ate, their furnishings, their thoughts, their interests, their very souls; it took him three hours of detailed elucidation, and having concluded this he said, "Ah, but you see what I wanted to REALLY tell you—much later—Arkansas, crossing on train—playing flute—play cards with boys, my dirty deck—won money, blew sweet-potato solo—for sailors. Long long awful trip five days and five nights just to SEE you, Sal."

"What about Camille?"

"Gave permission of course—waiting for me. Camille and I all straight forever-and-ever . . ."

"And Inez?"

"I—I—I want her to come back to Frisco with me live other side of town—don't you think? Don't know why I came." Later he said in a sudden moment of gaping wonder, "Well and yes, of course, I wanted to see your sweet girl and you—glad of you—love you as ever." He stayed in New York three days and hastily made preparations to get back on the train with his railroad passes and again recross the continent, five days and five nights in dusty coaches and hardbench crummies, and of course we had no money for a truck and couldn't go back with him. With Inez he spent one night explaining and sweating and fighting, and she threw him out. A letter came for him, care of me. I saw it. It was from Camille. "My heart broke when I saw you go across the tracks with your bag. I pray and pray you get back safe. . . . I do want Sal and his friend to come and live on the same street. . . . I know you'll make it but I can't help worrying—now that we've decided everything. . . . Dear Dean, it's the end of the first half of the century. Welcome with love and kisses to spend the other half with us. We all wait for you. [Signed] Camille, Amy, and Little Joanie." So Dean's life was settled with his most constant, most embittered, and best-knowing wife Camille, and I thanked God for him.

The last time I saw him it was under sad and strange circumstances. Remi Boncœur had arrived in New York after having gone around the world several times in ships. I wanted him to meet and know Dean. They did meet, but Dean couldn't talk any more and said nothing, and Remi turned away. Remi had gotten tickets for the Duke Ellington concert at the Metropolitan Opera and insisted Laura and I come with him and his girl. Remi was fat and sad now but still the eager and formal gentleman, and he wanted to do things the *right way*, as he emphasized. So he got his bookie to drive us to the concert in a Cadillac. It was a cold winter night. The Cadillac was parked and ready to go. Dean stood outside the windows with his bag, ready to go to Penn Station and on across the land.

"Good-by, Dean," I said. "I sure wish I didn't have to go to the concert."

"D'you think I can ride to Fortieth Street with you?" he whispered. "Want to be with you as much as possible, m'boy, and besides it's so durned cold in this here New Yawk . . ." I whispered to Remi. No, he wouldn't have it, he liked me but he didn't like my idiot friends. I wasn't going to start all over again ruining his planned evenings as I had done at Alfred's in San Francisco in 1947 with Roland Major.

"Absolutely out of the question, Sal!" Poor Remi, he had a special necktie made for this evening; on it was painted a replica of the concert tickets, and the names Sal and Laura and Remi and Vicki, the girl, together with a series of sad jokes and some of his favorite sayings such as "You can't teach the old maestro a new tune."

So Dean couldn't ride uptown with us and the only thing I could do was sit in the back of the Cadillac and wave at him. The bookie at the wheel also wanted nothing to do with Dean. Dean, ragged in a motheaten overcoat he brought specially for the freezing temperatures of the East, walked off alone, and the last I saw of him he rounded the corner of Seventh Avenue, eyes on the street ahead, and bent to it again. Poor little Laura, my baby, to whom I'd told everything about Dean, began almost to cry.

"Oh, we shouldn't let him go like this. What'll we do?"

Old Dean's gone, I thought, and out loud I said, "He'll be all right." And off we went to the sad and disinclined concert for which I had no stomach whatever and all the time I was thinking of Dean and how he got back on the train and rode over three thousand miles over that awful land and never knew why he had come anyway, except to see me.

So in America when the sun goes down and I sit on the old broken-down river pier watching the long, long skies over New Jersey and sense all that raw land that rolls in one unbelievable huge bulge over to the West Coast, and all that road going, all the people dreaming in the immensity of it, and in Iowa I know by now the children must be crying in the land where they let the children cry, and tonight the stars'll be out, and don't you know that God is Pooh Bear? the evening star must be drooping and shedding her sparkler dims on the prairie, which is just before the coming of complete night that blesses the earth, darkens all rivers, cups the peaks and folds the final shore in, and nobody, nobody knows what's going to happen to anybody besides the forlorn rags of growing old, I think of Dean Moriarty, I even think of Old Dean Moriarty the father we never found, I think of Dean Moriarty.

THE DHARMA BUMS

Dedicated to Han Shan

I

HOPPING a freight out of Los Angeles at high noon one day in late September 1955 I got on a gondola and lay down with my duffel bag under my head and my knees crossed and contemplated the clouds as we rolled north to Santa Barbara. It was a local and I intended to sleep on the beach at Santa Barbara that night and catch either another local to San Luis Obispo the next morning or the firstclass freight all the way to San Francisco at seven p.m. Somewhere near Camarillo where Charlie Parker'd been mad and relaxed back to normal health, a thin old little bum climbed into my gondola as we headed into a siding to give a train right of way and looked surprised to see me there. He established himself at the other end of the gondola and lay down, facing me, with his head on his own miserably small pack and said nothing. By and by they blew the highball whistle after the eastbound freight had smashed through on the main line and we pulled out as the air got colder and fog began to blow from the sea over the warm valleys of the coast. Both the little bum and I, after unsuccessful attempts to huddle on the cold steel in wraparounds, got up and paced back and forth and jumped and flapped arms at each our end of the gon. Pretty soon we headed into another siding at a small railroad town and I figured I needed a poorboy of Tokay wine to complete the cold dusk run to Santa Barbara. "Will you watch my pack while I run over there and get a bottle of wine?"

"Sure thing."

I jumped over the side and ran across Highway 101 to the store, and bought, besides wine, a little bread and candy. I ran back to my freight train which had another fifteen minutes to wait in the now warm sunny scene. But it was late afternoon and bound to get cold soon. The little bum was sitting cross-legged at his end before a pitiful repast of one can of sardines. I took pity on him and went over and said, "How about a little wine to warm you up? Maybe you'd like some bread and cheese with your sardines."

"Sure thing." He spoke from far away inside a little meek voice-box afraid or unwilling to assert himself. I'd bought the cheese three days ago in Mexico City before the long cheap bus trip across Zacatecas and Durango and Chihuahua two thousand long miles to the border at El Paso. He ate the cheese and bread and drank the wine with gusto and gratitude. I was pleased. I reminded myself of the line in the Diamond Sutra that says, "Practice charity without holding in mind any conceptions about charity, for charity after all is just a word." I was very devout in those days and was practicing my religious devotions almost to perfection. Since then I've become a little hypocritical about my lip-service and a little tired and cynical. Because now I am grown so old and neutral. . . . But then I really believed in the reality of charity and kindness and humility and zeal and neutral tranquillity and wisdom and ecstasy, and I believed that I was an oldtime bhikku in modern clothes wandering the world (usually the immense triangular arc of New York to Mexico City to San Francisco) in order to turn the wheel of the True Meaning, or Dharma, and gain merit for myself as a future Buddha (Awakener) and as a future Hero in Paradise. I had not met Japhy Ryder yet, I was about to the next week, or heard anything about "Dharma Bums" although at this time I was a perfect Dharma Bum myself and considered myself a religious wanderer. The little bum in the gondola solidified all my beliefs by warming up to the wine and talking and finally whipping out a tiny slip of paper which contained a prayer by Saint Teresa announcing that after her death she will return to the earth by showering it with roses from heaven, forever, for all living creatures.

"Where did you get this?" I asked.

"Oh, I cut it out of a reading-room magazine in Los Angeles couple of years ago. I always carry it with me."

"And you squat in boxcars and read it?"

"Most every day." He talked not much more than this, didn't amplify on the subject of Saint Teresa, and was very modest about his religion and told me little about his personal life. He is the kind of thin quiet little bum nobody pays much attention to even in Skid Row, let alone Main Street. If a cop hustled him off, he hustled, and disappeared, and if yard dicks were around in bigcity yards when a freight was pulling out, chances are they never got a sight of the little man hiding in the weeds and hopping on in the shadows. When I told him I was planning to hop the Zipper firstclass freight train the next night he said, "Ah you mean the Midnight Ghost."

"Is that what you call the Zipper?"

"You musta been a railroad man on that railroad."

"I was, I was a brakeman on the S.P."

"Well, we bums call it the Midnight Ghost cause you get on it at L.A. and nobody sees you till you get to San Francisco in the morning the thing flies so fast."

"Eighty miles an hour on the straightaways, pap."

"That's right but it gits mighty cold at night when you're flyin up that coast north of Gavioty and up around Surf."

"Surf that's right, then the mountains down south of Margarita."

"Margarity, that's right, but I've rid that Midnight Ghost more times'n I can count I guess."

"How many years been since you've been home?"

"More years than I care to count I guess. Ohio was where I was from."

But the train got started, the wind grew cold and foggy again, and we spent the following hour and a half doing everything in our power and will power not to freeze and chatter-teeth too much. I'd huddle and meditate on the warmth, the actual warmth of God, to obviate the cold; then I'd jump up and flap my arms and legs and sing. But the little bum had more patience than I had and just lay there most of the time chewing his cud in forlorn bitterlipped thought. My teeth were chattering, my lips blue. By dark we saw with relief the familiar mountains of Santa Barbara taking shape and soon we'd be stopped and warm in the warm starlit night by the tracks.

I bade farewell to the little bum of Saint Teresa at the crossing, where we jumped off, and went to sleep the night in the sand in my blankets, far down the beach at the foot of a cliff where cops wouldn't see me and drive me away. I cooked hotdogs on freshly cut and sharpened sticks over the coals of a big wood fire, and heated a can of beans and a can of cheese macaroni in the redhot hollows, and drank my newly bought wine, and exulted in one of the most pleasant nights of my life. I waded in the water and dunked a little and stood looking up at the splendorous night sky, Avalokitesvara's ten-wondered universe of dark and diamonds. "Well, Ray," sez I, glad, "only a few miles to go. You've done it again." Happy. Just in my swim shorts, barefooted, wild-haired, in the red fire dark, singing, swigging wine, spitting, jumping, running—that's the way to live. All alone and free in the soft sands of the beach by the sigh of the sea out there, with the Ma-Wink fallopian virgin warm stars reflecting on the outer channel fluid belly waters. And if your cans are redhot and you can't hold them in your hands, just use good old railroad gloves, that's all. I let the food cool a little to enjoy more wine and my thoughts. I sat crosslegged in the sand and contemplated my life. Well, there, and what difference did it make? "What's going to happen to me up ahead?" Then the wine got to work on my taste buds and before long I had to pitch into those hotdogs, biting them right off the end of the stick spit, and chomp chomp, and dig down into the two tasty cans with the old pack spoon, spooning up rich bites of hot beans and pork, or of macaroni with sizzling hot sauce, and maybe a little sand thrown in. "And how many grains of sand are there on this beach?" I think. "Why, as many grains of sand as there are stars in that sky!" (chomp chomp) and if so "How many human beings have there been, in fact how many living creatures have there been, since before the *less* part of beginningless time? Why, oy, I reckon you would have to calculate the number of grains of sand on this beach and on every star in the sky, in every one of the ten thousand great chilicosms, which would be a number of sand grains uncomputable by IBM and Burroughs too, why boy I don't rightly know" (swig of wine) "I don't rightly know but it must be a couple umpteen trillion sextillion infideled and busted up unnumberable number of roses that sweet Saint Teresa and that fine little old man are now this minute showering on your head, with lilies."

Then, meal done, wiping my lips with my red bandana, I washed up the dishes in the salt sea, kicked a few clods of sand, wandered around, wiped them, put them away, stuck the old spoon back in the salty pack, and lay down curled in my blanket for a night's good and just rest. Waking up in the middle of the night, "Wa? Where am I, what is the basketbally game of eternity the girls are playing here by me in the old house of my life, the house isn't on fire is it?" but it's only the banding rush of waves piling up higher closer high tide to my blanket bed. "I be as hard and old as a conch shell," and I go to sleep and dream that while sleeping I use up three slices of bread breathing. . . . Ah poor mind of man, and lonely man alone on the beach, and God watching with intent smile I'd say. . . . And I dreamed of home long ago in New England, my little kitkats trying to go a thousand miles following me on the road across America, and my mother with a pack on her back, and my father running after the ephemeral uncatchable train, and I dreamed and woke up to a gray dawn, saw it, sniffed (because I had seen all the horizon shift as if a sceneshifter had hurried to put it back in place and make me believe in its reality), and went back to sleep, turning over. "It's all the same thing," I heard my voice say in the void that's highly embraceable during sleep.

2

The little Saint Teresa bum was the first genuine Dharma Bum I'd met, and the second was the number one Dharma Bum of them all and in fact it was he, Japhy Ryder, who coined the phrase. Japhy Ryder was a kid from eastern Oregon brought up in a log cabin deep in the woods with his father and mother and sister, from the beginning a woods boy, an axman, farmer, interested in animals and Indian lore so that when he finally got to college by hook or crook he was already well equipped for his early studies in anthropology and later in Indian myth and in the actual texts of Indian mythology. Finally he learned Chinese and Japanese and became an Oriental scholar and discovered the greatest Dharma Bums of them all, the Zen Lunatics of China and Japan. At the same time, being a Northwest boy with idealistic tendencies, he got interested in old-fashioned I.W.W. anarchism and learned to play the guitar and sing old worker songs to go with his Indian songs and general folksong interests. I first saw him walking down the street in San Francisco the following week (after hitchhiking the rest of the way from Santa Barbara in one long zipping ride given me, as though anybody'll believe this, by a beautiful darling young blonde in a snow-white strapless bathing suit and barefooted with a gold bracelet on her ankle, driving a next-year's cinnamon-red Lincoln Mercury, who wanted benzedrine so she could drive all the way to the City and when I said I had some in my duffel bag yelled "Crazy!")—I saw Japhy loping along in that curious long stride of the mountainclimber, with a small knapsack on his back filled with books and toothbrushes and whatnot which was his small "goin-to-the-city" knapsack as apart from his big full rucksack complete with sleeping bag, poncho, and cookpots. He wore a little goatee, strangely Oriental-looking with his somewhat slanted green eyes, but he didn't look like a Bohemian at all, and was far from being a Bohemian (a hanger-onner around the arts). He was wiry, suntanned, vigorous, open, all howdies and glad talk and even yelling hello to bums on the street and when asked a question answered right off the bat from the top or bottom of his mind I don't know which and always in a sprightly sparkling way.

"Where did you meet Ray Smith?" they asked him when we walked into The Place, the favorite bar of the hepcats around the Beach.

"Oh I always meet my Bodhisattvas in the street!" he yelled, and ordered beers.

It was a great night, a historic night in more ways than one. He and some other poets (he also wrote poetry and translated Chinese and Japanese poetry into English) were scheduled to give a poetry reading at the Gallery Six in town. They were all meeting in the bar and getting high. But as they stood and sat around I saw that he was the only one who didn't look like a poet, though poet he was indeed. The other poets were either hornrimmed intellectual hepcats with wild black hair like Alvah Goldbook, or delicate pale handsome poets like Ike O'Shay (in a suit), or out-of-this-world genteel-looking Renaissance Italians like Francis DaPavia (who looks like a young priest), or bow-tied wild-haired old anarchist fuds like Rheinhold Cacoethes, or big fat bespectacled quiet booboos like Warren Coughlin. And all the other hopeful poets were standing around, in various costumes, worn-at-the-sleeves corduroy jackets, scuffly shoes, books sticking out of their pockets. But Japhy was in rough workingman's clothes he'd bought second-hand in Goodwill stores to serve him on mountain climbs and hikes and for sitting in the open at night, for campfires, for hitchhiking up and down the Coast. In fact in his little knapsack he also had a funny green alpine cap that he wore when he got to the foot of a mountain, usually with a yodel, before starting to tromp up a few thousand feet. He wore mountainclimbing boots, expensive ones, his pride and joy, Italian make, in which he clomped around over the sawdust floor of the bar like an oldtime lumberjack. Japhy wasn't big, just about five foot seven, but strong and wiry and fast and muscular. His face was a mask of woeful bone, but his eyes twinkled like the eyes of old giggling sages of China, over that little goatee, to offset the rough look of his handsome face. His teeth were a little brown, from early backwoods neglect, but you never noticed that and he opened his mouth wide to guffaw at jokes. Sometimes he'd quiet down and just stare sadly at the floor, like a man whittling. He was merry at times. He showed great sympathetic interest in me and in the story about the little Saint Teresa bum and the stories I told him about my own experiences hopping freights or hitchhiking or hiking in woods. He claimed at once that I was a great "Bodhisattva," meaning "great wise being" or "great wise angel," and that I was ornamenting this world with my sincerity. We had the same favorite Buddhist saint, too: Avalokitesvara, or, in Japanese, Kwannon the Eleven-Headed. He knew all the details of Tibetan, Chinese, Mahayana, Hinayana, Japanese and even Burmese Buddhism but I warned him at once I didn't give a goddamn about the mythology and all the names and national flavors of Buddhism, but was just interested in the first of Sakyamuni's four noble truths, *All life is suffering.* And to an extent interested in the third, *The suppression of suffering can be achieved,* which I didn't quite believe was possible then. (I hadn't yet digested the Lankavatara Scripture which eventually shows you that there's nothing in the world but the mind itself, and therefore all's possible including the suppression of suffering.) Japhy's buddy was the aforementioned booboo big old goodhearted Warren Coughlin a hundred and eighty pounds of poet meat, who was advertised by Japhy (privately in my ear) as being more than meets the eye.

"Who is he?"

"He's my big best friend from up in Oregon, we've known

each other a long time. At first you think he's slow and stupid but actually he's a shining diamond. You'll see. Don't let him cut you to ribbons. He'll make the top of your head fly away, boy, with a choice chance word."

"Why?"

"He's a great mysterious Bodhisattva I think maybe a reincarnation of Asagna the great Mahayana scholar of the old centuries."

"And who am I?"

"I dunno, maybe you're Goat."

"Goat?"

"Maybe you're Mudface."

"Who's Mudface?"

"Mudface is the mud in your goatface. What would you say if someone was asked the question 'Does a dog have the Buddha nature?' and said 'Woof!'"

"I'd say that was a lot of silly Zen Buddhism." This took Japhy back a bit. "Lissen Japhy," I said, "I'm not a Zen Buddhist, I'm a serious Buddhist, I'm an oldfashioned dreamy Hinayana coward of later Mahayanism," and so forth into the night, my contention being that Zen Buddhism didn't concentrate on kindness so much as on confusing the intellect to make it perceive the illusion of all sources of things. "It's *mean*," I complained. "All those Zen Masters throwing young kids in the mud because they can't answer their silly word questions."

"That's because they want them to realize mud is better than words, boy." But I can't recreate the exact (will try) brilliance of all Japhy's answers and come-backs and come-ons with which he had me on pins and needles all the time and did eventually stick something in my crystal head that made me change my plans in life.

Anyway I followed the whole gang of howling poets to the reading at Gallery Six that night, which was, among other important things, the night of the birth of the San Francisco Poetry Renaissance. Everyone was there. It was a mad night. And I was the one who got things jumping by going around collecting dimes and quarters from the rather stiff audience standing around in the gallery and coming back with three huge gallon jugs of California Burgundy and getting them all

piffed so that by eleven o'clock when Alvah Goldbook was
reading his, wailing his poem "Wail" drunk with arms outspread everybody was yelling "Go! Go! Go!" (like a jam session) and old Rheinhold Cacoethes the father of the Frisco
poetry scene was wiping his tears in gladness. Japhy himself
read his fine poems about Coyote the God of the North American Plateau Indians (I think), at least the God of the Northwest Indians, Kwakiutl and what-all. "Fuck you! sang Coyote,
and ran away!" read Japhy to the distinguished audience, making
them all howl with joy, it was so pure, fuck being a dirty word
that comes out clean. And he had his tender lyrical lines, like
the ones about bears eating berries, showing his love of
animals, and great mystery lines about oxen on the Mongolian
road showing his knowledge of Oriental literature even on to
Hsuan Tsung the great Chinese monk who walked from China
to Tibet, Lanchow to Kashgar and Mongolia carrying a stick
of incense in his hand. Then Japhy showed his sudden bar-
room humor with lines about Coyote bringing goodies. And
his anarchistic ideas about how Americans don't know how to
live, with lines about commuters being trapped in living rooms
that come from poor trees felled by chainsaws (showing here,
also, his background as a logger up north). His voice was deep
and resonant and somehow brave, like the voice of oldtime
American heroes and orators. Something earnest and strong
and humanly hopeful I liked about him, while the other poets
were either too dainty in their aestheticism, or too hysterically
cynical to hope for anything, or too abstract and indoorsy, or
too political, or like Coughlin too incomprehensible to understand (big Coughlin saying things about "unclarified pro-
cesses" though where Coughlin did say that revelation was a
personal thing I noticed the strong Buddhist and idealistic
feeling of Japhy, which he'd shared with goodhearted Coughlin in their buddy days at college, as I had shared mine with Alvah in the Eastern scene and with others less apocalyptical and
straighter but in no sense more sympathetic and tearful).

Meanwhile scores of people stood around in the darkened
gallery straining to hear every word of the amazing poetry
reading as I wandered from group to group, facing them and
facing away from the stage, urging them to glug a slug from
the jug, or wandered back and sat on the right side of the stage

giving out little wows and yesses of approval and even whole sentences of comment with nobody's invitation but in the general gaiety nobody's disapproval either. It was a great night. Delicate Francis DaPavia read, from delicate onionskin yellow pages, or pink, which he kept flipping carefully with long white fingers, the poems of his dead chum Altman who'd eaten too much peyote in Chihuahua (or died of polio, one) but read none of his own poems—a charming elegy in itself to the memory of the dead young poet, enough to draw tears from the Cervantes of Chapter Seven, and read them in a delicate Englishy voice that had me crying with inside laughter though I later got to know Francis and liked him.

Among the people standing in the audience was Rosie Buchanan, a girl with a short haircut, red-haired, bony, handsome, a real gone chick and friend of everybody of any consequence on the Beach, who'd been a painter's model and a writer herself and was bubbling over with excitement at that time because she was in love with my old buddy Cody. "Great, hey Rosie?" I yelled, and she took a big slug from my jug and shined eyes at me. Cody just stood behind her with both arms around her waist. Between poets, Rheinhold Cacoethes, in his bow tie and shabby old coat, would get up and make a little funny speech in his snide funny voice and introduce the next reader; but as I say come eleven-thirty when all the poems were read and everybody was milling around wondering what had happened and what would come next in American poetry, he was wiping his eyes with his handkerchief. And we all got together with him, the poets, and drove in several cars to Chinatown for a big fabulous dinner off the Chinese menu, with chopsticks, yelling conversation in the middle of the night in one of those freeswinging great Chinese restaurants of San Francisco. This happened to be Japhy's favorite Chinese restaurant, Nam Yuen, and he showed me how to order and how to eat with chopsticks and told anecdotes about the Zen Lunatics of the Orient and had me going so glad (and we had a bottle of wine on the table) that finally I went over to an old cook in the doorway of the kitchen and asked him "Why did Bodhidharma come from the West?" (Bodhidharma was the Indian who brought Buddhism eastward to China.)

"I don't care," said the old cook, with lidded eyes, and I

told Japhy and he said, "Perfect answer, absolutely perfect. Now you know what I mean by Zen."

I had a lot more to learn, too. Especially about how to handle girls—Japhy's incomparable Zen Lunatic way, which I got a chance to see firsthand the following week.

3

In Berkeley I was living with Alvah Goldbook in his little rose-covered cottage in the backyard of a bigger house on Milvia Street. The old rotten porch slanted forward to the ground, among vines, with a nice old rocking chair that I sat in every morning to read my Diamond Sutra. The yard was full of tomato plants about to ripen, and mint, mint, everything smelling of mint, and one fine old tree that I loved to sit under and meditate on those cool perfect starry California October nights unmatched anywhere in the world. We had a perfect little kitchen with a gas stove, but no icebox, but no matter. We also had a perfect little bathroom with a tub and hot water, and one main room, covered with pillows and floor mats of straw and mattresses to sleep on, and books, books, hundreds of books everything from Catullus to Pound to Blyth to albums of Bach and Beethoven (and even one swinging Ella Fitzgerald album with Clark Terry very interesting on trumpet) and a good three-speed Webcor phonograph that played loud enough to blast the roof off: and the roof nothing but plywood, the walls too, through which one night in one of our Zen Lunatic drunks I put my fist in glee and Coughlin saw me and put his head through about three inches.

About a mile from there, way down Milvia and then upslope toward the campus of the University of California, behind another big old house on a quiet street (Hillegass), Japhy lived in his own shack which was infinitely smaller than ours, about twelve by twelve, with nothing in it but typical Japhy appurtenances that showed his belief in the simple monastic life—no chairs at all, not even one sentimental rocking chair, but just straw mats. In the corner was his famous rucksack with cleaned-up pots and pans all fitting into one another in a compact unit and all tied and put away inside a knotted-up blue bandana. Then his Japanese wooden pata shoes, which he never used, and a pair of black inside-pata socks to pad around softly in over his pretty straw mats, just room for your four toes on one side and your big toe on the other. He had a slew of orange crates all filled with beautiful scholarly books, some of them in Oriental languages, all the great sutras, comments on sutras, the complete works of D. T. Suzuki and a fine quadruple-volume edition of Japanese haikus. He also had an immense collection of valuable general poetry. In fact if a thief should have broken in there the only things of real value were the books. Japhy's clothes were all old hand-me-downs bought secondhand with a bemused and happy expression in Goodwill and Salvation Army stores: wool socks darned, colored under-shirts, jeans, workshirts, moccasin shoes, and a few turtleneck sweaters that he wore one on top the other in the cold moun-tain nights of the High Sierras in California and the High Cas-cades of Washington and Oregon on the long incredible jaunts that sometimes lasted weeks and weeks with just a few pounds of dried food in his pack. A few orange crates made his table, on which, one late sunny afternoon as I arrived, was steaming a peaceful cup of tea at his side as he bent his serious head to the Chinese signs of the poet Han Shan. Coughlin had given me the address and I came there, seeing first Japhy's bicycle on the lawn in front of the big house out front (where his land-lady lived) then the few odd boulders and rocks and funny little trees he'd brought back from mountain jaunts to set out in his own "Japanese tea garden" or "tea-house garden," as there was a convenient pine tree soughing over his little domicile.

A peacefuller scene I never saw than when, in that rather nippy late red afternoon, I simply opened his little door and looked in and saw him at the end of the little shack, sitting crosslegged on a Paisley pillow on a straw mat, with his spectacles on, making him look old and scholarly and wise, with book on lap and the little tin teapot and porcelain cup steaming at his side. He looked up very peacefully, saw who it was, said, "Ray, come in," and bent his eyes again to the script.

"What you doing?"

"Translating Han Shan's great poem called 'Cold Mountain' written a thousand years ago some of it scribbled on the sides of cliffs hundreds of miles away from any other living beings."

"Wow."

"When you come into this house though you've got to take your shoes off, see those straw mats, you can ruin 'em with shoes." So I took my softsoled blue cloth shoes off and laid them dutifully by the door and he threw me a pillow and I sat crosslegged along the little wooden board wall and he offered me a cup of hot tea. "Did you ever read the Book of Tea?" said he.

"No, what's that?"

"It's a scholarly treatise on how to make tea utilizing all the knowledge of two thousand years about tea-brewing. Some of the descriptions of the effect of the first sip of tea, and the second, and the third, are really wild and ecstatic."

"Those guys got high on nothing, hey?"

"Sip your tea and you'll see; this is good green tea." It was good and I immediately felt calm and warm. "Want me to read you parts of this Han Shan poem? Want me to tell you about Han Shan?"

"Yeah."

"Han Shan you see was a Chinese scholar who got sick of the big city and the world and took off to hide in the mountains."

"Say, that sounds like you."

"In those days you could really do that. He stayed in caves not far from a Buddhist monastery in the T'ang Hsing district of T'ien Tai and his only human friend was the funny Zen Lunatic Shih-te who had a job sweeping out the monastery with a straw broom. Shih-te was a poet too but he never wrote much down. Every now and then Han Shan would come down from Cold Mountain in his bark clothing and come into the warm kitchen and wait for food, but none of the monks would ever feed him because he didn't want to join the order and answer the meditation bell three times a day. You see why in some of his utterances, like—listen and I'll look here and read from the Chinese," and I bent over his shoulder and watched him read from big wild crowtracks of Chinese signs: "Climbing up Cold Mountain path, Cold Mountain path goes on and on, long gorge choked with scree and boulders, wide creek and mist-blurred grass, moss is slippery though there's been no rain, pine sings but there's no wind, who can leap the world's ties and sit with me among white clouds?"

"Wow."

"Course that's my own translation into English, you see there are five signs for each line and I have to put in Western prepositions and articles and such."

"Why don't you just translate it as it is, five signs, five words? What's those first five signs?"

"Sign for climbing, sign for up, sign for cold, sign for mountain, sign for path."

"Well then, translate it 'Climbing up Cold Mountain path.'"

"Yeah, but what do you do with the sign for long, sign for gorge, sign for choke, sign for avalanche, sign for boulders?"

"Where's that?"

"That's the third line, would have to read 'Long gorge choke avalanche boulders.'"

"Well that's even better!"

"Well yeah, I thought of that, but I have to have this pass the approval of Chinese scholars here at the university and have it clear in English."

"Boy what a great thing this is," I said looking around at the little shack, "and you sitting here so very quietly at this very quiet hour studying all alone with your glasses. . . ."

"Ray what you got to do is go climb a mountain with me soon. How would you like to climb Matterhorn?"

"Great! Where's that?"

"Up in the High Sierras. We can go there with Henry Morley in his car and bring our packs and take off from the lake. I could carry all the food and stuff we need in my rucksack and you could borrow Alvah's small knapsack and carry extra socks and shoes and stuff."

"What's these signs mean?"

"These signs mean that Han Shan came down from the mountain after many years roaming around up there, to see his folks in town, says, 'Till recently I stayed at Cold Mountain, et cetera, yesterday I called on friends and family, more than half had gone to the Yellow Springs,' that means death, the Yellow Springs, 'now morning I face my lone shadow, I can't study with both eyes full of tears.'"

"That's like you too, Japhy, studying with eyes full of tears."

"My eyes aren't full of tears!"

"Aren't they going to be after a long long time?"

"They certainly will, Ray . . . and look here, 'In the mountains it's cold, it's always been cold not just this year,' see, he's real high, maybe twelve thousand or thirteen thousand feet or more, way up there, and says, 'Jagged scarps always snowed in, woods in the dark ravines spitting mist, grass is still sprouting at the end of June, leaves begin to fall in early August, and here am I high as a junkey—'"

"As a junkey!"

"That's my own translation, he actually says here am I as high as the sensualist in the city below, but I made it modern and high translation."

"Great." I wondered why Han Shan was Japhy's hero.

"Because," said he, "he was a poet, a mountain man, a Buddhist dedicated to the principle of meditation on the essence of all things, a vegetarian too by the way though I haven't got on that kick from figuring maybe in this modern world to be a vegetarian is to split hairs a little since all sentient beings eat what they can. And he was a man of solitude who could take off by himself and live purely and true to himself."

"That sounds like you too."

"And like you too, Ray, I haven't forgotten what you told me about how you made it in the woods meditating in North Carolina and all." Japhy was very sad, subdued, I'd never seen him so quiet, melancholy, thoughtful his voice was as tender as a mother's, he seemed to be talking from far away to a poor yearning creature (me) who needed to hear his message he wasn't putting anything on he was in a bit of a trance.

"Have you been meditating today?"

"Yeah I meditate first thing in the morning before breakfast and I always meditate a long time in the afternoon unless I'm interrupted."

"Who interrupts you?"

"Oh, people. Coughlin sometimes, and Alvah came yesterday, and Rol Sturlason, and I got this girl comes over to play yabyum."

"Yabyum? What's that?"

"Don't you know about yabyum, Smith? I'll tell you later."

He seemed to be too sad to talk about yabyum, which I found out about a couple of nights later. We talked a while longer about Han Shan and poems on cliffs and as I was going away his friend Rol Sturlason, a tall blond goodlooking kid, came in to discuss his coming trip to Japan with him. This Rol Sturlason was interested in the famous Ryoanji rock garden of Shokokuji monastery in Kyoto, which is nothing but old boulders placed in such a way, supposedly mystically aesthetic, as to cause thousands of tourists and monks every year to journey there to stare at the boulders in the sand and thereby gain peace of mind. I have never met such weird yet serious and earnest people. I never saw Rol Sturlason again, he went to Japan soon after, but I can't forget what he said about the boulders, to my question, "Well who placed them in that certain way that's so great?"

"Nobody knows, some monk, or monks, long ago. But there is a definite mysterious form in the arrangement of the rocks. It's only through form that we can realize emptiness." He showed me the picture of the boulders in well-raked sand, looking like islands in the sea, looking as though they had eyes (declivities) and surrounded by a neatly screened and architectural monastery patio. Then he showed me a diagram of the stone arrangement with the projection in silhouette and showed me the geometrical logics and all, and mentioned the phrases "lonely individuality" and the rocks as "bumps pushing into space," all meaning some kind of koan business I wasn't as much interested in as in him and especially in good kind Japhy who brewed more tea on his noisy gasoline primus and gave us added cups with almost a silent Oriental bow. It was quite different from the night of the poetry reading.

4

But the next night, about midnight, Coughlin and I and Alvah got together and decided to buy a big gallon jug of Burgundy and go bust in on Japhy in his shack.

"What's he doing tonight?" I asked.

"Oh," says Coughlin, "probably studying, probably screwing,

we'll go see." We bought the jug on Shattuck Avenue way down and went over and once more I saw his pitiful English bicycle on the lawn. "Japhy travels around on that bicycle with his little knapsack on his back all up and down Berkeley all day," said Coughlin. "He used to do the same thing at Reed College in Oregon. He was a regular fixture up there. Then we'd throw big wine parties and have girls and end up jumping out of windows and playing Joe College pranks all up and down town."

"Gee, he's strange," said Alvah, biting his lip, in a mood of marvel, and Alvah himself was making a careful interested study of our strange noisy-quiet friend. We came in the little door again, Japhy looked up from his crosslegged study over a book, American poetry this time, glasses on, and said nothing but "Ah" in a strangely cultured tone. We took off our shoes and padded across the little five feet of straw to sit by him, but I was last with my shoes off, and had the jug in my hand, which I turned to show him from across the shack, and from his crosslegged position Japhy suddenly roared "Yaaaaah!" and leaped up into the air and straight across the room to me, landing on his feet in a fencing position with a sudden dagger in his hand the tip of it just barely stabbing the glass of the bottle with a small distinct "clink." It was the most amazing leap I ever saw in my life, except by nutty acrobats, much like a mountain goat, which he was, it turned out. Also it reminded me of a Japanese Samurai warrior—the yelling roar, the leap, the position, and his expression of comic wrath his eyes bulging and making a big funny face at me. I had the feeling it was really a complaint against our breaking in on his studies and against wine itself which would get him drunk and make him miss his planned evening of reading. But without further ado he uncapped the bottle himself and took a big slug and we all sat crosslegged and spent four hours screaming news at one another, one of the funniest nights. Some of it went like this:

JAPHY: Well, Coughlin, you old fart, what you been doin?

COUGHLIN: Nothin.

ALVAH: What are all these strange books here? Hm, Pound, do you like Pound?

JAPHY: Except for the fact that that old fartface flubbed up the name of Li Po by calling him by his Japanese name and all such famous twaddle, he was all right—in fact he's my favorite poet.

RAY: Pound? Who wants to make a favorite poet out of that pretentious nut?

JAPHY: Have some more wine, Smith, you're not making sense. Who is your favorite poet, Alvah?

RAY: Why don't somebody ask me *my* favorite poet, I know more about poetry than all of you put together.

JAPHY: Is that true?

ALVAH: It might be. Haven't you seen Ray's new book of poems he just wrote in Mexico—"the wheel of the quivering meat conception turns in the void expelling tics, porcupines, elephants, people, stardusts, fools, nonsense . . ."

RAY: That's not it!

JAPHY: Speaking of meat, have you read the new poem of . . .

Etc., etc., then finally disintegrating into a wild talkfest and yellfast and finally songfest with people rolling on the floor in laughter and ending with Alvah and Coughlin and I going staggering up the quiet college street arm in arm singing "Eli Eli" at the top of our voices and dropping the empty jug right at our feet in a crash of glass, as Japhy laughed from his little door. But we'd made him miss his evening of study and I felt bad about that, till the following night when he suddenly appeared at our little cottage with a pretty girl and came in and told her to take her clothes off, which she did at once.

5

This was in keeping with Japhy's theories about women and lovemaking. I forgot to mention that the day the rock artist had called on him in the late afternoon, a girl had come right after, a blonde in rubber boots and a Tibetan coat with wooden buttons, and in the general talk she'd inquired about our plan to climb Mount Matterhorn and said "Can I come with ya?" as she was a bit of a mountainclimber herself.

"Shore," said Japhy, in his funny voice he used for joking, a big loud deep imitation of a lumberjack he knew in the Northwest, a ranger actually, old Burnie Byers, "shore, come on with us and we'll all screw ya at ten thousand feet" and the way he said it was so funny and casual, and in fact serious, that the girl wasn't shocked at all but somewhat pleased. In this same spirit he'd now brought this girl Princess to our cottage, it was about eight o'clock at night, dark, Alvah and I were quietly sipping tea and reading poems or typing poems at the typewriter and two bicycles came in the yard: Japhy on his, Princess on hers. Princess had gray eyes and yellow hair and was very beautiful and only twenty. I must say one thing about her, she was sex mad and man mad, so there wasn't much of a problem in persuading her to play yabyum. "Don't you know about yabyum, Smith?" said Japhy in his big booming voice striding in in his boots holding Princess's hand. "Princess and I come here to show ya, boy."

"Suits me," said I, "whatever it is." Also I'd known Princess before and had been mad about her, in the City, about a year ago. It was just another wild coincidence that she had happened to meet Japhy and fallen in love with him and madly too, she'd do anything he said. Whenever people dropped in to visit us at the cottage I'd always put my red bandana over the little wall lamp and put out the ceiling light to make a nice cool red dim scene to sit and drink wine and talk in. I did this, and went to get the bottle out of the kitchen and couldn't believe my eyes when I saw Japhy and Alvah taking their clothes off and throwing them every whichaway and I looked and Princess was stark naked, her skin white as snow when the red sun hits it at dusk, in the dim red light. "What the hell," I said.

"Here's what yabyum is, Smith," said Japhy, and he sat crosslegged on the pillow on the floor and motioned to Princess, who came over and sat down on him facing him with her arms about his neck and they sat like that saying nothing for a while. Japhy wasn't at all nervous and embarrassed and just sat there in perfect form just as he was supposed to do. "This is what they do in the temples of Tibet. It's a holy ceremony, it's done just like this in front of chanting priests. People pray and recite Om Mani Pahdme Hum, which means Amen the Thunderbolt in the Dark Void. I'm the thunderbolt and Princess is the dark void, you see."

"But what's she thinking?" I yelled almost in despair, I'd

had such idealistic longings for that girl in that past year and had conscience-stricken hours wondering if I should seduce her because she was so young and all.

"Oh this is lovely," said Princess. "Come on and try it."

"But I can't sit crosslegged like that." Japhy was sitting in the full lotus position, it's called, with both ankles over both thighs. Alvah was sitting on the mattress trying to yank his ankles over his thighs to do it. Finally Japhy's legs began to hurt and they just tumbled over on the mattress where both Alvah and Japhy began to explore the territory. I still couldn't believe it.

"Take your clothes off and join in, Smith!" But on top of all that, the feelings about Princess, I'd also gone through an entire year of celibacy based on my feeling that lust was the direct cause of birth which was the direct cause of suffering and death and I had really no lie come to a point where I regarded lust as offensive and even cruel.

"Pretty girls make graves," was my saying, whenever I'd had to turn my head around involuntarily to stare at the incomparable pretties of Indian Mexico. And the absence of active lust in me had also given me a new peaceful life that I was enjoying a great deal. But this was too much. I was still afraid to take my clothes off; also I never liked to do that in front of more than one person, especially with men around. But Japhy didn't give a goddamn hoot and holler about any of this and pretty soon he was making Princess happy and then Alvah had a turn (with his big serious eyes staring in the dim light, and him reading poems a minute ago). So I said "How about me startin to work on her arm?"

"Go ahead, great." Which I did, lying down on the floor with all my clothes on and kissing her hand, then her wrist, then up, to her body, as she laughed and almost cried with delight everybody everywhere working on her. All the peaceful celibacy of my Buddhism was going down the drain. "Smith, I distrust any kind of Buddhism or *any* kinda philosophy or social system that puts down sex," said Japhy quite scholarly now that he was done and sitting naked crosslegged rolling himself a Bull Durham cigarette (which he did as part of his "simplicity" life). It ended up with everybody naked and finally making gay pots of coffee in the kitchen and Princess on the kitchen floor naked with her knees clasped in her arms, lying on her side, just for nothing, just to do it, then finally she and I took a warm bath together in the bathtub and could hear Alvah and Japhy discussing Zen Free Love Lunacy orgies in the other room.

"Hey Princess we'll do this every Thursday night, hey?" yelled Japhy. "It'll be a regular function."

"Yeah," yelled Princess from the bathtub. I'm telling you she was actually glad to do all this and told me "You know, I feel like I'm the mother of all things and I have to take care of my little children."

"You're such a young pretty thing yourself."

"But I'm the old mother of earth. I'm a Bodhisattva." She was just a little off her nut but when I heard her say "Bodhisattva" I realized she wanted to be a big Buddhist like Japhy and being a girl the only way she could express it was this way, which had its traditional roots in the yabyum ceremony of Tibetan Buddhism, so everything was fine.

Alvah was immensely pleased and was all for the idea of "every Thursday night" and so was I by now.

"Alvah, Princess says she's a Bodhisattva."

"Of course she is."

"She says she's the mother of all of us."

"The Bodhisattva women of Tibet and parts of ancient India," said Japhy, "were taken and used as holy concubines in temples and sometimes in ritual caves and would get to lay up a stock of merit and they meditated too. All of them, men and women, they'd meditate, fast, have balls like this, go back to eating, drinking, talking, hike around, live in viharas in the rainy season and outdoors in the dry, there was no question of what to do about sex which is what I always liked about Oriental religion. And what I always dug about the Indians in our country . . . You know when I was a little kid in Oregon I didn't feel that I was an American at all, with all that suburban ideal and sex repression and general dreary newspaper gray censorship of all our real human values but and when I discovered Buddhism and all I suddenly felt that I had lived in a previous lifetime innumerable ages ago and now because of faults and sins in that lifetime I was being degraded to a more grievous domain of existence and my karma was to be born in

America where nobody has any fun or believes in anything, especially freedom. That's why I was always sympathetic to freedom movements, too, like anarchism in the Northwest, the oldtime heroes of Everett Massacre and all. . . ." It ended up with long earnest discussions about all these subjects and finally Princess got dressed and went home with Japhy on their bicycles and Alvah and I sat facing each other in the dim red light.

"But you know, Ray, Japhy is really sharp—he's really the wildest craziest sharpest cat we've ever met. And what I love about him is he's the big hero of the West Coast, do you realize I've been out here for two years now and hadn't met anybody worth knowing really or anybody with any truly illuminated intelligence and was giving up hope for the West Coast? Besides all the background he has, in Oriental scholarship, Pound, taking peyote and seeing visions, his mountainclimbing and bhikkuing, wow, Japhy Ryder is a great new hero of American culture."

"He's mad!" I agreed. "And other things I like about him, his quiet sad moments when he don't say much. . . ."

"Gee, I wonder what will happen to him in the end."

"I think he'll end up like Han Shan living alone in the mountains and writing poems on the walls of cliffs, or chanting them to crowds outside his cave."

"Or maybe he'll go to Hollywood and be a movie star, you know he said that the other day, he said 'Alvah you know I've never thought of going to the movies and becoming a star, I can do anything you know, I haven't tried that yet,' and I believe him, he *can* do anything. Did you see the way he had Princess all wrapped around him?"

"Aye indeed" and later that night as Alvah slept I sat under the tree in the yard and looked up at the stars or closed my eyes to meditate and tried to quiet myself down back to my normal self.

Alvah couldn't sleep and came out and lay flat on his back in the grass looking up at the sky, and said "Big steamy clouds going by in the dark up there, it makes me realize we live on an actual planet."

"Close your eyes and you'll see more than that."

"Oh I don't know what you mean by all that!" he said pettishly. He was always being bugged by my little lectures on Samadhi ecstasy, which is the state you reach when you stop everything and stop your mind and you actually with your eyes closed see a kind of eternal multiswarm of electrical Power of some kind ululating in place of just pitiful images and forms of objects, which are, after all, imaginary. And if you don't believe me come back in a billion years and deny it. For what is time? "Don't you think it's much more interesting just to be like Japhy and have girls and studies and good times and really be doing something, than all this silly sitting under trees?"

"Nope," I said, and meant it, and I knew Japhy would agree with me. "All Japhy's doing is amusing himself in the void."

"I don't think so."

"I bet he is. I'm going mountainclimbing with him next week and find out and tell you."

"Well" (sigh), "as for me, I'm just going to go on being Alvah Goldbook and to hell with all this Buddhist bullshit."

"You'll be sorry some day. Why don't you ever understand what I'm trying to tell you: it's with your six senses that you're fooled into believing not only that you have six senses, but that you contact an actual outside world with them. If it wasn't for your eyes, you wouldn't see me. If it wasn't for your ears, you wouldn't hear that airplane. If it wasn't for your nose, you wouldn't smell the midnight mint. If it wasn't for your tongue taster, you wouldn't taste the difference between A and B. If it wasn't for your body, you wouldn't feel Princess. There is no me, no airplane, no mind, no Princess, no nothing, you for krissakes do you want to go on being fooled every damn minute of your life?"

"Yes, that's all I want, I thank God that something has come out of nothing."

"Well, I got news for you, it's the other way around nothing has come out of something, and that something is Dharmakaya, the body of the True Meaning, and that nothing is this and all this twaddle and talk. I'm going to bed."

"Well sometimes I see a flash of illumination in what you're trying to say but believe me I get more of a satori out of Princess than out of words."

"It's a satori of your foolish flesh, you lecher."

"I know my redeemer liveth."

"What redeemer and what liveth?"

"Oh let's cut this out and just live!"

"Balls, when I thought like you, Alvah, I was just as miserable and graspy as you are now. All you want to do is run out there and get laid and get beat up and get screwed up and get old and sick and banged around by samsara, you fucking eternal meat of comeback you you'll deserve it too, I'll say."

"That's not nice. Everybody's tearful and trying to live with what they got. Your Buddhism has made you mean Ray and makes you even afraid to take your clothes off for a simple healthy orgy."

"Well, I did finally, didn't I?"

"But you were coming on so hincty about— Oh let's forget it."

Alvah went to bed and I sat and closed my eyes and thought "This thinking has stopped" but because I had to think it no thinking had stopped, but there did come over me a wave of gladness to know that all this perturbation was just a dream already ended and I didn't have to worry because I wasn't "I" and I prayed that God, or Tathagata, would give me enough time and enough sense and strength to be able to tell people what I knew (as I can't even do properly now) so they'd know what I know and not despair so much. The old tree brooded over me silently, a living thing. I heard a mouse snoring in the garden weeds. The rooftops of Berkeley looked like pitiful living meat sheltering grieving phantoms from the eternality of the heavens which they feared to face. By the time I went to bed I wasn't taken in by no Princess or no desire for no Princess and nobody's disapproval and I felt glad and slept well.

6

Now came the time for our big mountain climb. Japhy came over in late afternoon on his bike to get me. We took out Alvah's knapsack and put it in his bike basket. I took out socks and sweaters. But I had no climbing shoes and the only things that could serve were Japhy's tennis sneakers, old but firm. My own shoes were too floppy and torn. "That might be better, Ray, with sneakers your feet are light and you can jump from boulder to boulder with no trouble. Of course we'll swap shoes at certain times and make it."

"What about food? What are you bringing?"

"Well before I tell you about food, R-a-a-y" (sometimes he called me by my first name and always when he did so, it was a long-drawn-out sad "R-a-a-a-y" as though he was worried about my welfare), "I've got your sleeping bag, it's not a duck down like my own, and naturally a lot heavier, but with clothes on and a good big fire you'll be comfortable up there."

"Clothes on yeah, but why a big fire, it's only October."

"Yeah but it's below freezing up there, R-a-a-y, in October," he said sadly.

"At night?"

"Yeah at night and in the daytime it's real warm and pleasant. You know old John Muir used to go up to those mountains where we're going with nothing but his old Army coat and a paper bag full of dried bread and he slept in his coat and just soaked the old bread in water when he wanted to eat, and he roamed around like that for months before tramping back to the city."

"My goodness he musta been tough!"

"Now as for food, I went down to Market Street to the Crystal Palace market and bought my favorite dry cereal, bulgur, which is a kind of a Bulgarian cracked rough wheat and I'm going to stick pieces of bacon in it, little square chunks, that'll make a fine supper for all three of us, Morley and us. And I'm bringing tea, you always want a good cup of hot tea under those cold stars. And I'm bringing real chocolate pudding, not that instant phony stuff but good chocolate pudding that I'll bring to a boil and stir over the fire and then let it cool ice cold in the snow."

"Oh boy!"

"So insteada rice this time, which I usually bring, I thought I'd make a nice delicacy for you, R-a-a-y, and in the bulgur too I'm going to throw in all kinds of dried diced vegetables I bought at the Ski Shop. We'll have our supper and breakfast outa this, and for energy food this big bag of peanuts and raisins and another bag with dried apricot and dried prunes oughta fix us for the rest." And he showed me the very tiny bag in which all this important food for three grown men for twenty-four hours or more climbing at high altitudes was stored. "The main thing in going to mountains is to keep the weight as far down as possible, those packs get heavy."

"But my God there's not enough food in that little bag!"

"Yes there is, the water swells it up."

"Do we bring wine?"

"No it isn't any good up there and once you're at high altitude and tired you don't crave alcohol." I didn't believe this but said nothing. We put my own things on the bike and walked across the campus to his place pushing the bike along the edge of the sidewalk. It was a cool clear Arabian Night dusk with the tower clock of University of Cal a clean black shadow against a backdrop of cypress and eucalyptus and all kinds of trees, bells ringing somewhere, and the air crisp. "It's going to be cold up there," said Japhy, but he was feeling fine that night and laughed when I asked him about next Thursday with Princess. "You know we played yabyum twice more since that last night, she comes over to my shack any day or night any minute and man she won't take no for an answer. So I satisfy the Bodhisattva." And Japhy wanted to talk about everything, his boyhood in Oregon. "You know my mother and father and sister were living a real primitive life on that log-cabin farm and on cold winter mornings we'd all undress and dress in front of the fire, we had to, that's why I'm not like you about undressing, I mean I'm not bashful or anything like that."

"What'd you use to do around college?"

"In the summers I was always a government fire lookout— that's what you oughta do next summer, Smith—and in the winters I did a lot of skiing and used to walk around the campus on crutches real proud. I climbed some pretty big mountains up there, including a long haul up Rainier almost to the top where you sign your name. I finally made it one year. There are only a few names up there, you know. And I climbed all around the Cascades, off season and in season, and worked as a logger. Smith, I gotta tell you all about the romance of Northwest logging, like you keep talking about railroading, you shoulda seen the little narrow-gauge railways up there and those cold winter mornings with snow and your belly fulla pancakes and syrup and black coffee, boy, and you raise your doublebitted ax to your morning's first log there's nothing like it."

"That's just like my dream of the Great Northwest. The Kwakiutl Indians, the Northwest Mounted Police. . . ."

"Well, there in Canada they got them, over in British Columbia, I used to meet some on the trail." We pushed the bike down past the various college hangouts and cafeterias and looked into Robbie's to see if we knew anybody. Alvah was in there, working his part-time job as busboy. Japhy and I were kind of outlandish-looking on the campus in our old clothes in fact Japhy was considered an eccentric around the campus, which is the usual thing for campuses and college people to think whenever a real man appears on the scene—colleges being nothing but grooming schools for the middle-class non-identity which usually finds its perfect expression on the outskirts of the campus in rows of well-to-do houses with lawns and television sets in each living room with everybody looking at the same thing and thinking the same thing at the same time while the Japhies of the world go prowling in the wilderness to hear the voice crying in the wilderness, to find the ecstasy of the stars, to find the dark mysterious secret of the origin of faceless wonderless crapulous civilization. "All these people," said Japhy, "they all got white-tiled toilets and take big dirty craps like bears in the mountains, but it's all washed away to convenient supervised sewers and nobody thinks of crap any more or realizes that their origin is shit and civet and scum of the sea. They spend all day washing their hands with creamy soaps they secretly wanta eat in the bathroom." He had a million ideas, he had 'em all.

We got to his little shack as it grew dark and you could smell woodsmoke and smoke of leaves in the air, and packed everything up neat and went down the street to meet Henry Morley who had the car. Henry Morley was a bespectacled fellow of great learning but an eccentric himself, more eccentric and outré than Japhy on the campus, a librarian, with few friends, but a mountainclimber. His own little one-room cottage in a back lawn of Berkeley was filled with books and pictures of mountainclimbing and scattered all over with rucksacks, climbing boots, skis. I was amazed to hear him talk, he talked exactly like Rheinhold Cacoethes the critic, it turned out they'd been friends long ago and climbed mountains together and I couldn't tell whether Morley had influenced Cacoethes or the other way around. I felt it was Morley who had done the influencing—he had the same snide, sarcastic, extremely witty, well-formulated speech, with thousands of images, like, when Japhy and I walked in and there was a gathering of Morley's friends in there (a strange outlandish group including one Chinese and one German from Germany and several other students of some kind) Morley said "I'm bringing my air mattress, you guys can sleep on that hard cold ground if you want but I'm going to have pneumatic aid besides I went and spend sixteen dollars on it in the wilderness of Oakland Army Navy stores and drove around all day wondering if with rollerskates or suction cups you can technically call yourself a vehicle" or some such to-me-incomprehensible (to everybody else) secret-meaning joke of his own, to which nobody listened much anyway, he kept talking and talking as though to himself but I liked him right away. We sighed when we saw the huge amounts of junk he wanted to take on the climb: even canned goods, and besides his rubber air mattress a whole lot of pickax and whatnot equipment we'd really never need.

"You can carry that ax, Morley, but I don't think we'll need it, but canned goods is just a lot of water you have to lug on your back, don't you realize we got all the water we want waitin for us up there?"

"Well I just thought a can of this Chinese chop suey would be kinda tasty."

"I've got enough food for all of us. Let's go."

Morley spent a long time talking and fishing around and getting together his unwieldy packboard and finally we said goodbye to his friends and got into Morley's little English car and started off, about ten o'clock, toward Tracy and up to Bridgeport from where we would drive another eight miles to the foot of the trail at the lake.

I sat in the back seat and they talked up front. Morley was an actual madman who would come and get me (later) carrying a quart of eggnog expecting me to drink that, but I'd make him drive me to a liquor store, and the whole idea was to go out

and see some girl and he'd have me come along to act as paci-
fier of some kind: we came to her door, she opened it, when
she saw who it was she slammed the door and we drove back
to the cottage. "Well what was this?" "Well it's a long story,"
Morley would say vaguely, I never quite understood what he
was up to. Also, seeing Alvah had no spring bed in the cottage,
one day he appeared like a ghost in a doorway as we were in-
nocently getting up and brewing coffee and presented us with
a huge double-bed spring that, after he left, we struggled to
hide in the barn. And he'd bring odd assorted boards and whatnot, and impossible bookshelves, all kinds of things, and years
later I had further Three Stooges adventures with him going
out to his house in Contra Costa (which he owned and rented)
and spending impossible-to-believe afternoons when he paid
me two dollars an hour for hauling out bucket after bucket of
mudslime which he himself was doling out of a flooded cellar
by hand, black and mudcovered as Tartarilouak the King of
the Mudslimes of Paratioalaouakak Span, with a secret grin of
elfish delight on his face; and later, returning through some
little town and wanting ice-cream cones, we walked down Main
Street (had hiked on the highway with buckets and rakes) with
ice-cream cones in our hands knocking into people on the
little sidewalks like a couple of oldtime Hollywood silent film
comedians, whitewash and all. An extremely strange person
anyway, in any case, any old way you looked at, and drove the
car now out toward Tracy on the busy fourlaner highway and
did most of the talking, at everything Japhy said he had twelve
to say, and it went like this: Japhy would say something like
"By God I feel real studious lately, I think I'll read some ornithology next week." Morley would say, "Who doesn't feel
studious when he doesn't have a girl with a Riviera suntan?"

Every time he said something he would turn and look at
Japhy and deliver these rather brilliant inanities with a complete deadpan; I couldn't understand what kind of strange secret scholarly linguistic clown he really was under these
California skies. Or Japhy would mention sleeping bags, and
Morley would ramble in with "I'm going to be the possessor
of a pale blue French sleeping bag, light weight, goose down,
good buy I think, find 'em in Vancouver—good for Daisy
Mae. Completely wrong type for Canada. Everyone wants to

know if her grandfather was an explorer who met an Eskimo. I'm from the North Pole myself."

"What's he talking about?" I'd ask from the back seat, and Japhy: "He's just an interesting tape recorder."

I'd told the boys I had a touch of thrombophlebitis, blood clots in the veins in my feet, and was afraid about tomorrow's climb, not that it would hobble me but would get worse when we came down. Morley said "Is thrombophlebitis a peculiar rhythm for piss?" Or I'd say something about Westerners and he'd say, "I'm a dumb Westerner . . . look what preconceptions have done to England."

"You're crazy, Morley."

"I dunno, maybe I am, but if I am I'll leave a lovely will anyway." Then out of nowhere he would say "Well I'm very pleased to go climbing with two poets, I'm going to write a book myself, it'll be about Ragusa, a late medieval maritime city state republic which solved the class problem, offered the secretaryship to Machiavelli and for a generation had its language used as the diplomatic one for the Levant. This was because of pull with the Turks, of course."

"Of course," we'd say.

So he'd ask himself the question out loud: "Can you secure Christmas with an approximation only eighteen million seconds left of the original old red chimney?"

"Sure," says Japhy laughing.

"Sure," says Morley wheeling the car around increasing curves, "they're boarding reindeer Greyhound specials for a pre-season heart-to-heart Happiness Conference deep in Sierra wilderness ten thousand five hundred and sixty yards from a primitive motel. It's newer than analysis and deceptively simple. If you lost the roundtrip ticket you can become a gnome, the outfits are cute and there's a rumor that Actors Equity conventions sop up the overflow bounced from the Legion. Either way, of course, Smith" (turning to me in the back) "and in finding your way back to the emotional wilderness you're bound to get a present from . . . someone. Will some maple syrup help you feel better?"

"Sure, Henry."

And that was Morley. Meanwhile the car began climbing into the foothills somewhere and we came to sundry sullen

towns where we stopped for gas and nothing but bluejeaned
Elvis Presleys in the road, waiting to beat somebody up, but
down beyond them the roar of fresh creeks and the feel of the
high mountains not far away. A pure sweet night, and finally
we got out on a real narrow tar country road and headed up
toward the mountains for sure. Tall pine trees began to appear
at the side of the road and occasional rock cliffs. The air felt
nippy and grand. This also happened to be the opening eve of
the hunting season and in a bar where we stopped for a drink
there were many hunters in red caps and wool shirts looking
silly getting loaded, with all their guns and shells in their cars
and eagerly asking us if we'd seen any deer or not. We had,
certainly, seen a deer, just before we came to the bar. Morley
had been driving and talking, saying, "Well Ryder maybe you'll
be Alfred Lord Tennyson of our little tennis party here on the
Coast, they'll call you the New Bohemian and compare you to
the Knights of the Round Table minus Amadis the Great and
the extraordinary splendors of the little Moorish kingdom that
was sold round to Ethiopia for seventeen thousand camels and
sixteen hundred foot soldiers when Caesar was sucking on his
mammy's teat," and suddenly the deer was in the road, looking
at our headlamps, petrified, before leaping into the shrubbery
by the side of the road and disappearing into the sudden vast
diamond silence of the forest (which we heard as Morley cut the
motor) and just the scuffle of its hoofs running off to the haven
of the raw fish Indian up there in the mists. It was real country
we were in, Morley said about three thousand feet now. We
could hear creeks rushing coldly below on cold starlit rocks
without seeing them. "Hey little deer," I'd yelled to the
animal, "don't worry, we won't shoot you." Now in the bar,
where we'd stopped at my insistence ("In this kinda cold
northern upmountain country ain't nothin better for a man's
soul at midnight but a good warm glass of warmin red port
heavy as the syrups of Sir Arthur")—

"Okay Smith," said Japhy, "but seems to me we shouldn't
drink on a hiking trip."

"Ah who gives a damn?"

"Okay, but look at all the money we saved by buying cheap
dried foods for this weekend and all you're gonna do is drink it
right down."

"That's the story of my life rich or poor and mostly poor and truly poor." We went in the bar, which was a roadhouse all done up in the upcountry mountain style, like a Swiss chalet, with moose heads and designs of deer on the booths and the people in the bar itself an advertisement for the hunting season but all of them loaded, a weaving mass of shadows at the dim bar as we walked in and sat at three stools and ordered the port. The port was a strange request in the whisky country of hunters but the bartender rousted up an odd bottle of Christian Brothers port and poured us two shots in wide wineglasses (Morley a teetotaler actually) and Japhy and I drank and felt it fine.

"Ah," said Japhy warming up to his wine and midnight, "soon I'm going back north to visit my childhood wet woods and cloudy mountains and old bitter intellectual friends and old drunken logger friends, by God, Ray you ain't lived till you been up there with me, or without. And then I'm going to Japan and walk all over that hilly country finding ancient little temples hidden and forgotten in the mountains and old sages a hundred and nine years old praying to Kwannon in huts and meditating so much that when they come out of meditation they laugh at everything that moves. But that don't mean I don't love America, by God, though I hate these damn hunters, all they wanta do is level a gun at a helpless sentient being and murder it, for every sentient being or living creature these actual pricks kill they will be reborn a thousand times to suffer the horrors of samsara and damn good for 'em too."

"Hear that, Morley, Henry, what you think?"

"My Buddhism is nothing but a mild unhappy interest in some of the pictures they've drawn though I must say sometimes Cacoethes strikes a nutty note of Buddhism in his mountainclimbing poems though I'm not much interested in the belief part of it." In fact it didn't make a goddamn much of a difference to him. "I'm neutral," said he, laughing happily with a kind of an eager slaking leer, and Japhy yelled:

"Neutral is what Buddhism is!"

"Well, that port'll make you have to swear off yogurt. You know I am *a fortiori* disappointed because there's no Benedictine or Trappist wine, only Christian Brothers holy waters and spirits around here. Not that I feel very expansive about being here in this curious bar anyway, it looks like the homeplate for Ciardi and Bread Loaf writers, Armenian grocers all of 'em, well-meaning awkward Protestants who are on a group excursion for a binge and want to but don't understand how to insert the contraception. These people must be assholes," he added in a sudden straight revelation. "The milk around here must be fine but more cows than people. This must be a different race of Anglos up here, I don't particularly warm up to their appearance. The fast kids around here must go thirty-four miles. Well, Japhy," said he, concluding, "if you ever get an official job I hope you get a Brooks Brothers suit . . . hope you don't wind up in artsfartsy parties where it would— Say," as some girls walked in, "young hunters . . . must be why the baby wards are open all year."

But the hunters didn't like us to be huddled there talking close and friendly in low voices about sundry personal topics and joined us and pretty soon it was a long funny harangue up and down the oval bar about deer in the locality, where to go climb, what do do, and when they heard we were out in this country not to kill animals but just to climb mountains they took us to be hopeless eccentrics and left us alone. Japhy and I had two wines and felt fine and went back in the car with Morley and we drove away, higher and higher, the trees taller, the air colder, climbing, till finally it was almost two o'clock in the morning and they said we had a long way to go yet to Bridgeport and the foot of the trail so we might as well sleep out in these woods in our sleeping bags and call it a day.

"We'll get up at dawn and take off. Meanwhile we have this good brown bread and cheese too," said Japhy producing it, brown bread and cheese he'd thrown in at the last minute in his little shack, "and that'll make a fine breakfast and we'll save the bulgur and goodies for our breakfast tomorrow morning at ten thousand feet." Fine. Still talking and all, Morley drove the car a little way over some hard pine needles under an immense spread of natural park trees, firs and ponderosas a hundred feet high some of them, a great quiet starlit grove with frost on the ground and dead silence except for occasional little ticks of sound in the thickets where maybe a rabbit stood petrified hearing us. I got out my sleeping bag and spread it out and took off my shoes and just as I was sighing happily and slipping my stockinged feet into my sleeping bag and looking around gladly at the beautiful tall trees thinking "Ah what a night of true sweet sleep this will be, what meditations I can get into in this intense silence of Nowhere" Japhy yelled at me from the car: "Say, it appears Mr. Morley has forgotten his sleeping bag!"

"What . . . well now what?"

They discussed it awhile fiddling with flashlights in the frost and then Japhy came over and said "You'll have to crawl outa there Smith, all we have is two sleeping bags now and gotta zip 'em open and spread 'em out to form a blanket for three, god-dammit that'll be cold."

"What? And the cold'll slip in around the bottoms!"

"Well Henry can't sleep in that car, he'll freeze to death, no heater."

"But goddammit I was all ready to enjoy this so much," I whined getting out and putting on my shoes and pretty soon Japhy had fixed the two sleeping bags on top of ponchos and was already settled down to sleep and on toss it was me had to sleep in the middle, and it was way below freezing by now, and the stars were icicles of mockery. I got in and lay down and Morley, I could hear the maniac blowing up his ridiculous air mattress so he could lay beside me, but the moment he'd done so, he started at once to turn over and heave and sigh, and around the other side, and back toward me, and around the other side, all under the ice-cold stars and loveliness, while Japhy snored, Japhy who wasn't subjected to all the mad wig-gling. Finally Morley couldn't sleep at all and got up and went to the car probably to talk to himself in that mad way of his and I got a wink of sleep, but in a few minutes he was back, freezing, and got under the sleeping-bag blanket but started to turn and turn again, even curse once in a while, or sigh, and this went on for what seemed to be eternities and the first thing I knew Au-rora was paling the eastern hems of Amida and pretty soon we'd be getting up anyway. That mad Morley! And this was only the beginning of the misadventures of that most remark-able man (as you'll see now), that remarkable man who was probably the only mountainclimber in the history of the world who forgot to bring his sleeping bag. "Jesus," I thought, "why didn't he just forget his dreary air mattress instead."

7

From the very first moment we'd met Morley he'd kept emitting sudden yodels in keeping with our venture. This was a simple "Yodelayhee" but it came at the oddest moments and in oddest circumstances, like several times when his Chinese and German friends were still around, then later in the car, sitting with us enclosed, "Yodelayhee!" and then as we got out of the car to go in the bar, "Yodelayhee!" Now as Japhy woke up and saw it was dawn and jumped out of the bags and ran to gather firewood and shudder over a little preliminary fire, Morley woke up from his nervous small sleep of dawn, yawned, and yelled "Yodelayhee!" which echoed toward vales in the distance. I got up too; it was all we could do to hold together; the only thing to do was hop around and flap your arms, like me and my sad bum on the gon on the south coast. But soon Japhy got more logs on the fire and it was a roaring bonfire that we turned our backs to after a while and yelled and talked. A beautiful morning—red pristine shafts of sunlight coming in over the hill and slanting down into the cold trees like cathedral light, and the mists rising to meet the sun, and all the way around the giant secret roar of tumbling creeks probably with films of ice in the pools. Great fishing country. Pretty soon I was yelling "Yodelayhee" myself but when Japhy went to fetch more wood and we couldn't see him for a while and Morley yelled "Yodelayhee" Japhy answered back with a simple "Hoo" which he said was the Indian way to call in the mountains and much nicer. So I began to yell "Hoo" myself.

Then we got in the car and started off. We ate the bread and cheese. No difference between the Morley of this morning and the Morley of last night, except his voice as he rattled on yakking in that cultured snide funny way of his was sorta cute with that morning freshness, like the way people's voices sound after getting up early in the morning, something faintly wistful and hoarse and eager in it, ready for a new day. Soon the sun was warm. The black bread was good, it had been baked by Sean Monahan's wife, Sean who had a shack in Corte Madera we could all go live in free of rent some day. The cheese was sharp Cheddar. But it didn't satisfy me much and when we got out into country with no more houses and anything I began to yearn for a good old hot breakfast and suddenly after we'd gone over a little creek bridge we saw a merry little lodge by the side of the road under tremendous juniper trees with smoke boiling out of the chimney and neon signs outside and a sign in the window advertising pancakes and hot coffee.

"Let's go in there, by God we need a man's breakfast if we're gonna climb all day."

Nobody complained about my idea and we went in, and sat at booths, and a nice woman took our orders with that cheery loquaciousness of people in the backcountry. "Well you boys goin huntin this mornin?"

"No'm," said Japhy, "just climbing Matterhorn."

"*Matterhorn*, why I wouldn't do that if somebody paid me a thousand dollars!"

Meanwhile I went out to the log johns out back and washed from water in the tap which was delightfully cold and made my face tingle, then I drank some of it and it was like cool liquid ice in my stomach and sat there real nice, and I had more. Shaggy dogs were barking in the golden red sunlight slanting down from the hundred-foot branches of the firs and ponderosas. I could see snowcapped mountains glittering in the distance. One of them was Matterhorn. I went in and the pancakes were ready, hot and steaming, and poured syrup over my three pats of butter and cut them up and slurped hot coffee and ate. So did Henry and Japhy—for once no conversation. Then we washed it all down with that incomparable cold water as hunters came in in hunting boots with wool shirts but no giddy drunk hunters but serious hunters ready to go out there after breakfast. There was a bar adjoining but nobody cared about alcohol this morning.

We got in the car, crossed another creek bridge, crossed a meadow with a few cows and log cabins, and came out on a plain which clearly showed Matterhorn rising the highest most awful looking of the jagged peaks to the south. "There she is," said Morley really proud. "Isn't it beautiful, doesn't it remind you of the Alps? I've got a collection of snow covered mountain photos you should see sometime."

"I like the real thing meself," said Japhy, looking seriously at the mountains and in that far-off look in his eyes, that secret self-sigh, I saw he was back home again. Bridgeport is a little sleepy town, curiously New England-like, on that plain. Two restaurants, two gas stations, a school, all sidewalking Highway 395 as it comes through there running from down Bishop way up to Carson City Nevada.

8

Now another incredible delay was caused as Mr. Morley decided to see if he could find a store open in Bridgeport and buy a sleeping bag or at least a canvas cover or tarpaulin of some kind for tonight's sleep at nine thousand feet and judging from last night's sleep at four thousand it was bound to be pretty cold. Meanwhile Japhy and I waited, sitting in the now hot sun of ten a.m. on the grass of the school, watching occasional laconic traffic pass by on the not-busy highway and watching to see the fortunes of a young Indian hitchhiker pointed north. We discussed him warmly. "That's what I like, hitchhiking around, feeling free, imagine though being an Indian and doing all that. Dammit Smith, let's go talk to him and wish him luck." The Indian wasn't very talkative but not unfriendly and told us he'd been making pretty slow time on 395. We wished him luck. Meanwhile in the very tiny town Morley was nowhere to be seen.

"What's he doing, waking up some proprietor in his bed back there?"

Finally Morley came back and said there was nothing available and the only thing to do was to borrow a couple of blankets at the lake lodge. We got in the car, went back down the highway a few hundred yards, and turned south toward the glittering trackless snows high in the blue air. We drove along beautiful Twin Lakes and came to the lake lodge, which was a big white framehouse inn, Morley went in and deposited five dollars for the use of two blankets for one night. A woman was standing in the doorway arms akimbo, dogs barked. The road was dusty, a dirt road, but the lake was cerulean pure. In it the reflections of the cliffs and foothills showed perfectly. But the road was being repaired and we could see yellow dust boiling up ahead where we'd have to walk along the lake road awhile before cutting across a creek at the end of the lake and up through underbrush and up the beginning of the trail.

We parked the car and got all our gear out and arranged it in the warm sun. Japhy put things in my knapsack and told me I had to carry it or jump in the lake. He was being very serious and leaderly and it pleased me more than anything else. Then with the same boyish gravity he went over to the dust of the road with the pickax and drew a big circle and began drawing things in the circle.

"What's that?"

"I'm doin a magic mandala that'll not only help us on our climb but after a few more marks and chants I'll be able to predict the future from it."

"What's a mandala?"

"They're the Buddhist designs that are always circles filled with things, the circle representing the void and the things illusion, see. You sometimes see mandalas painted over a Bodhisattva's head and can tell his history from studying it. Tibetan in origin."

I had on the tennis sneakers and now I whipped out my mountainclimbing cap for the day, which Japhy had consigned to me, which was a little black French beret, which I put on at a jaunty angle and hitched the knapsack up and I was ready to go. In the sneakers and the beret I felt more like a Bohemian painter than a mountainclimber. But Japhy had on his fine big boots and his little green Swiss cap with feather, and looked elfin but rugged. I see the picture of him alone in the mountains in that outfit: the vision: it's pure morning in the high dry Sierras, far off clean firs can be seen shadowing the sides of rocky hills, further yet snowcapped pinpoints, nearer the big bushy forms of pines and there's Japhy in his little cap with a big rucksack on his back, clomping along, but with a flower in his left hand which is hooked to the strap of the rucksack at his breast; grass grows out between crowded rocks and boulders; distant sweeps of scree can be seen making gashes down the sides of morning, his eyes shine with joy, he's on his way, his heroes are John Muir and Han Shan and Shih-te and Li Po and John Burroughs and Paul Bunyan and Kropotkin; he's small and has a funny kind of belly coming out as he strides, but it's not because his belly is big, it's because his spine curves a bit, but that's offset by the vigorous long steps he takes, actually the long steps of a tall man (as I found out following him up-trail) and his chest is deep and shoulders broad.

"Goldangit Japhy I feel great this morning," I said as we locked the car and all three of us started swinging down the lake road with our packs, straggling a bit occupying side and center and other side of the road like straggling infantrymen. "Isn't this a hell of a lot greater than The Place? Gettin drunk in there on a fresh Saturday morning like this, all bleary and sick, and here we are by the fresh pure lake walkin along in this good air, by God it's a haiku in itself."

"Comparisons are odious, Smith," he sent sailing back to me, quoting Cervantes and making a Zen Buddhist observation to boot. "It don't make a damn frigging difference whether you're in The Place or hiking up Matterhorn, it's all the same old void, boy." And I mused about that and realized he was right, comparisons *are* odious, it's all the same, but it sure felt great and suddenly I realized this (in spite of my swollen foot veins) would do me a lot of good and get me away from drinking and maybe make me appreciate perhaps a whole new way of living.

"Japhy I'm glad I met you. I'm gonna learn all about how to pack rucksacks and what to do and hide in these mountains when I'm sick of civilization. In fact I'm grateful I met you."

"Well Smith I'm grateful I met you too, learnin about how to write spontaneously and all that."

"Ah that's nothing."

"To me it's a lot. Let's go boys, a little faster, we ain't got no time to waste."

By and by we reached the boiling yellow dust where caterpillars were churning around and great big fat sweaty operators who didn't even look at us were swearing and cussing on the job. For them to climb a mountain you'd have to pay them double time and quadruple time today, Saturday.

Japhy and I laughed to think of it. I felt a little embarrassed with my silly beret but the cat operators didn't even look and soon we left them behind and were approaching the final little store lodge at the foot of the trail. It was a log cabin, set right on the end of the lake, and it was enclosed in a V of pretty big foothills. Here we stopped and rested awhile on the steps, we'd hiked approximately four miles but on flat good road, and went in and bought candy and crackers and Cokes and stuff. Then suddenly Morley, who'd not been silent on the four-mile hike, and looked funny in his own outfit which was that immense packboard with air mattress and all (deflated now) and no hat at all, so that he looked just like he does in the library, but with big floppy pants of some kind, Morley suddenly remembered he'd forgotten to drain the crankcase.

"So he forgot to drain the crankcase," I said noticing their consternation and not knowing much about cars, "so he forgot to brain the drankbase."

"No, this means that if it gets below freezing tonight down here the goddamn radiator explodes and we can't drive back home and have to walk twelve miles to Bridgeport and all and get all hung-up."

"Well maybe it won't be so cold tonight."

"Can't take a chance," said Morley and by that time I was pretty mad at him for finding more ways than he could figure to forget, foul up, disturb, delay, and make go round in circles this relatively simple hiking trip we'd undertaken.

"What you gonna do? What we gonna do, walk back four miles?"

"Only thing to do, I'll walk back alone, drain the crankcase, walk back and follow you up the trail and meet you tonight at the camp."

"And I'll light a big bonfire," said Japhy, "and you'll see the glow and just yodel and we'll direct you in."

"That's simple."

"But you've got to step on it to make it by nightfall at camp."

"I will, I'll start back right now."

But then I felt sorry about poor old hapless funny Henry and said "Ah hell, you mean you're not going to climb with us today, the hell with the crankcase come on with us."

"It'd cost too much money if that thing froze tonight, Smith no I think I better go back. I've got plenty of nice thoughts to keep me acquainted with probably what you two'll be talking about all day, aw hell I'll just start back right now. Be sure not to roar at bees and don't hurt the cur and if the tennis party comes on with everybody shirtless don't make eyes at the searchlight or the sun'll kick a girl's ass right back at you, cats and all and boxes of fruit and oranges thrown in" and some such statement and with no ado or ceremony there he went down the road with just a little handwave, muttering and talking on to himself, so we had to yell "Well so long Henry, hurry up" and he didn't answer but just walked off shrugging.

"You know," I said, "I think it doesn't make any difference to him anyway. He's just satisfied to wander around and forget things."

"And pat his belly and look at things as they are, sorta like in Chuangtse" and Japhy and I had a good laugh watching forlorn Henry swaggering down all that road we'd only just negotiated, alone and mad.

"Well here we go" said Japhy. "When I get tired of this big rucksack we'll swap."

"I'm ready now. Man, come on, give it to me now, I feel like carrying something heavy. You don't realize how *good* I feel, man, come on!" So we swapped packs and started off.

Both of us were feeling fine and were talking a blue streak, about anything, literature, the mountains, girls, Princess, the poets, Japan, our past adventures in life, and I suddenly realized it was a kind of blessing in disguise Morley had forgotten to drain the crankcase, otherwise Japhy wouldn't have got in a word edgewise all the blessed day and now I had a chance to hear his ideas. In the way he did things, hiking, he reminded me of Mike my boyhood chum who also loved to lead the way, real grave like Buck Jones, eyes to the distant horizons, like Natty Bumppo, cautioning me about snapping twigs or "It's too deep here, let's go down the creek a ways to ford it," or "There'll be mud in that low bottom, we better skirt around" and dead serious and glad. I saw all Japhy's boyhood in those eastern Oregon forests the way he went about it. He walked like he talked, from behind I could see his toes pointed slightly inward, the way mine do, instead of out; but when it came time to climb he pointed his toes out, like Chaplin, to make a kind of easier flapthwap as he trudged. We went across a kind of muddy riverbottom through dense undergrowth and a few willow trees and came out on the other side a little wet and started up the trail, which was clearly marked and named and had been recently repaired by trail crews but as we hit parts where a rock had rolled on the trail he took great precaution to throw the rock off saying "I used to work on trail crews, I can't see a trail all mettlesome like that, Smith." As we climbed the lake began to appear below us and suddenly in its clear blue pool we could see the deep holes where the lake had its springs, like black wells, and we could see schools of fish skitter.

"Oh this is like an early morning in China and I'm five years old in beginningless time!" I sang out and felt like sitting by the trail and whipping out my little notebook and writing sketches about it.

"Look over there," sang Japhy, "yellow aspens. Just put me in the mind of a haiku . . . 'Talking about the literary life— the yellow aspens.'" Walking in this country you could understand the perfect gems of haikus the Oriental poets had written, never getting drunk in the mountains or anything but just going along as fresh as children writing down what they saw without literary devices or fanciness of expression. We made up haikus as we climbed, winding up and up now on the slopes of brush.

"Rocks on the side of the cliff," I said, "why don't they tumble down?"

"Maybe that's a haiku, maybe not, it might be a little too complicated," said Japhy. "A real haiku's gotta be as simple as porridge and yet make you see the real thing, like the greatest haiku of them all probably is the one that goes 'The sparrow hops along the veranda, with wet feet.' By Shiki. You see the wet footprints like a vision in your mind and yet in those few words you also see all the rain that's been falling that day and almost smell the wet pine needles."

"Let's have another."

"I'll make up one of my own this time, let's see, 'Lake below . . . the black holes the wells make,' no that's not a haiku goddammit, you never can be too careful about haiku."

"How about making them up real fast as you go along, spontaneously?"

"Look here," he cried happily, "mountain lupine, see the delicate blue color those little flowers have. And there's some California red poppy over there. The whole meadow is just powdered with color! Up there by the way is a genuine California white pine, you never see them much any more."

"You sure know a lot about birds and trees and stuff."

"I've studied it all my life." Then also as we went on climbing we began getting more casual and making funnier sillier talk and pretty soon we got to a bend in the trail where it was suddenly gladey and dark with shade and a tremendous cataracting stream was bashing and frothing over scummy rocks and tumbling on down, and over the stream was a perfect bridge formed by a fallen snag, we got on it and lay bellydown and dunked our heads down, hair wet, and drank deep as the water splashed in our faces, like sticking your head by the jet of a dam. I lay there a good long minute enjoying the sudden coolness.

"This is like an advertisement for Rainier Ale!" yelled Japhy.

"Let's sit awhile and enjoy it."

"Boy you don't know how far we got to go yet!"

"Well I'm not tired!"

"Well you'll be, Tiger."

9

We went on, and I was immensely pleased with the way the trail had a kind of immortal look to it, in the early afternoon now, the way the side of the grassy hill seemed to be clouded with ancient gold dust and the bugs flipped over rocks and the wind sighed in shimmering dances over the hot rocks, and the way the trail would suddenly come into a cool shady part with big trees overhead, and here the light deeper. And the way the lake below us soon became a toy lake with those black well holes perfectly visible still, and the giant cloud shadows on the lake, and the tragic little road winding away where poor Morley was walking back.

"Can you see Morl down back there?"

Japhy took a long look. "I see a little cloud of dust, maybe

that's him comin back already." But it seemed that I had seen
the ancient afternoon of that trail, from meadow rocks and
lupine posies, to sudden revisits with the roaring stream with
its splashed snag bridges and undersea greennesses, there was
something inexpressibly broken in my heart as though I'd lived
before and walked this trail, under similar circumstances with a
fellow Bodhisattva, but maybe on a more important journey, I
felt like lying down by the side of the trail and remembering it
all. The woods do that to you, they always look familiar, long
lost, like the face of a long-dead relative, like an old dream, like
a piece of forgotten song drifting across the water, most of all
like golden eternities of past childhood or past manhood and
all the living and the dying and the heartbreak that went on a
million years ago and the clouds as they pass overhead seem to
testify (by their own lonesome familiarity) to this feeling. Ecstasy, even, I felt, with flashes of sudden remembrance, and
feeling sweaty and drowsy I felt like sleeping and dreaming in
the grass. As we got higher we got more tired and now like
two true mountainclimbers we weren't talking any more and
didn't have to talk and were glad, in fact Japhy mentioned
that, turning to me after a half-hour's silence, "This is the way
I like it, when you get going there's just no need to talk, as if
we were animals and just communicated by silent telepathy."
So huddled in our own thoughts we tromped on, Japhy using
that gazotsky trudge I mentioned, and myself finding my own
true step, which was short steps slowly patiently going up the
mountain at one mile an hour, so I was always thirty yards
behind him and when we had any haikus now we'd yell them
fore and aft. Pretty soon we got to the top of the part of the
trail that was a trail no more, to the incomparable dreamy
meadow, which had a beautiful pond, and after that it was
boulders and nothing but boulders.

"Only sign we have now to know which way we're going, is
ducks."

"What's ducks?"

"See those boulders over there?"

"See those boulders over there! Why God man, I see five
miles of boulders leading up to that mountain."

"See the little pile of rocks on that near boulder there by the

pine? That's a duck, put up by other climbers, maybe that's one
I put up myself in 'fifty-four I'm not sure. We just go from
boulder to boulder from now on keeping a sharp eye for ducks
then we get a general idea how to raggle along. Although of
course we know which way we're going, that big cliff face up
there is where our plateau is."

"Plateau? My God you mean that ain't the top of the
mountain?"

"Of course not, after that we got a plateau and then scree and
then more rocks and we get to a final alpine lake no biggern this
pond and then comes the final climb over one thousand feet
almost straight up boy to the top of the world where you'll see
all California and parts of Nevada and the wind'll blow right
through your pants."

"Ow . . . How long does it all take?"

"Why the only thing we can expect to make tonight is our
camp up there on that plateau. I call it a plateau, it ain't that at
all, it's a shelf between heights."

But the top and the end of the trail was such a beautiful spot
I said: "Boy look at this . . ." A dreamy meadow, pines at
one end, the pond, the clear fresh air, the afternoon clouds
rushing golden . . . "Why don't we just sleep here tonight, I
don't think I've ever seen a more beautiful park."

"Ah this is nowhere. It's great of course, but we might wake
up tomorrow morning and find three dozen schoolteachers on
horseback frying bacon in our backyard. Where we're going
you can bet your ass there won't be one human being, and
if there is, I'll be a spotted horse's ass. Or maybe just one
mountainclimber, or two, but I don't expect so at this time of
the year. You know the snow's about to come here any time
now. If it comes tonight it's goodbye me and you."

"Well goodbye Japhy. But let's rest here and drink some
water and admire the meadow." We were feeling tired and
great. We spread out in the grass and rested and swapped packs
and strapped them on and were rarin to go. Almost instanta-
neously the grass ended and the boulders started; we got up
on the first one and from that point on it was just a matter
of jumping from boulder to boulder, gradually climbing,
climbing, five miles up a valley of boulders getting steeper and

steeper with immense crags on both sides forming the walls of the valley, till near the cliff face we'd be scrambling up the boulders, it seemed.

"And what's behind that cliff face?"

"There's high grass up there, shrubbery, scattered boulders, beautiful meandering creeks that have ice in 'em even in the afternoon, spots of snow, tremendous trees, and one boulder just about as big as two of Alvah's cottages piled on top the other which leans over and makes a kind of concave cave for us to camp at, lightin a big bonfire that'll throw heat against the wall. Then after that the grass and the timber ends. That'll be at nine thousand just about."

With my sneakers it was as easy as pie to just dance nimbly from boulder to boulder, but after a while I noticed how gracefully Japhy was doing it and he just ambled from boulder to boulder, sometimes in a deliberate dance with his legs crossing from right to left, right to left and for a while I followed his every step but then I learned it was better for me to just spontaneously pick my own boulders and make a ragged dance of my own.

"The secret of this kind of climbing," said Japhy, "is like Zen. Don't think. Just dance along. It's the easiest thing in the world, actually easier than walking on flat ground which is monotonous. The cute little problems present themselves at each step and yet you never hesitate and you find yourself on some other boulder you picked out for no special reason at all, just like Zen." Which it was.

We didn't talk much now. It got tiresome on the leg muscles. We spent hours, about three, going up that long, long valley. In that time it grew to late afternoon and the light was growing amber and shadows were falling ominously in the valley of dry boulders and instead, though, of making you feel scared it gave you that immortal feeling again. The ducks were all laid out easy to see: on top of a boulder you'd stand, and look ahead, and spot a duck (usually only two flat rocks on top of each other maybe with one round one on top for decoration) and you aimed in that general direction. The purpose of these ducks, as laid out by all previous climbers, was to save a mile or two of wandering around in the immense valley. Meanwhile our roaring creek was still at it, but thinner and more quiet now, running from the cliff face itself a mile up the valley in a big black stain I could see in the gray rock.

Jumping from boulder to boulder and never falling, with a heavy pack, is easier than it sounds; you just can't fall when you get into the rhythm of the dance. I looked back down the valley sometimes and was surprised to see how high we'd come, and to see farther horizons of mountains now back there. Our beautiful trail-top park was like a little glen of the Forest of Arden. Then the climbing got steeper, the sun got redder, and pretty soon I began to see patches of snow in the shade of some rocks. We got up to where the cliff face seemed to loom over us. At one point I saw Japhy throw down his pack and danced my way up to him.

"Well this is where we'll drop our gear and climb those few hundred feet up the side of that cliff, where you see there it's shallower, and find that camp. I remember it. In fact you can sit here and rest or beat your bishop while I go ramblin around there, I like to ramble by myself."

Okay. So I sat down and changed my wet socks and changed soaking undershirt for dry one and crossed my legs and rested and whistled for about a half-hour, a very pleasant occupation, and Japhy got back and said he'd found the camp. I thought it would be a little jaunt to our resting place but it took almost another hour to jump up the steep boulders, climb around some, get to the level of the cliff-face plateau, and there, on flat grass more or less, hike about two hundred yards to where a huge gray rock towered among pines. Here now the earth was a splendorous thing—snow on the ground, in melting patches in the grass, and gurgling creeks, and the huge silent rock mountains on both sides, and a wind blowing, and the smell of heather. We forded a lovely little creek, shallow as your hand, pearl pure lucid water, and got to the huge rock. Here were old charred logs where other mountainclimbers had camped.

"And where's Matterhorn mountain?"

"You can't see it from here, but"—pointing up the farther long plateau and a scree gorge twisting to the right—"around that draw and up two miles or so and then we'll be at the foot of it."

"Wow, heck, whoo, that'll take us a whole other day!"

"Not when you're travelin with me, Smith."

"Well Ryderee, that's okay with me."

"Okay Smithee and now how's about we relax and enjoy ourselves and cook up some supper and wait for ole Morleree?"

So we unpacked our packs and laid things out and smoked and had a good time. Now the mountains were getting that pink tinge, I mean the rocks, they were just solid rock covered with the atoms of dust accumulated there since beginningless time. In fact I was afraid of those jagged monstrosities all around and over our heads.

"They're so silent!" I said.

"Yeah man, you know to me a mountain is a Buddha. Think of the patience, hundreds of thousands of years just sittin there bein perfectly perfectly silent and like praying for all living creatures in that silence and just waitin for us to stop all our frettin and foolin." Japhy got out the tea, Chinese tea, and sprinkled some in a tin pot, and had the fire going meanwhile, a small one to begin with, the sun was still on us, and stuck a long stick tight down under a few big rocks and made himself something to hang the teapot on and pretty soon the water was boiling and he poured it out steaming into the tin pot and we had cups of tea with our tin cups. I myself'd gotten the water from the stream, which was cold and pure like snow and the crystal-lidded eyes of heaven. Therefore, the tea was by far the most pure and thirstquenching tea I ever drank in all my life, it made you want to drink more and more, it actually quenched your thirst and of course it swam around hot in your belly.

"Now you understand the Oriental passion for tea," said Japhy. "Remember that book I told you about the first sip is joy the second is gladness, the third is serenity, the fourth is madness, the fifth is ecstasy."

"Just about old buddy."

That rock we were camped against was a marvel. It was thirty feet high and thirty feet at base, a perfect square almost, and twisted trees arched over it and peeked down on us. From the base it went outward, forming a concave, so if rain came we'd be partially covered. "How did this immense sonumbitch ever get here?"

"It probably was left here by the retreating glacier. See over there that field of snow?"

"Yeah."

"That's the glacier what's left of it. Either that or this rock tumbled here from inconceivable prehistoric mountains we can't understand, or maybe it just landed here when the friggin mountain range itself burst out of the ground in the Jurassic upheaval. Ray when you're up here you're not sittin in a Berkeley tea room. This is the beginning and the end of the world right here. Look at all those patient Buddhas lookin at us saying nothing."

"And you come out here by yourself. . . ."

"For weeks on end, just like John Muir, climb around all by myself following quartzite veins or making posies of flowers for my camp, or just walking around naked singing, and cook my supper and laugh."

"Japhy I gotta hand it to you, you're the happiest little cat in the world and the greatest by God you are. I'm sure glad I'm learning all this. This place makes me feel devoted, too, I mean, you know I have a prayer, did you know the prayer I use?"

"What?"

"I sit down and say, and I run all my friends and relatives and enemies one by one in this, without entertaining any angers or gratitudes or anything, and I say, like 'Japhy Ryder, equally empty, equally to be loved, equally a coming Buddha,' then I run on, say, to 'David O. Selznick, equally empty, equally to be loved, equally a coming Buddha' though I don't use names like David O. Selznick, just people I know because when I say the words 'equally a coming Buddha' I want to be thinking of their eyes, like you take Morley, his blue eyes behind those glasses, when you think 'equally a coming Buddha' you think of those eyes and you really do suddenly see the true secret serenity and the truth of his coming Buddhahood. Then you think of your enemy's eyes."

"That's great, Ray," and Japhy took out his notebook and wrote down the prayer, and shook his head in wonder. "That's really really great. I'm going to teach this prayer to the monks I meet in Japan. There's nothing wrong with you Ray, your only trouble is you never learned to get out to spots like this, you've let the world drown you in its horseshit and you've been vexed . . . though as I say comparisons *are* odious, but what we're sayin now is true."

He took his bulgur rough cracked wheat and dumped a couple of packages of dried vegetables in and put it all in the pot to be ready to be boiled at dusk. We began listening for the yodels of Henry Morley, which didn't come. We began to worry about him.

"The trouble about all this, dammit, if he fell off a boulder and broke his leg there'd be no one to help him. It's dangerous to . . . I do it all by myself but I'm pretty good, I'm a mountain goat."

"I'm gettin hungry."

"Me too dammit, I wish he gets here soon. Let's ramble around and eat snowballs and drink water and wait."

We did this, investigating the upper end of the flat plateau, and came back. By now the sun was gone behind the western wall of our valley and it was getting darker, pinker, colder, more hues of purple began to steal across the jags. The sky was deep. We even began to see pale stars, at least one or two. Suddenly we heard a distant "Yodelayhee" and Japhy leaped up and jumped to the top of a boulder and yelled "Hoo hoo hoo!" The Yodelayhee came back.

"How far is he?"

"My God from the sound of it he's not even started. He's not even at the beginning of the valley of boulders. He can never make it tonight."

"What'll we do?"

"Let's go to the rock cliff and sit on the edge and call him in an hour. Let's bring these peanuts and raisins and munch on 'em and wait. Maybe he's not so far as I think."

We went over to the promontory where we could see the whole valley and Japhy sat down in full lotus posture cross-legged on a rock and took out his wooden juju prayerbeads and prayed. That is, he simply held the beads in his hands, the hands upsidedown with thumbs touching, and stared straight ahead and didn't move a bone. I sat down as best I could on another rock and we both said nothing and meditated. Only I meditated with my eyes closed. The silence was an intense roar. From where we were, the sound of the creek, the gurgle

and slapping talk of the creek, was blocked off by rocks. We
heard several more melancholy Yodelayhees and answered them
but it seemed farther and farther away each time. When I opened
my eyes the pink was more purple all the time. The stars began
to flash. I fell into deep meditation, felt that the mountains
were indeed Buddhas and our friends, and I felt the weird sensation that it was strange that there were only three men in this
whole immense valley: the mystic number three. Nirmanakaya,
Sambhogakaya, and Dharmakaya. I prayed for the safety and
in fact the eternal happiness of poor Morley. Once I opened
my eyes and saw Japhy sitting there rigid as a rock and I felt
like laughing he looked so funny. But the mountains were
mighty solemn, and so was Japhy, and for that matter so was I,
and in fact laughter is solemn.

It was beautiful. The pinkness vanished and then it was all
purple dusk and the roar of the silence was like a wash of diamond waves going through the liquid porches of our ears,
enough to soothe a man a thousand years. I prayed for Japhy,
for his future safety and happiness and eventual Buddhahood.
It was all completely serious, all completely hallucinated, all
completely happy.

"Rocks are space," I thought, "and space is illusion." I had
a million thoughts. Japhy had his. I was amazed at the way he
meditated with his eyes open. And I was mostly humanly
amazed that this tremendous little guy who eagerly studied
Oriental poetry and anthropology and ornithology and everything else in the books and was a tough little adventurer of
trails and mountains should also suddenly whip out his pitiful
beautiful wooden prayerbeads and solemnly pray there, like an
oldfashioned saint of the deserts certainly, but so amazing to
see it in America with its steel mills and airfields. The world
ain't so bad, when you got Japhies, I thought, and felt glad.
All the aching muscles and the hunger in my belly were bad
enough, and the surroundant dark rocks, the fact that there is
nothing there to soothe you with kisses and soft words, but
just to be sitting there meditating and praying for the world
with another earnest young man—'twere good enough to
have been born just to die, as we all are. Something will come
of it in the Milky Ways of eternity stretching in front of all our
phantom unjaundiced eyes, friends. I felt like telling Japhy

everything I thought but I knew it didn't matter and moreover he knew it anyway and silence is the golden mountain.

"Yodelayhee," sang Morley, and now it was dark, and Japhy said "Well, from the looks of things he's still far away. He has enough sense to pitch his own camp down there tonight so let's go back to our camp and cook supper."

"Okay." And we yelled "Hoo" a couple of times reassuringly and gave up poor Morl for the night. He did have enough sense, we knew. And as it turned out he did, and pitched his camp, wrapped up in his two blankets on top of the air mattress, and slept the night out in that incomparably happy meadow with the pond and the pines, telling us about it when he finally reached us the next day.

IO

I rousted about and got a lot of little pieces of wood to make kindling for the fire and then I went around gathering bigger pieces and finally I was hunting out huge logs, easy to find all over the place. We had a fire that Morley must have seen from five miles away, except we were way up behind the cliff face, cut off from his view. It cast mighty blasts of heat against our cliff, the cliff absorbed it and threw it back, we were in a hot room except that the ends of our noses were nippy from sticking them out of that area to get firewood and water. Japhy put the bulgur in the pot with water and started it boiling and stirred it around and meanwhile busied himself with the mixings for the chocolate pudding and started boiling that in a separate smaller pot out of my knapsack. He also brewed a fresh pot of tea. Then he whipped out his double set of chopsticks and pretty soon we had our supper ready and laughed over it. It was the most delicious supper of all time. Up out of the orange glow of our fire you could see immense systems of uncountable stars, either as individual blazers, or in low Venus droppers, or vast Milky Ways incommensurate with human understanding, all cold, blue, silver, but our food and our fire was pink and goodies. And true to what Japhy had predicted, I had absolutely not a jot of appetite for alcohol, I'd forgotten all about it, the altitude was too high, the exercise too heavy, the air too brisk, the air itself was enough to get your drunk ass drunk. It was a tremendous supper, food is always better eaten in doleful little pinchfuls off the ends of chopsticks, no gobbling, the reason why Darwin's law of survival applies best to China: if you don't know how to handle a chopstick and stick it in that family pot with the best of 'em, you'll starve. I ended up flupping it all up with my forefinger anyhow.

Supper done, Japhy assiduously got to scraping the pots with a wire scraper and got me to bring water, which I did dipping a leftover can from other campers into the fire pool of stars, and came back with a snowball to boot, and Japhy washed the dishes in preboiled water. "Usually I don't wash my dishes, I just wrap 'em up in my blue bandana, cause it really doesn't matter . . . though they don't appreciate this little bit of wisdom in the horse-soap building thar on Madison Avenue, what you call it, that English firm, Urber and Urber, whatall, damn hell and upsidedown boy I'll be as tight as Dick's hatband if I don't feel like takin out my star map and seein what the lay of the pack is tonight. That houndsapack up there more uncountable than all your favorite Surangamy sutries, boy." So he whips out his star map and turns it around a little, and adjusts, and looks, and says, "It's exactly eight-forty-eight p.m."

"How do you know."

"Sirius wouldn't be where Sirius is, if it wasn't eight-fortyeight p.m. . . . You know what I like about you, Ray, you've woke me up to the true language of this country which is the language of the working men, railroad men, loggers. D'yever hear them guys talk?"

"I shore did. I had a guy, an oil rig driver, truck, picked me up in Houston Texas one night round about midnight after some little faggot who owned some motel courts called of all things and rather appropriately my dear, Dandy Courts, had left me off and said if you can't get a ride come on in sleep on my floor, so I wait about an hour in the empty road and here comes this rig and it's driven by a Cherokee he said he was but his name was Johnson or Ally Reynolds or some damn thing and as he talked starting in with a speech like 'Well boy I left my mammy's cabin before you knew the smell of the river and came west to drive myself mad in the East Texas oilfield' and

all kinds of rhythmic talk and with every bang of rhythm he'd
ram at his clutch and his various gears and pop up the truck
and had her roaring down the road about seventy miles an
hour with momentum only when his story got rolling with
him, magnificent, that's what I call poetry."

"That's what I mean. You oughta hear old Burnie Byers talk
up that talk up in the Skagit country, Ray you just gotta go up
there."

"Okay I will."

Japhy, kneeling there studying his star map, leaning forward
slightly to peek up through the overhanging gnarled old rock
country trees, with his goatee and all, looked, with that mighty
grawfaced rock behind him, like, exactly like the vision I had of
the old Zen Masters of China out in the wilderness. He was
leaning forward on his knees, upward looking, as if with a holy
sutra in his hands. Pretty soon he went to the snowbank and
brought back the chocolate pudding which was now ice cold
and absolutely delicious beyond words. We ate it all up.

"Maybe we oughta leave some for Morley."

"Ah it won't keep, it'll melt in the morning sun."

As the fire stopped roaring and just got to be red coals, but
big ones six feet long, the night interposed its icy crystal feel
more and more but with the smell of smoking logs it was as
delicious as chocolate pudding. For a while I went on a little
walk by myself, out by the shallow iced creek, and sat meditating against a stump of dirt and the huge mountain walls on
both sides of our valley were silent masses. Too cold to do this
more than a minute. As I came back our orange fire casting its
glow on the big rock, and Japhy kneeling and peering up at
the sky, and all of it ten thousand feet above the gnashing world,
was a picture of peace and good sense. There was another aspect of Japhy that amazed me: his tremendous and tender
sense of charity. He was always giving things, always practicing
what the Buddhists call the Paramita of Dana, the perfection
of charity.

Now when I came back and sat down by the fire he said
"Well Smith it's about time you owned a set of juju beads you
can have these," and he handed me the brown wood beads run
together over a strong string with the string, black and shiny,
coming out at the large bead at the end in a pretty loop.

"Aw you can't give me something like this, these things come from Japan don't they?"

"I've got another set of black ones. Smith that prayer you gave me tonight is worth that set of juju beads, but you can have it anyway." A few minutes later he cleaned out the rest of the chocolate pudding but made sure that I got most of it. Then when he laid boughs over the rock of our clearing and the poncho over that he made sure his sleeping bag was farther away from the fire than mine so I would sure to be warm. He was always practicing charity. In fact he taught me, and a week later I was giving him nice new undershirts I'd discovered in the Goodwill store. He'd turn right around and make me a gift of a plastic container to keep food in. For a joke I'd give him a gift of a huge flower from Alvah's yard. Solemnly a day later he'd bring me a little bouquet of flowers picked in the street plots of Berkeley. "And you can keep the sneakers too," he said. "I've got another pair older than those but just as good."

"Aw I can't be taking all your things."

"Smith you don't realize it's a privilege to practice giving presents to others." The way he did it was charming; there was nothing glittery and Christmasy about it, but almost sad, and sometimes his gifts were old beat-up things but they had the charm of usefulness and sadness of his giving.

We rolled into our sleeping bags, it was freezing cold now, about eleven o'clock, and talked a while more before one of us just didn't answer from the pillow and pretty soon we were asleep. While he snored I woke up and just lay flat back with my eyes to the stars and thanked God I'd come on this mountain climb. My legs felt better, my whole body felt strong. The crack of the dying logs was like Japhy making little comments on my happiness. I looked at him, his head was buried way under inside his duck-down bag. His little huddled form was the only thing I could see for miles of darkness that was so packed and concentrated with eager desire to be good. I thought, "What a strange thing is man . . . like in the Bible it says, Who knoweth the spirit of man that looketh upward? This poor kid ten years younger than I am is making me look like a fool forgetting all the ideals and joys I knew before, in my recent years of drinking and disappointment, what does he care if he hasn't got any money: he doesn't need any money, all he needs is his rucksack with those little plastic bags of dried food and a good pair of shoes and off he goes and enjoys the privileges of a millionaire in surroundings like this. And what gouty millionaire could get up this rock anyhow? It took us all day to climb." And I promised myself that I would begin a new life. "All over the West, and the mountains in the East, and the desert, I'll tramp with a rucksack and make it the pure way." I went to sleep after burying my nose under the sleeping bag and woke up around dawn shivering, the ground cold had seeped through the poncho and through the bag and my ribs were up against a damper damp than the damp of a cold bed. My breath was coming out in steams. I rolled over to the other ribs and slept more: my dreams were pure cold dreams like ice water, happy dreams, no nightmares.

When I woke up again and the sunlight was a pristine orange pouring through the crags to the east and down through our fragrant pine boughs, I felt like I did when I was a boy and it was time to get up and go play all day Saturday, in overalls. Japhy was already up singing and blowing on his hands at a small fire. White frost was on the ground. He rushed out a way and yelled out "Yodelayhee" and by God we heard it come right back at us from Morley, closer than the night before. "He's on his way now. Wake up Smith and have a hot cupa tea, do you good!" I got up and fished my sneakers out of the sleeping bag where they'd been kept warm all night, and put them on, and put on my beret, and jumped up and ran a few blocks in the grass. The shallow creek was iced over except in the middle where a rill of gurgles rolled like tinkly tinkly. I fell down on my belly and took a deep drink, wetting my face. There's no feeling in the world like washing your face in cold water on a mountain morning. Then I went back and Japhy was heating up the remains of last night's supper and it was still good. Then we went out on the edge of the cliff and Hooed at Morley, and suddenly we could see him, a tiny figure two miles down the valley of boulders moving like a little animate being in the immense void. "That little dot down there is our witty friend Morley," said Japhy in his funny resounding voice of a lumberjack.

In about two hours Morley was within talking distance of us

and started right in talking as he negotiated the final boulders, to where we were sitting in the now warm sun on a rock waiting.

"The Ladies' Aid Society says I should come up and see if you boys would like to have blue ribbons pinned on your shirts, they say there's plenty of pink lemonade left and Lord Mountbatten is getting mighty impatient. You think they'll investigate the source of that recent trouble in the Mid-East, or learn to appreciate coffee better. I should think with a couple of literary gentlemen like you two they should learn to mind their manners . . ." and so on and so on, for no reason at all, yakking in the happy blue morning sky over rocks with his slaking grin, sweating a little from the long morning's work.

"Well Morley you ready to climb Matterhorn?"

"I'm ready just as soon as I can change these wet socks."

II

At about noon we started out, leaving our big packs at the camp where nobody was likely to be till next year anyway, and went up the scree valley with just some food and first-aid kits. The valley was longer than it looked. In no time at all it was two o'clock in the afternoon and the sun was getting that later more golden look and a wind was rising and I began to think "By gosh how we ever gonna climb that mountain, tonight?"

I put it up to Japhy who said: "You're right, we'll have to hurry."

"Why don't we just forget it and go on home?"

"Aw come on Tiger, we'll make a run up that hill and then we'll go home." The valley was long and long and long. And at the top end it got very steep and I began to be a little afraid of falling down, the rocks were small and it got slippery and my ankles were in pain from yesterday's muscle strain anyway. But Morley kept walking and talking and I noticed his tremendous endurance. Japhy took his pants off so he could look just like an Indian, I mean stark naked, except for a jockstrap, and hiked almost a quarter-mile ahead of us, sometimes waiting a while, to give us time to catch up, then went on, moving fast, wanting to climb the mountain today. Morley came second, about fifty yards ahead of me all the way. I was in no hurry. Then as it got later afternoon I went faster and decided to pass Morley and join Japhy. Now we were at about eleven thousand feet and it was cold and there was a lot of snow and to the east we could see immense snowcapped ranges and whooee levels of valleyland below them, we were already practically on top of California. At one point I had to scramble, like the others, on a narrow ledge, around a butte of rock, and it really scared me: the fall was a hundred feet, enough to break your neck, with another little ledge letting you bounce a minute preparatory to a nice goodbye one-thousand-foot drop. The wind was whipping now. Yet that whole afternoon, even more than the other, was filled with old premonitions or memories, as though I'd been there before, scrambling on these rocks, for other purposes more ancient, more serious, more simple. We finally got to the foot of Matterhorn where there was a most beautiful small lake unknown to the eyes of most men in this world, seen by only a handful of mountainclimbers, a small lake at eleven thousand some odd feet with snow on the edges of it and beautiful flowers and a beautiful meadow, an alpine meadow, flat and dreamy, upon which I immediately threw myself and took my shoes off. Japhy'd been there a half-hour when I made it, and it was cold now and his clothes were on again. Morley came up behind us smiling. We sat there looking up at the imminent steep scree slope of the final crag of Matterhorn.

"That don't look much, we can do it!" I said glad now.

"No, Ray, that's more than it looks. Do you realize that's a thousand feet more?"

"That much?"

"Unless we make a run up there, double-time, we'll never make it down again to our camp before nightfall and never make it down to the car at the lodge before tomorrow morning at, well at midnight."

"Phew."

"I'm tired," said Morley. "I don't think I'll try it."

"Well that's right," I said. "The whole purpose of mountainclimbing to me isn't just to show off you can get to the top, it's getting out to this wild country."

"Well I'm gonna go," said Japhy.

"Well if you're gonna go I'm goin with you."

"Morley?"

"I don't think I can make it. I'll wait here." And that wind was strong, too strong, I felt that as soon as we'd be a few hundred feet up the slope it might hamper our climbing.

Japhy took a small pack of peanuts and raisins and said "This'll be our gasoline, boy. You ready Ray to make a double-time run?"

"Ready. What would I say to the boys in The Place if I came all this way only to give up at the last minute?"

"It's late so let's hurry." Japhy started up walking very rapidly and then even running sometimes where the climb had to be to the right or left along ridges of scree. Scree is long land-slides of rocks and sand, very difficult to scramble through, always little avalanches going on. At every few steps we took it seemed we were going higher and higher on a terrifying elevator, I gulped when I turned around to look back and see all of the state of California it would seem stretching out in three directions under huge blue skies with frightening planetary space clouds and immense vistas of distant valleys and even plateaus and for all I knew whole Nevadas out there. It was terrifying to look down and see Morley a dreaming spot by the little lake waiting for us. "Oh why didn't I stay with old Henry?" I thought. I now began to be afraid to go any higher from sheer fear of being too high. I began to be afraid of being blown away by the wind. All the nightmares I'd ever had about falling off mountains and precipitous buildings ran through my head in perfect clarity. Also with every twenty steps we took upward we both became completely exhausted.

"That's because of the high altitude now Ray," said Japhy sitting beside me panting. "So have raisins and peanuts and you'll see what kick it gives you." And each time it gave us such a tremendous kick we both jumped up without a word and climbed another twenty, thirty steps. Then sat down again, panting, sweating in the cold wind, high on top of the world our noses sniffling like the noses of little boys playing late Saturday afternoon their final little games in winter. Now the wind began to howl like the wind in movies about the Shroud of Tibet. The steepness began to be too much for me;

I was afraid now to look back any more; I peeked: I couldn't even make out Morley by the tiny lake.

"Hurry it up," yelled Japhy from a hundred feet ahead. "It's getting awfully late." I looked up to the peak. It was right there, I'd be there in five minutes. "Only a half-hour to go!" yelled Japhy. I didn't believe it. In five minutes of scrambling angrily upward I fell down and looked up and it was still just as far away. What I didn't like about that peak-top was that the clouds of all the world were blowing right through it like fog.

"Wouldn't see anything up there anyway," I muttered. "Oh why did I ever let myself into this?" Japhy was way ahead of me now, he'd left the peanuts and raisins with me, it was with a kind of lonely solemnity now he had decided to rush to the top if it killed him. He didn't sit down any more. Soon he was a whole football field, a hundred yards ahead of me, getting smaller. I looked back and like Lot's wife that did it. "*This is too high!*" I yelled to Japhy in a panic. He didn't hear me. I raced a few more feet up and fell exhausted on my belly, slipping back just a little. "*This is too high!*" I yelled. I was really scared. Supposing I'd start to slip back for good, these screes might start sliding any time anyway. That damn mountain goat Japhy, I could see him jumping through the foggy air up ahead from rock to rock, up, up, just the flash of his boot bottoms. "How can I keep up with a maniac like that?" But with nutty desperation I followed him. Finally I came to a kind of ledge where I could sit at a level angle instead of having to cling not to slip, and I nudged my whole body inside the ledge just to hold me there tight, so the wind would not dislodge me, and I looked down and around and I had had it. "*I'm stayin here!*" I yelled to Japhy.

"Come on Smith, only another five minutes. I only got a hundred feet to go!"

"*I'm staying right here! It's too high!*"

He said nothing and went on. I saw him collapse and pant and get up and make his run again.

I nudged myself closer into the ledge and closed my eyes and thought "Oh what a life this is, why do we have to be born in the first place, and only so we can have our poor gentle flesh laid out to such impossible horrors as huge mountains and rock and empty space," and with horror I remembered the famous Zen saying, "When you get to the top of a mountain, keep climbing." The saying made my hair stand on end; it had been such cute poetry sitting on Alvah's straw mats. Now it was enough to make my heart pound and my heart bleed for being born at all. "In fact when Japhy gets to the top of that crag he *will* keep climbing, the way the wind's blowing. Well this old philosopher is staying right here," and I closed my eyes. "Besides," I thought, "rest and be kind, you don't have to prove anything." Suddenly I heard a beautiful broken yodel of a strange musical and mystical intensity in the wind, and looked up, and it was Japhy standing on top of Matterhorn peak letting out his triumphant mountain-conquering Buddha Mountain Smashing song of joy. It was beautiful. It was funny, too, up here on the not-so-funny top of California and in all that rushing fog. But I had to hand it to him, the guts, the endurance, the sweat, and now the crazy human singing: whipped cream on top of ice cream. I didn't have enough strength to answer his yodel. He ran around up there and went out of sight to investigate the little flat top of some kind (he said) that ran a few feet west and then dropped sheer back down maybe as far as I care to the sawdust floors of Virginia City. It was insane. I could hear him yelling at me but I just nudged farther in my protective nook, trembling. I looked down at the small lake where Morley was lying on his back with a blade of grass in his mouth and said out loud "Now there's the karma of these three men here: Japhy Ryder gets to his triumphant mountaintop and makes it, I almost make it and have to give up and huddle in a bloody cave, but the smartest of them all is that poet's poet lyin down there with his knees crossed to the sky chewing on a flower dreaming by a gurgling *plage*, goddammit they'll never get me up here again."

12

I really was amazed by the wisdom of Morley now: "Him with all his goddamn pictures of snowcapped Swiss Alps" I thought.

Then suddenly everything was just like jazz: it happened in one insane second or so: I looked up and saw Japhy *running down the mountain* in huge twenty-foot leaps, running, leaping, landing with a great drive of his booted heels, bouncing five feet or so, running, then taking another long crazy yelling yodelaying sail down the sides of the world and in that flash I realized *it's impossible to fall off mountains you fool* and with a yodel of my own I suddenly got up and began running down the mountain after him doing exactly the same huge leaps, the same fantastic runs and jumps, and in the space of about five minutes I'd guess Japhy Ryder and I (in my sneakers, driving the heels of my sneakers right into sand, rock, boulders, I didn't care any more I was so anxious to get down out of there) came leaping and yelling like mountain goats or I'd say like Chinese lunatics of a thousand years ago, enough to raise the hair on the head of the meditating Morley by the lake, who said he looked up and saw us flying down and couldn't believe it. In fact with one of my greatest leaps and loudest screams of joy I came flying right down to the edge of the lake and dug my sneakered heels into the mud and just fell sitting there, glad. Japhy was already taking his shoes off and pouring sand and pebbles out. It was great. I took off my sneakers and poured out a couple of buckets of lava dust and said "Ah Japhy you taught me the final lesson of them all, you can't fall off a mountain."

"And that's what they mean by the saying, When you get to the top of a mountain keep climbing, Smith."

"Dammit that yodel of triumph of yours was the most beautiful thing I ever heard in my life. I wish I'd a had a tape recorder to take it down."

"Those things aren't made to be heard by the people below," says Japhy dead serious.

"By God you're right, all those sedentary bums sitting around on pillows hearing the cry of the triumphant mountain smasher, they don't deserve it. But when I looked up and saw you running down that mountain I suddenly understood everything."

"Ah a little satori for Smith today," says Morley.

"What were you doing down here?"

"Sleeping, mostly."

"Well dammit I didn't get to the top. Now I'm ashamed of myself because now that I know how to come *down* a mountain I know how to go *up* and that I can't fall off, but now it's too late."

"We'll come back next summer Ray and climb it. Do you realize that this is the first time you've been mountainclimbin and you left old veteran Morley here way behind you?"

"Sure," said Morley. "Do you think, Japhy, they would assign Smith the title of Tiger for what he done today?"

"Oh sure," says Japhy, and I really felt proud. I was a Tiger.

"Well dammit I'll be a lion next time we get up here."

"Let's go men, now we've got a long long way to go back down this scree to our camp and down that valley of boulders and then down that lake trail, wow, I doubt if we can make it before pitch dark."

"It'll be mostly okay." Morley pointed to the sliver of moon in the pinkening deepening blue sky. "That oughta light us a way."

"Let's go." We all got up and started back. Now when I went around that ledge that had scared me it was just fun and a lark, I just skipped and jumped and danced along and I had really learned that you can't fall off a mountain. Whether you *can* fall off a mountain or not I don't know, but I had learned that you can't. That was the way it struck me.

It was a joy, though, to get down into the valley and lose sight of all that open sky space underneath everything and finally, as it got graying five o'clock, about a hundred yards from the other boys and walking alone, to just pick my way singing and thinking along the little black cruds of a deer trail through the rocks, no call to think or look ahead or worry, just follow the little balls of deer crud with your eyes cast down and enjoy life. At one point I looked and saw crazy Japhy who'd climbed for fun to the top of a snow slope and skied right down to the bottom, about a hundred yards, on his boots and the final few yards on his back, yippeeing and glad. Not only that but he'd taken off his pants again and wrapped them around his neck. This pants bit of his was simply he said for comfort, which is true, besides nobody around to see him anyway, though I figured that when he went mountainclimbing with girls it didn't make any difference to him. I could hear Morley talking to him in the great lonely valley: even across the rocks you could tell it was his voice. Finally I followed my

deer trail so assiduously I was by myself going along ridges and
down across creekbottoms completely out of sight of them,
though I could hear them, but I trusted the instinct of my
sweet little millennial deer and true enough, just as it was getting dark their ancient trail took me right to the edges of the
familiar shallow creek (where they stopped to drink for the last
five thousand years) and there was the glow of Japhy's bonfire
making the side of the big rock orange and gay. The moon was
bright high in the sky. "Well that moon's gonna save our ass,
we got eight miles to go downtrail boys."

We ate a little and drank a lot of tea and arranged all our
stuff. I had never had a happier moment in my life than those
lonely moments coming down that little deer trace and when
we hiked off with our packs I turned to take a final look up
that way, it was dark now, hoping to see a few dear little deer,
nothing in sight, and I thanked everything up that way. It had
been like when you're a little boy and have spent a whole day
rambling alone in the woods and fields and on the dusk homeward walk you did it all with your eyes to the ground, scuffling, thinking, whistling, like little Indian boys must feel when
they follow their striding fathers from Russian River to Shasta
two hundred years ago, like little Arab boys following their
fathers, their fathers' trails; that singsong little joyful solitude,
nose sniffling, like a little girl pulling her little brother home
on the sled and they're both singing little ditties of their imagination and making faces at the ground and just being themselves before they have to go in the kitchen and put on a straight
face again for the world of seriousness. "Yet what could be
more serious than to follow a deer trace to get to your water?"
I thought. We got to the cliff and started down the five-mile
valley of boulders, in clear moonlight now, it was quite easy to
dance down from boulder to boulder, the boulders were snow
white, with patches of deep black shadow. Everything was
cleanly whitely beautiful in the moonlight. Sometimes you
could see the silver flash of the creek. Far down were the pines
of the meadow park and the pool of the pond.

At this point my feet were unable to go on. I called Japhy
and apologized. I couldn't take any more jumps. There were
blisters not only on the bottoms but on the sides of my feet,

from there having been no protection all yesterday and today. So Japhy swapped and let me wear his boots.

With these big lightweight protective boots on I knew I could go on fine. It was a great new feeling to be able to jump from rock to rock without having to feel the pain through the thin sneakers. On the other hand, for Japhy, it was also a relief to be suddenly lightfooted and he enjoyed it. We made double-time down the valley. But every step was getting us bent, now, we were all really tired. With the heavy packs it was difficult to control those thigh muscles that you need to go *down* a mountain, which is sometimes harder than going up. And there were all those boulders to surmount, for sometimes we'd be walking in sand awhile and our path would be blocked by boulders and we had to climb them and jump from one to the other then suddenly no more boulders and we had to jump down to the sand. Then we'd be trapped in impassable thickets and had to go around them or try to crash through and sometimes I'd get stuck in a thicket with my rucksack, standing there cursing in the impossible moonlight. None of us were talking. I was angry too because Japhy and Morley were afraid to stop and rest, they said it was dangerous at this point to stop.

"What's the difference the moon's shining, we can even sleep."

"No, we've got to get down to that car tonight."

"Well let's stop a minute here. My legs can't take it."

"Okay, only a minute."

But they never rested long enough to suit me and it seemed to me they were getting hysterical. I even began to curse them and at one point I even gave Japhy hell: "What's the sense of killing yourself like this, you call this fun? Phooey." (Your ideas are a crock, I added to myself.) A little weariness'll change a lot of things. Eternities of moonlight rock and thickets and boulders and ducks and that horrifying valley with the two rim walls and finally it seemed we were almost out of there, but nope, not quite yet, and my legs screaming to stop, and me cursing and smashing at twigs and throwing myself on the ground to rest a minute.

"Come on Ray, everything comes to an end." In fact I realized I had no guts anyway, which I've long known. But I have joy. When we got to the alpine meadow I stretched out on my belly and drank water and enjoyed myself peacefully in silence while they talked and worried about getting down the rest of the trail in time.

"Ah don't worry, it's a beautiful night, you've driven yourself too hard. Drink some water and lie down here for about five even ten minutes, everything takes care of itself." Now I was being the philosopher. In fact Japhy agreed with me and we rested peacefully. That good long rest assured my bones I could make it down to the lake okay. It was beautiful going down the trail. The moonlight poured through thick foliage and made dapples on the backs of Morley and Japhy as they walked in front of me. With our packs we got into a good rhythmic walk and enjoying going "Hup hup" as we came to switchbacks and swiveled around, always down, down, the pleasant downgoing swinging rhythm trail. And that roaring creek was a beauty by moonlight, those flashes of flying moon water, that snow white foam, those black-as-pitch trees, regular elfin paradises of shadow and moon. The air began to get warmer and nicer and in fact I thought I could begin to smell people again. We could smell the nice raunchy tidesmell of the lake water, and flowers, and softer dust of down below. Everything up there had smelled of ice and snow and heartless spine rock. Here there was the smell of sun-heated wood, sunny dust resting in the moonlight, lake mud, flowers, straw, all those good things of the earth. The trail was fun coming down and yet at one point I was as tired as ever, more than in that endless valley of boulders, but you could see the lake lodge down below now, a sweet little lamp of light and so it didn't matter. Morley and Japhy were talking a blue streak and all we had to do was roll on down to the car. In fact suddenly, as in a happy dream, with the suddenness of waking up from an endless nightmare and it's all over, we were striding across the road and there were houses and there were automobiles parked under trees and Morley's car was sitting right there.

"From what I can tell by feeling this air," said Morley, leaning on the car as we slung our packs to the ground, "it mustn't have froze at all last night, I went back and drained the crankcase for nothing."

"Well maybe it did freeze." Morley went over and got motor oil at the lodge store and they told him it hadn't been freezing at all, but one of the warmest nights of the year.

"All that mad trouble for nothing," I said. But we didn't care. We were famished. I said "Let's go to Bridgeport and go in one of those lunchcarts there boy and eat hamburg and potatoes and hot coffee." We drove down the lakeside dirt road in the moonlight, stopped at the inn where Morley returned the blankets, and drove on into the little town and parked on the highway. Poor Japhy, it was here finally I found out his Achilles heel. This little tough guy who wasn't afraid of anything and could ramble around mountains for weeks alone and run down mountains, was afraid of going into a restaurant because the people in it were too well dressed. Morley and I laughed and said "What's the difference? We'll just go in and eat." But Japhy thought the place I chose looked too bourgeois and insisted on going to a more workingman-looking restaurant across the highway. We went in there and it was a desultory place with lazy waitresses letting us sit there five minutes without even bringing a menu. I got mad and said "Let's go to that other place. What you afraid of, Japhy, what's the difference? You may know all about mountains but I know about where to eat." In fact we got a little miffed at each other and I felt bad. But he came to the other place, which was the better restaurant of the two, with a bar on one side, many hunters drinking in the dim cocktail-lounge light, and the restaurant itself a long counter and a lot of tables with whole gay families eating from a very considerable selection. The menu was huge and good: mountain trout and everything. Japhy, I found, was also afraid of spending ten cents more for a good dinner. I went to the bar and bought a glass of port and brought it to our stool seats at the counter (Japhy: "You sure you can do that?") and I kidded Japhy awhile. He felt better now. "That's what's the trouble with you Japhy, you're just an old anarchist scared of society. What difference does it make? Comparisons are odious."

"Well Smith it just looked to me like this place was full of old rich farts and the prices would be too high, I admit it, I'm scared of all this American wealth, I'm just an old bhikku and I got nothin to do with all this high standard of living, goddammit, I've been a poor guy all my life and I can't get used to some things."

"Well your weaknesses are admirable. I'll buy 'em." And we had a raving great dinner of baked potatoes and porkchops and salad and hot buns and blueberry pie and the works. We were so honestly hungry it wasn't funny and it was honest. After dinner we went into a liquor store where I bought a bottle of muscatel and the old proprietor and his old fat buddy looked at us and said "Where you boys been?"

"Climbin Matterhorn out there," I said proudly. They only stared at us, gaping. But I felt great and bought a cigar and lit up and said "Twelve thousand feet and we come down outa there with such an appetite and feelin so good that now this wine is gonna hit us just right." The old men gaped. We were all sunburned and dirty and wildlooking, too. They didn't say anything. They thought we were crazy.

We got in the car and drove back to San Francisco drinking and laughing and telling long stories and Morley really drove beautifully that night and wheeled us silently through the graying dawn streets of Berkeley as Japhy and I slept dead to the world in the seats. At some point or other I woke up like a little child and was told I was home and staggered out of the car and went across the grass into the cottage and opened my blankets and curled up and slept till late the next afternoon a completely dreamless beautiful sleep. When I woke up the next day the veins in my feet were all cleared. I had worked the blood clots right out of existence. I felt very happy.

13

When I got up the next day I couldn't help smiling thinking of Japhy standing huddled in the night outside the fancy restaurant wondering if we would be let in or not. It was the first time I'd ever seen him afraid of anything. I planned to tell him about such things, that night, when he'd be coming over. But that night everything happened. First, Alvah left and went out for a few hours and I was alone reading when suddenly I heard a bike in the yard and I looked and it was Princess.

"Where's everybody?" says she.

"How long can you stay?"

"I've got to go right away, unless I call my mother."

"Let's call."

"Okay."

We went down to the corner gas station pay phone, and she said she'd be home in two hours, and as we walked back along the sidewalk I put my arm around her waist but way around with my fingers digging into her belly and she said "*Oooh*, I can't stand that!" and almost fell down on the sidewalk and bit my shirt just as an old woman was coming our way ogling us angrily and after she passed us we clinched in a big mad passionate kiss under the trees of evening. We rushed to the cottage where she spent an hour literally spinning in my arms and Alvah walked in right in the middle of our final ministrations of the Bodhisattva. We took our usual bath together. It was great sitting in the hot tub chatting and soaping each other's backs. Poor Princess, she meant every word she said. I really felt good about her, and compassionate, and even warned her: "Now don't go wild and get into orgies with fifteen guys on a mountaintop."

Japhy came after she left, and then Coughlin came and suddenly (we had wine) a mad party began in the cottage. It started off with Coughlin and me, drunk now, walking arm in arm down the main drag of town carrying huge, almost impossibly huge flowers of some kind we'd found in a garden, and a new jug of wine, shouting haikus and hoos and satoris at everybody we saw in the street and everybody was smiling at us. "Walked five miles carrying huge flower," yelled Coughlin, and I liked him now, he was deceptively scholarly looking or fatty-boomboom looking but he was a real man. We went to visit some professor of the English Department at U. of Cal. we knew and Coughlin left his shoes on the lawn and danced right into the astonished professor's house, in fact frightened him somewhat, though Coughlin was a fairly well known poet by now. Then barefooted with our huge flowers and jugs we went back to the cottage it was now about ten. I had just gotten some money in the mail that day, a fellowship of three hundred bucks, so I said to Japhy "Well I've learned everything now, I'm ready. How about driving me to Oakland tomorrow and helping me buy all my rucksack and gear and stuff so I can take off for the desert?"

"Good, I'll get Morley's car and be over to get you first thing in the morning, but right now how about some of that wine?" I turned on the little red bandana dimbulb and we poured wine and all sat around talking. It was a great night of talk. First Japhy started telling his later life story, like when he was a merchant seaman in New York port and went around with a dagger on his hip, 1948, which surprised Alvah and me, and then about the girl he was in love with who lived in California: "I had a hardon for her three thousand miles long, goodness!"

Then Coughlin said "Tell 'em about Great Plum, Japh."

Instantly Japhy said "Great Plum Zen Master was asked what the great meaning of Buddhism was, and he said rush flowers, willow catkins, bamboo needles, linen thread, in other words hang on boy, the ecstasy's general, 's what he means, ecstasy of the mind, the world is nothing but mind and what is the mind? The mind is nothing but the world, goddammit. Then Horse Ancestor said 'This mind is Buddha.' He also said 'No mind is Buddha.' Then finally talking about Great Plum his boy, 'The plum is ripe.'"

"Well that's pretty interesting," said Alvah, "but Où sont les neiges d'antan?"

"Well I sort of agree with you because the trouble is these people saw the flowers like they were in a dream but dammitall the world is *real* Smith and Goldbook and everybody carries on like it was a dream, shit, like they were themselves dreams or dots. Pain or love or danger makes you real again, ain't that right Ray like when you were scared on that ledge?"

"Everything was real, okay."

"That's why frontiersmen are always heroes and were always my real heroes and will always be. They're constantly on the alert in the realness which might as well be real as unreal, what difference does it make, Diamond Sutra says 'Make no formed conceptions about the realness of existence nor about the unrealness of existence,' or words like that. Handcuffs will get soft and billy clubs will topple over, let's go on being free anyhow."

"The President of the United States suddenly grows cross-eyed and floats away!" I yell.

"And anchovies will turn to dust!" yells Coughlin.

"The Golden Gate is creaking with sunset rust," says Alvah.

"And anchovies will turn to dust," insists Coughlin.

"Give me another slug of that jug. How! Ho! Hoo!" Japhy leaping up: "I've been reading Whitman, know what he says, *Cheer up slaves, and horrify foreign despots,* he means that's the attitude for the Bard, the Zen Lunacy bard of old desert paths, see the whole thing is a world full of rucksack wanderers, Dharma Bums refusing to subscribe to the general demand that they consume production and therefore have to work for the privilege of consuming, all that crap they didn't really want anyway such as refrigerators, TV sets, cars, at least new fancy cars, certain hair oils and deodorants and general junk you finally always see a week later in the garbage anyway, all of them imprisoned in a system of work, produce, consume, work, produce, consume, I see a vision of a great rucksack revolution thousands or even millions of young Americans wandering around with rucksacks, going up to mountains to pray, making children laugh and old men glad, making young girls happy and old girls happier, all of 'em Zen Lunatics who go about writing poems that happen to appear in their heads for no reason and also by being kind and also by strange unexpected acts keep giving visions of eternal freedom to everybody and to all living creatures, that's what I like about you Goldbook and Smith, you two guys from the East Coast which I thought was dead."

"We thought the *West* Coast was dead!"

"You've really brought a fresh wind around here. Why, do you realize the Jurassic pure granite of Sierra Nevada with the straggling high conifers of the last ice age and lakes we just saw is one of the greatest expressions on this earth, just think how truly great and wise America will be, with all this energy and exuberance and space focused into the Dharma."

"Oh"—Alvah—"balls on that old tired Dharma."

"Ho! What we need is a floating zendo, where an old Bodhisattva can wander from place to place and always be sure to find a spot to sleep in among friends and cook up mush."

" 'The boys was glad, and rested up for more, and Jack cooked mush, in honor of the door,' " I recited.

"What's that?"

"That's a poem I wrote. 'The boys was sittin in a grove of trees, listenin to Buddy explain the keys. Boys, sez he, the Dharma is a door . . . Let's see . . . Boys, I say the keys, cause there's lotsa keys, but only one door, one hive for the bees. So listen to me, and I'll try to tell all, as I heard it long ago, in the Pure Land Hall. For you good boys, with wine-soaked teeth, that can't understand these words on a heath, I'll make it simpler, like a bottle of wine, and a good woodfire, under stars divine. Now listen to me, and when you have learned the Dharma of the Buddhas of old and yearned, to sit down with the truth, under a lonesome tree, in Yuma Arizony, or anywhere you be, don't thank me for tellin, what was told me, this is the wheel I'm a-turnin, this is the reason I be: Mind is the Maker, for no reason at all, for all this creation, created to fall.'"

"Ah but that's too pessimistic and like dream gucky," says Alvah, "though the rhyme is pure like Melville."

"We'll have a floatin zendo for Buddy's winesoaked boys to come and lay up in and learn to drink tea like Ray did, learn to meditate like you should Alvah, and I'll be a head monk of a zendo with a big jar full of crickets."

"Crickets?"

"Yessir, that's what, a series of monasteries for fellows to go and monastate and meditate in, we can have groups of shacks up in the Sierras or the High Cascades or even Ray says down in Mexico and have big wild gangs of pure holy men getting together to drink and talk and pray, think of the waves of salvation can flow out of nights like that, and finally have women, too, wives, small huts with religious families, like the old days of the Puritans. Who's to say the cops of America and the Republicans and Democrats are gonna tell everybody what to do?"

"What's the crickets?"

"Big jar full of crickets, give me another drink Coughlin, about one tenth of an inch long with huge white antennae and hatch 'em myself, little sentient beings in a bottle that sing real good when they grow up. I wanta swim in rivers and drink goatmilk and talk with priests and just read Chinese books and amble around the valleys talking to farmers and their children. We've got to have mind-collecting weeks in our zendos where your mind tries to fly off like a Tinker Toy and like a good soldier you put it back together with your eyes closed except of course the whole thing is wrong. D'y'hear my latest poem Goldbook?"

"No what?"

"Mother of children, sister, daughter of sick old man, virgin your blouse is torn, hungry and barelegged, I'm hungry too, take these poems."

"Fine, fine."

"I wanta bicycle in hot afternoon heat, wear Pakistan leather sandals, shout in high voice at Zen monk buddies standing in thin hemp summer robes and stubble heads, wanta live in golden pavilion temples, drink beer, say goodbye, go Yokahama big buzz Asia port full of vassals and vessels, hope, work around, come back, go, go to Japan, come back to U.S.A., read Hakuin, grit my teeth and discipline myself all the time while getting nowhere and thereby learn . . . learn that my body and everything gets tired and ill and droopy and so find out all about Hakuyu."

"Who's Hakuyu?"

"His name meant White Obscurity, his name meant he who lived in the hills back of Northern-White-Water where I'm gonna go hiking, by God, it must be full of steep piney gorges and bamboo valleys and little cliffs."

"I'll go with you!" (me).

"I wanta read about Hakuin, who went to see this old man who lived in a cave, slept with deer and ate chestnuts and the old man told him to quit meditating and quit thinking about koans, as Ray says, and instead learn how to go to sleep and wake up, said, when you go to sleep you should put your legs together and take deep breaths and then concentrate your mind on a spot one and a half inches below your navel until you feel it get like a ball of power and then start breathing from your heels clear up and concentrate saying to yourself that that center just here is Amida's Pure Land, the center of the mind, and when you wake up you should start by consciously breathing and stretching a little and thinking the same thoughts, see, the rest of the time."

"That's what I like, see," says Alvah, "these actual signposts to something. What else?"

"The rest of the time he said don't bother about thinkin about nothin, just eat well, not too much, and sleep good, and old Hakuyu said he was three hundred friggin years old just then and figured he was good for five hundred more, by Gawd which makes me think he must still be up there if he's anybody at all."

"Or the sheepherder kicked his dog!" puts in Coughlin.

"I bet I can find that cave in Japan."

"You can't live in this world but there's nowhere else to go," laughs Coughlin.

"What's that mean?" I ask.

"It means the chair I sit in is a lion throne and the lion is walking, he roars."

"What's he say?"

"Says, Rahula! Rahula! Face of Glory! Universe chawed and swallowed!"

"Ah balls!" I yell.

"I'm goin to Marin County in a few weeks," said Japhy, "go walk a hunnerd times around Tamalpais and help purify the atmosphere and accustom the local spirits to the sound of sutra. What you think, Alvah?"

"I think it's all lovely hallucination but I love it sorta."

"Alvah, trouble with you is you don't do plenty night zazen especially when it's cold out, that's best, besides you should get married and have halfbreed babies, manuscripts, homespun blankets and mother's milk on your happy ragged mat floor like this one. Get yourself a hut house not too far from town, live cheap, go ball in the bars once in a while, write and rumble in the hills and learn how to saw boards and talk to grandmas you damn fool, carry loads of wood for them, clap your hands at shrines, get supernatural favors, take flower-arrangement lessons and grow chrysanthemums by the door, and get married for krissakes, get a friendly smart sensitive human-being gal who don't give a shit for martinis every night and all that dumb white machinery in the kitchen."

"Oh," says Alvah sitting up glad, "and what else?"

"Think of barn swallows and nighthawks filling the fields. Do you know, say Ray, since yesterday I translated another stanza of Han Shan, lissen, 'Cold Mountain is a house, without beams or walls, the six doors left and right are open, the hall is the blue sky, the rooms are vacant and empty, the east wall strikes the west wall, at the center not one thing. Borrowers don't trouble me, in the cold I build a little fire, when I'm hungry I boil up some greens, I've got no use for the kulak with his big barn and pasture . . . he just sets up a prison for himself, once in, he can't get out, think it over, it might happen to you.'"

Then Japhy picked up his guitar and got going on songs; finally I took the guitar and made up a song as I went along plucking on the strings any old way, actually drumming on them with my fingertips, drum drum drum, and sang the song of the Midnight Ghost freight train. "That's about the midnight ghost in California but you know what it made me think of Smith? Hot, very hot, bamboo growing up to forty feet out thar and whipping around in the breeze and hot and a bunch of monks are making a racket on their flutes somewhere and when they recite sutras with a steady Kwakiutl dance drumbeat and riffs on the bells and sticks it's something to hear like a big prehistoric coyote chanting. . . . Things tucked away in all you mad guys like that go back to the days when men married bears and talked to the buffalo by Gawd. Give me another drink. Keep your socks darned, boys, and your boots greased."

But as though that wasn't enough Coughlin says quite calmly crosslegged "Sharpen your pencils, straighten your ties, shine your shoes and button your flies, brush your teeth, comb your hair, sweep the floor, eat blueberry pies, open your eyes . . ."

"Eat blueberry spies is good," says Alvah fingering his lip seriously.

"Remembering all the while that I have tried very hard, but the rhododendron tree is only half enlightened, and ants and bees are communists and trolley cars are bored."

"And little Japanese boys in the F train sing Inky Dinky Parly Voo!" I yell.

"And the mountains live in total ignorance so I don't give up, take off your shoes and put 'em in your pocket. Now I've answered all your questions, too bad, give me a drink, mauvais sujet."

"Don't step on the ballsucker!" I yell drunk.

"Try to do it without stepping on the aardvark," says Coughlin. "Don't be a sucker all your life, dummy up, ya dope. Do you see what I mean? My lion is fed, I sleep at his side."

"Oh," says Alvah, "I wish I could take all this down." And I was amazed, pretty amazed, by the fast wonderful yak yak yak darts in my sleeping brain. We all got dizzy and drunk. It was a mad night. It ended up with Coughlin and me wrestling and making holes in the wall and almost knocking the little cottage down: Alvah was pretty mad the next day. During the wrestling match I practically broke poor Coughlin's leg; myself, I got a bad splinter of wood stuck an inch up into my skin and it didn't come out till almost a year later. Meanwhile, at some point, Morley appeared in the doorway like a ghost carrying two quarts of yogurt and wanting to know if we wanted some. Japhy left at about two a.m. saying he'd come back and get me in the morning for our big day outfitting me with full pack. Everything was fine with the Zen Lunatics, the nut wagon was too far away to hear us. But there was a wisdom in it all, as you'll see if you take a walk some night on a suburban street and pass house after house on both sides of the street each with the lamplight of the living room, shining golden, and inside the little blue square of the television, each living family riveting its attention on probably one show; nobody talking; silence in the yards; dogs barking at you because you pass on human feet instead of on wheels. You'll see what I mean, when it begins to appear like everybody in the world is soon going to be thinking the same way and the Zen Lunatics have long joined dust, laughter on their dust lips. Only one thing I'll say for the people watching television, the millions and millions of the One Eye: they're not hurting anyone while they're sitting in front of that Eye. But neither was Japhy. . . . I see him in future years stalking along with full rucksack, in suburban streets, passing the blue television windows of homes, alone, his thoughts the only thoughts not electrified to the Master Switch. As for me, maybe the answer was in my little Buddy poem that kept on: " 'Who played this cruel joke, on bloke after bloke, packing like a rat, across the desert flat?' asked Montana Slim, gesturing to him, the buddy of the men, in this lion's den. 'Was it God got mad, like the Indian cad, who was only a giver, crooked like the river? Gave you a garden, let it all harden, then comes the flood, and the loss of your blood? Pray tell us, good buddy, and don't make it muddy, who played this trick, on Harry and Dick, and why is so mean, this Eternal Scene, just what's the point, of this whole joint?' " I thought maybe I could find out at last from these Dharma Bums.

14

But I had my own little bangtail ideas and they had nothing to do with the "lunatic" part of all this. I wanted to get me a full pack complete with everything necessary to sleep, shelter, eat, cook, in fact a regular kitchen and bedroom right on my back, and go off somewhere and find perfect solitude and look into the perfect emptiness of my mind and be completely neutral from any and all ideas. I intended to pray, too, as my only activity, pray for all living creatures; I saw it was the only decent activity left in the world. To be in some riverbottom somewhere, or in a desert, or in mountains, or in some hut in Mexico or shack in Adirondack, and rest and be kind, and do nothing else, practice what the Chinese call "do-nothing." I didn't want to have anything to do, really, either with Japhy's ideas about society (I figured it would be better just to avoid it altogether, walk around it) or with any of Alvah's ideas about grasping after life as much as you can because of its sweet sadness and because you would be dead some day.

When Japhy came to get me the following morning I had all this in mind. He and I and Alvah drove to Oakland in Morley's car and went first to some Goodwill stores and Salvation Army stores to buy various flannel shirts (at fifty cents a crack) and undershirts. We were all hung-up on colored undershirts, just a minute after walking across the street in the clean morning sun Japhy'd said, "You know, the earth is a fresh planet, why worry about anything?" (which is true) now we were foraging with bemused countenances among all kinds of dusty old bins filled with the washed and mended shirts of all the old bums in the Skid Row universe. I bought socks, one pair of long woolen Scotch socks that go way up over your knees, which would be useful enough on a cold night meditating in the frost. And I bought a nice little canvas jacket with zipper for ninety cents.

Then we drove to the huge Army Navy store in Oakland and went way in the back where sleeping bags were hanging from hooks and all kinds of equipment, including Morley's famous air mattress, water cans, flashlights, tents, rifles, canteens, rubber boots, incredible doodas for hunters and fishermen, out of which Japhy and I found a lot of useful little things for bhikkus. He bought an aluminum pot holder and made me a gift of it; it never burns you, being aluminum, and you just pluck your pots right out of a campfire with it. He selected an excellent duck-down used sleeping bag for me, zipping it open and examining the inside. Then a brand new rucksack, of which I was so proud. "I'll give you my own old sleeping-bag cover," he said. Then I bought little plastic snow glasses just for the hell of it, and railroad gloves, new ones. I figured I had good enough boots back home east, where I was going for Christmas, otherwise I would have bought a pair of Italian mountain boots like Japhy had.

We drove from the Oakland store to Berkeley again to the Ski Shop, where, as we walked in and the clerk came over, Japhy said in his lumberjack voice "Outfittin me friends for the Apocalypse." And he led me to the back of the store and picked out a beautiful nylon poncho with hood, which you put over you and even over your rucksack (making a huge hunchbacked monk) and which completely protects you from the rain. It can also be made into a pup tent, and can also be used as your sleeping mat under the sleeping bag. I bought a polybdenum bottle, with screw top, which could be used (I said to myself) to carry honey up to the mountains. But I later used it as a canteen for wine more than anything else, and later when I made some money as a canteen for whisky. I also bought a plastic shaker which came in very handy, just a tablespoon of powdered milk and a little creek water and you shake yourself up a glass of milk. I bought a whole bunch of food wraps like Japhy's. I was all outfitted for the Apocalypse indeed, no joke about that; if an atom bomb should have hit San Francisco that night all I'd have to do is hike on out of there, if possible, and with my dried foods all packed tight and my bedroom and kitchen on my head, no trouble in the world. The final big purchases were my cookpots, two large pots fitting into each other, with a handled cover that was also the frying pan, and tin cups, and small fitted-together cutlery in aluminum. Japhy made me another present from his own pack, a regular tablespoon, but he took out his pliers and twisted the handle up back and said "See, when you wanta pluck a pot out of a big fire, just go flup." I felt like a new man.

15

I put on my new flannel shirt and new socks and underwear and my jeans and packed the rucksack tight and slung it on and went to San Francisco that night just to get the feel of walking around the city night with it on my back. I walked down Mission Street singing merrily. I went to Skid Row Third Street to enjoy my favorite fresh doughnuts and coffee and the bums in there were all fascinated and wanted to know if I was going uranium hunting. I didn't want to start making speeches about what I was going to hunt for was infinitely more valuable to mankind in the long run than ore, but let them tell me: "Boy, all you gotta do is go to that Colorady country and take off with your pack there and a nice little Geiger counter and you'll be a millionaire." Everybody in Skid Row wants to be a millionaire.

"Okay boys," I said, "mebbe I'll do that."

"Lotsa uranium up in the Yukon country too."

"And down in Chihuahua," said an old man. "Bet any dough that's uranium in Chihuahua."

I went out of there and walked around San Francisco with my huge pack, happy. I went over to Rosie's place to see Cody and Rosie. I was amazed to see her, she'd changed so suddenly, she was suddenly skinny and a skeleton and her eyes were huge with terror and popping out of her face. "What's the matter?"

Cody drew me into the other room and didn't want me to talk to her. "She's got like this in the last forty-eight hours," he whispered.

"What's the matter with her?"

"She says she wrote out a list of all our names and all our sins, she says, and then tried to flush them down the toilet where she works, and the long list of paper stuck in the toilet and they had to send for some sanitation character to clean up the mess and she claims he wore a uniform and was a cop and took it with him to the police station and we're all going to be arrested. She's just nuts, that's all." Cody was my old buddy who'd let me live in his attic in San Francisco years ago, an old trusted friend. "And did you see the marks on her arms?"

"Yes." I had seen her arms, which were all cut up.

"She tried to slash her wrists with some old knife that doesn't cut right. I'm worried about her. Will you watch her while I go to work tonight?"

"Oh man—"

"Oh you, oh man, don't be like that. You know what it says in the Bible, 'even unto the least of these . . .'"

"All right but I was planning on having fun tonight."

"Fun isn't everything. You've got some responsibilities sometimes, you know."

I didn't have a chance to show off my new pack in The Place. He drove me to the cafeteria on Van Ness where I got Rosie a bunch of sandwiches with his money and I went back alone and tried to make her eat. She sat in the kitchen staring at me.

"But you don't realize what this means!" she kept saying. "Now they know *everything* about you."

"Who?"

"You."

"Me?"

"You, and Alvah, and Cody, and that Japhy Ryder, all of you, and me. Everybody that hangs around The Place. We're all going to be arrested tomorrow if not sooner." She looked at the door in sheer terror.

"Why'd you try to cut your arms like that? Isn't that a mean thing to do to yourself?"

"Because I don't want to live. I'm telling you there's going to be a big new revolution of police now."

"No, there's going to be a rucksack revolution," I said laughing, not realizing how serious the situation was; in fact Cody and I had no sense, we should have known from her arms how far she wanted to go. "Listen to me," I began, but she wouldn't listen.

"Don't you *realize* what's happening?" she yelled staring at me with big wide sincere eyes trying by crazy telepathy to make me believe that what she was saying was absolutely *true*. She stood there in the kitchen of the little apartment with her skeletal hands held out in supplicatory explanation, her legs braced, her red hair all frizzly, trembling and shuddering and grabbing her face from time to time.

"It's nothing but bullshit!" I yelled and suddenly I had the feeling I always got when I tried to explain the Dharma to people, Alvah, my mother, my relatives, girl friends, everybody, they never listened, they always wanted me to listen to them, *they* knew, I didn't know anything, I was just a dumb young kid and impractical fool who didn't understand the serious significance of this very important, very real world.

"The police are going to swoop down and arrest us all and not only that but we're all going to be questioned for weeks and weeks and maybe even years till they find out *all* the crimes and sins that have been committed, it's a network, it runs in every direction, finally they'll arrest everybody in North Beach and even everybody in Greenwich Village and then Paris and then finally they'll have *everybody* in jail, you don't know, it's only the beginning." She kept jumping at sounds in the hall, thinking the cops were coming.

"Why don't you listen to me?" I kept pleading, but each time I said that, she hypnotized me with her staring eyes and almost had me for a while believing in what she believed from the sheer weight of her complete dedication to the discriminations her mind was making. "But you're getting these silly convictions and conceptions out of nowhere, don't you realize all this life is just a dream? Why don't you just relax and enjoy God? God is *you*, you fool!"

"Oh, they're going to destroy you, Ray, I can see it, they're going to fetch all the religious squares too and fix them good. It's only begun. It's all tied in with Russia though they won't say it . . . and there's something I heard about the sun's rays and something about what happens while we're all asleep. Oh Ray the world will never be the same!"

"What world? What difference does it make? Please stop, you're scaring me. By God in fact you're not scaring me and I won't listen to another word." I went out, angry, bought some wine and ran into Cowboy and some other musicians and ran back with the gang to watch her. "Have some wine, put some wisdom in your head."

"No, I'm laying off the lush, all that wine you drink is rotgut, it burns your stomach out, it makes your brain dull. I can tell there's something wrong with you, you're not sensitive, you don't *realize* what's going on!"

"Oh come on."

"This is my last night on earth," she added.

The musicians and I drank up all the wine and talked, till about midnight, and Rosie seemed to be all right now, lying on the couch, talking, even laughing a bit, eating her sandwiches and drinking some tea I'd brewed her. The musicians left and I slept on the kitchen floor in my new sleeping bag. But when Cody came home that night and I was gone she went up on the roof while he was asleep and broke the skylight to get jagged bits of glass to cut her wrists, and was sitting there bleeding at dawn when a neighbor saw her and sent for the cops and when the cops ran out on the roof to help her that was it: she saw the great cops who were going to arrest us all and made a run for the roof edge. The young Irish cop made a flying tackle and just got a hold of her bathrobe but she fell out of it and fell naked to the sidewalk six flights below. The musicians, who lived downstairs in a basement pad, and had been up all night talking and playing records, heard the thud. They looked out the basement window and saw that horrible sight. "Man it broke us up, we couldn't make the gig that night." They drew the shades and trembled. Cody was asleep. . . . When I heard about it the next day, when I saw the picture in the paper showing an X on the sidewalk where she had landed, one of my thoughts was: "And if she had only listened to me . . . Was I talking so dumb after all? Are my ideas about what to do so silly and stupid and childlike? Isn't this the time now to start following what I know to be true?"

And that had done it. The following week I packed up and decided to hit the road and get out of that city of ignorance which is the modern city. I said goodbye to Japhy and the others and hopped my freight back down the Coast to L.A. Poor Rosie—she had been absolutely *certain* that the world was real and fear was real and now what was real? "At least," I thought, "she's in Heaven now, and she knows."

16

And that's what I said to myself, "I am now on the road to Heaven." Suddenly it became clear to me that there was a lot of teaching for me to do in my lifetime. As I say, I saw Japhy before I left, we wandered sadly to the Chinatown park, had a dinner in Nam Yuen's, came out, sat in the Sunday morning grass and suddenly here was this group of Negro preachers standing in the grass preaching to desultory groups of uninterested Chinese families letting their kiddies romp in the grass and to bums who cared just a little bit more. A big fat woman like Ma Rainey was standing there with her legs outspread howling out a tremendous sermon in a booming voice that kept breaking from speech to blues-singing music, beautiful, and the reason why this woman, who was such a great preacher, was not preaching in a church was because every now and then she just simply had to go *sploosh* and spit as hard as she could off to the side in the grass, "And I'm tellin you, the Lawd will take care of you if you re-cognize that you have a *new field* . . . *Yes!*"—and sploosh, she turns and spits about ten feet away a great sploosh of spit. "See," I told Japhy, "she couldn't do that in a church, that's her flaw as a preacher as far as the churches are concerned but boy have you ever heard a greater preacher?"

"Yeah," says Japhy. "But I don't like all that Jesus stuff she's talking about."

"What's wrong with Jesus? Didn't Jesus speak of Heaven? Isn't Heaven Buddha's nirvana?"

"According to your own interpretation, Smith."

"Japhy, there were things I wanted to tell Rosie and I felt suppressed by this schism we have about separating Buddhism from Christianity, East from West, what the hell difference does it make? We're all in Heaven now, ain't we?"

"Who said so?"

"Is this nirvana we're in now or ain't it?"

"It's both nirvana and samsara we're in now."

"Words, words, what's in a word? Nirvana by any other name. Besides don't you hear that big old gal calling you and telling you you've got a *new field*, a new Buddha-field boy?" Japhy was so pleased he wrinkled his eyes and smiled. "Whole Buddha-fields in every direction for each one of us, and Rosie was a flower we let wither."

"Never spoke more truly, Ray."

The big old gal came up to us, too, noticing us, especially me. She called me darling, in fact. "I kin see from your eyes that you understand ever word I'm sayin, darling. I want you to know that I want you to go to Heaven and be happy. I want you to understand ever word I'm sayin."

"I hear and understand."

Across the street was the new Buddhist temple some young Chamber of Commerce Chinatown Chinese were trying to build, by themselves, one night I'd come by there and, drunk, pitched in with them with a wheelbarrow hauling sand from outside in, they were young Sinclair Lewis idealistic forward-looking kids who lived in nice homes but put on jeans to come down and work on the church, like you might expect in some midwest town some midwest kids with a bright-faced Richard Nixon leader, the prairie all around. Here in the heart of the tremendously sophisticated little city called San Francisco Chinatown they were doing the same thing but their church was the church of Buddha. Strangely Japhy wasn't interested in the Buddhism of San Francisco Chinatown because it was traditional Buddhism, not the Zen intellectual artistic Buddhism he loved—but I was trying to make him see that everything was the same. In the restaurant we'd eaten with chopsticks and enjoyed it. Now he was saying goodbye to me and I didn't know when I'd see him again.

Behind the colored woman was a man preacher who kept rocking with his eyes closed saying "That's right." She said to us "Bless both you boys for listenin to what I have to say. Remember that we know that all things work together for good to them that loves *God*, to them who *are* the called accordin to *His* purpose. Romans eight eighteen, younguns. And there's a *new field* a-waitin for ya, and be sure you live up to every one of your obligations. Hear now?"

"Yes, ma'am, be seein ya." I said goodbye to Japhy.

I spent a few days with Cody's family in the hills. He was tremendously sad about Rosie's suicide and kept saying he had to pray for her night and day at this particular crucial moment when because she was a suicide her soul was still flitting around the surface of the earth ready for either purgatory or hell. "We got to get her in purgatory, man." So I helped him pray when I slept on his lawn at night in my new sleeping bag. During the days I took down the little poems his children recited to me, in my little breastpocket notebooks. Yoo hoo . . .

yoo hoo . . . I come to you . . . Boo hoo . . . boo hoo
. . . I love you . . . Bloo bloo . . . the sky is blue . . .
I'm higher than you . . . boo hoo . . . boo hoo. Mean-
while Cody was saying "Don't drink so much of that old wine."

Late Monday afternoon I was at the San Jose yards and
waited for the afternoon Zipper due in at four-thirty. It was its
day off so I had to wait for the Midnight Ghost due in at
seven-thirty. Meanwhile as soon as it got dark I cooked my can
of macaroni on a little Indian fire of twigs among the deep
dense weeds by the track, and ate. The Ghost was coming in.
A friendly switchman told me I'd better not try to get on it as
there was a yard bull at the crossing with a big flashlight who
would see if anybody was riding away on it and would phone
ahead of Watsonville to have them thrown off. "Now that it's
winter the boys have been breaking into the sealed trucks and
breaking windows and leaving bottles on the floor, wreckin
that train."

I sneaked down to the east end of the yard with heavy pack
slung on, and caught the Ghost as she was coming out,
beyond the bull's crossing, and opened the sleeping bag and
took my shoes off, put them under my wrapped-up balled-up
coat and slipped in and slept beautiful joyous sleep all the way
to Watsonville where I hid by the weeds till highball, got on
again, and slept then all night long flying down the unbelievable coast and O Buddha thy moonlight O Christ thy starling
on the sea, the sea, Surf, Tangair, Gaviota, the train going
eighty miles an hour and me warm as toast in my sleeping bag
flying down and going home for Christmas. In fact I only
woke up at about seven o'clock in the morning when the train
was slowing down into the L.A. yards and the first thing I saw,
as I was putting my shoes on and getting my stuff ready to
jump off, was a yard worker waving at me and yelling "Welcome to L.A.!"

But I was bound to get out of there fast. The smog was
heavy, my eyes were weeping from it, the sun was hot, the air
stank, a regular hell is L.A. And I had caught a cold from Cody's
kids and had that old California virus and felt miserable now.
With the water dripping out of reefer refrigerators I gathered
up palmfuls and splashed it in my face and washed and washed
my teeth and combed my hair and walked into L.A. to wait

until seven-thirty in the evening when I planned to catch the Zipper firstclass freight to Yuma Arizona. It was a horrible day waiting. I drank coffee in Skid Row coffee houses, South Main Street, coffee-and, seventeen cents.

At nightfall I was lurking around waiting for my train. A bum was sitting in a doorway watching me with peculiar interest. I went over to talk to him. He said he was an ex-Marine from Paterson New Jersey and after a while he whipped out a little slip of paper he read sometimes on freight trains. I looked at it. It was a quotation from the Digha Nikaya, the words of Buddha. I smiled; I didn't say anything. He was a great voluble bum, and a bum who didn't drink, he was an idealistic hobo and said "That's all there is to it, that's what I like to do, I'd rather hop freights around the country and cook my food out of tin cans over wood fires, than be rich and have a home or work. I'm satisfied. I used to have arthritis, you know, I was in the hospital for years. I found out a way to cure it and then I hit the road and I been on it ever since."

"How'd you cure your arthritis? I got thrombophlebitis myself."

"You do? Well this'll work for you too. Just stand on your head three minutes a day, or mebbe five minutes. Every morning when I get up whether it's in a riverbottom or right on a train that's rollin along, I put a little mat on the floor and I stand on my head and count to five hundred, that's about three minutes isn't it?" He was very concerned about whether counting up to five hundred made it three minutes. That was strange. I figured he was worried about his arithmetic record in school.

"Yeah, about that."

"Just do that every day and your phlebitis will go away like my arthritis did. I'm forty, you know. Also, before you go to bed at night, have hot milk and honey, I always have a little jar of honey" (he fished one out from his pack) "and I put the milk in a can and the honey, and heat it over the fire, and drink it. Just those two things."

"Okay." I vowed to take his advice because he was Buddha. The result was that in about three months my phlebitis disappeared completely, and didn't show up ever again, which is amazing. In fact since that time I've tried to tell doctors about this but they seem to think I'm crazy. Dharma Bum, Dharma Bum. I'll never forget that intelligent Jewish ex-Marine bum from Paterson New Jersey, whoever he was, with *his* little slip of paper to read in the raw gon night by dripping reefer platforms in the nowhere industrial formations of an America that is still magic America.

At seven-thirty my Zipper came in and was being made up by the switchmen and I hid in the weeds to catch it, hiding partly behind a telephone pole. It pulled out, surprisingly fast I thought, and with my heavy fifty-pound rucksack I ran out and trotted along till I saw an agreeable drawbar and took a hold of it and hauled on and climbed straight to the top of the box to have a good look at the whole train and see where my flatcar'd be. Holy smokes goddamn and all ye falling candles of heaven smash, but as the train picked up tremendous momentum and tore out of that yard I saw it was a bloody no-good eighteen-car sealed sonofabitch and at almost twenty miles an hour it was do or die, get off or hang on to my life at eighty miles per (impossible on a boxcar top) so I had to scramble down the rungs again but first I had to untangle my strap clip from where it had got caught in the catwalk on top so by the time I was hanging from the lowest rung and ready to drop off we were going too fast now. Slinging the rucksack and holding it hard in one hand calmly and madly I stepped off hoping for the best and turned everything away and only staggered a few feet and I was safe on ground.

But now I was three miles into the industrial jungle of L.A. in mad sick sniffling smog night and had to sleep all that night by a wire fence in a ditch by the tracks being waked up all night by rackets of Southern Pacific and Santa Fe switchers bellyaching around, till fog and clear of midnight when I breathed better (thinking and praying in my sack) but then more fog and smog again and horrible damp white cloud of dawn and my bag too hot to sleep in and outside too raw to stand, nothing but horror all night long, except at dawn a little bird blessed me.

The only thing to do was to get out of L.A. According to my friend's instructions I stood on my head, using the wire fence to prevent me from falling over. It made my cold feel a little better. Then I walked to the bus station (through tracks and side streets) and caught a cheap bus twenty-five miles to Riverside. Cops kept looking at me suspiciously with that big bag on my back. Everything was far away from the easy purity of being with Japhy Ryder in that high rock camp under peaceful singing stars.

17

It took exactly the entire twenty-five miles to get out of the smog of Los Angeles; the sun was clear in Riverside. I exulted to see a beautiful dry riverbottom with white sand and just a trickle river in the middle as we rolled over the bridge into Riverside. I was looking for my first chance to camp out for the night and try out my new ideas. But at the hot bus station a Negro saw me with my pack and came over and said he was part Mohawk and when I told him I was going back up the road to sleep in that riverbottom he said "No sir, you can't do that, cops in this town are the toughest in the state. If they see you down there they'll pull you in. Boy," said he, "I'd like to sleep outdoor too tonight but's against the law."

"This ain't India, is it," I said, sore, and walked off anyway to try it. It was just like the cop in the San Jose yards, even though it was against the law and they were trying to catch you the only thing to do was do it anyway and keep hidden. I laughed thinking what would happen if I was Fuke the Chinese sage of the ninth century who wandered around China constantly ringing his bell. The only alternative to sleeping out, hopping freights, and doing what I wanted, I saw in a vision would be to just sit with a hundred other patients in front of a nice television set in a madhouse, where we could be "supervised." I went into a supermarket and bought some concentrated orange juice and nutted cream cheese and whole wheat bread, which would make nice meals till tomorrow, when I'd hitchhike on through the other side of town. I saw many cop cruising cars and they were looking at me suspiciously: sleek, well-paid cops in brand-new cars with all that expensive radio equipment to see that no bhikku slept in his grove tonight.

At the highway woods I took one good look to make sure no cruisers were up or down the road and I dove right in the woods. It was a lot of dry thickets I had to crash through, I didn't want to bother finding the Boy Scout trail. I aimed straight for the golden sands of the riverbottom I could see up ahead. Over the thickets ran the highway bridge, no one could see me unless they stopped and got out to stare down. Like a criminal I crashed through bright brittle thickets and came out sweating and stomped ankle deep in streams and then when I found a nice opening in a kind of bamboo grove I hesitated to light a fire till dusk when no one'd see my small smoke, and make sure to keep it low embers. I spread my poncho and sleeping bag out on some dry rackety grovebottom leaves and bamboo splitjoints. Yellow aspens filled the afternoon air with gold smoke and made my eyes quiver. It was a nice spot except for the roar of trucks on the river bridge. My head cold and sinus were bad and I stood on my head five minutes. I laughed. "What would people think if they saw me?" But it wasn't funny, I felt rather sad, in fact real sad, like the night before in that horrible fog wire-fence country in industrial L.A., when in fact I'd cried a little. After all a homeless man has reason to cry, everything in the world is pointed against him.

It got dark. I took my pot and went to get water but had to scramble through so much underbrush that when I got back to my camp most of the water had splashed out. I mixed it in my new plastic shaker with orange-juice concentrate and shook up an ice-cold orange, then I spread nutted cream cheese on the whole-wheat bread and ate content. "Tonight," I thought, "I sleep tight and long and pray under the stars for the Lord to bring me to Buddhahood after my Buddhawork is done, amen." And as it was Christmas, I added "Lord bless you all and merry tender Christmas on all your rooftops and I hope angels squat there the night of the big rich real Star, amen." And then I thought, later, lying on my bag smoking, "Everything is possible. I am God, I am Buddha, I am imperfect Ray Smith, all at the same time, I am empty space, I am all things. I have all the time in the world from life to life to do what is to do, to do what is done, to do the timeless doing, infinitely perfect within, why cry, why worry, perfect like mind essence and the minds of banana peels" I added laughing remembering my poetic Zen Lunatic Dharma Bum friends of San Francisco whom I was beginning to miss now. And I added a little prayer for Rosie.

"If she'd lived, and could have come here with me, maybe I could have told her something, made her feel different. Maybe I'd just make love to her and say nothing."

I spent a long time meditating crosslegged, but the truck growl bothered me. Soon the stars came out and my little Indian fire sent up some smoke to them. I slipped in my bag at eleven and slept well, except for the bamboo joints under the leaves that caused me to turn over all night. "Better to sleep in an uncomfortable bed free, than sleep in a comfortable bed unfree." I was making up all kinds of sayings as I went along. I was started on my new life with my new equipment: a regular Don Quixote of tenderness. In the morning I felt exhilarated and meditated first thing and made up a little prayer: "I bless you, all living things, I bless you in the endless past, I bless you in the endless present, I bless you in the endless future, amen."

This little prayer made me feel good and fool good as I packed up my things and took off to the tumbling water that came down from a rock across the highway, delicious spring water to bathe my face in and wash my teeth in and drink. Then I was ready for the three-thousand-mile hitchhike to Rocky Mount, North Carolina, where my mother was waiting, probably washing the dishes in her dear pitiful kitchen.

18

The current song at that time was Roy Hamilton singing "Everybody's Got a Home but Me." I kept singing that as I swung along. On the other side of Riverside I got on the highway and got a ride right away from a young couple, to an airfield five miles out of town, and from there a ride from a quiet man almost to Beaumont, California, but five miles short of it on a double-lane speed highway with nobody likely to stop so I hiked on in in beautiful sparkling air. At Beaumont I ate hotdogs, hamburgers and a bag of fries and added a big strawberry shake, all among giggling high-school children. Then, the other side of town, I got a ride from a Mexican called Jaimy who said he was the son of the governor of the state of Baja California, Mexico, which I didn't believe and was a wino and had me buy him wine which he only threw up out the window as he drove: a droopy, sad, helpless young man, very sad eyes, very nice, a bit nutty. He was driving clear to Mexicali, a little off my route but good enough and far enough out toward Arizona to suit me.

At Calexico it was Christmas shopping time on Main Street with incredible perfect astonished Mexican beauties who kept getting so much better that when the first ones had re-passed they'd already become capped and thin in my mind, I was standing there looking everywhichaway, eating an ice-cream cone, waiting for Jaimy who said he had an errand and would pick me up again and take me personally into Mexicali, Mexico, to meet his friends. My plan was to have a nice cheap supper in Mexico and then roll on that night. Jaimy didn't show up, of course. I crossed the border by myself and turned sharp right at the gate to avoid the hawker street and went immediately to relieve myself of water in construction dirt but a crazy Mexican watchman with an official uniform thought it was a big infringement and said something and when I said I didn't know (No se) he said "No sabes *police?*"—the nerve of him to call the cops because I peed on his dirt ground. But I did notice afterward and felt sad, that I had watered the spot where he sat to light a small fire nights because there were wood coals piled so I moved up the muddy street feeling meek and truly sorry, with the big pack on my back, as he stared after me with his doleful stare.

I came to a hill and saw great mudflat riverbottoms with stinks and tarns and awful paths with women and burros ambling in the dusk, an old Chinese Mexican beggar caught my eye and we stopped to chat, when I told him I might go Dormiendo sleep in those flats (I was really thinking of a little beyond the flats, in the foothills) he looked horrified and, being a deafmute, he demonstrated that I would be robbed of my pack and killed if I tried it, which I suddenly realized was true. I wasn't in America any more. Either side of the border, either way you slice the boloney, a homeless man was in hot water. Where would I find a quiet grove to meditate in, to live in forever? After the old man tried to tell me his life story by signs I walked away waving and smiling and crossed the flats and narrow board bridge over the yellow water and over to the poor adobe district of Mexicali where the Mexico gaiety as ever charmed me, and I ate a delicious tin bowl of garbanzo soup with pieces of cabeza (head) and cebolla (onion) raw, having cashed a quarter at the border gate for three paper pesos and a big pile of huge pennies. While eating at the little mud street counter I dug the street, the people, the poor bitch dogs, the cantinas, the whores, the music, men goofing in the narrow road wrestling, and across the street an unforgettable beauty parlor (Salon de Belleza) with a bare mirror on a bare wall and bare chairs and one little seventeen-year-old beauty with her hair in pins dreaming at the mirror, but an old plaster bust with periwig beside her, and a big man with a mustache in a Scandinavian ski sweater picking his teeth behind and a little boy at the next mirror chair eating a banana and out on the sidewalk some little children gathered like before a movie house and I thought "Oh all Mexicali on some Saturday afternoon! Thank you O Lord for returning me my zest for life, for Thy ever-recurring forms in Thy Womb of Exuberant Fertility." All my tears weren't in vain. It'll all work out finally.

Then, strolling, I bought a hot doughnut stick, then two oranges from a girl, and re-crossed the bridge in dust of evening and headed for the border gate happy. But here I was stopped by three unpleasant American guards and my whole rucksack was searched sullenly.

"What'd you buy in Mexico?"

"Nothing."

They didn't believe me. They fished around. After fingering my wraps of leftover frenchfries from Beaumont and raisins and peanuts and carrots, and cans of pork and beans I made sure to have for the road, and half-loaves of whole wheat bread they got disgusted and let me go. It was funny, really; they were expecting a rucksack full of opium from Sinaloa, no doubt, or weed from Mazatlan, or heroin from Panama. Maybe they thought I'd walked all the way from Panama. They couldn't figure me out.

I went to the Greyhound bus station and bought a short ticket to El Centro and the main highway. I figured I'd catch the Arizona Midnight Ghost and be in Yuma that same night and sleep in the Colorado riverbottom, which I'd noticed long ago. But it wound up, in El Centro I went to the yards and angled around and finally talked to a conductor passing the sign to a switch engine: "Where's the Zipper?"

"It don't come through El Centro."

I was surprised at my stupidity.

"Only freight you can catch goes through Mexico, then Yuma, but they'll find you and kick you out and you'll wind up in a Mexican calaboose boy."

"I've had enough of Mexico. Thanks." So I went to the big intersection in town with the cars turning for the eastward run to Yuma and started thumbing. I had no luck for an hour. Suddenly a big truck pulled up to the side; the driver got out and fiddled with his suitcase. "You goin on east?" I asked.

"Soon as I spend a little time in Mexicali. You know anything about Mexico?"

"Lived there for years." He looked me over. He was a good old joe, fat, happy, middlewestern. He liked me.

"How about showin me around Mexicali tonight then I'll drive you to Tucson."

"Great!" We got in the truck and went right back to Mexicali on the road I'd just covered in the bus. But it was worth it to get clear to Tucson. We parked the truck in Calexico, which was quiet now, at eleven, and went over into Mexicali and I took him away from tourist-trap honkytonks and led him to the good old saloons of real Mexico where there were girls at a peso a dance and raw tequila and lots of fun. It was a big night, he danced and enjoyed himself, had his picture taken with a senorita and drank about twenty shots of tequila. Somewhere during the night we hooked up with a colored guy who was some kind of queer but was awfully funny and led us to a whorehouse and then as we were coming out a Mexican cop relieved him of his snapknife.

"That's my third knife this month those bastards stole from me," he said.

In the morning Beaudry (the driver) and I got back to the truck bleary eyes and hungover and he wasted no time and drove right straight to Yuma, not going back to El Centro, but on the excellent no-traffic Highway 98 straight a hundred miles

after hitting 80 at Gray Wells. Soon we were in fact coming
into Tucson. We'd eaten a slight lunch outside Yuma and now
he said he was hungry for a good steak. "Only thing is these
truck stops ain't got big enough steaks to suit me."

"Well you just park your truck up one of these Tucson
supermarkets on the highway and I'll buy a two-inch thick
T-bone and we'll stop in the desert and I'll light a fire and broil
you the greatest steak of your life." He didn't really believe it
but I did it. Outside the lights of Tucson in a flaming red dusk
over the desert, he stopped and I lit a fire with mesquite
branches, adding bigger branches and logs later, as it got dark,
and when the coals were hot I tried to hold the steak over them
with a spit but the spit burned so I just fried the huge steaks in
their own fat in my lovely new potpan cover and handed him
my jackknife and he went to it and said "Hm, om, wow, that *is*
the best steak I ever et."

I'd also bought milk and we had just steak and milk, a great
protein feast, squatting there in the sand as highway cars
zipped by our little red fire. "Where'd you *learn* to do all these
funny things?" he laughed. "And you know I say funny but
there's sumpthin so durned sensible about 'em. Here I am
killin myself drivin this rig back and forth from Ohio to L.A.
and I make more money than you ever had in your whole life
as a hobo, but you're the one who enjoys life and not only that
but you do it without workin or a whole lot of money. Now
who's smart, you or me?" And he had a nice home in Ohio
with wife, daughter, Christmas tree, two cars, garage, lawn,
lawnmower, but he couldn't enjoy any of it because he really
wasn't free. It was sadly true. It didn't mean I was a better man
than he was, however, he was a great man and I liked him and
he liked me and said "Well I'll tell you, supposin I drive you all
the way to Ohio."

"Wow, great! That'll take me just about home! I'm goin
south of there to North Carolina."

"I was hesitatin at first on account of them Markell insurance men, see if they catch you ridin with me I'll lose my job."

"Oh hell . . . and ain't that somethin typical."

"It shore is, but I'll tell you sumpthin, after this steak you
made for me, even though I paid for it, but you cooked it and
here you are washin your dishes in sand, I'll just have to tell

them to stick the job up their ass because now you're my friend and I got a right to give my friend a ride."

"Okay," I said, "and I'll pray we don't get stopped by no Markell insurance men."

"Good chance of that because it's Saturday now and we'll be in Springfield Ohio at about dawn Tuesday if I push this rig and it's their weekend off more or less."

And did he ever push that rig! From that desert in Arizona he roared on up to New Mexico, took the cut through Las Cruces up to Alamogordo where the atom bomb was first blasted and where I had a strange vision as we drove along seeing in the clouds above the Alamogordo mountains the words as if imprinted in the sky: "This Is the Impossibility of the Existence of Anything" (which was a strange place for that strange true vision) and then he batted on through the beautiful Atascadero Indian country in the uphills of New Mexico beautiful green valleys and pines and New England-like rolling meadows and then down to Oklahoma (at outside Bowie Arizona we'd had a short nap at dawn, he in the truck, me in my bag in the cold red clay with just stars blazing silence overhead and a distant coyote), in no time at all he was going up through Arkansas and eating it up in one afternoon and then Missouri and St. Louis and finally on Monday night bashing across Illinois and Indiana and into old snowy Ohio with all the cute Christmas lights making my heart joy in the windows of old farms. "Wow," I thought, "all the way from the warm arms of the senoritas of Mexicali to the Christmas snows of Ohio in one fast ride." He had a radio on his dashboard and played it booming all the way, too. We didn't talk much, he just yelled once in a while, telling an anecdote, and had such a loud voice that he actually pierced my eardrum (the left one) and made it hurt, making me jump two feet in my seat. He was great. We had a lot of good meals, too, en route, in various favorite truckstops of his, one in Oklahoma where we had roast pork and yams worthy of my mother's own kitchen, we ate and ate, he was always hungry, in fact so was I, it was winter cold now and Christmas was on the fields and food was good.

In Independence Missouri we made our only stop to sleep in a room, in a hotel at almost five dollars apiece, which was robbery, but he needed the sleep and I couldn't wait in the below-zero truck. When I woke up in the morning, on Monday, I looked out and saw all the eager young men in business suits going to work in insurance offices hoping to be big Harry Trumans some day. By Tuesday dawn he let me off in downtown Springfield Ohio in a deep cold wave and we said goodbye just a little sadly.

I went to a lunchcart, drank tea, figured my budget, went to a hotel and had one good exhausted sleep. Then I bought a bus ticket to Rocky Mount, as it was impossible to hitchhike from Ohio to North Carolina in all that winter mountain country through the Blue Ridge and all. But I got impatient and decided to hitchhike anyway and asked the bus to stop on the outskirts and walked back to the bus station to cash my ticket. They wouldn't give me the money. The upshot of my insane impatience was that I had to wait eight more hours for the next slow bus to Charleston West Virginia. I started hitchhiking out of Springfield figuring to catch the bus in a town farther down, just for fun, and froze my feet and hands standing in dismal country roads in freezing dusk. One good ride took me to a little town and there I just waited around the tiny telegraph office which served as a station, till my bus arrived. Then it was a crowded bus going slowly over the mountains all night long and in the dawn the laborious climb over the Blue Ridge with beautiful timbered country in the snow, then after a whole day of stopping and starting, stopping and starting, down out of the mountains into Mount Airy and finally after ages Raleigh where I transferred to my local bus and instructed the driver to let me off at the country road that wound three miles through the piney woods to my mother's house in Big Easonburg Woods which is a country crossroad outside Rocky Mount.

He let me off, at about eight p.m., and I walked the three miles in silent freezing Carolina road of moon, watching a jet plane overhead, her stream drifting across the face of the moon and bisecting the snow circle. It was beautiful to be back east in the snow at Christmas time, the little lights in occasional farm windows, the quiet woods, the piney barrens so naked and drear, the railroad track that ran off into the gray blue woods toward my dream.

At nine o'clock I was stomping with full pack across my

mother's yard and there she was at the white tiled sink in the kitchen, washing her dishes, with a rueful expression waiting for me (I was late), worried I'd never even make it and probably thinking, "Poor Raymond, why does he always have to hitchhike and worry me to death, why isn't he like other men?" And I thought of Japhy as I stood there in the cold yard looking at her: "Why is he so mad about white tiled sinks and 'kitchen machinery' he calls it? People have good hearts whether or not they live like Dharma Bums. Compassion is the heart of Buddhism." Behind the house was a great pine forest where I would spend all that winter and spring meditating under the trees and finding out by myself the truth of all things. I was very happy. I walked around the house and looked at the Christmas tree in the window. A hundred yards down the road the two country stores made a bright warm scene in the otherwise bleak wooded void. I went to the dog house and found old Bob trembling and snorting in the cold. He whimpered glad to see me. I unleashed him and he yipped and leaped around and came into the house with me where I embraced my mother in the warm kitchen and my sister and brother-in-law came out of the parlor and greeted me, and little nephew Lou too, and I was home again.

19

They all wanted me to sleep on the couch in the parlor by the comfortable oil-burning stove but I insisted on making my room (as before) on the back porch with its six windows looking out on the winter barren cottonfield and the pine woods beyond, leaving all the windows open and stretching my good old sleeping bag on the couch there to sleep the pure sleep of winter nights with my head buried inside the smooth nylon duck-down warmth. After they'd gone to bed I put on my jacket and my earmuff cap and railroad gloves and over all that my nylon poncho and strode out in the cottonfield moonlight like a shroudy monk. The ground was covered with moonlit frost. The old cemetery down the road gleamed in the frost. The roofs of nearby farmhouses were like white panels of snow. I went through the cottonfield rows followed by Bob, a big bird dog, and little Sandy who belonged to the Joyners down the road, and a few other stray dogs (all dogs love me) and came to the edge of the forest. In there, the previous spring, I'd worn out a little path going to meditate under a favorite baby pine. The path was still there. My official entrance to the forest was still there, this being two evenly spaced young pines making kind of gate posts. I always bowed there and clasped my hands and thanked Avalokitesvara for the privilege of the wood. Then I went in, led moonwhite Bob direct to my pine, where my old bed of straw was still at the foot of the tree. I arranged my cape and legs and sat to meditate.

The dogs meditated on their paws. We were all absolutely quiet. The entire moony countryside was frosty silent, not even the little tick of rabbits or coons anywhere. An absolute cold blessed silence. Maybe a dog barking five miles away toward Sandy Cross. Just the faintest, faintest sound of big trucks rolling out the night on 301, about twelve miles away, and of course the distant occasional Diesel baugh of the Atlantic Coast Line passenger and freight trains going north and south to New York and Florida. A blessed night. I immediately fell into a blank thoughtless trance wherein it was again revealed to me "This thinking has stopped" and I sighed because I didn't have to think any more and felt my whole body sink into a blessedness surely to be believed, completely relaxed and at peace with all the ephemeral world of dream and dreamer and the dreaming itself. All kinds of thoughts, too, like "One man practicing kindness in the wilderness is worth all the temples this world pulls" and I reached out and stroked old Bob, who looked at me satisfied. "All living and dying things like these dogs and me coming and going without any duration or self substance, O God, and therefore we can't possibly exist. How strange, how worthy, how good for us! What a horror it would have been if the world was real, because if the world was real, it would be immortal." My nylon poncho protected me from the cold, like a fitted-on tent, and I stayed a long time sitting crosslegged in the winter midnight woods, about an hour. Then I went back to the house, warmed up by the fire in the living room while the others slept, then slipped into my bag on the porch and fell asleep.

The following night was Christmas Eve which I spent with a bottle of wine before the TV enjoying the shows and the midnight mass from Saint Patrick's Cathedral in New York with bishops ministering, and doctrines glistering, and congregations, the priests in their lacy snow vestments before great official altars not half as great as my straw mat beneath a little pine tree I figured. Then at midnight the breathless little parents, my sister and brother-in-law, laying out the presents under the tree and more gloriful than all the Gloria in Excelsis Deos of Rome Church and all its attendant bishops. "For after all," I thought, "Augustine was a spade and Francis my idiot brother." My cat Davey suddenly blessed me, sweet cat, with his arrival on my lap. I took out the Bible and read a little Saint Paul by the warm stove and the light of the tree, "Let him become a fool, that he may become wise," and I thought of good dear Japhy and wished he was enjoying the Christmas Eve with me. "Already are ye filled," says Saint Paul, "already are ye become rich. The saints shall judge the world." Then in a burst of beautiful poetry more beautiful than all the poetry readings of all the San Francisco Renaissances of Time: "Meats for the belly, and the belly for meats; but God shall bring to naught both it and them."

"Yep," I thought, "you pay through the nose for shortlived shows. . . ."

That week I was all alone in the house, my mother had to go to New York for a funeral, and the others worked. Every afternoon I went into the piney woods with my dogs, read, studied, meditated, in the warm winter southern sun, and came back and made supper for everybody at dusk. Also, I put up a basket and shot baskets every sundown. At night, after they went to bed, back I went to the woods in starlight or even in rain sometimes with my poncho. The woods received me well. I amused myself writing little Emily Dickinson poems like "Light a fire, fight a liar, what's the difference, in existence?" or "A watermelon seed, produces a need, large and juicy, such autocracy."

"Let there be blowing-out and bliss forevermore," I prayed in the woods at night. I kept making newer and better prayers. And more poems, like when the snow came, "Not oft, the holy snow, so soft, the holy bow," and at one point I wrote

"The Four Inevitabilities: 1. Musty Books. 2. Uninteresting Nature. 3. Dull Existence. 4. Blank Nirvana, buy that boy." Or I wrote, on dull afternoons when neither Buddhism nor poetry nor wine nor solitude nor basketball would avail my lazy but earnest flesh, "Nothin to do, Oh poo! Practically blue." One afternoon I watched the ducks in the pig field across the road and it was Sunday, and the hollering preachers were screaming on the Carolina radio and I wrote: "Imagine blessing all living and dying worms in eternity and the ducks that eat 'em . . . there's your Sunday school sermon." In a dream I heard the words, "Pain, 'tis but a concubine's puff." But in Shakespeare it would say, "Ay, by my faith, that bears a frosty sound." Then suddenly one night after supper as I was pacing in the cold windy darkness of the yard I felt tremendously depressed and threw myself right on the ground and cried "I'm gonna die!" because there was nothing else to do in the cold loneliness of this harsh inhospitable earth, and instantly the tender bliss of enlightenment was like milk in my eyelids and I was warm. And I realized that this was the truth Rosie knew now, and all the dead, my dead father and dead brother and dead uncles and cousins and aunts, the truth that is realizable in a dead man's bones and is beyond the Tree of Buddha as well as the Cross of Jesus. *Believe* that the world is an ethereal flower, and ye live. I knew this! I also knew that I was the worst bum in the world. The diamond light was in my eyes.

My cat meowed at the icebox, anxious to see what all the good dear delight was. I fed him.

20

After a while my meditations and studies began to bear fruit. It really started late in January, one frosty night in the woods in the dead silence it seemed I almost heard the words said: "Everything is all right forever and forever and forever." I let out a big Hoo, one o'clock in the morning, the dogs leaped up and exulted. I felt like yelling it to the stars. I clasped my hands and prayed, "O wise and serene spirit of Awakenerhood, everything's all right forever and forever and forever and thank

you thank you thank you amen." What'd I care about the
tower of ghouls, and sperm and bones and dust, I felt free and
therefore I *was* free.

I suddenly felt the desire to write to Warren Coughlin, who
was strong in my thoughts now as I recalled his modesty and
general silence among the vain screams of myself and Alvah
and Japhy: "Yes, Coughlin, it's a shining now-ness and we've
done it, carried America like a shining blanket into that
brighter nowhere Already."

It began to get warmer in February and the ground began
to melt a little and the nights in the woods were milder, my
sleeps on the porch more enjoyable. The stars seemed to
get wet in the sky, bigger. Under the stars I'd be dozing
crosslegged under my tree and in my half-asleep mind I'd be
saying "Moab? Who is Moab?" and I'd wake up with a burr in
my hand, a cotton burr off one of the dogs. So, awake, I'd
make thoughts like "It's all different appearances of the same
thing, my drowsiness, the burr, Moab, all one ephemeral
dream. All belongs to the same emptiness, glory be!" Then I'd
run these words through my mind to train myself: "I am
emptiness, I am not different from emptiness, neither is emptiness different from me; indeed, emptiness is me." There'd be a
puddle of water with a star shining in it, I'd spit in the puddle,
the star would be obliterated, I'd say "That star is real?"

I wasn't exactly unconscious of the fact that I had a good
warm fire to return to after these midnight meditations, pro-
vided kindly for me by my brother-in-law, who was getting a
little sick and tired of my hanging around not working. Once I
told him a line from something, about how one grows through
suffering, he said: "If you grow through suffering by this time
I oughta be as big as the side of the house."

When I'd go to the country store to buy bread and milk the
old boys there sitting around among bamboo poles and molasses barrels'd say, "What you do in those woods?"

"Oh I just go in there to study."

"Ain't you kinda old to be a college student?"

"Well I just go in there sometimes and just sleep."

But I'd watch them rambling around the fields all day
looking for something to do, so their wives would think they
were real busy hardworking men, and they weren't fooling me

either. I knew they secretly wanted to go sleep in the woods, or just sit and do nothing in the woods, like I wasn't too ashamed to do. They never bothered me. How could I tell them that my knowing was the knowing that the substance of my bones and their bones and the bones of dead men in the earth of rain at night is the common individual substance that is everlastingly tranquil and blissful? Whether they believed it or not makes no difference, too. One night in my rain cape I sat in a regular downpour and I had a little song to go with the pattering rain on my rubber hood: "Raindrops are ecstasy, raindrops are not different from ecstasy, neither is ecstasy different from raindrops, yea, ecstasy is raindrops, rain on, O cloud!" So what did I care what the old tobacco-chewing stickwhittlers at the crossroads store had to say about my mortal eccentricity, we all get to be gum in graves anyway. I even got a little drunk with one of the old men one time and we went driving around the country roads and I actually told him how I was sitting out in those woods meditating and he really rather understood and said he would like to try that if he had time, or if he could get up enough nerve, and had a little rueful envy in his voice. Everybody knows everything.

21

Spring came after heavy rains that washed everything, brown puddles were everywhere in moist, sere fields. Strong warm winds whipped snow white clouds across the sun and dry air. Golden days with beauteous moon at night, warm, one emboldened frog picking up a croak song at eleven p.m. in "Buddha Creek" where I had established my new straw sitting place under a twisted twin tree by a little opening in the pines and a dry stretch of grass and a tiny brook. There, one day, my nephew little Lou came with me and I took an object from the ground and raised it silently, sitting under the tree, and little Lou facing me asked "What's that?" and I said "That" and made a leveling motion with my hand, saying, "Tathata," repeating, "That . . . It's *that*" and only when I told him it was a pine cone did he make the imaginary judgment of the word "pine cone," for, indeed, as it says in the sutra: "Emptiness is discrimination," and he said "My head jumped out, and my brain went crooked and then my eyes started lookin like cucumbers and my hair'd a cowlick on it and the cowlick licked my chin." Then he said "Why don't I make up a poem?" He wanted to commemorate the moment.

"Okay, but make it up right away, just as you go along."

"Okay . . . 'The pine trees are wavin, the wind is tryin to whisper somethin, the birds are sayin drit-drit-drit, and the hawks are goin hark-hark-hark—' Oho, we're in for danger."

"Why?"

"Hawk—hark hark hark!"

"Then what?"

"Hark! Hark!—Nothin." I puffed on my silent pipe, peace and quiet in my heart.

I called my new grove "Twin Tree Grove," because of the two treetrunks I leaned against, that wound around each other, white spruce shining white in the night and showing me from hundreds of feet away where I was heading, although old Bob whitely showed me the way down the dark path. On that path one night I lost my juju beads Japhy'd given me, but the next day I found them right in the path, figuring, "The Dharma can't be lost, nothing can be lost, on a well-worn path."

There were now early spring mornings with the happy dogs, me forgetting the Path of Buddhism and just being glad; looking around at new little birds not yet summer fat; the dogs yawning and almost swallowing my Dharma; the grass waving, hens chuckling. Spring nights, practicing Dhyana under the cloudy moon. I'd see the truth: "Here, this, is *It*. The world as it is, is Heaven, I'm looking for a Heaven outside what there is, it's only this poor pitiful world that's Heaven. Ah, if I could realize, if I could forget myself and devote my meditations to the freeing, the awakening and the blessedness of all living creatures everywhere I'd realize what there is, *is* ecstasy."

Long afternoons just sitting in the straw until I was tired of "thinking nothing" and just going to sleep and having little flash dreams like the strange one I had once of being up in some kind of gray ghostly attic hauling up suitcases of gray meat my mother is handing up and I'm petulantly complaining: "I won't come down again!" (to do this work of the

world). I felt I was a blank being called upon to enjoy the ecstasy of the endless truebody.

Days tumbled on days, I was in my overalls, didn't comb my
hair, didn't shave much, consorted only with dogs and cats, I
was living the happy life of childhood again. Meanwhile I wrote
and got an assignment for the coming summer as a fire lookout for the U.S. Forest Service on Desolation Peak in the
High Cascades in Washington state. So I figured to set out for
Japhy's shack in March to be nearer Washington for my summer job.

Sunday afternoons my family would want me to go driving
with them but I preferred to stay home alone, and they'd get
mad and say "What's the matter with him anyway?" and I'd
hear them argue about the futility of my "Buddhism" in the
kitchen, then they'd all get in the car and leave and I'd go in
the kitchen and sing "The tables are empty, everybody's gone
over" to the tune of Frank Sinatra's "You're Learning the
Blues." I was as nutty as a fruitcake and happier. Sunday afternoon, then, I'd go to my woods with the dogs and sit and put
out my hands palms up and accept handfuls of sun boiling over
the palms. "Nirvana is the moving paw," I'd say, seeing the
first thing I saw as I opened my eyes from meditation, that
being Bob's paw moving in the grass as he dreamed. Then I'd
go back to the house on my clear, pure, well-traveled path,
waiting for the night when again I'd see the countless Buddhas
hiding in the moonlight air.

But my serenity was finally disturbed by a curious argument
with my brother-in-law; he began to resent my unshackling
Bob the dog and taking him in the woods with me. "I've got
too much money invested in that dog to untie him from his
chain."

I said "How would you like to be tied to a chain and cry all
day like the dog?"

He replied "It doesn't bother *me*" and my sister said "And *I*
don't care."

I got so mad I stomped off into the woods, it was a Sunday
afternoon, and resolved to sit there without food till midnight
and come back and pack my things in the night and leave. But
in a few hours my mother was calling me from the back porch

to supper, I wouldn't come; finally little Lou came out to my tree and begged me to come back.

I had frogs in the little brook that kept croaking at the oddest times, interrupting my meditations as if by design, once at high noon a frog croaked three times and was silent the rest of the day, as though expounding me the Triple Vehicle. Now my frog croaked once. I felt it was a signal meaning the One Vehicle of Compassion and went back determined to overlook the whole thing, even my pity about the dog. What a sad and bootless dream. In the woods again that night, fingering the juju beads, I went through curious prayers like these: "My pride is hurt, that is emptiness; my business is with the Dharma, that is emptiness; I'm proud of my kindness to animals, that is emptiness; my conception of the chain, that is emptiness; Ananda's pity, even that is emptiness." Perhaps if some old Zen Master had been on the scene, he would have gone out and kicked the dog on his chain to give everybody a sudden shot of awakening. My pain was in getting rid of the conception of people and dogs anyway, and of myself. I was hurting deep inside from the sad business of trying to *deny* what was. In any case it was a tender little drama in the Sunday countryside: "Raymond doesn't want the dog chained." But then suddenly under the tree at night, I had the astonishing idea: "Everything is empty but awake! Things are empty in time and space and mind." I figured it all out and the next day feeling very exhilarated I felt the time had come to explain everything to my family. They laughed more than anything else. "But listen! No! Look! It's simple, let me lay it out as simple and concise as I can. All things are empty, ain't they?"

"Whattayou mean, empty, I'm holding this orange in my hand, ain't I?"

"It's empty, everythin's empty, things come but to go, all things made have to be unmade, and they'll have to be unmade simply *because* they were made!"

Nobody would buy even that.

"You and your Buddha, why don't you stick to the religion you were born with?" my mother and sister said.

"Everything's gone, already gone, already come and gone," I yelled. "Ah," stomping around, coming back, "and things are empty because they appear, don't they, you see them, but they're made up of atoms that can't be measured or weighed or taken hold of, even the dumb scientists know that now, there *isn't* any finding of the farthest atom so-called, things are just empty arrangements of something that seems solid appearing in the space, they ain't either big or small, near or far, true or false, they're ghosts pure and simple."

"Ghostses!" yelled little Lou amazed. He really agreed with me but he was afraid of my insistence on "Ghostses."

"Look," said my brother-in-law, "if things were empty how could I feel this orange, in fact taste it and swallow it, answer me that one."

"Your mind makes out the orange by seeing it, hearing it, touching it, smelling it, tasting it and thinking about it but without this mind, you call it, the orange would not be seen or heard or smelled or tasted or even mentally noticed, it's actually, that orange, depending on your mind to exist! Don't you see that? By itself it's a no-thing, it's really mental, it's seen only of your mind. In other words it's empty and awake."

"Well, if that's so, I still don't care." All enthusiastic I went back to the woods that night and thought, "What does it mean that I am in this endless universe, thinking that I'm a man sitting under the stars on the terrace of the earth, but actually empty and awake throughout the emptiness and awakedness of everything? It means that I'm empty and awake, that I *know* I'm empty, awake, and that there's no difference between me and anything else. In other words it means that I've become the same as everything else. It means I've become a Buddha." I really felt that and believed it and exulted to think what I had to tell Japhy now when I got back to California. "At least *he'll* listen," I pouted. I felt great compassion for the trees because we were the same thing; I petted the dogs who didn't argue with me ever. All dogs love God. They're wiser than their masters. I told that to the dogs, too, they listened to me perking up their ears and licking my face. They didn't care one way or the other as long as I was there. St. Raymond of the Dogs is who I was that year, if no one or nothing else.

Sometimes in the woods I'd just sit and stare at things themselves, trying to divine the secret of existence anyway. I'd stare at the holy yellow long bowing weeds that faced my grass sitmat of Tathagata Seat of Purity as they pointed in all directions and hairily conversed as the winds dictated Ta Ta Ta, in gossip groups with some lone weeds proud to show off on the side, or sick ones and half-dead falling ones, the whole congregation of living weedhood in the wind suddenly ringing like bells and jumping to get excited and all made of yellow stuff and sticking to the ground and I'd think *This is it.* "Rop rop rop," I'd yell at the weeds, and they'd show windward pointing intelligent reachers to indicate and flail and finagle, some rooted in blossom imagination earth moist perturbation idea that had karmacized their very root-and-stem. . . . It was eerie. I'd fall asleep and dream the words "By this teaching the earth came to an end," and I'd dream of my Ma nodding solemnly with her whole head, umph, and eyes closed. What did I care about all the irking hurts and tedious wronks of the world, the human bones are but vain lines dawdling, the whole universe a blank mold of stars. "I am Bhikku Blank Rat!" I dreamed.

What did I care about the squawk of the little very self which wanders everywhere? I was dealing in outblownness, cutoff-ness, snipped, blownoutness, putoutness, turned-off-ness, nothing-happens-ness, gone-ness, gone-out-ness, the snapped link, nir, link, vana, snap! "The dust of my thoughts collected into a globe," I thought, "in this ageless solitude," I thought, and really smiled, because I was seeing the white light everywhere everything at last.

The warm wind made the pines talk deep one night when I began to experience what is called "Samapatti," which in Sanskrit means Transcendental Visits. I'd got a little drowsy in the mind but was somehow physically wide awake sitting erect under my tree when suddenly I saw flowers, pink worlds of walls of them, salmon pink, in the *Shh* of silent woods (obtaining nirvana is like locating silence) and I saw an ancient vision of Dipankara Buddha who was the Buddha who never said anything, Dipankara as a vast snowy Pyramid Buddha with bushy wild black eyebrows like John L. Lewis and a terrible stare, all in an old location, an ancient snowy field like Alban ("A *new* field!" had yelled the Negro preacherwoman), the whole vision making my hair rise. I remember the strange magic final cry that it evoked in me, whatever it means: *Colyalcolor.* It, the vision, was devoid of any sensation of I being myself, it was pure egolessness, just simply wild ethereal activities devoid of any wrong predicates . . . devoid of effort, devoid of mistake. "Everything's all right," I thought. "Form is emptiness and emptiness is form and we're here forever in one form or another which is empty. What the dead have accomplished, this rich silent hush of the Pure Awakened Land."

I felt like crying out over the woods and rooftops of North Carolina announcing the glorious and simple truth. Then I said "I've got my full rucksack pack and it's spring, I'm going to go south-west to the dry land, to the long lone land of Texas and Chihuahua and the gay streets of Mexico night, music coming out of doors, girls, wine, weed, wild hats, viva! What does it matter? Like the ants that have nothing to do but dig all day, I have nothing to do but do what I want and be kind and remain nevertheless uninfluenced by imaginary judgments and pray for the light." Sitting in my Buddha-arbor, therefore, in that "colyalcolor" wall of flowers pink and red and ivory white, among aviaries of magic transcendent birds recognizing my awakening mind with sweet weird cries (the pathless lark), in the ethereal perfume, mysteriously ancient, the bliss of the Buddha-fields, I saw that my life was a vast glowing empty page and I could do anything I wanted.

A strange thing happened the next day, to illustrate the true power I had gained from these magic visions. My mother had been coughing for five days and her nose was running and now her throat was beginning to hurt so much that her coughs were painful and sounded dangerous to me. I decided to go into a deep trance and hypnotize myself, reminding myself "All is empty and awake," to investigate the cause and cure of my mother's illness. Instantly, in my closed eyes, I saw a vision of a brandy bottle which then I saw to be "Heet" rubbing medicine and on top of that, superimposed like a movie fade-in, I saw a distinct picture of little white flowers, round, with small petals. I instantly got up, it was midnight, my mother was coughing in her bed, and I went and took several bowls of bachelor's buttons my sister had arranged around the house the week before and I set them outside. Then I took some "Heet" out of the medicine cabinet and told my mother to rub it on her neck. The next day her cough was gone. Later on, after I was gone hitchhiking west, a nurse friend of ours heard the story and said "Yes, it sounds like an allergy to the flowers." During this vision and this action I knew perfectly clearly that people get sick by utilizing physical opportunities to punish themselves because of their self-regulating God nature, or Buddha nature, or Allah nature, or any name you want to give God, and everything worked automatically that way. This was my first and last "miracle" because I was afraid of getting too interested in this and becoming vain. I was a little scared too, of all the responsibility.

Everybody in the family heard of my vision and what I did but they didn't seem to think much of it: in fact I didn't, either. And that was right. I was very rich now, a super myriad trillionaire in Samapatti transcendental graces, because of good humble karma, maybe because I had pitied the dog and forgiven men. But I knew now that I was a bliss heir, and that the final sin, the worst, is righteousness. So I would shut up and just hit the road and go see Japhy. "Don't let the blues make you bad," sings Frank Sinatra. On my final night in the woods, the eve of my departure by thumb, I heard the word "starbody" concerning how things don't have to be made to disappear but to awake, to their supremely pure truebody and starbody. I saw there was nothing to do because nothing ever happened, nothing ever would happen, all things were empty light. So I took off well fortified, with my pack, kissing my mother goodbye. She had paid five dollars to have brand new thick rubber soles with cleats put on the bottom of my old boots and now I was all set for a summer working in the mountains. Our old country-store friend, Buddhy Tom, a character in his own right, took me in his vehicle out to Highway 64 and there we waved goodbye and I started hitching three thousand miles back to California. I would be home again the next Christmas.

22

Meanwhile Japhy was waiting for me in his nice little shack in Corte Madera California. He was settled in Sean Monahan's hermitage, a wooden cabin built behind a cypress windrow on a steep little grassy hill also covered with eucalyptus and pine, behind Sean's main house. The shack had been built by an old man to die in, years ago. It was well built. I was invited to go live there as long as I wanted, rent free. The shack had been made habitable after years as a wreck, by Sean Monahan's brother-in-law Whitey Jones, a good young carpenter, who had put in burlap over the wood walls and a good woodstove and a kerosene lamp and then never lived in it, having to go to work out of town. So Japhy'd moved in to finish his studies and live the good solitary life. If anybody wanted to go see him it was a steep climb. On the floor were woven grass mats and Japhy said in a letter "I sit and smoke a pipe and drink tea and hear the wind beat the slender eucalyptus limbs like whips and the cypress windrow roars." He'd stay there until May 15, his sailing date for Japan, where he had been invited by an American foundation to stay in a monastery and study under a Master. "Meanwhile," wrote Japhy, "come share a wild man's dark cabin with wine and weekend girls and good pots of food and woodfire heat. Monahan will give us grocery bucks to fall a few trees in his big yard and buck and split 'em out for firewood and I'll teach you all about logging."

During that winter Japhy had hitchhiked up to his home-country in the Northwest, up through Portland in snow, farther up to the blue ice glacier country, finally northern Washington on the farm of a friend in the Nooksack Valley, a week in a berrypicker's splitshake cabin, and a few climbs around. The names like "Nooksack" and "Mount Baker National Forest" excited in my mind a beautiful crystal vision of snow and ice and pines in the Far North of my childhood dreams. . . . But I was standing on the very hot April road of North Carolina waiting for my first ride, which came very soon from a young high-school kid who took me to a country town called Nashville, where I broiled in the sun a half-hour till I got a ride from a taciturn but kindly naval officer who drove me clear to Greenville South Carolina. After that whole winter and early spring of incredible peace sleeping on my porch and resting in my woods, the stint of hitchhiking was harder than ever and more like hell than ever. In Greenville in fact I walked three miles in the burning sun for nothing, lost in the maze of down-town back streets, looking for a certain highway, and at one point passed a kind of forge where colored men were all black and sweaty and covered with coal and I cried "I'm suddenly in hell again!" as I felt the blast of heat.

But it began to rain on the road and few rides took me into the rainy night of Georgia, where I rested sitting on my pack under the overhanging sidewalk roofs of old hardware stores and drank a half pint of wine. A rainy night, no rides. When the Greyhound bus came I hailed it down and rode to Gaines-ville. In Gainesville I thought I'd sleep by the railroad tracks awhile but they were about a mile away and just as I thought of sleeping in the yard a local crew came out to switch and saw me, so I retired to an empty lot by the tracks, but the cop car kept circling around using its spot (had probably heard of me from the railroad men, probably not) so I gave it up, mosquitoes anyway, and went back to town and stood waiting for a ride in the bright lights by the luncheonettes of down-town, the cops seeing me plainly and therefore not searching for me or worrying about me.

But no ride, and dawn coming, so I slept in a four-dollar room in a hotel and showered and rested well. But what feelings of homelessness and bleak, again, as the Christmas trip east. All I had to be really proud of were my fine new thick-soled workshoes and my full pack. In the morning, after breakfast in a dismal Georgia restaurant with revolving fans on the ceiling and *mucho* flies, I went out on the broiling highway and got a ride from a truckdriver to Flowery Branch Georgia, then a few spot rides on through Atlanta to the other side at another small town called Stonewall, where I was picked up by a big fat Southerner with a broadbrimmed hat who reeked of whisky and kept telling jokes and turning to look at me to see if I laughed, meanwhile sending the car spurting into the soft shoulders and leaving big clouds of dust behind us, so that long before he reached his destination I begged off and said I wanted to get off to eat.

"Heck, boy, I'll eat with ya 'n' drive ya on." He was drunk and he drove very fast.

"Well I gotta go to the toilet," I said trailing off my voice. The experience had bugged me so I decided, "The hell with hitchhiking. I've got enough money to take a bus to El Paso and from there I'll hop Southern Pacific freights and be ten times safer." Besides the thought of being all the way out in El Paso Texas in that dry Southwest of clear blue skies and endless desert land to sleep in, no cops, made up my mind. I was anxious to get out of the South, out of chaingang Georgia.

The bus came at four o'clock and we were at Birmingham Alabama in the middle of the night, where I waited on a bench for my next bus trying to sleep on my arms on my rucksack but kept waking up to see the pale ghosts of American bus stations wandering around: in fact one woman streamed by like a wisp of smoke, I was definitely certain *she* didn't exist for sure. On her face the phantasmal belief in what she was doing . . . On my face, for that matter, too. After Birmingham it was soon Louisiana and then east Texas oilfields, then Dallas, then a long day's ride in a bus crowded with servicemen across the long immense waste of Texas, to the ends of it, El Paso, arriving at midnight, by now I being so exhausted all I wanted to do was sleep. But I didn't go to a hotel, I had to watch my money now, and instead I just hauled my pack to my back and walked straight for the railroad yards to stretch my bag out somewhere behind the tracks. It was then, that night, that I realized the dream that had made me want to buy the pack.

It was a beautiful night and the most beautiful sleep of my life. First I went to the yards and walked through, warily, behind lines of boxcars, and got out to the west end of the yard but kept going because suddenly I saw in the dark there was indeed a lot of desert land out there. I could see rocks, dry bushes, imminent mountains of them faintly in the starlight. "Why hang around viaducts and tracks," I reasoned, "when all I gotta do is exert a little footwork and I'll be safe out of reach of all yard cops and bums too for that matter." I just kept walking along the mainline track for a few miles and soon I was in the open desert mountain country. My thick boots walked well on the ties and rocks. It was now about one a.m., I longed to sleep off the long trip from Carolina. Finally I saw a mountain to the right I liked, after passing a long valley with many lights in it distinctly a penitentiary or prison. "Stay away from that yard, son," I thought. I went up a dry arroyo and in the starlight the sand and rocks were white. I climbed and climbed.

Suddenly I was exhilarated to realize I was completely alone and safe and nobody was going to wake me up all night long. What an amazing revelation! And I had everything I needed right on my back; I'd put fresh bus-station water in my polybdenum bottle before leaving. I climbed up the arroyo, so finally when I turned and looked back I could see all of Mexico, all of Chihuahua, the entire sand-glittering desert of it, under a late sinking moon that was huge and bright just over the Chihuahua mountains. The Southern Pacific rails run right along parallel to the Rio Grande River outside of El Paso, so from where I was, on the American side, I could see right down to the river itself separating the two borders. The sand in the arroyo was soft as silk. I spread my sleeping bag on it and took off my shoes and had a slug of water and lit my pipe and crossed my legs and felt glad. Not a sound; it was still winter in the desert. Far off, just the sound of the yards where they were kicking cuts of cars with a great *splowm* waking up all El Paso, but not me. All I had for companionship was that moon of Chihuahua sinking lower and lower as I looked, losing its white light and getting more and more yellow butter, yet when I turned in to sleep it was bright as a lamp in my face and I had to turn my face away to sleep. In keeping with my naming of little spots with personal names, I called this spot "Apache Gulch." I slept well indeed.

In the morning I discovered a rattlesnake trail in the sand but that might have been from the summer before. There were very few bootmarks, and those were hunters' boots. The sky was flawlessly blue in the morning, the sun hot, plenty of little dry wood to light a breakfast fire. I had cans of pork and beans in my spacious pack. I had a royal breakfast. The problem now was water, though, as I drank it all and the sun was hot and I got thirsty. I climbed up the arroyo investigating it further and came to the end of it, a solid wall of rock, and at the foot of it even deeper softer sand than that of the night before. I decided to camp there that night, after a pleasant day spent in old Juárez enjoying the church and streets and food of Mexico. For a while I contemplated leaving my pack hidden among rocks but the chances were slim yet possible that some old hobo or hunter would come along and find it so I hauled it on my back and went down the arroyo to the rails again and walked back three miles into El Paso and left the pack in a twenty-five-cent locker in the railroad station. Then I walked through the city and out to the border gate and crossed over for two pennies.

It turned out to be an insane day, starting sanely enough in the church of Mary Guadaloupe and a saunter in the Indian Markets and resting on park benches among the gay childlike Mexicans but later the bars and a few too many to drink, yelling at old mustachioed Mexican peons "Todas las granas de arena del desierto de Chihuahua son vacuidad!" and finally I ran into a bunch of evil Mexican Apaches of some kind who took me to their dripping stone pad and turned me on by candlelight and invited their friends and it was all a lot of shadowy heads by candlelight and smoke. In fact I got sick of it and remembered my perfect white sand gulch and the place where I would sleep tonight and I excused myself. But they didn't want me to leave. One of them stole a few things from my bag of purchases but I didn't care. One of the Mexican boys was queer and had fallen in love with me and wanted to go to California with me. It was night now in Juárez; all the nightclubs were wailing away. We went for a short beer in one nightclub which was exclusively Negro soldiers sprawling around with senoritas in their laps, a mad bar, with rock and roll on the jukebox, a regular paradise. The Mexican kid wanted me to go down alleys and go "sst" and tell American boys that I knew where there were some girls. "Then I bring them to my room, sst, *no gurls!*" said the Mexican kid. The only place I could shake him was at the border gate. We waved goodbye. But it was the evil city and I had my virtuous desert waiting for me.

I walked anxiously over the border and through El Paso and out to the railroad station, got my bag out, heaved a big sigh, and went right on down those three miles to the arroyo, which was easy to re-recognize in the moonlight, and on up, my feet making that lonely thwap thwap of Japhy's boots and I realized I had indeed learned from Japhy how to cast off the evils of the world and the city and find my true pure soul, just as long as I had a decent pack on my back. I got back to my camp and spread the sleeping bag and thanked the Lord for all He was giving me. Now the remembrance of the whole long evil afternoon smoking marijuana with slant-hatted Mexicans in a musty candlelit room was like a dream, a bad dream, like one of my dreams on the straw mat at Buddha Creek North Carolina. I meditated and prayed. There just isn't any kind of night's sleep in the world that can compare with the night's sleep you get in the desert winter night, providing you're good and warm in a duck-down bag. The silence is so intense that you can hear your own blood roar in your ears but louder than that by far is the mysterious roar which I always identify with the roaring of the diamond of wisdom, the mysterious roar of silence itself, which is a great Shhhh reminding you of something you've seemed to have forgotten in the stress of your days since birth. I wished I could explain it to those I loved, to my mother, to Japhy, but there just weren't any words to describe the nothingness and purity of it. "Is there a certain and definite teaching to be given to all living creatures?" was the question probably asked to beetlebrowed snowy Dipankara, and his answer was the roaring silence of the diamond.

23

In the morning I had to get the show on the road or never get to my protective shack in California. I had about eight dollars left of the cash I'd brought with me. I went down to the highway and started to hitchhike, hoping for quick luck. A salesman gave me a ride. He said "Three hundred and sixty days out of the year we get bright sunshine here in El Paso and my wife just bought a clothes dryer!" He took me to Las Cruces New Mexico and there I walked through the little town, following the highway, and came out on the other end and saw a big beautiful old tree and decided to just lay my pack down and rest anyhow. "Since it's a dream already ended, then I'm already in California, then I've already decided to rest under that tree at noon," which I did, on my back, even napping awhile, pleasantly.

Then I got up and walked over the railroad bridge, and just then a man saw me and said "How would you like to earn two dollars an hour helping me move a piano?" I needed the money and said okay. We left my rucksack in his moving storage room and went off in his little truck, to a home in the outskirts of

Las Cruces, where a lot of nice middleclass people were chatting on the porch, and the man and I got out of the truck with the handtruck and the pads and got the piano out, also a lot of other furniture, then transported it to their new house and got that in and that was that. Two hours, he gave me four dollars and I went into a truckstop diner and had a royal meal and was all set for that afternoon and night. Just then a car stopped, driven by a big Texan with a sombrero, with a poor Mexican couple, young, in the back seat, the girl carrying an infant, and he offered me a ride all the way to Los Angeles for ten dollars.

I said "I'll give you all I can, which is only four."

"Well goddammit come on anyway." He talked and talked and drove all night straight through Arizona and the California desert and left me off in Los Angeles a stone's throw from my railroad yards at nine o'clock in the morning, and the only disaster was the poor little Mexican wife had spilled some baby food on my rucksack on the floor of the car and I wiped it off angrily. But they had been nice people. In fact, driving through Arizona I'd explained a little Buddhism to them, specifically karma, reincarnation, and they all seemed pleased to hear the news.

"You mean other chance to come back and try again?" asked the poor little Mexican, who was all bandaged from a fight in Juárez the night before.

"That's what they say."

"Well goddammit next time I be born I hope I ain't who I am now."

And the big Texan, if anybody better get another chance it was him: his stories all night long were about how he slugged so-and-so for such-and-such, from what he said he had knocked enough men out to form Coxie's army of avenged phantasmal grievers crawling on to Texas-land. But I noticed he was more of a big fibber than anything else and didn't believe half his stories and stopped listening at midnight. Now, nine a.m. in L.A., I walked to the railroad yards, had a cheap breakfast of doughnuts and coffee in a bar sitting at the counter chatting with the Italian bartender who wanted to know what I was doing with the big rucksack, then I went to the yards and sat in the grass watching them make up the trains.

Proud of myself because I used to be a brakeman I made the mistake of wandering around the yards with my rucksack on my back chatting with the switchmen, asking about the next local, and suddenly here came a great big young cop with a gun swinging in a holster on his hip, all done up like on TV the Sheriff of Cochise and Wyatt Earp, and giving me a steely look through dark glasses orders me out of the yards. So he watches me as I go over the overpass to the highway, standing there arms akimbo. Mad, I went back down the highway and jumped over the railroad fence and lay flat in the grass awhile. Then I sat up and chewed grass, keeping low however, and waited. Soon I heard a highball blow and I knew what train was ready and I climbed over cars to my train and jumped on it as it was pulling out and rode right out of the L.A. yards lying on my back with a grass stem in my mouth right under the unforgiving gaze of my policeman, who was now arms akimbo for a different reason. In fact he scratched his head.

The local went to Santa Barbara where again I went to the beach, had a swim and some food over a fine woodfire in the sand, and came back to the yards with plenty of time to catch the Midnight Ghost. The Midnight Ghost is composed mainly of flatcars with truck trailers lashed on them by steel cables. The huge wheels of the trucks are encased in woodblocks. Since I always lay my head down right by those woodblocks, it would be goodbye Ray if there ever was a crash. I figured if it was my destiny to die on the Midnight Ghost it was my destiny. I figured God had work for me to do yet. The Ghost came right on schedule and I got on a flatcar, under a truck, spread out my bag, stuck my shoes under my balled coat for a pillow, and relaxed and sighed. Zoom, we were gone. And now I know why the bums call it the Midnight Ghost, because, exhausted, against all better judgment, I fell fast asleep and only woke up under the glare of the yard office lights in San Luis Obispo, a very dangerous situation, the train had stopped just in the wrong way. But there wasn't a soul in sight around the yard office, it was mid of night, besides just then, as I woke up from a perfect dreamless sleep the highball was going baugh baugh up front and we were already pulling out, exactly like ghosts. And I didn't wake up then till almost San Francisco in the morning. I had a dollar left and Japhy was waiting for me at the shack. The whole trip had been as swift and enlightening as a dream, and I was back.

24

If the Dharma Bums ever get lay brothers in America who live normal lives with wives and children and homes, they will be like Sean Monahan.

Sean was a young carpenter who lived in an old wooden house far up a country road from the huddled cottages of Corte Madera, drove an old jalopy, personally added a porch to the back of the house to make a nursery for later children, and had selected a wife who agreed with him in every detail about how to live the joyous life in America without much money. Sean liked to take days off from his job to just go up the hill to the shack, which belonged to the property he rented, and spend a day of meditation and study of the Buddhist sutras and just brewing himself pots of tea and taking naps. His wife was Christine, a beautiful young honey-haired girl, her hair falling way down over her shoulders, who wandered around the house and yard barefooted hanging up wash and baking her own brown bread and cookies. She was an expert on making food out of nothing. The year before Japhy had made them an anniversary gift which was a huge ten-pound bag of flour, and they were very glad to receive it. Sean in fact was just an oldtime patriarch; though he was only twenty-two he wore a full beard like Saint Joseph and in it you could see his pearly white teeth smiling and his young blue eyes twinkling. They already had two little daughters, who also wandered around barefooted in the house and yard and were brought up to take care of themselves. Sean's house had woven straw mats on the floor and there too when you came in you were required to take off your shoes. He had lots of books and the only extravagance was a hi-fi set so he could play his fine collection of Indian records and Flamenco records and jazz. He even had Chinese and Japanese records. The dining table was a low, black-lacquered, Japanese style table, and to eat in Sean's house you not only had to be in your socks but sitting on mats at this table, any way you could. Christine was a great one for delicious soups and fresh biscuits.

When I arrived there at noon that day, getting off the Greyhound bus and walking up the tar road about a mile, Christine immediately had me sit down to hot soup and hot bread with butter. She was a gentle creature. "Sean and Japhy are both working on his job at Sausalito. They'll be home about five."

"I'll go up to the shack and look at it and wait up there this afternoon."

"Well, you can stay down here and play records."

"Well, I'll get out of your way."

"You won't be in my way, all I'm gonna do is hang out the wash and bake some bread for tonight and mend a few things." With a wife like that Sean, working only desultorily at carpentry, had managed to put a few thousand dollars in the bank. And like a patriarch of old Sean was generous, he always insisted on feeding you and if twelve people were in the house he'd lay out a big dinner (a simple dinner but delicious) on a board outside in the yard, and always a big jug of red wine. It was a communal arrangement, though, he was strict about that: we'd make collections for the wine, and if people came, as they all did, for a long weekend, they were expected to bring food or food money. Then at night under the trees and the stars of his yard, with everybody well fed and drinking red wine, Sean would take out his guitar and sing folksongs. Whenever I got tired of it I'd climb my hill and go sleep.

After eating lunch and talking awhile to Christine, I went up the hill. It climbed steeply right at the back door. Huge ponderosas and other pines, and in the property adjoining Sean's a dreamy horse meadow with wild flowers and two beautiful bays with their sleek necks bent to the butterfat grass in the hot sun. "Boy, this is going to be greater than North Carolina woods!" I thought, starting up. In the slope of grass was where Sean and Japhy had felled three huge eucalyptus trees and had already bucked them (sawed whole logs) with a chain saw. Now the block was set and I could see where they had begun to split the logs with wedges and sledgehammers and doublebitted axes. The little trail up the hill went so steeply that you almost had to lean over and walk like a monkey. It followed a long cypress row that had been planted by the old man who had died on the hill a few years ago. This prevented the cold foggy winds from the ocean from blasting across the property unhindered. There were three stages to the climb: Sean's backyard; then a fence, forming a little pure deer park where I actually saw deer one night, five of them, resting (the whole area was a game refuge); then the final fence and the top grassy hill with its sudden hollow on the right where the shack was barely visible under trees and flowery bushes. Behind the shack, a well-built affair actually of three big rooms but only one room occupied by Japhy, was plenty of good firewood and a saw horse and axes and an outdoor privy with no roof, just a hole in the ground and a board. It was like the first morning in the world in fine yard, with the sun streaming in through the dense sea of leaves, and birds and butterflies jumping around, warm, sweet, the smell of higher-hill heathers and flowers beyond the barbed-wire fence which led to the very top of the mountain and showed you a vista of all the Marin County area. I went inside the shack.

On the door was a board with Chinese inscriptions on it; I never did find out what it meant: probably "Mara stay away" (Mara the Tempter). Inside I saw the beautiful simplicity of Japhy's way of living, neat, sensible, strangely rich without a cent having been spent on the decoration. Old clay jars exploded with bouquets of flowers picked around the yard. His books were neatly stacked in orange crates. The floor was covered with inexpensive straw mats. The walls, as I say, were lined with burlap, which is one of the finest wallpapers you can have, very attractive and nice smelling. Japhy's mat was covered with a thin mattress and a Paisley shawl over that, and at the head of it, neatly rolled for the day, his sleeping bag. Behind burlap drapes in a closet his rucksack and junk were put away from sight. From the burlap wall hung beautiful prints of old Chinese silk paintings and maps of Marin County and northwest Washington and various poems he'd written and just stuck on a nail for anybody to read. The latest poem superimposed over others on the nail said: "It started just now with a hummingbird stopping over the porch two yards away through the open door, then gone, it stopped me studying and I saw the old redwood post leaning in clod ground, tangled in a huge bush of yellow flowers higher than my head, through which I push every time I come inside. The shadow network of the sunshine through its vines. White-crowned sparrows make tremendous singings in the trees, the rooster down the valley crows and crows. Sean Monahan outside, behind my back, reads the Diamond Sutra in the sun. Yesterday I read Migration of Birds. The Golden Plover and the Arctic Tern, today that big abstraction's at my door, for juncoes and the robins soon will leave, and nesting scrabblers will pick up all the string, and soon in hazy day of April summer heat across the hill, without a book I'll know, the seabirds'll chase spring north along the coast: they'll be nesting in Alaska in six weeks." And it was signed: "Japheth M. Ryder, Cypress-Cabin, 18:III: 56."

I didn't want to disturb anything in the house till he got back from work so I went out and lay down in the tall green grass in the sun and waited all afternoon, dreaming. But then I realized, "I might as well make a nice supper for Japhy" and I went down the hill again and down the road to the store and bought beans, saltpork, various groceries and came back and lit a fire in the woodstove and boiled up a good pot of New England beans, with molasses and onions. I was amazed at the way Japhy stored his food: just on a shelf by the woodstove: two onions, an orange, a bag of wheat germ, cans of curry powder, rice, mysterious pieces of dried Chinese seaweed, a bottle of soy sauce (to make his mysterious Chinese dishes). His salt and pepper was all neatly wrapped up in little plastic wrappers bound with elastic. There wasn't anything in the world Japhy would ever waste, or lose. Now I was introducing into his kitchen all the big substantial pork-and-beans of the world, maybe he wouldn't like it. He also had a big chunk of Christine's fine brown bread, and his bread knife was a dagger simply stuck into the board.

It got dark and I waited in the yard, letting the pot of beans keep warm on the fire. I chopped some wood and added it to the pile behind the stove. The fog began to blow in from the Pacific, the trees bowed deeply and roared. From the top of the hill you could see nothing but trees, trees, a roaring sea of trees. It was paradise. As it got cold I went inside and stoked up the fire, singing, and closed the windows. The windows were simply removable opaque plastic pieces that had been cleverly carpentered by Whitey Jones, Christine's brother, they let in light but you couldn't see anything outdoors and they cut off the cold wind. Soon it was warm in the cozy cabin. By and by I heard a "Hoo" out in the roaring sea of fog trees and it was Japhy coming back.

I went out to greet him. He was coming across the tall final grass, weary from the day's work, clomping along in his boots, his coat over his back. "Well, Smith, here you are."

"I cooked up a nice pot of beans for you."

"You did?" He was tremendously grateful. "Boy, what a relief to come home from work and don't have to cook up a meal yourself. I'm starved." He pitched right into the beans with bread and hot coffee I made in a pan on the stove, just French style brewing coffee stirred with a spoon. We had a great supper and then lit up our pipes and talked with the fire roaring. "Ray, you're going to have a great summer up on that Desolation Peak. I'll tell you all about it."

"I'm gonna have a great spring right here in this shack."

"Durn right, first thing we do this weekend is invite some nice new girls I know, Psyche and Polly Whitmore, though wait a minute, hmm. I can't invite both of them they both love me and'll be jealous. Anyway we'll have big parties every weekend, starting downstairs at Sean's and ending up here. And I'm not workin tomorrow so we'll cut some firewood for Sean. That's all he wants you to do. Though, if you wanta work on that job of ours in Sausalito next week, you can make ten bucks a day."

"Fine . . . that'll buy a lotta pork and beans and wine."

Japhy pulled out a fine brush drawing of a mountain. "Here's your mountain that'll loom over you, Hozomeen. I drew it myself two summers ago from Crater Peak. In nineteen-fifty-two I first went into that Skagit country, hitched from Frisco to Seattle and then in, with a beard just started and a bare shaved head—"

"Bare shaved head! Why?"

"To be like a bhikku, you know what it says in the sutras."

"But what did people think about you hitchhiking around with a bare shaved head?"

"They thought I was crazy, but everybody that gave me a ride I'd spin 'em the Dharmy, boy, and leave 'em enlightened."

"I shoulda done a bit of that myself hitchin out here just now. . . . I gotta tell you about my arroyo in the desert mountains."

"Wait a minute, so they put me on Crater Mountain lookout but the snow was so deep in the high country that year I worked trail for a month first in Granite Creek gorge, you'll see all those places, and then with a string of mules we made it the final seven miles of winding Tibetan rocktrail above timber line over snowfields to the final jagged pinnacles, and then climbed the cliffs in a snowstorm and I opened my cabin and cooked my first dinner while the wind howled and the ice grew on two walls in the wind. Boy, wait'll you get up there. That year my friend Jack Joseph was on Desolation, where you'll be."

"What a name, Desolation, oo, wow, ugh, wait . . ."

"He was the first lookout to go up, I got him on my radio first off and he welcomed me to the community of lookouts. Later I contacted other mountains, see they give you a two-way radio, it's almost a ritual all the lookouts chat and talk about bears they've seen or sometimes ask instructions for how to bake muffins on a woodstove and so on, and there we all were in a high world talking on a net of wireless across hundreds of miles of wilderness. It's a primitive area, where you're going boy. From my cabin I could see the lamps of Desolation after dark, Jack Joseph reading his geology books and in the day we flashed by mirror to align our firefinder transits, accurate to the compass."

"Gee, how'll I ever learn all that, I'm just a simple poet bum."

"Oh you'll learn, the magnetic pole, the pole star and the northern lights. Every night Jack Joseph and I talked: one day he got a swarm of ladybugs on the lookout that covered the roof and filled up his water cistern, another day he went for a walk along the ridge and stepped right on a sleeping bear."

"Oho, I thought *this* place was wild."

"This is nothin . . . and when the lightning storm came by, closer and closer, he called to finally say he was going off the air because the storm was too close to leave his radio on, he disappeared from sound and then sight as the black clouds swept over and the lightning danced on his hill. But as the summer passed Desolation got dry and flowery and Blakey

lambs and he wandered the cliffs and I was on Crater Mountain in my jockstrap and boots hunting out ptarmigan nests
out of curiosity, climbing and pooking about, gettin bit by
bees. . . . Desolation's way up there, Ray, six thousand feet
or so up looking into Canada and the Chelan highlands, the
wilds of the Pickett range, and mountains like Challenger, Terror, Fury, Despair and the name of your own ridge is Starvation Ridge and the upcountry of the Boston Peak and Buckner
Peak range to the south thousands of miles of mountains,
deer, bear, conies, hawks, trout, chipmunks. It'll be great for
you Ray."

"I look forward to it okay. I bet no bee bites me."

Then he took out his books and read awhile, and I read too,
both of us with separate oil lamps banked low, a quiet evening
at home as the foggy wind roared in the trees outside and
across the valley a mournful mule heehawed in one of the most
tremendously heartbroken cries I've ever heard. "When that
mule weeps like that," says Japhy, "I feel like praying for all
sentient beings." Then for a while he meditated motionless in
the full lotus position on his mat and then said "Well, time for
bed." But now I wanted to tell him all the things I'd discovered that winter meditating in the woods. "Ah, it's just a
lot of words," he said, sadly, surprising me. "I don't wanta
hear all your word descriptions of words words words you
made up all winter, man I wanta be enlightened by actions."
Japhy had changed since the year before, too. He no longer
had his goatee, which had removed the funny merry little look
of his face but left him looking gaunt and rocky faced. Also
he'd cut his hair in a close crew cut and looked Germanic and
stern and above all sad. There seemed to be some kind of disappointment in his face now, and certainly in his soul, he
wouldn't listen to my eager explanations that everything was
all right forever and forever and forever. Suddenly he said "I'm
gonna get married, soon, I think, I'm gettin tired of battin
around like this."

"But I thought you'd discovered the Zen ideal of poverty
and freedom."

"Aw maybe I'm gettin tired of all that. After I come back
from the monastery in Japan I'll probably have my fill of it

anyhow. Maybe I'll be rich and work and make a lot of money and live in a big house." But a minute later: "And who wants to enslave himself to a lot of all that, though? I dunno, Smith, I'm just depressed and everything you're saying just depresses me further. My sister's back in town you know."

"Who's that?"

"That's Rhoda, my sister, I grew up with her in the woods in Oregon. She's gonna marry this rich jerk from Chicago, a real square. My father's having trouble with his sister, too, my Aunt Noss. She's an old bitch from way back."

"You shouldn't have cut off your goatee, you used to look like a happy little sage."

"Well I ain't happy little sage no mo' and I'm tired." He was exhausted from a long hard day's work. We decided to go to sleep and forget it. In fact we were a bit sad and sore at each other. During the day I had discovered a spot by a wild rosebush in the yard where I planned to lay out my sleeping bag. I'd covered it a foot deep with fresh pulled grass. Now, with my flashlight and my bottle of cold water from the sink tap, I went out there and rolled into a beautiful night's rest under the sighing trees, meditating awhile first. I couldn't meditate indoors any more like Japhy had just done, after all that winter in the woods of night I had to hear the little sounds of animals and birds and feel the cold sighing earth under me before I could rightly get to feel a kinship with all living things as being empty and awake and saved already. I prayed for Japhy: it looked like he was changing for the worse. At dawn a little rain pattered on my sleeping bag and I put my poncho over me instead of under me, cursing, and slept on. At seven in the morning the sun was out and the butterflies were in the roses by my head and a hummingbird did a jet dive right down at me, whistling, and darted away happily. But I was mistaken about Japhy changing. It was one of the greatest mornings in our lives. There he was standing in the doorway of the shack with a big frying pan in his hand banging on it and chanting "Buddham saranam gocchami . . . Dhammam saranam gocchami . . . Sangham saranam gocchami" and yelling "Come on, boy, your pancakes are ready! Come and get it! Bang bang bang" and the orange sun was pouring in through the pines

and everything was fine again, in fact Japhy had contemplated
that night and decided I was right about hewing to the good
old Dharma.

25

Japhy had cooked up some good buckwheat pancakes and we
had Log Cabin syrup to go with them and a little butter. I
asked him what the "Gocchami" chant meant. "That's the
chant they give out for the three meals in Buddhist monasteries in Japan. It means, Buddham Saranam Gocchami, I take
refuge in the Buddha, Sangham, I take refuge in the church,
Dhammam, I take refuge in the Dharma, the truth. Tomorrow
morning I'll make you another nice breakfast, slumgullion,
d'yever eat good oldfashioned slumgullion boy, 'taint nothin
but scrambled eggs and potatoes all scrambled up together."

"It's a lumberjack meal?"

"There ain't no such thing as *lumber*jack, that must be a
Back East expression. Up here we call 'em loggers. Come on
eat up your pancakes and we'll go down and split logs and I'll
show you how to handle a doublebitted ax." He took the ax
out and sharpened it and showed me how to sharpen it. "And
don't ever use this ax on a piece of wood that's on the ground,
you'll hit rocks and blunt it, always have a log or sumpthin for
a block."

I went out to the privy and, coming back, wishing to surprise Japhy with a Zen trick I threw the roll of toilet paper
through the open window and he let out a big Samurai Warrior roar and appeared on the windowsill in his boots and
shorts with a dagger in his hand and jumped fifteen feet down
into the loggy yard. It was crazy. We started downhill feeling
high. All the logs that had been bucked had more or less of a
crack in them, where you more or less inserted the heavy iron
wedge, and then, raising a five-pound sledgehammer over
your head, standing way back so's not to hit your own ankle,
you brought it down konko on the wedge and split the log
clean in half. Then you'd sit the half-logs up on a block-log
and let down with the doublebitted ax, a long beautiful ax,

sharp as a razor, and fawap, you had quarter-logs. Then you set up a quarter-log and brought down to an eighth. He showed me how to swing the sledge and the ax, not too hard, but when he got mad himself I noticed he swung the ax as hard as he could, roaring his famous cry, or cursing. Pretty soon I had the knack and was going along as though I'd been doing it all my life.

Christine came out in the yard to watch us and called "I'll have some nice lunch for ya."

"Okay." Japhy and Christine were like brother and sister.

We split a lot of logs. It was great swinging down the sledge-hammer, all the weight clank on top of a wedge and feeling that log give, if not the first time the second time. The smell of sawdust, pine trees, the breeze blowing over the placid mountains from the sea, the meadowlarks singing, the butterflies in the grass, it was perfect. Then we went in and ate a good lunch of hotdogs and rice and soup and red wine and Christine's fresh biscuits and sat there crosslegged and barefoot thumbing through Sean's vast library.

"Did ya hear about the disciple who asked the Zen master 'What is the Buddha?'"

"No, what?"

"'The Buddha is a dried piece of turd,' was the answer. The disciple experienced sudden enlightenment."

"Simple shit," I said.

"Do you know what sudden enlightenment is? One disciple came to a Master and answered his koan and the Master hit him with a stick and knocked him off the veranda ten feet into a mud puddle. The disciple got up and laughed. He later became a Master himself. 'Twasn't by words he was enlightened, but by that great healthy push off the porch."

"All wallowing in mud to prove the crystal truth of compassion," I thought, I wasn't about to start advertising my "words" out loud any more to Japhy.

"Woo!" he yelled throwing a flower at my head. "Do you know how Kasyapa became the First Patriarch? The Buddha was about to start expounding a sutra and twelve hundred and fifty bhikkus were waiting with their garments arranged and their feet crossed, and all the Buddha did was raise a flower. Everybody was perturbed. The Buddha didn't say nothin. Only

Kasyapa smiled. That was how the Buddha selected Kasyapa. That's known as the flower sermon, boy."

I went in the kitchen and got a banana and came out and said, "Well, I'll tell you what nirvana is."

"What?"

I ate the banana and threw the peel away and said nothing. "That's the banana sermon."

"Hoo!" yelled Japhy. "D'I ever tell you about Coyote Old Man and how him and Silver Fox started the world by stomping in empty space till a little ground appeared beneath their feet? Look at this picture, by the way. This is the famous Bulls." It was an ancient Chinese cartoon showing first a young boy going out into the wilderness with a small staff and pack, like an American Nat Wills tramp of 1905, and in later panels he discovers an ox, tries to tame, tries to ride it, finally does tame it and ride it but then abandons the ox and just sits in the moonlight meditating, finally you see him coming down from the mountain of enlightenment and then suddenly the next panel shows absolutely nothing at all, followed by a panel showing blossoms in a tree, then the last picture you see the young boy is a big fat old laughing wizard with a huge bag on his back and he's going into the city to get drunk with the butchers, enlightened, and another new young boy is going up to the mountain with a little pack and staff.

"It goes on and on, the disciples and the Masters go through the same thing, first they have to find and tame the ox of their mind essence, and then abandon that, then finally they attain to nothing, as represented by this empty panel, then having attained nothing they attain everything which is springtime blossoms in the trees so they end up coming down to the city to get drunk with the butchers like Li Po." That was a very wise cartoon, it reminded me of my own experience, trying to tame my mind in the woods, then realizing it was all empty and awake and I didn't have to do anything, and now I was getting drunk with the butcher Japhy. We played records and lounged around smoking then went out and cut more wood.

Then as it got cool late afternoon we went up to the shack and washed and dressed up for the big Saturday night party. During the day Japhy went up and down the hill at least ten times to make phone calls and see Christine and get bread and bring up sheets for his girl that night (when he had a girl he put out clean sheets on his thin mattress on the straw mats, a ritual). But I just sat around in the grass doing nothing, or writing haikus, or watching the old vulture circling the hill. "Must be something dead around here," I figured.

Japhy said "Why do you sit on your ass all day?"

"I practice do-nothing."

"What's the difference? Burn it, my Buddhism is activity," said Japhy rushing off down the hill again. Then I could hear him sawing wood and whistling in the distance. He couldn't stop jiggling for a minute. His meditations were regular things, by the clock, he'd meditated first thing waking in the morning then he had his mid-afternoon meditation, only about three minutes long, then before going to bed and that was that. But I just ambled and dreamed around. We were two strange dissimilar monks on the same path. I took a shovel, however, and leveled the ground near the rosebush where my bed of grass was: it was a little too slanty for comfort: I fixed it just right and that night I slept well after the big wine party.

The big party was wild. Japhy had a girl called Polly Whitmore come out to see him, a beautiful brunette with a Spanish hairdo and dark eyes, a regular raving beauty actually, a mountainclimber too. She'd just been divorced and lived alone in Millbrae. And Christine's brother Whitey Jones brought his fiancée Patsy. And of course Sean came home from work and cleaned up for the party. Another guy came out for the weekend, big blond Bud Diefendorf who worked as the janitor in the Buddhist Association to earn his rent and attend classes free, a big mild pipesmoking Buddha with all kinds of strange ideas. I liked Bud, he was intelligent, and I liked the fact that he had started out as a physicist at the University of Chicago then gone from that to philosophy and finally now to philosophy's dreadful murderer, Buddha. He said "I had a dream one time that I was sitting under a tree picking on a lute and singing 'I ain't got no name.' I was the no-name bhikku." It was so pleasing to meet so many Buddhists after that harsh road hitchhiking.

Sean was a strange mystical Buddhist with a mind full of superstitions and premonitions. "I believe in devils," he said.

"Well," I said, stroking his little daughter's hair, "all little children know that everybody goes to Heaven" to which he assented tenderly with a sad nod of his bearded skull. He was very kind. He kept saying "Aye" all the time, which went with his old boat that was anchored out in the bay and kept being scuttled by storms and we had to row out and bail it out in the cold gray fog. Just a little old wreck of a boat about twelve feet long, with no cabin to speak of, nothing but a ragged hull floating in the water around a rusty anchor. Whitey Jones, Christine's brother, was a sweet young kid of twenty who never said anything and just smiled and took ribbings without complaint. For instance the party finally got pretty wild and the three couples took all their clothes off and danced a kind of quaint innocent polka all hand-in-hand around the parlor, as the kiddies slept in their cribs. This didn't disturb Bud and me at all, we went right on smoking our pipes and discussing Buddhism in the corner, in fact that was best because we didn't have girls of our own. And those were three well stacked nymphs dancing there. But Japhy and Sean dragged Patsy into the bedroom and pretended to be trying to make her, to bug Whitey, who blushed all red, stark naked, and there were wrestlings and laughs all around the house. Bud and I were sitting there crosslegged with naked dancing girls in front of us and laughed to realize that it was a mighty familiar occasion.

"Seems like in some previous lifetime, Ray," said Bud, "you and I were monks in some monastery in Tibet where the girls danced for us before yabyum."

"Yeh, and we were the old monks who weren't interested in sex any more but Sean and Japhy and Whitey were the young monks and were still full of the fire of evil and still had a lot to learn." Every now and then Bud and I looked at all that flesh and licked our lips in secret. But most of the time, actually, during these naked revels, I just kept my eyes closed and listened to the music: I was really sincerely keeping lust out of my mind by main force and gritting of my teeth. And the best way was to keep my eyes closed. In spite of the nakedness and all it was really a gentle little home party and everybody began yawning for time for bed. Whitey went off with Patsy, Japhy went up the hill with Polly and took her to his fresh sheets, and I unrolled my sleeping bag by the rosebush and slept. Bud had brought his own sleeping bag and rolled out on Sean's straw mat floor.

In the morning Bud came up and lit his pipe and sat in the grass chatting to me as I rubbed my eyes to waking. During the day, Sunday, all kinds of other people came calling on the Monahans and half of them came up the hill to see the pretty shack and the two crazy famous bhikkus Japhy and Ray. Among them were Princess, Alvah, and Warren Coughlin. Sean spread out a board in the yard and put out a royal table of wine and hamburgers and pickles and lit a big bonfire and took out his two guitars and it was really a magnificent kind of way to live in Sunny California, I realized, with all this fine Dharma connected with it, and mountainclimbing, all of them had rucksacks and sleeping bags and some of them were going hiking that next day on the Marin County trails, which are beautiful. So the party was divided into three parts all the time: those in the living room listening to the hi-fi or thumbing through books, those in the yard eating and listening to the guitar music, and those on the hilltop in the shack brewing pots of tea and sitting crosslegged discussing poetry and things and the Dharma or wandering around in the high meadow to go see the children fly kites or old ladies ride by on horseback. Every weekend was the same mild picnic, a regular classical scene of angels and dolls having a kind flowery time in the void like the void in the cartoon of the Bulls, the blossom branch.

Bud and I sat on the hill watching kites. "That kite won't go high enough, it hasn't got a long enough tail," I said.

Bud said, "Say, that's great, that reminds me of my main problem in my meditations. The reason why I can't get really high into nirvana is because my tail isn't long enough." He puffed and pondered seriously over this. He was the most serious guy in the world. He pondered it all night and the next morning said "Last night I saw myself as a fish swimming through the void of the sea, going left and right in the water without knowing the meaning of left and right, but because of my fin I did so, that is, my kite tail, so I'm a Buddhafish and my fin is my wisdom."

"That was pretty infinyte, that kyte," says I.

Throughout all these parties I always stole off for a nap under the eucalyptus trees, instead of by my rosebush, which was all hot sun all day; in the shade of the trees I rested well. One afternoon as I just gazed at the topmost branches of those immensely tall trees I began to notice that the uppermost twigs and leaves were lyrical happy dancers glad that they had been apportioned the top, with all that rumbling experience of the whole tree swaying beneath them making their dance, their every jiggle, a huge and communal and mysterious necessity dance, and so just floating up there in the void dancing the meaning of the tree. I noticed how the leaves almost looked human the way they bowed and then leaped up and then swayed lyrically side to side. It was a crazy vision in my mind but beautiful. Another time under those trees I dreamt I saw a purple throne all covered with gold, some kind of Eternity Pope or Patriarch in it, and Rosie somewhere, and at that moment Cody was in the shack yakking to some guys and it seemed that he was to the left of this vision as some kind of Archangel, and when I opened my eyes I saw it was only the sun against my eyelids. And as I say, that hummingbird, a beautiful little blue hummingbird no bigger than a dragonfly, kept making a whistling jet dive at me, definitely saying hello to me, every day, usually in the morning, and I always yelled back at him a greeting. Finally he began to hover in the open window of the shack, buzzing there with his furious wings, looking at me beadily, then, flash, he was gone. That California humming guy . . .

Though sometimes I was afraid he would drive right into my head with his long beaker like a hatpin. There was also an old rat scrambling in the cellar under the shack and it was a good thing to keep the door closed at night. My other great friends were the ants, a colony of them that wanted to come in the shack and find the honey ("Calling all ants, calling all ants, come and get your ho-ney!" sang a little boy one day in the shack), so I went out to their anthill and made a trail of honey leading them into the back garden, and they were at that new vein of joy for a week. I even got down on my knees and talked to the ants. There were beautiful flowers all around the shack, red, purple, pink, white, we kept making bouquets but the prettiest of all was the one Japhy made of just pine cones and a sprig of pine needles. It had that simple look that characterized all his life. He'd come barging into the shack with his saw and see me sitting there and say "Why did you sit around all day?"

"I am the Buddha known as the Quitter."

Then it would be when Japhy's face would crease up in that funny littleboy laugh of his, like a Chinese boy laughing, crow's tracks appearing on each side of his eyes and his long mouth cracking open. He was so pleased with me sometimes.

Everybody loved Japhy, the girls Polly and Princess and even married Christine were all madly in love with him and they were all secretly jealous of Japhy's favorite doll Psyche, who came the following weekend real cute in jeans and a little white collar falling over her black turtleneck sweater and a tender little body and face. Japhy had told me he was a bit in love with her himself. But he had a hard time convincing her to make love he had to get her drunk, once she got drinking she couldn't stop. That weekend she came Japhy made slumgullion for all the three of us in the shack then we borrowed Sean's jalopy and drove about a hundred miles up the seacoast to an isolated beach where we picked mussels right off the washed rocks of the sea and smoked them in a big woodfire covered with seaweed. We had wine and bread and cheese and Psyche spent the whole day lying on her stomach in her jeans and sweater, saying nothing. But once she looked up with her little blue eyes and said "How oral you are, Smith, you're always eating and drinking."

"I am Buddha Empty-Eat," I said.

"Ain't she cute?" said Japhy.

"Psyche," I said, "this world is the movie of what everything is, it is one movie, made of the same stuff throughout, belonging to nobody, which is what everything is."

"Ah boloney."

We ran around the beach. At one point Japhy and Psyche were hiking up ahead on the beach and I was walking alone whistling Stan Getz's "Stella" and a couple of beautiful girls up front with their boyfriends heard me and one girl turned and said "Swing." There were natural caves on that beach where Japhy had once brought big parties of people and had organized naked bonfire dances.

Then the weekdays would come again and the parties were

over and Japhy and I would sweep out the shack, wee dried
bums dusting small temples. I still had a little left of my grant
from last fall, in traveler's checks, and I took one and went to
the supermarket down on the highway and bought flour, oatmeal, sugar, molasses, honey, salt, pepper, onions, rice, dried
milk, bread, beans, black-eyed peas, potatoes, carrots, cabbage,
lettuce, coffee, big wood matches for our woodstove and came
staggering back up the hill with all that and a half-gallon of red
port. Japhy's neat little spare foodshelf was suddenly loaded
with too much food. "What we gonna do with all this? We'll
have to feed all the bhikkus." In due time we had more
bhikkus than we could handle: poor drunken Joe Mahoney, a
friend of mine from the year before, would come out and sleep
for three days and recuperate for another crack at North Beach
and The Place. I'd bring him his breakfast in bed. On weekends sometimes there'd be twelve guys in the shack all arguing
and yakking and I'd take some yellow corn meal and mix it
with chopped onions and salt and water and pour out little
johnnycake tablespoons in the hot frying pan (with oil) and
provide the whole gang with delicious hots to go with their
tea. In the Chinese Book of Changes a year ago I had tossed a
couple of pennies to see what the prediction of my fortune was
and it had come out, "You will feed others." In fact I was
always standing over a hot stove.

"What does it mean that those trees and mountains out
there are not magic but real?" I'd yell, pointing outdoors.

"What?" they'd say.

"It means that those trees and mountains out there are not
magic but real."

"Yeah?"

Then I'd say, "What does it mean that those trees and mountains aren't real at all, just magic?"

"Oh come on."

"It means that those trees and mountains aren't real at all,
just magic."

"Well which is it, goddammit!"

"What does it mean that you ask, well which is it goddammit?" I yelled.

"Well what?"

"It means that you ask well which is it goddammit."

"Oh go bury your head in your sleeping bag, bring me a cup of that hot coffee." I was always boiling big pots of coffee on the stove.

"Oh cut it out," yelled Warren Coughlin. "The chariot will wear down!"

One afternoon I was sitting with some children in the grass and they asked me "Why is the sky blue?"

"Because the sky is blue."

"I wanta know *why* the sky is blue."

"The sky is blue because you wanta know why the sky is blue."

"Blue blue you," they said.

There were also some little kids who came around throwing rocks on our shack roof, thinking it was abandoned. One afternoon, at the time when Japhy and I had a little jet-black cat, they came sneaking to the door to look in. Just as they were about to open the door I opened it, with the black cat in my arms, and said in a low voice "I am the ghost."

They gulped and looked at me and believed me and said "Yeah." Pretty soon they were over the other side of the hill. They never came around throwing rocks again. They thought I was a witch for sure.

26

Plans were being made for Japhy's big farewell party a few days before his boat sailed for Japan. He was scheduled to leave on a Japanese freighter. It was going to be the biggest party of all time, spilling out of Sean's hi-fi living room right out into the bonfire yard and up the hill and even over it. Japhy and I had had our fill of parties and were not looking forward to it too happily. But everybody was going to be there: all his girls, including Psyche, and the poet Cacoethes, and Coughlin, and Alvah, and Princess and her new boyfriend, and even the director of the Buddhist Association Arthur Whane and his wife and sons, and even Japhy's father, and of course Bud, and unspecified couples from everywhere who would come with wine and food and guitars. Japhy said "I'm gettin sick and tired of these parties. How about you and me taking off for the Marin trails after the party, it'll go on for days, we'll just bring our packs and take off for Potrero Meadows camp or Laurel Dell."

"Good."

Meanwhile, suddenly one afternoon Japhy's sister Rhoda appeared on the scene with her fiancé. She was going to be married in Japhy's father's house in Mill Valley, big reception and all. Japhy and I were sitting around in the shack in a drowsy afternoon and suddenly she was in the door, slim and blond and pretty, with her well-dressed Chicago fiancé, a very handsome man. "Hoo!" yelled Japhy jumping up and kissing her in a big passionate embrace, which she returned whole-heartedly. And the way they talked!

"Well is your husband gonna be a good bang?"

"He damn well is, I picked him out real careful, ya grunge-jumper!"

"He'd better be or you'll have to call on me!"

Then to show off Japhy started a woodfire and said "Here's what we do up in that real country up north," and dumped too much kerosene into the fire but ran away from the stove and waited like a mischievous little boy and *broom!* the stove let out a deep rumbling explosion way inside that I could feel the shock of clear across the room. He'd almost done it that time. Then he said to her poor fiancé "Well you know any good positions for honeymoon night?" The poor guy had just come back from being a serviceman in Burma and tried to talk about Burma but couldn't get a word in edgewise. Japhy was mad as hell and really jealous. He was invited to the fancy reception and he said "Can I show up nekkid?"

"Anything you want, but come."

"I can just see it now, the punchbowl and all the ladies in their lawn hats and the hi-fi playing hearts and flowers organ music and everybody wipin their eyes cause the bride is so beautiful. What you wanta get all involved in the middle class for, Rhoda?"

She said "Ah I don't care, I wanta start living." Her fiancé had a lot of money. Actually he was a nice guy and I felt sorry for him having to smile through all this.

After they left Japhy said "She won't stay with him more

than six months. Rhoda's a real mad girl, she'd rather put on jeans and go hiking than sit around Chicago apartments."

"You love her, don't you?"

"You damn right, I oughta marry her myself."

"But she's your sister."

"I don't give a goddamn. She needs a real man like me. You don't know how wild she is, you weren't brought up with her in the woods." Rhoda was real nice and I wished she hadn't shown up with a fiancé. In all this welter of women I still hadn't got one for myself, not that I was trying too hard, but sometimes I felt lonely to see everybody paired off and having a good time and all I did was curl up in my sleeping bag in the rosebushes and sigh and say bah. For me it was just red wine in my mouth and a pile of firewood.

But then I'd find something like a dead crow in the deer park and think "That's a pretty sight for sensitive human eyes, and all of it comes out of sex." So I put sex out of my mind again. As long as the sun shined then blinked and shined again, I was satisfied. I would be kind and remain in solitude, I wouldn't pook about, I'd rest and be kind. "Compassion is the guide star," said Buddha. "Don't dispute with the authorities or with women. Beg. Be humble." I wrote a pretty poem addressed to all the people coming to the party: "Are in your eyelids wars, and silk . . . but the saints are gone, all gone, safe to that other." I really thought myself a kind of crazy saint. And it was based on telling myself "Ray, don't run after liquor and excitement of women and talk, stay in your shack and enjoy natural relationship of things as they are" but it was hard to live up to this with all kinds of pretty broads coming up the hill every weekend and even on weeknights. One time a beautiful brunette finally consented to go up the hill with me and we were there in the dark on my mattress day-mat when suddenly the door burst open and Sean and Joe Mahoney danced in laughing, deliberately trying to make me mad . . . either that or they really believed in my effort at asceticism and were like angels coming in to drive away the devil woman. Which they did, all right. Sometimes when I was really drunk and high and sitting crosslegged in the midst of the mad parties I really did see visions of holy empty snow in my eyelids and when I opened them I'd see all these good friends sitting around waiting for me to explain; and nobody ever considered my behavior strange, quite natural among Buddhists; and whether I opened my eyes to explain something or not they were satisfied. During that whole season, in fact, I had an over-whelming urge to close my eyes in company. I think the girls were terrified of this. "What's he always sitting with his eyes closed for?"

Little Prajna, Sean's two-year-old daughter, would come and poke at my closed eyelids and say "Booba. Hack!" Some-times I preferred taking her for little magic walks in the yard, holding her hand, to sitting yakking in the living room.

As for Japhy he was quite pleased with anything I did pro-vided I didn't pull any boners like making the kerosene lamp smoke from turning the wick too far up, or failing to sharpen the ax properly. He was very stern on those subjects. "You've got to learn!" he'd say. "Dammit, if there's anything I can't stand is when things ain't done right." It was amazing the suppers he'd roust up out of his own part of the food shelf, all kinds of weeds and dry roots bought in Chinatown and he'd boil up a mess of stuff, just a little, with soy sauce, and that went on top of freshly boiled rice and was delicious indeed, eaten with chopsticks. There we were sitting in the roar of trees at dusk with our windows wide open still, cold, but going chomp-chomp on delicious home-made Chinese dinners. Japhy really knew how to handle chopsticks and shoveled it in with a will. Then I'd sometimes wash the dishes and go out to meditate awhile on my mat beneath the eucalypti, and in the window of the shack I'd see the brown glow of Japhy's kerosene lamp as he sat reading and picking his teeth. Some-times he'd come to the door of the shack and yell "Hoo!" and I wouldn't answer and I could hear him mutter "Where the hell is he?" and see him peering out into the night for his bhikku. One night I was sitting meditating when I heard a loud crack to my right and I looked and it was a deer, coming to re-visit the ancient deer park and munch awhile in the dry foliage. Across the evening valley the old mule went with his heartbroken "Hee haw" broken like a yodel in the wind: like a horn blown by some terribly sad angel: like a reminder to people digesting dinners at home that all was not as well as they thought. Yet it was just a love cry for another mule. But that was why . . .

One night I was meditating in such perfect stillness that two mosquitoes came and sat on each of my cheekbones and stayed there a long time without biting and then went away without biting.

27

A few days before his big farewell party Japhy and I had an argument. We went into San Francisco to deliver his bike to the freighter at the pier and then went up to Skid Row in a drizzling rain to get cheap haircuts at the barber college and pook around Salvation Army and Goodwill stores in search of long underwear and stuff. As we were walking in the drizzly exciting streets ("Reminds me of Seattle!" he yelled) I got the overwhelming urge to get drunk and feel good. I bought a poorboy of ruby port and uncapped it and dragged Japhy into an alley and we drank. "You better not drink too much," he said, "you know we gotta go to Berkeley after this and attend a lecture and discussion at the Buddhist Center."

"Aw I don't wanta go to no such thing, I just wanta drink in alleys."

"But they're expecting you, I read all your poems there last year."

"I don't care. Look at that fog flyin over the alley and look at this warm ruby red port, don't it make ya feel like singing in the wind?"

"No it doesn't. You know, Ray, Cacoethes says you drink too much."

"And him with his ulcer! Why do you think he has an ulcer? Because he drank too much himself. Do I have an ulcer? Not on your life! I drink for joy! If you don't like my drinking you can go to the lecture by yourself. I'll wait at Coughlin's cottage."

"But you'll miss all that, just for some old wine."

"There's wisdom in wine, goddam it!" I yelled. "Have a shot!"

"No I won't!"

"Well then I'll drink it!" and I drained the bottle and we went back on Sixth Street where I immediately jumped back into the same store and bought another poorboy. I was feeling fine now.

Japhy was sad and disappointed. "How do you expect to become a good bhikku or even a Bodhisattva Mahasattva always getting drunk like that?"

"Have you forgotten the last of the Bulls, where he gets drunk with the butchers?"

"Ah so what, how can you understand your own mind essence with your head all muddled and your teeth all stained and your belly all sick?"

"I'm not sick, I'm fine. I could just float up into that gray fog and fly around San Francisco like a seagull. D'I ever tell you about Skid Row here, I used to live here—"

"I lived on Skid Road in Seattle myself, I know all about all that."

The neons of stores and bars were glowing in the gray gloom of rainy afternoon, I felt great. After we had our haircuts we went into a Goodwill store and fished around bins, pulling out socks and undershirts and various belts and junk that we bought for a few pennies. I kept taking surreptitious slugs of wine out of my bottle which I had wedged in my belt. Japhy was disgusted. Then we got in the jalopy and drove to Berkeley, across the rainy bridge, to the cottages of Oakland and then downtown Oakland, where Japhy wanted to find a pair of jeans that fitted me. We'd been looking all day for used jeans that would fit me. I kept giving him wine and finally he relented a little and drank some and showed me the poem he had written while I was getting my haircut in Skid Row: "Modern barber college, Smith eyes closed suffers a haircut fearing its ugliness 50 cents, a barber student olive-skinned 'Garcia' on his coat, two blond small boys one with feared face and big ears watching from seats, tell him 'You're ugly little boy & you've got big ears' he'd weep and suffer and it wouldn't even be true, the other thinfaced conscious concentrated patched bluejeans and scuffed shoes who watches me delicate, suffering child that grows hard and greedy with puberty, Ray and I with poorboy of ruby port in us rainy May day no used levis in this town, our size, and old barber college t and g crappers skidrow haircuts middleage barber careers start out now flowering."

"See," I said, "you wouldn't have even written that poem if it wasn't for the wine made you feel good!"

"Ah I would have written it anyway. You're just drinking too much all the time, I don't see how you're even going to gain enlightenment and manage to stay out in the mountains, you'll always be coming down the hill spending your bean money on wine and finally you'll end up lying in the street in the rain, dead drunk, and then they'll take you away and you'll have to be reborn a teetotalin bartender to atone for your karma." He was really sad about it, and worried about me, but I just went on drinking.

When we got to Alvah's cottage and it was time to leave for the Buddhist Center lecture I said "I'll just sit here and get drunk and wait for you."

"Okay," said Japhy, looking at me darkly. "It's your life."

He was gone for two hours. I felt sad and drank too much and was dizzy. But I was determined not to pass out and stick it out and prove something to Japhy. Suddenly, at dusk, he came running back into the cottage drunk as a hoot owl yelling "You know what happened Smith? I went to the Buddhist lecture and they were all drinking white raw saki out of teacups and everybody got drunk. All those crazy Japanese saints! You were right! It doesn't make any difference! We all got drunk and discussed prajna! It was great!" And after that Japhy and I never had an argument again.

28

The night of the big party came. I could practically hear the hubbubs of preparation going on down the hill and felt depressed. "Oh my God, sociability is just a big smile and a big smile is nothing but teeth, I wish I could just stay up here and rest and be kind." But somebody brought up some wine and that started me off.

That night the wine flowed down the hill like a river. Sean

had put together a lot of big logs for an immense bonfire in the yard. It was a clear starry night, warm and pleasant, in May. Everybody came. The party soon became clearly divided into three parts again. I spent most of my time in the living room where we had Cal Tjader records on the hi-fi and a lot of girls were dancing as Bud and I and Sean and sometimes Alvah and his new buddy George played bongo drums on inverted cans.

Out in the yard it was a quieter scene, with the glow of the fire and lots of people sitting on the long logs Sean had placed around the fire, and on the board a spread fit for a king and his hungry retinue. Here, by the fire, far from the freneticism of the bongo-ing living room, Cacoethes held forth discussing poetry with the local wits, in tones about like this: "Marshall Dashiell is too busy cultivating his beard and driving his Mercedes Benz around cocktail parties in Chevy Chase and up Cleopatra's needle, O. O. Dowler is being carried around Long Island in limousines and spending his summers shrieking on St. Mark's Place, and Tough Shit Short alas successfully manages to be a Savile Row fop with bowler and waistcoat, and as for Manuel Drubbing he just flips quarters to see who'll flop in the little reviews, and Omar Tott I got nothing to say. Albert Law Livingston is busy signing autograph copies of his novels and sending Christmas cards to Sarah Vaughan; Ariadne Jones is importuned by the Ford Company; Leontine McGee says she's old, and who does that leave?"

"Ronald Firbank," said Coughlin.

"I guess the only real poets in the country, outside the orbit of this little backyard, are Doctor Musial, who's probably muttering behind his living-room curtains right now, and Dee Sampson, who's too rich. That leaves us dear old Japhy here who's going away to Japan, and our wailing friend Goldbook and our Mr. Coughlin, who has a sharp tongue. By God, I'm the only good one here. At least I've got an honest anarchist background. At least I had frost on my nose, boots on my feet, and protest in my mouth." He stroked his mustache.

"What about Smith?"

"Well I guess he's a Bodhisattva in its frightful aspect, 'ts about all I can say." (Aside, sneering: "He's too drrronk all the time.")

Henry Morley also came that night, only for a short while,

and acted very strange sitting in the background reading *Mad* comic books and the new magazine called *Hip*, and left early with the remark "The hotdogs are too thin, do you think that's a sign of the times or are Armour and Swift using stray Mexicans you think?" Nobody talked to him except me and Japhy. I was sorry to see him leave so soon, he was ungraspable as a ghost, as ever. Nevertheless he had worn a brand-new brown suit for the occasion, and suddenly he was gone.

Up the hill meanwhile, where the stars nodded on trees, occasional couples were sneaking up to neck or just brought jugs of wine and guitars up and had separate little parties in our shack. It was a great night. Japhy's father finally came, after work, and he was a tight-built little tough guy just like Japhy, balding a little, but completely energetic and crazy just like his son. He immediately began dancing wild mambos with the girls while I beat madly on a can. "Go, man!" You never saw a more frantic dancer: he stood there, bending way back till he was almost falling over, moving his loins at the girl, sweating, eager, grinning, glad, the maddest father I ever saw. Just recently at his daughter's wedding he had broken up the lawn reception by rushing out on his hands and knees with a tiger skin on his back, snapping at the ladies' heels and barking. Now he took a tall almost sixfoot gal by the name of Jane and swung her around and almost knocked over the bookcase. Japhy kept wandering to all sections of the party with a big jug in his hand, his face beaming with happiness. For a while the party in the living room emptied out the bonfire clique and soon Psyche and Japhy were doing a mad dance, then Sean leaped up and whirled her around and she made as if to swoon and fell right in between Bud and me sitting on the floor drumming (Bud and I who never had girls of our own and ignored everything) and lay there a second sleeping on our laps. We puffed on our pipes and drummed on. Polly Whitmore kept hanging around the kitchen helping Christine with the cooking and even turning out a batch of delicious cookies of her own. I saw she was lonely because Psyche was there and Japhy wasn't hers so I went over to grab her by the waist but she looked at me with such fear I didn't do anything. She seemed to be terrified of me. Princess was there with her new boyfriend and she too was pouting in a corner.

I said to Japhy "What the hell you gonna do with all these broads? Ain't you gonna give me one?"

"Take whichever one you want. I'm neutral tonight."

I went out to the bonfire to hear Cacoethes' latest witticisms. Arthur Whane was sitting on a log, well dressed, necktie and suit, and I went over and asked him "Well what is Buddhism? Is it fantastic imagination magic of the lightning flash, is it plays, dreams, not even plays, dreams?"

"No, to me Buddhism is getting to know as many people as possible." And there he was going around the party real affable shaking hands with everybody and chatting, a regular cocktail party. The party inside was getting more and more frantic. I began to dance with the tall girl myself. She was wild. I wanted to sneak her up on the hill with a jug but her husband was there. Later in the night a crazy colored guy showed up and began playing bongos on his own head and cheeks and mouth and chest, whacking himself with real loud sounds, and a great beat, a tremendous beat. Everybody was delighted and declared he must be a Bodhisattva.

People of all kinds were pouring in from the city, where news of the great party was going the rounds of our bars. Suddenly I looked up and Alvah and George were walking around naked.

"What are you doing?"

"Oh, we just decided to take our clothes off."

Nobody seemed to mind. In fact I saw Cacoethes and Arthur Whane well dressed standing having a polite conversation in the firelight with the two naked madmen, a kind of serious conversation about world affairs. Finally Japhy also got naked and wandered around with his jug. Every time one of his girls looked at him he gave a loud roar and leaped at them and they ran out of the house squealing. It was insane. I wondered what would ever happen if the cops in Corte Madera got wind of this and came roarin up the hill in their squad cars. The bonfire was bright, anybody down the road could see everything that was going on in the yard. Nevertheless it was strangely not out of place to see the bonfire, the food on the board, hear the guitar players, see the dense trees swaying in the breeze and a few naked men in the party.

I talked to Japhy's father and said "What you think about Japhy bein naked?"

"Oh I don't give a damn, Japh can do anything he wants far as I'm concerned. Say where's that big old tall gal we was dancin with?" He was a pure Dharma Bum father. He had had it rough too, in his early years in the Oregon woods, taking care of a whole family in a cabin he'd built himself and all the horny-headed troubles of trying to raise crops in merciless country, and the cold winters. Now he was a well-to-do painting contractor and had built himself one of the finest houses in Mill Valley and took good care of his sister. Japhy's own mother was alone living in a rooming house in the north. Japhy was going to take care of her when he got back from Japan. I had seen a lonely letter from her. Japhy said his parents had separated with a great deal of finality but when he got back from the monastery he would see what he could do to take care of her. Japhy didn't like to talk about her, and his father of course never mentioned her at all. But I liked Japhy's father, the way he danced sweating and mad, the way he didn't mind any of the eccentric sights he saw, the way he let everybody do what they wanted anyway and went home around midnight in a shower of thrown flowers dancing off down to his car parked in the road.

Al Lark was another nice guy who was there, just kept sitting sprawled with his guitar plucking out rumbling rambling blues chords or sometimes flamenco and looking off into space, and when the party was over at three a.m. he and his wife went to sleep in sleeping bags in the yard and I could hear them goofing in the grass. "Let's dance," she said. "Ah, go to sleep!" he said.

Psyche and Japhy were sore at each other that night and she didn't want to come up the hill and honor his new white sheets and stomped off to leave. I watched Japhy going up the hill, weaving drunk, the party was over.

I went with Psyche to her car and said "Come on, why do you make Japhy unhappy on his farewell night?"

"Oh he was mean to me, the hell with him."

"Aw come on, nobody'll eat you up the hill."

"I don't care, I'm driving back to the city."

"Well, that's not nice, and Japhy told me he loved you."

"I don't believe it."

"That's the story of life," I said walking away with a huge jug of wine hooked in my forefinger and I started up the hill and heard Psyche trying to back up her car and do a U-turn in the narrow road and the back end landed in the ditch and she couldn't get out and had to sleep on Christine's floor anyway. Meanwhile Bud and Coughlin and Alvah and George were all up in the shack sprawled out in various blankets and sleeping bags on the floors. I put my bag down in the sweet grass and felt I was the most fortunate person of the lot. So the party was over and all the screaming was done and what was accomplished? I began to sing in the night, enjoying myself with the jug. The stars were blinding bright.

"A mosquito as big as Mount Sumeru is much bigger than you think!" yelled Coughlin from inside the shack, hearing me sing.

I yelled back, "A horse's hoof is more delicate than it looks!"

Alvah came running out in his long underwear and did a big dance and howled long poems in the grass. Finally we had Bud up talking earnestly about his latest idea. We had a kind of a new party up there. "Let's go down see how many gals are left!" I went down the hill rolling half the way and tried to make Psyche come up again but she was out like a light on the floor. The embers of the big bonfire were still red hot and plenty of heat was being given off. Sean was snoring in his wife's bedroom. I took some bread from the board and spread cottage cheese on it and ate, and drank wine. I was all alone by the fire and it was getting gray dawn in the east. "Boy, am I drunk!" I said. "Wake up! wake up!" I yelled. "The goat of day is butting dawn! No ifs or buts! Bang! Come on, you girls! gimps! punks! thieves! pimps! hangmen! Run!" Then I suddenly had the most tremendous feeling of the pitifulness of human beings, whatever they were, their faces, pained mouths, personalities, attempts to be gay, little petulances, feelings of loss, their dull and empty witticisms so soon forgotten: Ah, for what? I knew that the sound of silence was everywhere and therefore everything everywhere was silence. Suppose we suddenly wake up and see that what we thought to be this and that, ain't this and that at all? I staggered up the hill, greeted by birds, and looked at all the huddled sleeping figures on the floor. Who were all these strange ghosts rooted to the silly little adventure of earth with me? And who was I? Poor Japhy, at eight a.m. he got up and banged on his frying pan and chanted the "Gocchami" chant and called everybody to pancakes.

29

The party went on for days; the morning of the third day people were still sprawled about the grounds when Japhy and I sneaked our rucksacks out, with a few choice groceries, and started down the road in the orange early-morning sun of California golden days. It was going to be a great day, we were back in our element: trails.

Japhy was in high spirits. "Goddammit it feels good to get away from dissipation and go in the woods. When I get back from Japan, Ray, when the weather gets really cold we'll put on our long underwear and hitchhike through the land. Think if you can of ocean to mountain Alaska to Klamath a solid forest of fir to bhikku in, a lake of a million wild geese. Woo! You know what woo means in Chinese?"

"What?"

"Fog. These woods are great here in Marin, I'll show you Muir Woods today, but up north is all that real old Pacific Coast mountain and ocean land, the future home of the Dharma-body. Know what I'm gonna do? I'll do a new long poem called 'Rivers and Mountains Without End' and just write it on and on on a scroll and unfold on and on with new surprises and always what went before forgotten, see, like a river, or like one of them real long Chinese silk paintings that show two little men hiking in an endless landscape of gnarled old trees and mountains so high they merge with the fog in the upper silk void. I'll spend three thousand years writing it, it'll be packed full of information on soil conservation, the Tennessee Valley Authority, astronomy, geology, Hsuan Tsung's travels, Chinese painting theory, reforestation, Oceanic ecology and food chains."

"Go to it, boy." As ever I strode on behind him and when we began to climb, with our packs feeling good on our backs as though we were pack animals and didn't feel right without a burden, it was that same old lonesome old good old thwap thwap up the trail, slowly, a mile an hour. We came to the end of the steep road where we had to go through a few houses built near steep bushy cliffs with waterfalls trickling down, then up to a high steep meadow, full of butterflies and hay and a little seven a.m. dew, and down to a dirt road, then to the end of the dirt road, which rose higher and higher till we could see vistas of Corte Madera and Mill Valley far away and even the red top of Golden Gate Bridge.

"Tomorrow afternoon on our run to Stimson Beach," said Japhy, "you'll see the whole white city of San Francisco miles away in the blue bay. Ray, by God, later on in our future life we can have a fine free-wheeling tribe in these California hills, get girls and have dozens of radiant enlightened brats, live like Indians in hogans and eat berries and buds."

"No beans?"

"We'll write poems, we'll get a printing press and print our own poems, the Dharma Press, we'll poetize the lot and make a fat book of icy bombs for the booby public."

"Ah the public ain't so bad, they suffer too. You always read about some tarpaper shack burning somewhere in the Middlewest with three little children perishing and you see a picture of the parents crying. Even the kitty was burned. Japhy, do you think God made the world to amuse himself because he was bored? Because if so he would have to be mean."

"Ho, who would you mean by God?"

"Just Tathagata, if you will."

"Well it says in the sutra that God, or Tathagata, doesn't himself emanate a world from his womb but it just appears due to the ignorance of sentient beings."

"But he emanated the sentient beings and their ignorance too. It's all too pitiful. I ain't gonna rest till I find out *why*, Japhy, *why*."

"Ah don't trouble your mind essence. Remember that in pure Tathagata mind essence there is no asking of the question why and not even any significance attached to it."

"Well, then nothing's really happening, then."

He threw a stick at me and hit me on the foot.

"Well, that didn't happen," I said.

"I really don't know, Ray, but I appreciate your sadness about the world. 'Tis indeed. Look at that party the other night. Everybody wanted to have a good time and tried real hard but we all woke up the next day feeling sorta sad and separate. What do you think about death, Ray?"

"I think death is our reward. When we die we go straight to nirvana Heaven and that's that."

"But supposing you're reborn in the lower hells and have hot redhot balls of iron shoved down your throat by devils."

"Life's already shoved an iron foot down *my* mouth. But I don't think that's anything but a dream cooked up by some hysterical monks who didn't understand Buddha's peace under the Bo Tree or for that matter Christ's peace looking down on the heads of his tormentors and forgiving them."

"You really like Christ, don't you?"

"Of course I do. And after all, a lot of people say he is Maitreya, the Buddha prophesied to appear after Sakyamuni, you know, Maitreya means 'Love' in Sanskrit and that's all Christ talked about was love."

"Oh, don't start preaching Christianity to me, I can just see you on your deathbed kissing the cross like some old Karamazov or like our old friend Dwight Goddard who spent his life as a Buddhist and suddenly returned to Christianity in his last days. Ah that's not for me, I want to spend hours every day in a lonely temple meditating in front of a sealed statue of Kwannon which no one is ever allowed to see because it's too powerful. Strike hard, old diamond!"

"It'll all come out in the wash."

"You remember Rol Sturlason my buddy who went to Japan to study those rocks of Ryoanji. He went over on a freighter named *Sea Serpent* so he painted a big mural of a sea serpent and mermaids on a bulkhead in the messhall to the delight of the crew who dug him like crazy and all wanted to become Dharma Bums right there. Now he's climbing up holy Mount Hiei in Kyoto through a foot of snow probably, straight up where there are no trails, steep steep, through bamboo thickets and twisty pine like in brush drawings. Feet wet and lunch forgot, that's the way to climb."

"What are you going to wear in the monastery, anyway?"

"Oh man, the works, old T'ang Dynasty style things long black floppy with huge droopy sleeves and funny pleats, make you feel real Oriental."

"Alvah says that while guys like us are all excited about being real Orientals and wearing robes, actual Orientals over there are reading surrealism and Charles Darwin and mad about Western business suits."

"East'll meet West anyway. Think what a great world revolution will take place when East meets West finally, and it'll be guys like us that can start the thing. Think of millions of guys all over the world with rucksacks on their backs tramping around the back country and hitchhiking and bringing the word down to everybody."

"That's a lot like the early days of the Crusades, Walter the Penniless and Peter the Hermit leading ragged bands of believers to the Holy Land."

"Yeah but that was all such European gloom and crap, I want my Dharma Bums to have springtime in their hearts when the blooms are girling and the birds are dropping little fresh turds surprising cats who wanted to eat them a moment ago."

"What are you thinking about?"

"Just makin up poems in my head as I climb toward Mount Tamalpais. See up there ahead, as beautiful a mountain as you'll see anywhere in the world, a beautiful shape to it, I really love Tamalpais. We'll sleep tonight way around the back of it. Take us till late afternoon to get there."

The Marin country was much more rustic and kindly than the rough Sierra country we'd climbed last fall: it was all flowers, flowers, trees, bushes, but also a great deal of poison oak by the side of the trail. When we got to the end of the high dirt road we suddenly plunged into the dense redwood forest and went along following a pipeline through glades that were so deep the fresh morning sun barely penetrated and it was cold and damp. But the odor was pure deep rich pine and wet logs. Japhy was all talk this morning. He was like a little kid again now that he was out on the trail. "The only thing wrong with that monastery shot in Japan for me, is, though for all their intelligence and good intentions, the Americans out there, they have so little real sense of America and who the people are who really dig Buddhism here, and they don't have any use for poetry."

"Who?"

"Well, the people who are sending me out there and finance things. They spend their good money fixing elegant scenes of gardens and books and Japanese architecture and all that crap which nobody will like or be able to use anyway but rich American divorcees on Japanese cruises and all they really should do is just build or buy an old Jap house and vegetable garden and have a place there for cats to hang out in and be Buddhists, I mean have a real flower of something and not just the usual American middleclass fuggup with appearances. Anyway I'm looking forward to it, oh boy I can just see myself in the morning sitting on the mats with a low table at my side, typing on my portable, and my hibachi nearby with a pot of hot water on it keeping hot and all my papers and maps and pipe and flashlight neatly packed away and outside plum trees and pines with snow on the boughs and up on Mount Hieizan the snow getting deep and sugi and hinoki all around, them's redwoods, boy, and cedars. Little tucked-away temples down the rocky trails, cold mossy ancient places where frogs croak, and inside small statues and hanging buttery lamps and gold lotuses and paintings and ancient incense-soaked smells and lacquer chests with statues." His boat was leaving in two days. "But I'm sad too about leaving California . . . s'why I wanted to take one last long look at it today with ya, Ray."

We came up out of the gladey redwood forest onto a road, where there was a mountain lodge, then crossed the road and dipped down again through bushes to a trail that probably nobody even knew was there except a few hikers, and we were in Muir Woods. It extended, a vast valley, for miles before us. An old logger road led us for two miles then Japhy got off and scrambled up the slope and got onto another trail nobody dreamed was there. We hiked on this one, up and down along a tumbling creek, with fallen logs again where you crossed the creek, and sometimes bridges that had been built Japhy said by the Boy Scouts, trees sawed in half the flat surface for walking. Then we climbed up a steep pine slope and came out to the highway and went up the side of a hill of grass and came out in some outdoor theater, done up Greek style with stone seats all

around a bare stone arrangement for four-dimensional pre-
sentations of Aeschylus and Sophocles. We drank water and sat
down and took our shoes off and watched the silent play from
the upper stone seats. Far away you could see the Golden Gate
Bridge and the whiteness of San Francisco.

Japhy began to shriek and hoot and whistle and sing, full of
pure gladness. Nobody around to hear him. "This is the way
you'll be on top of Mount Desolation, this summer, Ray."

"I'll sing at the top of my voice for the first time in my life."

"If anybody hears ya it'll just be the conies, or maybe a critic
bear. Ray that Skagit country where you're going is the greatest place in America, that snaky river running back through
gorges and into its own unpeopled watershed, wet snowy
mountains fading into dry pine mountains and deep valleys
like Big Beaver and Little Beaver with some of the best virgin
stands of red cedar left in the world. I keep thinking of my
abandoned Crater Mountain Lookout house sitting up there
with nobody but the conies in the howling winds, getting old,
the conies down in their furry nests deep under boulders, and
warm, eating seeds or whatever they eat. The closer you get to
real matter, rock air fire and wood, boy, the more spiritual the
world is. All these people thinking they're hardheaded materi-
alistic practical types, they don't know shit about matter, their
heads are full of dreamy ideas and notions." He raised his hand.
"Listen to that quail calling."

"I wonder what everybody's doing back at Sean's."

"Well they're all up now and starting on that sour old red
wine again and sitting around talking nothing. They should
have all come with us and learnt something." He picked up his
pack and started off. In a half-hour we were in a beautiful
meadow following a dusty little trail over shallow creeks and
finally we were at Potrero Meadows camp. It was a National
Forest camp with a stone fireplace and picnic tables and everything but no one would be there till the weekend. A few miles
away, the lookout shack on top of Tamalpais looked right down
on us. We undid our packs and spent a quiet late afternoon
dozing in the sun or Japhy ran around looking at butterflies
and birds and making notes in his notebook and I hiked alone
down the other side, north, where a desolate rocky country
much like the Sierras stretched out toward the sea.

At dusk Japhy lit a good big fire and started supper. We were very tired and happy. He made a soup that night that I shall never forget and was really the best soup I'd eaten since I was a lionized young author in New York eating lunch at the Chambord or in Henri Cru's kitchen. This was nothing but a couple of envelopes of dried pea soup thrown into a pot of water with fried bacon, fat and all, and stirred till boiling. It was rich, real pea taste, with that smoky bacon and bacon fat, just the thing to drink in the cold gathering darkness by a sparkling fire. Also while pooking about he'd found puffballs, natural mushrooms, not the umbrella type, just round grapefruit-size puffs of white firm meat, and these he sliced and fried in bacon fat and we had them on the side with fried rice. It was a great supper. We washed the dishes in the gurgling creek. The roaring bonfire kept the mosquitoes away. A new moon peeked down through the pine boughs. We rolled out our sleeping bags in the meadow grass and went to bed early, bone weary.

"Well Ray," said Japhy, "pretty soon I'll be far out to sea and you'll be hitchhiking up the coast to Seattle and on through the Skagit country. I wonder what'll happen to all of us."

We went to sleep on this dreamy theme. During the night I had a vivid dream, one of the most distinct dreams I ever had, I clearly saw a crowded dirty smoky Chinese market with beggars and vendors and pack horses and mud and smokepots and piles of rubbish and vegetables for sale in dirty clay pans on the ground and suddenly from the mountains a ragged hobo, a little seamed brown unimaginable Chinese hobo, had come down and was just standing at the end of the market, surveying it with an expressionless humor. He was short, wiry, his face leathered hard and dark red by the sun of the desert and the mountains; his clothes were nothing but gathered rags; he had a pack of leather on his back; he was barefooted. I had seen guys like that only seldom, and only in Mexico, maybe coming into Monterrey out of those stark rock mountains, beggars who probably live in caves. But this one was a Chinese twice-as-poor, twice-as-tough and infinitely mysterious tramp and it was Japhy for sure. It was the same broad mouth, merry twinkling eyes, bony face (a face like Dostoevsky's death mask, with prominent eyebrow bones and square head); and he was short and compact like Japhy. I woke up at dawn, thinking

"Wow, is *that* what'll happen to Japhy? Maybe he'll leave that monastery and just disappear and we'll never see him again, and he'll be the Han Shan ghost of the Orient mountains and even the Chinese'll be afraid of him he'll be so raggedy and beat."

I told Japhy about it. He was already up stoking the fire and whistling. "Well don't just lay there in your sleeping bag pullin your puddin, get up and fetch some water. Yodelayhee hoo! Ray, I will bring you incense sticks from the coldwater temple of Kiyomizu and set them one by one in a big brass incense bowl and do the proper bows, how's about that. That was some dream you had. If that's me, then it's me. Ever weeping, ever youthful, hoo!" He got out the hand-ax from the rucksack and hammered at boughs and got a crackling fire going. There was still mist in the trees and fog on the ground. "Let's pack up and take off and dig Laurel Dell camp. Then we'll hike over the trails down to the sea and swim."

"Great." On this trip Japhy had brought along a delicious combination for hiking energy: Ry-Krisp crackers, good sharp Cheddar cheese a wedge of that, and a roll of salami. We had this for breakfast with hot fresh tea and felt great. Two grown men could live two days on that concentrated bread and that salami (concentrated meat) and cheese and the whole thing only weighed about a pound and a half. Japhy was full of great ideas like that. What hope, what human energy, what truly American optimism was packed in that neat little frame of his! There he was clomping along in front of me on the trail and shouting back "Try the meditation of the trail, just walk along looking at the trail at your feet and don't look about and just fall into a trance as the ground zips by."

We arrived at Laurel Dell camp at about ten, it was also supplied with stone fireplaces with grates, and picnic tables, but the surroundings were infinitely more beautiful than Potrero Meadows. Here were the real meadows: dreamy beauties with soft grass sloping all around, fringed by heavy deep green timber, the whole scene of waving grass and brooks and nothing in sight.

"By God, I'm gonna come back here and bring nothing but food and gasoline and a primus and cook my suppers smokeless and the Forest Service won't even know the difference."

"Yeah, but if they ever catch you cooking away from these stone places they put you out, Smith."

"But what would I do on weekends, join the merry picnickers? I'd just hide up there beyond that beautiful meadow. I'd stay there forever."

"And you'd only have two miles of trail down to Stimson Beach and your grocery store down there." At noon we started for the beach. It was a tremendously grinding trip. We climbed way up high on meadows, where again we could see San Francisco far away, then dipped down into a steep trail that seemed to fall directly down to sea level; you had sometimes to run down the trail or slide on your back, one. A torrent of water fell down at the side of the trail. I went ahead of Japhy and began swinging down the trail so fast, singing happily, I left him behind about a mile and had to wait for him at the bottom. He was taking his time enjoying the ferns and flowers. We stashed our rucksacks in the fallen leaves under bushes and hiked freely down the sea meadows and past seaside farmhouses with cows browsing, to the beach community, where we bought wine in a grocery store and stomped on out into the sand and the waves. It was a chill day with only occasional flashes of sun. But we were making it. We jumped into the ocean in our shorts and swam swiftly around then came out and spread out some of our salami and Ry-Krisp and cheese on a piece of paper in the sand and drank wine and talked. At one point I even took a nap. Japhy was feeling very good. "Goddammit, Ray, you'll never know how happy I am we decided to have these last two days hiking. I feel good all over again. I *know* somethin good's gonna come out of all this!"

"All what?"

"I dunno—out of the way we feel about life. You and I ain't out to bust anybody's skull, or cut someone's throat in an economic way, we've dedicated ourselves to prayer for all sentient beings and when we're strong enough we'll really be able to do it, too, like the old saints. Who knows, the world might wake up and burst out into a beautiful flower of Dharma everywhere."

After dozing awhile he woke up and looked and said, "Look at all that water out there stretching all the way to Japan." He was getting sadder and sadder about leaving.

30

We started back and found our packs and went back up that trail that had dropped straight down to sea level, a sheer crawling handgrasping climb among rocks and little trees that exhausted us, but finally we came out on a beautiful meadow and climbed it and again saw all San Francisco in the distance. "Jack London used to walk this trail," said Japhy. We proceeded along the south slope of a beautiful mountain that afforded us a view of the Golden Gate and even of Oakland miles away for hours on end as we trudged. There were beautiful natural parks of serene oaks, all golden and green in the late afternoon, and many wild flowers. Once we saw a fawn standing at a nub of grass, staring at us with wonder. We came down off this meadow down deep into a redwood forest then up again, again so steeply that we were cursing and sweating in the dust. Trails are like that: you're floating along in a Shakespearean Arden paradise and expect to see nymphs and fluteboys, then suddenly you're struggling in a hot broiling sun of hell in dust and nettles and poison oak . . . just like life. "Bad karma automatically produces good karma," said Japhy, "don't cuss so much and come on, we'll soon be sitting pretty on a flat hill."

The last two miles of the hill were terrible and I said "Japhy there's one thing I would like right now more than anything in the world—more than anything I've ever wanted all my life." Cold dusk winds were blowing, we hurried bent with our packs on the endless trail.

"What?"

"A nice big Hershey bar or even a little one. For some reason or other, a Hershey bar would save my soul right now."

"There's your Buddhism, a Hershey bar. How about moonlight in an orange grove and a vanilla ice-cream cone?"

"Too cold. What I need, want, pray for, yearn for, dying for, right now, is a Hershey bar . . . with nuts." We were very tired and trudging along home talking like two children. I kept repeating and repeating about my good old Hershey bar. I really meant it. I needed the energy anyway, I was a little woozy and needed sugar, but to think of chocolate and peanuts all melting in my mouth in that cold wind, it was too much.

Soon we were climbing over the corral fence that led to the horse meadow over our shack and then climbing over the barbed-wire fence right in our yard and trudging down the final twenty feet of high grass past my rosebush bed to the door of the good old little shack. It was our last night home together. We sat sadly in the dark shack taking off our boots and sighing. I couldn't do anything but sit on my feet, sitting on my feet took the pain out of them. "No more hikes for me forever," I said.

Japhy said "Well we still have to get supper and I see where we used up everything this weekend. I'll have to go down the road to the supermarket and get some food."

"Oh, man, aren't you tired? Just go to bed, we'll eat tomorrow." But he sadly put on his boots again and went out. Everybody was gone, the party had ended when it was found that Japhy and I had disappeared. I lit the fire and lay down and even slept awhile and suddenly it was dark and Japhy came in and lit the kerosene lamp and dumped the groceries on the table, and among them were three bars of Hershey chocolate just for me. It was the greatest Hershey bar I ever ate. He'd also brought my favorite wine, red port, just for me.

"I'm leaving, Ray, and I figured you and me might celebrate a little. . . ." His voice trailed off sadly and tiredly. When Japhy was tired, and he often wore himself out completely hiking or working, his voice sounded far-off and small. But pretty soon he roused his resources together and began cooking a supper and singing at the stove like a millionaire, stomping around in his boots on the resounding wood floor, arranging bouquets of flowers in the clay pots, boiling water for tea, plucking on his guitar, trying to cheer me up as I lay there staring sadly at the burlap ceiling. It was our last night, we both felt it.

"I wonder which one of us'll die first," I mused out loud. "Whoever it is, come on back, ghost, and give 'em the key."

"Ha!" He brought me my supper and we sat crosslegged and chomped away as on so many nights before: just the wind furying in the ocean of trees and our teeth going chomp chomp over good simple mournful bhikku food. "Just think, Ray, what it was like right here on this hill where our shack stands thirty thousand years ago in the time of the Neanderthal man. And do you realize that they say in the sutras there was a Buddha of that time, Dipankara?"

"The one who never said anything!"

"Can't you just see all those enlightened monkey men sitting around a roaring woodfire around their Buddha saying nothing and knowing everything?"

"The stars were the same then as they are tonight."

Later that night Sean came up and sat crosslegged and talked briefly and sadly with Japhy. It was all over. Then Christine came up with both children in her arms, she was a good strong girl and could climb hills with great burdens. That night I went to sleep in my bag by the rosebush and rued the sudden cold darkness that had fallen over the shack. It reminded me of the early chapters in the life of Buddha, when he decides to leave the Palace, leaving his mourning wife and child and his poor father and riding away on a white horse to go cut off his golden hair in the woods and send the horse back with the weeping servant, and embarks on a mournful journey through the forest to find the truth forever. "Like as the birds that gather in the trees of afternoon," wrote Ashvhaghosha almost two thousand years ago, "then at nightfall vanish all away, so are the separations of the world."

The next day I figured to give Japhy some kind of strange little going-away gift and didn't have much money or any ideas particularly so I took a little piece of paper about as big as a thumbnail and carefully printed on it: MAY YOU USE THE DIAMONDCUTTER OF MERCY and when I said goodbye to him at the pier I handed it to him, and he read it, put it right in his pocket, and said nothing.

The last thing he was seen doing in San Francisco: Psyche had finally melted and written him a note saying "Meet me on your ship in your cabin and I'll give you what you want," or words to that effect, so that was why none of us went on board to see him off in his cabin, Psyche was waiting there for a final passionate love scene. Only Sean was allowed to go aboard and hover around for whatever was going to happen. So after we all waved goodbye and went away, Japhy and Psyche presum-

ably made love in the cabin and then she began to cry and insist she wanted to go to Japan too and the captain ordered
everybody off but she wouldn't get off and the last thing was:
the boat was pulling away from the pier and Japhy came out
on deck with Psyche in his arms and threw her clean off the
boat, he was strong enough to throw a girl ten feet, right on
the pier, where Sean helped catch her. And though it wasn't
exactly in keeping with the diamondcutter of mercy it was
good enough, he wanted to get to that other shore and get on
to his business. His business was with the Dharma. And the
freighter sailed away out the Golden Gate and out to the deep
swells of the gray Pacific, westward across. Psyche cried, Sean
cried, everybody felt sad.

Warren Coughlin said "Too bad, he'll probably disappear
into Central Asia marching about on a quiet but steady round
from Kashgar to Lanchow via Lhasa with a string of yaks
selling popcorn, safety-pins, and assorted colors of sewing-
thread and occasionally climb a Himalaya and end up enlightening the Dalai Lama and all the gang for miles around and
never be heard of again."

"No he won't," I said, "he loves us too much."

Alvah said, "It all ends in tears anyway."

31

Now, as though Japhy's finger were pointing me the way, I
started north to my mountain.

It was the morning of June 18, 1956. I came down and said
goodbye to Christine and thanked her for everything and
walked down the road. She waved from the grassy yard. "It's
going to be lonely around here with everybody gone and no
big huge parties on weekends." She really enjoyed everything
that had gone on. There she was standing in the yard barefooted, with little barefooted Prajna, as I walked off along the
horse meadow.

I had an easy trip north, as though Japhy's best wishes for
me to get to my mountain that could be kept forever, were
with me. On 101 I immediately got a ride from a teacher of

social studies, from Boston originally, who used to sing on
Cape Cod and had fainted just yesterday at his buddy's wedding because he'd been fasting. When he left me off at
Cloverdale I bought my supplies for the road: a salami, Cheddar cheese wedge, Ry-Krisp and also some dates for dessert, all
put away neatly in my foodwrappers. I still had peanuts and
raisins left over from our last hike together. Japhy had said, "I
won't be needing those peanuts and raisins on that freighter."
I recalled with a twinge of sadness how Japhy was always so
dead serious about food, and I wished the whole world was
dead serious about food instead of silly rockets and machines
and explosives using everybody's food money to blow their
heads off anyway.

I hiked about a mile after eating my lunch in back of a
garage, up to a bridge on the Russian River, where, in gray
gloom, I was stuck for as much as three hours. But suddenly I
got an unexpected short ride from a farmer with a tic that
made his face twitch, with his wife and boy, to a small town,
Preston, where a truckdriver offered me a ride all the way to
Eureka ("Eureka!" I yelled) and then he got talking to me and
said "Goldang it I get lonesome driving this rig, I want someone to talk to all night, I'll take you all the way to Crescent
City if you want." This was a little off my route but farther
north than Eureka so I said okay. The guy's name was Ray
Breton, he drove me two hundred and eighty miles all night in
the rain, talking ceaselessly about his whole life, his brothers,
his wives, sons, his father and at Humboldt Redwood Forest in
a restaurant called Forest of Arden I had a fabulous dinner of
fried shrimp with huge strawberry pie and vanilla ice cream for
dessert and a whole pot of coffee and he paid for the whole
works. I got him off talking about his troubles to talk about
the Last Things and he said, "Yeah, those who're good stay in
Heaven, they've been in Heaven from the beginning," which
was very wise.

We drove through the rainy night and arrived at Crescent
City at dawn in a gray fog, a small town by the sea, and parked
the truck in the sand by the beach and slept an hour. Then he
left me after buying me a breakfast of pancakes and eggs, probably sick and tired of paying for all my meals, and I started
walking out of Crescent City and over on an eastward road,

Highway 199, to get back to big-shot 99 that would shoot me to Portland and Seattle faster than the more picturesque but slower coast road.

Suddenly I felt so free I began to walk on the wrong side of the road and sticking out my thumb from that side, hiking like a Chinese Saint to Nowhere for no reason, going to my mountain to rejoice. Poor little angel world! I suddenly didn't care any more, I'd walk all the way. But just because I was dancing along on the wrong side of the road and didn't care, anybody began to pick me up immediately, a goldminer with a small caterpillar up front being hauled by his son, and we had a long talk about the woods, the Siskiyou Mountains (through which we were driving, toward Grants Pass Oregon), and how to make good baked fish, he said, just by lighting a fire in the clean yellow sand by a creek and then burying the fish in the hot sand after you've scraped away the fire and just leaving it there a few hours then taking it out and cleaning it of sand. He was very interested in my rucksack and my plans.

He left me off at a mountain village very similar to Bridgeport California where Japhy and I had sat in the sun. I walked out a mile and took a nap in the woods, right in the heart of the Siskiyou Range. I woke up from my nap feeling very strange in the Chinese unknown fog. I walked on the same way, wrong side, got a ride at Kerby from a blond used-car dealer to Grants Pass, and there, after a fat cowboy in a gravel truck with a malicious grin on his face deliberately tried to run over my rucksack in the road, I got a ride from a sad logger boy in a tin hat going very fast across a great swooping up and down dream valley thruway to Canyonville, where, as in a dream, a crazy store-truck full of gloves for sale stopped and the driver, Ernest Petersen, chatting amiably all the way and insisting that I sit on the seat that faced him (so that I was being zoomed down the road backward) took me to Eugene Oregon. He talked about everything under the sun, bought me two beers, and even stopped at several gas stations and hung out displays of gloves. He said, "My father was a great man, his saying was 'There are more horses' asses than horses in this world.'" He was a mad sports fan and timed outdoor track meets with a stopwatch and rushed around fearlessly and independently in his own truck defying local attempts to get him in the unions.

At red nightfall he bade me farewell near a sweet pond out-side Eugene. There I intended to spend the night. I spread my bag out under a pine in a dense thicket across the road from cute suburban cottages that couldn't see me and wouldn't see me because they were all looking at television anyway, and ate my supper and slept twelve hours in the bag, waking up only once in the middle of the night to put on mosquito repellent.

At morning I could see the mighty beginnings of the Cascade Range, the northernmost end of which would be my mountain on the skirt of Canada, four hundred more miles north. The morning brook was smoky because of the lumber mill across the highway. I washed up in the brook and took off after one short prayer over the beads Japhy had given me in Matterhorn camp: "Adoration to emptiness of the divine Buddha bead."

I immediately got a ride on the open highway from two tough young hombres to outside Junction City where I had coffee and walked two miles to a roadside restaurant that looked better and had pancakes and then walking along the highway rocks, cars zipping by, wondering how I'd ever get to Portland let alone Seattle, I got a ride from a little funny lighthaired housepainter with spattered shoes and four pint cans of cold beer who also stopped at a roadside tavern for more beer and finally we were in Portland crossing vast eternity bridges as draws went up behind us to allow crane barges through in the big smoky river city scene surrounded by pine ridges. In downtown Portland I took the twenty-five-cent bus to Vancouver Washington, ate a Coney Island hamburger there, then out on the road, 99, where a sweet young mustached one-kidney Bodhisattva Okie picked me up and said "I'm s'proud I picked you up, someone to talk to," and everywhere we stopped for coffee he played the pinball machines with dead seriousness and also he picked up all hitchhikers on the road, first a big drawling Okie from Alabama then a crazy sailor from Montana who was full of crazed intelligent talk and we balled right up to Olympia Washington at eighty m.p.h. then up Olympic Peninsula on curvy woodsroads to the Naval Base at Bremerton Washington where a fifty-cent ferry ride was all that separated me from Seattle!

We said goodbye and the Okie bum and I went on the ferry,

I paid his fare in gratitude for my terrific good luck on the road, and even gave him handfuls of peanuts and raisins which he devoured hungrily so I also gave him salami and cheese.

Then, while he sat in the main room, I went topdeck as the ferry pulled out in a cold drizzle to dig and enjoy Puget Sound. It was one hour sailing to the Port of Seattle and I found a half-pint of vodka stuck in the deck rail concealed under a *Time* magazine and just casually drank it and opened my rucksack and took out my warm sweater to go under my rain jacket and paced up and down all alone on the cold fogswept deck feeling wild and lyrical. And suddenly I saw that the Northwest was a great deal more than the little vision I had of it of Japhy in my mind. It was miles and miles of unbelievable mountains grooking on all horizons in the wild broken clouds, Mount Olympus and Mount Baker, a giant orange sash in the gloom over the Pacific-ward skies that led I knew toward the Hokkaido Siberian desolations of the world. I huddled against the bridgehouse hearing the Mark Twain talk of the skipper and the wheelman inside. In the deepened dusk fog ahead the big red neons saying: PORT OF SEATTLE. And suddenly everything Japhy had ever told me about Seattle began to seep into me like cold rain, I could feel it and see it now, and not just think it. It was exactly like he'd said: wet, immense, timbered, mountainous, cold, exhilarating, challenging. The ferry nosed in at the pier on Alaskan Way and immediately I saw the totem poles in old stores and the ancient 1880-style switch goat with sleepy firemen chug chugging up and down the waterfront spur like a scene from my own dreams, the old Casey Jones locomotive of America, the only one I ever saw that old outside of Western movies, but actually working and hauling boxcars in the smoky gloom of the magic city.

I immediately went to a good clean skid row hotel, the Hotel Stevens, got a room for the night for a dollar seventy-five and had a hot tub bath and a good long sleep and in the morning I shaved and walked out First Avenue and accidentally found all kinds of Goodwill stores with wonderful sweaters and red underwear for sale and I had a big breakfast with five-cent coffee in the crowded market morning with blue sky and clouds scudding overhead and waters of Puget Sound sparkling and dancing under old piers. It was real true Northwest. At noon I checked out of the hotel, with my new wool socks and bandanas and things all packed in gladly, and walked out to 99 a few miles out of town and got many short rides.

Now I was beginning to see the Cascades on the northeast horizon, unbelievable jags and twisted rock and snow-covered immensities, enough to make you gulp. The road ran right through the dreamy fertile valleys of the Stilaquamish and the Skagit, rich butterfat valleys with farms and cows browsing under that tremendous background of snow-pure heaps. The further north I hitched the bigger the mountains got till I finally began to feel afraid. I got a ride from a fellow who looked like a bespectacled careful lawyer in a conservative car, but turned out he was the famous Bat Lindstrom the hardtop racing champion and his conservative automobile had in it a souped-up motor that could make it go a hundred and seventy miles an hour. But he just demonstrated it by gunning it at a red light to let me hear the deep hum of power. Then I got a ride from a lumberman who said he knew the forest rangers where I was going and said "The Skagit Valley is second only to the Nile for fertility." He left me off at Highway 1-G, which was the little highway to 17-A that wound into the heart of the mountains and in fact would come to a dead-end as a dirt road at Diablo Dam. Now I was really in the mountain country. The fellows who picked me up were loggers, uranium prospectors, farmers, they drove me through the final big town of Skagit Valley, Sedro Woolley, a farming market town, and then out as the road got narrower and more curved among cliffs and the Skagit River, which we'd crossed on 99 as a dreaming belly river with meadows on both sides, was now a pure torrent of melted snow pouring narrow and fast between muddy snag shores. Cliffs began to appear on both sides. The snow-covered mountains themselves had disappeared, receded from my view, I couldn't see them any more but now I was beginning to feel them more.

32

In an old tavern I saw an old decrepit man who could hardly move around to get me a beer behind the bar, I thought "I'd rather die in a glacial cave than in an eternity afternoon room of dust like this." A Min 'n' Bill couple left me off at a grocery store in Sauk and there I got my final ride from a mad drunk fastswerving dark long-sideburned guitarplaying Skagit Valley wrangler who came to a dusty flying stop at the Marblemount Ranger Station and had me home.

The assistant ranger was standing there watching. "Are you Smith?"

"Yeah."

"That a friend of yours?"

"No, just a ride he gave me."

"Who does he think he is speeding on government property."

I gulped, I wasn't a free bhikku any more. Not until I'd get to my hideaway mountain that next week. I had to spend a whole week at Fire School with whole bunches of young kids, all of us in tin hats which we wore either straight on our heads or as I did at a rakish tilt, and we dug fire lines in the wet woods or felled trees or put out experimental small fires and I met the oldtimer ranger and onetime logger Burnie Byers, the "lumberjack" that Japhy was always imitating with his big deep funny voice.

Burnie and I sat in his truck in the woods and discussed Japhy. "It's a damn shame Japhy ain't come back this year. He was the best lookout we ever had and by God he was the best trailworker *I* ever seen. Just eager and anxious to go climbin around and so durn cheerful, I ain't never seen a better kid. And he wasn't afraid of nobody, he'd just come right out with it. That's what I like, cause when the time comes when a man can't say whatever he pleases I guess that'll be when I'm gonna go up in the backcountry and finish my life out in a lean-to. One thing about Japhy, though, wherever he'll be all the resta his life, I don't care how old he gets, he'll always have a good time." Burnie was about sixty-five and really spoke very paternally about Japhy. Some of the other kids also remembered

Japhy and wondered why he wasn't back. That night, because it was Burnie's fortieth anniversary in the Forest Service, the other rangers voted him a gift, which was a brand new big leather belt. Old Burnie was always having trouble with belts and was wearing a kind of cord at the time. So he put on his new belt and said something funny about how he'd better not eat too much and everybody applauded and cheered. I figured Burnie and Japhy were probably the two best men that had ever worked in this country.

After Fire School I spent some time hiking up the mountains in back of the Ranger Station or just sitting by the rushing Skagit with my pipe in my mouth and a bottle of wine between my crossed legs, afternoons and also moonlit nights, while the other kids went beering at local carnivals. The Skagit River at Marblemount was a rushing clear snowmelt of pure green; above, Pacific Northwest pines were shrouded in clouds; and further beyond were peak tops with clouds going right through them and then fitfully the sun would shine through. It was the work of the quiet mountains, this torrent of purity at my feet. The sun shined on the roils, fighting snags held on. Birds scouted over the water looking for secret smiling fish that only occasionally suddenly leaped flying out of the water and arched their backs and fell in again into water that rushed on and obliterated their loophole, and everything was swept along. Logs and snags came floating down at twenty-five miles an hour. I figured if I should try to swim across the narrow river I'd be a half-mile downstream before I kicked to the other shore. It was a river wonderland, the emptiness of the golden eternity, odors of moss and bark and twigs and mud, all ululating mysterious visionstuff before my eyes, tranquil and everlasting nevertheless, the hillhairing trees, the dancing sunlight. As I looked up the clouds assumed, as I assumed, faces of hermits. The pine boughs looked satisfied washing in the waters. The top trees shrouded in gray fog looked content. The jiggling sunshine leaves of Northwest breeze seemed bred to rejoice. The upper snows on the horizon, the trackless, seemed cradled and warm. Everything was everlastingly loose and responsive, it was all everywhere beyond the truth, beyond emptyspace blue. "The mountains are mighty patient, Buddha-man," I said out loud and took a drink. It was coldish, but when the sun peeped out the tree stump I was sitting on turned into a red oven. When I went back in the moonlight to my same old tree stump the world was like a dream, like a phantom, like a bubble, like a shadow, like a vanishing dew, like a lightning's flash.

Time came finally for me to be packed up into my mountain. I bought forty-five dollars' worth of groceries on credit in the little Marblemount grocery store and we packed that in the truck, Happy the muleskinner and I, and drove on up the river to Diablo Dam. As we proceeded the Skagit got narrower and more like a torrent, finally it was crashing over rocks and being fed by side-falls of water from heavy timbered shores, it was getting wilder and craggier all the time. The Skagit River was dammed back at Newhalem, then again at Diablo Dam, where a giant Pittsburgh-type lift took you up on a platform to the level of Diablo Lake. There'd been a gold rush in the 1890s in this country, the prospectors had built a trail through the solid rock cliffs of the gorge between Newhalem and what was now Ross Lake, the final dam, and dotted the drainages of Ruby Creek, Granite Creek, and Canyon Creek with claims that never paid off. Now most of this trail was under water anyway. In 1919 a fire had raged in the Upper Skagit and all the country around Desolation, my mountain, had burned and burned for two months and filled the skies of northern Washington and British Columbia with smoke that blotted out the sun. The government had tried to fight it, sent a thousand men in with pack string supply lines that then took three weeks from Marblemount fire camp, but only the fall rains had stopped that blaze and the charred snags, I was told, were still standing on Desolation Peak and in some valleys. That was the reason for the name: Desolation.

"Boy," said funny old Happy the muleskinner, who still wore his old floppy cowboy hat from Wyoming days and rolled his own butts and kept making jokes, "don't be like the kid we had a few years ago up on Desolation, we took him up there and he was the greenest kid I ever saw, I packed him into his lookout and he tried to fry an egg for supper and broke it and missed the friggin fryingpan and missed the stove and it landed on his boot, he didn't know whether to run shit or go blind and when I left I told him not to flog his damn dummy too much and the sucker says to me 'Yes sir, yes sir.'"

"Well I don't care, all I want is to be alone up there this summer."

"You're sayin that now but you'll change your tune soon enough. They all talk brave. But then you get to talkin to yourself. That ain't so bad but don't start *answerin* yourself, son." Old Happy drove the pack mules on the gorge trail while I rode the boat from Diablo Dam, to the foot of Ross Dam where you could see immense dazzling openings of vistas that showed the Mount Baker National Forest mountains in wide panorama around Ross Lake that extended shiningly all the way back to Canada. At Ross Dam the Forest Service floats were lashed a little way off from the steep timbered shore. It was hard sleeping on those bunks at night, they swayed with the float and the log and the wave combined to make a booming slapping noise that kept you awake.

The moon was full the night I slept there, it was dancing on the waters. One of the lookouts said "The moon is right on the mountain, when I see that I always imagine I see a coyote silhouettin."

Finally came the gray rainy day of my departure to Desolation Peak. The assistant ranger was with us, the three of us were going up and it wasn't going to be a pleasant day's horseback riding in all that downpour. "Boy, you shoulda put a couple quarts of brandy in your grocery list, you're gonna need it up there in the cold," said Happy looking at me with his big red nose. We were standing by the corral, Happy was giving the animals bags of feed and tying it around their necks and they were chomping away unmindful of the rain. We came plowing to the log gate and bumped through and went around under the immense shrouds of Sourdough and Ruby mountains. The waves were crashing up and spraying back at us. We went inside to the pilot's cabin and he had a pot of coffee ready. Firs on steep banks you could barely see on the lake shore were like ranged ghosts in the mist. It was the real Northwest grim and bitter misery.

"Where's Desolation?" I asked.

"You ain't about to see it today till you're practically on top of it," said Happy, "and then you won't like it much. It's snowin and hailin up there right now. Boy, ain't you sure you didn't sneak a little bottle of brandy in your pack somewheres?" We'd already downed a quart of blackberry wine he'd bought in Marblemount.

"Happy when I get down from this mountain in September I'll buy you a whole quart of scotch." I was going to be paid good money for finding the mountain I wanted.

"That's a promise and don't you forget it." Japhy had told me a lot about Happy the Packer, he was called. Happy was a good man; he and old Burnie Byers were the best oldtimers on the scene. They knew the mountains and they knew pack animals and they weren't ambitious to become forestry supervisors either.

Happy remembered Japhy too, wistfully. "That boy used to know an awful lot of funny songs and stuff. He shore loved to go out loggin out trails. He had himself a Chinee girlfriend one time down in Seattle, I seen her in his hotel room, that Japhy I'm tellin you he shore was a grunge-jumper with the women." I could hear Japhy's voice singing gay songs with his guitar as the wind howled around our barge and the gray waves plashed up against the windows of the pilot house.

"And this is Japhy's lake, and these are Japhy's mountains," I thought, and wished Japhy were there to see me doing everything he wanted me to do.

In two hours we eased over to the steep timbered shore eight miles uplake and jumped off and lashed the float to old stumps and Happy whacked the first mule, and she scampered off the wood with her doublesided load and charged up the slippery bank, legs thrashing and almost falling back in the lake with all my groceries, but made it and went off clomping in the mist to wait on the trail for her master. Then the other mules with batteries and various equipment, then finally Happy leading the way on his horse and then myself on the mare Mabel and then Wally the assistant ranger.

We waved goodbye to the tugboat man and started up a sad and dripping party in a hard Arctic climb in heavy foggy rain up narrow rocky trails with trees and underbrush wetting us clean to the skin when we brushed by. I had my nylon poncho tied around the pommel of the saddle and soon took it out and put it over me, a shroudy monk on a horse. Happy and Wally didn't put on anything and just rode wet with heads bowed. The horse slipped occasionally in the rocks of the trail. We went on and on, up and up, and finally we came to a snag that had fallen across the trail and Happy dismounted and took out his doublebitted ax and went to work cursing and sweating and hacking out a new shortcut trail around it with Wally while I was delegated to watch the animals, which I did in a rather comfortable way sitting under a bush and rolling a cigarette. The mules were afraid of the steepness and roughness of the shortcut trail and Happy cursed at me "Goddammit it grab 'im by the hair and drag 'im up here." Then the mare was afraid. "Bring up that mare! You expect me to do everything around here by myself?"

We finally got out of there and climbed on up, soon leaving the shrubbery and entering a new alpine height of rocky meadow with blue lupine and red poppy feathering the gray mist with lovely vaguenesses of color and the wind blowing hard now and with sleet. "Five thousand feet now!" yelled Happy from up front, turning in the saddle with his old hat furling in the wind, rolling himself a cigarette, sitting easy in his saddle from a whole lifetime on horses. The heather wildflower drizzly meadows wound up and up, on switchback trails, the wind getting harder all the time, finally Happy yelled: "See that big rock face up thar?" I looked up and saw a goopy shroud of gray rock in the fog, just above. "That's another thousand feet though you might think you can reach up and touch it. When we get there we're almost in. Only another half hour after that."

"You sure you didn't bring just a *little* extry bottle of brandy boy?" he yelled back a minute later. He was wet and miserable but he didn't care and I could hear him singing in the wind. By and by we were up above timberline practically, the meadow gave way to grim rocks and suddenly there was snow on the ground to the right and to the left, the horses were slowshing in a sleety foot of it, you could see the water holes their hoofs left, we were really way up there now. Yet on all sides I could see nothing but fog and white snow and blowing mists. On a clear day I would have been able to see the sheer drops from the side of the trail and would have been scared for my horse's slips of hoof; but now all I saw were vague intimations of tree-tops way below that looked like little clumps of grasses. "O Japhy," I thought, "and there you are sailing across the ocean safe on a ship, warm in a cabin, writing letters to Psyche and Sean and Christine."

The snow deepened and hail began to pelt our red weather-beaten faces and finally Happy yelled from up ahead "We're almost there now." I was cold and wet: I got off the horse and simply led her up the trail, she grunted a kind of groan of relief to be rid of the weight and followed me obediently. She already had quite a load of supplies, anyway. "There she is!" yelled Happy and in the swirled-across top-of-the-world fog I saw a funny little peaked almost Chinese cabin among little pointy firs and boulders standing on a bald rock top surrounded by snowbanks and patches of wet grass with tiny flowers.

I gulped. It was too dark and dismal to like it. "This will be my home and restingplace all summer?"

We trudged on to the log corral built by some old lookout of the thirties and tethered the animals and took down the packs. Happy went up and took the weather door off and got the keys and opened her up and inside it was all gray dank gloomy muddy floor with rain-stained walls and a dismal wooden bunk with a mattress made of ropes (so as not to at-tract lightning) and the windows completely impenetrable with dust and worst of all the floor littered with magazines torn and chewed up by mice and pieces of groceries too and uncount-able little black balls of rat turd.

"Well," said Wally showing his long teeth at me, "it's gonna take you a long time to clean up this mess, hey? Start in right now by taking all those leftover canned goods off the shelf and running a wet soapy rag over that filthy shelf." Which I did, and I had to do, I was getting paid.

But good old Happy got a roaring woodfire going in the potbelly stove and put on a pot of water and dumped half a can of coffee in it and yelled "Ain't nothing like real strong coffee, up in this country boy we want coffee that'll make your hair stand on end."

I looked out the windows: fog. "How high are we?"

"Six thousand and a half feet."

"Well how can I see any fires? There's nothing but fog out there."

"In a couple of days it'll all blow away and you'll be able to see for a hundred miles in every direction, don't worry."

But I didn't believe it. I remembered Han Shan talking about the fog on Cold Mountain, how it never went away; I began to appreciate Han Shan's hardihood. Happy and Wally went out with me and we spent some time putting up the anemometer pole and doing other chores, then Happy went in and started a crackling supper on the stove frying Spam with eggs. We drank coffee deep, and had a rich good meal. Wally unpacked the two-way battery radio and contacted Ross Float. Then they curled up in their sleeping bags for a night's rest, on the floor, while I slept on the damp bunk in my own bag.

In the morning it was still gray fog and wind. They got the animals ready and before leaving turned and said to me, "Well, do you still like Desolation Peak?"

And Happy: "Don't forget what I told ya about answerin your own questions now. And if a bar comes by and looks in your window just close your eyes."

The windows howled as they rode out of sight in the mist among the gnarled rock-top trees and pretty soon I couldn't see them any more and I was alone on Desolation Peak for all I knew for eternity, I was sure I wasn't going to come out of there alive anyway. I was trying to see the mountains but only occasional gaps in the blowing fog would reveal distant dim shapes. I gave up and went in and spent a whole day cleaning out the mess in the cabin.

At night I put on my poncho over my rain jacket and warm clothing and went out to meditate on the foggy top of the world. Here indeed was the Great Truth Cloud, Dharma-mega, the ultimate goal. I began to see my first star at ten, and suddenly some of the white mist parted and I thought I saw mountains, immense black gooky shapes across the way, stark black and white with snow on top, so near, suddenly, I almost jumped. At eleven I could see the evening star over Canada, north way, and thought I could detect an orange sash of sunset behind the fog but all this was taken out of my mind by the sound of pack rats scratching at my cellar door. In the attic little diamond mice skittered on black feet among oats and bits of rice and old rigs left up there by a generation of Desolation losers. "Ugh, ow," I thought, "will I get to like this? And if I don't, how do I get to leave?" The only thing was to go to bed and stick my head under the down.

In the middle of the night while half asleep I had apparently opened my eyes a bit, and then suddenly I woke up with my hair standing on end, I had just seen a huge black monster standing in my window, and I looked, and it had a star over it, and it was Mount Hozomeen miles away by Canada leaning over my backyard and staring in my window. The fog had all blown away and it was perfect starry night. What a mountain! It had that same unmistakable witches' tower shape Japhy had given it in his brush drawing of it that used to hang on the burlap wall in the flowery shack in Corte Madera. It was built with a kind of winding rock-ledge road going around and around, spiraling to the very top where a perfect witches' tower peakied up and pointed to all infinity. Hozomeen, Hozomeen, the most mournful mountain I ever seen, and the most beautiful as soon as I got to know it and saw the Northern Lights behind it reflecting all the ice of the North Pole from the other side of the world.

33

Lo, in the morning I woke up and it was beautiful blue sunshine sky and I went out in my alpine yard and there it was, everything Japhy said it was, hundreds of miles of pure snow-covered rocks and virgin lakes and high timber, and below, instead of the world, I saw a sea of marshmallow clouds flat as a roof and extending miles and miles in every direction, creaming all the valleys, what they call low-level clouds, on my 6600-foot pinnacle it was all far below me. I brewed coffee on the stove and came out and warmed my mist-drenched bones in the hot sun of my little woodsteps. I said "Tee tee" to a big furry cony and he calmly enjoyed a minute with me gazing at the sea of clouds. I made bacon and eggs, dug a garbage pit a hundred yards down the trail, hauled wood and identified landmarks with my panoramic and firefinder and named all the magic rocks and clefts, names Japhy had sung to me so often: Jack Mountain, Mount Terror, Mount Fury, Mount Challenger, Mount Despair, Golden Horn, Sourdough, Crater Peak, Ruby, Mount Baker bigger than the world in the western distance, Jackass Mountain, Crooked Thumb Peak, and the fabulous names of the creeks: Three Fools, Cinnamon, Trouble, Lightning and Freezeout. And it was all mine, not another human pair of eyes in the world were looking at this immense cycloramic universe of matter. I had a tremendous sensation of its dreamlikeness which never left me all that summer and in fact grew and grew, especially when I stood on my head to circulate my blood, right on top of the mountain, using a burlap bag for a head mat, and then the mountains looked like little bubbles hanging in the void upsidedown. In fact I realized they were upsidedown and I was upsidedown! There was nothing here to hide the fact of gravity holding us all intact upsidedown against a surface globe of earth in infinite empty space. And suddenly I realized I was truly alone and had nothing to do but feed myself and rest and amuse myself, and nobody could criticize. The little flowers grew everywhere around the rocks, and no one had asked them to grow, or me to grow.

In the afternoon the marshmallow roof of clouds blew away in patches and Ross Lake was open to my sight, a beautiful cerulean pool far below with tiny toy boats of vacationists, the boats themselves too far to see, just the pitiful little tracks they left rilling in the mirror lake. You could see pines reflected upsidedown in the lake pointing to infinity. Late afternoon I lay in the grass with all that glory before me and grew a little bored and thought "There's nothing there because I don't care." Then I jumped up and began singing and dancing and whistling through my teeth far across Lightning Gorge and it was too immense for an echo. Behind the shack was a huge snowfield that would provide me with fresh drinking water till September, just a bucket a day let melt in the house, to dip into with a tin cup, cold ice water. I was feeling happier than in years and years, since childhood, I felt deliberate and glad and solitary. "Buddy-o, yiddam, diddam dee," I sang, walking around kicking rocks. Then my first sunset came and it was unbelievable. The mountains were covered with pink snow, the clouds were distant and frilly and like ancient remote cities of Buddhaland splendor, the wind worked incessantly, whish, whish, booming at times, rattling my ship. The new moon disk was prognathic and secretly funny in the pale plank of blue over the monstrous shoulders of haze that rose from Ross Lake. Sharp jags popped up from behind slopes, like childhood mountains I grayly drew. Somewhere, it seemed, a golden festival of rejoicement was taking place. In my diary I wrote, "Oh I'm happy!" In the late day peaks I saw the hope. Japhy had been right.

As darkness enveloped my mountain and soon it would be night again and stars and Abominable Snowman stalking on Hozomeen, I started a cracking fire in the stove and baked delicious rye muffins and mixed up a good beef stew. A high west wind buffeted the shack, it was well built with steel rods going down into concrete pourings, it wouldn't blow away. I was satisfied. Every time I'd look out the windows I'd see alpine firs with snowcapped backgrounds, blinding mists, or the lake below all riffled and moony like a toy bathtub lake. I made myself a little bouquet of lupine and mountain posies and put them in a coffee cup with water. The top of Jack Mountain was done in by silver clouds. Sometimes I'd see flashes of lightning far away, illuminating suddenly the unbelievable horizons. Some mornings there was fog and my ridge, Starvation Ridge, would be milkied over completely.

On the dot the following Sunday morning, just like the first, daybreak revealed the sea of flat shining clouds a thousand feet below me. Every time I felt bored I rolled another cigarette out of my can of Prince Albert; there's nothing better in the world than a roll-your-own deeply enjoyed without hurry. I paced in the bright silver stillness with pink horizons in the west, and all the insects ceased in honor of the moon. There were days that were hot and miserable with locusts of plagues of insects, winged ants, heat, no air, no clouds, I couldn't understand how the top of a mountain in the North could be so hot. At noon the only sound in the world was the symphonic hum of a million insects, my friends. But night would come and with it the mountain moon and the lake would be moonlaned and I'd go out and sit in the grass and meditate facing west, wishing there were a Personal God in all this impersonal matter. I'd go out to my snowfield and dig out my jar of purple Jello and look at the white moon through it. I could feel the world rolling toward the moon. At night while I was in my bag, the deer would come up from the lower timber and nibble at leftovers in tin plates in the yard: bucks with wide antlers, does, and cute little fawns looking like otherworldly mammals on another planet with all that moonlight rock behind them.

Then would come wild lyrical drizzling rain, from the south, in the wind, and I'd say "The taste of rain, why kneel?" and I'd say "Time for hot coffee and a cigarette, boys," addressing my imaginary bhikkus. The moon became full and huge and with it came Aurora Borealis over Mount Hozomeen ("Look at the void and it is even stiller," Han Shan had said in Japhy's translation); and in fact I was so still all I had to do was shift my crossed legs in the alpine grass and I could hear the hoofs of deers running away somewhere. Standing on my head before bedtime on that rock roof of the moonlight I could indeed see that the earth was truly upsidedown and man a weird vain beetle full of strange ideas walking around upsidedown and boasting, and I could realize that man remembered why this dream of planets and plants and Plantagenets was built out of the primordial essence. Sometimes I'd get mad because things didn't work out well, I'd spoil a flapjack, or slip in the snowfield while getting water, or one time my shovel went sailing down into the gorge, and I'd be so mad I'd want to bite the mountaintops and would come in the shack and kick the cupboard and hurt my toe. But let the mind beware, that though the flesh be bugged, the circumstances of existence are pretty glorious.

All I had to do was keep an eye on all horizons for smoke and run the two-way radio and sweep the floor. The radio didn't bother me much; there were no fires close enough for me to report ahead of anybody else and I didn't participate in the lookout chats. They dropped me a couple of radio batteries by parachute but my own batteries were still in good shape.

One night in a meditation vision Avalokitesvara the Hearer and Answerer of Prayer said to me "You are empowered to remind people that they are utterly free" so I laid my hand on myself to remind myself first and then felt gay, yelled "Ta," opened my eyes, and a shooting star shot. The innumerable worlds in the Milky Way, *words.* I ate my soup in little doleful bowlfuls and it tasted much better than in some vast tureen . . . my Japhy pea-and-bacon soup. I took two-hour naps every afternoon, waking up and realizing "none of this ever happened" as I looked around my mountaintop. The world was upsidedown hanging in an ocean of endless space and here were all these people sitting in theaters watching movies, down there in the world to which I would return. . . . Pacing in the yard at dusk, singing "Wee Small Hours," when I came to the lines "when the whole wide world is fast asleep" my eyes filled with tears. "Okay world," I said, "I'll love ya." In bed at night, warm and happy in my bag on the good hemp bunk, I'd see my table and my clothes in the moonlight and feel, "Poor Raymond boy, his day is so sorrowful and worried, his reasons are so ephemeral, it's such a haunted and pitiful thing to have to live" and on this I'd go to sleep like a lamb. Are we fallen angels who didn't want to believe that nothing *is* nothing and so were born to lose our loved ones and dear friends one by one and finally our own life, to see it proved? . . . But cold morning would return, with clouds billowing out of Lightning Gorge like giant smoke, the lake below still cerulean neutral, and empty space the same as ever. O gnashing teeth of earth, where would it all lead to but some sweet golden eternity, to prove that we've all been wrong, to prove that the proving itself was nil . . .

34

August finally came in with a blast that shook my house and augured little augusticity. I made raspberry Jello the color of rubies in the setting sun. Mad raging sunsets poured in seafoams of cloud through unimaginable crags, with every rose tint of hope beyond, I felt just like it, brilliant and bleak beyond words. Everywhere awful ice fields and snow straws; one blade of grass jiggling in the winds of infinity, anchored to a rock. To the east, it was gray; to the north, awful; to the west, raging mad, hard iron fools wrestling in the groomian gloom; to the south, my father's mist. Jack Mountain, his thousand-foot rock hat overlooked a hundred football fields of snow. Cinnamon Creek was an eyrie of Scottish fog. Shull lost itself in the Golden Horn of Bleak. My oil lamp burned in infinity. "Poor gentle flesh," I realized, "there is no answer." I didn't know anything any more, I didn't care, and it didn't matter, and suddenly I felt really free. Then would come really freezing mornings, cracking fire, I'd chop wood with my hat on (earmuff cap), and would feel lazy and wonderful indoors, fogged in by icy clouds. Rain, thunder in the mountains, but in front of the stove I read my Western magazines. Everywhere snowy air and woodsmoke. Finally the snow came, in a whirling shroud from Hozomeen by Canada, it came surling my way sending radiant white heralds through which I saw the angel of light peep, and the wind rose, dark low clouds rushed up as out of a forge, Canada was a sea of meaningless mist; it came in a general fanning attack advertised by the sing in my stovepipe; it rammed it, to absorb my old blue sky view which had been all thoughtful clouds of gold; far, the rum dum dum of Canadian thunder; and to the south another vaster darker storm closing in like a pincer; but Hozomeen mountain stood there returning the attack with a surl of silence. And nothing could induce the gay golden horizons far northeast where there was no storm, to change places with Desolation. Suddenly a green and rose rainbow shafted right down into Starvation Ridge not three hundred yards away from my door, like a bolt, like a pillar: it came among steaming clouds and orange sun turmoiling.

What is a rainbow, Lord?

A hoop

For the lowly.

It hooped right into Lightning Creek, rain and snow fell simultaneous, the lake was milkwhite a mile below, it was just too crazy. I went outside and suddenly my shadow was ringed by the rainbow as I walked on the hilltop, a lovely-haloed mystery making me want to pray. "O Ray, the career of your life is like a raindrop in the illimitable ocean which is eternal awakenerhood. Why worry ever any more? Write and tell Japhy that." The storm went away as swiftly as it came and the late afternoon lake-sparkle blinded me. Late afternoon, my mop drying on the rock. Late afternoon, my bare back cold as I stood above the world in a snowfield digging shovelsful into a pail. Late afternoon, it was I not the void that changed. Warm rose dusk, I meditated in the yellow half moon of August. Whenever I heard thunder in the mountains it was like the iron of my mother's love. "Thunder and snow, how we shall go!" I'd sing. Suddenly came the drenching fall rains, all-night rain, millions of acres of Bo-trees being washed and washed, and in my attic millennial rats wisely sleeping.

Morning, the definite feel of autumn coming, the end of my job coming, wild windy cloud-crazed days now, a definite golden look in the high noon haze. Night, made hot cocoa and sang by the woodfire. I called Han Shan in the mountains: there was no answer. I called Han Shan in the morning fog: silence, it said. I called: Dipankara instructed me by saying nothing. Mists blew by, I closed my eyes, the stove did the talking. "Woo!" I yelled, and the bird of perfect balance on the fir point just moved his tail; then he was gone and distance grew immensely white. Dark wild nights with hint of bears: down in my garbage pit old soured solidified cans of evaporated milk bitten into and torn apart by mighty behemoth paws: Avalokitesvara the Bear. Wild cold fogs with awesome holes. On my calendar I ringed off the fifty-fifth day.

My hair was long, my eyes pure blue in the mirror, my skin tanned and happy. All night gales of soaking rain again, autumn rain, but I warm as toast in my bag dreaming of long infantry-scouting movements in the mountains; cold wild morning with high wind, racing fogs, racing clouds, sudden bright suns, the pristine light on hill patches and my fire roaring with three big logs as I exulted to hear Burnie Byers over the radio telling all his lookouts to come down that very day. The season was over. I paced in the windy yard with cup of coffee forked in my thumb singing "Blubbery dubbery the chipmunk's in the grass." There he was, my chipmunk, in the bright clear windy sunny air staring on the rock; hands clasping he sat up straight, some little oat between his paws; he nibbled, he darted away, the little nutty lord of all he surveyed. At dusk, big wall of clouds from the north coming in. "Brrr," I said. And I'd sing "Yar, but my she was yar!" meaning my shack all summer, how the wind hadn't blown it away, and I said "Pass pass pass, that which passes through everything!" Sixty sunsets had I seen revolve on that perpendicular hill. The vision of the freedom of eternity was mine forever. The chipmunk ran into the rocks and a butterfly came out. It was as simple as that. Birds flew over the shack rejoicing; they had a mile-long patch of sweet blueberries all the way down to the timberline. For the last time I went out to the edge of Lightning Gorge where the little outhouse was built right on the precipice of a steep gulch. Here, sitting every day for sixty days, in fog or in moonlight or in sunny day or in darkest night, I had always seen the little twisted gnarly trees that seemed to grow right out of the midair rock.

And suddenly it seemed I saw that unimaginable little Chinese bum standing there, in the fog, with that expressionless humor on his seamed face. It wasn't the real-life Japhy of rucksacks and Buddhism studies and big mad parties at Corte Madera, it was the realer-than life Japhy of my dreams, and he stood there saying nothing. "Go away, thieves of the mind!" he cried down the hollows of the unbelievable Cascades. It was Japhy who had advised me to come here and now though he was seven thousand miles away in Japan answering the meditation bell (a little bell he later sent to my mother in the mail, just because she was my mother, a gift to please her) he seemed to be standing on Desolation Peak by the gnarled old rocky trees certifying and justifying all that was here. "Japhy," I said out loud, "I don't know when we'll meet again or what'll happen in the future, but Desolation, Desolation, I owe so much to Desolation, thank you forever for guiding me to the place where I learned all. Now comes the sadness of coming back to cities and I've grown two months older and there's all that humanity of bars and burlesque shows and gritty love, all upsidedown in the void God bless them, but Japhy you and me forever we know, O ever youthful, O ever weeping." Down on the lake rosy reflections of celestial vapor appeared, and I said "God, I love you" and looked up to the sky and really meant it. "I have fallen in love with you, God. Take care of us all, one way or the other."

To the children and the innocent it's all the same.

And in keeping with Japhy's habit of always getting down

on one knee and delivering a little prayer to the camp we left, to the one in the Sierra, and the others in Marin, and the little prayer of gratitude he had delivered to Sean's shack the day he sailed away, as I was hiking down the mountain with my pack I turned and knelt on the trail and said "Thank you, shack." Then I added "Blah," with a little grin, because I knew that shack and that mountain would understand what that meant, and turned and went on down the trail back to this world.

THE SUBTERRANEANS

ONCE I WAS YOUNG and had so much more orientation and could talk with nervous intelligence about everything and with clarity and without as much literary preambling as this; in other words this is the story of an unself-confident man, at the same time of an egomaniac, naturally, facetious won't do—just to start at the beginning and let the truth seep out, that's what I'll do—. It began on a warm summernight—ah, she was sitting on a fender with Julien Alexander who is . . . let me begin with the history of the subterraneans of San Francisco . . .

Julien Alexander is the angel of the subterraneans, the subterraneans is a name invented by Adam Moorad who is a poet and friend of mine who said "They are hip without being slick, they are intelligent without being corny, they are intellectual as hell and know all about Pound without being pretentious or talking too much about it, they are very quiet, they are very Christlike." Julien certainly is Christlike. I was coming down the street with Larry O'Hara old drinking buddy of mine from all the times in San Francisco in my long and nervous and mad careers I've gotten drunk and in fact cadged drinks off friends with such "genial" regularity nobody really cared to notice or announce that I am developing or was developing, in my youth, such bad freeloading habits though of course they did notice but liked me and as Sam said "Everybody comes to you for your gasoline boy, that's some filling station you got there" or say words to that effect—old Larry O'Hara always nice to me, a crazy Irish young businessman of San Francisco with Balzacian backroom in his bookstore where they'd smoke tea and talk of the old days of the great Basie band or the days of the great Chu Berry—of whom more anon since she got involved with him too as she had to get involved with everyone because of knowing me who am nervous and many leveled and not in the least one-souled—not a piece of my pain has showed yet—or suffering—Angels, bear with me—I'm not even looking at the page but straight ahead into the sadglint of my wallroom and at a Sarah Vaughan Gerry Mulligan Radio KROW show on the desk in the form of a radio, in other words, they were sitting on the fender of a car in front of the Black Mask bar on Montgomery Street, Julien Alexander the Christlike unshaved thin youthful quiet strange almost as you or as Adam might say apocalyptic angel or saint of the subterraneans, certainly star (now), and she, Mardou Fox, whose face when first I saw it in Dante's bar around the corner made me think, "By God, I've got to get involved with that little woman" and maybe too because she was Negro. Also she had the same face that Rita Savage a girlhood girlfriend of my sister's had, and of whom among other things I used to have daydreams of her between my legs while kneeling on the floor of the toilet, I on the seat, with her special cool lips and Indian-like hard high soft cheekbones—same face, but dark, sweet, with little eyes honest glittering and intense she Mardou was leaning saying something extremely earnestly to Ross Wallenstein (Julien's friend) leaning over the table, deep—"I got to get involved with her"—I tried to shoot her the glad eye the sex eye she never had a notion of looking up or seeing—I must explain, I'd just come off a ship in New York, paid off before the trip to Kobe Japan because of trouble with the steward and my inability to be gracious and in fact human and like an ordinary guy while performing my chores as saloon messman (and you must admit now I'm sticking to the facts), a thing typical of me, I would treat the first engineer and the other officers with backwards-falling politeness, it finally drove them angry, they wanted me to say something, maybe gruff, in the morning, while setting their coffee down and instead of which silently on crepefeet I rushed to do their bidding and never cracked a smile or if so a sick one, a superior one, all having to do with that loneliness angel riding on my shoulder as I came down warm Montgomery Street that night and saw Mardou on the fender with Julien, remembering, "O there's the girl I gotta get involved with, I wonder if she's going with any of these boys" —dark, you could barely see her in the dim street—her feet in thongs of sandals of such sexuality-looking greatness I wanted to kiss her, them—having no notion of anything though.

The subterraneans were hanging outside the Mask in the

warm night, Julien on the fender, Ross Wallenstein standing
up, Roger Beloit the great bop tenorman, Walt Fitzpatrick who
was the son of a famous director and had grown up in Hollywood in an atmosphere of Greta Garbo parties at dawn and
Chaplin falling in the door drunk, several other girls, Harriet
the ex-wife of Ross Wallenstein a kind of blonde with soft
expressionless features and wearing a simple almost housewife-
in-the-kitchen cotton dress but softly bellysweet to look at—as
another confession must be made, as many I must make ere
time's sup—I am crudely malely sexual and cannot help myself
and have lecherous and so on propensities as almost all my
male readers no doubt are the same—confession after confession, I am a Canuck, I could not speak English till I was 5 or 6,
at 16 I spoke with a halting accent and was a big blue baby in
school though varsity basketball later and if not for that no one
would have noticed I could cope in any way with the world
(underself-confidence) and would have been put in the madhouse for some kind of inadequacy—

But now let me tell Mardou herself (difficult to make a real
confession and show what happened when you're such an egomaniac all you can do is take off on big paragraphs about minor details about yourself and the big soul details about others
go sitting and waiting around)—in any case, therefore, also
there was Fritz Nicholas the titular leader of the subterraneans,
to whom I said (having met him New Year's Eve in a Nob Hill
swank apartment sitting crosslegged like a peote Indian on a
thick rug wearing a kind of clean white Russian shirt and a
crazy Isadora Duncan girl with long blue hair on his shoulder
smoking pot and talking about Pound and peote) (thin also
Christlike with a faun's look and young and serious and like
the father of the group, as say, suddenly you'd see him in the
Black Mask sitting there with head thrown back thin dark eyes
watching everybody as if in sudden slow astonishment and
"Here we are little ones and now what my dears," but also a
great dope man, anything in the form of kicks he would want
at any time and very intense) I said to him, "Do you know this
girl, the dark one?"— "Mardou?"—"That her name? Who she
go with?"—"No one in particular just now, this has been an
incestuous group in its time," a very strange thing he said to
me there, as we walked to his old beat 36 Chevvy with no

backseat parked across from the bar for the purpose of picking
up some tea for the group to get all together, as, I told Larry,
"Man, let's get some tea."—"And what for you want all those
people?"—"I want to dig them as a group," saying this, too, in
front of Nicholas so perhaps he might appreciate my sensitivity
being a stranger to the group and yet immediately, etc., perceiving their value—facts, facts, sweet philosophy long deserted
me with the juices of other years fled—incestuous—there was
another final great figure in the group who was however now
this summer not here but in Paris, Jack Steen, very interesting
Leslie-Howard-like little guy who walked (as Mardou later imitated for me) like a Viennese philosopher with soft arms
swinging slight side flow and long slow flowing strides, coming
to a stop on corner with imperious soft pose—he too had had
to do with Mardou and as I learned later most weirdly—but
now my first crumb of information concerning this girl I was
SEEKING to get involved with as if not enough trouble
already or other old romances hadn't taught me that message
of pain, keep asking for it, for life—

Out of the bar were pouring interesting people, the night
making a great impression on me, some kind of Truman-
Capote-haired dark Marlon Brando with a beautiful thin birl
or girl in boy slacks with stars in her eyes and hips that seemed
so soft when she put her hands in her slacks I could see the
change—and dark thin slackpant legs dropping down to little
feet, and that face, and with them a guy with another beautiful
doll, the guy's name Rob and he's some kind of adventurous
Israeli soldier with a British accent whom I suppose you might
find in some Riviera bar at 5 A.M. drinking everything in sight
alphabetically with a bunch of interesting crazy international-
set friends on a spree—Larry O'Hara introducing me to Roger
Beloit (I did not believe that this young man with ordinary
face in front of me was that great poet I'd revered in my youth,
my youth, my youth, that is, 1948, I keep saying my youth)—
"This is Roger Beloit?—I'm Bennett Fitzpatrick" (Walt's
father) which brought a smile to Roger Beloit's face—Adam
Moorad by now having emerged from the night was also there
and the night would open—

So we all did go to Larry's and Julien sat on the floor in
front of an open newspaper in which was the tea (poor quality

L.A. but good enough) and rolled, or "twisted," as Jack Steen, the absent one, had said to me the previous New Year's and that having been my first contact with the subterraneans, he'd asked to roll a stick for me and I'd said really coldly "What for? I roll my own" and immediately the cloud crossed his sensitive little face, etc., and he hated me—and so cut me all the night when he had a chance—but now Julien was on the floor, cross-legged, and himself now twisting for the group and everybody droned the conversations which I certainly won't repeat, except, it was, like, "I'm looking at this book by Percepied— who's Percepied, has he been busted yet?" and such small talk, or, while listening to Stan Kenton talking about the music of tomorrow and we hear a new young tenorman come on, Ricci Comucca, Roger Beloit says, moving back expressive thin purple lips, "This is the music of tomorrow?" and Larry O'Hara telling his usual stock repertoire anecdotes. In the 36 Chevvy on the way, Julien, sitting beside me on the floor, had stuck out his hand and said, "My name's Julien Alexander, I have something, I conquered Egypt," and then Mardou stuck her hand out to Adam Moorad and introduced herself, saying, "Mardou Fox," but didn't think of doing it to me which should have been my first inkling of the prophecy of what was to come, so I had to stick my hand at her and say, "Leo Per-cepied my name" and shake—ah, you always go for the ones who don't really want you—she really wanted Adam Moorad, she had just been rejected coldly and subterraneanly by Julien —she was interested in thin ascetic strange intellectuals of San Francisco and Berkeley and not in big paranoiac bums of ships and railroads and novels and all that hatefulness which in my-self is to myself so evident and so to others too—though and because ten years younger than I seeing none of my virtues which anyway had long been drowned under years of drug-taking and desiring to die, to give up, to give it all up and for-get it all, to die in the dark star—it was I stuck out my hand, not she—ah time.

But in eying her little charms I only had the foremost one idea that I had to immerse my lonely being ("A big sad lonely man," is what she said to me one night later, seeing me sud-denly in the chair) in the warm bath and salvation of her thighs—the intimacies of younglovers in a bed, high, facing eye to eye, breast to breast naked, organ to organ, knee to shivering goosepimpled knee, exchanging existential and lover-acts for a crack at making it—"making it" the big expression with her, I can see the little out-pushing teeth through the little redlips seeing "making it"—the key to pain—she sat in the corner, by the window, she was being "separated" or "aloof" or "prepared to cut out from this group" for her own reasons.—In the corner I went, not leaning my head on her but on the wall and tried silent communication, then quiet words (as befit party) and North Beach words, "What are you reading?" and for the first time she opened her mouth and spoke to me communicating a full thought and my heart didn't exactly sink but wondered when I heard the cultured funny tones of part Beach, part I. Magnin model, part Berke-ley, part Negro highclass, something, a mixture of *langue* and style of talking and use of words I'd never heard before except in certain rare girls of course *white* and so strange even Adam at once noticed and commented with me that night—but def-initely the new bop generation way of speaking, you don't say *I*, you say "ahy" or "Oy" and long ways, like oft or erstwhile "effeminate" way of speaking so when you hear it in men at first it has a disagreeable sound and when you hear it in women it's charming but much too strange, and a sound I had already definitely and wonderingly heard in the voice of new bop singers like Jerry Winters especially with Kenton band on the record *Yes Daddy Yes* and maybe in Jeri Southern too—but my heart sank for the Beach has always hated me, cast me out, overlooked me, shat on me, from the beginning in 1943 on in—for look, coming down the street I am some kind of hood-lum and then when they learn I'm not a hoodlum but some kind of crazy saint they don't like it and moreover they're afraid I'll suddenly become a hoodlum anyway and slug them and break things and this I have almost done anyway and in my adolescence did so, as one time I roamed through North Beach with the Stanford basketball team, specifically with Red Kelly whose wife (rightly?) died in Redwood City in 1946, the whole team behind us, the Garetta brothers besides, he pushed a violinist a queer into a doorway and I pushed another one in, he slugged his, I glared at mine, I was 18, I was a nannybeater and fresh as a daisy too—now, seeing this past in the scowl and glare and horror and the beat of my brow-pride they wanted nothing to do with me, and so I of course also knew that Mardou had real genuine distrust and dislike of me as I sat there "trying to (not make IT) but make her"—unhiplike, brash, smiling, the false hysterical "compulsive" smiling they call it—me hot—them cool—and also I had on a very noxious unbeachlike shirt, bought on Broadway in New York when I thought I'd be cutting down the gangplanks in Kobe, a foolish Crosby Hawaiian shirt with designs, which malelike and vain after the original honest humilities of my regular self (really) with the smoking of two drags of tea I felt constrained to open an extra button down and so show my tanned, hairy chest—which must have disgusted her—in any case she didn't look, and spoke little and low—and was intent on Julien who was squatting with his back to her—and she listened and murmured the laughter in the general talk—most of the talk being conducted by O'Hara and loudspeaking Roger Beloit and that intelligent adventurous Rob and I, too silent, listening, digging, but in the tea vanity occasionally throwing in "perfect" (I thought) remarks which were "too perfect" but to Adam Moorad who'd known me all the time clear indication of my awe and listening and respect of the group in fact, and to them this new person throwing in remarks intended to sow his hipness—all horrible, and unredeemable.—Although at first, before the puffs, which were passed around Indian style, I had the definite sensation of being able to come close with Mardou and involved and making her that very first night, that is taking off with her alone if only for coffee but with the puffs which made me pray reverently and in serious secrecy for the return of my pre-puff "sanity" I became extremely unself-confident, overtrying, positive she didn't like me, hating the facts—remembering now the first night I met my Nicki Peters love in 1948 in Adam Moorad's pad in (then) the Fillmore, I was standing unconcerned and beerdrinking in the kitchen as ever (and at home working furiously on a huge novel, mad, cracked, confident, young, talented as never since) when she pointed to my profile shadow on the pale green wall and said, "How beautiful your profile is," which so nonplussed me and (like the tea) made me unself-confident, attentive, attempting to "begin to make her," to act in that way which by her almost hypnotic suggestion now led to the first preliminary probings into pride vs. pride and beauty or beatitude or sensitivity *versus* the stupid neurotic nervousness of the phallic type, forever conscious of his phallus, his tower, of women as wells—the truth of the matter being there, but the man unhinged, unrelaxed, and now it is no longer 1948 but 1953 with cool generations and I five years older, or younger, having to make it (or make the women) with a new style and stow the nervousness —in any case, I gave up consciously trying to make Mardou and settled down to a night of digging the great new perplexing group of subterraneans Adam had discovered and named on the Beach.

But from the first Mardou was indeed self-dependent and independent announcing she wanted no one, nothing to do with anyone, ending (after me) with same—which now in the cold unblessing night I feel in the air, this announcement of hers, and that her little teeth are no longer mine but probably my enemy's lapping at them and giving her the sadistic treatment she probably loves as I had given her none—murders in the air—and that bleak corner where a lamp shines, and winds swirl, a paper, fog, I see the great discouraged face of myself and my so-called love drooping in the lane, no good—as before it had been melancholy droopings in hot chairs, downcast by moons (though tonight's the great night of the harvest moon)—as where then, before, it was the recognition of the need for my return to worldwide love as a great writer should do, like a Luther, a Wagner, now this warm thought of greatness is a big chill in the wind—for greatness dies too—ah and who said I was great—and supposing one were a great writer, a secret Shakespeare of the pillow night? or really so—a Baudelaire's poem is not worth his grief—his grief—(It was Mardou finally said to me, "I would have preferred the happy man to the unhappy poems he's left us," which I agree with and I am Baudelaire, and love my brown mistress and I too leaned to her belly and listened to the rumbling underground)—but I should have known from her original announcement of independence to believe in the sincerity of her distaste for involvement, instead hurling on at her as if and because in fact I wanted to be hurt and "lacerate" myself—one more laceration yet and they'll pull the blue sod on, and make my box plop

boy—for now death bends big wings over my window, I see it,
I hear it, I smell it, I see it in the limp hang of my shirts des-
tined to be not worn, new-old, stylish-out-of-date, neckties
snakelike behung I don't even use any more, new blankets for
autumn peace beds now writhing rushing cots on the sea of
self-murder—loss—hate—paranoia—it was her little face I
wanted to enter, and did—

That morning when the party was at its pitch I was in Larry's
bedroom again admiring the red light and remembering the
night we'd had Micky in there the three of us, Adam and Larry
and myself, and had benny and a big sexball amazing to describe in itself—when Larry ran in and said, "Man you gonna
make it with her tonight?"—"I'd shore like to—I dunno."—
"Well man find out, ain't much time left, whatsamatter with
you, we bring all these people to the house and give em all that
tea and now all my beer from the icebox, man we gotta get
something out of it, work on it—." "Oh, you like her?"—"I
like anybody as far as that goes man—but I *mean*, after all."—
Which led me to a short unwillful abortive fresh effort, some
look, glance, remark, sitting next to her in corner, I gave up
and at dawn she cut out with the others who all went for coffee and I went down there with Adam to see her again (following the group down the stairs five minutes later) and they
were there but she wasn't, independently darkly brooding,
she'd gone off to her stuffy little place in Heavenly Lane on
Telegraph Hill.

So I went home and for several days in sexual phantasies it
was she, her dark feet, thongs of sandals, dark eyes, little soft
brown face, Rita-Savage-like cheeks and lips, little secretive in-
timacy and somehow now softly snakelike charm as befits a
little thin brown woman disposed to wearing dark clothes,
poor beat subterranean clothes. . . .

A few nights later Adam with an evil smile announced he
had run into her in a Third Street bus and they'd gone to his
place to talk and drink and had a big long talk which Leroy-
like culminated in Adam sitting naked reading Chinese poetry
and passing the stick and ending up laying in the bed, "And
she's very affectionate, God, the way suddenly she wraps her
arms around you as if for no other reason but pure sudden
affection."—"Are you going to make it? have an affair with

her?"—"Well now let me—actually I tell you—she's a whole lot and not a little crazy—she's having therapy, has apparently very seriously flipped only very recently, something to do with Julien, has been having therapy but not showing up, sits or lies down reading or doing nothing but staring at the ceiling all day long in her place, eighteen dollars a month in Heavenly Lane, gets, apparently, some kind of allowance tied up somehow by her doctors or somebody with her inadequacy to work or something—is always talking about it and really too much for my likings—has apparently real hallucinations concerning nuns in the orphanage where she was raised and has seen them and felt actual threat—and also other things, like the sensation of taking junk although she's never had junk but only known junkies." —"Julien?"—"Julien takes junk whenever he can which is not often because he has no money and his ambition like is to be a real junkey—but in any case she had hallucinations of not being properly contact high but actually somehow secretly injected by someone or something, people who follow her down the street, say, and is really crazy—and it's too much for me—and finally being a Negro I don't want to get all involved."—"Is she pretty?"—"Beautiful—but I can't make it."—"But boy I sure dig her looks and everything else." —"Well allright man then you'll make it—go over there, I'll give you the address, or better yet when, I'll invite her here and we'll talk, you can try if you want but although I have a hot feeling sexually and all that for her I really don't want to get any further into her not only for these reasons but finally, the big one, if I'm going to get involved with a girl now I want to be permanent like permanent and serious and long termed and I can't do that with her."—"I'd like a long permanent, et cetera."—"Well we'll see."

He told me of a night she'd be coming for a little snack dinner he'd cook for her so I was there, smoking tea in the red livingroom, with a dim red bulb light on, and she came in looking the same but now I was wearing a plain blue silk sports shirt and fancy slacks and I sat back cool to pretend to be cool hoping she would notice this with the result, when the lady entered the parlor I did not rise.

While they ate in the kitchen I pretended to read. I pretended to pay no attention whatever. We went out for a walk

the three of us and by now all of us vying to talk like three
good friends who want to get in and say everything on their
minds, a friendly rivalry—we went to the Red Drum to hear
the jazz which that night was Charlie Parker with Honduras
Jones on drums and others interesting, probably Roger Beloit
too, whom I wanted to see now, and that excitement of soft-
night San Francisco bop in the air but all in the cool sweet un-
exerting Beach—so we in fact ran, from Adam's on Telegraph
Hill, down the white street under lamps, ran, jumped, showed
off, had fun—felt gleeful and something was throbbing and I
was pleased that she was able to walk as fast as we were—a nice
thin strong little beauty to cut along the street with and so
striking everyone turned to see, the strange bearded Adam,
dark Mardou in strange slacks, and me, big gleeful hood.

So there we were at the Red Drum, a tableful of beers a few
that is and all the gangs cutting in and out, paying a dollar
quarter at the door, the little hip-pretending weazel there
taking tickets, Paddy Cordavan floating in as prophesied (a big
tall blond brakeman type subterranean from Eastern Washington cowboy-looking in jeans coming in to a wild generation
party all smoky and mad and I yelled "Paddy Cordavan?" and
"Yeah?" and he'd come over)—all sitting together, interesting
groups at various tables, Julien, Roxanne (a woman of 25
prophesying the future style of America with short almost
crewcut but with curls black snaky hair, snaky walk, pale pale
junkey anemic face and we say junkey when once Dostoevsky
would have said what? if not ascetic or saintly? but not in the
least? but the cold pale booster face of the cold blue girl and
wearing a man's white shirt but with the cuffs undone untied
at the buttons so I remember her leaning over talking to someone after having slinked across the floor with flowing propelled
shoulders, bending to talk with her hand holding a short butt
and the neat little flick she was giving it to knock ashes but repeatedly with long long fingernails an inch long and also orient and snakelike)—groups of all kinds, and Ross Wallenstein,
the crowd, and up on the stand Bird Parker with solemn eyes
who'd been busted fairly recently and had now returned to a
kind of bop dead Frisco but had just discovered or been told
about the Red Drum, the great new generation gang wailing
and gathering there, so here he was on the stand, examining

them with his eyes as he blew his now-settled-down-into-regulated-design "crazy" notes—the booming drums, the high ceiling—Adam for my sake dutifully cutting out at about 11 o'clock so he could go to bed and get to work in the morning, after a brief cutout with Paddy and myself for a quick ten-cent beer at roaring Pantera's, where Paddy and I in our first talk and laughter together pulled wrists—now Mardou cut out with me, glee eyed, between sets, for quick beers, but at her insistence at the Mask instead where they were fifteen cents, but she had a few pennies herself and we went there and began earnestly talking and getting hightingled on the beer and now it was the beginning—returning to the Red Drum for sets, to hear Bird, whom I saw distinctly digging Mardou several times also myself directly into my eye looking to search if really I was that great writer I thought myself to be as if he knew my thoughts and ambitions or remembered me from other night clubs and other coasts, other Chicagos—not a challenging look but the king and founder of the bop generation at least the sound of it in digging his audience digging the eyes, the secret eyes him-watching, as he just pursed his lips and let great lungs and immortal fingers work, his eyes separate and interested and humane, the kindest jazz musician there could be while being and therefore naturally the greatest—watching Mardou and me in the infancy of our love and probably wondering why, or knowing it wouldn't last, or seeing who it was would be hurt, as now, obviously, but not quite yet, it was Mardou whose eyes were shining in my direction, though I could not have known and now do not definitely know—except the one fact, on the way home, the session over the beer in the Mask drunk we went home on the Third Street bus sadly through night and throb knock neons and when I suddenly leaned over her to shout something further (in her secret self as later confessed) her heart leapt to smell the "sweetness of my breath" (quote) and suddenly she almost loved me—I not knowing this, as we found the Russian dark sad door of Heavenly Lane a great iron gate rasping on the sidewalk to the pull, the insides of smelling garbage cans sad-leaning together, fish heads, cats, and then the Lane itself, my first view of it (the long history and hugeness of it in my soul, as in 1951 cutting along with my sketchbook on a wild October evening when I was discovering my own writing soul at last I saw the subterranean Victor who'd come to Big Sur once on a motorcycle, was reputed to have gone to Alaska on same, with little subterranean chick Dorie Kiehl, there he was in striding Jesus coat heading north to Heavenly Lane to his pad and I followed him awhile, wondering about Heavenly Lane and all the long talks I'd been having for years with people like Mac Jones about the mystery, the silence of the subterraneans, "urban Thoreaus" Mac called them, as from Alfred Kazin in New York New School lectures back East commenting on all the students being interested in Whitman from a sexual revolution standpoint and in Thoreau from a contemplative mystic and antimaterialistic as if existentialist or whatever standpoint, the *Pierre*-of-Melville goof and wonder of it, the dark little beat burlap dresses, the stories you'd heard about great tenormen shooting junk by broken windows and starting at their horns, or great young poets with bears lying high in Rouault-like saintly obscurities, Heavenly Lane the famous Heavenly Lane where they'd all at one time or another the bat subterraneans lived, like Alfred and his little sickly wife something straight out of Dostoevsky's Petersburg slums you'd think but really the American lost bearded idealistic—the whole thing in any case), seeing it for the first time, but with Mardou, the wash hung over the court, actually the back courtyard of a big 20-family tenement with bay windows, the wash hung out and in the afternoon the great symphony of Italian mothers, children, fathers BeFinneganing and yelling from stepladders, smells, cats mewing, Mexicans, the music from all the radios whether bolero of Mexican or Italian tenor of spaghetti eaters or loud suddenly turned-up KPFA symphonies of Vivaldi harpsichord intellectuals performances boom blam the tremendous sound of it which I then came to hear all the summer wrapt in the arms of my love—walking in there now, and going up the narrow musty stairs like in a hovel, and her door.

Plotting I demanded we dance—previously she'd been hungry so I'd suggested and we'd actually gone and bought egg foo young at Jackson and Kearny and now she heated this (later confession she'd hated it though it's one of my favorite dishes and typical of my later behavior I was already forcing down her throat that which she in subterranean sorrow wanted to endure alone if at all ever), ah.—Dancing, I had put the light out, so, in the dark, dancing, I kissed her—it was giddy, whirling to the dance, the beginning, the usual beginning of lovers kissing standing up in a dark room the room being the woman's the man all designs—ending up later in wild dances she on my lap or thigh as I danced her around bent back for balance and she around my neck her arms that came to warm so much the *me* that then was only hot—

And soon enough I'd learn she had no belief and had had no place to get it from—Negro mother dead for birth of her—unknown Cherokee-halfbreed father a hobo who'd come throwing torn shoes across gray plains of fall in black sombrero and pink scarf squatting by hotdog fires casting Tokay empties into the night "Yaa Calexico!"

Quick to plunge, bite, put the light out, hide my face in shame, make love to her tremendously because of lack of love for a year almost and the need pushing me down—our little agreements in the dark, the really should-not-be-tolds—for it was she who later said "Men are so crazy, they want the essence, the woman is the essence, there it is right in their hands but they rush off erecting big abstract constructions."—"You mean they should just stay home with the essence, that is lie under a tree all day with the woman but Mardou that's an old idea of mine, a lovely idea, I never heard it better expressed and never dreamed."—"Instead they rush off and have big wars and consider women as prizes instead of human beings, well man I may be in the middle of all this shit but I certainly don't want any part of it" (in her sweet cultured hip tones of new generation).—And so having had the essence of her love now I erect big word constructions and thereby betray it really —telling tales of every gossip sheet the washline of the world —and hers, ours, in all the two months of our love (I thought) only once-washed as she being a lonely subterranean spent mooningdays and would go to the laundry with them but suddenly it's dank late afternoon and too late and the sheets are gray, lovely to me—because soft.—But I cannot in this confession betray the innermosts, the thighs, what the thighs contain —and yet why write?—the thighs contain the essence—yet tho there I should stay and from there I came and'll eventually return, still I have to rush off and construct construct—for nothing—for Baudelaire poems—

Never did she use the word love, even that first moment after our wild dance when I carried her still on my lap and hanging clear to the bed and slowly dumped her, suffered to find her, which she loved, and being unsexual in her entire life (except for the first 15-year-old conjugality which for some reason consummated her and never since) (O the pain of telling these secrets which are so necessary to tell, or why write or live) now "*casus in eventu est*" but glad to have me losing my mind in the slight way egomaniacally I might on a few beers.— Lying then in the dark, soft, tentacled, waiting, till sleep—so in the morning I wake from the scream of beermares and see beside me the Negro woman with parted lips sleeping, and little bits of white pillow stuffing in her black hair, feel almost revulsion, realize what a beast I am for feeling anything near it, grape little sweetbody naked on the restless sheets of the nightbefore excitement, the noise in Heavenly Lane sneaking in through the gray window, a gray doomsday in August so I feel like leaving at once to get "back to my work" the chimera of not the chimera but the orderly advancing sense of work and duty which I had worked up and developed at home (in South City) humble as it is, the comforts there too, the solitude which I wanted and now can't stand.—I got up and began to dress, apologize, she lay like a little mummy in the sheet and cast the serious brown eyes on me, like eyes of Indian watchfulness in a wood, like with the brown lashes suddenly rising with black lashes to reveal sudden fantastic whites of eye with the brown glittering iris center, the seriousness of her face accentuated by the slightly Mongoloid as if of a boxer nose and the cheeks puffed a little from sleep, like the face on a beautiful porphyry mask found long ago and Aztecan.—"But why do you have to rush off so fast, as though almost hysterical or worried?"—"Well I do I have work to do and I have to straighten out—hangover—" and she barely awake, so I sneak out with a few words in fact when she lapses almost into sleep and I don't see her again for a few days—

The adolescent cocksman having made his conquest barely broods at home the loss of the love of the conquered lass, the blacklash lovely—no confession there.—It was on a morning when I slept at Adam's that I saw her again, I was going to rise, do some typing and coffee drinking in the kitchen all day since at that time work, work was my dominant thought, not love—not the pain which impels me to write this even while I don't want to, the pain which won't be eased by the writing of this but heightened, but which will be redeemed, and if only it were a dignified pain and could be placed somewhere other than in this black gutter of shame and loss and noisemaking folly in the night and poor sweat on my brow—Adam rising to go to work, I too, washing, mumbling talk, when the phone rang and it was Mardou, who was going to her therapist, but needed a dime for the bus, living around the corner, "Okay come on over but quick I'm going to work or I'll leave the dime with Leo."—"O is he there?"—"Yes."—In my mind man-thoughts of doing it again and actually looking forward to seeing her suddenly, as if I'd felt she was displeased with our first night (no reason to feel that, previous to the balling she'd lain on my chest eating the egg foo young and dug me with glittering glee eyes) (that tonight my enemy devour?) the thought of which makes me drop my greasy hot brow into a tired hand—O love, fled me—or do telepathies cross sympathetically in the night?—Such cacoëthes him befalls—that the cold lover of lust will earn the warm bleed of spirit—so she came in, 8 A.M., Adam went to work and we were alone and immediately she curled up in my lap, at my invite, in the big stuffed chair and we began to talk, she began to tell her story and I turned on (in the gray day) the dim red bulblight and thus began our true love—

She had to tell me everything—no doubt just the other day she'd already told her whole story to Adam and he'd listened tweaking his beard with a dream in his far-off eye to look attentive and loverman in the bleak eternity, nodding—now with me she was starting all over again but as if (as I thought) to a brother of Adam's a greater lover and bigger, more awful listener and worrier.—There we were in all gray San Francisco of the gray West, you could almost smell rain in the air and far across the land, over the mountains beyond Oakland and out beyond Donner and Truckee was the great desert of Nevada, the wastes leading to Utah, to Colorado, to the cold cold come fall plains where I kept imagining that Cherokee-halfbreed hobo father of hers lying bellydown on a flatcar with the wind furling back his rags and black hat, his brown sad face facing all that land and desolation.—At other moments I imagined him instead working as a picker around Indio and on a hot night he's sitting on a chair on the sidewalk among the joking shirtsleeved men, and he spits and they say, "Hey Hawk Taw, tell us that story agin about the time you stole a taxicab and drove it clear to Manitoba, Canada—d'jever hear him tell that one, Cy?"—I saw the vision of her father, he's standing straight up, proudly, handsome, in the bleak dim red light of America on a corner, nobody knows his name, nobody cares—

Her own little stories about flipping and her minor fugues, cutting across boundaries of the city, and smoking too much marijuana, which held so much terror for her (in the light of my own absorptions concerning her father the founder of her flesh and predecessor terror-ee of her terrors and knower of much greater flips and madness than she in psychoanalytic-induced anxieties could ever even summon up to just imag-ine), formed just the background for thoughts about the Negroes and Indians and America in general but with all the overtones of 'new generation' and other historical concerns in which she was now swirled just like all of us in the Wig and Eu-rope Sadness of us all, the innocent seriousness with which she told her story and I'd listened to so often and myself told—wide eyed hugging in heaven together—hipsters of America in the 1950's sitting in a dim room—the clash of the streets beyond the window's bare soft sill.—Concern for her father, because I'd been out there and sat down on the ground and seen the rail the steel of America covering the ground filled with the bones of old Indians and Original Americans.—In the cold gray fall in Colorado and Wyoming I'd worked on the land and watched Indian hoboes come suddenly out of brush by the track and move slowly, hawk lipped, rill-jawed and wrinkled, into the great shadow of the light bearing burden-bags and junk talking quietly to one another and so distant from the absorptions of the field hands, even the Negroes of Cheyenne and Denver streets, the Japs, the general minority Armenians and Mexicans of the whole West that to look at a three-or-foursome of Indians crossing a field and a railroad

track is to the senses like something unbelievable as a dream—
you think, "They must be Indians—ain't a soul looking at 'em
—they're goin' that way—nobody notices—doesn't matter
much which way they go—reservation? What have they got in
those brown paper bags?" and only with a great amount of
effort you realize "But they were the inhabitors of this land
and under these huge skies they were the worriers and keeners
and protectors of wives in whole nations gathered around
tents—now the rail that runs over their forefathers' bones
leads them onward pointing into infinity, wraiths of humanity
treading lightly the surface of the ground so deeply suppurated with the stock of their suffering you only have to dig a
foot down to find a baby's hand.—The hotshot passenger train
with grashing diesel balls by, browm, browm, the Indians just
look up—I see them vanishing like spots—" and sitting in the
redbulb room in San Francisco now with sweet Mardou I
think, "And this is your father I saw in the gray waste, swallowed by night—from his juices came your lips, your eyes full
of suffering and sorrow, and we're not to know his name or
name his destiny?"—Her little brown hand is curled in mine,
her fingernails are paler than her skin, on her toes too and with
her shoes off she has one foot curled in between my thighs for
warmth and we talk, we begin our romance on the deeper level
of love and histories of respect and shame.—For the greatest
key to courage is shame and the blurfaces in the passing train
see nothing out on the plain but figures of hoboes rolling out
of sight—

"I remember one Sunday, Mike and Rita were over, we had
some very strong tea—they said it had volcanic ash in it and it
was the strongest they'd ever had."—"Came from L.A.?"—
"From Mexico—some guys had driven down in the station
wagon and pooled their money, or Tijuana or something, I
dunno—Rita was flipping at the time—when we were practically stoned she rose very dramatically and stood there in the
middle of the room man saying she felt her nerves burning
thru her bones—To see her *flip* right before my eyes—I got
nervous and had some kind of idea about Mike, he kept
looking at me like he wanted to kill me—he has such a funny
look anyway—I got out of the house and walked along and
didn't know which way to go, my mind kept turning into the

several directions that I was thinking of going but my body kept walking straight along Columbus altho I felt the sensation of each of the directions I mentally and emotionally turned into, amazed at all the possible directions you can take with different motives that come in, like it can make you a different *person*—I've often thought of this since childhood, of suppose instead of going up Columbus as I usually did I'd turn into Filbert would something happen that at the time is insignificant enough but would be like enough to influence my whole life in the end?—What's in store for me in the direction I *don't* take?—and all that, so if this had not been such a constant preoccupation that accompanied me in my solitude which I played upon in as many different ways as possible I wouldn't bother now except but seeing the horrible roads this pure *supposing* goes to it took me to *frights,* if I wasn't so damned *persistent*—" and so on deep into the day, a long confusing story only pieces of which and imperfectly I remember, just the mass of the misery in connective form—

Flips in gloomy afternoons in Julien's room and Julien sitting paying no attention to her but staring in the gray moth void stirring only occasionally to close the window or change his knee crossings, eyes round staring in a meditation so long and so mysterious and as I say so Christlike really outwardly lamby it was enough to drive anybody crazy I'd say to live there even one day with Julien or Wallenstein (same type) or Mike Murphy (same type), the subterraneans their gloomy long-thoughts enduring.—And the meekened girl waiting in a dark corner, as I remembered so well the time I was at Big Sur and Victor arrived on his literally homemade motorcycle with little Dorie Kiehl, there was a party in Patsy's cottage, beer, candlelight, radio, talk, yet for the first hour the newcomers in their funny ragged clothes and he with that beard and she with those somber serious eyes had sat practically out of sight behind the candlelight shadows so no one could see them and since they said nothing whatever but just (if not listened) meditated, gloomed, endured, finally I even forgot they were there—and later that night they slept in a pup tent in the field in the foggy dew of Pacific Coast Starry Night and with the same humble silence mentioned nothing in the morn—Victor so much in my mind always the central exaggerator of subterranean hip generation tendencies to silence, bohemian mystery, drugs, beard, semi-holiness and, as I came to find later, insurpassable nastiness (like George Sanders in *The Moon and Sixpence*)—so Mardou a healthy girl in her own right and from the windy open ready for love now hid in a musty corner waiting for Julien to speak.—Occasionally in the general "incest" she'd been slyly silently by some consenting arrangement or secret statesmanship shifted or probably just "Hey Ross you take Mardou home tonight I wanta make it with Rita for a change,"—and staying at Ross's for a week, smoking the volcanic ash, she was flipping—(the tense anxiety of improper sex additionally, the premature ejaculations of these anemic *maquereaux* leaving her suspended in tension and wonder).—"I was just an innocent chick when I met them, independent and like well not happy or anything but feeling that I had something to do, I wanted to go to night school, I had several jobs at my trade, binding in Olstad's and small places down around Harrison, the art teacher the old gal at school was saying I could become a great sculptress and I was living with various roommates and buying clothes and making it"—(sucking in her little lip, and that slick 'cuk' in the throat of drawing in breath quickly in sadness and as if with a cold, like in the throats of great drinkers, but she not a drinker but saddener of self) (supreme, dark)—(twining warm arm farther around me) "and he's lying there saying whatsamatter and I can't understand—." She can't understand suddenly what has happened because she's lost her mind, her usual recognition of self, and feels the eerie buzz of mystery, she really does not know who she is and what for and where she is, she looks out the window and this city San Francisco is the big bleak bare stage of some giant joke being perpetrated on her.—"With my back turned I didn't know what Ross was thinking—even doing."—She had no clothes on, she'd risen out of his satisfied sheets to stand in the wash of gray gloomtime thinking what to do, where to go.—And the longer she stood there finger-in-mouth and the more the man said, "What's the matter ba-by" (finally he stopped asking and just let her stand there) the more she could feel the pressure from inside towards bursting and explosion coming on, finally she took a giant step forward with a gulp of fear—everything was clear: danger in the air—it was writ in the shadows, in the gloomy dust behind the drawing table in the corner, in the garbage bags, the gray drain of day seeping down the wall and into the window—in the hollow eyes of people—she ran out of the room.—"What'd he say?"

"Nothing—he didn't move but was just with his head off the pillow when I glanced back in closing the door—I had no clothes on in the alley, it didn't disturb me, I was so intent on this realization of everything I knew I was an innocent child." —"The naked babe, wow."—(And to myself: "My God, this girl, Adam's right she's crazy, like I'd do that, I'd flip like I did on Benzedrine with Honey in 1945 and thought she wanted to use my body for the gang car and the wrecking and flames but I'd certainly never run out into the streets of San Francisco naked tho I might have maybe if I really felt there was need for action, yah") and I looked at her wondering if she, was she telling the truth.—She was in the alley, wondering who she was, night, a thin drizzle of mist, silence of sleeping Frisco, the B-O boats in the bay, the shroud over the bay of great clawmouth fogs, the aureola of funny eerie light being sent up in the middle by the Arcade Hood Droops of the Pillar-templed Alcatraz—her heart thumping in the stillness, the cool dark peace.—Up on a wood fence, waiting—to see if some idea from outside would be sent telling her what to do next and full of import and omen because it had to be right and just once— "One slip in the wrong direction . . . ," her direction kick, should she jump down on one side of fence or other, endless space reaching out in four directions, bleak-hatted men going to work in glistening streets uncaring of the naked girl hiding in the mist or if they'd been there and seen her would in a circle stand not touching her just waiting for the cop-authorities to come and cart her away and all their uninterested weary eyes flat with blank shame watching every part of her body— the naked babe.—The longer she hangs on the fence the less power she'll have finally to really get down and decide, and upstairs Ross Wallenstein doesn't even move from that junk-high bed, thinking her in the hall huddling, or he's gone to sleep anyhow in his own skin and bone.—The rainy night blooping all over, kissing everywhere men women and cities in one wash of sad poetry, with honey lines of high-shelved Angels trumpet-blowing up above the final Orient-shroud

Pacific-huge songs of Paradise, an end to fear below.—She squats on the fence, the thin drizzle making beads on her brown shoulders, stars in her hair, her wild now-Indian eyes now staring into the Black with a little fog emanating from her brown mouth, the misery like ice crystals on the blankets on the ponies of her Indian ancestors, the drizzle on the village long ago and the poorsmoke crawling out of the underground and when a mournful mother pounded acorns and made mush in hopeless millenniums—the song of the Asia hunting gang clanking down the final Alaskan rib of earth to New World Howls (in their eyes and in Mardou's eyes now the eventual Kingdom of Inca Maya and vast Azteca shining of gold snake and temples as noble as Greek, Egypt, the long sleek crack jaws and flattened noses of Mongolian geniuses creating arts in temple rooms and the leap of their jaws to speak, till the Cortez Spaniards, the Pizarro weary old-world sissified pantalooned Dutch bums came smashing canebrake in savannahs to find shining cities of Indian Eyes high, landscaped, boulevarded, ritualled, heralded, beflagged in that selfsame New World Sun the beating heart held up to it)—her heart beating in the Frisco rain, on the fence, facing last facts, ready to go run down the land now and go back and fold in again where she was and where was all—consoling herself with visions of truth—coming down off the fence, on tiptoe moving ahead, finding a hall, shuddering, sneaking—

"I'd made up my mind, I'd erected some structure, it was like, but I can't—." Making a new start, starting from flesh in the rain, "Why should anyone want to harm my little heart, my feet, my little hands, my skin that I'm wrapt in because God wants me warm and Inside, my toes—why did God make all this all so decayable and dieable and harmable and wants to make me realize and scream—why the wild ground and bodies bare and breaks—I quaked when the giver creamed, when my father screamed, my mother dreamed—I started small and ballooned up and now I'm big and a naked child again and only to cry and fear. —Ah—Protect yourself, angel of no harm, you who've never and could never harm and crack another innocent its shell and thin veiled pain—wrap a robe around you, honey lamb—protect yourself from rain and wait, till Daddy comes again, and Mama throws you warm inside her valley of the moon, loom at the loom of patient time, be happy in the mornings."—Making a new start, shivering, out of the alley night naked in the skin and on wood feet to the stained door of some neighbor—knocking—the woman coming to the door in answer to the frightened butter knock knuckles, sees the naked browngirl, frightened—("Here is a woman, a soul in my rain, she looks at me, she is frightened.")—"Knocking on this perfect stranger's door, sure."—"Thinking I was just going down the street to Betty's and back, promised her *meaning* it deeply I'd bring the clothes back and she did let me in and she got a blanket and wrapped it around me, then the clothes, and luckily she was alone—an Italian woman.—And in the alley I'd all come out and *on*, it was now first clothes, then I'd go to Betty's and get two bucks—then buy this brooch I'd seen that afternoon at some place with old sea-wood in the window, at North Beach, art handicraft ironwork like, a shoppey, it was the first symbol I was going to allow myself."—"Sure."—Out of the naked rain to a robe, to inno-cence shrouding in, then the decoration of God and religious sweetness.—"Like when I had that fist fight with Jack Steen it was in my mind strongly."—"Fist fight with Jack Steen?"—"This was earlier, all the junkies in Ross's room, tying up and shooting with Pusher, you know Pusher, well I took my clothes off there too—it was . . . all . . . part of the same . . . flip . . ."—"But this *clothes*, this *clothes*!" (to myself).—"I stood in the middle of the room flipping and Pusher was plucking at the guitar, just one string, and I went up to him and said, 'Man don't pluck those dirty notes at ME,' and like he just got up without a word and left."—And Jack Steen was furious at her and thought if he hit her and knocked her out with his fists she'd come to her senses so he slugged at her but she was just as strong as he (anemic pale 110 lb. junkey ascetics of America), blam, they fought it out before the weary others. —She'd pulled wrists with Jack, Julien, beat them practically— "Like Julien finally won at wrists but he really furiously had to put me down to do it and hurt me and was really upset" (glee-ful little shniffle thru the little out-teeth)—so there she'd been fighting it out with Jack Steen and really almost licking him but he was furious and neighbors downstairs called cops who came and had to be explained to—"dancing."—"But that day

I'd seen this iron thing, a little brooch with a beautiful dull sheen, to be worn around the neck, you know how nice that would look on my breast."—"On your brown breastbone a dull gold beautiful it would be baby, go on with your amazing story."—"So I immediately needed this brooch in spite of the time, 4 A.M. now, and I had that old coat and shoes and an old dress she gave me, I felt like a streetwalker but I felt no one could tell—I ran to Betty's for the two bucks, woke her up—." She demanded the money, she was coming out of death and money was just the means to get the shiny brooch (the silly means invented by inventors of barter and haggle and styles of who owns who, who owns what—). Then she was running down the street with her $2, going to the store long before it opened, going for coffee in the cafeteria, sitting at the table alone, digging the world at last, the gloomy hats, the glistening sidewalks, the signs announcing baked flounder, the reflections of rain in paneglass and in pillar mirror, the beauty of the food counters displaying cold spreads and mountains of crullers and the steam of the coffee urn.—"How warm the world is, all you gotta do is get little symbolic coins—they'll let you in for all the warmth and food you want—you don't have to strip your skin off and chew your bone in alleyways— these places were designed to house and comfort bag-and-bone people come to cry for consolation."—She is sitting there staring at everyone, the usual sexfiends are afraid to stare back because the vibration from her eyes is wild, they sense some living danger in the apocalypse of her tense avid neck and trembling wiry hands.—"This ain't no woman."—"That crazy Indian she'll kill somebody."—Morning coming, Mardou hurrying gleeful and mindswum, absorbed, to the store, to buy the brooch—standing then in a drugstore at the picture postcard swiveller for a solid two hours examining each one over and over again minutely because she only had ten cents left and could only buy two and those two must be perfect private talismans of the new important meaning, personal omen emblems —her avid lips slack to see the little corner meanings of the cable-car shadows, Chinatown, flower stalls, blue, the clerks wondering: "Two hours she's been in here, no stockings on, dirty knees, looking at cards, some Third Street Wino's wife run away, came to the big whiteman drugstore, never saw a shiny sheen postcard before—." In the night before they would have seen her up Market Street in Foster's with her last (again) dime and a glass of milk, crying into her milk, and men always looking at her, always trying to make her but now doing nothing because frightened, because she was like a child —and because: "Why didn't Julien or Jack Steen or Walt Fitzpatrick give you a place to stay and leave you alone in the corner, or lend you a couple bucks?"—"But they didn't care, they were frightened of me, they *really* didn't want me around, they had like distant objectivity, watching me, asking *nasty* questions—a couple times Julien went into his head-against-mine act like you know 'Whatsamatter, Mardou,' and his routines like that and phony sympathy but he really just was curious to find out why I was flipping—none of them'd ever give me *money*, man."—"Those guys really treated you bad, do you know that?"—"Yeah well they never treat anyone—like they never do anything—you take care of yourself, I'll take care of me."—"Existentialism."—"But American worse cool existentialism and of junkies man, I hung around with them, it was for almost a year by then and I was getting, every time they turned on, a kind of a contact high."—She'd sit with them, they'd go on the nod, in the dead silence she'd wait, sensing the slow snakelike waves of vibration struggling across the room, the eyelids falling, the heads nodding and jerking up again, someone mumbling some disagreeable complaint, "Ma-a-n, I'm drug by that son of a bitch MacDoud with all his routines about how he ain't got enough money for one cap, could he get a half a cap or pay a half—m-a-a-n, I never seen such nowhereness, no s-h-i-t, why don't he just go somewhere and *fade*, um." (That junkey 'um' that follows any out-on-the-limb, and anything one says is out-on-the-limb statement, *um*, *he-um*, the self-indulgent baby sob inkept from exploding to the big bawl mawk crackfaced WAAA they feel from the junk regressing their systems to the crib.)—Mardou would be sitting there, and finally high on tea or benny she'd begin to feel like she'd been injected, she'd walk down the street in her flip and actually feel the electric contact with other human beings (in her sensitivity recognizing a fact) but some times she was suspicious because it was someone secretly injecting her and following her down the street who was really responsible for the electric sensation and so independent of any natural law of the universe.—"But you really didn't believe that—but you did—when I flipped on benny in 1945 I really believed the girl wanted to use my body to burn it and put her boy's papers in my pocket so the cops'd think he was dead—I told her, too." —"Oh what did she do?"—"She said, 'Ooo daddy,' and hugged me and took care of me, Honey was a wild bitch, she put pancake makeup on my pale—I'd lost thirty, ten, fifteen pounds—but what happened?"—"I wandered around with my brooch."—She went into some kind of gift shop and there was a man in a wheel chair there. (She wandered into a doorway with cages and green canaries in the glass, she wanted to touch the beads, watch goldfish, caress the old fat cat sunning on the floor, stand in the cool green parakeet jungle of the store high on the green out-of-this-world dart eyes of parrots swivelling witless necks to cake and burrow in the mad feather and to feel that definite communication from them of birdy terror, the electric spasms of their notice, s q u a w k, l a w k, l e e k, and the man was exremely strange.)—"Why?"—"I dunno he was just very strange, he wanted, he talked with me very clearly and insisting —like intensely looking right at me and at great length but smiling about the simplest commonplace subjects but we both knew we meant everything else that we said—you know life—actually it was about the tunnels, the Stockton Street tunnel and the one they just built on Broadway, that's the one we talked of the most, but as we talked this a great electrical current of real understanding passed between us and I could feel the other levels the infinite number of them of every intonation in his speech and mine and the world of meaning in every *word*—I'd never realized before how much is *happening* all the time, and people *know* it—in their eyes they show it, they *refuse* to show it by any other—I stayed a very long time."—"He must have been a weirdy himself."—"You know, balding, and queer like, and middleaged, and with that with-neck-cut-off look or head-on-air," (witless, peaked) "looking all over, I guess it was his mother, the old lady with the Paisley shawl—but my god it would take me all day."— "Wow."—"Out on the street this beautiful old woman with white hair had come up to me and saw me, but was asking directions, but liked to talk—." (On the sunny now lyrical

Sunday morning after-rain sidewalk, Easter in Frisco and all
the purple hats out and the lavender coats parading in the cool
gusts and the little girls so tiny with their just whitened shoes
and hopeful coats going slowly in the white hill streets,
churches of old bells busy and downtown around Market
where our tattered holy Negro Joan of Arc wandered hosan-
nahing in her brown borrowed-from-night skin and heart,
flutters of betting sheets at corner newsstands, watchers at nude
magazines, the flowers on the corner in baskets and the old
Italian in his apron with the newspapers kneeling to water, and
the Chinese father in tight ecstatic suit wheeling the basket-
carriaged baby down Powell with his pink-spot-cheeked wife
of glitter brown eyes in her new bonnet rippling to flap in sun,
there stands Mardou smiling intensely and strangely and the
old eccentric lady not any more conscious of her Negroness
than the kind cripple of the store and because of her out and
open face now, the clear indications of a troubled pure innocent spirit just risen from a pit in pockmarked earth and by
own broken hands self-pulled to safety and salvation, the two
women Mardou and the old lady in the incredibly sad empty
streets of Sunday after the excitements of Saturday night the
great glitter up and down Market like wash gold dusting and
the throb of neons at O'Farrell and Mason bars with cocktail
glass cherrysticks winking invitation to the open hungering
hearts of Saturday and actually leading only finally to Sunday-
morning blue emptiness just the flutter of a few papers in the
gutter and the long white view to Oakland Sabbath haunted,
still—Easter sidewalk of Frisco as white ships cut in clean blue
lines from Sasebo beneath the Golden Gate's span, the wind
that sparkles all the leaves of Marin here laving the washed glitter of the white kind city, in the lostpurity clouds high above
redbrick track and Embarcadero pier, the haunted broken hint
of song of old Pomos the once onlywanderers of these eleven
last American now white-behoused hills, the face of Mardou's
father himself now as she raises her face to draw breath to
speak in the streets of life materializing huge above America,
fading—.) "And like I told her but talked too and when she
left she gave me her flower and pinned it on me and called me
honey."—"Was she white?"—"Yeah, like, she was very affectionate, very plea-*sant* she seemed to love me—like save me,

bring me out—I walked up a hill, up California past Chinatown, someplace I came to a white garage like with a big
garage wall and this guy in a swivel chair wanted to know what
I wanted, I understood all of my moves as one obligation after
another to communicate to whoever not accidentally but by
arrangement was placed before me, communicate and exchange this news, the vibration and new meaning that I had,
about everything happening to everyone all the time everywhere and for them not to worry, nobody as mean as you
think or—a colored guy, in the swivel chair, and we had a long
confused talk and he was reluctant, I remember, to look in my
eyes and really listen to what I was saying."—"But what were
you saying?"—"But it's all forgotten now—something as simple and like you'd never expect like those tunnels or the old
lady and I hanging-up on streets and directions—but the guy
wanted to make it with me, I saw him open his zipper but suddenly he got ashamed, I was turned around and could see it in
the glass." (In the white planes of wall garage morning, the
phantom man and the girl turned slumped watching in the
window that not only reflected the black strange sheepish man
secretly staring but the whole office, the chair, the safe, the
dank concrete back interiors of garage and dull sheen autos,
showing up also unwashed specks of dust from last night's
rainsplash and thru the glass the across-the-street immortal
balcony of wooden bay-window tenement where suddenly she
saw three Negro children in strange attire waving but without
yelling at a Negro man four stories below in overalls and therefore apparently working on Easter, who waved back as he
walked in his own strange direction that bisected suddenly the
slow direction being taken by two men, two hatted, coated ordinary men but carrying one a bottle, the other a boy of three,
stopping now and then to raise the bottle of Four Star California Sherry and drink as the Frisco A.M. All Morn Sun wind
flapped their tragic topcoats to the side, the boy bawling, their
shadows on the street like shadows of gulls the color of hand-
made Italian cigars of deep brown stores at Columbus and Pacific, now the passage of a fishtail Cadillac in second gear
headed for hilltop houses bay-viewing and some scented visit
of relatives bringing the funny papers, news of old aunts,
candy to some unhappy little boy waiting for Sunday to end,

for the sun to cease pouring thru the French blinds and paling the potted plants but rather rain and Monday again and the joy of the woodfence alley where only last night poor Mardou'd almost lost.)—"What'd the colored guy do?"—"He zipped up again, he wouldn't look at me, he turned away, it was strange he got ashamed and sat down—it reminded me too when I was a little girl in Oakland and this man would send us to the store and give us dimes then he'd open his bathrobe and show us himself."—"Negro?"—"Yea, in my neighborhood where I lived—I remember I used to never stay there but my girlfriend did and I think she even did something with him one time."—"What'd you do about the guy in the swivel chair?"— "Well, like I wandered out of there and it was a beautiful day, Easter, man."—"Gad, Easter where was I?"—"The soft sun, the flowers and here I was going down the street and thinking 'Why did I allow myself to be bored ever in the past and to compensate for it got high or drunk or rages or all the tricks people have because they want anything but serene understanding of just what there is, which is after all so much, and thinking like angry social deals,—like angry—kicks—like hasseling over social problems and my race problem, it meant so little and I could feel that great confidence and gold of the morning would slip away eventually and had already started— I could have made my whole life like that morning just on the strength of pure understanding and willingness to live and go along, God it was all the most beautiful thing that ever happened to me in its own way—but it was all sinister."—Ended when she got home to her sisters' house in Oakland and they were furious at her anyway but she told them off and did strange things; she noticed for instance the complicated wiring her eldest sister had done to connect the TV and the radio to the kitchen plug in the ramshackle wood upstairs of their cottage near Seventh and Pine the railroad sooty wood and gargoyle porches like tinder in the sham scrapple slums, the yard nothing but a lot with broken rocks and black wood showing where hoboes Tokay'd last night before moving off across the meatpacking yard to the Mainline rail Tracy-bound thru vast endless impossible Brooklyn-Oakland full of telephone poles and crap and on Saturday nights the wild Negro bars full of whores and the Mexicans Ya-Yaaing in their own saloons and the cop car cruising the long sad avenue riddled with drinkers and the glitter of broken bottles (now in the wood house where she was raised in terror Mardou is squatting against the wall looking at the wires in the half dark and she hears herself speak and doesn't understand why she's saying it except that it must be said, come out, because that day earlier when in her wandering she finally got to wild Third Street among the lines of slugging winos and the bloody drunken Indians with bandages rolling out of alleys and the 10¢ movie house with three features and little children of skid row hotels running on the sidewalk and the pawnshops and the Negro chickenshack jukeboxes and she stood in drowsy sun suddenly listening to bop as if for the first time as it poured out, the intention of the musicians and of the horns and instruments suddenly a mystical unity expressing itself in waves like sinister and again electricity but screaming with palpable aliveness the direct *word* from the vibration, the interchanges of statement, the levels of waving intimation, the smile in sound, the same living insinuation in the way her sister'd arranged those wires wriggled entangled and fraught with intention, innocent looking but actually behind the mask of casual life completely by agreement the mawkish mouth almost sneering snakes of electricity purposely placed she'd been seeing all day and hearing in the music and saw now in the wires), "What are you trying to do actually electrocute me?" so the sisters could see something was really wrong, worse than the youngest of the Fox sisters who was alcoholic and made the wild street and got arrested regularly by the vice squad, some nameless horrible yawning *wrong*, "She smokes dope, she hangs out with all those queer guys with beards in the City."—They called the police and Mardou was taken to the hospital—realizing now, "God, I saw how awful what was really happening and about to happen to me and man I pulled out of it fast, and talked sanely with everyone possible and did everything right, they let me out in 48 hours —the other women were with me, we'd look out the windows and the things they said, they made me see the preciousness of really being *out* of those damn bathrobes and *out* of there and out on the street, the sun, we could see ships, out and FREE man to roam around, how great it really is and how we never appreciate it all glum inside our worries and skins, like *fools*

really, or blind spoiled detestable children pouting because
. . . they can't get . . . all . . . the . . . candy . . . they
want, so I talked to the doctors and told them—." "And you
had no place to stay, where was your clothes?"—"Scattered all
over—all over the Beach—I had to do something—they let me
have this place, some friends of mine, for the summer, I'll have
to get out in October."—"In the Lane?"—"Yah."—"Honey
let's you and me—would you go to Mexico with me?"—"Yes!"
—"If I go to Mexico? that is, if I get the money? altho I do
have a hunnerd eighty now and we really actually could go tomorrow and make it—like Indians—I mean cheap and living
in the country or in the slums."—"Yes—it would be so nice to
get away now."—"But we could or should really wait till I
get—I'm supposed to get five hundred see—and—" (and that
was when I would have whisked her off into the bosom of my
own life)—she saying "I really don't want anything more to do
with the Beach or any of that gang, man, that's why—I guess I
spoke or agreed too soon, you don't seem so sure now"
(laughing to see me ponder).—"But I'm only pondering practical problems."—"Nevertheless if I'd have said 'maybe' I
bet—oooo that awright," kissing me—the gray day, the red
bulblight, I had never heard such a story from such a soul except from the great men I had known in my youth, great
heroes of America I'd been buddies with, with whom I'd ad-
ventured and gone to jail and known in raggedy dawns, the
boys beat on curbstones seeing symbols in the saturated gutter,
the Rimbauds and Verlaines of America on Times Square,
kids—no girl had ever moved me with a story of spiritual suffering and so beautifully her soul showing out radiant as an angel wandering in hell and the hell the selfsame streets I'd
roamed in watching, watching for someone just like her and
never dreaming the darkness and the mystery and eventuality
of our meeting in eternity, the hugeness of her face now like
the sudden vast Tiger head on a poster on the back of a woodfence in the smoky dumpyards Saturday no-school mornings,
direct, beautiful, insane, in the rain.—We hugged, we held
close—it was like love now, I was amazed—we made it in the
livingroom, gladly, in chairs, on the bed, slept entwined,
satisfied—I would show her more sexuality—

*

We woke up late, she'd not gone to her psychoanalyst, she'd "wasted" her day and when Adam came home and saw us in the chair again still talking and with the house belittered (coffee cups, crumbs of cakes I'd bought down on tragic Broadway in the gray Italianness which was so much like the lost Indianness of Mardou, tragic America-Frisco with its gray fences, gloomy sidewalks, doorways of dank, I from the small town and more recently from sunny Florida East Coast found so frightening).—"Mardou, you wasted your visit to a therapist, really Leo you should be ashamed and feel a little responsible, after all—" "You mean I'm making her lay off her duties . . . I used to do it with all my girls . . . ah it'll be good for her to miss" (not knowing her need).—Adam almost joking but also most serious, "Mardou you must write a letter or call—why don't you call him now?"—"It's a she doctor, up at City & County."—"Well call now, here's a dime."—"But I can do it tomorrow, but it's too late."—"How do you know it's too late—no really, you really goofed today, and you too Leo you're awfully responsible you rat." And then a gay supper, two girls coming from outside (gray crazy outside) to join us, one of them fresh from an overland drive from New York with Buddy Pond, the doll an L.A. hip type with short haircut who immediately pitched into the dirty kitchen and cooked everybody a delicious supper of black bean soup (all out of cans) with a few groceries while the other girl, Adam's, goofed on the phone and Mardou and I sat around guiltily, darkly in the kitchen drinking stale beer and wondering if Adam wasn't perhaps really right about what should be done, how one should pull oneself together, but our stories told, our love solidified, and something sad come into both our eyes—the evening proceeding with the gay supper, five of us, the girl with the short haircut saying later that I was so beautiful she couldn't look (which later turned out to be an East Coast saying of hers and Buddy Pond's), "beautiful" so amazing to me, unbelievable, but must have impressed Mardou, who was anyway during the supper jealous of the girl's attentions to me and later said so—my position so airy, secure—and we all went driving in her foreign convertible car, through now clearing Frisco streets not gray but opening soft hot reds in the sky between the homes Mardou and I lying back in the open backseat digging them,

the soft shades, commenting, holding hands—they up front
like gay young international Paris sets driving through town,
the short hair girl driving solemnly, Adam pointing out—
going to visit some guy on Russian Hill packing for a New
York train and France-bound ship where a few beers, small
talk, later troopings on foot with Buddy Pond to some literary
friend of Adam's Aylward So-and-So famous for the dialogs in
Current Review, possessor of a magnificent library, then
around the corner to (as I told Aylward) America's greatest
wit, Charles Bernard, who had gin, and an old gray queer, and
others, and sundry suchlike parties, ending late at night as I
made my first foolish mistake in my life and love with Mardou,
refusing to go home with all the others at 3 A.M., insisting, tho
at Charles' invite, to stay till dawn studying his pornographic
(homo male sexual) pictures and listening to Marlene Dietrich
records, with Aylward—the others leaving, Mardou tired and
too much to drink looking at me meekly and not protesting
and seeing how I was, a drunk really, always staying late, freeloading, shouting, foolish—but now loving me so not complaining and on her little bare thonged brown feet padding
around the kitchen after me as we mix drinks and even when
Bernard claims a pornographic picture has been stolen by her
(as she's in the bathroom and he's telling me confidentially,
"My dear, I saw her slip it into her pocket, her waist I mean
her breast pocket") so that when she comes out of bathroom
she senses some of this, the queers around her, the strange
drunkard she's with, she complains not—the first of so many
indignities piled on her, not on her capacity for suffering but
gratuitously on her little female dignities.—Ah I shouldn't
have done it, goofed, the long list of parties and drinkings and
downcrashings and times I ran out on her, the final shocker
being when in a cab together she's insisting I take her home
(to sleep) and I can go see Sam alone (in bar) but I jump out
of cab, madly ("I never saw anything so maniacal"), and run
into another cab and zoom off, leaving her in the night—so
when Yuri bangs on her door the following night, and I'm not
around, and he's drunk and insists, and jumps on her as he'd
been doing, she gave in, she gave in—she gave up—jumping
ahead of my story, naming my enemy at once—the pain, why
should "the sweet ram of their lunge in love" which has really

nothing to do with me in time or space, be like a dagger in my throat?

Waking up, then, from the partying, in Heavenly Lane, again I have the beer nightmare (now a little gin too) and with remorse and again almost and now for no reason revulsion the little white woolly particles from the pillow stuffing in her black almost wiry hair, and her puffed cheeks and little puffed lips, the gloom and dank of Heavenly Lane, and once more "I gotta go home, straighten out"—as tho never I was straight with her, but crooked—never away from my chimerical work room and comfort home, in the alien gray of the world city, in a state of WELL-BEING—. "But why do you always want to rush off so soon?"—"I guess a feeling of well-being at home, that I need, to be straight—like—." "I know baby—but I'm, I miss you in a way I'm jealous that you have a home and a mother who irons your clothes and all that and I haven't—." "When shall I come back, Friday night?"—"But baby it's up to you—to say when."—"But tell me what YOU want."—"But I'm not supposed to."—"But what do you mean s'posed?" —"It's like what they say—about—oh, I dunno" (sighing, turning over in the bed, hiding, burrowing little grape body around, so I go, turn her over, flop on bed, kiss the straight line that runs from her breastbone, a depression there, straight, clear down to her bellybutton where it becomes an infinitesimal line and proceeds like as if ruled with pencil on down and then continues just as straight underneath, and need a man get well-being from history and thought as she herself said when he has that, the essence, but still).—The weight of my need to go home, my neurotic fears, hangovers, horrors— "I shouldna—we shouldn't a gone to Bernard's at all last night —at least we shoulda come home at three with the others."— "That's what I say baby—but God" (laughing the shnuffle and making little funny imitation voice of slurring) "you never do what I ash you t'do."—"Aw I'm sorry—I love you—do you love me?"—"Man," laughing, "what do you *mean*"—looking at me warily—"I mean do you feel affection for me?" even as she's putting brown arm around my tense big neck.— "Naturally baby."—"But what is the—?" I want to ask every-thing, can't, don't know how, what is the mystery of what I want from you, what is man or woman, love, what do I mean by love or why do I have to insist and ask and why do I go and leave you because in your poor wretched little quarters—"It's the place depresses me—at home I sit in the yard, under trees, feed my cat."—"Oh man I know it's stuffy in here—shall I open the blind?"—"No everybody'll see you—I'll be so glad when the summer's over—when I get that dough and we go to Mexico."—"Well man, let's like you say go now on your money that you have now, you say we can really make it."— "Okay! Okay!" an idea which gains power in my brain as I take a few swigs of stale beer and consider a dobe hut say outside Texcoco at five dollars a month and we go to the market in the early dewy morning she in her sweet brown feet on sandals padding wifelike Ruthlike to follow me, we come, buy or-anges, load up on bread, even wine, local white, we go home and cook it up cleanly on our little cooker, we sit together over coffee writing down our dreams, analyzing them, we make love on our little bed.—Now Mardou and I are sitting there talking all this over, daydreaming, a big phantasy—"Well man," with little teeth outlaughing, "WHEN do we do this—like it's been a minor flip our whole relationship, all this indecisive clouds and planning—God."—"Maybe we should wait till I get that royalty dough—yep! really! it'll be better, cause like that we can get a typewriter and a three-speed machine and Gerry Mulligan records and clothes for you and everything we need, like the way it is now we can't do anything."—"Yeah—I dunno" (brooding) "Man you know I don't have any eyes for that hysterical poverty deal"—(statements of such sudden pith and hip I get mad and go home and brood about it for days). "When will you be back?"—"Well okay, then we'll make it Thursday."—"But if you really want to make it Friday—don't let me interfere with your work, baby—maybe you'd like it better to be away longer times."—"After what you—O I love you—you—." I undress and stay another three hours, and leave guiltily because the well-being, the sense of doing what I should has been sacrificed, but tho sacrificed to healthy love, something is sick in me, lost, fears—I realize too I have not given Mardou a dime, a loaf of bread literally, but talk, hugs, kisses, I leave the house and her unemployment check hasn't come and she has nothing to eat—"What will you eat?"—"O there's some cans—or I can go to Adam's maybe—but I don't wanta go there too often—I feel he resents me now, your friendship has been, I've come between that certain something you had sort of—." "No you didn't."—"But it's something else—I don't want to go out, I want to stay in, see no one"—"Not even me?"—"Not even you, sometimes God I feel that."—"Ah Mardou, I'm all mixed up—I can't make up my mind—we ought to do something together—I know what, I'll get a job on the railroad and we'll live together—" this is the great new idea.

(And Charles Bernard, the vastness of the name in the cosmogony of my brain, a hero of the Proustian past in the scheme as I knew it, in the Frisco-alone branch of it, Charles Bernard who'd been Jane's lover, Jane who'd been shot by Frank, Jane whom I'd lived with, Marie's best friend, the cold winter rainy nights when Charles would be crossing the campus saying something witty, the great epics almost here sounding phantom like and uninteresting if at all believable but the true position and bigburn importance of not only Charles but a good dozen others in the light rack of my brain, so Mardou seen in this light, is a little brown body in a gray sheet bed in the slums of Telegraph Hill, huge figure in the history of the night yes but only one among many, the asexuality of the WORK—also the sudden gut joy of beer when the visions of great words in rhythmic order all in one giant archangel book go roaring thru my brain, so I lie in the dark also seeing also hearing the jargon of the future worlds—damajehe eleout ekeke dhdkdk dldoud, ——d, ekeoeu dhdhdkehgyt—better not a more than lther ehe the macmurphy out of that dgardent that which strangely he doth mdodudltkdip—baseeaatra—poor examples because of mechanical needs of typing, of the flow of river sounds, words, dark, leading to the future and attesting to the madness, hollowness, ring and roar of my mind which blessed or unblessed is where trees sing—in a funny wind—well-being believes he'll go to heaven—a word to the wise is enough—"Smart went Crazy," wrote Allen Ginsberg.)

Reason why I didn't go home at 3 A.M.—and example.

2

At first I had doubts, because she was Negro, because she was sloppy (always putting off everything till tomorrow, the dirty room, unwashed sheets—what do I really for Christ's sake care about sheets)—doubts because I knew she'd been seriously insane and could very well be again and one of the first things we did, the first nights, she was going into the bathroom naked in the abandoned hall but the door of her place having a strange squeak it sounded to me (high on tea) like suddenly someone had come up and was standing in the stairwell (like maybe Gonzalez the Mexican sort of bum or hanger-on sort of faggish who kept coming up to her place on the strength of some old friendship she'd had with some Tracy Pachucos to bum little 7 centses from her or two cigarettes and all the time usually when she was at her lowest, sometimes even to take negotiable bottles away), thinking it might be him, or some of the subterraneans, in the hall asking "Is anybody with you?" and she naked, unconcernedly, and like in the alley just stands there saying, "No man, you better come back tomorrow I'm busy I'm not alone," this my tea-revery as I lay there, because the moansqueak of the door had that moan of voices in it, so when she got back from the toilet I told her this (reasoning honesty anyway) (and believing it had been really so, almost, and still believing her actively insane, as on the fence in the alley) but when she heard my confession she said she almost flipped again and was frightened of me and almost got up and ran out—for reasons like this, madness, repeated chances of more madness, I had my "doubts" my male self-contained doubts about her, so reasoned, "I'll just at some time cut out and get me another girl, white, white thighs, etc., and it'll have been a grand affair and I hope I don't hurt her tho."—Ha!— doubts because she cooked sloppily and never cleaned up dishes right away, which as first I didn't like and then came to see she really didn't cook sloppily and did wash the dishes after awhile and at the age of six (she later told me) she was forced to wash dishes for her tyrannical uncle's family and all the time on top of that forced to go out in alley in dark night with garbage pan every night same time where she was convinced the same ghost lurked for her—doubts, doubts—which I have not now in the luxury of time-past.—What a luxury it is to know that now I want her forever to my breast my prize my own woman whom I would defend from all Yuries and any-bodies with my fists and anything else, *her* time has come to claim independence, announcing, only yesterday ere I began this tearbook, "I want to be an independent chick with money and cuttin' around."—"Yeah, and knowing and screwing everybody, Wanderingfoot," I'm thinking, wandering foot from when we—I'd stood at the bus stop in the cold wind and there were a lot of men there and instead of standing at my side she wandered off in little funny red raincoat and black slacks and went into a shoestore doorway (ALWAYS DO WHAT YOU WANT TO DO AIN'T NOTHIN' I LIKE BETTER THAN A GUY DOIN' WHAT HE WANTS, Leroy always said) so I follow her reluctantly thinking, "She sure has wandering feet to hell with her I'll get another chick" (weak-ening at this point as reader can tell from tone) but turns out she knew I had only shirt no undershirt and should stand where no wind was, telling me later, the realization that she did not talk naked to anyone in the hall any more than it was wanderingfoot to walk away to lead me to a warmer waiting-place, that it was no more than shit, still making no impression on my eager impressionable ready-to-create construct destroy and die brain—as will be seen in the great construction of jeal-ousy which I later from a dream and for reasons of self-laceration recreated. . . . Bear with me all lover readers who've suffered pangs, bear with me men who understand that the sea of blackness in a darkeyed woman's eyes is the lonely sea itself and would you go ask the sea to explain itself, or ask woman why she crosseth hands on lap over rose? no—

Doubts, therefore, of, well, Mardou's Negro, naturally not only my mother but my sister whom I may have to live with some day and her husband a Southerner and everybody con-cerned, would be mortified to hell and have nothing to do with us—like it would preclude completely the possibility of living in the South, like in that Faulknerian pillar homestead in the Old Granddad moonlight I'd so long envisioned for myself and there I am with Doctor Whitley pulling out the panel of my rolltop desk and we drink to great books and outside the

cobwebs on the pines and old mules clop in soft roads, what
would they say if my mansion lady wife was a black Cherokee,
it would cut my life in half, and all such sundry awful American
as if to say white ambition thoughts or white daydreams.—
Doubts galore too about her body itself, again, and in a funny
way really relaxing now to her love so surprising myself I
couldn't believe it, I'd seen it in the light one playful night so
I—walking through the Fillmore she insisted we confess everything we'd been hiding for this first week of our relationship,
in order to see and understand and I gave my first confession,
haltingly, "I thought I saw some kind of black thing I've never
seen before, hanging, like it *scared* me" (laughing)—it must
have stabbed her heart to hear, it seemed to me I felt some
kind of shock in her being at my side as she walked as I divulged this secret thought—but later in the house with light
on we both of us childlike examined said body and looked
closely and it wasn't anything pernicious and pizen juices but
just bluedark as in all kinds of women and I was really and
truly reassured to actually see and make the study with her—
but this being a doubt that, confessed, warmed her heart to
me and made her see that fundamentally I would never snakelike hide the furthest, not the—but no need to defend, I cannot at all possibly begin to understand who I am or what I am
any more, my love for Mardou has completely separated me
from any previous phantasies valuable and otherwise—The
thing therefore that kept these outburst doubts from holding
upper sway in my activity in relating with her was the realization not only that she was sexy and sweet and good for me and
I was cutting quite a figure with her on the Beach anyway (and
in a sense too now cutting the subterraneans who were becoming progressively deeply colder in their looks towards me
in Dante's and on street from natural reasons that I had taken
over their play doll and one of their really if not the most brilliant gals in their orbit)—Adam also saying, "You go well together and it's good for you," he being at the time and still my
artistic and paternal manager—not only this, but, hard to confess, to show how abstract the life in the city of the Talking
Class to which we all belong, the Talking Class trying to ra-
tionalize itself I suppose out of a really base almost lecherous
lustful materialism—it was the reading, the sudden illuminated

glad wondrous discovery of Wilhelm Reich, his book *The Function of the Orgasm*, clarity as I had not seen in a long time, not since perhaps the clarity of personal modern grief of Céline, or, say, the clarity of Carmody's mind in 1945 when I first sat at his feet, the clarity of the poesy of Wolfe (at 19 it was clarity for me), the clarity here tho was scientific, Germanic, beautiful, true—something I'd always known and closely in- deed connected to my 1948 sudden notion that the only thing that really mattered was love, the lovers going to and fro beneath the boughs in the Forest of Arden of the World, here magnified and at the same time microcosmed and pointed in and maled into: orgasm—the reflexes of the orgasm—you can't be healthy without normal sex love and orgasm—I won't go into Reich's theory since it is available in his own book— but at the same time Mardou kept saying "O don't pull that Reich on me in bed, I read his damn book, I don't want our relationship all pointed out and f . . . . d up with what HE said," (and I'd noticed that all the subterraneans and practi- cally all intellectuals I have known have really in the strangest way always put down Reich if not at first, after awhile)— besides which, Mardou did not gain orgasm from normal cop- ulation and only after awhile from stimulation as applied by myself (an old trick that I had learned with a previous frigid wife) so it wasn't so great of me to make her come but as she finally only yesterday said "You're doing this just to give me the pleasure of coming, you're so kind," which was a state- ment suddenly hard for either one of us to believe and came on the heels of her "I think we ought to break up, we never do anything together, and I want to be indep—" and so doubts I had of Mardou, that I the great Finn Macpossipy should take her for my long love wife here there or anywhere and with all the objections my family, especially my really but sweetly but nevertheless really tyrannical (because of my subjective view of her and her influence) mother's sway over me—sway or what- ever.—"Leo, I don't think it's good for you to live with your mother always," Mardou, a statement that in my early confi- dence only made me think, "Well naturally she, she's just jeal- ous, and has no folks herself, and is one of those modern psychoanalyzed people who hate mothers anyway"—out loud saying, "I really do really love her and love you too and don't you see how hard I try to spend my time, divide my time between the two of you—over there it's my writing work, my well-being and when she comes home from work at night, tired, from the store, mind you, I feel very good making her supper, having the supper and a martini ready when she walks in so by 8 o'clock the dishes are all cleared, see, and she has more time to look at her television—which I worked on the railroad six months to buy her, see."—"Well you've done a lot of things for her," and Adam Moorad (whom my mother considered mad and evil) too had once said "You've really done a lot for her, Leo, forget her for a while, you've got your own life to live," which is exactly what my mother always was telling me in the dark of the South San Francisco night when we relaxed with Tom Collinses under the moon and neighbors would join us, "You have your own life to live, I won't interfere, Ti Leo, with anything you want to do, you decide, of course it will be all right with me," me sitting there goopy realizing it's all myself, a big subjective phantasy that my mother really needs me and would die if I weren't around, and nevertheless having a bellyful of other rationalizations allowing me to rush off two or three times a year on gigantic voyages to Mexico or New York or Panama Canal on ships—A million doubts of Mardou, now dispelled, now (and even without the help of Reich who shows how life is simply the man entering the woman and the rubbing of the two in soft—that essence, that dingdong essence—something making me now almost so mad as to shout, I GOT MY OWN LITTLE BANGTAIL ESSENCE AND THAT ESSENCE IS MIND RECOGNITION—) now no more doubts. Even, a thousand times, I without even remembering later asked her if she'd really stolen the pornographic picture from Bernard and the last time finally she fired "But I've told you and told you, about eight times in all, I did not take that picture and I told you too a thousand times I don't even didn't even have any pockets whatever in that particular suit I was wearing that night—no pockets at all," yet it never making an impression (in feverish folly brain me) that it was Bernard now who was really crazy, Bernard had gotten older and developed some personal sad foible, accusing others of stealing, solemnly—"Leo don't you see and you keep asking it"—this being the last deepest final doubt I wanted about Mardou that she was really a thief of some sort and therefore was out to steal my heart, my white man heart, a Negress sneaking in the world sneaking the holy white men for sacrificial rituals later when they'll be roasted and roiled (remembering the Tennessee Williams story about the Negro Turkish bath attendant and the little white fag) because, not only Ross Wallenstein had called me to my face a fag—"Man what are you, a fag? you talk you just like a fag," saying this after I'd said to him in what I hoped were cultured tones, "You're on goofballs tonight? you ought to try three sometimes, they'll really knock you out and have a few beers too, but don't take four, just three," it insulting him completely since he is the veteran hipster of the Beach and for anyone especially a brash newcomer stealing Mardou from his group and at the same time hoodlum-looking with a reputation as a great writer, which he didn't see, from only published book—the whole mess of it, Mardou becoming the big buck nigger Turkish bath attendant, and I the little fag who's broken to bits in the love affair and carried to the bay in a burlap bag, there to be distributed piece by piece and broken bone by bone to the fish if there are still fish in that sad water)—so she'd thieve my soul and eat it—so told me a thousand times, "I did not steal that picture and I'm sure Aylward whatshisname didn't and you didn't it's just Bernard, he's got some kind of fetish there"—But it never impressed and stayed till the last, only the other night, time—that deepest doubt about her arising too from the time, (which she'd told me about) she was living in Jack Steen's pad in a crazy loft down on Commercial Street near the seamen's union halls, in the glooms, had sat in front of his suitcase an hour thinking whether she ought to look in it to see what he had there, then Jack came home and rummaged in it and thought or saw something was missing and said, sinister, sullen, "Have you been going thru my bag?" and she almost leaped up and cried YES because she HAD—"Man I had, in Mind, been going thru that bag all day and suddenly he was looking at me, with that look—I almost flipped"—that story also not impressing into my rigid paranoia-ridden brain, so for two months I went around thinking she'd told me, "Yes, I did go thru his bag but of course took nothing," but so I saw she'd lied to Jack Steen in reality—but in reality now, the facts, she had only thought to do so, and so on—my doubts all of them hastily ably assisted by a driving paranoia, which is really my confession—doubts, then, all gone.

For now I want Mardou—she just told me that six months ago a disease took root deeply in her soul, and forever now—doesn't this make her more beautiful?—But I want Mardou—because I see her standing, with her black velvet slacks, handsapockets, thin, slouched, cig hanging from lips, the smoke itself curling up, her little black back hairs of short hair-cut combed down fine and sleek, her lipstick, pale brown skin, dark eyes, the way shadows play on her high cheekbones, the nose, the little soft shape of chin to neck, the little Adam's apple, so hip, so cool, so beautiful, so modern, so new, so un-attainable to sad bagpants me in my shack in the middle of the woods—I want her because of the way she imitated Jack Steen that time on the street and it amazed me so much but Adam Moorad was solemn watching the imitation as if perhaps en-grossed in the thing itself, or just skeptical, but she disengaged herself from the two men she was walking with and went ahead of them showing the walk (among crowds) the soft swing of arms, the long cool strides, the stop on the corner to hang and softly face up to birds with like as I say Viennese philosopher—but to see her do it, and to a T, (as I'd seen his walk indeed across the park), the fact of her—I love her but this song is . . . broken—but in French now . . . in French I can sing her on and on. . . .

Our little pleasures at home at night, she eats an orange, she makes a lot of noise sucking it—

When I laugh she looks at me with little round black eyes that hide themselves in her lids because she laughs hard (con-torting all her face, showing the little teeth, making lights everywhere) (the first time I saw her, at Larry O'Hara's, in the corner, I remember, I'd put my face close to hers to talk about books, she'd turned her face to me close, it was an ocean of melting things and drowning, I could have swimmed in it, I was afraid of all that richness and looked away)—

With her rose bandana she always puts on for the pleasures of the bed, like a gypsy, rose, and then later the purple one, and the little hairs falling black from the phosphorescent pur-ple in her brow as brown as wood—

Her little eyes moving like cats—

We play Gerry Mulligan loud when he arrives in the night, she listens and chews her fingernails, her head moves slowly side to side like a nun in profound prayer—

When she smokes she raises the cigarette to her mouth and slits her eyes—

She reads till gray dawn, head on one arm, *Don Quixote*, Proust, anything—

We lie down, look at each other seriously saying nothing, head to head on the pillow—

Sometimes when she speaks and I have my head under hers on the pillow and I see her jaw the dimple the woman in her neck, I see her deeply, richly, the neck, the deep chin, I know she's one of the most *enwomaned* women I've seen, a brunette of eternity incomprehensibly beautiful and for always sad, profound, calm—

When I catch her in the house, small, squeeze her, she yells out, tickles me furiously, I laugh, she laughs, her eyes shine, she punches me, she wants to beat me with a switch, she says she likes me—

I'm hiding with her in the secret house of the night—

Dawn finds us mystical in our shrouds, heart to heart—

'My sister!' I'd thought suddenly the first time I saw her—

The light is out.

Daydreams of she and I bowing at big fellaheen cocktail parties somehow with glittering Parises in the horizon and in the forefront—she's crossing the long planks of my floor with a smile.

Always putting her to a test, which goes with "doubts"— doubts indeed—and I would like to accuse myself of bastardliness—such tests—briefly I can name two, the night Arial Lavalina the famous young writer suddenly was standing in the Mask and I was sitting with Carmody also now famous writer in a way who'd just arrived from North Africa, Mardou around the corner in Dante's cutting back and forth as was our wont all around, from bar to bar, and sometimes she'd cut unescorted there to see the Juliens and others—I saw Lavalina and called his name and he came over.—When Mardou came to get me to go home I wouldn't go, I kept insisting it was an important literary moment, the meeting of those two (Carmody having plotted with me a year earlier in dark Mexico when we'd lived poor and beat and he's a junkey, "Write a letter to Ralph Lowry find out how I can get to meet this here good-looking Arial Lavalina, man, look at that picture on the back of *Recognition of Rome*, ain't that something?" my sympathies with him in the matter being personal and again like Bernard also queer he was connected with the legend of the bigbrain of myself which was my WORK, that all consuming work, so wrote the letter and all that) but now suddenly (after of course no reply from the Ischia and otherwise grapevines and certainly just as well for me at least) he was standing there and I recognized him from the night I'd met him at the Met ballet when—in New York in tux I'd cut out with tuxed editor to see glitter nightworld New York of letters and wit, and Leon Danillian, so I yelled "Arial Lavalina! come here!" which he did.—When Mardou came I said whispering gleefully "This is Arial Lavalina ain't that mad!"—"Yeh man but I want to go home."—And in those days her love meaning no more to me than that I had a nice convenient dog chasing after me (much like in my real secretive Mexican vision of her following me down dark dobe streets of slums of Mexico City not walking with me but following, like Indian woman) I just goofed and said "But wait, you go home and wait for me, I want to dig Arial and then I'll be home."—"But baby you said that the other night and you were two hours late and you don't know what pain it caused me to wait." (Pain!)—"I know but look," and so I took her around the block to persuade her, and drunk as usual at one point to prove something I stood on my head in the pavement of Montgomery or Clay Street and some hoodlums passed by, saw this, saying "That's right"—finally (she laughing) depositing her in a cab, to get home, wait for me—going back to Lavalina and Carmody whom gleefully and now alone back in my big world night adolescent literary vision of the world, with nose pressed to window glass, "Will you look at that, Carmody and Lavalina, the great Arial Lavalina tho not a great great writer like me nevertheless so famous and glamorous etc. together in the Mask and I arranged it and everything ties together, the myth of the rainy night, Master Mad, Raw Road, going back to 1949 and 1950 and all things grand great the Mask of old history crusts"—(this my feeling

and I go in) and sit with them and drink further—repairing the
three of us to 13 Pater a lesbian joint down Columbus, Carmody, high, leaving us to go enjoy it, and we sitting in there,
further beers, the horror the unspeakable horror of myself
suddenly finding in myself a kind of perhaps William Blake or
Crazy Jane or really Christopher Smart alcoholic humility
grabbing and kissing Arial's hand and exclaiming "Oh Arial
you dear—you are going to be—you are so famous—you wrote
so well— I remember you—what—" whatever and now unrememberable and drunkenness, and there he is a well-known
and perfectly obvious homosexual of the first water, my roaring brain— we go to his suite in some hotel—I wake up in the
morning on the couch, filled with the first horrible recognition, "I didn't go back to Mardou's at all" so in the cab he
gives me—I ask for fifty cents but he gives me a dollar saying
"You owe me a dollar" and I rush out and walk fast in the hot
sun face all broken from drinking and chagrin to her place
down in Heavenly Lane arriving just as she's dressing up to go
to the therapist.—Ah sad Mardou with little dark eyes looking
with pain and had waited all night in a dark bed and the
drunken man leering in and I rushed down in fact at once to
get two cans of beer to straighten up ("To curb the fearful
hounds of hair" Old Bull Balloon would say), so as she abluted
to go out I yelled and cavorted—went to sleep, to wait for her
return, which was in the late afternoon, waking to hear the cry
of pure children in the alleyways down there—the horror the
horror, and deciding, "I'll write a letter at once to Lavalina,"
enclosing a dollar and apologizing for getting so drunk and
acting in such a way as to mislead him—Mardou returning, no
complaints, only a few a little later, and the days rolling and
passing and still she forgives me enough or is humble enough
in the wake of my crashing star in fact to write me, a few nights
later, this letter:

DEAR BABY,
    Isn't it good to know winter is coming—

as we'd been complaining so much about heat and now the
heat was ended, a coolness came into the air, you could feel it in
the draining gray airshaft of Heavenly Lane and in the look of
the sky and nights with a greater wavy glitter in streetlights—

—and that life will be a little more quiet—and you will be home writing and eating well and we will be spending pleasant nights wrapped round one another—and you are home now, rested and eating well because you should not become too sad—

written after, one night, in the Mask with her and newly arrived and future enemy Yuri erstwhile close lil brother I'd suddenly said "I feel impossibly sad and like I'll die, what can we do?" and Yuri'd suggested "Call Sam," which, in my sadness, I did, and so earnestly, as otherwise he'd pay no attention being a newspaper man and new father and no time to goof, but so earnestly he accepted us, the three, to come at once, from the Mask, to his apartment on Russian Hill, where we went, I getting drunker than ever, Sam as ever punching me and saying "The trouble with you, Percepied," and, "You've got rotten bags in the bottom of your store," and, "You Canucks are really all alike and I don't even believe you'll admit it when you die"—Mardou watching amused, drinking a little, Sam finally, as always falling over drunk, but not really, drunk-desiring, over a little lowtable covered a foot high with ashtrays piled three inches high and drinks and doodads, crash, his wife, with baby just from crib, sighing—Yuri, who didn't drink but only watched bead-eyed, after having said to me the first day of his arrival, "You know Percepied I really like you now, I really feel like communicating with you now," which I should have suspected, in him, as constituting a new kind of sinister interest in the innocence of my activities, that being by the name of, Mardou—

—because you should not become too sad

was only sweet comment heartbreakable Mardou made about that disastrous awful night—similar to example 2, one following the one with Lavalina, the night of the beautiful faun boy who'd been in bed with Micky two years before at a great depraved wildparty I'd myself arranged in days when living with Micky the great doll of the roaring legend night, seeing him in the Mask, and being with Frank Carmody and everybody, tugging at his shirt, insisting he follow us to other bars, follow us around, Mardou finally in the blur and roar of the night yelling at me "It's him or me goddamit," but not really serious (herself usually not a drinker because a subterranean but in her affair with Percepied a big drinker now)—she left, I heard her say "We're through" but never for a moment believed it and it was not so, she came back later, I saw her again, we swayed together, once more I'd been a bad boy and again ludicrously like a fag, this distressing me again in waking in gray Heavenly Lane in the morning beer roared.—This is the confession of a man who can't drink.—And so her letter saying:

> *because you should not become too sad—and I feel better when you are well—*

forgiving, forgetting all this sad folly when all she wants to do, "I don't want to go out drinking and getting drunk with all your friends and keep going to Dante's and see all those Juliens and everybody again, I want us to stay quiet at home, listen to KPFA and read or something, or go to a show, baby I like shows, movies on Market Street, I really do."—"But I hate movies, life's more interesting!" (another putdown)—her sweet letter continuing:

> *I am full of strange feelings, reliving and refashioning many old things*

—when she was 14 or 13 maybe she'd play hookey from school in Oakland and take the ferry to Market Street and spend all day in one movie, wandering around having hallucinated phantasies, looking at all the eyes, a little Negro girl roaming the shuffle restless street of winos, hoodlums, sams, cops, paper peddlers, the mad mixup there the crowd eying looking everywhere the sexfiend crowd and all of it in the gray rain of hookey days—poor Mardou—"I'd get sexual phantasies the strangest kind, not with like sex acts with people but strange situations that I'd spend all day working out as I walked, and my orgasms the few I had only came, because I never masturbated or even knew how, when I dreamed that my father or somebody was leaving me, running away from me, I'd wake up with a funny convulsion and wetness in myself, in my thighs, and on Market Street the same way but different and anxiety

dreams woven out of the movies I saw."—Me thinking *O
grayscreen gangster cocktail rainyday roaring gunshot spectral
immortality B movie tire pile black-in-the-mist Wildamerica
but it's a crazy world!*—"Honey" (out loud) "wished I could
have seen you walking around Market like that—I bet I DID
see you—I bet I did—you were thirteen and I was twenty-
two—1944, yeah I bet I saw you, I was a seaman, I was always
there, I knew the gangs around the bars—" So in her letter
saying:

reliving and refashioning many old things

probably reliving those days and phantasies, and earlier cruder
horrors of home in Oakland where her aunt hysterically beat
her or hysterically tried and her sisters (tho occasional little-
sister tenderness like dutiful kisses before bed and writing on
one another's backs) giving her a bad time, and she roaming
the street late, deep in broodthoughts, and men trying to make
her, the dark men of dark colored-district doors—so going on,

*and feeling the cold and the quietude even in the midst of
my forebodings and fears—which clear nights soothe and
make more sharp and real—tangible and easier to cope with*

—said indeed with a nice rhythm, too, so I remember admiring her intelligence even then—but at the same time darkening at home there at my desk of well-being and thinking,
"But cope that old psychoanalytic cope, she talks like all of em,
the city decadent intellectual dead-ended in cause-and-effect
analysis and solution of so-called problems instead of the great
JOY of being and will and fearlessness—rupture's their rap-
ture—that's her trouble, she's just like Adam, like Julien, the
lot, afraid of madness, the fear of madness haunts her—not Me
Not Me by God"—

*But why am I writing to say these things to you. But all
feelings are real and you probably discern or feel too what I
am saying and why I need to write it—*

—a sentiment of mystery and charm—but, as I told her often,
not enough detail, the details are the life of it, I insist, say
everything on your mind, don't hold it back, don't analyze or

anything as you go along, say it out, "That's" (I now say in reading letter) "a typical example—but no mind, she's just a girl—humph"—

My image of you now is strange

—I see the bough of that statement, it waves on the tree—

I feel a distance from you which you might feel too which gives me a picture of you that is warm and friendly

and then inserts, in smaller writing,

(*and loving*)

to obviate my feeling depressed probably over seeing in a letter from lover only word "friendly"—but that whole complicated phrase further complicated by the fact it is presented in originally written form under the marks and additions of a rewrite, which is not as interesting to me, naturally—the rewrite being

I feel a distance from you which you might feel too with pictures of you that are warm and friendly (*and loving*)
—and because of the anxieties we are experiencing but never speak of really, and are similar too—

a piece of communication making me suddenly by some majesty of her pen feel sorry for myself, seeing myself like her lost in the suffering ignorant sea of human life feeling distant from she who should be closest and not knowing (no not under the sun) why the distance instead is the feeling, the both of us entwined and lost in that, as under the sea—

I am going to sleep to dream, to wake

—hints of our business of writing down dreams or telling dreams on waking, all the strange dreams indeed and (later will show) the further brain communicating we did, telepathizing images together with eyes closed, where it will be shown, all thoughts meet in the crystal chandelier of eternity—Jim— yet I also like the rhythm of *to dream, to wake*, and flatter myself I have a rhythmic girl in any case, at my metaphysical homedesk—

You have a very beautiful face and I like to see it as I do now—

—echoes of that New York girl's statement and now coming from humble meek Mardou not so unbelievable and I actually begin to preen and believe in this (O humble paper of letters, O the time I sat on a log near Idlewild airport in New York and watched the helicopter flying in with the mail and as I looked I saw the smile of all the angels of earth who'd written the letters which were packed in its hold, the smiles of them, specifically of my mother, bending over sweet paper and pen to communicate by mail with her daughter, the angelical smile like the smiles of workingwomen in factories, the world-wide bliss of it and the courage and beauty of it, recognition of which facts I shouldn't even deserve, treating Mardou as I have done) (O forgive me angels of the heaven and of the earth—even Ross Wallenstein will go to heaven)—

Forgive the conjunctions and double infinitives and the not said

—again I'm impressed and I think, she too there, for the first time self-conscious of writing to an author—

I don't know really what I wanted to say but want you to have a few words from me this Wednesday morning

and the mail only carried it in much later, after I saw her, the letter losing therefore its hopeful impactedness

We are like two animals escaping to dark warm holes and live our pains alone

—at this time my dumb phantasy of the two of us (after all the drunks making me drunksick city sick) was, a shack in the middle of the Mississippi woods, Mardou with me, damn the lynchers, the not-likings, so I wrote back: "I hope you meant by that line (*animals to dark warm holes*) you'll turn out to be the woman who can really live with me in profound solitude of woods finally and at same time make the glittering Parises (there it is) and grow old with me in my cottage of peace" (suddenly seeing myself as William Blake with the meek wife in the middle of London early dewy morning, Crabbe Robinson is coming with some more etching work but Blake is lost in the vision of the Lamb at breakfast leavings table).—Ah regrettable Mardou, and never a thought of that thing beats in your

brow, that I should kiss, the pain of your own pride, enough
19th-century romantic general talk—the details are the life of
it—(a man may act stupid and top tippity and bigtime 19th-
century boss type dominant with a woman but it won't help
him when the chips are down—the loss lass'll make it back, it's
hidden in her eyes, her future triumph and strength—on his
lips we hear nothing but "of course love").—Her closing
words a beautiful pastichepattisee, or pie, of—

> *Write to me   anything   Please Stay Well Your Freind*
> [misspelled]   *And my love   And   Oh*   [over some kind
> of hiddenforever erasures] [and many X's for of course
> kisses]   *And Love for You*   MARDOU [underlined]

and weirdest, most strange, central of all—ringed by itself, the
word, PLEASE—her lastplea neither one of us knowing—Answering this letter myself with a dull boloney bullshit rising out
of my anger with the incident of the pushcart.

(And tonight this letter is my last hope.)

The incident of the pushcart began, again as usual, in the
Mask and Dante's, drinking, I'd come in to see Mardou from
my work, we were in a drinking mood, for some reason suddenly I wanted to drink red Burgundy wine which I'd tasted
with Frank and Adam and Yuri the Sunday before—another,
and first, worthy of mention incident, being—but that's the
crux of it all—THE DREAM. Oh the bloody dream! In which
there was a pushcart, and everything else prophesied. This too
after a night of severe drinking, the night of the redshirt faun
boy—where everybody afterward of course said "You made a
fool of yourself, Leo, you're making yourself a reputation on
the Beach as a big fag tugging at the shirts of well-known
punks."—"But I only wanted him for you to dig."—"Nevertheless" (Adam) "*really.*"—And Frank: "You really makin a
horrible reputation."—Me: "I don't care, you remember 1948
when Sylvester Strauss that fag composer got sore at me
because I wouldn't go to bed with him because he'd read my
novel and submitted it, yelled at me 'I know all about you and
your awful reputation.'—'What?'—'You and that there Sam
Vedder go around the Beach picking up sailors and giving them
dope and he makes them only so he can bite, I've heard about

you.'—'Where did you hear this fantastic tale?'—you know that story, Frank."—"I should imagine" (Frank laughing) "what with all the things you do right there in the Mask, drunk, in front of everybody, if I didn't know you I'd swear you were the craziest piece of rough trade that ever walked" (a typical Carmodian pithy statement) and Adam "Really that's true."—After the night of the redshirt boy, drunk, I'd slept with Mardou and had the worst nightmare of all, which was, everybody, the whole world was around our bed, we lay there and everything was happening. Dead Jane was there, had a big bottle of Tokay wine hidden in Mardou's dresser for me and got it out and poured me a big slug and spilled a lot out of the waterglass on the bed (a symbol of even further drinking, more wine, to come)—and Frank with her—and Adam, who went out the door to the dark tragic Italian pushcart Telegraph Hill street, going down the rickety wooden Shatov stairs where the subterraneans were "digging an old Jewish patriarch just arrived from Russia" who is holding some ritual by the barrels of the fish head cats (the fish heads, in the height of the hot days Mardou had a fish head for our crazy little visiting cat who was almost human in his insistence to be loved his scrolling of neck and purring to be against you, for him she had a fish head which smelled so horrible in the almost airless night I threw part of it out in the barrel downstairs after first throwing a piece of slimy gut unbeknownst I'd put my hands against in the dark icebox where was a small piece of ice I wanted to chill my sauterne with, smack against a great soft mass, the guts or mouth of a fish, this being left in the icebox after disposal of fish I threw it out, the piece draped over fire escape and was there all hotnight and so in the morning when waking I was being bitten by gigantic big blue flies that had been attracted by the fish, I was naked and they were biting like mad, which annoyed me, as the pieces of pillow had annoyed me and somehow I tied it up with Mardou's Indianness, the fish heads the awful sloppy way to dispose of fish, she sensing my annoyance but laughing, ah bird)—that alley, out there, in the dream, Adam, and in the house, the actual room and bed of Mardou and I the whole world roaring around us, back ass flat—Yuri also there, and when I turn my head (after nameless events of the millionfold mothswarms) suddenly he's got Mardou on the bed laid out and wiggling and is necking furiously with her—at first I say nothing—when I look again, again they're at it, I get mad—I'm beginning to wake up, just as I give Mardou a rabbit punch in the back of her neck, which causes Yuri to reach a hand for me—I wake up I'm swinging Yuri by the heels against the brick fireplace wall.—On waking from this dream I told all to Mardou except the part where I hit her or Yuri—and she too (in tying in with our telepathies already experienced that sad summer season now autumn mooned to death, we'd communicated many feelings of empathy and I'd come running to see her on nights when she sensed it) had been dreaming like me of the whole world around our bed, of Frank, Adam, others, her recurrent dream of her father rushing off, in a train, the spasm of almost orgasm.—"Ah honey I want to stop all this drinking these nightmares'll kill me—you don't know how jealous I was in that dream" (a feeling I'd not yet had about Mardou)—the energy behind this anxious dream had obtained from her reaction to my foolishness with the red-shirt boy (Absolutely insufferable type anyway" Carmody had commented "tho obviously good-looking, really Leo you were funny" and Mardou: "Acting like a little boy but I like it.")— Her reaction had of course been violent, on arriving home, after she'd tugged me in the Mask in front of everyone including her Berkeley friends who saw her and probably even heard "It's me or him!" and the madness humor futility of that— arriving in Heavenly Lane she'd found a balloon in the hall, nice young writer John Golz who lived downstairs had been playing balloons with the kids of the Lane all day and some were in the hall, with the balloon Mardou had (drunk) danced around the floor, puffing and poooshing and flupping it up with dance interpretive gestures and said something that not only made me fear her madness, her hospital type insanity, but cut my heart deeply, and so deeply that she could not therefore have been insane, in communicating something so exactly, with precise—whatever—"You can go now I have this balloon."— "What do you mean?" (I, drunk, on floor blearing).—"I have this balloon now—I don't need you any more—goodbye—goo away—leave me alone"—a statement that even in my drunkenness made me heavy as lead and I lay there, on the floor, where I slept an hour while she played with the balloon and finally went to bed, waking me up at dawn to undress and get in—both of us dreaming the nightmare of the world around our bed—and that GUILT-Jealousy entering into my mind for the first time—the crux of this entire tale being: I want Mardou because she has begun to reject me—BECAUSE—"But baby that was a mad dream."—"I was so jealous—I was sick." —I harkened suddenly now to what Mardou'd said the first week of our relationship, when, I thought secretly, in my mind I had privately superseded her importance with the importance of my writing work, as, in every romance, the first week is so intense all previous worlds are eligible for throwover, but when the energy (of mystery, pride) begins to wane, elder worlds of sanity, well-being, common sense, etc., return, so I had secretly told myself: "My work's more important than Mardou."—Nevertheless she'd sensed it, that first week, and now said, "Leo there's something different now—in you—I feel it in me—I don't know what it is." I knew very well what it was and pretended not to be able to articulate with myself and least of all with her anyway—I remembered now, in the waking from the jealousy nightmare, where she necks with Yuri, something had changed, I could sense it, something in me was cracked, there was a new loss, a new Mardou even— and, again, the difference was not isolated in myself who had dreamed the cuckold dream, but in she, the subject, who'd not dreamed it, but participated somehow in the general rueful mixed up dream of all this life with me—so I felt she could now this morning look at me and tell that something had died—not due to the balloon and "You can go now"—but the dream—and so the dream, the dream, I kept harping on it, desperately I kept chewing and telling about it, over coffee, to her, finally when Carmody and Adam and Yuri came (in themselves lonely and looking to come get juices from that great current between Mardou and me running, a current everybody I found out later wanted to get in on, the act) I began telling *them* about the dream, stressing, stressing, stressing the Yuri part, where Yuri "every time I turn my back" is kissing her—naturally the others wanting to know their parts, which I told with less vigor—a sad Sunday afternoon, Yuri going out to get beer, a spread, bread—eating a little—and in fact a few wrestling matches that broke my heart. For when I saw Mardou for fun wrestling with Adam (who was not the villain of the dream tho now I figured I must have switched persons) I was pierced with that pain that's now all over me, that firstpain, how cute she looked in her jeans wrestling and struggling (I'd said "She's strong as hell, d'jever hear of her fight with Jack Steen? try her Adam")—Adam having already started to wrestle with Frank on some impetus from some talk about holds, now Adam had her pinned in the coitus position on the floor (which in itself didn't hurt me)—it was her beautifulness, her game guts wrestling, I felt proud, I wanted to know how Carmody felt NOW (feeling he must have been at the outset critical of her for being a Negro, he being a Texan and a Texas gentleman-type at that) to see her be so great, buddy like, joining in, humble and meek too and a real woman. Even somehow the presence of Yuri, whose personality was energized already in my mind from the energy of the dream, added to my love of Mardou—I suddenly loved her.—They wanted me to go with them, sit in the park—as agreed in solemn sober conclaves Mardou said "But I'll stay here and read and do things, Leo, you go with them like we said"—as they left and trooped down the stairs I stayed behind to tell her I loved her now—she was not as surprised, or pleased, as I wished—she had looked at Yuri now already with the point of view eyes not only of my dream but had seen him in a new light as a possible successor to me because of my continual betrayal and getting drunk.

Yuri Gligoric: a young poet, 22, had just come down from apple-picking Oregon, before that a waiter in a big dude ranch dininghall—tall thin blond Yugoslavian, good-looking, very brash and above all trying to cut Adam and myself and Carmody, all the time knowing us as an old revered trinity, wanting, naturally, as a young unpublished unknown but very genius poet to destroy the big established gods and raise himself—wanting therefore their women too, being uninhibited, or unsaddened, yet, at least.—I liked him, considered him another new "young brother" (as Leroy and Adam before, whom I'd "shown" writing tricks) and now I would show Yuri and he would be a buddy with me and walk around with me and Mardou—his own lover, June, had left him, he'd treated her badly, he wanted her back, she was with another life in Compton, I sympathized with him and asked about the progress of his letters and phonecalls to Compton, and, most important, as I say, he was now for the first time suddenly looking at me and saying "Percepied I want to talk to you—suddenly I want to really know you."—In a joke at the Sunday wine in Dante's I'd said "Frank's leching after Adam. Adam's leching after Yuri" and Yuri'd thrown in "And I'm leching after you."

Indeed he was indeed. On this mournful Sunday of my first pained love of Mardou after sitting in the park with the boys as agreed, I dragged myself again home, to work, to Sunday dinner, guiltily, arriving late, finding my mother glum and all-weekend-alone in a chair with her shawl . . . and my thoughts rich on Mardou now—not thinking it of any importance whatever that I had told young Yuri not only "I dreamed you were necking with Mardou" but also, at a soda fountain en route to the park when Adam wanted to call Sam and we all sat at counter waiting, with limeades, "Since I saw you last I've fallen in love with that girl," information which he received without comment and which I hope he still remembers, and of course does.

And so now brooding over her, valuing the precious good moments we'd had that heretofore I'd avoided thinking of, came the fact, ballooning in importance, the amazing fact she is the only girl I've ever known who could really understand bop and sing it, she'd said that first cuddly day of the redbulb at Adam's "While I was flipping I heard bop, on juke boxes and in the Red Drum and wherever I was happening to hear it, with an entirely new and different sense, which tho, I really can't describe."—"But what was it like?"—"But I can't describe it, it not only sent waves—went through me—I can't, like, *make* it, in telling it in words, you know? OO dee bee dee dee" singing a few notes, so cutely.—The night we walked swiftly down Larkin past the Blackhawk with Adam actually but he was following and listening, close head to head, singing wild choruses of jazz and bop, at times I'd phrase and she did perfect in fact interesting modern and advanced chords (like I'd never heard anywhere and which bore resemblance to Bartok modern chords but were hep wise to bop) and at other times she just did her chords as I did the bass fiddle, in the old great legend (again of the roaring high davenport amazing smash-afternoon which I expect no one to understand) before, I'd with Ossip Popper sung bop, made records, always taking the part of the bass fiddle thum thum to his phrasing (so much I see now like Billy Eckstine's bop phrasing)—the two of us arm in arm rushing longstrides down Market the hip old apple of the California Apple singing bop and well too—the glee of it, and coming after an awful party at Roger Walker's where (Adam's arrangement and my acquiescence) instead of a regular party were just boys and all queer including one Mexican younghustler and Mardou far from being nonplused enjoyed herself and talked—nevertheless of it all, rushing home to the Third Street bus singing gleeful—

The time we read Faulkner together, I read her *Spotted Horses*, out loud—when Mike Murphy came in she told him to sit and listen as I'd go on but then I was different and I couldn't read the same and stopped—but next day in her gloomy solitude Mardou sat down and read the entire Faulkner portable.

The time we went to a French movie on Larkin, the Vogue, saw *The Lower Depths*, held hands, smoked, felt close—tho out on Market Street she would not have me hold her arm for fear people of the street there would think her a hustler, which it would look like but I felt mad but let it go and we walked along, I wanted to go into a bar for a wine, she was afraid of all the behatted men ranged at the bar, now I saw her Negro fear of American society she was always talking about but palpably in the streets which never gave me any concern—tried to console her, show her she could do anything with me, "In fact baby I'll be a famous man and you'll be the dignified wife of a famous man so don't worry" but she said "You don't understand" but her little girl-like fear so cute, so edible, I let it go, we went home, to tender love scenes together in our own and secret dark—

Fact, the time, one of those fine times when we, or that is, I didn't drink and we spent the whole night together in bed, this time telling ghost stories, the tales of Poe I could remember, then we made some up, and finally we were making madhouse eyes at each other and trying to frighten with round stares, she showed me how one of her Market Street reveries had been that she was a catatonic ("Tho then I didn't know what the word meant, but like, I walked stiffly hang arming arms hanging and man not a soul dared to speak to me and some were afraid to look, there I was walking along zombie-like and just thirteen.") (Oh gleeful shnuff-fleeflue in fluffle in her little lips, I see the outthrust teeth, I say sternly, "Mardou you must get your teeth cleaned at once, at that hospital there, the therapist, get a dentist too—it's all free so do it—" because I see beginnings of bad congestion at the corners of her pearlies which would lead to decay)—and she makes the madwoman face at me, the face rigid, the eyes shining shining shining like the stars of heaven and far from being frightened I am utterly amazed at the beauty of her and I say "And I also see the earth in your eyes that's what I think of you, you have a certain kind of beauty, not that I'm hung-up on the earth and Indians and all that and wanta harp all the time about you and us, but I see in your eyes such warm—but when you make the madwoman I don't see madness but glee glee—it's like the ragamuffin dusts in the little kid's corner and he's asleep in his crib now and I love you, rain'll fall on our eaves some day sweetheart"—and we have just candlelight so the mad acts are funnier and the ghost stories more chilling—the one about the—but a lack, a lark, I go larking in the good things and don't and do forget my pain—

Extending the eye business, the time we closed our eyes (again not drinking because of broke, poverty would have saved this romance) and I sent her messages, "Are you ready," and I see the first thing in my black eye world and ask her to describe it, amazing how we came to the same thing, it was some rapport, I saw crystal chandeliers and she saw white petals in a black bog just after some melding of images as amazing as the accurate images I'd exchange with Carmody in Mexico—Mardou and I both seeing the same thing, some madness shape, some fountain, now by me forgotten and really not important yet, come together in mutual descriptions of it and joy and glee in this telepathic triumph of ours, ending where our thoughts meet at the crystal white and petals, the mystery—I see the gleeful hunger of her face devouring the sight of mine, I could die, don't break my heart radio with beautiful music, O world—the candlelight again, flickering, I'd bought a slue of candles in the store, the corners of our room in darkness, her shadow naked brown as she hurries to the sink—our use of the sink—my fear of communicating WHITE images to her in our telepathies for fear she'll be (in her fun) reminded of our racial difference, at that time making me feel guilty, now I realize it was one love's gentility on my part—Lord.

The good ones—going up on the top of Nob Hill at night with a fifth of Royal Chalice Tokay, sweet, rich, potent, the lights of the city and of the bay beneath us, the sad mystery—sitting on a bench there, lovers, loners pass, we pass the bottle, talk—she tells all her little girlhood in Oakland.—It's like Paris—it's soft, the breeze blows, the city may swelter but the hillers do fly—and over the bay is Oakland (ah me Hart Crane Melville and all ye assorted brother poets of the American night that once I thought would be my sacrificial altar and now it is but who's to care, know, and I lost love because of it—drunkard, dullard, poet)—returning via Van Ness to Aquatic Park beach, sitting in the sand, as I pass Mexicans I feel that great hepness I'd been having all summer on the street with Mardou my old dream of wanting to be vital, alive like a Negro or an Indian or a Denver Jap or a New York Puerto Rican come true, with her by my side so young, sexy, slender, strange, hip, myself in jeans and casual and both of us as if young (I say as if, to my 31)—the cops telling us to leave the beach, a lonely Negro passing us twice and staring—we walk along the waterslap, she laughs to see the crazy figures of reflected light of the moon dancing so bug-like in the ululating cool smooth water of the night—we smell harbors, we dance—

The time I walked her in broad sweet dry Mexico plateau-like or Arizona-like morning to her appointment with thera-pist at the hospital, along the Embarcadero, denying the bus, hand in hand—I proud, thinking, "In Mexico she'll look just like this and not a soul'll know I'm not an Indian by God and we'll go along"—and I point out the purity and clarity of the clouds, "Just like Mexico honey, O you'll love it" and we go up the busy street to the big grimbrick hospital and I'm sup-posed to be going home from there but she lingers, sad smile, love smile, when I give in and agree to wait for her 20-minute interview and her coming out she radiantly breaks out glad and rushes to the gate which we've already passed in her

almost therapy-giving-up strolling-with-me meandering, men
—love—not for sale—my prize—possession—nobody gets it
but gets a Sicilian line down his middle—a German boot in the
kisser, an axe Canuck—I'll pin them wriggling poets to some
London wall right here, explained.—And as I wait for her to
come out, I sit on side of water, in Mexico-like gravel and grass
and concrete blocks and take out sketchbooks and draw big
word pictures of the skyline and of the bay, putting in a little
mention of the great fact of the huge all-world with its infinite
levels, from Standard Oil top down to waterslap at barges
where old bargemen dream, the difference between men, the
difference so vast between concerns of executives in skyscrapers
and seadogs on harbor and psychoanalysts in stuffy offices in
great grim buildings full of dead bodies in the morgue below
and madwomen at windows, hoping thereby to instill in Mardou recognition of fact it's a big world and psychoanalysis is a
small way to explain it since it only scratches the surface, which
is, analysis, cause and effect, why instead of what—when she
comes out I read it to her, not impressing her too much but
she loves me, holds my hand as we cut down along Embarcadero towards her place and when I leave her at Third and
Townsend train in warm clear afternoon she says "O I hate to
see you go, I really miss you now."—"But I gotta be home in
time to make the supper—and write— so honey I'll be back,
tomorrow remember promptly at ten."—And tomorrow I arrive at midnight instead.

The time we had a shuddering come together and she said
"I was lost suddenly" and she was lost with me tho not coming
herself but frantic in my franticness (Reich's beclouding of the
senses) and how she loved it—all our teachings in bed, I explain
me to her, she explains her to me, we work, we wail, we bop—
we throw clothes off and jump at each other (after always her
little trip to the diaphragm sink and I have to wait holding softer
and making goofy remarks and she laughs and trickles water)
then here she comes padding to me across the Garden of
Eden, and I reach up and help her down to my side on the soft
bed, I pull her little body to me and it is warm, her warm spot
is hot, I kiss her brown breasts both of them, I kiss her love-
shoulders—she keeps with her lips going "ps ps ps" little kiss
sounds where actually no contact is made with my face except

when haphazardly while doing something else I do move it against her and her little ps ps kisses connect and are as sad and soft as when they don't—it's her little litany of night—and when she's sick and we're worried, then she takes me on her, on her arm, on mine—she services the mad unthinking beast —I spend long nights and many hours making her, finally I have her, I pray for it to come, I can hear her breathing harder, I hope against hope it's time, a noise in the hall (or whoop of drunkards next door) takes her mind off and she can't make it and laughs—but when she does make it I hear her crying, whimpering, the shuddering electrical female orgasm makes her sound like a little girl crying, moaning in the night, it lasts a good twenty seconds and when it's over she moans, "O why can't it last longer," and, "O when will I when you do?"— "Soon now I bet," I say, "you're getting closer and closer"— sweating against her in the warm sad Frisco with its damn old scows mooing on the tide out there, voom, voooom, and stars flickering on the water even where it waves beneath the pier-head where you expect gangsters dropping encemented bodies, or rats, or The Shadow—my little Mardou whom I love, who'd never read my unpublished works but only the first novel, which has guts but has a dreary prose to it when all's said and done and so now holding her and spent with sex I dream of the day she'll read great works by me and admire me, remembering the time Adam had said in sudden strangeness in his kitchen, "Mardou, what do you really think of Leo and myself as writers, our positions in the world, the rack of time," asking her that, knowing that her thinking is in accord in some ways more or less with the subterraneans whom he admires and fears, whose opinions he values with wonder—Mardou not really replying but evading the issue, but old man me plots greatbooks for her amaze—all those good things, good times we had, others I am now in the heat of my frenzy forgetting but I must tell all, but angels know all and record it in books—

But think of all the bad times—I have a list of bad times to make the good times, the times I was good to her and like I should be, to make it sick—when early in our love I was three hours late which is a lot of hours of lateness for younglovers, and so she wigged, got frightened, walked around the church handsapockets brooding looking for me in the mist of dawn and I ran out (seeing her note saying "I am gone out to look for you") (in all Frisco yet! that east and west, north and south of soulless loveless bleak she'd seen from the fence, all the countless men in hats going into buses and not caring about the naked girl on the fence, why)—when I saw her, I myself running out to find her, I opened my arms a halfmile away—

The worst almost worst time of all when a red flame crossed my brain, I was sitting with her and Larry O'Hara in his pad, we'd been drinking French Bordeaux and blasting, a subject was up, I had a hand on Larry's knee shouting "But listen to me, but listen to me!" wanting to make my point so bad there was a big crazy plead in the tone and Larry deeply engrossed in what Mardou is saying simultaneously and feeding a few words to her dialog, in the emptiness after the red flame I suddenly leap up and rush to the door and tug at it, ugh, locked, the in-door chain lock, I slide and undo it and with another try I lunge out in the hall and down the stairs as fast as my thieves' quick crepesoul shoes'll take me, putt pitterpit, floor after floor reeling around me as I round the stairwell, leaving them agape up there—calling back in half hour, meeting her on the street three blocks away—there is no hope—

The time even when we'd agreed she needed money for food, that I'd go home and get it and just bring it back and stay a short while, but I'm at this time far from in love, but bugged, not only her pitiful demands for money but that doubt, that old Mardou-doubt, and so rush into her pad, Alice her friend is there, I use that as an excuse (because Alice dike-like silent unpleasant and strange and likes no one) to lay the two bills on Mardou's dishes at sink, kiss a quick peck in the malt of her ear, say "I'll be back tomorrow" and run right out again without even asking her opinion—as if the whore'd made me for two bucks and I was sore.

How clear the realization one is going mad—the mind has a silence, nothing happens in the physique, urine gathers in your loins, your ribs contract.

Bad time she asked me, "What does Adam really think of me, you never told me, I know he resents us together but—" and I told her substantially what Adam had told me, of which none should have been divulged to her for the sake of her peace of mind, "He said it was just a social question of his not now wanting to get hung-up with you lovewise because you're Negro"—feeling again her telepathic little shock cross the room to me, it sunk deep, I question my motives for telling her this.

The time her cheerful little neighbor young writer John Golz came up (he dutifully eight hours a day types working on magazine stories, admirer of Hemingway, often feeds Mardou and is a nice Indiana boy and means no harm and certainly not a slinky snaky interesting subterranean but openfaced, jovial, plays with children in the court for God's sake)—came up to see Mardou, I was there alone (for some reason, Mardou at a bar with our accord arrangement, the night she went out with a Negro boy she didn't like too much but just for fun and told Adam she was doing it because she wanted to make it with a Negro boy again, which made me jealous, but Adam said "If I should if she should hear that you went out with a white girl to see if you could make it again she'd sure be flattered, Leo")—that night, I was at her place waiting, reading, young John Golz came in to borrow cigarettes and seeing I was alone wanted to talk literature—"Well I believe that the most important thing is selectivity," and I blew up and said "Ah don't give me all that high school stuff I've heard it and heard it long before you were born almost for krissakes and really now, say something interesting and new about writing"—putting him down, sullen, for reasons mainly of irritation and because he seemed harmless and therefore could be counted on to be safe to yell at, which he was—putting him down, her friend, was not nice—no, the world's no fit place for this kind of activity, and what we gonna do, and where? when? wha wha wha, the baby bawls in the midnight boom.

Nor could it have been charming and helpful to her fears and anxieties to have me start out, at the outset of our romance, "kissing her down between the stems"—starting and then suddenly quitting so later in an unguarded drinking-moment she said, "You suddenly stopped as tho I was—" and the reason I stopped being in itself not as significant as the reason I did it at all, to secure her greater sexual interest, which once tied on with a bow knot, I could dally out of—the warm lovemouth of the woman, the womb, being the place for men

who love, not . . . this immature drunkard and egomaniacal
. . . this . . . knowing as I do from past experience and interior sense, you've got to fall down on your knees and beg the
woman's permission, beg the woman's forgiveness for all your
sins, protect her, support her, doing everything for her, die for
her but for God's sake love her and love her all the way in and
every way you can—yes psychoanalysis, I hear (fearing secretly
the few times I had come into contact with the rough stubble-
like quality of the pubic, which was Negroid and therefore a
little rougher, tho not enough to make any difference, and the
insides itself I should say the best, the richest, most fecund
moist warm and full of hidden soft slidy mountains, also the pull
and force of the muscles being so powerful she unknowing
often vice-like closes over and makes a dam-up and hurt, tho
this I only realized the other night, too late—). And so the final lingering physiological doubt I have that this contraction
and greatstrength of womb, responsible I think now in retro-
spect for the time when Adam in his first encounter with her
experienced piercing unsupportable screamingsudden pain, so
he had to go to the doctor and have himself bandaged and all
(and even later when Carmody arrived and made a local orgone accumulator out of a big old watercan and burlap and
vegetative materials placing the nozzle of himself into the nozzle of the can to heal), I now wonder and suspect if our little
chick didn't really intend to bust us in half, if Adam isn't
thinking it's his own fault and doesn't know, but she contracted mightily there (the lesbian!) (always knew it) and
busted him and fixed him and couldn't do it to me but tried
enough till she threw me over a dead hulk that now I am—
psychoanalyst, I'm serious!

It's too much. Beginning, as I say with the pushcart incident
—the night we drank red wine at Dante's and were in a drinking
mood now both of us so disgusted—Yuri came with us, Ross
Wallenstein was in there and maybe to show off to Mardou
Yuri acted like a kid all night and kept hitting Wallenstein on
the back of his head with little finger taps like goofing in a bar
but Wallenstein (who's always being beaten up by hoodlums
because of this) turned around a stiff death's-head gaze with
big eyes glaring behind glasses, his Christlike blue unshaven

cheeks, staring rigidly as tho the stare itself will floor Yuri, not
speaking for a long time, finally saying, "Man, don't bug me,"
and turning back to his conversation with friends and Yuri
does it again and Ross turns again the same pitiless awful subterranean sort of nonviolent Indian Mahatma Gandhi defense
of some kind (which I'd suspected that first time he talked to
me saying, "Are you a fag you talk like a fag" a remark coming
from him so absurd because so inflammable and me 170
pounds to his 130 or 120 for God's sake so I thought secretly
"No you can't fight this man he will only scream and yell and
call cops and let you hit him again and haunt all your dreams,
there is no way to put a subterranean down on the floor or for
that matter put em down at all, they are the most unputdown-
able in this world and new culture")—finally Wallenstein
going to the head for a leak and Yuri says to me, Mardou being
at the bar gathering three more wines, "Come on let's go in
the john and bust him up," and I get up to go with Yuri but
not to bust up Ross rather to stop anything might happen
there—Yuri having been in his own in fact realer way than
mine almost a hoodlum, imprisoned in Soledad for defending
himself in some vicious fight in reform school—Mardou stopping us both as we head to the head, saying, "My God if I
hadn't stopped you" (laughing embarrassed little Mardou
smile and shniffle) "you'd actually have gone in there"—a former love of Ross's and now the bottomless toilet of Ross's position in her affections I think probably equal to mine now, O
damblast the thorny flaps of the pap time page—

Going thence to the Mask as usual, beers, get worse drunk,
then out to walk home, Yuri having just arrived from Oregon
having no place to sleep is asking if it's allright to sleep at our
place, I let Mardou speak for her own house, tho feebly say
some "okay" in the middle of the confusion, and Yuri comes
heading homeward with us—en route finds a pushcart, says
"Get in, I'll be a taxicab and push you both home up the
hill."—Okay we get in, and lie on our backs drunk as only you
can get drunk on red wine, and he pushes us from the Beach at
that fateful park (where we'd sat that first sad Sunday
afternoon of my dream and premonitions) and we ride along
in the pushcart of eternity, Angel Yuri pushing it, I can only
see stars and occasional rooftops of blocks—no thought in any

mind (except briefly in mine, possibly in others) of the sin, the
loss entailed for the poor Italian beggar losing his cart there—
on down Broadway clear to Mardou's, in the pushcart, at one
point I push and they ride, Mardou and I singing bop and also
bop to the tune *Are the Stars Out Tonight* and just drunk—
parking it foolishly in front of Adam's and rushing up, making
noise.—Next day, after sleeping on floor with Yuri snoring on
the couch, waiting up for Adam as if beaming to hear told
about our exploit, Adam comes home blackfaced mad from
work and says "Really you have no idea the pain you're causin'
some poor old Armenian peddler you never think that—but
jeopardizing my pad with that thing in front, supposing the
cops find it, and what's the matter with you." And Carmody
saying to me "Leo I think you perpetrated this masterpiece"
or "You masterminded this brilliant move" or such which I
really didn't—and all day we've been cutting up and down
stairs looking at pushcart which far from being cop-discovered
still sits there but with Adam's landlord teetering in front of it,
waiting to see who's going to claim it, sensing something fishy,
and of all things Mardou's poor purse still in it where drunkenly we'd left it and the landlord finally confiscating IT and
waiting for further development (she lost a few dollars and her
only purse).—"Only thing that can happen, Adam, is the cops'll
find the pushcart, they can very well see the purse, the address,
and take it to Mardou's but all she has to say is 'O I found my
purse,' and that's that, and nothing'll happen." But Adam
cries, "O you even if nothing'll happen you screw up the security of my pad, come in making noise, leave a licensed vehicle
out front, and tell me nothing'll happen."—And I had sensed
he'd be mad and am prepared and say, "To hell with that, you
can give hell to these but you won't give hell to me, I won't
take it from you—that was just a drunken prank," I add, and
Adam says, "This is my house and I can get mad when it's—"
so I up and throw his keys (the keys he'd had made for me to
walk in and out any time) at him but they're entwined with the
chain of my mother's keys and for a moment we fumble seriously at the mixed keys on the floor disengaging them and he
gets his and I say "No that, that's mine, there," and he puts it
in his pocket and there we are.—I want to rush up and leave,
like at Larry's.—Mardou is there seeing me flip again—far

from helping her from flips. (Once she'd asked me "If I ever flip what will you do, will you help me?—Supposing I think you're trying to harm me?"—"Honey," I said, "I'll try in fact I'll reassure you I'm not harming you and you'd come to your senses, I'll protect you," the confidence of the old man—but in reality himself flipping more often.)—I feel great waves of dark hostility, I mean hate, malice, destructiveness flowing out of Adam in his corner chair, I can hardly sit under the withering telepathic blast and there's all that *yage* of Carmody's around the pad, in suitcases, it's too much—(it's a comedy tho, we agree it will be a comedy later)—we talk of other things —Adam suddenly flips the key back at me, it lands in my thighs, and instead of dangling it in my finger (as if considering, as if a wily Canuck calculating advantages) I boy-like jump up and throw the key back in my pocket with a little giggle, to make Adam feel better, also to impress Mardou with my "fairness"— but she never noticed, was watching something else—so now that peace is restored I say "And in any case it was Yuri's fault it isn't at all as Frank says my unqualified masterminding"— (this pushcart, this darkness, the same as when Adam in the prophetic dream descended the wood steps to see the "Russian Patriarch", there were pushcarts there)—So in the letter that I write to Mardou answering her beauty which I have paraphrased, I make stupid angry but "pretending to be fair," "to be calm, deep, poetic" statements, like, "Yes, I got mad and threw Adam's keys back at him, because 'friendship, admiration, poetry sleep in the respectful mystery' and the invisible world is too beatific to have to be dragged before the court of social realities," or some such twaddle that Mardou must have glanced at with one eye—the letter, which was supposed to match the warmth of hers, her cuddly-in-October masterpiece, beginning with the inane-if-at-all confession: "The last time I wrote a love note it turned out to be boloney" (referring to an earlier in the year half-romance with Arlene Wohlstetter) "and I am glad you are honest," or "have honest eyes," the next sentence said—the letter intended to arrive Saturday morning to make her feel my warm presence while I was out taking my hardworking and deserving mother to her bi-six-monthlial show and shopping on Market Street (old Canuck working-woman completely ignorant of arrangement of mingled streets of San Francisco) but arriving long after I saw her and read while I was there, and dull—this not a literary complaint, but something that must have pained Mardou, the lack of reciprocity and the stupidity regarding my attack at Adam—"Man, you had no right to yell at him, really, it's his pad, his right"—but the letter a big defense of this "right to yell at Adam" and not at all response to her love notes—

The pushcart incident not important in itself, but what I saw, what my quick eye and hungry paranoia ate—a gesture of Mardou's that made my heart sink even as I doubted maybe I wasn't seeing, interpreting right, as so oft I do.—We'd come in and run upstairs and jumped on the big double bed waking Adam up and yelling and tousling and Carmody too sitting on the edge as if to say "Now children now children," just a lot of drunken lushes—at one time in the play back and forth between the rooms Mardou and Yuri ended on the couch together in front, where I think all three of us had flopped—but I ran to the bedroom for further business, talking, coming back I saw Yuri who knew I was coming flop off the couch onto the floor and as he did so Mardou (who probably didn't know I was coming) shot out her hand at him as if to say OH YOU RASCAL as if almost he'd before rolling off the couch goosed her or done something playful—I saw for the first time their youthful playfulness which I in my scowlingness and writer-ness had not participated in and my old man-ness about which I kept telling myself "You're old you old sonofabitch you're lucky to have such a young sweet thing" (while nevertheless at the same time plotting, as I'd been doing for about three weeks now, to get rid of Mardou, without her being hurt, even if possible "without her noticing" so as to get back to more comfortable modes of life, like say, stay at home all week and write and work on the three novels to make a lot of money and come in to town only for good times if not to see Mardou then any other chick will do, this was my three week thought and really the energy behind or the surface one behind the creation of the Jealousy Phantasy in the Gray Guilt dream of the World Around Our Bed)—now I saw Mardou pushing Yuri with a O H Y O U and I shuddered to think something maybe was going on behind my back—felt warned too by the quick and immediate manner Yuri heard me

coming and rolled off but as if guiltily as I say after some kind
of goose or feel up some illegal touch of Mardou which made
her purse little love loff lips at him and push at him and like
kids.—Mardou was just like a kid I remember the first night I
met her when Julien, rolling joints on the floor, she behind
him hunched, I'd explained to them why that week I wasn't
drinking at all (true at the time, and due to events on the ship
in New York, scaring me, saying to myself "If you keep on
drinking like that you'll die you can't even hold a simple job
any more," so returning to Frisco and not drinking at all and
everybody exclaiming "O you look wonderful"), telling that
first night almost heads together with Mardou and Julien, they
so kidlike in their naive WHY when I told them I wasn't drinking any more, so kidlike listening to my explanation about the
one can of beer leading to the second, the sudden gut explo-
sions and glitters, the third can, the fourth, "And then I go off
and drink for days and I'm gone man, like, I'm afraid I'm an
alcoholic" and they kidlike and othergenerationey making no
comment, but awed, curious—in the same rapport with young
Yuri here (her age) pushing at him, Oh You, which in drunkenness I paid not too much attention to, and we slept, Mardou
and I on the floor, Yuri on the couch (so kidlike, indulgent,
funny of him, all that)—this first exposure of the realization of
the mysteries of the guilt jealousy dream leading, from the
pushcart time, to the night we went to Bromberg's, most awful of all.

Beginning as usual in the Mask.

Nights that begin so glitter clear with hope, let's go see our
friends, things, phones ring, people come and go, coats, hats,
statements, bright reports, metropolitan excitements, a round
of beers, another round of beers, the talk gets more beautiful,
more excited, flushed, another round, the midnight hour,
later, the flushed happy faces are now wild and soon there's the
swaying buddy da day oobab bab smash smoke drunken latenight goof leading finally to the bartender, like a seer in Eliot,
TIME TO CLOSE UP—in this manner more or less arriving
at the Mask where a kid called Harold Sand came in, a chance
acquaintance of Mardou's from a year ago, a young novelist
looking like Leslie Howard who'd just had a manuscript accepted and so acquired a strange grace in my eyes I wanted to

devour—interested in him for same reasons as Lavalina, literary avidity, envy—as usual paying less attention therefore to
Mardou (at table) than Yuri whose continual presence with us
now did not raise my suspicions, whose complaints "I don't
have a place to stay—do you realize Percepied what it is not to
even have a place to write? I have not girls, nothing, Carmody
and Moorad won't let me stay up there any more, they're a
couple of old sisters," not sinking in, and already the only
comment I'd made to Mardou about Yuri had been, after his
leaving, "He's just like that Mexican stud comes up here and
grabs up your last cigarettes," both of us laughing because
whenever she was at her lowest financial ebb, bang, somebody
who needed a "mooch" was there—not that I would call Yuri
a mooch in the least (I'll tread lightly on him on this point, for
obvious reasons).—(Yuri and I'd had a long talk that week in a
bar, over port wines, he claimed everything was poetry, I tried
to make the common old distinction between verse and prose,
he said, "Lissen Percepied do you believe in freedom?—then
say what you want, it's poetry, poetry, all of it is poetry, great
prose is poetry, great verse is poetry."—"Yes" I said "but verse
is verse and prose is prose."—"No no" he yelled "it's all
poetry."—"Okay," I said, "I believe in you believing in freedom and maybe you're right, have another wine." And he read
me his "best line" which was something to do with "seldom
nocturne" that I said sounded like small magazine poetry and
wasn't his best—as already I'd seen some much better poetry
by him concerning his tough boyhood, about cats, mothers in
gutters, Jesus striding in the ashcan, appearing incarnate shining on the blowers of slum tenements or that is making great
steps across the light—the sum of it something he could do,
and did, well—"No, seldom nocturne isn't your meat" but he
claimed it was great, "I would say rather it was great if you'd
written it suddenly on the spur of the moment."—"But I
did—right out of my mind it flowed and I threw it down, it
sounds like it's been planned but it wasn't, it was bang! just
like you say, spontaneous vision!"—Which I now doubt tho
his saying "seldom nocturne" came to him spontaneously made
me suddenly respect it more, some falsehood hiding beneath
our wine yells in a saloon on Kearney.) Yuri hanging out with
Mardou and me every night almost—like a shadow—and

knowing Sand himself from before, so he, Sand, walking into the Mask, flushed successful young author but "ironic" looking and with a big parkingticket sticking out of his coat lapel, was set upon by the three of us with avidity, made to sit at our table—made to talk.—Around the corner from Mask to 13 Pater thence the lot of us going, and en route (reminiscent now more strongly and now with hints of pain of the pushcart night and Mardou's OH YOU) Yuri and Mardou start racing, pushing, shoving, wrestling on the sidewalk and finally she lofts a big empty cardboard box and throws it at him and he throws it back, they're like kids again—I walk on ahead in serious tone conversation with Sand tho—he too has eyes for Mardou—somehow I'm not able (at least haven't tried) to communicate to him that she is my love and I would prefer if he didn't have eyes for her so obviously, just as Jimmy Lowell, a colored seaman who'd suddenly phoned in the midst of an Adam party, and came, with a Scandinavian shipmate, looking at Mardou and me wondering, asking me "Do you make it with her sex?" and I saying yes and the night after the Red Drum session where Art Blakey was whaling like mad and Thelonious Monk sweating leading the generation with his elbow chords, eying the band madly to lead them on, *the monk and saint of bop* I kept telling Yuri, smooth sharp hep Jimmy Lowell leans to me and says "I would like to make it with your chick," (like in the old days Leroy and I always swapping so I'm not shocked), "would it be okay if I asked her?" and I saying "She's not that kind of girl, I'm sure she believes in one at a time, if you ask her that's what she'll tell you man" (at that time still feeling no pain or jealousy, this incidentally the night before the Jealousy Dream)—not able to communicate to Lowell that's—that I wanted her—to stay—to be stammer stammer be mine—not being able to come right out and say, "Lissen this is my girl, what are you talking about, if you want to try to make her you'll have to tangle with me, you understand that pops as well as I do."—In that way with a stud, in another way with polite dignified Sand a very interesting young fellow, like, "Sand, Mardou is my girl and I would prefer, etc."—but he has eyes for her and the reason he stays with us and goes around the corner to 13 Pater, but it's Yuri starts wrestling with her and goofing in the streets—so when we leave 13 Pater later on (a dike bar slummish now and nothing to it, where a year ago there were angels in red shirts straight out of Genet and Djuna Barnes) I get in the front seat of Sand's old car, he's going at least to drive us home, I sit next to him at the clutch in front for purposes of talking better and in drunkenness again avoiding Mardou's womanness, leaving room for her to sit beside me at front window—instead of which, no sooner plops her ass behind me, jumps over seat and dives into backseat with Yuri who is alone back there, to wrestle again and goof with him and now with such intensity I'm afraid to look back and see with my own eyes what's happening and how the dream (the dream I announced to everyone and made big issues of and told even Yuri about) is coming true.

We pull up at Mardou's door at Heavenly Lane and drunkly now she says (Sand and I having decided drunkenly to drive down to Los Altos the lot of us and crash in on old Austin Bromberg and have big further parties) "If you're going down to Bromberg's in Los Altos you two go out, Yuri and I'll stay here"—my heart sank deep—it sank so I gloated to hear it for the first time and the confirmation of it crowned me and blessed me.

And I thought, "Well boy here's your chance to get rid of her" (which I'd plotted for three weeks now) but the sound of this in my own ears sounded awfully false, I didn't believe it, myself, any more.

But on the sidewalk going in flushed Yuri takes my arm as Mardou and Sand go on ahead up the fish head stairs, "Lissen, Leo I don't want to make Mardou at all, she's all over me, I want you to know that I don't want to make her, all I want to do if you're going out there is go to sleep in your bed because I have an appointment tomorrow."—But now I myself feel reluctant to stay in Heavenly Lane for the night because Yuri will be there, in fact now is already on the bed tacitly as if, one would have to say, "Get off the bed so we can get in, go to that uncomfortable chair for the night."—So this more than anything else (in my tiredness and growing wisdom and patience) makes me agree with Sand (also reluctant) that we might as well drive down to Los Altos and wake up good old Bromberg, and I turn to Mardou with eyes saying or suggesting, "You can stay with Yuri you bitch" but she's already got her little traveling basket or weekend bag and is putting my toothbrush hairbrush and her things in and the idea is we three drive out—which we do, leaving Yuri in the bed.—En route, at near Bayshore in the great highway roadlamp night, which is now nothing but a bleakness for me and the prospect of the "weekend" at Bromberg's a horror of shame, I can't stand it any more and look at Mardou as soon as Sand gets out to buy hamburgs in the diner, "You jumped in the backseat with Yuri why'd you do that? and why'd you say you wanted to stay with him?"—"It was silly of me, I was just high baby." But I don't darkly any more now want to believe her—art is short, life is long—now I've got in full dragon bloom the monster of jealousy as green as in any cliché cartoon rising in my being, "You and Yuri play together all the time, it's just like the dream I told you about, that's what's horrible—O I'll never believe in dreams come true again."—"But baby it isn't anything like that" but I don't believe her—I can tell by looking at her she's got eyes for the youth—you can't fool an old hand who at the age of sixteen before even the juice was wiped off his heart by the Great Imperial World Wiper with Sadcloth fell in love with an impossible flirt and cheater, this is a boast—I feel so sick I can't stand it, curl up in the back seat, alone—they drive on, and Sand having anticipated a gay talkative weekend now finds himself with a couple of grim lover worriers, hears in fact the fragment "But I didn't mean you to think that baby" so obviously harkening to his mind the Yuri incident—finds himself with this pair of bores and has to drive all the way down to Los Altos, and so with the same grit that made him write the half million words of his novel bends to it and pushes the car through the Peninsula night and on into the dawn.

Arriving at Bromberg's house in Los Altos at gray dawn, parking, and ringing the doorbell the three of us sheepishly I most sheepish of all—and Bromberg comes right down, at once, with great roars of approval cries "Leo I didn't know you knew each other" (meaning Sand, whom Bromberg admired very much) and in we go to rum and coffee in the crazy famous Bromberg kitchen.—You might say, Bromberg the most amazing guy in the world with small dark curly hair like the hip girl Roxanne making little garter snakes over his brow and his great really angelic eyes shining, rolling, a big burbling baby, a great genius of talk really, wrote research and essays and has (and is famous for) the greatest possible private library in the world, right there in that house, library due to his erudition and this no reflection also on his big income—the house inherited from father—was also the sudden new bosom friend of Carmody and about to go to Peru with him, they'd go dig Indian boys and talk about it and discuss art and visit literaries and things of that nature, all matters so much had been dinning in Mardou's ear (queer, cultured matters) in her love affair with me that by now she was quite tired of cultured tones and fancy explicity, emphatic daintiness of expression, of which roll-eyed ecstatic almost spastic big Bromberg almost the pastmaster, "O my dear it's such a charming thing and I think much MUCH better than the Gascoyne translation tho I do believe—" and Sand imitating him to a T, from some recent great meeting and mutual admiration—so the two of them there in the once-to-me adventurous gray dawn of the Metropolitan Great-Rome Frisco talking of literary and musical and artistic matters, the kitchen littered, Bromberg rushing up (in pajamas) to fetch three-inch thick French editions of Genet or old editions of Chaucer or whatever he and Sand'd come to, Mardou darklashed and still thinking of Yuri (as I'm thinking to myself) sitting at the corner of the kitchen table, with her getting-cold rum and coffee—O I on a stool, hurt, broken, injured, about to get worse, drinking cup after cup and loading up on the great heavy brew—the birds beginning to sing finally at about eight and Bromberg's great voice, one of the mightiest you can hear, making the walls of the kitchen throw back great shudders of deep ecstatic sound—turning on the phonograph, an expensive well-furnished completely appointed house, with French wine, refrigerators, three-speed machines with speakers, cellar, etc.—I want to look at Mardou I don't know with what expression—I am afraid in fact to look only to find there the supplication in her eyes saying "Don't worry baby, I told you, I confessed to you I was silly, I'm sorry sorry sorry—" that "I'm-sorry" look hurting me the most as I glance side eyes to see it. . . .

It won't do when the very bluebirds are bleak, which I mention to Bromberg, he asking, "Whatsamatter with you this morning Leo?" (with burbling peek under eyebrows to see me better and make me laugh).—"Nothing, Austin, just that when I look out the window this morning the birds are bleak."— (And earlier when Mardou went upstairs to toilet I did mention, bearded, gaunt, foolish drunkard, to these erudite gentlemen, something about 'inconstancy,' which must have surprised them tho)—O inconstancy!

So they try anyway to make the best of it in spite of my palpable unhappy brooding all over the place, while listening to Verdi and Puccini opera recordings in the great upstairs library (four walls from rug to ceiling with things like *The Explanation of the Apocalypse* in three volumes, the complete works and poems of Chris Smart, the complete this and that, the apology of so-and-so written obscurely to you-know-who in 1839, in 1638—). I jump at the chance to say, "I'm going to sleep," it's now eleven, I have a right to be tired, been sitting on the floor and Mardou with dame-like majesty all this time in the easy chair in the corner of the library (where once I'd seen the famous one-armed Nick Spain sit when Bromberg on a happier early time in the year played for us the original recording of *The Rake's Progress*) and looking so, herself, tragic, lost—hurt so much by my hurt—by my sorriness from her sorriness borrowing—I think sensitive—that at one point in a burst of forgiveness, need, I run and sit at her feet and lean head on her knee in front of the others who by now don't care any more, that is Sand does not care about these things now, deeply engrossed in the music, the books, the brilliant conversation (the likes of which cannot be surpassed anywhere in the world, incidentally, and this too, tho now tiredly, crosses by my epic-wanting brain and I see the scheme of all my life, all acquaintances, loves, worries, travels rising again in a big symphonic mass but now I'm beginning not to care so much any more because of this 105 pounds of woman and brown at that whose little toenails, red in the thonged sandals, make my throat gulp)—"O dear Leo, you DO seem to be bored."— "Not bored! how could I be bored here!"—I wish I had some sympathetic way to tell Bromberg, "Every time I come here there's something wrong with me, it must seem like some awful comment on your house and hospitality and it isn't at all, can't you understand that this morning my heart is broken and out the window is bleak" (and how explain to him the other time I was a guest at his place, again uninvited but breaking in at gray dawn with Charley Krasner and the kids were there, and Mary, and the others came, gin and Schweppes, I became so drunk, disorderly, lost, I then too brooded and slept in fact on the floor in the middle of the room in front of everybody in the height of day—and for reasons so far removed from now, tho still as tho an adverse comment on the quality of Bromberg's weekend)—"No Austin I'm just sick—." No doubt, too, Sand must have hipped him quietly in a whisper somewhere what was happening with the lovers, Mardou also being silent—one of the strangest guests ever to hit Bromberg's, a poor subterranean beat Negro girl with no clothes on her back worth a twopenny (I saw to that generously), and yet so strange faced, solemn, serious, like a funny solemn unwanted probably angel in the house—feeling, as she told me, later, really unwanted because of the circumstances.—So I cop out, from the lot, from life, all of it, go to sleep in the bedroom (where Charley and I that earlier time had danced the mambo naked with Mary) and fall exhausted into new nightmares waking up about three hours later, in the heartbreakingly pure, clear, sane, happy afternoon, birds still singing, now kids singing, as if I was a spider waking up in a dusty bin and the world wasn't for me but for other airier creatures and more constant themselves and also less liable to the stains of inconstancy too—

While sleeping they three get in Sand's car and (properly) drive out to the beach, twenty miles, the boys jump in, swim, Mardou wanders on the shores of eternity her toes and feet that I love pressing down in the pale sand against the little shells and anemones and paupered dry seaweed long washed up and the wind blowing back her short haircut, as if Eternity'd met Heavenly Lane (as I thought of it in my bed) (seeing her also wandering around pouting, not knowing what to do next, abandoned by Suffering Leo and really alone and incapable of chatting about every tom dick and harry in art with Bromberg and Sand, what to do?)—So when they return she comes to the bed (after Bromberg's preliminary wild bound up the stairs and bursting in of door and "WAKE up Leo you don't want to sleep all day we've been to the beach, really it's not fair!")—"Leo," says Mardou, "I didn't want to sleep with you because I didn't want to wake up in Bromberg's bed at seven o'clock in the evening, it would be too much to cope with, I can't—" meaning her therapy (which she hadn't been going to any more out of sheer paralysis with me and my gang and cups), her inadequacy, the great now-crushing weight and fear of madness increasing in this disorderly awful life and unloved affair with me, to wake up horrified from hangover in a stranger's (a kind but nevertheless not altogether whole-heartedwelcoming stranger's) bed, with poor incapable Leo.— I suddenly looked at her, listening not to these real poor pleas so much as digging in her eyes that light that had shined on Yuri and it wasn't her fault it could shine on all the world all the time, my light o love—

"Are you sincere?"—("God you frighten me," she said later, "you make me think suddenly I've been two people and betrayed you in one way, with one person, and this other person—it really frightened me—") but as I ask that, "Are you sincere?" the pain I feel is so great, it has just risen fresh from that disordered roaring dream ("God is so disposed as to make our lives less cruel than our dreams," is a quote I saw the other day God knows where)—feeling all that and harkening to other horrified hangover awakenings in Bromberg's and all the hangover awakenings in my life, feeling now, "Boy, this is the real real beginning of the end, you can't go on much further, how much more vagueness can your positive flesh take and how long will it stay positive if your psyche keeps blamming on it—boy, you are going to die, when birds get bleak—that's the sign—." But thinking more roars than that, visions of my work neglected, my well-being (so-called old well-being again) smashed, brain permanently injured now—ideas for working on the railroad—O God the whole host and foolish illusion and entire rigamarole and madness that we erect in the place of onelove, in our sadness—but now with Mardou leaning over me, tired, solemn, somber, capable as she played with the little unshaven uglies of my chin of seeing right through my flesh into my horror and capable of feeling every vibration of pain and futility I could send, as, too, attested by her recognition of "Are you sincere?" as the deepwell sounded call from the bottom—"Baby, let's go home."

"We'll have to wait till Bromberg goes, take the train with him—I guess—." So I get up, go into the bathroom (where I'd been earlier while they were at the beach and sex-phantasized in remembrance of the time, on another even wilder and further back Bromberg weekend, poor Annie with her hair done up in curlers and her face no makeup and Leroy poor Leroy in the other room wondering what his wife's doing in there, and Leroy later driving off desperately into the night realizing we were up to something in the bathroom and so remembering myself now the pain I had caused Leroy that morning just for the sake of a little bit of sate for that worm and snake called sex)—I go into the bathroom and wash up and come down, trying to be cheerful.

Still I can't look at Mardou straight in the eye—in my heart, "O why did you do it?"—sensing, in my desperation, the prophecy of what's to come.

As if not enough this was the day of the night of the great Jones party, which was the night I jumped out of Mardou's cab and abandoned her to the dogs of war—the war man Yuri wages gainst man Leo, each one.—Beginning, Bromberg making phonecalls and gathering birthday gifts and getting ready to take the bus to make old 151 at 4:47 for the city, Sand driving us (a sorry lot indeed) to bus stop, where we have quick one in bar across street while Mardou by now ashamed not only of herself but me too stays in back seat of car (tho exhausted) but in broad daylight, trying to catch a wink—really trying to think her way out of trap only I could help her out of if I'm given one more chance—in the bar, parenthetically amazed I am to hear Bromberg going right on with big booming burbling comments on art and literature and even in fact by God queer anecdotes as sullen Santa Clara Valley farmers guzzle at rail, Bromberg doesn't even have consciousness of his fantastic impact on the ordinary—and Sand enjoying, himself in fact also weird—but minor details.—I come out to tell Mardou we have decided to take later train in order to go back to house to pick up forgotten package which is just another ringaround-therosy of futility for her, she receives this news with solemn lips—ah my love and lost darling (out of date word)—if then I'd known what I know now, instead of returning to bar, for further talks, and looking at her with hurt eyes, etc., and let her lay there in the bleak sea of time untended and unsolaced and unforgiven for the sin of the sea of time I'd have gone in and sat down with her, taken her hand, promised her my life and protection—"Because I love you and there's no reason"—but then far from having completely successfully realized this love, I was still in the act of thinking I was climbing out of my doubt about her—but the train came, finally, 153 at 5:31 after all our delays, we got in, and rode to the city—through South San Francisco and past my house, facing one another in coach seats, riding by the big yards in Bayshore and I gleefully (trying to be gleeful) point out a kicked boxcar ramming a hopper and you see the tinscrap shuddering far off, wow—but most of the time sitting bleakly under either stare and saying, finally, "I really do feel I must be getting a rummy nose"—anything I could think of saying to ease the pressure of what I really wanted to weep about—but in the main the three of us really sad, riding together on a train to gayety, horror, the eventual H bomb.

—Bidding Austin adieu finally at some teeming corner on Market where Mardou and I wandered among great sad sullen crowds in a confusion mass, as if we were suddenly lost in the actual physical manifestation of the mental condition we'd been in now together for two months, not even holding hands but I anxiously leading the way through crowds (so's to get out fast, hated it) but really because I was too "hurt" to hold her hand and remembering (now with greater pain) her usual insistence that I not hold her in the street or people'll think she's a hustler—ending up, in bright lost sad afternoon, down Price Street (O fated Price Street) towards Heavenly Lane, among the children, the young good-looking Mex chicks each one making me say to myself with contempt "Ah they're almost all of 'em better than Mardou, all I gotta do is get one of them . . . but O, but O"—neither one of us speaking much, and such chagrin in her eyes that in the original place where I had seen that Indian warmth which had originally prompted me to say to her, on some happy candlelit night, "Honey what I see in your eyes is a lifetime of affection not only from the Indian in you but because as part Negro somehow you are the first, the essential woman, and therefore the most, most originally most fully affectionate and maternal"—there now is the chagrin too, some lost American addition and mood with it—"Eden's in Africa," I'd added one time—but now in my hurt hate turning the other way and so walking down Price with her every time I see a Mexican gal or Negress I say to myself, "hustlers," they're all the same, always trying to cheat and rob you—harking back to all relations in the past with them—Mardou sensing these waves of hostility from me and silent.

And who's in our bed in Heavenly Lane but Yuri—cheerful —"Hey I been workin' all day, so tired I had to come back and get some more rest."—I decide to tell him everything, try to form the words in my mouth, Yuri sees my eyes, senses the tenseness, Mardou senses the tenseness, a knock on the door brings in John Golz (always romantically interested in Mardou in a naiver way), he senses the tenseness, "I've come to borrow a book"—grim expression on his face and remembering how I'd put him down about selectivity—so leaves at once, with book, and Yuri in getting up from bed (while Mardou hides behind screen to change from party dress to home jeans)— "Leo hand me my pants."—"Get up and get 'em yourself, they're right there on the chair, she can't see you"—a funny statement, and my mind feels funny and I look at Mardou who is silent and inward.

The moment she goes to the bathroom I say to Yuri "I'm very jealous about you and Mardou in the backseat last night man, I really am."—"It's not my fault, it was her started it."— "Lissen, you're such—like don't let her, keep away—you're such a lady-killer they all fall for you"—saying this just as Mardou returns, looking up sharply not hearing the words but seeing them in the air, and Yuri at once grabs the still open door and says "Well anyway I'm going to Adam's I'll see you there later."

"What did you tell Yuri—?" —I tell her word for word— "God the tenseness in here was unbearable"—(sheepishly I review the fact that instead of being stern and Moses-like in my jealousy and position I'd instead chatted with nervous "poet" talk with Yuri, as always, giving him the tension but not the positiveness of my feelings in words—sheepishly I review my sheepishness—I get sad to see old Carmody somehow—

"Baby I'm gonna—you think they got chickens on Columbus?—I've seen some—And cook it, see, we'll have a nice chicken supper."—"And," I say to myself, "what good is a nice domestic chicken supper when you love Yuri so much he has to leave the moment you walk in because of the pressure of my jealousy and your possibility as prophesied in a dream?" "I want" (out loud) "to see Carmody, I'm sad—you stay here, cook the chicken, eat—alone—I'll come back later and get you."—"But it always starts off like this, we always go away, we never stay alone."—"I know but tonight I'm sad I gotta see Carmody, for some reason don't ask me I have a tremendous sad desire and reason just to—after all I drew his picture the other day" (I had drawn my first pencil sketches of human figures reclining and they were greeted with amazement by Carmody and Adam and so I was proud) "and after all in drawing those shots of Frank the other day I saw such great sadness in the lines under his eyes that I know he—" (to myself: I know he'll understand how sad I am now, I know he has suffered on four continents this way).—Pondering Mardou does not know which way to turn but suddenly I tell her of my quick talk with Yuri the part I'd forgotten in the first report (and here too) "He said to me 'Leo I don't want to make your girl Mardou, after all I have no eyes—'." "Oh, so he has no eyes! A hell of a thing to say!" (the same teeth of glee now the portals where pass angry winds, and her eyes glitter) and I hear that junkey-like emphasis on the *ings* where she presses down on her *ings* like many junkies I know, from some inside heavy somnolent reason, which in Mardou I'd attributed to her amazing modernness culled (as I once asked her) "From where? where did you learn all you know and that amazing way you speak?" but now to hear that interesting *ing* only makes me mad as it's coming in a transparent speech about Yuri where she shows she's not really against seeing Yuri again at party or otherwise, "if he's gonna talk like that about no eyes," she's gonna tell him.—"O," I say, "now you WANT to come to the party at Adam's, because there you can get even with Yuri and tell him off—you're so transparent."

"Jesus," as we're walking along the benches of the church park sad park of the whole summer season, "now you're calling me names, transparent."

"Well that's what it is, you think I can't see through that, at first you didn't want to go to Adam's at all and now that you hear—well the hell with that if it ain't transparent I don't know what is."—"Calling me names, Jesus" (shnuffling to laugh) and both of us actually hysterically smiling and as tho nothing had happened at all and in fact like happy unconcerned people you see in newsreels busy going down the street to their chores and where-go's and we're in the same rainy newsreel mystery sad but inside of us (as must then be so inside the puppet filmdolls of screen) the great tumescent turbulent turmoil alliterative as a hammer on the brain bone bag and balls, bang I'm sorry I was ever born. . . .

To cap everything, as if it wasn't enough, the whole world opens up as Adam opens the door bowing solemnly but with a glint and secret in his eye and some kind of unwelcomeness I bristle at the sight of—"What's the matter?" Then I sense the presence of more people in there than Frank and Adam and Yuri.—"We have visitors."—"Oh," I say, "distinguished visitors?"—"I think so."—"Who?"—"Mac Jones and Phyllis." —"What?" (the great moment has come when I'm to come face to face, or leave, with my arch literary enemy Balliol MacJones erstwhile so close to me we used to slop beer on each other's knees in leaning-over talk excitement, we'd talked and exchanged and borrowed and read books and literarized so much the poor innocent had actually come under some kind of influence from me, that is, in the sense, only, that he learned the talk and style, mainly the history of the hip or beat generation or subterranean generation and I'd told him "Mac, write a great book about everything that happened when Leroy came to New York in 1949 and don't leave a word out and blow, go!" which he did, and I read it, critically Adam and I in visits to his place both critical of the manuscript but when it came out they guarantee him 20,000 dollars an unheard of sum and all of us beat types wandering the Beach and Market Street and Times Square when in New York, tho Adam and I had solemnly admitted, quote, "Jones is not of us—but from another world—the midtown sillies world" (an Adamism). And so his great success coming at the moment when I was poorest and most neglected by publishers and worse than that hung-up on paranoiac drug habits I became incensed but I didn't get too mad, but stayed black about it, changing my mind after father time's few local scythes and various misfortunes and trips around, writing him apologetic letters on ships which I tore up, he too writing them meanwhile, and then, Adam acting a year later as some kind of saint and mediator reported favorable inclinations on both our parts, to both parties —the great moment when I would have to face old Mac and shake with him and call it quits, let go all the rancor—making as little impression on Mardou, who is so independent and unavailable in that new heartbreaking way. Anyway MacJones was there, immediately I said out loud "Good, great, I been wantin' to see him," and I rushed into the livingroom and over someone's head who was getting up (Yuri it was) I shook hands firmly with Balliol, sat brooding awhile, didn't even notice how poor Mardou had managed to position herself (here as at Bromberg's as everywhere poor dark angel)—finally going to the bedroom unable to bear the polite conversation under which not only Yuri but Jones (and also Phyllis his woman who kept staring at me to see if it was still crazy) rumbled, I ran to the bedroom and lay in the dark and at the first opportunity tried to get Mardou to lie down with me but she said "Leo I don't want to lay around in here in the dark."—Yuri then coming over, putting on one of Adam's ties, saying, "I'm going out and find me a girl," and we have a kind of whispering rapport now away from them in the parlor—all's forgiven.— But I feel that because Jones does not move from his couch he really doesn't want to talk to me and probably wishes secretly I'd leave, when Mardou roams back again to my bed of shame and sorrow and hidingplace, I say, "What are you talking about in there, bop? Don't tell *him* anything about music."— (Let him find out for himself! I say to myself pettishly)—*I'm* the bop writer!—But as I'm commissioned to get the beer downstairs, when I come in again with beer in arms they're all in the kitchen, Mac foremost, smiling, and saying, "Leo! let me see those drawings they told me you did, I want to see them."—So we become friends again bending over drawings and Yuri has to be showing his too (he draws) and Mardou is in the other room, again forgotten—but it is a historic moment and as we also, with Carmody, study Carmody's South American bleak pictures of high jungle villages and Andean towns where you can see the clouds pass, I notice Mac's expensive goodlooking clothes, wrist watch, I feel proud of him and now he has an attractive little mustache that makes his maturity—which I announce to everyone—the beer by now warming us all up, and then his wife Phyllis begins a supper and the conviviality flows back and forth—

In the red bulblight parlor in fact I see Jones alone with Mardou questioning, as if interviewing her, I see that he's grinning and saying to himself 'Old Percepied's got himself another amazing doll' and I inside yearn to myself, "Yeah, for how long"—and he's listening to Mardou, who, impressed, forewarned, understanding everything, makes solemn statements about bop, like, "I don't like bop, I really don't, it's like junk to me, too many junkies are bop men and I hear the junk in it."—"Well," Mac adjusting glasses, "that's interesting."—And I go up and say, "But you never like what you come from" (looking at Mardou).—"What do you mean?"—"You're the child of Bop," or the children of bop, some such statement, which Mac and I agree on—so that later when we all the whole gang troop out to further festivities of the night, and Mardou, wearing Adam's long black velvet jacket (for her long) and a mad long scarf too, looking like a little Polish underground girl or boy in a sewer beneath the city and cute and hip, and in the street rushes up from one group to the one I'm in, and I reach out as she reaches me (I'm wearing Carmody's felt hat straight on my head like hipster for joke and my red shirt still, now defunct from weekends) and sweep her littleness off her feet and up against me and go on walking carrying her, I hear Mac's appreciative "Wow" and "Go" laugh in the background and I think proudly "He sees now that I have a real great chick—that I am not dead but going on—old continuous Percepied—never getting older, always in there, always with the young, the new generations—." A motley group in any case going down the street what with Adam Moorad wearing a full tuxedo borrowed from Sam the night before so he could attend some opening with tickets free from his office—trooping down to Dante's and Mask again—that Mask, that old po mask all the time—Dante's where in the rise and roar of the social and gab excitement I looked up many times to catch Mardou's eyes and play eyes with her but she seemed reluctant, abstract, brooding—no longer affectionate of me—sick of all our talk, with Bromberg re-arriving and great further discourses and that particular noxious group-enthusiasm that you're supposed to feel when like Mardou you're with a star of the group or even I mean just a member of that constellation, how noisome, tiresome it must have been to her to have to appreciate all we were saying, to be amazed by the latest quip from the lips of the one and only, the newest manifestation of the same old dreary mystery of personality in KaJa the great—disgusted she seemed indeed, and looking into space.

So later when in my drunkenness I managed to get Paddy Cordavan over to our table and he invited us all to his place for further drinking (the usually unattainable social Paddy Cordavan due to his woman who always wanted to go home alone with him, Paddy Cordavan of whom Buddy Pond had said, "He's too beautiful I can't look," tall, blond, big-jawed somber Montana cowboy slowmoving, slow talking, slow shouldered) Mardou wasn't impressed, as she wanted to get away from Paddy and all the other subterraneans of Dante's anyway, whom I had just freshly annoyed by yelling again at Julien, "Come here, we're all going to Paddy's party and Julien's coming," at which Julien immediately leaped up and rushed back to Ross Wallenstein and the others at their own booth, thinking, "God that awful Percepied is screaming at me and trying to drag me to his silly places again, I wish someone would do something about him." And Mardou wasn't any further impressed when, at Yuri's insistence, I went to the phone and spoke to Sam (calling from work) and agreed to meet him later at the bar across from the office—"We'll all go! we'll all go!" I'm screaming by now and even Adam and Frank are yawning ready to go home and Jones is long gone—rushing around up and down Paddy's stairs for further calls with Sam and at one point here I am rushing into Paddy's kitchen to get Mardou to come meet Sam with me and Ross Wallenstein having arrived while I was in the bar calling says, looking up, "Who let this guy in, hey, who is this? how'd you get in here! Hey Paddy!" in serious continuation of his original dislike and "are-you-a-fag" come-on, which I ignored, saying, "Brother I'll take the fuzz off your peach if you don't shut up," or some such putdown, can't remember, strong enough to make him swivel like a soldier, the way he does, stiff necked, and retire—I dragging Mardou down to a cab to rush to Sam's and all this wild world swirling night and she in her little voice I hear protesting from far away, "But Leo, dear Leo, I want to go home and sleep."—"Ah hell!" and I give Sam's address to the taxidriver, she says NO, insists, gives Heavenly Lane, "Take me there first and then go to Sam's" but I'm really seriously hung-up on the undeniable fact that if I take her to Heavenly Lane first the cab will never make it to Sam's waiting bar before closing time, so I argue, we harangue hurling different addresses at the cab driver who like in a movie waits, but suddenly, with that red flame that same red flame (for want of a better image) I leap out of the cab and rush out and there's another one, I jump in, give Sam's address and off he guns her—Mardou left in the night, in a cab, sick, and tired, and me intending to pay the second cab with the buck she'd entrusted to Adam to get her a sandwich but which in the turmoil had been forgotten but he gave it to me for her—poor Mardou going home alone, again, and drunken maniac was gone.

Well, I thought, this is the end—I finally made the step and by God I paid her back for what she done to me—it had to come and this is it—ploop.

> *Isn't is good to know winter is coming—*
> *and that life will be a little*
> *more quiet—and you will be home*
> *writing and eating well and we will*
> *be spending pleasant nights wrapped*
> *round one another—and you are home*
> *now, rested and eating well because you*
> *should not become too sad—and I feel*
> *better when I know you are well.*

and

> *Write to me   Anything.*
> *Please stay well*
> *Your Freind*
> *And my love*
> *And Oh*
> *And Love for You*
>   MARDOU
> *Please*

But the deepest premonition and prophesy of all had always

been, that when I walked into Heavenly Lane, cutting in sharply from sidewalk, I'd look up, and if Mardou's light was on Mardou's light was on—"But some day, dear Leo, that light will not shine for you"—this a prophesy irrespective of all your Yuris and attenuations in the snake of time.—"Someday she won't be there when you want her to be there, the light'll be out and you'll be looking up and it will be dark in Heavenly Lane and Mardou'll be gone, and it'll be when you least expect it and want it."—Always I knew this—it crossed my mind that night when I ran up, met Sam in the bar, he was with two newspaperman, we bought drinks, I spilled money on the floor, I hurried to get drunk (through with my baby!), rushed up to Adam and Frank's, woke them up again, wrestled on the floor, made noise, Sam tore my T-shirt off, bashed the lamp in, drank a fifth of bourbon as of old in our tremendous days together, it was just another big downcrashing in the night and all for nothing . . . waking up, I, in the morning with the final hangover that said to me, "Too late"—and got up and staggered to the door through the debris, and opened it, and went home, Adam saying to me as he heard me fiddle with the groaning faucet, "Leo go home and recuperate well," sensing how sick I was tho not knowing about Mardou and me—and at home I wandered around, couldn't stay in the house, couldn't stop, had to walk, as if someone was going to die soon, as if I could smell the flowers of death in the air, and I went in the South San Francisco railyard and cried.

Cried in the railyard sitting on an old piece of iron under the new moon and on the side of the old Southern Pacific tracks, cried because not only I had cast off Mardou whom now I was not so sure I wanted to cast off but the die'd been thrown, feeling too her empathetic tears across the night and the final horror both of us round-eyed realizing we part—but seeing suddenly not in the face of the moon but somewhere in the sky as I looked up and hoped to figure, the face of my mother—remembering it in fact from a haunted nap just after supper that same restless unable-to-stay-in-a-chair or on-earth day—just as I woke to some Arthur Godfrey program on the TV, I saw bending over me the visage of my mother, with impenetrable eyes and moveless lips and round cheekbones and glasses that glinted and hid the major part of her expression which at first I thought was a vision of horror that I might shudder at, but it didn't make me shudder—wondering about it on the walk and suddenly now in the railyards weeping for my lost Mardou and so stupidly because I'd decided to throw her away myself, it had been a vision of my mother's love for me—that expressionless and expressionless-because-so-profound face bending over me in the vision of my sleep, and with lips not so pressed together as enduring and as if to say, "*Pauvre Ti Leo, pauvre Ti Leo, tu souffri, les hommes souffri tant, y'ainque toi dans le monde j'va't prendre soin, j'aim'ra beaucoup t'prendre soin tous tes jours mon ange.*"—"Poor Little Leo, poor Little Leo, you suffer, men suffer so, you're all alone in the world I'll take care of you, I would very much like to take care of you all your days my angel."—My mother an angel too—the tears welled up in my eyes, something broke, I cracked—I had been sitting for an hour, in front of me was Butler Road and the gigantic rose neon ten blocks long BETHLEHEM WEST COAST STEEL with stars above and the smashby Zipper and the fragrance of locomotive coalsmoke as I sit there and let them pass and far down the line in the night around that South San Francisco airport you can see that sonofabitch red light waving Mars signal light swimming in the dark big red markers blowing up and down and sending fires in the keen-pure lostpurity lovelyskies of old California in the late sad night of autumn spring comefall winter's summertime tall, like trees —the only man in South City who ever walked from the neat suburban homes and went and hid by boxcars to think—broke. —Something fell loose in me—O blood of my soul I thought and the Good Lord or whatever's put me here to suffer and groan and on top of that be guilty and gives me the flesh and blood that is so painful the—women all mean well—this I knew—women love, bend over you—you'd as soon betray a woman's love as spit on your own feet, clay—

That sudden short crying in the railyard and for a reason I really didn't fathom, and couldn't—saying to myself in the bottom, "You see a vision of the face of the woman who is your mother who loves you so much she has supported you and protected you for years, you a bum, a drunkard—never complained a jot—because she knows that in your present state you can't go out in the world and make a living and take care of yourself and even find and hold the love of another protecting woman—and all because you are poor stupid Ti Leo—deep in the dark pit of night under the stars of the world you are lost, poor, no one cares, and now you threw away a little woman's love because you wanted another drink with a rowdy fiend from the other side of your insanity."

And as always.

Ending with the great sorrow of Price Street when Mardou and I, reunited on Sunday night according to my schedule (I'd made up the schedule that week thinking in a yard tea-reverie, "This is the cleverest arrangement I ever made, why with this thing I can live a full love-life," conscious of Mardou's Reichian worth, and at the same time write those three novels and be a big—etc.) (schedule all written out, and delivered to Mardou for her perusal, it said, "Go to Mardou at 9 in the evening, sleep, return following noon for afternoon of writing and evening supper and aftersupper rest and then return at 9 P.M. again," with holes in the schedule left open on weekends for "possible going out") (getting plastered)—with this schedule still in mind and after spending the weekend at home steeped in that awful—I rushed anyway to Mardou's on Sunday night at 9 P.M., as scheduled, there was no light in her window ("Just as I knew it would happen someday")—but on the door a note, and for me, which I read after quick leak in the hall john —"Dear Leo, I'll be back at 10:30," and the door (as always) unlocked and I go in to wait and read Reich—carrying again my big forwardlooking healthybook Reich and ready at least to "throw a good one in her" in case it's all bound to end this very night and sitting there eyes shifting around and plotting —11:30 and she hasn't come yet—fearing me—missing— ("Leo," later, she told me, "I really thought we were through, that you wouldn't come back at all")—nevertheless she'd left that Bird of Paradise note for me, always and still hoping and not aiming to hurt me and keep me waiting in dark—but because she does not return at 11:30 I cut out, to Adam's, leaving message for her to call, with ramifications that I erase after a while—all a host of minor details leading to the great sorrow of Price Street taking place after we spend a night of "successful" sex, when I tell her, "Mardou you've become much more precious to me since everything that happened," and because of that, as we agree, I am able to make her fulfill better, which she does—twice, in fact, and for the first time—spending a whole sweet afternoon as if reunited but at intervals poor Mardou looking up and saying, "But we should really break up, we've never done anything together, we were going to Mexico, and then you were going to get a job and we'd live together, then remember the loft idea, all big phantasm that like haven't worked out because you haven't pushed them from your mind out into the open world, haven't acted on them, and like, me, I don't—I've missed my therapist for weeks." (She'd written a fine letter that very day to the therapist begging forgiveness and permission to come back in a few weeks and advice for her lostness and I'd approved of it.)—All of this unreal from the moment I walked into Heavenly Lane after my crying-in-the-railyard lonely dark sojourn at home to see her light was out at last (as deeply promised), but the note, saving us awhile, my finding her a little later that night as she did finally call me at Adam's and told me to come to Rita's, where I brought beer, then Mike Murphy came and he brought beer too—ending with another silly yelling conversation drunk night.—Mardou saying in the morning, "Do you remember anything you said last night to Mike and Rita?" and me, "Of course not."—The whole day, borrowed from the sky day, sweet—we make love and try to make promises of little kinds—no go, as in the evening she says "Let's go to a show" (with her pitiful check money).—"Jesus, we'll spend all your money."—"Well goddamit I don't care, I'm going to spend that money and that's all there is to it," with great emphasis—so she puts on her black velvet slacks and some perfume and I go up and smell her neck and God, how sweet can you smell—and I want her more than ever, in my arms she's gone—in my hand she's as slippy as dust—something's wrong.—"Did I cut you when I jumped out of the cab?"—"Leo, it was baby, it was the most maniacal thing I ever saw."—"I'm sorry."—"I know you're sorry but it was the most maniacal thing I ever *saw* and it keeps happening and getting worse and like, now, oh hell—let's go to a show."—So we go out, and she has on this little heartbreaking never-seen-by-me before red raincoat over the black velvet slacks and cuts along, with black short hair making her look so strange, like a—like someone in Paris—I have on just my old ex-brakeman railroad Cant Bust Ems and a work-shirt without undershirt and suddenly it's cold October out there, and with gusts of rain, so I shiver at her side as we hurry up Price Street—towards Market, shows—I remember that afternoon returning from the Bromberg weekend—something is caught in both our throats, I don't know what, she does.

"Baby I'm going to tell you something and if I tell it to you I want you to promise nevertheless you'll come to the movie with me."—"Okay."—And naturally I add, after pause, "What is it?"—I think it has something to do with "Let's break up really and truly, I don't want to make it, not because I don't like you but it's by now or should be obvious to both of us by now—" that kind of argument that I can, as of yore and again, break, by saying, "But let's, look, I have, wait—" for always the man can make the little woman bend, she was made to bend, the little woman was—so I wait confidently for this kind of talk, tho feel bleak, tragic, grim, and the air cold.—"You know the other night" (she spends some time trying to order confused nights of recent—and I help her straighten them out, and have my arm around her waist, as we cut along we come closer to the brittle jewel lights of Price and Columbus that old North Beach corner so weird and ever weirder now and I have my private thoughts about it as from older scenes in my San Francisco life, in brief, almost smug and snug in the rug of myself—in any case we agree that the night she means to tell me about is Saturday night, which was the night I cried in the railyards—that short sudden, as I say, crying, that vision—I'm trying in fact to interpose and tell her about it, trying also to figure out if she means now that on Saturday night something awful happened that I should know—).

"Well I went to Dante's and didn't want to stay, and tried to leave—and Yuri was trying to hang around—and he called somebody—and I was at the phone—and told Yuri he was wanted" (as incoherent as that) "and while he is in the booth I cut on home, because I was tired—baby at two o'clock in the morning he came and knocked on the door—"

"Why?"—"For a place to sleep, he was drunk, he rushed in —and—well—."

"Huh?"

"Well baby we made it together,"—that hip word—at the

sound of which even as I walked and my legs propelled under me and my feet felt firm, the lower part of my stomach sagged into my pants or loins and the body experienced a sensation of deep melting downgoing into some soft somewhere, nowhere—suddenly the streets were so bleak, the people passing so beastly, the lights so unnecessary just to illumine this . . . this cutting world—it was going across the cobbles when she said it, "made it together," I had (locomotive wise) to concentrate on getting up on the curb again and I didn't look at her—I looked down Columbus and thought of walking away, rapidly, as I'd done at Larry's—I didn't—I said "I don't want to live in this beastly world"—but so low she barely if at all heard me and if so never commented, but after a pause she added a few things, like, "There are other details, like, what—but I won't go into them—like," stammering, and slow—yet both of us swinging along in the street to the show—the show being *Brave Bulls* (I cried to see the grief in the matador when he heard his best friend and girl had gone off the mountain in his own car, I cried to see even the bull that I knew would die and I knew the big deaths bulls do die in their trap called bull-ring)—I wanted to run away from Mardou. ("Look man," she'd said only a week before when I'd suddenly started talking about Adam and Eve and referred to her as Eve, the woman who by her beauty is able to make the man do anything, "don't call me Eve.")—But now no matter—walking along, at one point so irritable to my senses she stopped short on the rainy sidewalk and coolly said "I need a neckerchief" and turned to go into the store and I turned and followed her from reluctant ten feet back realizing I hadn't known what was going on in my mind really ever since Price and Columbus and here we were on Market—while she's in the store I keep haggling with myself, shall I just go now, I have my fare, just cut down the street swiftly and go home and when she comes out she'll see you're gone, she'll know you broke the promise to go to the movies just like you broke a lot of promises but this time she'll know you have a big male right to—but none of this is enough—I feel stabbed by Yuri—by Mardou I feel forsaken and shamed—I turn to look in the store blindly at anything and there she comes at just that moment wearing a phosphorescent purple bandana (because big raindrops had just started flying and she didn't want the rain to string out her carefully combed for the movies hair and here she was spending her small monies on kerchiefs.) —In the movie I hold her hand, after a fifteen-minute wait, not thinking to at all not because I was mad but I felt she would feel it was too subservient at this time to take her hand in the movieshow, like lovers—but I took her hand, she was warm, lost—ask not the sea why the eyes of the dark-eyed woman are strange and lost —came out of the movie, I glum, she businesslike to get through the cold to the bus, where, at the bus stop, she walked away from me to lead me to a warmer waiting place and (as I said) I'd mentally accused her of wanderingfoot.

Arriving home, where we sat, she on my lap, after a long warm talk with John Golz, who came in to see her, but found me too, and might have left, but in my new spirit I wanted at once to show him that I respected and liked him, and talked with him, and he stayed two hours—in fact I saw how he annoyed Mardou by talking literature with her beyond the point where she was interested and also about things she'd long known about—poor Mardou.

So he left, and I curled her on my lap, and she talked about the war between men—"They have a war, to them a woman is a prize, to Yuri it's just that your prize has less value now."

"Yeah," I say, sad, "but I should have paid more attention to the old junkey nevertheless, who said there's a lover on every corner—they're all the same, boy, don't get hung-up on one."

"It isn't true, it isn't true, that's just what Yuri wants is for you to go down to Dante's now and the two of you'll laugh and talk me over and agree that women are good lays and there are a lot of them.—I think you're like me—you want one love —like, men have the essence in the woman, there's an essence" ("Yes," I thought, "there's an essence, and that is your womb") "and the man has it in his hand, but rushes off to build big constructions." (I'd just read her the first few pages of *Finnegans Wake* and explained them and where Finnegan is always putting up "buildung supra buildung supra buildung" on the banks of the Liffey—dung!)

"I will say nothing," I thought—"Will you think I am not a man if I don't get mad?"

"Just like that war I told you about."

"Women have wars too—"

Oh what'll we do? I think—now I go home, and it's all over for sure, not only now is she bored and has had enough but has pierced me with an adultery of a kind, has been inconstant, as prophesied in a dream, the dream the bloody dream—I see myself grabbing Yuri by the shirt and throwing him on the floor, he pulls out a Yugoslavian knife, I pick up a chair to bash him with, everybody's watching . . . but I continue the daydream and I look into his eyes and I see suddenly the glare of a jester angel who made his presence on earth all a joke and I realize that this too with Mardou was a joke and I think, "Funny Angel, elevated amongst the subterraneans."

"Baby it's up to you," is what she's actually saying, "about how many times you wanta see me and all that—but I want to be independent like I say."

And I go home having lost her love.

And write this book.

TRISTESSA

Part One
Trembling and Chaste

I'M riding along with Tristessa in the cab, drunk, with big
bottle of Juarez Bourbon whiskey in the till-bag railroad
lootbag they'd accused me of holding in railroad 1952—here I
am in Mexico City, rainy Saturday night, mysteries, old dream
sidestreets with no names reeling in, the little street where I'd
walked through crowds of gloomy Hobo Indians wrapped in
tragic shawls enough to make you cry and you thought you saw
knives flashing beneath the folds—lugubrious dreams as tragic
as the one of Old Railroad Night where my father sits big of
thighs in smoking car of night, outside's a brakeman with red
light and white light, lumbering in the sad vast mist tracks of
life—but now I'm up on that Vegetable plateau Mexico, the
moon of Citlapol a few nights earlier I'd stumbled to on the
sleepy roof on the way to the ancient dripping stone toilet—
Tristessa is high, beautiful as ever, goin home gayly to go to
bed and enjoy her morphine.

Night before I've in a quiet hassel in the rain sat with her
darkly at Midnight counters eating bread and soup and
drinking Delaware Punch, and I'd come out of that interview
with a vision of Tristessa in my bed in my arms, the strangeness
of her love-cheek, Azteca, Indian girl with mysterious lidded
Billy Holliday eyes and spoke with great melancholic voice like
Luise Rainer sadfaced Viennese actresses that made all Ukraine
cry in 1910.

Gorgeous ripples of pear shape her skin to her cheekbones,
and long sad eyelids, and Virgin Mary resignation, and peachy
coffee complexion and eyes of astonishing mystery with
nothing-but-earth-depth expressionless half disdain and half
mournful lamentation of pain. "I am seek," she's always saying
to me and Bull at the pad—I'm in Mexico City wildhaired and
mad riding in a cab down past the Ciné Mexico in rainy traffic
jams, I'm swigging from the bottle, Tristessa is trying long harangues to explain that the night before when I put her in the
cab the driver'd tried to make her and she hit him with her fist,

news which the present driver receives without comment—
We're going down to Tristessa's house to sit and get high—
Tristessa has warned me that the house will be a mess because
her sister is drunk and sick, and El Indio will be there standing
majestically with morphine needle downward in the big brown
arm, glitter-eyed looking right at you or expecting the prick of
the needle to bring the wanted flame itself and going "Hm-za
. . . the Aztec needle in my flesh of flame" looking all a whole
lot like the big cat in Culiao who presented me the o the time I
came down to Mexico to see other visions—My whiskey bottle
has strange Mexican soft covercap that I keep worrying will slip
off and all my bag be drowned in Bourbon 86 proof whiskey.

Through the crazy Saturday night drizzle streets like Hong
Kong our cab pushes slowly through the Market ways and we
come out on the whore street district and get off behind the
fruity fruitstands and tortilla beans and tacos shacks with fixed
wood benches—It's the poor district of Rome.

I pay the cab 3.33 by giving cabbie 10 pesos and asking "seis"
for change, which I get without comment and wonder if
Tristessa thinks I am too splurgy like big John Drunk in Mexico
—But no time to think, we are hurrying through the slicky
sidewalks of glisten-neon reflections and candle lights of little
sidewalk sitters with walnuts on a towel for sale—turn quickly
at the stinky alleyway of her tenement cell-house one story
high —We go through dripping faucets and pails and boys and
duck under wash and come to her iron door, which from
adobe withins is unlocked and we step in the kitchen the rain
still falling from the leaves and boards that served as the
kitchen roof—allowing little drizzles to fizzle in the kitchen
over the chicken garbage in the damp corner—Where, miraculously, now, I see the little pink cat taking a little pee on piles of
okra and chickenfeed—The inside bedroom is littered completely and ransacked as by madmen with torn newspapers and
the chicken's pecking at the rice and the bits of sandwiches on
the floor—On the bed lay Tristessa's "sister" sick, wrapped in
pink coverlet—it's as tragic as the night Eddy was shot on the
rainy Russia Street—

Tristessa is sitting on the edge of the bed adjusting her nylon
stockings, she pulls them awkwardly from her shoes with big

sad face overlooking her endeavors with pursy lips, I watch the way she twists her feet inward convulsively when she looks at her shoes.

She is such a beautiful girl, I wonder what all my friends would say back in New York and up in San Francisco, and what would happen down in Nola when you see her cutting down Canal Street in the hot sun and she has dark glasses and a lazy walk and keeps trying to tie her kimono to her thin overcoat as though the kimono was supposed to tie to the coat, tugging convulsively at it and goofing in the street saying "Here ees the cab—hey hees hey who—there you go—I breeng you back the m o a - n y." Money's moany. She makes money sound like my old French Canadian Aunt in Lawrence "It's not you moany, that I want, it's you l o a v e"—Love is loave. "Eets you l a w v." The law is lawv.—Same with Tristessa, she is so high all the time, and sick, shooting ten gramos of morphine per month,—staggering down the city streets yet so beautiful people keep turning and looking at her—Her eyes are radiant and shining and her cheek is wet from the mist and her Indian hair is black and cool and slick hangin in 2 pigtails behind with the roll-sod hairdo behind (the correct Cathedral Indian hairdo)—Her shoes she keeps looking at are brand new not scrawny, but she lets her nylons keep falling and keeps pulling on them and convulsively twisting her feet—You picture what a beautiful girl in New York, wearing a flowery wide skirt a la New Look with Dior flat bosomed pink cashmere sweater, and her lips and eyes do the same and do the rest. Here she is reduced to impoverished Indian Lady gloomclothes—You see the Indian ladies in the inscrutable dark of doorways, looking like holes in the wall not women—their clothes—and you look again and see the brave, the noble *mujer*, the mother, the woman, the Virgin Mary of Mexico.—Tristessa has a huge ikon in a corner of her bedroom.

It faces the room, back to the kitchen wall, in right hand corner as you face the woesome kitchen with its drizzle showering ineffably from the roof tree twigs and hammmberboards (bombed out shelter roof)—Her ikon represents the Holy Mother staring out of her blue charaderees, her robes and Damema arrangements, at which El Indio prays devoutly when going out to get some junk. El Indio is a vendor of curios,

allegedly,—I never see him on San Juan Letran selling crucifixes, I never see El Indio in the street, no Redondas, no
anywhere—The Virgin Mary has a candle, a bunch of glass-
fulla-wax economical burners that go for weeks on end, like
Tibetan prayerwheels the inexhaustible aid from our Amida—
I smile to see this lovely ikon—

Around it are pictures of the dead—When Tristessa wants to
say "dead" she clasps her hands in holy attitude, indicating her
Aztecan belief in the holiness of death, by same token the holiness of the essence—So she has photo of dead Dave my old
buddy of previous years now dead of high blood pressure at
age 55—His vague Greek-Indian face looks out from pale indefinable photograph. I can't see him in all that snow. He's in
heaven for sure, hands V-clasped in eternity ecstasy of Nirvana.
That's why Tristessa keeps clasping her hands and praying,
saying, too, "I love Dave," she had loved her former master—
He had been an old man in love with a young girl. At 16 she
was an addict. He took her off the street and, himself an addict
of the street, redoubled his energies, finally made contact with
wealthy junkies and showed her how to live—once a year together they'd taken hikes to Chalmas to the mountain to climb
part of it on their knees to come to the shrine of piled crutches
left there by pilgrims healed of disease, the thousand *tapete*-
straws laid out in the mist where they sleep the night out in
blankets and raincoats—returning, devout, hungry, healthy, to
light new candles to the Mother and hitting the street again
for their morphine—God knows where they got it.

I sit admiring that majestical mother of lovers.

There's no describing the awfulness of that gloom in the holes
in the ceiling, the brown halo of the night city lost in a green
vegetable height above the Wheels of the Blakean adobe
rooftops—Rain is blearing now on the green endlessness of the
Valley Plain north of Actopan—pretty girls are dashing over
gutters full of pools—Dogs bark at hirshing cars—The drizzle
empties eerily into the kitchen's stone Dank, and the door glis-
tens (iron) all shiney and wet—The dog is howling in pain on
the bed.—The dog is the little Chihuahua mother 12 inches
long, with fine little feet with black toes and toenails, such a
"fine" and delicate dog you couldnt touch her without she'd

squeal in pain—"Y - e e e - p " All you could do was snap your finger gently at her and allow her to nip-nose her cold little wet snout (black as a bull's) against your fingernails and thumb. Sweet little dog—Tristessa says she's in heat and that's why she cries—The rooster screams beneath the bed.

All this time the rooster's been listening under the springs, meditating, turning to look all around in his quiet darkness, the noise of the golden humans above "B e u - v e u - VA A !" he screams, he howls, he interrupts a half a dozen simultaneous conversations raging like torn paper above—The hen chuckles.

The hen is outside, wandering among our feet, pecking gently at the floor—She digs the people. She wants to come up near me and rub illimitably against my pant leg, but I dont give her encouragement, in fact havent noticed her yet and it's like the dream of the vast mad father of the wild barn in howling Nova Scotia with the floodwaters of the sea about to engulf the town and surrounding pine countrysides in the endless north—It was Tristessa, Cruz on the bed, El Indio, the cock, the dove on the mantelpiece top (never a sound except occasional wing flap practice), the cat, the hen, and the bloody howling woman dog blacky Espana Chihuahua pooch bitch.

El Indio's eyedropper is completely full, he jabs in the needle hard and it's dull and it wont penetrate the skin and he jabs in harder and works it in but instead of wincing waits open mouthed with ecstasy and gets the dropful in, down, standing, —"You've got to do me a favor Mr. Gazookus," says Old Bull Gaines interrupting my thought, "come down to Tristessa's with me—I've run short—" but I'm bursting to explode out of sight of Mexico City with walking in the rain splashing through puddles not cursing nor interested but just trying to get home to bed, dead.

It's the raving bloody book of dreams of the cursing world, full of suits, dishonesties and written agreements. And briberies, to children for their sweets, to children for their sweets. "Morphine is for pain," I keep thinking, "and the rest is rest. It is what it is, I am what I am, Adoration to Tathagata, Sugata, Buddha, perfect in Wisdom and Compassion who has accomplished, and is accomplishing, and will accomplish, all these words of mystery."

—Reason I bring the whiskey, to drink, to crash through the

black curtain—At same time a comedian in the city in the
night—Bepestered by glooms and lull intervenes, bored,
drinking, curtsying, crashing, "Where I'm gonna do,"—I pull
the chair up to the corner of the foot of the bed so I can sit
between the kitty and the Virgin Mary. The kitty, *la gata* in
Spanish, the little Tathagata of the night, golden pink colored,
3 weeks old, crazy pink nose, crazy face, eyes of green, mustachio'd golden lion forceps and whiskers—I run my finger over
her little skull and she pops up purring and the little purring-
machine is started for awhile and she looks around the room
glad watching what we're all doing.—"She's having golden
thoughts," I'm thinking.—Tristessa likes eggs otherwise she
wouldnt allow a male rooster in this female establishment?
How should I know how eggs are made. On my right the de-
votional candles flame before the clay wall.

It's infinitely worse than the sleeping dream I've had of Mexico
City where I go dreary along empty white apartments, gray,
alone, or where the marble steps of a hotel horrify me—It's
the rainy night in Mexico City and I'm in the middle of Mexico Thieves Market district and El Indio is a wellknown thief
and even Tristessa was a pickpocket but I dont do more than
flick my backhand against the bulge of my folded money
sailorwise stowed in the railroad watchpocket of my jeans—
And in shirtpocket I have the travelers checks which are un-
stealable in a sense—That, Ah that side street where the gang
of Mexicans stop me and rifle through my dufflebag and take
what they want and take me along for a drink—It's gloom as
unpredicted on this earth, I realize all the uncountable mani-
festations the thinking-mind invents to place wall of horror
before its pure perfect realization that there is no wall and no
horror just Transcendental Empty Kissable Milk Light of Everlasting Eternity's true and perfectly empty nature.—I know
everything's alright but I want proof and the Buddhas and the
Virgin Marys are there reminding me of the solemn pledge of
faith in this harsh and stupid earth where we rage our so-called
lives in a sea of worry, meat for Chicagos of Graves—right this
minute my very father and my very brother lie side by side in
mud in the North and I'm supposed to be smarter than they
are—being quick I am dead. I look up at the others glooping,

they see I've been lost in thought in my corner chair but are pursuing endless wild worries (all mental 100%) of their own —They're yakking in Spanish, I only understand snatches of that virile conversation—Tristessa keeps saying "chinga" at every other sentence, a swearing Marine,—she says it with scorn and her teeth bite and it makes me worry 'Do you know women as well as you think you do?'—The rooster is unperturbed and lets go a blast.

I take out my whiskey bottle from the bag, the Canady Dry, open both, and pour me a hiball in a cup—making one too for Cruz who has just jumped outa bed to throw up on the kitchen floor and now wants another drink, she's been in the cantina for women all day somewhere back near the whore district of Panama Street and sinister Rayon Street with its dead dog in the gutter and beggars on the sidewalk with no hats looking at you helplessly—Cruz is a little Indian woman with no chin and bright eyes and wears high heel pumps without stockings and battered dresses, what a wild crew of people, in America a cop would have to do a double take seeing them pass all be-wrongled and arguing and staggering on the sidewalk, like apparitions of poverty—Cruz takes a hiball and throws it up too. Nobody notices, El Indio is holding eyedropper in one hand and little piece of paper in the other arguing, tense necked, red, fullblast at a screaming Tristessa whose bright eyes dance to fight it out—The old lady Cruz groans from the riot of it and buries back in her bed, the only bed, under her blanket, her face bandaged and greasy, the little black dog curling against her, and the cat, and she is lamenting something, her drink sickness, and El Indio's constant harassing for more of Tristessa's supply of morphine—I gulp my drink.

Next door the mother's made the little daughter cry, we can hear her praying little woeful squeals enough to make a father's heart break and maybe it might be,—Trucks pass, buses, loud, growling, loaded to the springs with people riding to Tacuyaba and Rastro and Circumvalacion round-routeries of town—the streets of mess puddles that I am going to walk home in at 2 AM splashing without care through streetpools, looking along lone fences at the dismal glimmer of the wet rain shining in the streetlight—The pit and horror of my grit, the Virya tense-neck muscles that a man needs to steel his teeth together to press through lonely roads of rain at night with no hope of a warm bed—My head falls and wearies to think of it. Tristessa says "How is Jack,—?—" She always asks: "Why are you so sad??—'Muy dolorosa'" and as though to mean "You are very full of pain," for pain means *dolor*—"I am sad because all la vida es dolorosa," I keep replying, hoping to teach her Number One of the Four Great Truths,—Besides, what could be truer? With her heavy purple eyes she lids at me the nodding reprisal, 'ha-hum,' Indian-wise understanding the tone of what I said, and nodding over it, making me suspicious of the bridge of her nose where it looks evil and conniving and I think of her as a Houri Hari Salesman in the hellbottoms Kshitigarbha never dreamed to redeem.—When she looks like an evil Indian Joe of Huckleberry Finn, plotting my demise— El Indio, standing, watching through sad blackened-blue eye flesh, hard and sharp and clear the side of his face, darkly hearing that I say All Life is Sad, nods, agreeing, no comment to make to me or to anyone about it.

Tristessa is bending over the spoon boiling morphine in it with a match boilerfactory. She looks awkward and lean and you see the lean hocks of her rear, in the kimono-like crazy-dress, as she kneels prayer fashion over the bed boiling her bang over the chair which is cluttered with ashes, hairpins, cottons, Konk material like strange Mexican eyelash lippmakers and teasies and greases—one jiblet of a whole bone of junk, that, had it been knocked down would have added to the mess on the floor only a minor further amount of confusion.—"I raced to find that Tarzan," I'm thinking, remembering boyhood and home as they lament in the Mexican Saturday Night Bedroom, "but the bushes and the rocks weren't real and the beauty of things must be that they end."

I wail on my cup of hiball so much they see I'm going to get drunk so they all permit me and beseech me to take a shot of morphine which I accept without fear because I am drunk— Worse sensation in the world, to take morphine when you're drunk, the result knots in your forehead like a rock and makes great pain there warring in that one field for dominion and none to be had because they've cancelled out each other the alcohol and the alkaloid. But I accept, and as soon as I begin to feel its warning effect and warm effect I look down and perceive that the chicken, the hen, wants to make friends with me —She's walking up close with bobbing neck, looking at my knee cap, looking at my hanging hands, wants to come close but has no authority—So I stick my hand out to its beak to be pecked, to let her know I'm not afraid because I trust her not to hurt me really—which she doesn't—just stares at my hand reasonably and doubtfully and suddenly almost tenderly and I pull away my hand with a sense of the victory. She contentedly chuckles, plucks up a piece of something from the floor, throws it away, a piece of linen thread hangs in her beak, she tosses it away, looks around, walks around the golden kitchen of Time in huge Nirvana glare of Saturday night and all the rivers roaring in the rain, the crash inside my soul when I think of babyhood and you watch the big adults in the room, the wave and gnash of their shadowy hands, as they harangue about time and responsibility, in a Golden Movie inside my own mind without substance not even gelatinous—the hope and horror of the void—great phantoms screeching inside mind with the yawk photograph VLORK of the Rooster as he now ups and emits from his throat intended for open fences of Missouri explodes gunpowder blurts of morningshame, reverend for man —At dawn in impenetrable bleak Oceanities of Undersunk gloom, he blows his rosy morn Collario and still the farmer knows it wont tend that rosy way. Then he chuckles, rooster chuckles, comments on something crazy we might have said, and chuckles—poor sentient noticing being, the beast he knows his time is up in the Chickenshacks of Lenox Avenue— chuckles like we do—yells louder if a man, with special rooster jowls and jinglets—Hen, his wife, she wears her adjustible hat falling from one side of her pretty beak to the other. "Good *morn* ing Mrs. Gazookas," I tell her, having fun by myself watching the chickens as I'd done as a boy in New Hampshire in farmhouses at night waiting for the talk to be done and the wood to be taken in. Worked hard for my father in the Pure Land, was strong and true, went to the city to see Tathagata, leveled the ground for his feet, saw bumps everywhere and leveled the ground, he passed by and saw me and said "First level your own mind, and then the earth will be level, even unto

Mount Sumeru" (the ancient name for Everest in Old Magadha) (India).

I wanta make friends with the rooster too, by now I'm sitting
in front of the bed in the other chair as El Indio has just gone
out with a bunch of suspicious men with mustaches one of
whom stared at me curiously and with pleased proud grin as I
stood with cup in hand acting drunk before the ladies for his
and his friends' edification—Alone in the house with the two
women I sit politely before them and we talk earnestly and
eagerly about God. "My friends ees seek, I geev them shot,"
beautiful Tristessa of Dolours is telling me with her long damp
expressive fingers dancing little India-Tinkle dances before my
haunted eyes."—Eees when, *cuando*, my friend does not pays
me back, don I dont care. Because" pointing up with a straight
expression into my eyes, finger aloft, "my Lord pay me—and
he pay me *more*—M-o-r-e"—she leans quickly emphasizing
more, and I wish I could tell her in Spanish the illimitable and
inestimable blessing she will get anyway in Nirvana. But I love
her, I fall in love with her. She strokes my arm with thin finger.
I love it. I'm trying to remember my place and my position in
eternity. I have sworn off lust with women,—sworn off lust for
lust's sake,—sworn off sexuality and the inhibiting impulse—I
want to enter the Holy Stream and be safe on my way to the
other shore, but would as lief leave a kiss to Tristessa for her
hark of my heart's sake. She knows I admire and love her with
all my heart and that I'm holding myself back. "You have you
life," she says to Old Bull (of whom in a minute) "and I haff
mind, mine, and Jack has hees life" indicating me, she is giving
me my life back and not claiming it for herself as so many of
the women you love do claim.—I love her but I want to leave.
She says: "I know it, a man and women iss dead,—" "when they
want to be dead"—She nods, confirms within herself some dark
Aztecan instinctual belief, wise—a wise woman, who would
have graced the herds of Bhikshunis in very Yasodhara's time
and made a divine additional nun. With her lidded eyes and
clasped hands, a Madonna. It makes me cry to realize Tristessa
has never had a child and probably never will because of her
morphine sickness (a sickness that goes on as long as the need
and feeds off the need and fills in the need simultaneously, so

that she moans from pain all day and the pain is real, like abcesses in the shoulder and neuralgia down the side of the head and in 1952 just before Christmas she was supposed to be dying), holy Tristessa will not be cause of further rebirth and will go straight to her God and He will recompense her multi-billionfold in aeons and aeons of dead Karma time. She understands Karma, she says: "What I do, I *reap*" she says in Spanish —"Men and women have *errores*—errors, faults, sins, *faltas*," humanbeings sow their own ground of trouble and stumble over the rocks of their own false erroring imagination, and life is hard. She knows, I know, you know.—"Bot—I weeling to haff jonk—morfina—and be no-seek any more." And she hunches her elbows with peasant face, understanding herself in a way that I cannot and as I gaze at her the candlelight flickers on the high cheekbones of her face and she looks as beautiful as Ava Gardner and even better like a Black Ava Gardner, a Brown Ava with long face and long bones and long lowered lids—Only Tristessa hasnt got that expression of sex-smile, it has the expression of mawkfaced downmouthed Indian disregard for what you think about its own pluperfect beauty. Not that it's perfect beauty like Ava, it's got faults, errors, but all men and women have them and so all women forgive men and men forgive women and go their own holy ways to death. Tristessa loves death, she goes to the ikon and adjusts flowers and prays,—She bends over a sandwich and prays, looking sideways at the ikon, sitting Burmese fashion in the bed (knee in front of knee) (down) (sitting), she makes a long prayer to Mary to ask blessing or thanks for the food, I wait in respectful silence, take a quick peek at El Indio, who is also devout and even on the point of crying from junk his eyes moist and reverent and sometimes like especially when Tristessa removes her stockings to get in the bed-blankets an undercurrent of reverent love sayings under his breath ("Tristessa, O Yé, comme t'est Belle") (which is certainly what I'm thinking but afraid to look and watch Tristessa remove her nylons for fear I will get a flash sight of her creamy coffee thighs and go mad)—But El Indio is too loaded with the poison solution of morphine to really care and follow up his reverence for Tristessa, he is busy, sometimes busy being sick, has a wife, two children (down the other side of town), has to work, has to cajole stuff off

Tristessa when he himself is out (as now)—(reason for his
presence in the house)—I see the whole thing popping and
parenthesizing in every direction, the story of that house and
that kitchen.

In the kitchen is hanging pictures of Mexican Pornography
Girls, with black lace and big thighs and revealing clouds of
bosom and pelvic drapery, that I study intently, in the right
places, but the pictures (2) are all roiled and rain-stained and
roll-spanned and hanging protruding from the wall so you
have to straighten them down to study, and even then the rain
is misting down through the cabbage leaves above and the
soggy cardboard—Who might have tried to make a roof for
Fellaheena?—"My Lord, he pay me back *more*"—

So now El Indio is back and standing at the head of the bed as
I sit there, and I turn to look at the rooster ("to tame him")—
I put my hand out exactly as I had done for the hen and allow
it to see I'm not scared if it pecks me, and I will pat it and
make it free from fear of me—The Rooster gazes at my hand
without comment, and looks away, and looks back, and gazes
at my hand (the seminal gysmal champion who dreams a daily
egg for Tristessa that she sucks out the end after a little punc-
ture, fresh)—he looks at my hand tenderly but majestically
moreover as the hen can't make that same majestical appraisal,
he's crowned and cocky and can howl, he is the King Fencer
biting the duel with that mosey morn. He chuckles at sight of
my hand, meaning Yeh and turns away—and I look proudly
around to see if Tristessa and El Indio heard my wild *estupi-
ante*—They rave to notice me with avid lips, "Yes we been talkin
about the ten gram-mos we gonna get tomorrar— Yeh—" and
I feel proud to've made the Rooster, now all the little animals
in the room know me and love me and I love them though
may not know them. All except The Crooner on the roof, on
the clothes closet, in the corner away from the edge, against
the wall just under the ceiling, cozy cooing Dove is sitting in
nest, ever contemplating the entire scene forever without comment. I look up, my Lord is flapping his wings and coo doving
white and I look at Tristessa to know why she got a dove and
Tristessa lifts up her tender hands helplessly and looks at me
affectionately and sadly, to indicate, "It is my Pigeon"—"my

pretty white Pigeon—what can I do about it?" "I love it so"—
"It is so sweet and white"—"It never make a noise"—"It got
soch prurty eyes you look you see the prurty eyes" and I look
into the eyes of the dove and they are dove's eyes, lidded, perfect, dark, pools, mysterious, almost Oriental, unbearable to
withstand the surge of such purity out of eyes—Yet so much
like Tristessa's eyes that I wish I could comment and tell
Tristessa 'Thou hast the dove's eyes'—

Or every now and then the Dove rises and flaps her wings
for exercise, instead of flying through the bleak air she waits in
her golden corner of the world waiting for perfect purity of
death, the Dove in the grave is a dark thing to rave—the raven
in the grave is no white light illuminating the Worlds pointing
up and pointing down throughout uppity ten sides of Eternity
—Poor Dove, poor eyes,—her breast white snow, her milk, her
rain of pity over me, her even gentle eye-gaze into mine from
rosy heights on a position in a rack and Arcabus in the Ope
Heavens of the Mind World,—rosy golden angel of my days,
and I can't touch her, wouldn't dare get up on a chair and trap
her in her corner and make her leery human teeth-grins trying
to impress it to my bloodstained heart—her blood.

El Indio has brought sandwiches back and the little cat is
going crazy for some meat and El Indio gets mad and slaps it
off the bed and I throw both hands up at him "Non" "Don't
do that" and he doesn't even hear me as Tristessa yells at him
—the great Man Beast raging in the kitchen meat and slapping
his daughter in her chair clear across the room to tumble on
the floor her tears start starting as she realizes what he's done
—I don't like El Indio for hitting the cat. But he isn't vicious
about it, just merely reprimandatory, stern, justified, dealing
with the cat, kicking the cat out of his way in the parlor as he
walks to his cigars and Television—Old Father Time is El Indio,
with the kids, the wife, the evenings at the supper table slapping the kids away and yornching on great meaty dinners in
the dim light—"Blurp, blap," he lets go before the kids who
look at him with shining and admiring eyes. Now it's Saturday
night and he's dealing with Tristessa and wrangling to explain
her, suddenly the old Cruz (who is not old, just 40) jumps up
crying "Yeh, with our money, Si, con nuestra dinero" and

repeating twice and sobbing and El Indio warns her I might understand (as I look up with imperial magnificence of unconcern tinged by regard for the scene) and as if to say "This woman is crying because you take all their money,—what is this? Russia? Mussia? Matamorapussia?" as if I didn't care anyway which I couldnt. All I wanted to do was get away. I had completely forgotten about the dove and only remembered it days later.

The wild way Tristessa stands legs spread in the middle of the room to explain something, like a junkey on a corner in Harlem or anyplace, Cairo, Bang Bombayo and the whole Fellah Ollah Lot from Tip of Bermudy to wings of albatross ledge befeathering the Arctic Coastline, only the poison they serve out of Eskimo Gloogloo seals and eagles of Greenland, ain't as bad as that German Civilization morphine she (an Indian) is forced to subdue and die to, in her native earth.

Meanwhile the cat is comfortably ensconced at Cruz's face place where she lies at the foot of the bed, curled, the way she sleeps all night while Tristessa curls at the head and they hook feet like sisters or like mother and daughter and make one little bed do comfortably for two—The little pink kitkat is so certain (despite all his fleas crossing the bridge of his nose or wandering over his eyelids)—that everything is alright—that all is well in the world (at least now)—he wants to be near Cruz's face, where all is well—He (it's a little She) he doesnt notice the bandages and the sorrow and the drunksick horrors she's having, he just knows she's the lady all day her legs are in the kitchen and every now and then she dumps him food, and besides she plays with him on the bed and pretends she's gonna beat him up and holds and scolds him and he yurks in little face into little head and blinks his eyes and flaps back his ears to wait for the beating but she's only playing with him— So now he sits in front of Cruz and even though we may gesture like maniacs as we talk and occasionally a rough hand is waved right by its whiskers almost hitting it or El Indio might roughly decide to throw a newspaper on the bed and land it right on his head, still he sits digging all of us with eyes closed and curled up under Cat Buddha style, meditating among our mad endeavors like the Dove above—I wonder: "Does kittykat know there's a pigeon on the clothes closet." I wish my relatives from Lowell were here to see how people and animals live in Mexico—

But the poor little cat is one mass of fleas, but he doesnt mind, he doesnt keep scratching like American cats but just endures—I pick him up and he's just a skinny little skeleton with great balloons of fur—Everything is so poor in Mexico, people are poor, and yet everything they do is happy and carefree, no matter what is—Tristessa is a junkey and she goes about it skinny and carefree, where an American would be gloomy—But she coughs and complains all day, and by same law, at intervals, the cat explodes into furious scratching that doesnt help—

Meanwhile I keep smoking, my cigarette goes out, and I reach into the ikon for a light from the candle flame, in a glass—I hear Tristessa say something that I interpret to mean "Ack, that stupid fool is using our altar for a light"—To me it's nothing unusual or strange, I just want a light—but perceiving the remark or maintaining belief in the remark without knowing what it was, I ulp and hold back and instead get a light from El Indio, who then shows me later, by quick devout prayer-ito with a piece of newspaper, getting his light indirectly and with a touch and a prayer—Perceiving the ritual I do it too, to get my light a few minutes later—I make a little French prayer: "*Excuse mué ma Dame*"—making emphasis on *Dame* because of Damema the Mother of Buddhas.

So I feel less guilty about my smoke and I know all of a sudden all of us will go to heaven straight up from where we are, like golden phantoms of Angels in Gold Strap we go hitch hiking the Deus Ex Machina to heights Apocalyptic, Eucalyptic, Aristophaneac and Divine—I suppose, and I wonder what the cat might think—To Cruz I say "Your cat is having golden thoughts (su gata tienes pensas de or)" but she doesnt understand for a thousand and one billion manifold reasons swimming in the swarm of her milk thoughts Buddha-buried in the stress of her illness enduring—"What's *pensas*?" she yells to the others, she doesnt know that the cat is having golden thoughts —But the cat loves her so, and stays there, little behind to her chin, purring, glad, eyes X-closed and stoopy, kitty kitkat like the Pinky I'd just lost in New York run over on Atlantic Avenue by the swerve dim madtraffics of Brooklyn and Queens, the automatons sitting at wheels automatically killing cats every day about five or six a day on the same road. "But this cat will die the normal Mexican death—by old age or disease—and be a wise old big bum in the alleys around, and you'll see him (dirty as rags) flitting by the garbage heap like a rat, if Cruz ever gets to throw it out—But Cruz won't, and so cat stays at her chin-point like a little sign of her good intentions."

El Indio goes out and gets meat sandwiches and now the cat goes mad yelling and mewing for some and El Indio throws her off the bed—but Cat finally gets a bite of meat and ronches at it like a mad little Tiger and I think "If she was as big as the one in the Zoo, she'd look at me with big green eyes before eating me." I'm having the fairy tale of Saturday night, having a good time actually because of the booze and the good cheer and the careless people—enjoying the little animals—noticing the little Chihuahua pup now meekly waiting for a bite of meat or bread with her tail curled in and woe, if she ever inherits the earth it'll be because of meek—Ears curled back and even whimpering the little Chihuahua smalldog fear-cry—Nevertheless she's been alternately watching us and sleeping all night, and her own reflections on the subject of Nirvana and death and mortals biding time till death, are of a whimpering high frequency terrified tender variety—and the kind that says 'Leave me alone, I am so delicate' and you leave her alone in her little fragile shell like the shell of canoes over the ocean deeps—I wish I could communicate to all these creatures and people, in the flush of my moonshine goodtimes, the cloudy mystery of the magic milk to be seen in Mind's Deep Imagery where we learn that everything is nothing—in which case they wouldnt worry any more, except after the instant they think to worry again—All of us trembling in our mortality boots, born to die, BORN TO DIE I could write it on the wall and on Walls all over America—Dove in wings of peace, with her Noah Menagery Moonshine eyes; dog with clitty claws black and shiny, to die is born, trembles in her purple eyes, her little weak bloodvessels down the ribs; yea the ribs of Chi-

huahua, and Tristessa's ribs too, beautiful ribs, her with her
aunts in Chihuahua also born to die, beautiful to be ugly, quick
to be dead, glad to be sad, mad to be had—and the El Indio
death, born to die, the man, so he plies the needle of Saturday
Night every night is Saturday night and goes wild to wait,
what else can he do,—The death of Cruz, the drizzles of religion falling on her burial fields, the grim mouth planted in the
satin of the earth coffin, . . . I moan to recover all that
magic, remembering my own *impending* death, 'If only I had
the magic self of babyhood when I remembered what it was
like before I was born, I wouldnt worry about death now
knowing both to be the same empty dream'—But what will
the Rooster say when it dies, and someone hacks a knife at its
fragile chin—And sweet Hen, she who eats out of Tristessa's
paw a globule of beer, her beak miffling like human lips to
churn up the milk of the beer—when she dies, sweet hen,
Tristessa who loves her will save her lucky bone and wrap it in
red thread and keep it in her belongings, nevertheless sweet
Mother Hen of our Arc of Noah Night, she the golden pur-
veyor and reaches so far back you can't find the egg that
prompted her outward through the first original shell, they'll
hack and whack at her tail with hacksaws and make mincemeat
out of her that you run through an iron grinder turning handle, and would you wonder why she trembles from fear of
punishment too? And the death of the cat, little dead rat in the
gutter with twisted yickface—I wish I could communicate to
all their combined fears of death the Teaching that I have
heard from Ages of Old, that recompenses all that pain with
soft reward of perfect silent love abiding up and down and in
and out everywhere past, present, and future in the Void unknown where nothing happens and all simply is what it is. But
they know that themselves, beast and jackal and love woman,
and my Teaching of Old is indeed so old they've heard it long
ago before my time.

I become depressed and I gotta go home. Everyone of us,
born to die.

Bright explanation of the crystal clarity of all the Worlds, I need,
to show that we'll all be all right—The measurement of robot
machines at this time is rather irrelevant or at any time—The

fact that Cruz cooked with a smoky kerosene stove big pot-
tery-fulls of carne meat-general from a whole heifer, bites of
veal, pieces of veal tripe and heifer brains and heifer forehead
bones . . . this wouldn't ever send Cruz to hell because no
one's told her to stop the slaying, and even if someone had,
Christ or Buddha or Holy Mohammed, she would still be safe
from harm—though by God the heifer ain't—

The little kitty is mewing rapidly for meat—himself a little
piece of quivering meat—soul eats soul in the general emptiness.

"Stop complainin!" I yell to the cat as he raves on the floor and
finally jumps and joins us on the bed—The hen is rubbing her
long feathery side gently imperceptibly against my shoe-tip
and I can barely feel it and look in time to recognize, what a
gentle touch it is from Mother Maya—She's the Magic hen-
layer without origin, the limitless chicken with its head cut off
—The cat is mewing so violently I begin to worry for the
chicken, but no the cat is merely meditating now quietly over
a piece of smell on the floor, and I give the poor little fellow a
whirr a purr on the thin sticky shoulders with my fingertip—
Time to go, I've petted the cat, said goodbye to God the Dove,
and wanta leave the heinous kitchen in the middle of a vicious
golden dream—It's all taking place in one vast mind, us in the
kitchen, I don't believe a word of it or a substantial atom-
empty hunk of flesh of it, I see right through it, right through
our fleshy forms (hens and all) at the bright amethyst future
whiteness of reality—I am worried but I aint glad—"Foo," I
say, and rooster looks at me, "what z he mean by *foo!*" and
Rooster goes "Cork a Loodle Doo" a real Sunday morning
(which it is now, 2 AM) Squawk and I see the brown corners of
the dream house and remember my mother's dark kitchen
long ago on cold streets in the other part of the same dream as
this cold present kitchen with its drip-pots and horrors of Indian Mexico City—Cruz is feebly trying to say goodnight to
me as I prepare to go, I've petted her several times a pat on the
shoulder thinking that's what she wanted at the right moments and reassured her I loved her and was on her side "but I
had no side of my own," I lie to myself—I've wondered what
Tristessa thought of my patting her—for awhile I almost
thought she was her mother, one wild moment I divined this:

'Tristessa and El Indio are brother and sister, and this is their Mother, and they're driving her crazy yakking in the night about poison and morphine'—Then I realize: "Cruz is a junkey too, uses three gramos a month, she'll be on the same time and antenna of their dream trouble, moaning and groaning they'll all three go through the rest of their lives sick. Addiction and affliction. Like diseases of the mad, insane inside encephalitises of the brain where you knock out your health purposely to hold a feeling of feeble chemical gladness that has no basis in anything but the thinking-mind—Gnosis, they will certainly change me the day they try to lay morphine on me. And on ye."

Though the shot has done me some good and I haven't touched the bottle since, a kind of weary gladness has come over me tinged with wild strength—the morphine has gentlized my concerns but I'd rather not have it for the weakness it brings to my ribs,—I shall have them bashed in—"I don't want no more morphine after this," I vow, and I yearn to get away from all the morphine talk which, after sporadic listens, has finally wearied me.

I get up to go, El Indio will go with me, walk me to the corner, though at first he argues with them as though he wanted to stay or wanted something further—We go out quickly, Tristessa closes the door in back of us, I don't even give her a close look, just a glance as she closes indicating I'll see her later —El Indio and I walk vigorously down the slimey rainy aisles, turn right, and cut out to the market street, I've already commented on his black hat, and now here I am on the street with the famous Black Bastard—I've already laughed and said "You're just like Dave" (Tristessa's ex husband) "you even wear the black hat" as I'd seen Dave one time, on Redondas—in the moil and wild of a warm Friday night with buses parading slowly by and mobs on the sidewalk; Dave hands the package to his boy, the seller calls the cop, cop comes running, boy hands it back to Dave, Dave says 'Okay take it and ron' and tosses it back and boy hits ledge of a flying bus and hangs in to the crowd with his loins his body hanging over the street and his arms rigidly holding the bus door pole, the cops can't catch, Dave meanwhile has vamoosed into a saloon, removed his legendary black hat, and sat at the counter with other men looking straight ahead—cops no find—I had admired Dave for his guts, now admire El Indio for *his*—As we come out of the Tristessa tenement he lets loose a whistle and a shout at a bunch of men on the corner, we walk right along and they spread and we come up to the corner and walk right on talking, I've not paid attention to what he's done, all I wanta do is go straight home—It's started to drizzle—

"Ya voy dormiendo, I go sleep now" says El Indio putting his palms together at side of his mouth—I say "Okay" then he makes a further elaborate statement I think repeating in words what done before by sign, I fail to acknowledge complete understanding of his new statement, he disappointedly says "Yo un untiende" (you dont understand) but I do understand that he wants to go home and go to bed—"Okay" I say—We shake—We then go through an elaborate smiling routine on the streets of man, in fact on broken cobbles of Redondas—

To reassure him I give him a parting smile and start off but he keeps alertly watching every flicker of my smiler and eye-lash, I can't turn away with an arbitrary leer, I want to smile him on his way, he replies by smiles of his own equally elaborate and psychologically corroborative, we swing informations back and forth with crazy smiles of farewell, so much so, El Indio stumbles in the extreme strain of this, over a rock, and throws still a further parting smile of reassurance capping my own, till no end in sight, but we stumble in our opposite directions as though reluctant—which reluctance lasts a brief second, the fresh air of the night hits your newborn solitude and both you and your Indio go off in a new man and the smile, part of the old, is removed, no longer necessita—He to his home, I to mine, why smile about it all night long except in company—The dreariness of the world politely—

I go down the Wild Street of Redondas, in the rain, it hasn't started increasing yet, I push through and dodge through moils of activity with whores by the hundreds lined up along the walls of Panama Street in front of their crib cells where big Mamacita sits near the cocina pig pottery, as you leave they ask a little for the pig who also represents the kitchen, the chow, *cocina*,—Taxis are slanting by, plotters are aiming for their dark, the whores are nooking the night with their crooking fingers of Come On, young men pass and give em the once over, arm in arm in crowds the young Mexicans are Casbah buddying down their main girl street, hair hanging over their eyes, drunk, borracho, longlegged brunettes in tight yellow dresses grab them and sock their pelvics in, and pull their lapels, and plead—the boys wobble—the cops down the street pass idly like figures on little wheel-thucks rolling by invisibly under the sidewalk—One look through the bar where the children gape and one through the whoreboy bar of queers where spidery heroes perform whore dances in turtleneck sweaters for assembled critical elders of 22—look through both holes and see the eye of the criminal, criminal in heaven.—I plow through digging the scene, swinging my bag with the bottle in it, I twist and give the whores a few twisting looks as I walk, they send me stereotyped soundwaves of scorn from cussin doorways—I am starving, I start eating El Indio's sandwich he gave me which at first I'd sought to refuse so as to leave it for the cat but El Indio insisted it was a present for me, so I nakedly breast-high in one delicate hold as I walk along the street—seeing the sandwich I begin to eat it—finishing it, I start buying tacos as I run by, any kind, any stand where they yell "Joven!"—I buy stinking livers of sausages chopped in black white onions steaming hot in grease that crackles on the inverted fender of the grille—I munch down on heats and hot-sauce salsas and come to devouring whole mouthloads of fire and rush along—nevertheless I buy another one, further, two, of broken cow-meat hacked on the woodblock, head and all it seems, bits of grit and gristle, all mungied together on a mangy tortilla and chewed down with salt, onions, and green leaf—diced—a delicious sandwich when you get a good stand —The stands are 1,2,3 in a row a half mile down the street, tragically lit by candles and dim bulbs and strange lanterns, the whole of Mexico a Bohemian Adventure in the great outdoor plateau night of stones, candle and mist—I pass Plaza Gari-baldi the hot spot of the police, strange crowds are grouping in narrow streets around quiet musicians that only later faintly you hear corneting round the block—Marimbas are drumming in the big bars—Rich men, poor men, in wide hats mingle—Come out of swinging doors spitting cigar butts and clapping big hands over their jock as though they were about to dive in a cold brook—guilty—Up the side streets dead buses waddling in the mud holes, spots of fiery yellow whoredress in the dark, assembled leaners and up against the wall lovers of the loving Mexican night—Pretty girls passing, every age, all the comic Gordos and me turn big heads to watch them, they're too beautiful to bear—

I rock right by the Post Office, cross the bottom of Juarez, the Palace of Fine Arts sinking nearby,—yoke myself to San Juan Letran and fall to hiking up fifteen blocks of it fast passing delicious places where they make the churros and cut you hot salt sugar butter bites of fresh hot donut from the grease basket, that you crunch freshly as you cover the Peruvian night ahead of your enemies on the sidewalk—All kinds of crazy gangs are assembled, chief gleeful leaders getting high on gang leadership wear crazy woollen Scandanavian Ski hats over their zoot paraphenalias and Pachuco haircuts—Other day here I'd passed a gang of children in a gutter their leader dressed as a clown (with nylon stocking over head) and wide rings painted around the eyes, the littler kids have imitated him and attempted similar clown outfits, the whole thing gray and blackened eyes with white loops, like silks of great racetracks the little gang of Pinocchioan heroes (and Genet) paraphernaliaing on the street curb, an older boy making fun of the Clown Hero "What are you doing clowning, Clown Hero?—There ain't no Heaven anywhere?" "There ain't no Santa Claus of Clown Heroes, mad boy"—Other gangs of semi-hipsters hide in front of nightclub bars with wronks and noise inside, I fly by with one quick Walt Whitman look at all that file deroll —It starts raining harder, I've got a long way to go walking and pushing that sore leg right along in the gathering rain, no chance no intention whatever of hailing a cab, the whiskey and the Morphine have made me unruffled by the sickness of the poison in my heart

When you have no more numbers in Nirvana then there won't be such a thing as "numberless" but the crowds on San Juan Letran were like numberless—I say "Count all these sufferings from here to the end of the endless sky which is no sky and see how many you can add together to make a figure to impress the Boss of Dead Souls in the Meat Manufactory in city City

CITY everyone of them in pain and born to die, milling in the streets at 2 AM underneath those imponderable skies"—their enormous endlessness, the sweep of the Mexican plateau away from the Moon—living but to die, the sad song of it I hear sometimes on my roof in the Tejado district, rooftop cell, with candles, waiting for my Nirvana or my Tristessa—neither come, at noon I hear "La Paloma" being played on mental radios in the fallways between the tenement windows—the crazy kid next door sings, the dream is taking place right now, the music is so sad, the French horns ache, the high whiney violins and the deberratarra-rabaratarara of the Indian Spanish announcer. Living but to die, here we wait on this shelf, and up in heaven is all that gold open caramel, ope my door—Diamond Sutra is the sky.

I crash along drunkenly and bleakly and hard with kicking feet over the precarious sidewalk slick of vegetable oil Tehuantepec, green sidewalks, swarmed with scumworm invisible but in high—dead women hiding in my hair, passing underneath the sandwich and chair—"You're nuts!" I yell to the crowds in English "You don't know what in a hell you're doing in this eternity bell rope tower swing to the puppeteer of Magadha, Mara the Tempter, insane, . . . And you all eagle and you beagle and you buy—All you bingle you baffle and you lie— You poor motherin bloaks pourin through the juice parade of your Main Street Night you don't know that the Lord has arranged everything in sight." "Includin your death." "And nothing's happening. I am not me, you are not ye, they unnumbered are not they, and One Un-Number Self there is no such thing."

I pray at the feet of man, waiting, as they.

As they? As Man? As he? There is no He. There is only the unsayable divine word. Which is not a Word, but a Mystery.

At the root of the Mystery the separation of one world from another by a sword of light.—

The winners of tonight's ball game in the open mist outside Tacabatabavac are romping by in the street swinging their baseball bats at the crowd showing how great they can hit and the crowd walks unconcernedly around because they are children not juvenile delinquents. They pull their beak baseball hats tight-hawk down their faces, in the drizzle, tapping their glove they wonder "Did I make a bad play in the fifth inning? Didn't I make it up with that *heet* in the seventh inning?"

At the end of San Juan Letran is that last series of bars that end in a ruined mist, fields of broken adobe, no bums hidden, all wood, Gorky, Dank, with sewers and puddles, ditches in the street five feet deep with water in the bottom—powdery tenements against the light of the nearby city—I watch the final sad bar-doors, where flashes of women golden shining lace behinds I can see and feel like flying in yet like a bird in flight twist on. Kids are in the doorway in goof suits, the band is wailing a chachacha inside, everybody's knee is knocking to bend as they pop and wail with the mad music, the whole club is rocking, *down*, an American Negro walking with me would have said "These cats are stoning themselves on some real hip kicks, they are goofing all the time, they wail, they spend all the time knocking and knocking for that *bread*, for that *girl*, they're up in against the doorways, man, wailing all—you know? They don't know when to stop. It's like Omar Khayyam, I wonder what the vintners buy, one half so precious, as what they sell." (My boy Al Damlette.)

I turn off at these last bars and it really starts raining hard and I walk fast as I can and come to a big puddle and jump out of it all wet and jump right in again and cross it—The morphine prevents me from feeling the wet, my skin and limbs are numb,—like a kid when he goes skating in winter, falls through ice, runs home with skates under his arm so he won't catch cold, I kept plowing through the Pan American rain and above is the gigantic roar of a Pan American Airplane coming in to land at Mexico City Airport with passengers from New York looking for to find the other end of dreams. I look up into the drizzle and watch their tail firespark—you won't find me landing over great cities and all I do is clutch the side of the seat and wobble as the air pilot expertly leads us into a tremendous flaming crash against the side of warehouses in the slum district of Old Indian Town—what? with all them rat tat tans with revolvers in their pockets pushing through my foggy bones looking for something made of gold, and then rats gnaw ya.

I'd rather walk than ride the airplane, I can fall on the ground flat on my face and die that way.—With a watermelon under my arm. *Mira*.

I come up gorgeous Orizaba Street (after crossing wide muddy parks near Ciné Mexico and the dismal trolley street called after dismal General Obregon in the rainy night, with roses in his mother's hair—) Orizaba Street has a magnificent fountain and pool in a green park at a round O-turn in residential splendid shape of stone and glass and old grills and scrolly worly lovely majesties that when looked at by the moon blend with magic inner Spanish gardens of an architecture (if architecture you will) designed for lovely nights at home. Andalusian in intention.

The fountain is not spraying water at 2 AM and as though it would have to, in the driving rain, and me rolling by there sitting on my railroad switchblock passing over pinking sparking switches on tracks of underneath-the-earth like the cops on the little whorestreet 35 blocks back and way downtown—

It's the dismal rainy night caught up with me—my hair is dripping water, my shoes are slopping—but I have my jacket on, and it is soaking on the outside—but it is rain repellent—"Why I bought it back in the Richmond Bank" I'm tellin heroes about it later, in a littlekid dream.—I run on home, walking past the bakery where they don't at 2 AM anymore make latenight donuts, twisters taken out of ovens and soaked in syrup and sold to you through the bakery window for two cents apiece and I'd buy baskets of them in my younger days—closed now, rainy night Mexico City of the present contains no roses and no fresh hot donuts and it's bleak. I cross the last street, slow down and relax letting out breath and stumbling on my muscles, now I go in, death or no death, and sleep the sweet sleep of white angels.

But my door is locked, my street door, I have no key for it, all lights are out, I stand there dripping in the rain with no place to dry up and sleep—I see there's a light in Old Bull Gaines' window and I go over and amazedly look in, just see his golden curtain, I realize "If I can't get in my own place then I'll just knock on Bull's window and sleep in his easy chair." Which I do, knocking, and he comes out of the dark establishment of about 20 people and in his bathrobe walks through the little bit of rain between building and the door—comes and snaps open the iron door. I go in after him—"Can't go in my own place" I say—He wants to know what Tristessa said about tomorrow, when they get more stuff from the Black Market, the Red Market, the Indian Market—So it's alright with Old Bull I sleep and stay in his room—"Till the street door is opened at 8 AM" I add, and suddenly decide to curl up on the floor with a flimsy coverlet, which, instantly as done, is like a bed of soft fleece and I lay there divine, legs all tired and clothes partly wet (am wrapped in Old Bull's big towel robe like a ghost in a Turkish bath) and the whole journey in the rain done, all I have to do is lie dreaming on the floor. I curl up and start sleeping. In the middle of the night now, with the small yellowbulb on, and rain crashing outside, Old Bull Gaines has closed shutters tight, is smoking cigarette after cigarette and I can't breathe in the room and he's coughing "K e-h e!" the dry junkey cough, like a protest, like yelling *Wake Up!* —he lies there, thin, emaciated, long nosed, strangely handsome and gray haired and lean and mangy 22 in his derelict worldling ("student of souls and cities" he calls himself) decapitated and bombed out by morphine frame—Yet all the guts in the world. He starts munching on candy, I lay there waking up realizing that Old Bull is munching on candy noisily in the night—All the sides to this dream—Annoyed, I glance anxiously around and see him myorking and monching on condy after condy, what a preposterous thing to do at 4 AM in your bed—Then at 4:30 he's up and boiling down a couple of capsules of morphine in a spoon,—you see him, after the shot has been sucked in and siphoned out, with big glad tongue licking so he can spit on the blackened bottom of the spoon and rub it clean and silver with a piece of paper, using, to really polish the spoon, a pinch of ashes—And he lays back, feeling it a little, it takes ten minutes, a muscle bang,—by about twenty minutes he might feel alright—if not, there he is rustling in his drawer waking me up again, he's looking for his goofballs—"So he can sleep."

So *I* can sleep. But no. Immediately he wants another jolt of some kind, he ups and opes his drawer and pulls out a tube of codeine pills and counts out ten and pops that in with a slug of cold coffee from his old cup that sits on the chair by the bed—and he endures in the night, with the light on, and lights further cigarettes—At some time or other, around dawn, he falls asleep—I get up after some reflections at 9 or 8, or 7, and quickly put my wet clothes on to rush upstairs to my warm bed and dry clothes—Old Bull is sleeping, he finally made it, Nirvana, he's snoring and he's out, I hate to wake him up but he'll have to lock himself in, with his bolt and slider—It's gray outside, rain has finally stopped after heaviest surge at dawn. 40,000 families were flooded out in the Northwestern part of Mexico City that storm. Old Bull, far from floods and storms with his needles and his powders beside the bed and cottons and eyedroppers and paraphernalias—"When you got morphine, you dont need anything else, me boy," he says to me in the daytime all combed and high sitting in his easy chair with papers the picture of glad health—"Madame Poppy, I call her. When you've got Opium you've got all you need.—All that good *O* goes down in your veins and you feel like singin Hallelujah!" And he laughs. "Bring me Grace Kelly on this chair, Morphine on that chair, I'll take Morphine."

"Ava Gardner *too?*"

"Ava GVavna and all the bazotzkas in all the countries so far—if I can have my M in the morning and my M in the afternoon and my M in the evening before going to bed, I dont even need to know what time it is on the City Hall Clock—" He tells me all this and more nodding vigorously and sincerely. His jaw quivers with emotion. "Why for krissakes if I had no junk I'd be bored to death, I'd die of *boredom*" he complains, almost crying—"I read Rimbaud and Verlaine, I know what I'm talking about—Junk is the only thing I want—You've never been junksick, you don't know what it's like—Boy when you wake up in the morning sick and take a good bang, boy, that feels good." I can picture myself and Tristessa waking up in our nuptial madbed of blankets and dogs and cats and canaries and dots of whoreplant in the coverlet and naked shoulder to shoulder (under the gentle eyes of the Dove) she shoots me in or I shoot myself in a big bang of waterycolored poison

straight into the flesh of your arm and into your system which
it instantly proclaims *its*—you feel the weak fall of your body
to the disease in the solution—but never having been junksick,
I don't know the horror of the disease—A story Old Bull
could tell much better than I—

He lets me out, but not until he's muttered and sputtered out
of bed—holding his pajamas and bathrobe, pushing in his
belly where it hurts, where some kind of hernia cave-in annoys
him,—poor sick fella, almost 60 years old and hanging on to
his diseases without bothering anybody—Born in Cincinnati,
brought up in the Red River Steamboats. (redlegged? his legs
as white as snow)—

    I see that it's stopped raining and I'm thirsty and have drunk
Old Bull's two cups of water (boiled, and kept in a jar)—I go
across the street in my damp sopping shoes and buy an ice-cold
Spur Cola and gobble it down on my way to my room—The
skies are opening up, there might be sunshine in afternoon,
the day is almost wild and Atlantican, like a day at sea off the
coast of the Firth of Scotland—I yell imperial flags in my
thoughts and rush up the two flights to my room, the final
flight a ricket of iron tin-spans creaking and cracking on nails
and full of sand, I get on the hard adobe floor of the roof, the
Tejado, and walk on slippery little puddles around the air of
the courtyard rail only two foot high so you can just easily fall
down three flights and crack your skull on tile Espaniala floors
where Americans gnash and fight sometimes in raucous parties
early in the twilight of the morning,—I could fall, Old Bull
almost fell over when he lived on the roof a month, the children sit on the soft stone of the 2 foot rail and goof and talk,
all day running around the thing and skidding and I never like
to watch—I come to my room around two curves of the Hole
and unlock my padlock which is hooked to decaying half-out
nails (one time left the room open and unattended all day)—I
go in and jam the door in the rain damp wood and rain has
swollen the wood and the door barely tightens at the top—I
get in my dry hobo pants and two big hobo shirts and go
to bed with thick socks on and finish the Spur and lay it on
the table and say "Ah" and wipe the back of my mouth and

look awhile at holes in my door showing the outside Sunday morning sky and I hear churchbells down Orizaba lane and people are going to church and I'm going to sleep and I'll make up for it later, goodnight.

"Blessed Lord, Thou lovedest all sentient life."

Why do I have to sin and do the sign of the Cross?

"Not one of the vast accumulation of conceptions from beginningless time, through the present and into the never ending future, not one of them is graspable."

It's the old question of "Yes life's not real" but you see a beautiful woman or something you can't get away from wanting because it is there in front of you—This beautiful woman of 28 standing in front of me with her fragile body ("I put thees in my neck [a dicky] so nobody look and see my beautiful body," she thinks she jokes, not regarding herself as beautiful) and that face so expressive of the pain and loveliness that went no doubt into the making of this fatal world,—a beautiful sunrise, that makes you stop on the sands and gaze out to sea hearing Wagner's Magic Fire Music in your thoughts—the fragile and holy countenance of poor Tristessa, the tremulous bravery of her little junk-racked body that a man could throw up in the air ten feet—the bundle of death and beauty—all pure Form standing in front of me, all the racks and tortures of sexual beauty, the breast, the limb of the middle body, the whole huggable mess of a woman some of them even though 6 feet high you can slumber on their bellies in the night like a nap on a dreaming bankside of a woman—Like Goethe at 80, you know the futility of love and you shrug—You shrug away the warm kiss, the tongue and lips, the tug at the thin waist, the whole warm floating thing against you held tight— the little woman—for which rivers flow and men fall down stepladders —The thin cold long brown fingers of Tristessa, slow, and casual and lazy, like the meeting of lips—The Tristessa Spanish Night of her deep love hole, the bullfights in her dreams of you, the lazy rainy rose against the idle cheek—And all the concomitant lovelinesses of a lovely woman a young man in a far-off country should yearn to stay for—I was traveling around in circles in North America in many a gray tragedy

*

I stand looking at Tristessa, she's come to visit me in my room, she won't sit down, she stands and talks—in the candle light she is excited and eager and beautiful and radiant—I sit down on the bed, looking down on the stony floor, while she talks —I don't even listen to what she's saying, about junk, Old Bull, how she's tired—"I go to the do it to-*morra*—TO-MORRAR—" she taps to emphasize me with her hand, so I have to say "Yeh Yeh go ahead" and she goes on with her story, which I don't understand—I just can't look at her for fear of thoughts I'll get—But she takes care of all of that for me, she says "Yes, we are in pain—" I say "La Vida es dolor" (life is pain), she agrees, she says life is love too. "When you got one million pesos I dont care how many, they dont move" —she says, indicating my paraphernalia of leather-covered scriptures and Sears Roebuck envelopes with stamps and air-mail envelopes inside—as though I had a million pesos hiding in time in my floor—"A million pesos does not move—but when you got the friend, the friend give it to you in the bed" she says, legs spread a little, pumping with her loins at the air in the direction of my bed to indicate how much better a human being is than a million paper pesos—I think of the inexpressible tenderness of receiving this holy friendship from the sacrificial sick body of Tristessa and I almost feel crying or grabbing her and kissing her—A wave of loneliness passes over me, remembering past loves and bodies in beds and the unbeatable surge when you go into your beloved deep and the whole world goes with you—Though we know that Mara the Tempter is evil, his fields of temptation are innocent—How could Tristessa, rousing passion in me, have anything to do, except as a field of merit or a dupe of innocence or a material witness to my murderous lust, how could she be blamed and how could she be sweeter than standing there explaining my love directly with her pantomiming thighs. She's high, she keeps trying at the lapel of her kimono (underneath's a slip that shows) and trying to attach it unattachably to an inexistent button of the coat. I look into her eyes deep, meaning "Would you be my friend like that?" and she looks straight at me pools of neither this or that, her combination of reluctance to break her personal disgust covenant moreover lodged in the

Virgin Mary, and her love of wish-for-me, makes her as mysterious as the Tathagata whose form is described as being as inexistent, rather as inscrutable as the direction in which a put-out fire has gone. I can't get a yes or no out of her eyes for the time I allot to them. Very nervous, I sit, stand, sit, she stands explaining further things. I am amazed by the way her skin wrinkles O so sensitively down the bridge of her nose in even clean lines, and her little laugh of delight that comes so rarely and so's littlegirlish, child of glee,—It's all my own sin if I make a play for her.

I want to take her in both hands by the waist and pull her slowly close with a few choice words of sudden endearment like "Mi gloria angela" or "Mi whichever it is" but I have no language to cover my embarrassment—Worst of all, would it be, to have her push me aside and say "No, no, no" like disappointed mustachio'd heroes in French movies being turned out by the little blonde who is the brakeman's wife, by a fence, in smoke, midnight, in the French railroad yards, and I turn away big pained loverface and apologize,—going away thence with the sensation that I have a beastly streak in me I didn't notice, conceptions common to all young lovers and old. I don't want to disgust Tristessa—It would horrify me to cause her ruinous fleshpetal tender secrets and have her wake up in the morning lodged against the back of some unwelcome man who loves by night and sleeps it off, and wakes up blearing to shave and by his very presence causes consternation where before there was absolute perfect purity of nobody.

But what I've missed when I don't get that friend lunge of the lover's body, coming right at me, all mine, but it was a slaughterhouse for meat and all you do is bend to wreak havocs in somethings-gotta-give of girlihood.—When Tristessa was 12 years old suitors twisted her arm in the sun outside the mother's cooking door—I've seen it a million times, in Mexico the young men want the young girls—Their birthrate is terrific —They turn em out wailing and dying by the golden tons in vats of semiwinery messaferies of oy Ole Tokyo birthcrib.—I lost track of my thought there,—

Yes, the thighs of Tristessa and the golden flesh all mine, what am I a Caveman? Am a Caveman.

Caveman buried deep under ground.

It would just be the coronna of her cheeks pulsing to mouth, and my rememberance of her splendid eyes, like sitting in a box the lovely latest in France enters the crashing orchestra and I turn to Monsieur next to me whispering "She is *splendide*, non?"—With Johnny Walker Scotch in my tuxedo coat-pocket.

I stand up. I must see her.

Poor Tristessa is swaying there explaining all her troubles, how she hasn't got enough money, she's sick, she'll be sick in the morning and in the look of her eye I caught perhaps the gesture of a shadow of acceptance of the idea of me as a lover— Only time I ever saw Tristessa cry, was when she was junk sick on the edge of Old Bull's bed, like a woman in the back pew of a church in daily novena she dabs at her eyes—She points to the sky again, "If my friend dont pay me back," looking at me straight, "my Lord pay me back—*more*" and I can feel the spirit enter the room as she stands, waiting with her finger pointed up, on her spread legs, confidently, for her Lord to pay her back—"So I geev every-things I have to my friend, and eef he doan pay me back"—she shrugs—"my Lord pay me back"—standing alert again—"*More*" and as the spirit swims around the room I can tell the effective mournful horror of it (her reward is so thin) now I see radiating from the crown of her head innumerable hands that have come from all ten quarters of the Universe to bless her and pronounce her Bodhisat for saying and knowing that so well.

Her Enlightenment is perfect,—"And we are nothing, you and me"—she pokes at my chest, "Jew—Jew—" (Mexican saying "You") "—and *me*"—pointing at herself—"We are *nothing*. Tomorrar we may be die, and so we are nothing—" I agree with her, I feel the strangeness of that truth, I feel we are two empty phantoms of light or like ghosts in old haunted-house stories diaphanous and precious and white and not-there,—She says "I know you want to sleep."

"No no" I say, seeing she wants to leave—

"I go to it sleep, early in the mawnins I go get see for the mans and I get the morfina and com bock for Old Bool"—and since we are *nada*, nothing, I forget what she said about friends all lost in the beauty of her strange intelligent imagery, every bit true—"She's an Angel," I think secretly, and escort her to the door with movement of arm as she leans to the door talking to go out—We are careful not to touch each other—I tremble, once I jumped a mile when her fingertip hit my knee in conversations, at chairs—the first afternoon I'd seen her, in dark glasses, in the sunny afternoon window, by a candle light lit for kicks, sick kicks of life, smoking, beautiful, like the Owner Damsel of Las Vegas, or the Revolutionary Heroine of Marlon Brando Zapata Mexico—with Culiacan heroes and all—That's when she got me—In afternoon space of gold the look, the sheer beauty, like silk, the children giggling, me blushing, at guy's house, where we first found Tristessa and started all this—Sympaticus Tristessa with her heart a gold gate, I'd first dug to be an evil enchantress—I'd run across a Saint in Modern Mexico and here I was fantasizing dreams away about foreordained orders for nothing and necessary betrayals—the betrayal of the old father when he entices by ruse the three little crazy kids screaming and playing in the burning house, "I'll give each one your favorite cart," out they come running for the carts, he gives them the High Incomparable Great Cart of the Single Vehicle White Bullock which they're too young to appreciate—with that greatcart command, he'd made me an offer—I look at Tristessa's leg and decide to avoid the issue of fate and rest beyond heaven.

I play games with her fabulous eyes and she longs to be in a monastery.

"Leave Tristessa alone" I say, anyway, like I'd say "Leave the kitty alone, don't hurt it"—and I open her the door, so we can go out, at midnight, from my room— In my hand I stumble-awkwardly hold big railroad brakeman lantern to her feet as we descend the perilous needless to say steps, she'd almost tripped coming up, she moaned and she groaned coming up, she smiled and minced with her hand on her skirt going down, with that majestical lovely slowness of woman, like a Chinese Victoria.

"We are nothing."

"Tomorrow we may be die."

"We are nothing."

"You and Me."

I politely lead all the way down by light and lead her out to street where I hail her a white taxi for her home.

Since beginningless time and into the never-ending future, men have loved women without telling them, and the Lord has loved them without telling, and the void is not the void because there's nothing to be empty of.

Art there, Lord Star?—Diminished is the drizzle that broke my calm.

Part Two
A Year Later . . .

Diminish'd never is the drizzle that broke no calm—I didnt
tell her I loved her but when I left Mexico I began to
think on her and then I began to tell her I loved her in letters,
and almost did, and she wrote too, pretty Spanish letters,
saying I was sweet, and please hurry back—I hurried back too
late, I should have come back in the Spring, almost did, had
no money, just touched the border of Mexico and felt that
vomity feeling of Mexico—went on to California and lived in a
shack with young monk Buddhist type visitors every day and
went north to Desolation Peak and spent a summer surling in
the Wilderness, eating and sleeping alone—said, "Soon I go
back, to the warm arms of Tristessa"—but waited too long.

O Lord, why have you done this to your angel-selves, this
blight life, this ugh raggedy crap scene full of puke and thieves
and dying?—couldnt you have placed us in a dismal heaven
where all was glad anyhow?—Art thou Masochist, Lord, art
thou Indian Giver, art thou Hater?

Finally I was back in Bull's room after a four thousand mile
voyage from the mountain peak near Canada, a terrible
enough trip in itself, not worth moot herein—and he went out
and got her.

Already he'd warned me: "I dont know what's the matter
with her, she's changed in the past two weeks, the *past week*
even—"

"Is that because she knew I was coming?" I thought
darkly—

"She throws fits and hits me over the head with coffee cups
and loses my money and falls in the street—"

"What's the *matter* with her?"

"Goofballs—I told her not to take too many—You know it
takes an old junkey with many years of experience to know how
to handle sleeping pills,—she wont listen, she dont know
how to use em, three, four, sometimes five, once twelve, it's
not the same Tristessa—What I wanta do is *marry* her and get

my citizenship, see, you think that's a good idea?—After all, she's my life, I'm her life—"

I could see Old Bull had fallen in love—with a woman not named Morphina.

"I never touch her—it's just a marriage of convenience—you know what I mean—I cant be getting stuff on the black market myself, I dont know how, I need her and she needs my money."

Bull got $150 a month from a trust fund established by his father before he died—his father had loved him, and I could know why, for Bull is a sweet and tender person, though just a little of the con man, for years in New York he supported his junk habit by stealing about $30 every day, twenty years—He'd been in jail a few times when they'd found him with wrong merchandise—In jail he was always the librarian, he is a great scholar, in many ways, with a marvelous interest in history and anthropology and of all things French Symbolist poetry, Mallarmé above all—I'm not talking of the other Bull who is the great writer who wrote "Junkey"—This is another Bull, older, almost 60, I wrote poems in his room all last summer when Tristessa was *mine, mine,* and I wouldnt take her—I had some silly ascetic or celibacious notion that I must not touch a woman—My touch might have saved her—

Now too late—

He brings her home and right away I see something is wrong—She comes tottering in on his arm and gives a weak (thank God for that) smile and holds out her arm rigidly, I dont know what to do but hold her arm up, "What's the matter with Tristessa is she sick?"

"All last month she was paralyzed down one whole leg and her arms were covered with cysts, O she was an awful sick girl last month"

"What's the matter with her now?"

"Shh—let her sit down—"

Tristessa is holding me and slowly levels her sweet brown cheek against mine, with a rare smile, and I'm playing the befuddled American almost consciously—

Look, I'll save her yet—

*

Trouble is, what would I do with her once I'd won her?—it's like winning an angel in hell and you are then entitled to go down with her to where it's worse or maybe there'll be light, some, down there, maybe it's me's crazy—

"She's going crazy," says Bull, "those goofballs'll do it to everybody, to you, anybody I dont care who."

In fact Bull himself took too many two nights later and proved it—

The problem of junkies, narcotic addicts bless their soul, bless their quiet thoughtful souls, is to get it—On all sides they're balked, they are continually unhappy—"If the government gave me enough morphine every day I would be completely happy and I would be completely willing to work as a male nurse in a hospital—I even sent the government my ideas on the subject, in a letter in 1938 from Lexington, how to solve the narcotic problem, by putting junkies to work, with their daily doses, cleaning the subways, anything—as long as they get their medicine they're all right, just like any other sick people—It's like alcoholics, they need medicine—"

I cant remember everything that happened except for last night so fateful, so horrible, so sad and mad—Better to do it that way, why build up?

It all started out with Bull being out of morphine, sick, a little too many goofballs he'd taken (secanols) to make up for the morphine lack and so he is acting like a baby, sloppy, like senile, not quite as bad as the night he slept in my bed on the roof because Tristessa had gone mad and was breaking everything in his room and hitting him and falling on the floor right on her head, goofballs she bought in a drugstore, Bull would give her no more—The anxious landladies are hovering at the door thinking we're beating her up but she's beating us up—

The things she said to me, what she really thought of me, now came out, a year later, a year too late, and all I should have done was *tell her* I loved her—She accused me of being a filthy teahead, she ordered me out of Bull's room, she tried to hit me with a bottle, she tried to take my tobacco pouch and keep it, I had to struggle with her—Bull and I hid the bread knife under the rug—She just sits there on the floor like an idiot baby, doodling with objects—She accuses me of trying to smoke marijuana out of my tobacco pouch but it is only Bull Durham tobacco for my roll-me-owns because commercial cigarettes have a chemical in them to keep them firm that damaged my susceptible phlebitic veins and arteries—

So Bull is afraid she'll kill him in the night, we cant get her out, previously (a week ago) he'd called cops and ambulances and even they wouldnt get her out, Mexico—So he comes sleep in my new room bed, with clean sheets, forgets that he's already taken two goofballs and takes two more and thereupon goes blind, cant find his cigarettes, gropes and knocks down everything, pees in the bed, spills coffee I bring him, I have to sleep on the floor of stone among bedbugs and cockroaches, I revile him all night poutingly: "Look what you're doing to my nice clean bed"

"I cant help it—I gotta find another cap—Is this a cap?" He holds up a matchstick and thinks it's a capsule of morphine. "Bring me your spoon"—He's going to boil it down and shoot it—Lord—In the morning at gray time he finally leaves and goes down to his room, stumbling with all his things including a Newsweek he could have never read—I dump his cans of pee in the toilet, it's all pure blue like the blue Sir of Joshua Reynolds, I think: "MY GOD, he's gotta be dying!" but turns out they were cans of washing blueing—Meanwhile Tristessa has slept and feels better and somehow they stumble around and get their shots and next day she returns tapping in Bull's window, pale and beautiful, no more an Aztec witch, and apologizes sweetly—

"She'll be back on goofballs in a week," says Bull—"But I'm not giving her any more"—He swallows one himself—

"Why do *you* take em!" I yell.

"Because I know how, I've been a junkey for forty years"

Comes then the fateful night—

I've already finally in a cab and once on the street told Tristessa I love her—"Yo te amo"—No reply—She lies to Bull and tells him I propositioned her saying "You've slept with a lot of men, why not sleep with me"—No such thing I ever said, just "Yo te amo"—Because I do love her—But what to do with her—She never used to lie before the goofballs—In fact she used to pray and go to church—

I've given up on Tristessa and this afternoon, Bull sick, we get a cab and go down into the slums to find El Indio (the Black Bastard he's called in the trade), who always has something— It's always been my secret hunch that El Indio loves Tristessa too—He has beautiful grown daughters, he lies in a bed behind flimsy curtains with the door wide open to the world, high on M, his elder wife sits anxiously in a chair, ikons burn, arguments take place, groans, all under the endless Mexican skies— We come to his pad and his old wife tells us she is his wife (we didnt know) and he's not in so we sit on the stone steps of the crazy courtyard full of screaming children and drunks and women with wash and banana peels you'd think, and wait there—Bull is so sick he has to go home—Tall, humped, wizard cadaver-like he goes, leaving me sitting drunk on the stone drawing pictures of the children in my little notebook—

Then out comes a host of some kind, a portly friendly man, with a waterglass of pulque, two glasses, he insists I chugalug mine with his, I do, bang, down, the cactus juice dripping from our lips, he beats me to the draw—Women laugh— There's a big kitchen—He brings me more—I drink and draw the children—I offer money for the pulque but they wont take it—It starts to grow dark in the courtyard—

I've already swallowed a fifth of wine on the way down, it's one of my drinking days, I've been bored and sad and lost— too, for three days I've been painting and drawing with pencil, chalk and watercolors (my first formal try) and I'm exhausted —I've sketched a little bearded Mexican artist in his roof hut and he tore the picture out of the big notebook to keep it— We drank tequila in the morning and drew each other—Of me he drew a kind of tourist sketch showing how young and handsome and American I am, I dont understand (he wants me to buy it?)—Of him I draw a terrible apocalyptic black bearded face, also his body tinily twisted on the edge of the couch, O heaven and posterity will judge all this art, whatever it is—So I'm drawing one particular little boy who wont stand still then I start drawing the Virgin Madonna—

More fellows appear and they invite me into a big room where a big white table is covered with pulque cups and on the floor open urns of it—Amazing the faces in there—I think "I'll have a good time and meanwhile I'm right on El Indio's

doorstep and I'll catch him for Bull when he comes home—
and Tristessa'll come too—"

Borracho, we drain big cups of cactus juice and there's an
old singer with guitar with his young disciple boy with thick
sensitive lips and a big fat hostess woman like out of Rabelais
and Rembrandt Middle Ages who sings—The leader of this
huge gang of fifteen appears to be Pancho Villa at the table
end, red clay face, perfectly round and jocund, but Mexican
owlish, with crazy blue eyes (I think) and a wild red checked
shirt and like always ecstatically happy—But beside him other
more sinister lieutenants of some sort, to them I look down-
table right dead in the eye and toast and even ask "Que es la
vida? What is life?"—(to prove I'm philosophical and smart)—
Meanwhile a man in a blue suit and blue hat appears the most
friendly, he beckons me to the toilet for a swaying talk over
urine—He locks the door—His eyes are sunken deep in pudgy
battered W.C. Fields sockets—"sockets" too clean a word—
but a wicked pair of funny eyes, also a hypnotist, I keep staring
at him, I keep *liking* him—I like him so much that when he
takes my wallet out and counts my money I laugh, I fiddle a
little bit trying to get it back, he holds off counting—Others
are trying to get in the toilet—"This is Mexico!" says he. "We
stay here if we like"—When he hands me back my wallet I see
my money's still in it but I swear on the Bible on God on Buddha on all that was supposed to be holy, in real life there was
no more money in that wallet (wallet, shwallet, just a leather
foldcase for travelers checks)—He leaves me *some* money
because later I give twenty pesos to a big fat guy and tell him
to go out and get some marijuana for the whole group—He
too keeps taking me to the toilet for earnest confabs, somehow
my dark glasses disappear—

Finally Blue Hat in front of everybody simply snatches my
notebook out of my (Bull's) coat, like a joke, pencil and all,
and slips it in his own coat and stares at me, wicked and funny
—I really cant help laughing but then I do say "Come on,
come on, give me back my poems" and I reach into his coat
and he twists away, and I reach again and he wont—I turn to
the most distinguished-looking man there, in fact the only one,
who is sitting next to me, "Will you undertake the responsibility of getting my poems back."

He says he will, without understanding what I'm saying, but I drunkenly assume he will—Meanwhile in a blind dazzle of ecstasy I throw fifty pesos on the floor to prove something— Later I throw two pesos on the floor saying "It's for the music"—They end up feeding that to the two musicians but I'm too proud after reconsideration to start looking around for my 50 pesos too but you will see that this is just a case of wanting to be robbed, a strange kind of exultation and drunken power, "I dont care about money, I am the King of the world, I will lead your little revolutions myself"—This I begin to work on by making friends with Pancho Villa, and brother there's a lot of knocking of cups and arm-around-chugalugs down, and song—And by this time I'm too stupid to check my wallet but every cent is gone—I take great pride meanwhile in showing how I appreciate the music, I even drum on the table—Finally I go out with Fat Boy to talk in the toilet and as we're coming out here comes a strange woman up the steps, unearthly and pale, slow, majestic, neither young nor old, I cant help staring at her and even when I realize it's Tristessa I keep staring and wondering at this strange woman and it seems that she has come to save me but she's only coming for a shot from El Indio (who, by the way, had by now, on his own accord, gone to Bull's two miles away)—I leave the gay gang of thieves and follow my love.

She is wearing a long dirty dress and a shawl and her face is pale, little rings under the eyes, that thin patrician slowly hawked nose, those luscious lips, those sad eyes—and the music of her voice, the complaint of her song, when she talks in Spanish to others . . .

Ah Sacristi—the sad mutilated blue Madonna, is Tristessa, and for me to keep saying that I love her is a bleeding lie—She hates me and I hate her, make no bones about it—I hate her because she hates me, no other reason—She hates me because I dont know, I guess I was too pious last year—She keeps yelling "*I dunt care!*" and hits us over the head and goes out and sits on the curb in the street and doodles and sways—Nobody dares approach the woman with her head between her knees— Tonight though I can see she's alright, quiet, pale, walking straight, coming up the stone steps of the thieves—

El Indio aint in, we go down again—I had already twice visited El Indio's to check on him, not there, but his brown daughter with the beautiful brown sad eyes staring out into the night as I question her, "Non, non," is all she can say, she is staring at some fixed point in the garbage of the sky, so all I do is stare at her eyes and I have never seen such a girl—Her eyes seem to say "I love my father even tho he takes narcoticas, but please dont come here, leave him alone"—

Tristessa and I go down to the slippery garbage street of dull brown cokestand lights and distant dim blue and rose neons (like rubbed chalk crayon) of Santa Maria de Redondas, where we hook up with poor bedraggled wild looking Cruz and start off somewhere—

I have my arm around Tristessa's waist and walk sadly with her—Tonight she doesnt hate me—Cruz always liked me and still does—In the past year she has caused poor old Bull every kind of trouble with her drunk shenanigans—O there's been pulque and vomiting in the streets and groans under heaven, spattered angel wings covered with the pale blue dirt of heaven —Angels in hell, our wings huge in the dark, the three of us start off, and from the Golden Eternal Heaven bends God blessing us with his face which I can only describe as being infinitely sorry (compassionate), that is, infinite with understanding of suffering, the sight of that Face would make you cry—I've seen it, in a vision, it will cancel all in the end—No tears, just the lips, O I can show you!—No woman could be that sad, God is like a man—It's all a blank how we go up the street to some small narrow dark street where two women are sitting with steaming cauldrons of some kind, or steamcups, where we sit on wood crates, I with my head on Tristessa's shoulder, Cruz at my feet, and they give me a drink of hot punch—I look in my wallet, no more money, I tell Tristessa, she pays for the drinks, or talks, or runs the whole show, maybe she's the leader of the gang of thieves even—

The drinks dont help much, it's getting late, towards dawn, the chill of the high plateau gets into my little sleeveless shirt and loose sports coat and shino pants and I start shivering uncontrollably—Nothing helps, drink after drink, nothing helps—

Two young Mexican cats attracted by Tristessa come and

stand there drinking and talking all night, both have mustaches, one of them is very short with a round baby face with pear-like cheeks—The other is taller, with wings of newspaper stuck somehow in his jacket to protect him from the cold—Cruz just stretches out right in the road in her topcoat and goes to sleep, head on the ground, on the stone—A cop arrests somebody at the head of the alley, we around the little candle flames and steampots watch without much interest—At one point Tristessa kisses me gently on the lips, the softest, just-touchingest kiss in the world—Aye, and I receive it with amazement—I've made up my mind to stay with her and sleep where she sleeps, even if she sleeps in a garbage can, in a stone cell with rats—But I keep shivering, no amount of wrapping in can do it, for a year now I've been spending every night in my sleeping bag and I'm no longer inured to ordinary dawn chills of the earth—At one point I fall right off the crate I occupy with Tristessa, land in the sidewalk, stay there—Other times I'm up haranguing long mysterious conversations with the two cats—What on earth are they trying to say and do?—Cruz sleeps in the street—

Her hair hangs out all black across the road, people step over her.—It's the end.

Dawn comes gray.

People start passing to go to work, soon the pale light begins to reveal the incredible colors of Mexico, the pale blue shawls of women, the deep purple shawls, the lips of people faintly roseate in general aubeal blue—

"What we waitin for? Where we goin?" I'd kept asking—

"I go get my shot," she says—gets me another hot punch, which goes down shivering through me—One of the ladies is asleep, the dealer with ladle is beginning to get sore because apparently I've drank more than Tristessa paid or the two cats or something—

Many people and carts pass—

"Vamonos," says Tristessa getting up, and we wake up ragged Cruz and waver a minute standing, and go off in the streets—

Now you can see to the ends of the streets, no more garbanzo darkness, it's all pale blue churches and pale people and pink shawls—We move along and come to rubbly fields and cross and come to a settlement of adobe huts—

It's a village in the city by itself—

We meet a woman and go into a room and I figure we'll finally sleep in here but the two beds are loaded with sleepers and wakers, we just stand there talking, leave and go down the alley past waking-up doors—Everybody curious to see the two ragged girls and the raggedy man, stumbling like a slow team in the dawn—The sun comes up orange over piles of red brick and plaster dust somewhere, it's the wee North America of my Indian Dreams but now I'm too gone to realize anything or understand, all I wanta do is sleep, next to Tristessa—She in her skimpy pink dress, her little breastless body, her thin shanks, her beautiful thighs, but I'm willing to just sleep but I'd like to hold her and stop shivering under some vast dark brown Mexican Blanket with Cruz too, on the other side, to chaperone, I just wanta stop this insane wandering in the streets—

No soap, at the end of the village, in the final house, beyond which is fields of dumps and distant Church tops and the bleary city, we go in—

What a scene! I jump to rejoice to see a huge bed—"We're coming to sleep here!"

But in the bed is a big fat woman with black hair, and beside her some guy with a ski cap, both awake, and simultaneously a brunette girl looking like some artist gal beatnik gal in Greenwich Village comes in—Then I see ten, maybe eight other people all milling around in the corners with spoons and matches—One of them is a typical junkey, that rugged tenderness, those rough and suffering features covered with a gray sick slick, the eyes certainly alert, the mouth alert, hat, suit, watch, spoon, heroin, working swiftly at shots—Everybody is shooting up—Tristessa is called by one of the men and she rolls up her coat sleeve—Cruz too—The ski cap has jumped out of bed and is doing the same—The Greenwich Village gal has somehow slipt into the bed, at the foot, got her big sensuous body under the sheets from the other end, and lies there, glad, on a pillow, watching—People come in and out from the village outdoors—I expect to get a shot too and I say to one of the cats "Poquito gote" which I imagine means little taste but really means "little leak"—Leak indeed, I get nothing, all my money's gone—

The activity is furious, interesting, human, I watch truly amazed, stoned as I am I can see this must be the biggest junk den in Latin America—What interesting types!—Tristessa is talking a mile a minute—The behatted junkey with rough and tender features, with little sandy mustache and faintly blue eyes and high cheekbones, is a Mexican but looks just like any junkey in New York—He wont give me a shot either—I just sit and wait—At my feet I have a half full bottle of beer Tristessa had bought me en route, which I'd cached in clothes, now I sip it in front of all these junkies and that finishes my chances —I keep a sharp eye on the bed expecting the fat lady to get up and leave, and the artist gal at her feet, but only the men hustle and dress and get out and finally we leave too—

"Where we goin?"

We walk outa there through a saddler's prompt line of crossed sword eyes of miux ow you know, the old gantlet line, of respectable bourgeois Mexicans in the morning, but nobody stops us, no cops, we stumble out and down a narrow dirt street and up to another door and inside a little old court where an old man is sweeping with a broom and inside you hear many voices—

He pleads with me with his eyes about something, like, "Dont start trouble," I make the sign "*Me* start trouble?" but he insists so I hesitate to go in but Tristessa and Cruz drag me confidently and I look back at the old man who has given his consent but is still pleading with his eyes—Great God, he knew!

The place is a kind of unofficial morning snort-bar, Cruz goes into dark noisy interiors and comes out with a kind of weak anisette in a waterglass and I taste—I dont want any particularly—I just stand against the dobe wall looking at the yellow light—Cruz looks absolutely crazy now, with high hairy bestial nostrils like in Orozco the women screaming in revolutions but nevertheless she manages to look dainty too— Besides she is a dainty little person, I mean her heart, all night long she has been very nice to me and she likes me—In fact she'd screamed in a drunk one time "Tristessa you're jealous because Yack wanted to marry me!"—and but she knows I love unlovable Tristessa—so she's sistered me and I liked it—

some people have vibrations that come straight from the vibrating heart of the sun, unjaded . . .

But as we're standing there Tristessa suddenly says: "Yack" (me) "all night"—and she starts imitating my shiver in the all-night street, at first I laugh, sun's yellow hot now on my coat, but I feel alarmed to see her imitate my shiver with such convulsive earnestness and Cruz notices too and says "Stop Tristessa!" but she goes on, her eyes wild and white, shivering her thin body in the coat, her legs begin to crumple—I reach out laughing "Ah come on"—she gets more shivery and convulsive and suddenly (as I'm thinking "How can she love me making fun of me *seriously* like that") she starts to fall, which imitation is going too far, I try to grab her, she bends way down to the ground and hangs a minute (just like descriptions Bull had just given me of heroin addicts nodding down to their shoetops on Fifth Avenue in the 20's Era, way down till their head hung completely from the necks and there was nowhere to go but up or flat down on the head) and to my pain and crash Tristessa just bonks her skull and falls headlong on it right on the harsh stone and collapses.

"*Oh no Tristessa!*" I cry and grab her under the arms and twist her over and sit her in my haunches as I hunch against the wall—She is breathing heavily and suddenly I see blood all over her coat—

"She's dying," I think, "suddenly she's decided now to die . . . This insane morning, this insane minute"—And here's the old man with the pleading eyes still looking at me with his broom and men and women going in for anisette stepping right over us (with gingerly unconcern but slowly, scarcely glancing down)—I put my head to hers, cheek to cheek, and hold her tight, and say "*Non non non non*" and what I mean is "Dont die"—Cruz is on the ground with us on the other side, crying—I hold Tristessa by her little ribs and pray—Blood now trickles out of her nose and mouth—

No one's gonna move us outa that doorway—this I swear—
I realize I'm there to refuse to let her die—

We get water, on my big red bandana, and mop her a little—After whiles of convulsive shuddering suddenly she becomes extremely calm and opens her eyes and even looks up—She wont die—I feel it, she wont die, not in my arms nor right now, but I feel too "She must know that I refused and now she'll be expecting me to show her something better than that—than death's eternal ecstasy"—O Golden Eternity, and as I know death is best but "Non, I love you, dont die, dont leave me. . . . I love you too much"—"Because I love you isnt that enough reason to try to live?"—O the gruesome destiny of we human beings, each one of us will suddenly at some terrible moment die and frighten all our lovers and carrion the world—and crack the world—and all the heroin addicts in all the yellow cities and sandy deserts cannot care—and they'll die too—

Tristessa now tries to get up, I raise her by little broken armpits, she leans, we adjust her coat, poor coat, we wipe off a little blood—Start off—Start off in the yellow Mexican morning, not dead—I let her walk by herself ahead of us, lead the Way, she does so through incredibly dirty staring streets full of dead dogs, past gawking children and old women and old men in dirty rags, out to a field of rocks, across that we stumble—Slowly—I can sense it now in her silence, "*This* is what you give me instead of death?"—I try to know what to give her instead—No such thing better than death—All I can do is stumble behind her, sometimes I briefly lead the way but I'm not much the figure of the man, The Man Who Leads The Way—But I know she is dying now, either from epilepsy or heart, shock, or goofball convulsion, and because of that no landlady is going to stop me from taking her home to my room on the roof and letting her sleep and rest under my open sleepbag, with Cruz and me both,—I tell her that, we get a cab and start to Bull's—We get off there, they wait in the cab as I knock on his window for the money for the cab—

"*You cant bring Cruz here!*" he yells. "Neither one of em!" He hands me the money, I pay the cab, the girls get out, and there's Bull's big sleepy face in the door saying "No No—the kitchen is full of women, they'll never let you through!"

"But she's *dying!* I've got to take care of her!"

I turn and I see both their coats, the back of their coats, have majestically Mexicanly womanly turned, with immense dignity, streaks of dust and all street plaster and all, together, the two ladies go down the sidewalk slowly, the way Mexican women aye French Canadian women go to church in the morning—There is something unalterable in the way both their coats have turned on the women in the kitchen, on Bull's worried face, on me—I run after them—Tristessa looks at me seriously: "I go down to Indio for to get a shot" and in that way that normal way she always says that, as if (I guess, I'm a liar, watch out!) as if she means it and really wants to go get that shot—

And I had said to her "I wanta sleep where you sleep tonight" but fat chance of me getting into Indio's or even herself, his wife hates her—They walk majestically, I hesitate majestically, with majestic cowardice, fearing the women in the kitchen who have barred Tristessa from the house (for breaking everything in her goofball fits) and barred her above all from passing through that kitchen (the only way to my room) up narrow ivory-tower winding iron steps that shiver and shake—

"They'd never let you through!" yells Bull from the door. "Let em go!"

One of the landladies is on the sidewalk, I'm too ashamed and drunk to look her in the eye—

"But I'll tell them she's dying!"

"Come *in* here! Come *in* here!" yells Bull.

I turn, they've got their bus at the corner, she's gone—

Either she'll die in my arms or I'll hear about it—

What shroud was the reason why darkness and heaven commingled to come and lay the mantle of sorrow on the hearts of Bull, El Indio and me, who all three love her and weep in our thoughts and know she will die—Three men, from three different nations, in the yellow morning of black shawls, what was the angelic demonic power that devised this?—What's going to happen?

At night little Mexican cop whistles blow that all is well, and all is all wrong, all is tragic,—I dont know what to say.

I'm only waiting to see her again—

And only last year she'd stood in my room and said "A friend is better than pesos, a friend that geev it to you in the bed" when still she believed anyway we'd get our tortured bellies together and get rid of some of the pain—Now too late, too late—

In my room at night, the door open, I watch to see her come in, as if she could get through that kitchen of women—

And for me to go looking for her in Mexico Thieves' Market, that's I suppose what I'll have to do—

Liar! Liar! I'm a liar!

And supposing I go find her and she wants to hit me over the head again, I know it's not her it's the goofballs—but where could I take her, and what would it solve to sleep with her?—a softest kiss from pale-rosest lips I did get, in the street, another one of those and I'm gone—

My poems stolen, my money stolen, my Tristessa dying, Mexican buses trying to run me down, grit in the sky, agh, I never dreamed it could be this bad—

And she hates me—Why does she hate me?

Because I'm so smart

"As sure as you're sittin there," Bull keeps saying since that morning, "Tristessa'll be back tapping on that window on the thirteenth for money for her connection"—

He wants her to come back—

El Indio comes over, in black hat, sad, manly, Mayan stern, preoccupied, "Where is Tristessa?" I ask, he says, hands out, "I dont know."

Her blood is on my pants like my conscience—

But she comes back sooner than we expect, on the night of the 9th—Right while we're sitting there talking about her— She taps on the window but not only that in a crazy brown hand through the old hole (where El Indio's a month ago put his fist through in a rage over junkless), she grabs the great rosy curtains that Bull junkey-wise hangs from ceiling to sill, she shivers and shakes them and sweeps them aside and looks in and as if to see we're not sneaking morphine shots on her—The first thing she sees is my smiling turned face—It must of disgusted the hell out of her—"Bool—Bool—"

Bool hastily dresses to go out and talk to her in the bar across the street, she's not allowed in the house.

"Aw let her in"

"I *cant*"

We both go out, I first while he locks, and there confronted by my "great love" on the sidewalk in the dim evening lights all I can do is shuffle awhile and wait in the line of time— "How you?" I do say—

"Okay"

Her left side of face is one big dirty bandage with black caked blood, she has it hidden under her head-shawl, holds it draped there—

"Where that happen, with me?"

"No, after I leave you, *tree times* I fall"—She holds up three fingers—She's had three further convulsions—The cotton batting hangs down and there are long strip tails down to almost her chin—She would look awful if she wasnt holy Tristessa—

Bull comes out and slowly we go across the street to the bar, I run to her other side to gentleman her, O what an old sister I am—It's like Hong Kong, the poorest sampan maids and mothers of the river in Chinee slacks propelling with the Venetian steer-pole and no rice in the bowl, even they, in fact they especially have their pride and would put down an old sister like me and O their beautiful little cans in sleek shiney silk, O—their sad faces, high cheekbones, brown color, eyes, they look at me in the night, at all Johns in the night, it's their last resort—O I wish I could write!—Only a beautiful poem could do it!

How frail, beat, final, is Tristessa as we load her into the quiet hostile bar where Madame X sits counting her pesos in the back room, facing all, and lil mustachio'd anxious bartender darts furtively to serve us, and I offer Tristessa a chair that will hide her sad mutilated face from Madame X but she refuses and sits any old way—What a threesome in a bar usually reserved for Army officers and Mex businessmen foaming their mustaches at mugs of afternoon!—Tall bony frightening humpbacked Bull (what do the Mexicans think of him?) with his owlish glasses and his slow shaky but firm-going walk and me the baggy-trousered gringo jerk with combed hair and blood and paint on his jeans, and she, Tristessa, wrapt in a purple shawl, skinny,—poor,—like a vendor of lotteria tickets in the street, like doom in Mexico—I order a glass of beer to make it look good, Bull condescends to coffee, the waiter is nervous—

O headache, but there she is sitting next to me, I drink her in—Occasionally she turns those purple eyes at me—She is sick and wants a shot, Bull no got—But she will now go get three gramos on the black market—I show her the pictures I've been painting, of Bull in his chair in purple celestial opium pajamas, of me and my first wife ("Mi primera esposa," she makes no comment, her eyes look briefly at each picture)—Finally when I show her my painting "candle burning at night" she doesnt even look—They're talking about junk—All the time I feel like taking her in my arms and squeezing her, squeezing that little frail unobtainable not-there body—

The shawl falls a little and her bandage shows in the bar—miserable—I dont know what to do—I begin to get mad—

Finally she's talking about her friend's husband who's put her out of the house that day by calling the cops (he a cop himself), "He call cops because I no give im my *body*" she says nastily—

Ah, so she thinks of her body as some prize she shant give away, to hell with her—I pivot in my feelings and brood—I look at her feelingless eyes—

Meanwhile Bull is warning her about goofballs and I remind her that her old ex-lover (now dead junkey) had told me too never to touch them—Suddenly I look at the wall and there are the pictures of the beautiful broads of the calendar (that Al Damlette had in his room in Frisco, one for each month, over tokay wine we used to revere them), I bring Tristessa's attention to them, she looks away, the bartender notices, I feel like a beast—

And all the previous ensalchichas and papas fritas of the year before, Ah Above, what you doin with your children?—You with your sad compassionate and nay-would-I-ever-say unbeautiful face, what you doin with your stolen children you stole from your mind to think a thought because you were bored or you were Mind—shouldna done it, Lord, Awakenerhood, shouldna played the suffering-and-dying game with the children in your own mind, shouldna slept, shoulda whistled for the music and danced, alone, on a cloud, yelling to the stars you made, God, but never shouldna thought up and topped up tippy top Toonerville tweaky little sorrowers like us, the children—Poor crying Bull—child, when's sick, and I cry too, and Tristessa who wont even let herself cry . . .

Oh what was the racket that backeted and smashed in raging might, to make this oil-puddle world?—

Because Tristessa needs my help but wont take it and I wont give—yet, supposing everybody in the world devoted himself to helping others all day long, because of a dream or a vision of the freedom of eternity, then wouldnt the world be a garden? A Garden of Arden, full of lovers and louts in clouds, young drinkers dreaming and boasting on clouds, gods—Still the god's'd'a fought? Devote themselves to gods-dont-fight and bang! Miss Goofball would ope her rosy lips and kiss in the World all day, and men would sleep—And there wouldnt be men or women, but just one sex, the original sex of the mind—But that day's so close I could snap my finger and it would show, what does *it* care? . . . About this recent little event called the world.

"I love Tristessa," nevertheless I have the gall to stay and say, to both of them—"I woulda told the landladies I love Tristessa—I can tell them she's sick—She needs help—She can come sleep in my room tonight"—

Bull is alarmed, his mouth opens—O the old cage, he loves her!—You should see her puttering around the room cleaning up while he sits and cuts up his junk with a razorblade, or just sits saying "M-m-m-m-m-m-m-m" in long low groans that arent groans but his message and song, now I begin to realize Tristessa wants Bull to be her husband—

"I wanted Tristessa to be my third wife," I say later—"I didnt come to Mexico to be told what to do by old sisters? Right in front of the faculty, shooting?—Listen Bull and Tristessa, if Tristessa dont care then I dont care—" At this she looks at me, with surprised not-surprised round she-doesnt-care-eyes—"Give me a shot of morphine so I can think the way you do."

They promptly give me that, in the room later on, meanwhile I've been drinking mescal again—"All or nothing at all," says I to Bull, who repeats it—

"I'm not a whore," I add—And I also want to say "Tristessa is not a whore" but I dont want to bring up the subject—Meanwhile she changes completely with her shot, feels better, combs her hair to a beautiful black sheen, washes her blood, washes her whole face and hands in a soapy washtub like Long Jim Beaver up on the Cascades by his campfire—Swoosh—And she rubs the soap thoroughly in her ears and twists finger-

tips in there and makes squishy sounds, wow, washing, Charley
didnt have a beard last night—She cowls her head again with
the now-brushed shawl and turns to present us, in the light-
bulbed highceiling room, a charming Spanish beauty with a
little scar on her brow—The color of her face is really tan (she
calls herself dark, "As Negra as *me*?") but in the lights that
shine her face keeps changing, sometimes it is jet-brown
almost black-blue (beautiful) with outlines of sheeny cheek
and long sad mouth and the bump on her nose which is like
Indian women in the morning in Nogales on a high dry hill,
the women of the various guitar—The Castilian touch, though
it may be only as Castilian as old Zacatecas it is fitting—
She turns, neat, and I notice she *has* no body at all, it is utterly
lost in a little skimpy dress, then I realize she never eats,
"her body" (I think) "must be beautiful"—"beautiful little
thing"—

But then Bull explains: "She dont want love—You put
Grace Kelly in this chair, Muckymuck's morphine on that
chair, Jack, I take the morphine, I no take the Grace Kelly."

"Yes," asserts Tristessa, "and me, I no awanta love."

I dont say nothin about love, like I dont start singing "Love
is a completely endless thing, it's the April row when feelers
reach for everything" and I dont sing "Embraceable You" like
Frank Sinatra nor that "Towering Feeling" Vic Damone says
"the touch of your hand upon my brow, the look in your eyes
I see," wow, no, I wont disagree or agree with this pair of love-
thieves, let em get married and get under—go under the sheets
—go bateau'ing in Roma—Gallo—anywhere—me, I'm not
going to marry Tristessa, Bull is— —She putters around him
endlessly, how strangely while I'm lying on the bed junk-high
she comes over and cleans up the headboard with her thighs
practically in my face and I study them and old Bull is watching out of the top of his glasses to the side—Min n Bill n
Mamie n Ike n Maroney Maroney Izzy and Bizzy and Dizzy
and Bessy Fall-me-my-closer Martarky and Bee, O god their
names, their names, I want their names, Amie n Bill, not Amos
n Andy, open the mayor (my father did love them) open the
crocus the mokus in the closet (this Freudian sloop of the
mind) (O slip slop) (slap) this old guy that's always—Molly!—
Fibber M'Gee be jesus and Molly—Bull and Tristessa, sitting

there in the house all night, moaning over their razor-blades and white junk and pieces of broken mirror to act as the pan (the diamond sharp junk that cuts into glass)—Quiet evenings at home—Clark Gable and Mona Lisa—

Yet—"Hey, Tristessa I live with you and Bull pay" I say finally—

"I dont care," she says, turning to me on the stool—"It's awright with me."

"Wont you at least pay half of her rent?" asks Bull, noting in his notebook figures he keeps all the time. "Will you say yes or no."

"You can go see her when you want," he adds.

"No, I wanted to live with her."

"Well, you cant do that—you havent got the money."

But Tristessa keeps looking at me and I keep staring at her, suddenly we love each other as Bull drones on and I admire her openly and she shines openly—Earlier, I'd grabbed her, when she said "You remember everything the other night?"— "Yes"—"in the street, how you kiss me"—And I show her how she'd kissed me.

That little gentle brush of the lips on the lips, with just the slightest kiss, to indicate kiss—She'd shined on that one—She didnt care—

She had no money to take the cab home, no bus was running, we had no more money any of us (except money in the bloodbank) (money in the mudbank, Charley)—"Yes, I walk home."

"Three miles, two miles," I say, and there was that long walk through the rain I remembered—"You can come up there," pointing to my room on the roof, "I wont bother you, no te molesta."

"No te molesta" but I would leave her molest me—Old Bull is glancing over his glasses and paper, I've screwed everything up with the mama again, Oedipus Rex, I'll tear out my eyes in the morning—San Francisco, New York, Padici, Medu, Mantua or anywhere, I'm always the King sucker who was made out to be the positional son in woman and man relationships, Ahh-yaaaaa—(Indian howl in the night, to campo-country sweet musica)—"King, bing, I'm always in the way for momma and poppa—When am *I* gonna be poppa?"

*

"No te molesta," and too, for Bull, my poppa,—I said: "I'd have to be a junkey to live with Tristessa, and I cant be a junkey."

"Aint nobody knows junkies like another junkey."

I gulp to hear the truth, too—

"Besides, too, Tristessa is an oldtime junkey, like me, she no chicken—in junk—Junkies are very strange persons."

Then he would launch into a long story about the strange persons he's known, in Riker's Island, in Lexington, in New York, in Panama—in Mexico City, in Annapolis—In keeping with his strange history, which included opium dreams of strange tiered racks where girls are being fed opium through dreamy blue tubes, and similar strange episodes like all the innocent *faux pas* he'd made, tho always with an evil greed just before it, he'd thrown up at Annapolis after a binge, in the showers, and to conceal it from his officers he'd tried to wash it down with the hot water, with the result the smell permeated "all of Bradley Hall" and there was a beautiful poem written about it in the newspaper of the Navy Goats—He would launch into long stories but she was there and with her he just conducted routine junkey talk in baby Spanish, like, "You no go tomorrow good look like that."

"Yes, I clean my face now."

"It no look good—They take one look at you and they know you takin too many secanols"

"Yes, I go"

"I brush your coat—" Bull gets up and helps clean her things—

To me he says, "Them artists and writers, they dont like to work—Dont believe in work" (as the year before, as Tristessa and Cruz and I chatted gayly with the gaiety I had last year, in the room, he's banging with a Mayan stone statue about the size of a big fist trying to fix the door he'd broken down the night before because he took too many goofballs and went out of his room and locked-clicked the padlock, key in the room and him in his pajamas at One A M)—wow, I do gossippy—(So he'd yelled at me "Come help me fix this door, I cant do this by myself"—"Oh yes you can, I'm talking"—"You artists are all lazy bums")

Now to prove I'm not like that I get up slowly, dizzy from that shot of their love stuff, and get some water in the tin pitcher to heat on the upturned ray-lamp so's Tristessa can have hot water for her wound-wash—but I hand him the pitcher because I cant go thru the hassle of balancing it on the flimsy wires and anyway he's the old master Old Wizard old Water Witch Doctor who can do it and wont let me try it— Then I get back on the bed, prostrate—prostate gland too, as morphine takes all the sex out of your parts and leaves it somewhere else, in your gut—Some people are all guts and no heart —I take heart—You shoot spades—You drink clubs—You blast oranges—I take heart and bat—Two—Three—Ten trillion million dizzying powder of stars fermangitatin in the high blue Jack Shaft—prop—I dont drown no buddies in oil—I got no guts to do it—Got heart not to—But the sex, when the morphine is loosed in your flesh, and slowly spreads, hot, and headies your brain, the sex recedes into the gut, most junkies are thin, Bull and Tristessa are both bags of bones—

But O the grace of some bones, that milt a little flesh hang-on, like Tristessa, and makes a woman—And Old Bull, spite of his thin hawky body nobody, his gray hair is well slicked and his cheek is youthful and sometimes he looks positively pretty, and in fact Tristessa had finally one night decided to make it and he was there and they made it, good—I wanted some of that too, seein's how Bull didnt rise to the issue except once every twenty years or so—

But no, that's enough, hear no more, Min n Molly n Bill n Gregory Pegory Fibber McGoy, oy, I'd leave them be and go my own way—"Find me a Mimi in Paris, a Nicole, a sweet Tathagata Pure Pretty Piti"—Like poems spoke by old Italians in South American palm mud, flat, who wanta go back to Palabbrio, reggi, and stroll the beauteous bell-ringing girl-walking boulevard and drink aperitif with the coffee muggers of the card street—O movie—A movie by God, showing us him—him,—and us showing him,—him which is us—for how can there be two, not-one? Palmsunday me that, Bishop San Jose . . .

I'll go light candles to the Madonna, I'll paint the Madonna, and eat ice cream, benny and bread—"Dope and saltpork," as Bhikku Booboo said—I'll go to the South of Sicily in the winter, and paint memories of Arles—I'll buy a piano and Mozart me that—I'll write long sad tales about people in the legend of my life—This part is my part of the movie, let's hear yours

Solo

LONESOME TRAVELER

CONTENTS

AUTHOR'S INTRODUCTION

NAME   Jack Kerouac

NATIONALITY   Franco-American

PLACE OF BIRTH   Lowell, Massachusetts

DATE OF BIRTH   March 12, 1922

EDUCATION   (*schools attended, special courses of study, degrees and years*)

Lowell (Mass.) High School; Horace Mann School for Boys; Columbia College (1940–42); New School for Social Research (1948–49). Liberal arts, no degrees (1936–1949). Got an A from Mark Van Doren in English at Columbia (Shakespeare course). —Flunked chemistry at Columbia.—Had a 92 average at Horace Mann School (1939–40). Played football on varsities. Also track, baseball, chess teams.

MARRIED   Nah

CHILDREN   No

SUMMARY OF PRINCIPAL OCCUPATIONS AND/OR JOBS

Everything: Let's elucidate: scullion on ships, gas station attendant, deckhand on ships, newspaper sportswriter (*Lowell Sun*), railroad brakeman, script synopsizer for 20th Century Fox in N.Y., soda jerk, railroad yardclerk, also railroad baggagehandler, cottonpicker, assistant furniture mover, sheet metal apprentice on the Pentagon in 1942, forest service fire lookout 1956, construction laborer (1941).

INTERESTS

HOBBIES   I invented my own baseball game, on cards, extremely complicated, and am in the process of playing a whole 154-game season among eight clubs, with all the works, batting averages, E.R.A. averages, etc.

SPORTS   Played all of them except tennis and lacrosse and skull.

SPECIAL   Girls

PLEASE GIVE A BRIEF RESUME OF YOUR LIFE

Had beautiful childhood, my father a printer in Lowell, Mass., roamed fields and riverbanks day and night, wrote little novels in my room, first novel written at age 11, also kept extensive diaries and "newspapers" covering my own-invented horse-racing and baseball and football worlds (as recorded in novel *Doctor Sax*).—Had good early education from Jesuit brothers at St. Joseph's Parochial School in Lowell making me jump sixth grade in public school later on; as child traveled to Montreal, Quebec, with family; was given a horse at age 11 by mayor of Lawrence (Mass.), Billy White, gave rides to all kids in neighborhood; horse ran away. Took long walks under old trees of New England at night with my mother and aunt. Listened to their gossip attentively. Decided to become a writer at age 17 under influence of Sebastian Sampas, local young poet who later died on Anzio beach head; read the life of Jack London at 18 and decided to also be an adventurer, a lonesome traveler; early literary influences Saroyan and Hemingway; later Wolfe (after I had broken leg in Freshman football at Columbia read Tom Wolfe and roamed his New York on crutches).—Influenced by older brother Gerard Kerouac who died at age 9 in 1926 when I was 4, was great painter and drawer in childhood (he was) — (also said to be a saint by the nuns) — (recorded in forthcoming novel *Visions of Gerard*).—My father was completely honest man full of gaiety; soured in last years over Roosevelt and World War II and died of cancer of the spleen. —Mother still living, I live with her a kind of monastic life that has enabled me to write as much as I did.—But also wrote on the road, as hobo, railroader, Mexican exile, Europe travel (as shown in *Lonesome Traveler*).—One sister, Caroline, now married to Paul E. Blake Jr. of Henderson N.C., a government anti-missile technician—she has one son, Paul Jr., my nephew, who calls me Uncle Jack and loves me.—My mother's name Gabrielle, learned all about natural story-telling from her long stories about Montreal and New Hampshire.—My people go back to Breton France, first North American ancestor Baron Alexandre Louis Lebris de Kérouac of Cornwall, Brittany, 1750 or so, was granted land along the Rivière du Loop after victory of Wolfe over Montcalm; his descendants married Indians (Mohawk and Caughnawaga) and became potato farmers; first United States descendant my grandfather Jean-Baptiste Kérouac, carpenter, Nashua N.H.—My father's mother a Bernier related to explorer Bernier—all Bretons on father's side—My mother has a Norman name, L'Evesque.—

First formal novel *The Town and the City* written in tradition of long work and revision, from 1946 to 1948, three years, published by Harcourt Brace in 1950.—Then discovered "spontaneous" prose and wrote, say, *The Subterraneans* in 3 nights—wrote *On the Road* in 3 weeks—

Read and studied alone all my life.—Set a record at Columbia College cutting classes in order to stay in dormitory room to write a daily play and read, say, Louis Ferdinand Céline, instead of "classics" of the course.—

Had own mind.—Am known as "madman bum and angel" with "naked endless head" of "prose."—Also a verse poet, *Mexico City Blues* (Grove, 1959).—Always considered writing my duty on earth. Also the preachment of universal kindness, which hysterical critics have failed to notice beneath frenetic activity of my true-story novels about the "beat" generation.—Am actually not "beat" but strange solitary crazy Catholic mystic . . .

Final plans: hermitage in the woods, quiet writing of old age, mellow hopes of Paradise (which comes to everybody anyway) . . .

Favorite complaint about contemporary world: the facetiousness of "respectable" people . . . who, because not taking anything seriously, are destroying old human feelings older than *Time Magazine* . . . Dave Garroways laughing at white doves . . .

PLEASE GIVE A SHORT DESCRIPTION OF THE BOOK, ITS SCOPE AND PURPOSE AS YOU SEE THEM

Lonesome Traveler is a collection of published and unpublished pieces connected together because they have a common theme: Traveling.

The travels cover the United States from the south to the east coast to the west coast to the far northwest, cover Mexico, Morocco Africa, Paris, London, both the Atlantic and Pacific oceans at sea in ships, and various interesting people and cities therein included.

Railroad work, sea work, mysticism, mountain work, lasciviousness, solepsism, self-indulgence, bullfights, drugs, churches, art museums, streets of cities, a mishmosh of life as lived by an independent educated penniless rake going anywhere.

Its scope and purpose is simply poetry, or, natural description.

I.

Piers of the Homeless Night

HERE DOWN ON DARK EARTH
    before we all go to Heaven
VISIONS OF AMERICA
All that hitchhikin
All that railroadin
All that comin back
    to America
Via Mexican & Canadian borders . . .

Less begin with the sight of me with collar huddled up close to neck and tied around with a handkerchief to keep it tight and snug, as I go trudging across the bleak, dark warehouse lots of the ever lovin San Pedro waterfront, the oil refineries smelling in the damp foggish night of Christmas 1951 just like burning rubber and the brought-up mysteries of Sea Hag Pacific, where just off to my left as I trudge you can see the oily skeel of old bay waters marching up to hug the scummy posts and out on over the flatiron waters are the lights ululating in the moving tide and also lights of ships and bum boats themselves moving and closing in and leaving this last lip of American land.—Out on that dark ocean, that wild dark sea, where the worm invisibly rides to come, like a hag flying and laid out as if casually on sad sofa but her hair flying and she's on her way to find the crimson joy of lovers and eat it up, Death by name, the doom and death ship the S.S. *Roamer*, painted black with orange booms, was coming now like a ghost and without a sound except for its vastly shuddering engine, to be warped & wailed in at the Pedro pier, fresh from a run from New York through the Panamy canal, and aboard's my ole buddy Deni Bleu let's call him who had me travel 3,000 miles overland on buses with the promise he will get me on and I sail the rest of the trip around the world.—And since I'm well and on the bum again & aint got nothing else to do, but roam, longfaced, the real America, with my unreal heart, here I am eager and ready to be a big busted nose scullion or dishwasher on the old scoff scow s'long as I can buy my next fancy shirt in a Hong Kong haberdashery or wave a polo mallet in some old Singapore bar or play the horses in Australian, it's all the same to me as long as it can be exciting and goes around the world.

For weeks I have been traveling on the road, west from New York, and waiting up in Frisco at a friend's house meanwhile earning an extra 50 bucks working the Christmas rush as a baggagehandler with the old sop out railroad, have just now come the 500 miles down from Frisco as an honored secret guest in the caboose of the Zipper first class freight train thanx to my connections on the railroad up there and now I think I'm going to be a big seaman, I'll get on the *Roamer* right here in Pedro, so I think fondly, anyway if it wasnt for this shipping I'd sure like it maybe to be a railroad man, learn to be a brakeman, and get paid to ride that old zooming Zipper.—But I'd been sick, a sudden choking awful cold of the virus X type California style, and could hardly see out the dusty window of the caboose as it flashed past the snowy breaking surf at Surf and Tangair and Gaviota on the division that runs that moony rail between San Luis Obispo and Santa Barbara.—I'd tried my best to appreciate a good ride but could only lay flat on the caboose seat with my face buried in my bundled jacket and every conductor from San Jose to Los Angeles had had to wake me up to ask about my qualifications, I was a brakeman's brother and a brakeman in Texas Division myself, so whenever I looked up thinking "Ole Jack you are now actually riding in a caboose and going along the surf on the spectrallest railroad you'd ever in your wildest little dreams wanta ride, like a kid's dream, why is it you cant lift your head and look out there and appreciate the feathery shore of California the last land being feathered by fine powdery skeel of doorstop sills of doorstep water weaving in from every Orient and bay boom shroud from here to Catteras Flapperas Voldivious and Gratteras, boy," but I'd raise my head, and nothing there was to see, except my bloodshot soul, and vague hints of an unreal moon shinin on an unreal sea, and the flashby quick of the pebbles of the road bed, the rail in the starlight.—Arriving in L.A. in the morning and I stagger with full huge cuddlebag on shoulder from the L.A. yards clear into downtown Main Street L.A. where I laid up in a hotel room 24 hours drinking bourbon lemon juice and anacin and seeing as I lay on my back a vision of America that had no end—which was only beginning—thinking, tho, "I'll get on the *Roamer* at Pedro and be gone for Japan before you can say boo."—Looking out the window when I felt a little better and digging the hot sunny streets of L.A. Christmas, going down finally to the skid row poolhalls and shoe shine joints and gouging around, waiting for the time when the *Roamer* would warp in at the Pedro pier, where I was to meet Deni right at the gangplank with the gun he'd sent ahead.

More reasons than one for the meeting in Pedro—he'd sent a gun ahead inside of a book which he'd carefully cut and hollowed out and made into a tight neat package covered with brown paper and tied with string, addressed to a girl in Hollywood, Helen something, with address which he gave me, "Now Kerouac when you get to Hollywood you go immediately to Helen's and ask her for that package I sent her, then you carefully open it in your hotel room and there's the gun and it's loaded so be careful dont shoot your finger off, then you put it in your pocket, do you hear me Kerouac, has it gotten into your heskefuffle frantic imagination—but now you've got a little errand to do for me, for your boy Denny Blue, remember we went to school together, we thought up ways to survive together to scrounge for pennies we were even cops together we even married the same woman," (cough) "I mean, —we both wanted the same woman, Kerouac, it's up to you now now to help defend me against the evil of Matthew Peters, you bring that gun with you" poking me and emphatically pronouncing each word and poking me with each word "and bring it on you and dont get caught and dont miss the boat whatever you do."—A plan so absurd, so typical of this maniac, I came of course without the gun, without even looking up Helen, but just in my beatup jacket hurrying, almost late, I could see her masts close in against the pier, night, spotlights everywhere, down that dismal long plaza of refineries and oil storage tanks, on my poor scuffledown shoes that had begun a real journey now—starting in New York to follow the fool ship but it was about to be made plain to me in the first 24 hours I'd never get on no ship—didnt know it then, but was doomed to stay in America, always, road rail or waterscrew, it'll always be

America (Orient-bound ships chugging up the Mississippi, as will be shown later.)—No gun, huddled against the awful winter damp of Pedro and Long Beach, in the night, passing the Puss n' Boots factory on a corner with little lawn out front and American flagpoles and a big tuna fish ad inside the same building they make fish for humans and for cats—passing the Matson piers, the Lurline not in.—Eyes peeled for Matthew Peters the villain who was behind the need for the gun.

It went back, maniacally, to further earlier events in this gnashing huge movie of earth only a piece of which here's offered by me, long tho it is, how wild can the world be until finally you realize "O well it's just repetitious anyway."—But Deni had deliberately wrecked this Matthew Peters' car. It seems they had lived together and with a bunch of girls in Hollywood. They were seamen. You saw snapshots of them sitting around sunny pools in bathingsuits and with blondes and in big hugging poses. Deni tall, fattish, dark, smiling white teeth hypocrite's smile, Matthew Peters an extremely handsome blond with a self-assured grim expression or (morbid) expression of sin and silence, the hero—of the group, of the time—so that you hear it always spoken behind the hand, the confidential stories told to you by every drunk and non-drunk in every bar and non-bar from here to the other side of all the Tathagata worlds in the 10 Quarters of the universe, it's like the ghosts of all the mosquitos that had ever lived, the density of the story of the world all of it would be enough to drown the Pacific as many times as you could remove a grain of sand from its sandy bed. The big story was, the big complaint, that I heard chanted, from Deni, an old complainer and chanter and one of the most vituperative of complainers, "While I was scrounging around in the garbage cans and barrels of Hollywood mind you, going behind those very fancy apartment houses and at night, late, very quietly sneaking around, getting bottles for 5 cent deposits and putting them in my little bag, for extra money, when we couldnt get longshore work and nor get a ship for love nor money, Matthew, with his airy ways, was having big parties and spending every cent he could get from my grimy hands and not once, NO TTT Once, did I hear one WORD of appreciation—you can imagine how I felt when finally he took my best girl and took off with her for a night—

I sneaked to his garage where he had his car parked, I very quietly backed it out without starting the motor, I let it roll down the street, and then man I was on my way to Frisco, drinking beer from cans—I could tell you a story—" and so he goes on with his story, told in his own inimitable way, how he wrecked the car in Cucamonga California, a head-on crash into some tree, how he almost got killed, how the cops were, and lawyers, and papers, and troubles, and how he finally got to Frisco, and got another ship, and how Matthew Peters who knew he was on the *Roamer*, would be waiting at the pierhead this very same clammy cold night in Pedro with a gun, a knife, henchmen, friends, anything and everything.—Deni was going to step off the ship looking in all directions, ready to throw himself flat on the ground, and I was to be waiting there at the foot of the gangplank and hand him the gun real quick—all in the foggy foggy night—

"Alright tell me a story."

"Gently now."

"Well you're the one who started all this."

"Gently, gently" says Deni in his own peculiar way saying "JHENT" very loud with mouth moawed like a radio announcer to pronounce every sound and then the "LY" is just said English-wise, it was a trick we'd both picked up at a certain madcap prep school where everybody went around talking like very high smotche smahz, . . . now shmuz, SHmazaa zzz, inexplicable the foolish tricks of schoolboys long ago, lost,—which Deni now in the absurd San Pedro night was still quipping up to fogs, as if it didnt make any difference.— "GENT ly" says Deni taking a firm grip on my arm and holding me tight and looking at me seriously, he's about six-three and he's looking down at little five-nine me and his eyes are dark, glittering, you can see he's mad, you can see his conception of life is something no one else has ever had and ever will have tho just as seriously he can go around believing and claiming his theory about me for instance, "Kerouac is a victim, a VIC timm of his own i ma JHI NA Tion."—Or his favorite joke about me, which is supposed to be so funny and is the saddest story he ever told or anyone ever told, "Kerouac wouldnt accept a leg of fried chicken one night and when I asked him why he said 'I'm thinking about the poor starving people of Europe'. . . Hyaa WA W W W" and he goes off on his fantastic laugh which is a great shrieking lofter into a sky designed specially for him and which I always see over him when I think of him, the black night, the around the world night, the night he stood on the pier in Honolulu with contraband Japanese kimonos on, four of them, and the customs guards made him undress down to em and there he stands at night on the platform in Japanese kimonos, big huge Deni Bleu, downcast & very very unhappy—"I could tell you a story that's so long I couldnt finish telling it to you if we took a trip around the world, Kerouac, you but you dont you wont you never liste—Kerouac what WHAT are you going to tell the poor people starving in Europe about the Puss n' Boots plant there with the tuna fish in back, H MHmmh Ya aYYaawww Yawww, *they make the same food for cats and people,* Yyorr yhOOOOOOOOOO!"—And when he laughed like that you know he was having a hell of a good time and lonely in it, because I never saw it to fail, the fellas on the ship and all ships he ever sailed on couldnt see what was so funny what with all, also, his practical joking, which I'll show.—"I wrecked Matthew Peters' car you understand—now let me say of course I didnt do it deliberately, Matthew Peters would like to think so, a lot of evil skulls like to believe so, Paul Lyman likes to believe so so he can also believe I stole his wife which I assure you Kerouac I ding e do, it was my buddy Harry Mc-Kinley who stole Paul Lyman's wife—I drove Matthew's car to Frisco, I was going to leave it there on the street and ship out, he would have got the thing back but unfortunately, Kerouac, life isnt always outcome could coming the way we like and tie but the name of the town I can never and I shall never be able to—there, up, er, Kerouac, you're not listening," gripping my arm "Gently now, are you listening to what I'm SAYING to you!"

"Of course I'm listening."

"Then why are you going myu, m, hu, what's up there, the birds up there, you heard the bird up there, mmmmy" turning away with a little shnuffle lonely laugh, this is when I see the true Deni, now, when he turns away, it isnt a big joke, there was no way to make it a big joke, he was talking to me and then he tried to make a joke out of my seeming not-listening and it wasnt funny because I was listening, in fact I was seriously listening as always to all his complaints and songs and but he turned away and had tried and in a forlorn little look into his own, as if, past, you see the double chin or dimplechin of some big baby nature folding up and with rue, with a heartbreaking, French giving-up, humility, meekness even, he ran the gamut from absolutely malicious plotting and scheming and practical joking, to big angel Ananda baby mourning in the night, I saw him I know.—"Cucamonga, Practamonga, Calamongonata, I shall shall never remember the name of that town, but I ran the car head-on into a tree, Jack, and that was that and I was set upon by every scroungy cop lawyer judge doctor indian chief insurance salesman conman type in the—I tell you I was lucky to get away alive I had to wire home for all kinds of money, as you know my mother in Vermont has all my savings and when I'm in a real pinch I always wire home, it's my money."

"Yes Deni." But to cap everything there was Matthew Peters' buddy Paul Lyman, who had a wife, who ran away with Harry McKinley or in some way that I could never understand, they took a lot of money and got on an Orient bound passenger vessel and were now living with an alcoholic major in a villa in Singapore and having a big time in white duck trousers and tennis shoes but Lyman the husband, also a seaman and in fact a shipmate of Matthew Peters' and (tho Den didn't know at this time, aboard the Lurline both of them) (keep that) bang, he was convinced Deni was behind that too, and so the both of them had sworn to kill Deni or get Deni and according to Deni they were going to be on the pier when the ship came in that night, with guns and friends, and I was to be there, ready, when Deni comes off the gangplank swiftly and all dressed up to go to Hollywood to see his stars and girls and all the big things he'd written me I'm to step up quickly and hand him the gun, loaded and cocked, and Deni, looking around carefully to see no shadows leap up, ready to throw himself flat on the ground, takes the gun from me and together we cut into the darkness of the waterfront and rush to town—for further events, developments—

So now the *Roamer* was coming in, it was being straightened out along the concrete pier, I stood and spoke quietly to one of the after deckhands struggling with ropes, "Where's the carpenter?"

"Who Blue? the—I'll see him in a minute." A few other requests and out comes Deni just as the ship is being winched and secured and the ordinary's putting out the rat guards and the captain's blowed his little whistle and that incomprehensible slow huge slowmotion eternity move of ships is done, you hear the churns the backwater churns, the pissing of scuppers —the big ghostly trip is done, the ship is in—the same human faces are on the deck—and here comes Deni in his dungarees and unbelievably in the foggy night he sees his boy standing right there on the quai, just as planned, with hands-a-pockets, almost could reach out and touch him.

"There you are Kerouac, I never thought you'd be here."

"You told me to, didnt you—"

"Wait, another half hour to finish up and clean up and dress, I'll be right with you—anybody around?"

"I dont know." I looked around. I had been looking around for a half hour, at parked cars, dark corners, holes of sheds, door holes, niches, crypts of Egypt, waterfront rat holes, crapule doorholes, and beercan clouts, midmast booms and fishing eagles—bah, nowhere, the heroes were nowhere to be seen.

Two of the saddest dogs you ever saw (haw haw haw) walking off that pier, in the dark, past a few customs guards who gave Deni a customary little look and wouldnt have found the gun in his pocket anyway but he'd taken all those pains to mail it in that hollowed-out tome and now as we peered around together he whispered "Well have you got it?"

"Yea yea in my pocket."

"Hang on to it, give to me outside on the street."

"Dont worry."

"I guess they're not here, but you never can tell."

"I looked everywhere."

"We'll get outa here and make tracks—I've got it all planned Kerouac what we're gonna do tonight tomorrow and the whole weekend; I've been talking to all the cooks, we've got it all planned, a letter for you down to Jim Jackson at the hall and you're going to sleep in the cadets' stateroom on board, think of it Kerouac a whole stateroom to yourself, and Mr. Smith has agreed to come with us and celebrate, hm a mahya." —Mr. Smith was the fat pale potbellied wizard of the bottom skeels of the engine room, a wiper or oiler or general water-tender, he was the funniest old guy you'd ever wish to see and already Deni was laughing and feeling good and forgetting the imaginary enemies—out on the pier street it was evident we were in the clear. Deni was wearing an expensive Hong Kong blue serge suit, with soldiers in his shoulder pads and a fine drape, a beautiful suit, in which, now, beside mine in my road rags, he stomped along like a French farmer throwing his biggest brogans over the rows *de bledeine*, like a Boston hood-lum scuffling along the Common on Saturday night to see the guys at the poolhall but in his own way, with cherubic Deni smile that was heightened tonight by the fog making his face jovial round and red, tho not old, but what with the sun shine of the trip thru the canal he looked like a Dickens character stepping to his post chaise and dusty roads, only what a dismal scene spread before us as we walked.—Always with Deni it's walking, long long walks, he wouldnt spend a dollar on a cab because he likes to walk but also there were those days when he went out with my first wife and used to shove her right through the subway turnstile before she could realize what happened, from the back naturally—a charming little trick—to save a nickel—a pastime at which old Den's unbeatable, as could be shown—We came to the Pacific Red Car tracks after a fast hike of about 20 minutes along those dreary refineries and waterskeel slaphouse stop holes, under impossible skies laden I suppose with stars but you could just see their dirty blur in the Southern California Christmas—"Kerouac we are now at the Pacific Red Car tracks, do you have any faint idea as to what that thing is can you tell that you think you can, but Kerouac you have always struck me as being the funniest man I have ever known . . ."

"No, Deni YOU are the funniest man I ever known—"

"Dont interrupt, dont drool, dont—" the way he answered and always talked and he's leading the way across the Red Car tracks, to a hotel, in downtown long Pedro where someone was supposed to meet us with blondes and so he bought en-route a couple of small hand cases of beer for us to portable around with, and when we got to the hotel, which had potted palms and potted barfronts and cars parked, and everything dead and windless with that dead California sad windless smoke-smog, and the Pachucos going by in a hot road and Deni says "You see that bunch of Mexicans in that car with their blue jeans, they got one of our seamen here last Christmas, about a year ago today, he was doing nothing but minding his own business, but they jumped right out that car and beat the living hell out of him—they take his money—no money, it's just to be mean, they're Pachucos, they just like to beat up on people for the hell of it—"

"When I was in Mexico it didnt seem to me the Mexicans there were like that—"

"The Mexicans in the U.S. is another matter Kerouac, if you'd a been around the world like I have you could see as I do a few of the rough facts of life that apparently with you and the poor people starving in Europe you'll never NEVER under STAAANNND . . ." gripping my arm again, swinging as he walks, like in our prep school days when we used to go up the sunny morning hill, to Horace Mann, at 246th in Manhattan, on the rock cliffs over by the Van Cortlandt park, the little road, going up thru English halftimber cottages and apartment houses, to the ivied school on top, the whole bunch swinging uphill to school but nobody ever went as fast as Deni as he never paused to take a breath, the climb was very sharp, most had to wind and work and whine and moan along but Deni swung it with his big glad laugh—In those days he'd sell daggers to the rich little fourth formers, in back of the toilets—He was up to more tricks tonight—"Kerouac I'm going to introduce you to two cucamongas in Hollywood tonight if we can get there on time, tomorrow for sure . . . two cucamongas living in a house, in an apartment house, the whole thing built clear around a swimmingpool, do you understand what I said, Kerouac? . . . a swimmingpool, that you go swimming in—"

"I know, I know, I seen it in that picture of you and Matthew Peters and all the blondes, great . . . What we do, work on em?"

"Wait, a minute, before I explain the rest of the story to you, hand me the gun."

"I havent got the gun you fool, I was only saying that so you'd get off the ship . . . I was ready to help you if anything happened."

"YOU HAVENT GOT IT?" It dawned on him he had boasted to the whole crew "My boy's out there on the pier with the gun, what did I tell ya" and he had earler, when the ship left New York, posted a big absurd typically Deni ridiculous poster printed in red ink on a piece of letter paper, "WARNING, THERE ARE FELLOWS ON THE WEST COAST BY THE NAMES OF MATTHEW PETERS AND PAUL LYMAN WOULD LIKE NOTHING BETTER THAN TO CLOBBER THE CARPENTER OF THE ROAMER DENI E. BLEU IF ONLY THEY COULD BUT ANY SHIP-MATES OF BLEU WHO WANT TO HELP BE ON THE LOOKOUT FOR THOSE TWO EVIL SCROUNGERS WHEN THE SHIP PUTS IN AT PEDRO AND THERE WILL BE APPRECIATION SIGNED CARPT. FREE DRINKS IN THE CARPT. TONIGHT"—and then by word in the messroom he'd loudly boasted his boy.

"I knew you'd tell everybody I had the gun, so I said I did. Didnt you feel better walking off the ship?"

"Where is it?"

"I didnt even go."

"Then it's still there. We'll have to pick it up tonight." He was lost in thought—it was okay.

Deni had big plans for what was going to happen at the hotel, which was the El Carrido Per to Motpaotta Calfiornia potator hotel as I say with potted palmettos and seamen inside and also hotrod champion sons of aircraft computators of Long Beach, the whole general and really dismal California culture a palpable hangout for it, where you saw the dim interiors where you saw the Hawaiian shirted and be-wristwatched, tanned strong young men tilting long thin beers to their mouths and leering and mincing with broads in fancy necklaces and with little white ivory things at their tanned ears and a whole blank blue in their eyes that you saw, also a bestial cruelty hidden and the smell of the beer and smoke and smart smell of the cool in-side plush cocktail lounge all that Americanness that in my youth had me get wild to be in it and leave my home and go off be big hero in the American romance-me-jazz night.— That had made Deni lose his head too, at one time he had been a sad infuriated French boy brought over on a ship to attend American private schools at which time hate smoldered in his bones and in his dark eyes and he wanted to kill the world—but a little of the Sage and Wisdom education from the Masters of the High West and he wanted to do his hating and killing in cocktail lounges learned from Franchot Tone movies and God knows where and what else.—We come up to this thing down the drear boulevard, phantasm street with its very bright street lamps and very bright but somber palms jutting out of the sidewalk all pineapple-ribbed and rising into the indefinable California night sky and no wind.—Inside there was no one to meet Deni as usual mistaken and completely ignored by everyone (good for him but he dont know it) so we have a couple beers, ostensibly waiting, Deni outlines me more facts & personal sophistries, there aint no one coming, no friends, no enemies either, Deni is a perfect Taoist, nothing happens to him, the trouble runs off his shoulders like water, as if he had pig grease on em, he dont know how luck he is, and here he's got his boy at his side old Ti Jean who'll go anywhere follow anyone for adventure.—Suddenly in the middle of our third or so beer he whoops and realizes we missed the hourly Red Car train and that is going to hold us up another hour in dismal Pedro, we want to get to the glitters of Los Angeles if possible or Hollywood before all the bars closed, in my mind's eye I see all the wonderful things Deni has planned for us there and see, incomprehensible, unrememberable what the images were I was now inventing ere we got going and arrived at the actual scene, not the screen but the dismal four-dimensional scene itself.—Bang, Deni wants to take a cab and chase the Red Car also with our beer cans in hand cartons we go jogging down the street to a cab stand and hire one to chase the Red Car, which the guy does without comment, knowing the egocentricities of seamen as a O how dismal cabdriver in a O how dismal pierhead jumpin town.—Off we go—it's my suspicion he isnt really driving as fast as he ought to actually catch the Red Car, which hiballs right down that line, towards Compton and environs of L.A., at 60 per.—My suspicion is he doesnt want to get a ticket and at the same time seem to go fast enough to satisfy the whims of the seamen in the back—it's my suspicion he's just gonna gyp old Den out of a 5 dollar bill.—Nothing Den likes better than throw away his

5 dollar bills, too—He thrives on it, he lives for it, he'll take voyages around the world working belowdecks among electrical equipment but worse than that take the abuse off officers and men (at four o'clock in the Morning he's asleep in his bunk, "Hey Carptenter, are you the carpenter or are you the chief bottlestopper or shithouse watcher, that goddam forward boom light is out again, I dont know who is using slingshots around here, and but I want that goddam light fixed we'll pulling into Penang in 2 hours and goddam it if it's still dark at that time and I, and we dong got no light it's your ass not mine, see the chief about it") so Deni has to get up, and I can just see him do it, rub the innocent sleep from his eyes and wake to the cold howling world and wish he had a sword so he could cut the man's head off but at the same time he doesnt want to spend the rest of his life in a prison either, or get his own head partially cut off and spend the rest of his life paralyzed with a shoe brace in his neck and people bring him crap pans, so he crawls outa bed and does the bidding of every beast that has every yell to throw at him for every reason in the thousand and one electrical apparati on the goddamn stinking steel jail which as far as I'm concerned, and floating on water too, is what they call a ship.—What is 5 dollars to a martyr?— "Step on the gas, we gotta catch that car."

"I'm going fast enough you'll get it." He passes right through Cucamonga. "At exactly 11:38 in 1947 or 1948, one, now I cant remember which one exactly, but I remember I done this for another seaman couple years ago and he passed right through—" and he goes on talking easing up so's not to pass through the insulting part of just barely beating a red light and I lay back in the seat and say:

"You coulda made that red light, we'll never make it now."

"Listen Jack you wanta make it dontcha and not get fined by some traffic cop."

"Where?" I say looking out the window and all over the horizon at those marshes of night for signs of a cop on a motorcycle or a cruiser—all you see is marshes and great black distances of night and far off, on hills, the little communities with Christmas lights in their windows blearing red, blearing green, blearing blue, suddenly sending pangs thru me and I think, "Ah America, so big, so sad, so black, you're like the leafs of a dry summer that go crinkly ere August found its end, you're hopeless, everyone you look on you, there's nothing but the dry drear hopelessness, the knowledge of impending death, the suffering of present life, lights of Christmas wont save you or anybody, any more you could put Christmas lights on a dead bush in August, at night, and make it look like something, what is this Christmas you profess, in this void? . . . in this nebulous cloud?"

"That's perfectly alright" says Deni. "Move right along, we'll make it."—He beats the next light to make it look good but eases up for the next, and up the track and back, you can't see any sign of the rear or the front of no Red Car, shoot—he comes to his place where coupla years ago he'd dropped that seaman, no Red Car, you can feel its absence, it's come and gone, empty smell—You can tell by the electric stillness on the corner that something just was, & aint.

"Well I guess I missed it, goldang it," says the cabdriver pushing his hat back to apologize and looking real hypocritical about it, so Deni gives him five dollars and we get out and Deni says:

"Kerouac this means we have an hour to wait here by the cold tracks, in the cold foggy night, for the next train to L.A."

"That's okay" I say "we got beer aint we, open one up" and Deni fishes down for the old copper churchkey and up comes two cans of beer spissing all over the sad night and we up end the tin, and go slurp—two cans each and we start throwing rocks at signs, dancing around to keep warm, squatting, telling jokes, remembering the past, Deni's going "Hyra rrour Hoo" and again I hear his great laugh ringing in the American night and I try to tell him "Deni the reason I followed the ship all the way 3,200 miles from Staten Island to goddam Pedro is not only because I wanta get on and be seen going around the world and have myself a ball in Port Swettenham and pick up on gangee in Bombay and find the sleepers and the fluteplayers in filthy Karachi and start revolutions of my own in the Cairo Casbah and make it from Marseilles to the other side, but because if you, because, the things we used to do, where, I have a hell of a good time with you Den, there's no two ways about . . . I never have any money that I admit, I already owe you sixty for the bus fare, but you must admit I try . . . I'm sorry that I dont have any money ever, but you know I tried with you, that time . . . Well goddam, wa ahoo, shit, I want get drunk tonight.—" And Deni says "We dont have to hang around in the cold like this Jack, look there's a bar, over there" (a roadhouse gleaming redly in the misty night) "it may be a Mexican Pachuco bar and we might get the hell beat out of us but let's go in there and wait the half hour we got with a few beers . . . and see if there're any cucamongas" so we head out to there, across an empty lot. Deni is meanwhile very busy tellin me what a mess I've made of my life but I've heard that from every body coast to coast and I dont care generally and I dont care tonight and this is my way of doing and saying things.

A coupla days later the S.S. *Roamer* sails away without me because they wouldnt let me get on at the union hall, I had no seniority, all I had to do they said was hang around a couple of months and work on the waterfront or something and wait for a coastwise ship to Seattle and I thought "So if I'm gonna travel coasts I'm going to go down the coast I covet."—So I see the Roamer slipping out of Pedro bay, at night again, the red port light and the green starboard light sneaking across the water with attendant ghostly following mast lights, vup! (the whistle of the little tug)—then the ever Gandharva-like, illusion-and-Maya-like dimlights of the portholes where some members of the crew are reading in bunks, others eating snacks in the crew mess, and others, like Deni, eagerly writing letters with a big red ink fountain pen assuring me that next time around the world I will get on the Roamer.—"But I dont care, I'll go to Mexico" says I and walk off to the Pacific Red Car waving at Deni's ship vanishing out there . . .

Among the madcap pranks we'd pulled after that first night I told you about, we carried a huge tumbleweed up the gangplank at 3 AM Christmas Eve and shoved it into the engine crew foc'sle (where they were all snoring) and left it there.— When they woke up in the morning they thought they were somewhere else, in the jungle or something, and all went back to bed.—So when the Chief Engineer is yelling "Who the hell put that tree on board!" (it was ten feet by ten feet, a big ball of dry twigs), way off across and down the ship's iron heart you hear Deni howling "Hoo hoo hoo! *Who the hell put that tree on board!* Oh that Chief Engineer is a very funny m-a-h-n!"

2.

Mexico Fellaheen

WHEN you go across the border at Nogales Arizona some very severe looking American guards, some of them pasty faced with sinister steelrim spectacles go scrounging through all your beat baggage for signs of the scorpion of scofflaw.—You just wait patiently like you always do in America among those apparently endless policemen and their endless laws *against* (no laws *for*)—but the moment you cross the little wire gate and you're in Mexico, you feel like you just sneaked out of school when you told the teacher you were sick and she told you you could go home, 2 o'clock in the afternoon.—You feel as though you just come home from Sunday morning church and you take off your suit and slip into your soft worn smooth cool overalls, to play—you look around and you see happy smiling faces, or the absorbed dark faces of worried lovers and fathers and policemen, you hear cantina music from across the little park of balloons and popsicles. —In the middle of the little park is a bandstand for concerts, actual concerts for the people, free—generations of marimba players maybe, or an Orozco jazzband playing Mexican anthems to El Presidente.—You walk thirsty through the swinging doors of a saloon and get a bar beer, and turn around and there's fellas shooting pool, cooking tacos, wearing sombreros, some wearing guns on their rancher hips, and gangs of singing businessmen throwing pesos at the standing musicians who wander up and down the room.—It's a great feeling of entering the Pure Land, especially because it's so close to dry faced Arizona and Texas and all over the Southwest—but you can find it, this feeling, this fellaheen feeling about life, that timeless gayety of people not involved in great cultural and civilization issues—you can find it almost anywhere else, in Morocco, in Latin America entire, in Dakar, in Kurd land.—

There is no "violence" in Mexico, that was all a lot of bull written up by Hollywood writers or writers who went to

Mexico to "be violent"—I know of an American who went to
Mexico for bar brawls because you dont usually get arrested
there for disorderly conduct, my God I've seen men wrestle
playfully in the middle of the road blocking traffic, screaming
with laughter, as people walked by smiling—Mexico is generally gentle and fine, even when you travel among the dangerous characters as I did—"dangerous" in the sense we mean in
America—in fact the further you go away from the border, and
deeper down, the finer it is, as though the influence of civilizations hung over the border like a cloud.

The earth is an Indian thing—I squatted on it, rolled thick
sticks of marijuana on sod floors of stick huts not far from
Mazatlan near the opium center of the world and we sprinkled
opium in our masterjoints—we had black heels. We talked
about Revolution. The host was of the opinion the Indians
originally owned North America just as well as South America,
about time to come out and say "*La tierra esta la notre*"—(the
earth is ours) —which he did, clacking his tongue and with a
hip sneer hunching up his mad shoulders for us to see his
doubt and mistrust of anyone understanding what he meant
but I was there and understood quite well.—In the corner an
Indian woman, 18, sat, partly behind the table, her face in the
shadows of the candle glow—she was watching us high either
on "O" or herself as wife of a man who in the morning went
out in the yard with a spear and split sticks on the ground idly
languidly throwing it ground down half-turning to gesture
and say something to his partner.—The drowsy hum of Fellaheen Village at noon—not far away was the sea, warm, the
tropical Pacific of Cancer.—Spine-ribbed mountains all the
way from Calexico and Shasta and Modoc and Columbia River
Pasco-viewing sat rumped behind the plain upon which this
coast was laid.—A one thousand mile dirt road led there—
quiet buses 1931 thin high style goofy with oldfashioned clutch
handles leading to floor holes, old side benches for seats,
turned around, solid wood, bouncing in interminable dust
down past the Navajoas, Margaritas and general pig desert dry
huts of Doctor Pepper and pig's eye on tortilla half burned—
tortured road—led to this the capital of the world kingdom of
opium—Ah Jesus—I looked at my host.—On the sod floor, in

a corner, snored a soldier of the Mexican Army, it was a revolution. The Indian was mad. "*La Tierra esta la notre—*"

Enrique my guide and buddy who couldnt say "H" but had to say "K"—because his nativity was not buried in the Spanish name of Vera Cruz his hometown, in the Mixtecan Tongue instead.—On buses joggling in eternity he kept yelling at me "HK-o-t? HK-o-t? Is means *caliente*. Unnerstan?"

"Yeah yeah."

"Is k-o-t . . . is k-o-t . . . is means *caliente*— HK-eat . . . eat . . ."

"H-eat!"

"Is what letter—alphabay?"

"H"

"Is . . . HK . . . ?"

"No . . . H . . ."

"Is Kard for me to pronouse. I can' do it."

When he said "K" his whole jaw leaped out, I saw the Indian in his face. He now squatted in the sod explaining eagerly to the host who by his tremendous demeanor I knew to be the King of some regal gang laid out in the desert, by his complete sneering speech concerning every subject brought up, as if by blood king by right, trying to persuade, or protect, or ask for something, I sat, said nothing, watched, like Gerardo in the corner.—Gerardo was listening with astonished air at his big brother make a mad speech in front of the King and under the circumstances of the strange Americano Gringo with his seabag. He nodded and leered like an old merchant the host to hear it and turned to his wife and showed his tongue and licked his lower teeth and then damped top teeth on lip, to make a quick sneer into the unknown Mexican dark overhead the candlelight hut under Pacific Coast Tropic of Cancer stars like in Acapulco fighting name.—The moon washed rocks from El Capitan on down—The swamps of Panama later on and soon enough.

Pointing, with huge arm, finger, the host:—"Is in the rib of mountains of the big plateau! the golds of war are buried deep! the caves bleed! we'll take the snake out of the woods! we'll tear the wings off the great bird! we shall live in the iron houses overturned in fields of rags!"

"*Si!*" said our quiet friend from the edge of the pallet cot.

Estrando.—Goatee, hip eyes drooping brown sad and narcotic, opium, hands falling, strange witchdoctor sitter-next-to of this King—threw in occasional remarks that had the others listening but whenever he tried to follow through it was no go, he overdid something, he dulled them, they refused to listen to his elaborations and artistic touches in the brew.—Primeval carnal sacrifice is what they wanted. No anthropologist should forget the cannibals, or avoid the Auca. Get me a bow and arrow and I'll go; I'm ready now; plane fare please; plain fare; vacuous is the list; knights grow bold growing old; young knights dream.

Soft.—Our Indian King wanted nothing to do with tentative ideas; he listened to Enrique's real pleas, took note of Estrando's hallucinated sayings, guttural remarks spicy thrown in pithy like madness inward and from which the King had learned all he knew of what reality would think of him—he eyed me with honest suspicion.

In Spanish I heard him ask if this Gringo was some cop following him from L.A., some F.B.I. man. I heard and said no. Enrique tried to tell him I was *interessa* pointing at his own head to mean I was interested in things—I was trying to learn Spanish, I was a head, *cabeza*, also *chucharro*—(potsmoker).—*Chucharro* didnt interest King. In L.A. he'd gone walking in from the Mexican darkness on bare feet palms out black face to the lights—somebody's ripped a crucifix chain from his neck, some cop or hoodlum, he snarled remembering it, his revenge was either silent or someone was left dead and I was the F.B.I. man—the weird follower of Mexican suspects with records of having left feet prints on the sidewalks of Iron L.A. and chains in jailhouses and potential revolutionary heroes of late afternoon mustaches in the reddy soft light.—

He showed me a pellet of O.—I named it.—Partially satisfied. Enrique pleaded further in my defense. The witchdoctor smiled inwardly, he had no time to goof or do court dances or sing of drink in whore alleys looking for pimps—he was Goethe in the court of Fredericko Weimar.—Vibrations of television telepathy surrounded the room as silently the King decided to accept me—when he did I heard the sceptre drop in all their thoughts.

And O the holy sea of Mazatlan and the great red plain of eve with burros and aznos and red and brown horses and green cactus pulque.

The three *muchachas* two miles away in a little group talking in the exact concentric center of the circle of the red universe—the softness of their speech could never reach us, nor these waves of Mazatlan destroy it by their bark—soft sea winds to beautify the weed—three islands one mile out—rocks—the Fellaheen City's muddy rooftops dusk in back . . .

To explain, I'd missed the ship in San Pedro and this was the midway point of the trip from the Mexican border at Nogales Arizona that I had undertaken on cheap second class buses all the way down the West Coast to Mexico City.—I'd met Enrique and his kid brother Gerardo while the passengers were stretching their legs at desert huts in the Sonora desert where big fat Indian ladies served hot tortillas and meat off stone stoves and as you stood there waiting for your sandwich the little pigs grazed lovingly against your legs.—Enrique was a great sweet kid with black hair and black eyes who was making this epic journey all the way to Vera Cruz two thousand miles away on the Gulf of Mexico with his kid brother for some reason I never found out—all he let me know was that inside his home made wooden radio set was hidden about a half a pound of strong dark green marijuana with the moss still in it and long black hairs in it, the sign of good pot.—We immediately started blasting among the cacti in the back of the desert waystations, squatting there in the hot sun laughing, as Gerardo watched (he was only 18 and wasnt allowed to smoke by his older brother)—"Is why? because marijuana is bad for the eye and bad for *la ley*" (bad for the eyesight and bad for the law) —"But jew!" pointing at me (Mexican saying "you"), "and *me*!" pointing at himself, "we alright." He undertook to be my guide in the great trip through the continental spaces of Mexico—he spoke some English and tried to explain to me the epic grandeur of his land and I certainly agreed with him.—"See?" he'd say pointing at distant mountain ranges. "*Mehico!*"

The bus was an old high thin affair with wooden benches, as I say, and passengers in shawls and straw hats got on with their goats or pigs or chickens while kids rode on the roof or hung on singing and screaming from the tailgate.—We bounced and bounced over that one thousand mile dirt road and when we came to rivers the driver just plowed through the shallow water, washing off the dust, and bounced on.—Strange towns like Navajoa where I took a walk by myself and saw, in the market outdoor affair, a butcher standing in front of a pile of lousy beef for sale, flies swarming all over it while mangy skinny fellaheen dogs scrounged around under the table—and towns like Los Mochis (The Flies) where we sat drinking Orange Crush like grandees at sticky little tables, where the day's headline in the Los Mochis newspaper told of a midnight gun duel between the Chief of Police and the Mayor—it was all over town, some excitement in the white alleys—both of them with revolvers on their hips, bang, blam, right in the muddy street outside the cantina.—Now we were in a town further south in Sinaloa and had gotten off the old bus at midnight to walk single file through the slums and past the bars ("Ees no good you and me and Gerardo go into cantina, ees bad for *la ley*" said Enrique) and then, Gerardo carrying my seabag on his back like a true friend and brother, we crossed a great empty plaza of dirt and came to a bunch of stick huts forming a little village not far from the soft starlit surf, and there we knocked on the door of that mustachio'd wild man with the opium and were admitted to his candlelit kitchen where he and his witchdoctor goatee Estrando were sprinkling red pinches of pure opium into huge cigarettes of marijuana the size of a cigar.

The host allowed us to sleep the night in the little grass hut nearby—this hermitage belonged to Estrando, who was very kind to let us sleep there—he showed us in by candlelight, removed his only belongings which consisted of his opium stash under the pallet on the sod where he slept, and crept off to sleep somewhere else.—We had only one blanket and tossed to see who would have to sleep in the middle: it was the kid Gerardo, who didnt complain.—In the morning I got up and peeked out through the sticks: it was a drowsy sweet little grass hut village with lovely brown maids carrying jugs of water from the main well on their shoulders—smoke of tortillas rose among the trees—dogs barked, children played, and as I say

our host was up and splitting twigs with a spear by throwing
the spear to the ground neatly parting the twigs (or thin
boughs) clean in half, an amazing sight.—And when I wanted
to go to the john I was directed to an ancient stone seat which
overlorded the entire village like some king's throne and there
I had to sit in full sight of everybody, it was completely in the
open—mothers passing by smiled politely, children stared with
fingers in mouth, young girls hummed at their work.

We began packing to get back on the bus and carry on to
Mexico City but first I bought a quarter pound of marijuana
but as soon as the deal was done in the hut a file of Mexican
soldiers and a few seedy policemen came in with sad eyes.—I
said to Enrique: "Hey, are we going to be arrested?" He said
no, they just wanted some of the marijuana for themselves,
free, and would let us go peaceably.—So Enrique cut them
into about half of what we had and they squatted all around
the hut and rolled joints on the ground.—I was so sick on an
opium hangover I lay there staring at everybody feeling like I
was about to be skewered, have my arms cut off, hung upsidedown on the cross and burned at the stake on that high stone
john.—Boys brought me soup with hot peppers in it and
everybody smiled as I sipped it, lying on my side—it burned
into my throat, made me gasp, cough and sneeze, and instantly I felt better.

We got up and Gerardo again heaved my seabag to his back,
Enrique hid the marijuana in his wooden radio, we shook
hands with our host and the witchdoctor solemnly, shook
hands seriously and solemnly with every one of the ten policemen and cop soldiers and off we went single file again in the
hot sun towards the bus station in town.—"Now," said Enrique patting the home made radio, "see, *mir*, we all set to get
high."

The sun was very hot and we were sweating—we came to a
large beautiful church in the old Spanish Mission style and Enrique said: "We go in here now"—it amazed me to remember
that we were all Catholics.—We went inside and Gerardo
kneeled first, then Enrique and I kneed the pews and did the
sign of the cross and he whispered in my ear "See? is cool in
the chorch. Is good to get away from the sun a *minuto*."

At Mazatlan at dusk we stopped for awhile for a swim in our

underwear in that magnificent surf and it was there, on the beach, with a big joint smoking in his hand where Enrique turned and pointed inland at the beautiful green fields of Mexico and said "See the three girls in the middle of the field far away?" and I looked and looked and only barely saw three dots in the middle of a distant pasture. "Three muchachas," said Enrique. "Is mean: *Mehico!*"

He wanted me to go to Vera Cruz with him. "I am a shoemaker by trade. You stay home with the gurls while I work, *mir*? You write you *interessa* books and we get lots of gurls."

I never saw him after Mexico City because I had no money absolutely and I had to stay on William Seward Burroughs' couch. And Burroughs didnt want Enrique around: "You shouldnt hang around with these Mexicans, they're all a bunch of con men."

I still have the rabbit's foot Enrique gave me when he left.

A few weeks later I go to see my first bullfight, which I must confess is a *novillera*, a novice fight, and not the real thing they show in the winter which is supposed to be so artistic. Inside it is a perfect round bowl with a neat circle of brown dirt being harrowed and raked by expert loving rakers like the man who rakes second base in Yankee Stadium only this is Bite-the-Dust Stadium.—When I sat down the bull had just come in and the orchestra was sitting down again.—Fine embroidered clothes tightly fitted to boys behind a fence.—Solemn they were, as a big beautiful shiny black bull rushed out gallumphing from a corner I hadnt looked, where he'd been apparently mooing for help, black nostrils and big white eyes and outspread horns, all chest no belly, stove polish thin legs seeking to drive the earth down with all that locomotive weight above—some people sniggered—bull galloped and flashed, you saw the riddled-up muscle holes in his perfect prize skin.—Matador stepped out and invited and the bull charged and slammed in, matador sneered his cape, let pass the horns by his loins a foot or two, got the bull revolved around by cape, and walked away like a Grandee—and stood his back to the dumb perfect bull who didnt charge like in "Blood & Sand" and lift Señor Grandee into the upper deck. Then business got underway. Out comes the old pirate horse with patch on eye, picador KNIGHT aboard with a lance, to come and dart a few slivers of steel in the bull's shoulderblade who responds by trying to lift the horse but the horse is mailed (thank God)—a historical and crazy scene except suddenly you realize the picador has started the bull on his interminable bleeding. The blinding of the poor bull in mindless vertigo is continued by the brave bow-legged little dart man carrying two darts with ribbon, here he comes head-on at the bull, the bull head-on for him, wham, no head-on crash for the dart man has stung with dart and darted away before you can say boo (& I did say boo), because a bull is hard to dodge? Good enough, but the darts now have the bull streaming with blood like Marlowe's Christ in the heavens.—An old matador comes out and tests the bull with a few capes' turn then another set of darts, a battleflag now shining down the living breathing suffering bull's side and everybody *glad.*—And now the bull's charge is just a stagger and so now the serious hero matador comes out for the kill as the orchestra goes one boom-lick on bass drum, it get quiet like a cloud passing over the sun, you hear a drunkard's bottle smash a mile away in the cruel Spanish green aromatic coun-tryside—children pause over tortas—the bull stands in the sun head-bowed, panting for life, his sides actually *flapping* against his ribs, his shoulders barbed like San Sebastian.—The careful footed matador youth, brave enough in his own right, ap-proaches and curses and the bull rolls around and comes stog-gling on wobbly feet at the red cape, dives in with blood streaming everywhichaway and the boy just accommodates him through the imaginary hoop and circles and hangs on tip-toe, knockkneed. And Lord, I didnt want to see his smooth tight belly ranted by no horn.—He rippled his cape again at the bull who just stood there thinking "O why cant I go home?" and the matador moved closer and now the animal bunched tired legs to run but one leg slipped throwing up a cloud of dust.—But he dove in and flounced off to rest.—The matador draped his sword and called the humble bull with glazed eyes.—The bull pricked his ears and didnt move.—The matador's whole body stiffened like a board that shakes under the trample of many feet—a muscle showed in his stocking.— Bull plunged a feeble three feet and turned in dust and the matador arched his back in front of him like a man leaning over a hot stove to reach for something on the other side and flipped his sword a yard deep into the bull's shoulderblade separation.—Matador walked one way, bull the other with sword to hilt and staggered, started to run, looked up with human surprise at the sky & sun, and then gargled—O go see it folks!—He threw up ten gallons of blood into the air and it splashed all over—he fell on his knees choking on his own blood and spewed and twisted his neck around and suddenly got floppy doll and his head blammed flat.—He still wasnt dead, an extra idiot rushed out and knifed him with a wren-like dagger in the neck nerve and still the bull dug the sides of his poor mouth in the sand and chewed old blood.—His eyes! O his eyes!—Idiots sniggered because the dagger did this, as though it would not.—A team of hysterical horses were rushed out to chain and drag the bull away, they galloped off but the chain broke and the bull slid in dust like a dead fly kicked unconsciously by a foot.—Off, off with him!—He's gone, white eyes staring the last thing you see.—Next bull!—First the old boys shovel blood in a wheel-barrow and rush off with it. The quiet raker returns with his rake—"Ole!," girls throwing flowers at the animal-murder in the fine britches.—And I saw how everybody dies and nobody's going to care, I felt how awful it is to live just so you can die like a bull trapped in a screaming human ring.—

Jai Alai, Mexico, Jai Alai!

The last day I'm in Mexico I'm in the little church near Redondas in Mexico City, 4 o'clock in the gray afternoon, I've walked all over town delivering packages at the Post Offices and I've munched on fudge candy for breakfast and now, with two beers under me, I'm resting in the church contemplating the void.

Right above me is a great tormented statue of Christ on the Cross, when I first saw it I instantly sat under it, after brief standing hand-clasped look at it—("Jeanne!" they call me in the courtyard and it's for some other Lady, I run to the door and look out).—"*Mon Jésus*," I'm saying, and I look up and there He is, they've put on Him a handsome face like young Robert Mitchum and have closed His eyes in death tho one of them is slightly open you think and it also looks like young

Robert Mitchum or Enrique high on tea looking at you thru
the smoke and saying "Hombre, man, this is the end."—His
knees are all scratched so hard sore they're scathed wore out
through, an inch deep the hole where His kneecap's been
wailed away by flailing falls on them with the big Flail Cross a
hundred miles long on His back, and as He leans there with
the Cross on rocks they goad Him on to slide on His knees
and He's worn them out by the time He's nailed to the cross
—I was there.—Shows the big rip in His ribs where the sword-
tips of lancers were stuck up at Him.—I was not there, had I
been there I would have yelled "Stop it" and got crucified
too.—Here Holy Spain has sent the bloodheart sacrifice
Aztecs of Mexico a picture of tenderness and pity, saying,
"This you would do to Man? I am the Son of Man, I am of
Man, I am Man and this you would do to Me, Who Am Man
and God—I am God, and you would pierce my feet bound together with long nails with big stayfast points on the end
slightly blunted by the hammerer's might—this you did to
Me, and I preached Love?"

He Preached love, and you would have him bound to a tree
and hammered into it with nails, you fools, you should be
forgiven.

It shows the blood running from His hands to His armpits
and down His sides.—The Mexicans have hung a graceful
canopy of red velvet around His loins, it's too high a statue for
there to have been pinners of medals on That Holy Victory
Cloth—

What a Victory, the Victory of Christ! Victory over madness, mankind's blight. "Kill him!" they still roar at fights,
cockfights, bullfights, prizefights, streetfights, fieldfights, air-
fights, wordfights—"Kill him!"—Kill the Fox, the Pig and the
Pox.

Christ in His Agony, pray for me.

It shows His body falling from the Cross on His hand of
nails, the perfect slump built in by the artist, the devout sculp-
tor who worked on this with all his heart, the Compassion and
tenacity of a Christ—a sweet perhaps Indian Spanish Catholic
of the 15th century, among ruins of adobe and mud and
stinksmokes of Indian mid millenium in North America, devised this *statuo del Cristo* and pinned it up in the new church

which now, 1950's, four hundred years later or five, has lost portions of the ceiling where some Spanish Michelangelo has run up cherubs and angelkins for the edification of upward gazers on Sunday mornings when the kind Padre expostulates on the details of the law religious.

I pray on my knees so long, looking up sideways at my Christ, I suddenly wake up in a trance in the church with my knees aching and a sudden realization that I've been listening to a profound buzz in my ears that permeates throughout the church and throughout my ears and head and throughout the universe, the intrinsic silence of Purity (which is Divine). I sit in the pew quietly, rubbing my knees, the silence is roaring.—

Ahead is the Altar, the Virgin Mary is white in a field of blue-and-white-and-golden arrangements—it's too far to see adequately, I promise myself to go forward to the altar as soon as some of the people leave.—The people are all women, young and old, and suddenly here come two children in rags and blankets and barefooted walking slowly down the right hand aisle with the big boy laying his hand anxiously holding something on his little brother's head, I wonder why—they're both barefooted but I hear the clack of heels, I wonder why—they go forward to the altar, come around the side to the glass coffin of a saint statue, all the time walking slowly, anxiously, touching everything, looking up, crawling infinitesimally around the church and taking it all in completely.—At the coffin the littler boy (3 years old) touches the glass and goes around to the foot of the dead and touches the glass and I think "They understand death, they stand there in the church under the skies that have a beginningless past and go into the never-ending future, waiting themselves for death, at the foot of the dead, in a holy temple."—I get a vision of myself and the two little boys hung up in a great endless universe with nothing overhead and nothing under but the Infinite Nothingness, the Enormousness of it, the dead without number in all directions of existence whether inward into the atomworlds of your own body or outward to the universe which may only be one atom in an infinity of atomworlds and each atom world only a figure of speech—inward, outward, up and down, nothing but emptiness and divine majesty and silence for the two little boys and me.—Anxiously I watch them leave, to my amaze I see a little tiny girl one foot or and-a-half high, two years old, or one-and-a-half, waddling tinily lowly beneath them, a meek little lamb on the floor of the church. Anxiousness of big brother was to hold a shawl over her head, he wanted little brother to hold *his* end, between them and under the canopy marched Princessa Sweetheart examining the church with her big brown eyes, her little heels clacking.

As soon as they're outside, they play with the other children. Many children are playing in the garden-enclosed entryway, some of them are standing and staring at the upper front of the church at images of angels in rain dimmed stone.

I bow to all this, kneel at my pew entryway, and go out, taking one last look at St. Antoine de Padue (St. Anthony) Santo Antonio de Padua.—Everything is perfect on the street again, the world is permeated with roses of happiness all the time, but none of us know it. The happiness consists in realizing that it is all a great strange dream.

Cut-lover

3

The Railroad Earth

THERE was a little alley in San Francisco back of the Southern Pacific station at Third and Townsend in redbrick of drowsy lazy afternoons with everybody at work in offices in the air you feel the impending rush of their commuter frenzy as soon they'll be charging en masse from Market and Sansome buildings on foot and in buses and all well-dressed thru workingman Frisco of Walkup ?? truck drivers and even the poor grime-bemarked Third Steet of lost bums even Negroes so hopeless and long left East and meanings of responsibility and *try* that now all they do is stand there spitting in the broken glass sometimes fifty in one afternoon against one wall at Third and Howard and here's all these Millbrae and San Carlos neat-necktied producers and commuters of America and Steel civilization rushing by with San Francisco *Chronicles* and green *Call-Bulletins* not even enough time to be disdainful, they've got to catch 130, 132, 134, 136 all the way up to 146 till the time of evening supper in homes of the railroad earth when high in the sky the magic stars ride above the following hotshot freight trains.—It's all in California, it's all a sea, I swim out of it in afternoons of sun hot meditation in my jeans with head on handkerchief on brakeman's lantern or (if not working) on books, I look up at blue sky of perfect lostpurity and feel the warp of wood of old America beneath me and have insane conversations with Negroes in several-story windows above and everything is pouring in, the switching moves of boxcars in that little alley which is so much like the alleys of Lowell and I hear far off in the sense of coming night that engine calling our mountains.

But it was that beautiful cut of clouds I could always see above the little S.P. alley, puffs floating by from Oakland or the Gate of Marin to the north or San Jose south, the clarity of Cal to break your heart. It was the fantastic drowse and drum hum of lum mum afternoon nathin' to do, ole Frisco with end of land sadness—the people—the alley full of trucks and cars of businesses nearabouts and nobody knew or far from cared who I was all my life three thousand five hundred miles from birth-O opened up and at last belonged to me in Great America.

Now it's night in Third Street the keen little neons and also yellow bulblights of impossible-to-believe flops with dark ruined shadows moving back of torn yellow shades like a degenerate China with no money—the cats in Annie's Alley, the flop comes on, moans, rolls, the street is loaded with darkness. Blue sky above with stars hanging high over old hotel roofs and blowers of hotels moaning out dusts of interior, the grime inside the word in mouths falling out tooth by tooth, the reading rooms tick tock bigclock with creak chair and slantboards and old faces looking up over rimless spectacles bought in some West Virginia or Florida or Liverpool England pawnshop long before I was born and across rains they've come to the end of the land sadness end of the world gladness all you San Franciscos will have to fall eventually and burn again. But I'm walking and one night a bum fell into the hole of the construction job where theyre tearing a sewer by day the husky Pacific & Electric youths in torn jeans who work there often I think of going up to some of em like say blond ones with wild hair and torn shirts and say "You oughta apply for the railroad its much easier work you dont stand around the street all day and you get much more pay" but this bum fell in the hole you saw his foot stick out, a British MG also driven by some eccentric once backed into the hole and as I came home from a long Saturday afternoon local to Hollister out of San Jose miles away across verdurous fields of prune and juice joy here's this British MG backed and legs up wheels up into a pit and bums and cops standing around right outside the coffee shop—it was the way they fenced it but he never had the nerve to do it due to the fact that he had no money and nowhere to go and O his father was dead and O his mother was dead and O his sister was dead and O his whereabout was dead was dead.— But and then at that time also I lay in my room on long Saturday afternoons listening to Jumpin' George with my fifth of tokay no tea and just under the sheets laughed to hear the crazy music "Mama, he treats your daughter mean," Mama, Papa,

and dont you come in here I'll kill you etc. getting high by
myself in room glooms and all wondrous knowing about the
Negro the essential American out there always finding his sol-
ace his meaning in the fellaheen street and not in abstract
morality and even when he has a church you see the pastor out
front bowing to the ladies on the make you hear his great vi-
brant voice on the sunny Sunday afternoon sidewalk full of
sexual vibratos saying "Why yes Mam but de gospel do say that
man was born of woman's womb—" and no and so by that
time I come crawling out of my warmsack and hit the street
when I see the railroad ain't gonna call me till 5 AM Sunday
morn probably for a local out of Bayshore in fact always for a
local out of Bayshore and I go to the wailbar of all the wildbars
in the world the one and only Third-and-Howard and there I
go in and drink with the madmen and if I get drunk I git.

The whore who come up to me in there the night I was
there with Al Buckle and said to me "You wanta play with me
tonight Jim, and?" and I didnt think I had enough money and
later told this to Charley Low and he laughed and said "How
do you know she wanted money always take the chance that
she might be out just for love or just out for love you know
what I mean man dont be a sucker." She was a goodlooking
doll and said "How would you like to oolyakoo with me
mon?" and I stood there like a jerk and in fact bought drink
got drink drunk that night and in the 299 Club I was hit by the
proprietor the band breaking up the fight before I had a
chance to decide to hit him back which I didnt do and out on
the street I tried to rush back in but they had locked the door
and were looking at me thru the forbidden glass in the
door with faces like undersea—I should have played with her
shurrouruuruuruuruuruuruurkdiei.

Despite the fact I was a brakeman making 600 a month I kept
going to the Public restaurant on Howard Street which was
three eggs for 26 cents 2 eggs for 21 this with toast (hardly no
butter) coffee (hardly no coffee and sugar rationed) oatmeal
with dash of milk and sugar the smell of soured old shirts lingering above the cookpot steams as if they were making
skidrow lumberjack stews out of San Francisco ancient Chinese mildewed laundries with poker games in the back among

the barrels and the rats of the earthquake days, but actually the
food somewhat on the level of an oldtime 1890 or 1910 section-
gang cook of lumber camps far in the North with an oldtime
pigtail Chinaman cooking it and cussing out those who didnt
like it. The prices were incredible but one time I had the beefstew and it was absolutely the worst beefstew I ever et, it was
incredible I tell you—and as they often did that to me it
was with the most intensest regret that I tried to convey to the
geek back of counter what I wanted but he was a tough sonofabitch, ech, ti-ti, I thought the counterman was kind of
queer especially he handled gruffly the hopeless drooldrunks,
"What now you doing you think you can come in here and cut
like that for God's sake act like a man won't you and eat or get
out-t-t-t-"—I always did wonder what a guy like that was
doing working in a place like that because, but why some sympathy in his horny heart for the busted wrecks, all up and
down the street were restaurants like the Public catering exclusively to bums of the black, winos with no money, who found
21 cents left over from wine panhandlings and so stumbled in
for their third or fourth touch of food in a week, as sometimes
they didnt eat at all and so you'd see them in the corner puking
white liquid which was a couple quarts of rancid sauterne
rotgut or sweet white sherry and they had nothing on their
stomachs, most of them had one leg or were on crutches and
had bandages around their feet, from nicotine and alcohol poi-
soning together, and one time finally on my way up Third near
Market across the street from Breens, when in early 1952 I lived
on Russian Hill and didnt quite dig the complete horror and
humor of railroad's Third Street, a bum a thin sickly littlebum
like Anton Abraham lay face down on the pavement with crutch
aside and some old remnant newspaper sticking out and it
seemed to me he was dead. I looked closely to see if he was
breathing and he was not, another man with me was looking
down and we agreed he was dead, and soon a cop came over
and took and agreed and called the wagon, the little wretch
weighed about 50 pounds in his bleeding count and was stone
mackerel snotnose cold dead as a bleeding doornail—ah I tell
you—and who could notice but other half dead deadbums
bums bums bums dead dead times X times X times all dead
bums forever dead with nothing and all finished and out—

there.—And this was the clientele in the Public Hair restaurant where I ate many's the morn a 3-egg breakfast with almost dry toast and oatmeal a little saucer of, and thin sickly dishwater coffee, all to save 14 cents so in my little book proudly I could make a notation and of the day and prove that I could live comfortably in America while working seven days a week and earning 600 a month I could live on less than 17 a week which with my rent of 4.20 was okay as I had also to spend money to eat and sleep sometimes on the other end of my Watsonville chaingang run but preferred most times to sleep free of charge and uncomfortable in cabooses of the crummy rack—my 26-cent breakfast, my pride.—And that incredible semiqueer counterman who dished out the food, threw it at you, slammed it, had a languid frank expression straight in your eyes like a 1930's lunchcart heroine in Steinbeck and at the steamtable itself labored coolly a junkey-looking Chinese with an actual stocking in his hair as if they'd just Shanghai'd him off the foot of Commercial Street before the Ferry Building was up but forgot it was 1952, dreamed it was 1860 goldrush Frisco—and on rainy days you felt they had ships in the back room.

I'd take walks up Harrison and the boomcrash of truck traffic towards the glorious girders of the Oakland Bay Bridge that you could see after climbing Harrison Hill a little like radar machine of eternity in the sky, huge, in the blue, by pure clouds crossed, gulls, idiot cars streaking to destinations on its undinal boom across shmoshwaters flocked up by winds and news of San Rafael storms and flash boats.—There O I always came and walked and negotiated whole Friscos in one after-noon from the overlooking hills of the high Fillmore where Orient-bound vessels you can see on drowsy Sunday mornings of poolhall goof like after a whole night playing drums in a jam session and a morn in the hall of cuesticks I went by the rich homes of old ladies supported by daughters or female secre-taries with immense ugly gargoyle Frisco millions fronts of other days and way below is the blue passage of the Gate, the Alcatraz mad rock, the mouths of Tamalpais, San Pablo Bay, Sausalito sleepy hemming the rock and bush over yonder, and the sweet white ships cleanly cutting a path to Sasebo.—Over Harrison and down to the Embarcadero and around Tele-

graph Hill and up the back of Russian Hill and down to the
play streets of Chinatown and down Kearney back across Market to Third and my wild-night neon twinkle fate there, ah,
and then finally at dawn of a Sunday and they did call me, the
immense girders of Oakland Bay still haunting me and all that
eternity too much to swallow and not knowing who I am at all
but like a big plump longhaired baby walking up in the dark
trying to wonder who I am the door knocks and it's the desk
keeper of the flop hotel with silver rims and white hair and
clean clothes and sickly potbelly said he was from Rocky
Mount and looked like yes, he had been desk clerk of the Nash
Buncome Association hotel down there in 50 successive heat-
wave summers without the sun and only palmos of the lobby
with cigar crutches in the albums of the South and him with
his dear mother waiting in a buried log cabin of graves with all
that mashed past historied underground afoot with the stain of
the bear the blood of the tree and cornfields long plowed
under and Negroes whose voices long faded from the middle
of the wood and the dog barked his last, this man had voy-
ageured to the West Coast too like all the other loose American
elements and was pale and sixty and complaining of sickness,
might at one time been a handsome squire to women with
money but now a forgotten clerk and maybe spent a little time
in jail for a few forgeries or harmless cons and might also have
been a railroad clerk and might have wept and might have never
made it, and that day I'd say he saw the bridgegirders up over
the hill of traffic of Harrison like me and woke up mornings
with same lost, is now beckoning on my door and breaking in
the world on me and he is standing on the frayed carpet of the
hall all worn down by black steps of sunken old men for last 40
years since earthquake and the toilet stained, beyond the last
toilet bowl and the last stink and stain I guess yes is the end of
the world the bloody end of the world, so now knocks on my
door and I wake up, saying "How what howp howelk howel of
the knavery they've meaking, ek and wont let me slepit? Whey
they dool? Whand out wisis thing that comes flarminging
around my dooring in the mouth of the night and there everything knows that I have no mother, and no sister, and no
father and no bot sosstle, but not crib" I get up and sit up and
says "Howowow?" and he says "Telephone?" and I have to

put on my jeans heavy with knife, wallet, I look closely at my railroad watch hanging on little door flicker of closet door face to me ticking silent the time, it says 4:30 AM of a Sunday morn, I go down the carpet of the skidrow hall in jeans and with no shirt and yes with shirt tails hanging gray workshirt and pick up phone and ticky sleepy night desk with cage and spittoons and keys hanging and old towels piled clean ones but frayed at edges and bearing names of every hotel of the moving prime, on the phone is the Crew Clerk, "Kerroway?" "Yeah." "Kerroway it's gonna be the Sherman Local at 7 AM this morning." "Sherman Local right." "Out of Bayshore, you know the way?" "Yeah." "You had that same job last Sunday—Okay Keroway-y-y-y." And we mutually hang up and I say to myself okay it's the Bayshore bloody old dirty hagglous old coveted old madman Sherman who hates me so much especially when we were at Redwood Junction kicking boxcars and he always insists I work the rear end tho as one-year man it would be easier for me to follow pot but I work rear and he wants me to be right there with a block of wood when a car or cut of cars kicked stops, so they wont roll down that incline and start catastrophes, O well anyway I'll be learning eventually to like the railroad and Sherman will like me some day, and anyway another day another dollar.

And there's my room, small, gray in the Sunday morning, now all the franticness of the street and night before is done with, bums sleep, maybe one or two sprawled on sidewalk with empty poorboy on a sill—my mind whirls with life.

So there I am in dawn in my dim cell—2½ hours to go till the time I have to stick my railroad watch in my jean watchpocket and cut out allowing myself exactly 8 minutes to the station and the 7:15 train No. 112 I have to catch for the ride five miles to Bayshore through four tunnels, emerging from the sad Rath scene of Frisco gloom gleak in the rainymouth fogmorning to a sudden valley with grim hills rising to the sea, bay on left, the fog rolling in like demented in the draws that have little white cottages disposed real-estatically for come-Christmas blue sad lights—my whole soul and concomitant eyes looking out on this reality of living and working in San Francisco with that pleased semi-loin-located shudder, energy for sex changing to pain at the portals of work and culture and natural foggy fear.—There I am in my little room wondering how I'll really manage to fool myself into feeling that these next 2½ hours will be well filled, fed, with work and pleasure thoughts.—It's so thrilling to feel the coldness of the morning wrap around my thickquilt blankets as I lay there, watch facing and ticking me, legs spread in comfy skidrow soft sheets with soft tears or sew lines in 'em, huddled in my own skin and rich and not spending a cent on—I look at my littlebook—and I stare at the words of the Bible.—On the floor I find last red afternoon Saturday's *Chronicle* sports page with news of football games in Great America the end of which I bleakly see in the gray light entering.—The fact that Frisco is built of wood satisfies me in my peace, I know nobody'll disturb me for 2½ hours and all bums are asleep in their own bed of eternity awake or not, bottle or not—it's the joy I feel that counts for me.—On the floor's my shoes, big lumberboot flopjack workshoes to colomp over rockbed with and not turn the ankle—solidity shoes that when you put them on, yokewise, you know you're working now and so for same reason shoes not be worn for any reason like joys of restaurant and shows.—Night-before shoes are on the floor beside the clunkershoes a pair of blue canvas shoes à la 1952 style, in them I'd trod soft as ghost the indented hill sidewalks of Ah Me Frisco all in the glitter night, from the top of Russian Hill I'd looked down at one point on all roofs of North Beach and the Mexican nightclub neons, I'd descended to them on the old steps of Broadway under which they were newly laboring a mountain tunnel—shoes fit for watersides, embarcaderos, hill and plot lawns of park and tiptop vista.—Workshoes covered with dust and some oil of engines—the crumpled jeans nearby, belt, blue railroad hank, knife, comb, keys, switch keys and caboose coach key, the knees white from Pajaro Riverbottom finedusts, the ass black from slick sandboxes in yardgoat after yardgoat—the gray workshorts, the dirty undershirt, sad shorts, tortured socks of my life.—And the Bible on my desk next to the peanut butter, the lettuce, the raisin bread, the crack in the plaster, the stiff-with-old-dust lace drape now no longer laceable but hard as—after all those years of hard dust eternity in that Cameo skid inn with red eyes of rheumy oldmen dying there staring without hope out on the dead wall you can hardly see thru windowdusts and all you heard lately in the shaft of the rooftop middle way was the cries of a Chinese child whose father and mother were always telling him to shush and then screaming at him, he was a pest and his tears from China were most persistent and worldwide and represented all our feelings in broken-down Cameo tho this was not admitted by bum one except for an occasional harsh clearing of throat in the halls or moan of nightmarer—by things like this and neglect of a hard-eyed alcoholic oldtime chorusgirl maid the curtains had now absorbed all the iron they could take and hung stiff and even the dust in them was iron, if you shook them they'd crack and fall in tatters to the floor and spatter like wings of iron on the bong and the dust would fly into your nose like filings of steel and choke you to death, so I never touched them. My little room at 6 in the comfy dawn (at 4:30) and before me all that time, that fresh-eyed time for a little coffee to boil water on my hot plate, throw some coffee in, stir it, French style, slowly carefully pour it in my white tin cup, throw sugar in (not California beet sugar like I should have been using but New Orleans cane sugar, because beet racks I carried from Oakland out to Watsonville many's the time, a 80-car freight train with nothing but gondolas loaded with sad beets looking like the heads of decapitated women).—Ah me how but it was a hell and now I had the whole thing to myself, and make my raisin toast by sitting it on a little wire I'd especially bent to place over the hotplate, the toast crackled up, there, I spread the margarine on the still red hot toast and it too would crackle and sink in golden, among burnt raisins and this was my toast.—Then two eggs gently slowly fried in soft margarine in my little skidrow frying pan about half as thick as a dime in fact less, a little piece of tiny tin you could bring on a camp trip—the eggs slowly fluffled in there and swelled from butter steams and I threw garlic salt on them, and when they were ready the yellow of them had been slightly filmed with a cooked white at the top from the tin cover I'd put over the frying pan, so now they were ready, and out they came, I spread them out on top of my already prepared potatoes which had been boiled in small pieces and then mixed with the bacon I'd already fried in small pieces, kind of raggely mashed bacon potatoes, with eggs on top steaming, and on the side lettuce, with peanut butter dab nearby on side.—I had heard that peanut butter and lettuce contained all the vitamins you should want, this after I had originally started to eat this combination because of the deliciousness and nostalgia of the taste—my breakfast ready at about 6:45 and as I eat already I'm dressing to go piece by piece and by the time the last dish is washed in the little sink at the boiling hotwater tap and I'm taking my lastquick slug of coffee and quickly rinsing the cup in the hot water spout and rushing to dry it and plop it in its place by the hot plate and the brown carton in which all the groceries sit tightly wrapped in brown paper, I'm already picking up my brakeman's lantern from where it's been hanging on the door handle and my tattered timetable's long been in my back-pocket folded and ready to go, everything tight, keys, time-table, lantern, knife, handkerchief, wallet, comb, railroad keys, change and myself. I put the light out on the sad dab mad grub little diving room and hustle out into the fog of the flow, descending the creak hall steps where the old men are not yet sitting with Sunday morn papers because still asleep or some of them I can now as I leave hear beginning to disfawdle to wake in their rooms with their moans and yorks and scrapings and horror sounds, I'm going down the steps to work, glance to check time of watch with clerk cage clock.—A hardy two or three oldtimers sitting already in the dark brown lobby under the tockboom clock, toothless, or grim, or elegantly mustached —what thought in the world swirling in them as they see the young eager brakeman bum hurrying to his thirty dollars of the Sunday—what memories of old homesteads, built without sympathy, hornyhanded fate dealt them the loss of wives, childs, moons—libraries collapsed in their time—oldtimers of the telegraph wired wood Frisco in the fog gray top time sitting in their brown sunk sea and will be there when this afternoon my face flushed from the sun, which at eight'll flame out and make sunbaths for us at Redwood, they'll still be here the color of paste in the green underworld and still reading the same editorial over again and wont understand where I've been or what for or what.—I have to get out of there or suffocate, out of Third Street or become a worm, it's alright to live and bed-wine in and play the radio and cook little breakfasts and rest in but O my I've got to go now to work, I hurry down Third to Townsend for my 7:15 train—it's 3 minutes to go, I start in a panic to jog, goddam it I didnt give myself enough time this morning, I hurry down under the Harrison ramp to the Oakland-Bay Bridge, down past Schweibacker-Frey the great dim red neon printshop always spectrally my father the dead executive I see there, I run and hurry past the beat Negro grocery stores where I buy all my peanut butter and raisin bread, past the redbrick railroad alley now mist and wet, across Townsend, the train is leaving!

Fatuous railroad men, the conductor old John J. Coppertwang 35 years pure service on ye olde S.P. is there in the gray Sunday morning with his gold watch out peering at it, he's standing by the engine yelling up pleasantries at old hoghead Jones and young fireman Smith with the baseball cap is at the fireman's seat munching sandwich—"We'll how'd ye like old Johnny O yestiddy, I guess he didnt score so many touchdowns like we thought." "Smith bet six dollars on the pool down in Watsonville and said he's rakin' in thirty four." "I've been in that Watsonville pool—." They've been in the pool of life fleartiming with one another, all the long pokerplaying nights in brownwood railroad places, you can smell the mashed cigar in the wood, the spittoon's been there for more than 750,099 yars and the dog's been in and out and these old boys by old shaded brown light have bent and muttered and young boys too with their new brakeman passenger uniform the tie undone the coat thrown back the flashing youth smile of happy fatuous well-fed goodjobbed careered futured pensioned hospitalized taken-care-of railroad men.—35, 40 years of it and then they get to be conductors and in the middle of the night they've been for years called by the Crew Clerk yelling "Cassady? It's the Maximush localized week do you for the right lead" but now as old men all they have is a regular job, a regular train, conductor of the 112 with goldwatch is helling up his pleasantries at all fire dog crazy Satan hoghead Willis why the wildest man this side of France and Frankincense, he was known once to take his engine up that steep grade . . . 7:15, time to pull, as I'm running thru the station hearing the bell jangling and the steam chuff they're pulling out, O I come

flying out on the platform and forget momentarily or that is
never did know what track it was and whirl in confusion a
while wondering what track and cant see no train and this is
the time I lose there, 5, 6, 7 seconds when the train tho underway is only slowly upchugging to go and a man a fat executive
could easily run up and grab it but when I yell to Assistant
Stationmaster "Where's 112?" and he tells me the last track
which is the track I never dreamed I run to it fast as I can go
and dodge people à la Columbia halfback and cut into track
fast as off-tackle where you carry the ball with you to the left
and feint with neck and head and push of ball as tho you're
gonna throw yourself all out to fly around that left end and
everybody psychologically chuffs with you that way and suddenly you contract and you like whiff of smoke are buried in
the hole in tackle, cutback play, you're flying into the hole
almost before you yourself know it, flying into the track I am
and there's the train about 30 yards away even as I look picking
up tremendously momentum the kind of momentum I would
have been able to catch if I'd a looked a second earlier—but I
run, I know I can catch it. Standing on the back platform are
the rear brakeman and an old deadheading conductor ole
Charley W. Jones, why he had seven wives and six kids and one
time out at Lick no I guess it was Coyote he couldnt see on account of the steam and out he come and found his lantern in
the igloo regular anglecock of my herald and they gave him fifteen benefits so now there he is in the Sunday har har owlala
morning and he and young rear man watch incredulously his
student brakeman running like a crazy trackman after their departing train. I feel like yelling "Make your airtest now make
your airtest now!" knowing that when a passenger pulls out
just about at the first crossing east of the station they pull the
air a little bit to test the brakes, on signal from the engine, and
this momentarily slows up the train and I could manage it, and
could catch it, but they're not making no airtest the bastards,
and I hek knowing I'm going to have to run like a sonofabitch.
But suddenly I get embarrassed thinking what are all the
people of the world gonna say to see a man running so devil-
ishly fast with all his might sprinting thru life like Jesse Owens
just to catch a goddam train and all of them with their hysteria wondering if I'll get killed when I catch the back platform

and blam, I fall down and go boom and lay supine across the crossing, so the old flagman when the train has flowed by will see that everything lies on the earth in the same stew, all of us angels will die and we dont ever know how or our own diamond, O heaven will enlighten us and open your eyes—open our eyes, open our eyes.—I know I wont get hurt, I trust my shoes, hand grip, feet, solidity of yipe and cripe of gripe and grip and strength and need no mystic strength to measure the musculature in my rib rack—but damn it all it's a social embarrassment to be caught sprinting like a maniac after a train especially with two men gaping at me from rear of train and shaking their heads and yelling I cant make it even as I half-heartedly sprint after them with open eyes trying to communicate that I can and not for them to get hysterical or laugh, but I realize it's all too much for me, not the run, not the speed of the train which anyway two seconds after I gave up the complicated chase did indeed slow down at the crossing in the airtest before chugging up again for good and Bayshore. So I was late for work, and old Sherman hated me and was about to hate me more.

The ground I would have eaten in solitude, cronch—the railroad earth, the flat stretches of long Bayshore that I have to negotiate to get to Sherman's bloody caboose on track 17 ready to go with pot pointed to Redwood and the morning's 3-hour work.—I get off the bus at Bayshore Highway and rush down the little street and turn in—boys riding the pot of a switcheroo in the yardgoat day come yelling by at me from the headboards and footboards "Come on down ride with us" otherwise I would have been about 3 minutes even later to my work but now I hop on the little engine that momentarily slows up to pick me up and it's alone not pulling anything but tender, the guys have been up to the other end of the yard to get back on some track of necessity.—That boy will have to learn to flag himself without nobody helping him as many's the time I've seen some of these young goats think they have everything but the plan is late, the word will have to wait, the massive arboreal thief with the crime of the kind, and air and all kinds of ghouls—ZONKed! made tremendous by the flare of the whole crime and encrudalatures of all kinds—San Fran-

ciscos and shroudband Bayshores the last and the last furbelow
of the eek plot pall prime tit top work oil twicks and wouldn't
you?—the railroad earth I would have eaten alone, cronch, on
foot head bent to get to Sherman who ticking watch observes
with finicky eyes the time to go to give the hiball sign get on
going it's Sunday no time to waste the only day of his long
seven-day-a-week worklife he gets a chance to rest a little bit at
home when "Eee Christ" when "Tell that sonofabitch student
this is no party picnic damn this shit and throb tit you tell
them something and how do you what the hell expect to
underdries out tit all you bright tremendous trouble anyway,
we's LATE" and this is the way I come rushing up late. Old
Sherman is sitting in the crummy over his switch lists, when he
sees me with cold blue eyes he says "You know you're supposed to be here 7:30 dont you so what the hell you doing gettin' in here at 7:50 you're twenty goddam minutes late, what
the fuck you think this your birthday?" and he gets up and
leans off the rear bleak platform and gives the high sign to the
enginemen up front we have a cut of about 12 cars and they say
it easy and off we go slowly at first, picking up momentum to
the work, "Light that goddam fire" says Sherman he's wearing
brandnew workshoes just about bought yestiddy and I notice
his clean coveralls that his wife washed and set on his chair just
that morning probably and I rush up and throw coal in the
potbelly flop and take a fusee and two fusees and light them
crack em. Ah fourth of the July when the angels would smile
on the horizon and all the racks where the mad are lost are returned to us forever from Lowell of my soul prime and single
meditated longsong hope to heaven of prayers and angels and
of course the sleep and interested eye of images and but now
we detect the missing buffoon there's the poor goodman rear
man aint even on the train yet and Sherman looks out sulkily
the back door and sees his rear man waving from fifteen yards
aways to stop and wait for him and being an old railroad man
he certainly isnt going to run or even walk fast, it's well
understood, conductor Sherman's got to get up off his switch-
list desk chair and pull the air and stop the goddam train for
rear man Arkansaw Charley, who sees this done and just come
up lopin' in his flop overalls without no care, so he was late
too, or at least had gone gossiping in the yard office while

waiting for the stupid head brakeman, the tagman's up in front on the presumably pot. "First thing we do is pick up a car in front at Redwood so all's you do get off at the crossing and stand back to flag, not too far." "Dont I work the head end?" "You work the hind end we got not much to do and I wanna get it done fast," snarls the conductor. "Just take it easy and do what we say and watch and flag." So it's peaceful Sunday morning in California and off we go, tack-a-tick, lao-tichi-couch, out of the Bayshore yards, pause momentarily at the main line for the green, ole 71 or ole whatever been by and now we get out and go swamming up the tree valleys and town vale hollows and main street crossing parking-lot last-night attendant plots and Stanford lots of the world—to our destination in the Pooh which I can see, and, so to while the time I'm up in the cupolo and with my newspaper dig the latest news on the front page and also consider and make notations of the money I spent already for this day Sunday absolutely not jot spend a nothing—California rushes by and with sad eyes we watch it reel the whole bay and the discourse falling off to gradual gils that ease and graduate to Santa Clara Valley then and the fig and behind is the fog immemoriate while the mist closes and we come running out to the bright sun of the Sabbath Californiay—

At Redwood I get off and standing on sad oily ties of the brakie railroad earth with red flag and torpedoes attached and fusees in backpocket with timetable crushed against and I leave my hot jacket in crummy standing there then with sleeves rolled up and there's the porch of a Negro home, the brothers are sitting in shirtsleeves talking with cigarettes and laughing and little daughter standing amongst the weeds of the garden with her playpail and pigtails and we the railroad men with soft signs and no sound pick up our flower, according to same goodman train order that for the last entire lifetime of attentions ole conductor industrial worker harlotized Sherman has been reading carefully son so's not to make a mistake:

"Sunday morning October 15 pick up flower
car at Redwood, Dispatcher M.M.S."

I'd put a block of wood under the wheels of the car and watch it writhe and crack as the car eased up on it and stopped and

sometimes didnt at all but just rolled on leaving the wood flattened to the level of the rail with upthrusted crackee ends.—
Afternoons in Lowell long ago I'd wondered what the grimy
men were doing with big boxcars and blocks of wood in their
hands and when far above the ramps and rooftops of the great
gray warehouse of eternity I'd see the immortal canal clouds of
redbrick time, the drowse so heavy in the whole July city it
would hang even in the dank gloom of my father's shop outside where they kept big rolltrucks with little wheels and flat
silvery platforms and junk in corners and boards, the ink dyed
into the oily wood as deep as a black river folded therein forever, contrasts for the whitepuff creamclouds outdoors that
you just can see standing in the dust moted hall door over the
old 1830 Lowell Dickens redbrick floating like in an old cartoon with little bird designs floating by too, all of a gray da-
guerrotype mystery in the whorly spermy waters of the canal.
—Thus in the same way the afternoons in the S.P. redbrick
alley, remembering my wonder at the slow grinding movement and squee of gigantic boxcars and flats and gons rolling
by with that overpowering steel dust crenching closh and clack
of steel on steel, the shudder of the whole steely proposition, a
car going by with a brake on and so the whole brakebar—
monstre empoudrement de fer en enfer the frightening fog nights
in California when you can see thru the mist the monsters
slowly passing and hear the whee whee squee, those merciless
wheels that one time Conductor Ray Miles on my student
trips said, "When those wheels go over your leg they dont care
about you" same way with that wood that I sacrifice.—What
those grimy men had been doing some of em standing on top
of the boxcars and signalling far down the redbrick canal alleys
of Lowell and some old men slowly like bums moving around
over rails with nothing to do, the big cut of cars squeeing by
with that teethgritting cree cree and gigantic hugsteel bending
rails into earth and making ties move, now I knew from
working as on the Sherman Local on Sundays we dealt with
blocks of wood because of an incline in the ground that made
kicked cars keep going and you had to ride them brake them
and stop them up with blocks. Lessons I learned there, like,
"Put, tie a good brake on him, we dont want to start chasin
the sonofabitch back to the City when we kick a car again

him," okay, but I'm playing the safety rules of the safety book
to the T and so now here I am the rear man on the Sherman
Local, we've set out our Sunday morning preacher blossom
flower car and made curtsies bows to the sabbath God in the
dark everything has been arranged in that fashion and according to old traditions reaching back to Sutter's Mill and the
times when the pioneers sick of hanging around the hardware
store all week had put on their best vestments and smoked and
jaw-bleaked in front of the wooden church and old railroad
men of the 19th century the inconceivably ancient S.P. of another era with stovepipe hats and flowers in their lapels and
had made the moves with the few cars into the goldtown milk-
bottle with the formality and the different chew the thinky
thought,—They give the sign and kick a car, with wood in
hand I run out, the old conductor yells "You'd better brake
him he's going too fast can you get im?" "Okay" and I run
and take it easy on a jog and wait and here's the big car looming
over me has just switched into its track from the locomotive
tracks where (the lead) all the angling and arrowing's been
done by the conductor who throws the switch, reads the
taglist, throws the switch—so up the rungs I go and according
to safety rules with one hand I hang on, with the other I brake,
slowly, according to a joint, easing up, till I reach the cut of
cars waiting and into it gently my braked boxcar bangs,
zommm—vibrations, things inside shake, the cradle rockababy
merchandise zomms with it, all the cars at this impact go forward about a foot and crush woodblocks earlier placed, I jump
down and place a block of wood and just neatly glue it under
the steel lip of that monstrous wheel and everything stops.
And so I turn back to take care of the next kicked car which is
going down the other track and also quite fast, I jog, finding
wood en route, run up the rung, stop it, safety rule hanging
on one hand forgetting the conductor's "Tie a good brake on
it," something I should have learned then as a year later in
Guadaloupe hundreds of miles down the line I tied poor
brakes on three flats, the flat handbrakes that have old rust and
loose chains, poorly with one hand safety wise hanging on in
case unexpected joint would jolt me off and under merciless
wheels whose action with blocks of wood my bones would
belie—bam, at Guadaloupe they kicked a cut of cars against

my poorly braked flats and everything began parading down the incline back to San Luis Obispo, if it hadn't been for the alert old conductor looking out of the crummy switch lists to see this parade and running out to throw switches in front of it and unlocking switch locks as fast as the cars kept coming, a kind of comic circus act with him in floppy clown pants and hysterical horror darting from switch stand to switch stand and the guys in back hollering, the pot taking off after the cut and catching it almost pushing it but the couplers closing just in time and the engine braking everything to a stop, 30 feet almost in front of the final derail which the old winded conductor couldnt have finally made, we'd all have lost our jobs, my safety rule brakes had not taken momentum of steel and slight land inclines into consideration . . . if it had been Sherman at Guadaloupe I would have been hated Keeroo-waaayy.

Guadaloupe is 275.5 miles down the shining rail from San Francisco, down on the subdivision named after it, the Guadaloupe—the whole Coast Division begins at those sad dead end blocks of Third and Townsend where grass grows from soot beds like green hair of old tokay heroes long slanted into the ground like the railroad men of the 19th century whom I saw in the Colorado plains at little train order stations slanted into the ground of the hard dry dustcake, boxed, mawk-lipped, puking grit, fondled by the cricket, gone aslant so far sunk gravewise boxdeep into the foot of the sole of the earth Oh, you'd think they had never suffered and dropped real sweats to that unhumped earth, had never voiced juicy sorrow words from blackcaked lips now make no more noise than the tire of an old tin lizzy the tin of which is zinging in the sun winds this afternoon, ah spectral Cheyenne Wellses and train order Denver Rio Grandes Northern Pacifics and Atlantic Coast Lines and Wunposts of America, all gone.—The Coast Division of the ole S.P. which was built in umpteen o too too and used to run a little crazy crooked mainline up and down the hills of Bayshore like a crazy cross country track for European runners, this was their gold carrying bandito held up railroad of the old Zorro night of inks and furly caped riders.—But now 'tis the modern ole Coast Division S.P. and

begins at those dead end blocks and at 4:30 the frantic Market
Street and Sansome Street commuters as I say come hysterically running for their 112 to get home on time for the 5:30 tel-
evisions Howdy Doody of their gun toting Neal Cassady'd
Hopalong childrens. 1.9 miles to 23rd Street, another 1.2 New-
comb, another 1.0 to Paul Avenue and etcetera these being the
little piss stops on that 5 miles short run thru 4 tunnels to
mighty Bayshore, Bayshore at milepost 5.2 shows you as I say
that gigantic valley wall sloping in with sometimes in extinct
winter dusks the huge fogs milking furling meerolling in without a sound but as if you could hear the radar hum, the old-
fashioned dullmasks mouth of Potato Patch Jack London old
scrollwaves crawling in across the gray bleak North Pacific
with a wild fleck, a fish, the wall of a cabin, the old arranged
wallworks of a sunken ship, the fish swimming in the pelvic
bones of old lovers lay tangled at the bottom of the sea like
slugs no longer discernible bone by bone but melted into one
squid of time, that fog, that terrible and bleak Seattleish fog
that potatopatch wise comes bringing messages from Alaska
and from the Aleutian mongol, and from the seal, and from
the wave, and from the smiling porpoise, that fog at Bayshore
you can see waving in and filling in rills and rolling down and
making milk on hillsides and you think, "It's hypocrisy of men
makes these hills grim."—To the left at the Bayshore mountain wall there's all your San Fran Bay pointing across the
broadflat blues to the Oakland lostness and the train the mainline train runs and clack and clackity clicks and makes the little
Bayshore yard office a passing fancy things so important to the
railroad men the little yellowish shack of clerks and paper
onion skin train order lips and clearances of conductors and
waybills tacked and typed and stamped from Kearney Neb. on
in with mooing cows that have moved over 3 different railroads and all ye such facts, that passed in a flash and the train
negotiates, on, passing Visitacion Tower, that by old Okie railroad men of now-California aint at all mexicanized in pronun-
ciation, Vi Zi Tah Sioh, but is simply called, Visitation, like on
Sunday morning, and oft you hear, "Visitation Tower, Visitation Tower," ah ah ah ah aha.—Mile post 6.9, the following
8.6 Butler Road far from being a mystery to me by the time I
became a brakeman was the great sad scene of yard clerking

nights when at the far end of a 80 car freight the numbers of which with my little lamp I was taking down as I crunched over the gravel and all backtired, measuring how far I had to go by the sad streetlamp of Butler Road shining up ahead at the wall's end of long black sadmouth longcars of ye iron red-dark railroad night—with stars above, and the smashby Zipper and the fragrance of locomotive coalsmoke as I stand aside and let them pass and far down the line at night around that South San Fran airport you can see that sonofabitch red light waving Mars signal light waving in the dark big red markers blowing up and down and sending fires in the keenpure lostpurity lovelyskies of old California in the late sad night of autumn spring comefall winter's summertime tall, like trees.—all of it, and Butler Road no mystery to me, no blind spot in this song, but well known, I could also measure how far I had to go by the end of the gigantic rose neon six miles long you'd think saying WEST COAST BETHLEHEM STEEL as I'd be taking down the numbers of boxcars JC 74635 (Jersey Central) D&RG 38376 and NYC and PR and all the others, my work almost done when that huge neon was even with me and at the same time this meant the sad little streetlamp of Butler Road was only 50 feet away and no cars beyond that because that was the crossing where they'd cut them and then fold them over into another track of the South City yards, things of brake significance switch significance I only got to learn later.—So SF milepost 9.3 and what a bleak little main street, o my goodness, the fog'd roll in fine from there and the little neon cocktails with a little cherry on a toothpick and the bleak foglike green Chronicles in 10¢ sidewalk tin clonks, and yr bars with fat slick haired ex troopers inside drinking and October in the poolhall and all, where I'd go for a few bars of candy or desultory soups between chores as yardclerk when I was a yardclerk digging the lostness on that side, the human, and then having to go to the other end, a mile towards the Bay, to the great Armour & Swift slaughterplants where I'd take down the numbers of meat reefers and sometimes have to step aside and wait while the local came in and did some switching and the tagman or conductor would always tell me which ones were staying, which ones going.—Always at night, and always soft ground of like manure but really rat ground underneath, the

countless rats I saw and threw rocks at till I felt like being sick,
I'd hurry fleeing as from nightmare from that hole and sometimes fabricated phoney numbers instead of going too near
a gigantic woodpile which was so full of rats it was like their
tenement.—And the sad cows mooing inside where little ratty
Mexicans and Californians with bleak unpleasant unfriendly
faces and going-to-work jalopies were milling around in their
bloody work—till finally I worked it on a Sunday, the Armour
& Swift yards, and saw that the Bay was 60 feet away and I'd
never known it, but a dump yard a recka of crap and rat havens
worse than ever tho beyond it the waters did ripple bluely and
did in the sad morning clarity show clear flat mirrors clear to
Oakland and the Alameda places across the way.—And in the
hard wind of the Sunday morning I heard the mutter of the
tinware walls of brokendown abandoned slaughter house
warehouses, the crap inside and dead rats killed by that local
on off nights and some even I might have hit with my jacketful
of protective rocks, but mostly systematically killed rats laying
around in the keen heartbreaking cloud haunted wildwind day
with big silver airplanes of civilized hope taking off across the
stinking swamp and filthy tin flats for places in the air.—Gah,
bah, ieoeoeoeoe—it has a horrible filthy moaning sound you'd
hear eiderdowning in that flydung those hideaway silos and
murdered tinpaint aisles, scum, of salt, and bah oh bah and
harbors of the rat, the axe, the sledgehammer, the moo cows
and all that, one big South San Francisco horror there's your
milepost 9.3.—After that the rushing train takes you to San
Bruno clear and far around a long bend circling the marsh of
the SSF airport and then on in to Lomita Park milepost 12.1
where the sweet commuter trees are and the redwoods crash
and talk about you when you pass in the engine the boilers of
which redly cast your omnipotent shadow out on the night.—
You see all the lil ranchstyle California homes and in the
evening people sipping in livingrooms open to the sweetness,
the stars, the hope that lil children must see when they lay in
little beds and bedtime and look up and a star throbs for them
above the railroad earth, and the train calls, and they think
tonite the stars will be out, they come, they leave, they lave,
they angelicize, ah me, I must come from a land where they let
the children cry, ah me I wish I was a child in California when

the sun's gone down and the Zipper crashes by and I could see thru the redwood or the fig tree my throbbing hope-light shining just for me and making milk on Permanente hillsides horrible Kafka cement factories or no, rats of South City slaughterhouses or no, no, or no, I wish I was a little child in a crib in a little ranchstyle sweet house with my parents sipping in the livingroom with their picture window pointing out on the little backyard of lawning chairs and the fence, the ranchstyle brown pointed full fence, the stars above, the pure dry golden smelling night, and just beyond a few weeds, and blocks of wood, and rubber tires, bam the main line of the Ole SP and the train flashing by, toom, tboom, the great crash of the black engine, the grimy red men inside, the tender, then the long snake freighttrain and all the numbers and all the whole thing flashing by, gcrachs, thunder, the world is going by all of it finally terminated by the sweet little caboose with its brown smoky light inside where old conductor bends over waybills and up in the cupola the rear man sits looking out once in a while and saying to himself all black, and the rear markers, red, the lamps in the caboose rear porch, and the thing all gone howling around the bend to Burlingame to Mountain View to the sweet San Joses of the night the further down Gilroys Carnaderos Corporals and that bird of Chittenden of the dawn, your Logans of the strange night all be-lit and insected and mad, your Watsonvilles sea marshes your long long line and mainline track sticky to the touch in the midnight star.

Mile post 46.9 is San Jose scene of a hundred interested bums lounging in the weeds along the track with their packs of junk, their buddies, their private watertanks, their cans of water to make coffee or tea or soup with, and their bottle of tokay wine or usually muskatel.—The Muskat California is all around them, in the sky blue, tatteredly white clouds are being shoved across the top of the Santa Clara Valley from Bayshore where a high fogwind came and thru South City gaps too and the peace lies heavy in the sheltered valley where the bums have found a temporary rest.—Hot drowse in the dry weeds, just hollows of dry reed stick up and you walk against them crashing.—"Well boy, how's about a shot of rum to Watsonville." "This aint rum boy, this is a new kinda shit"—a colored hobo sitting on a shitty old newspaper of last year and's been used by Rat Eye Jim of the Denver viaducts who came thru here last spring with a package of dates on his back—"Things aint been as bad as this since 1906!" Now it's 1952 October and the dew is on the grain of this real ground. One of the boys picks up a piece of tin from the ground (that got bounced off a gon in a sudden sprrram of freights ramming together in the yard from the bucklin slack) (bowm!)—pieces of tin go flying off, fall in the weeds, outside track No. 1.—The hobo puts the tin on rocks over the fire and uses it to toast some bread but's drinking tokay and talking to the other boys and toast burns just like in tile kitchen tragedies.—The bum comes curses angrily because he lost some bread, and kicks a rock, and says "Twenty eight years I spent inside the walls of Dannemora and I had my fill of excitin panoramas of the great actions like when drunken Canneman wrote me that letter fum minneapoly and it was jess about chicago sponges—I turd him looka jock you caint— well I wrote im a letter ennyways." Aint been a soul listening because no one listens to a bum all the other bums are blagdengabsting and you cant find nor finangilate yr way out of that—all talking at the same time and all of them confused. You have to go back to the railroad man to understand.—Like, say, you ask a man "Where's track 109?"—nu—if it's a bum he'll say "Cart right over there dadday, and see if the old boy in the blue bandana knows, I'm Slim Holmes Hubbard from Ruston Louisiana and I got no time and got no knowledge to make me ways of knowin what where that track 109—only thing's I got, is— I want a dime, if you can spare a dime I'll go along my way peacefully —if you cant I'll go along my way peacefully—ya cant win—ya cant lose—and from between here to Bismarck Idaho I got nothing but lost and lost and lost everything I ever had." You've got to admit these bums into your soul when they talk like that—most of them rasp "Track 109 Chillicothe Ioway" thru the stubbles and spits of their beard—and wander off dragassing packs so huge, profound, heavy—dismembered bodies are in there you'd think—red eyes, wild wild hair, the railroad men look at them with amazement and at first sight then never look again—what would wives say?—If you ask a railroad man what track is 109, he stop, stop chewing his gum, shift his package his coatlamp or lunch and turn, and spit, and squint at the mountains to the east and roll his eyes very slowly in the private cavern of his eyebone between brow bone and cheek, bone, and say, still deliberating and having deliberated "They call it track 109 but they should call it 110, it's right next to the ice platform you know the icehouse up there—" "Yeah—" "There it is, from track one on the main line here we start the numbers but the ice house make em jump they make a turn and you have to go across track 110 to get to 109—But you never have to go to 109 too often—so it's just like 109 was jess missing from the yard . . . numbers, see . . ." "Yeah"—I know it for sure—"I know it for sure now." "And there she is—" "Thanks—I gotta get there fast"—"That's the trouble with the railroad, you always gotta get there fast—'cause if you dont it's like turning down a local on the phone and say you want to turn over and go to sleep (like Mike Ryan did last Monday)" he's sayin to himself.—And we walk wave and are gone.

This is the cricket in the reed. I sat down in the Pajaro riverbottoms and lit fires and slept with my coat on top of my brakeman's lantern and considered the California life staring at the blue sky—

The conductor is in there hanging around waiting for his train orders—when he gets them he'll give the engineer the hiball sign, a little side to side wave of the palmed hand, and off we go—the old hoghead gives orders for steam, the young fireman complies, the hoghead kicks and pulls at his big lever throttle and sometimes jumps up to wrestle with it like hugely an angel in hell and pulls the whistle twice toot toot we're leaving, and you hear the first chug of the engine—chug—a failure like—chug a lut—zoom—chug CHUG—the first movement—the train's underway.—

San Jose—because the soul of the railroad is the chain gang run, the long freight train you see snaking down the track with a puff puff en jyne pulling is the traveler the winner the arterial moody mainline maker of the rail —San Jose is 50 miles south of Frisco and is the center of the Coast Division chain gang or long road run activity, known as the horn because the pivot point for rails going down from Frisco toward Santa Barbara and L.A. and rails going and shining back to Oakland via Newark and Niles on sub lines that also cross the mighty main line of the Fresno bound Valley Division.—San Jose is where I should have been living instead of Third Street Frisco, for these reasons: 4 o'clock in the morning, in San Jose, comes a call on the phone it is the Chief Dispatcher calling from 4th and Townsend in the Sad Frisco, "Keroowayyyy? it's deadhead on 112 to San Jose for a drag east with Conductor Degnan got that?" "Yeh deadahead 112 drag east right," meaning, go back to bed and rise again around 9, you're being paid all this time and boy dont worry about a durg and doo-gaddm things, at 9 all's you gotta do is get ups and you already done made how many dollars? anyways in your sleep and put on your gig clothes and cut out and take a little bus and go down to the San Jose yard office down by the airport there and in the yard office are hundreds of interested railroad men and tackings of tickers and telegraph and the engines are being lined up and numbered and markered out there, and new engines keep rushing up from the roundhouse, & everywhere in the gray air tremendous excitements of movement of rolling stocks and the making of great wages.—You go down there, find your conductor who'll just be some old baggypants circus comedian with a turned up hatbrim and red face and red handkerchief and grimy waybills and switchlists in his hand and far from carrying a student big brakeman lantern like you's got his little old 10 year old tiny lantern from some old boomer bought and the batteries of which he has to keep buying at Davegas instead of like the student getting free at the yard office, because after 20 years on the rr you gotta find some way to be different and also t'lighten the burdens you carry around with yourself, he's there, leaning, by spittoons, with others, you go up hat over eyes, say "Conductor Degnan?" "I'm Degnan, well it doesnt look like anything'll bevore noon so just take it easy and be around" so you go into the blue room they call it, where blue flies buzz and hum around old zawful dirty couch tops stretched on benches with the stuffing coming out and attracting and probably breeding further flies, and there you lie down if it ain't already full of sleeping brakemen and you turn your shoetops up to the dirty old brown sad ceiling of time there, haunted by the clack of telegraphs and the chug of engines outdoors enough to make you go in your pants, and turns your hatbrim over yr eyes, and go ahead and sleep.— Since 4 in the morning, since 6 in the morning when still the sleep was on yr eyes in that dark dream house you've been getting 1.90 per hour and it is now 10 AM and the train aint even made up and "not before noon" says Degnan so that by noon you'll already have been working (because counting from time of 112, deadhead time) six hours and so you'll leave San Jose with your train around noon or maybe further at one and not get to the terminal great chaingang town of Watsonville where everything's going (L.A. ward) till 3 in the afternoon and with happy mishaps 4 or 5, nightfall, when down there waiting for the herder's sign enginemen and trainmen see the long red sad sun of waning day falling on the lovely old landmark milepost 98.2. farm and day's done, run's done, they been being paid since down dawn of that day and only traveled about 50 miles. —This will be so, so sleep in the blue room, dream of 1.90 per hour and also of your dead father and your dead love and the mouldering in your bones and the eventual Fall of you—the train wont be made up till noon and no one wants to bother you *till*—lucky child and railroad angel softly in your steel propositioned sleep.

So much more to Jan Jose.

So if you live in San Jose you have the advantage of 3 hours of extra sleep at home not counting the further sleep on the blue room rot puff leather couch—nevertheless I was using the 50 mile ride from 3rd Street as my library, bringing books and papers in a little tattered black bag already 10 years old which I'd originally bought on a pristine morning in Lowell in 1942 to go to sea with, arriving in Greenland that summer, and so a bag so bad a brakeman seeing me with it in the San Jose yard coffee shop said whooping loud "A railroad loot bag if I ever saw one!" and I didnt even smile or acknowledge and that was the beginning middle and extent of my social rapport on the railroad with the good old boys who worked it, thereafter becoming known as Kerouaayyy the Indian with the phony name and everytime we went by the Pomo Indians working sectionhand tracks, gandy dancers with greasy black hair I waved and smiled and was the only man on the S.P. who did so

except old hogheads always do wave and smile and sectionhand bosses who are old white bespectacled respectable old
toppers and topers of time and everybody respects, but the
dark Indian and the eastern Negro, with sledgehammers and
dirtypants to them I waved and shortly thereafter I read a
book and found out that the Pomo Indian battle cry is Ya Ya
Henna, which I thought once of yelling as the engine crash-
boomed by but what would I be starting but derailments of
my own self and engineer.—All the railroad opening up and
vaster and vaster until finally when I did quit it a year later I
saw it again but now over the waves of the sea, the entire Coast
Division winding down along the dun walls of bleak headland
balboa amerikay, from a ship, and so the railroad opens up on
the waves that are Chinese and on the orient shroud and
sea.—It runs ragged to the plateau clouds and Pucalpas and
lost Andean heights far below the world rim, it also bores a
deep hole in the mind of man and freights a lot of interesting
cargo in and out the holes precipitate and otherwise hiding-
places and imitative cauchemar of eternity, as you'll see.

So one morning they called me at 3rd Street at about 4 AM
and I took the early morning train to San Jose, arriving there
7:30 was told not to worry about anything till about 10 so I
went out in my inconceivably bum's existence went looking
for pieces of wire that I could bend in such a way over my hotplate so they would support little raisin breads to make toast
and also looking if possible for better than that a chickenwire
arrangement on which I could sit pots to heat water and pans
to fry eggs since the hotplate was so powerful it often burned
and blackcaked the bottom of my eggs if by chance I'd overlook the possibility while busy peeling my potatoes or
otherwise involved—I'd walk around, San Jose had a junk yard
across the track, I went in there and lookt around, stuff in
there so useless the proprietor never came out, I who was
earning 600 a month made off with a piece of chicken wire for
my hotplate.—Here it was 11 and still no train made up, gray,
gloomy, wonderful day—I wandered down the little street of
cottages to the big boulevard of Jose and had Carnation ice
cream and coffee in the morning, whole bevies and classrooms
of girls came in with tightfitting and sloosesucking sweaters

and everything on earth on, it was some academy of dames suddenly come to gossip coffee and I was there in my baseball hat black slick oiled and rusted jacket weather jacket with fur collar that I had used to lean my head on in the sands of Watsonville riverbottoms and grits of Sunnyvale across from Westinghouse near Schukl's student days ground where my first great moment of the railroad had taken place over by Del Monte's when I kicked my first car and Whitey said "You're the boss do it pull the pin with a will put your hand in there and pull 'cause you're the boss" and it was October night, dark, clean, clear, dry, piles of leaves by the track in the sweet scented dark and beyond them crates of the Del Monte fruit and workers going around in crate wagons with under reaching stuckers and—never will forget Whitey saying that.—By same reminiscence of doubt, in spite and because of, wanted to save all me money for Mexico, I also refused to spend 75 cents or even 35 cents less for a pair of workgloves, instead, after initial losing of my first bought workglove while setting out that sweet San Mateo flower car on Sunday morning with the Sherman local I resolved to get all my other gloves from the ground and so went for weeks with my black hand clutching sticky cold iron of engines in the dewy cold night, till I finally found the first glove outside the San Jose yard office, a brown cloth glove with red Mephistophelean lining, picking it up limp and damp from the ground and smashed it on my knee and let it dry and wore it.—Final other glove found outside Watsonville yard office, a little leather imitation outside glove with inside warm lining and cut with scissors or razor at the wrist to facilitate putting it on and obviate yanking and yunking.—These were my gloves, I'd lost as I say my first glove in San Mateo, the second with Conductor Degnan while waiting for the all clear signal from the pot (working rear because of his fear) by the track at Lick, the long curve, the traffic on 101 making it difficult to hear and in fact it was the old conductor who in the dark of that Saturday night did finally hear, I heard nothing, I ran to the caboose as it leapt ahead with the slack and got on counting my red lamps gloves fusees and whatnots and realizing with horror as the train pulled along I had dropped one of my gloves at Lick, damn!—now I had two new gloves from off the ground pickied.—At noon of that day the engine still wasnt on, the old hoghead hadnt left home yet where he'd picked up his kid on a sunny sidewalk with open arms and kissed him the late red john time of afternoon before, so I was there sleeping on the horrible old couch when by god in some way or other and after I'd gone out several times to check and climb around the pot which was now tied on and the conductor and rear man having coffee in the shop and even the fireman and then I went back for further musings or nappings on the seat cover expecting them to call me, when in my dreams I hear a double toot toot and hear a great anxiety engine taking off and it's my engine but I dont realize it right away, I think it's some slomming woeful old blacktrackpot whack cracking along in a dream or dream reality when suddenly I wake up to the fact they didnt know I was sleeping in the blue room, and they got their orders, and gave the hiball, and there they go to Watsonville leaving the head man behind—as tradition goes, fireman and engineer if they dont see the head man on the engine and they've gotten the sign, off they go, they have nothing to do with these sleepy trainmen.— I leap up grab lamp and in the gray day and running precisely over the spot where I'd found that brown glove with red lining and thinking of it in the fury of my worry and as I dash I see the engine way down the line 50 years picking up and chufgffouffing and the whole train's rumbling after and cars waiting at the crossing for the event, it's MY TRAIN!—Off I go loping and running fast over the glove place, and over the road, and over the corner of the junk field where I'd searched for tin also that lazy morning, amazied mouth-gagaped railroad men about five of them are watching this crazy student running after his engine as it leaves for Watsonville—is he going to make it? Inside 30 seconds I was abreast with the iron ladder and shifting lantern t'other hand to grab holt of and get on and climb, and anyway the whole shebang restopped again at a red to allow old I think 71 get through the station yards, it was I think by now almost 3 o'clock I'd slept and earned or started to earn incredible overtimes and this nightmare transpiring. —So they got the red and stopped anyway and I had my train made and sat on the sand box to catch my breath, no comment whatever in the world on the bleak jawbones and cold blue okie eyes of that engineer and fireman they must have been holding some protocol with the iron railroad in their hearts for all they cared about this softheaded kid who'd run down the cinders to his late lost work

Forgive me o Lord

At the rickety fenceback Del Monte Fruitpacking Company which is directly across the track from the San Jose passenger station there is a curve in the track, a curve shmurve of eternity rememberable from the dreams of the railroad dark I had where I'm working unspeakable locals with Indians and suddenly we come upon a great Indian caucus in an underground subterraneana somewhere right there in the vicinity of the Del Monte curve (where Indians work anyway) (packing the crates, the cans, the fruit in cans with syrup) and I'm with the heroes of the Portuguese bars of San Francisco watching dances and hearing revolutionary speeches like the speeches of the revolutionary sod squat down heroes of Culiacan where by the bark of the wave in the drearylit drolling night I have heard them say *la tierra esta la notre* and knew they mean it and for this reason the dream of the Indians revolutionary meeting and celebrating in the bottom lip cellar of the railroad earth.—The train goes around the curve there and gently I lean out of the grabiron darks and look and there's our little clearance and train order sitting in a piece of string which is stretched between the two train order bamrods, as the train passes the trainmen simply (usually the fireman) reaches out with whole arm so to make sure not to miss and hooks the string in passing (the string being taut) and off comes the string and the two bows which are rigid sorta ping a little and in yr arm is looped the train orders on yellow onionskin tied by string, the engineer upon receipt of this freight takes the string and slowly according to years of personal habit in the manner of undoing train order strings undoes the string and then according again to habit unfolds the paper to read and sometimes they even put glasses on like great professors of ivy universities to read as that big engine goes chug chugging across and down the green land of California and Mexicans of railside mexshacks standing with eyes shaded watching us past, see the great bespectacled monk student in engineer of the night peering learnedly at his little slip in big grimy paw and it reads, date,

"Oct 3 1952, Train Orders, to Train 2-9222, issued 2:04 PM, wait at Rucker till 3:58 for eastbound 914, do not go beyond Corporal till 4:08 and etc." all the various orders which the train order dispatchers and various thinking officials at switch towers and telephones are thinking up in the great metaphysical passage of iron traffics of the rail—we all take turns reading, like they say to young students "Read it carefully dont leave it up to us to decide if there are any mistakes many's the time a student found a mistake that the engineer and fireman out of years of habit didnt see so read it carefully" so I go over the whole thing reading even over and over again checking dates the time, like, the time of the order should certainly be not later than time of departure from station (when I went loping over the junkfield with lantern and loot bag racing to catch my guilt late in the gray candy gloom) and ah but all of it sweet. The little curve at Del Monte, the train orders, then the train goes on to mile post 49.1 to the Western Pacific RR crossing, where you always see the track goes directly vertically across this alien track so there is a definite hump in the rail bed, but chickaluck, as we go over, sometimes at dawn returning from Watsonville I'd be dozing in the engine and wondering just about where we were not knowing generally we were in the vicinity of San Jose or Lick and I'd hear the brock a brock and say to myself "The Western Pacific crossing!" and remember how one time a brakee said to me, "Cant sleep nights in this here new house I got here out on Santa Clara avenue for the clatter and racket of that damn engine out there in the midnight" "Why I thought you loved the railroad" "Well to tell you the fact of the matter, is the Western Pacific happens to have a rail running out there" and with such, as tho it was inconceivable that there could be other railroads than the Southern Pacific.—On we go across the crossing and there we go along the stream, the Oconee of old Jose the little blank blank Guadaloupe river dry and with Indians standing on the banks, that is Mexican children watching the train, and great fields of prickly pear cactus and all green and sweet in the gray afternoon and gonna be golden brown and rich when the sun at five flames flares to throw the California wine over the rearwestern licks into the pacific brine.—On we go to Lick, always I take my looks at favorite landmarks, some school where boys are practising football in varsity and sub varsity and freshman and sub freshman squads, four of em, under tutelage of raven priests with piping glad voices in the wind, for it's October of footingball heavening rooting root to you.—Then at Lick there is on a hill a kind of monastery, you barefly see the dreaming marijuana walls of it as you pass, up there, with a bird wheeling to peace, there a field, cloisters, work, cloisterous prayers and every form known to man of sweet mediating going on as we wrangle and backgiggle by with a bursting engine and long knocking space-taking-up half mile long freight any minute I expect a hotbox in, as I look back anxiously, fit to work.—The dreams of monastery men up there on the hill at Lick, and I think, "Ah creamy walls of either Rome, civilizations, or the last monasterial mediation with God in the didoudkekeghgj" god knows what I'm thinking, and then and my thoughts rapidly change as 101 rears into sight, and Coyote, and the beginning of the sweet fruit fields and prune orchards and the great strawberry fields and the vast fields where you see far off the humble squatting figures of Mexican brazeros in the great haze working to pluck from the earth that which the America with his vast iron wages no longer thinks feasible as an activity yet eats, yet goes on eating, and the brass backs with arms of iron Mexico in the cactus plateau love, they'll do it for us, the railroad freight train and concomitant racks of beets is not even, the men on it, are not even mindful of how those beets or in what mood, sweat, sweetness, were picked—and laid to rest out of the earth in the steely cradle.—I see them their bent humble backs remembering my own cotton picking days in Selma California and I see far off across the grapevines the hills to the west, then the sea, the great sweet hills and further along you begin to see the familiar hill of Morgan Hill, we pass the fields of Perry and Madrone and where they make wine, and it's all there, all sweet the furrows of brown, with blossoms and one time we took a siding to wait for 98 and I ran out there like the hound of the Baskervilles and got me a few old prunes not longer fitten to eat—the proprietor seeing me, trainman running guiltily back to engine with a stolen prune, always I was running, always was running, running to throw switches, running in my sleep and running now—happy.

*

The sweetness of the fields unspeakable—the names themselves bloody edible like Lick Coyote Perry Madrone Morgan
Hill San Martin Rucker Gilroy o sleepy Gilroy Carnadero Corporal Sargent Chittenden Logan Aromas and Watsonville
Junction with the Pajaro River passing thru it and we of the
railroad pass over its wooded dry Indian draws at somewhere
outside Chittenden where one morning all dew pink I saw a
little bird sitting on a piece of stanchion straight up wood in
the wild tangle, and it was the Bird of Chittenden, and the
meaning of morning.—Sweet enough the fields outside San
Jose like at say Lawrence and Sunnyvale and where they have
vast harvest and fields with the bentback sad mexicano labori-
oring in his primavery.—But once past San Jose somehow the
whole California opens ever further, at sunset at Perry or
Madrone it is like a dream, you see the little rickety farmhouse,
the fields, the rows of green planted fruit, and beyond the
green pale mist of hills and over that the red aureoles of pacific
sunfall and in the silence the bark of a duog and that fine California night dew already rising ere maw's done wiped the hamburg juice off the frying pan and later on tonite beautiful little
Carmelita O' Jose will be gomezing along the road with her
brown breasts inside cashmere sweater bouncing ever so
slightly even with maidenform bra and her brown feet in
thonged sandals also brown, and her dark eyes with pools in
em of you wonder what mad meaning, and her arms like arms
of handmaidens in the Plutonian bible—and ladles for her
arms, in the form of trees; with juice, take a peach, take the ful-
some orange, bit a hole in in, take the orange throw your head
back use all your strength and drink and squeeze out the orange thru the hole, all the juice runs down your lip and on her
arms.—she has dust on her toes, and toe nail polish—she has a
tiny brown waist, a little soft chin, soft neck like swan, little
voice, little femininity and doesn't know it—her little voice is
littletinkled.— Along comes the tired field hand Jose Camero
and he see her in the vast sun red in the fruit field moving
queen majesty to the well, the tower, he runs for her, the railroad crashes by he pays no attention standing on the engine
student brakeman J. L. Kerouac and old hoghead W. H. Sears
12 years in California since leaving the packed Oklahoma dust
farms, his father'd in a broken down okie truck ordered depar-

tures from there, for the first nonces they were and tried to be cottonpickers and were mighty good at it but one day somebody told Sears to try railroading which he did and then he was now after several years a young fireman, an engineer—the beautify of the salvation fields of California making no difference to the stone of his eye as with glove framed throttle hand he guides the black beast down the star rail.—Switches rush up and melt into the rail, sidings part from it like lips, return like lover arms.—My mind is on the brown knees of Carmelity, the dark spltot between her thighs where creation hides its majesty and all the boys with eager head do rush suffering and want the whole the hole the works the hair the seekme membrane the lovey sucky ducky workjohn, the equalled you, she never able and down goes the sun and it's dark and they're layin in a grape row, nobody can see, or hear, only the dog hears OOO slowly against the dust of that railroad earth he presses her little behind down to form a little depression in the earth from the force and weight of his tears slowly lunging her downthru and into the portals of her sweetness, and slowly the blood pounds in his indian head and comes to a rise and she softly pants with parted brownly lips and with little pear teeth showing and sticking out just far and just so gently almost biting, burning in the burn of his own, lips—he drives and thrives to pound, the grain, the grape nod in unison, the wine is springing from the noggin of the ground, bottles will roll on 3rd Street to the sands of Santa Barbara, he's making it with the wouldyou seek it then would and wouldn't you if you too could—the sweet flesh intermingling, the flowing blood wine dry husk leaf bepiled earth with the hard iron passages going oer, the engine's saying K RRRR OOO AAAWWOOOO and the crossing it's ye famous Krrot Krroot Krroo ooooaaaawwww Kroot—2 short one long, one short, 'sa thing I got to learn as one time the hoghead was busy telling a joke in the fireman's ear and we were coming to a crossing and he yelled at me "Go ahead go ahead" and made a pull sign with his hand and I lookied up and grabbed the string and looked out, big engineer, saw the crossing racing up and girls in sandals and tight ass dresses waiting at the flashby RR crossing boards of Carnadero and I let it to, two short pulls, one long, one short, Krroo Krroo Krrrooooa Krut.—So now it's purple in the sky, the whole rim

America falling spilling over the west mountains into the eternal and orient sea, and there's your sad field and lovers twined and the wine is in the earth already and in Watsonville up ahead at the end of my grimy run among a million others sits a bottle of tokay wine which I am going to buy to put some of that earth back in my belly after all this shudder of ferrous knock klock against my soft flesh and bone exultation—in other words, when work's done, I'm gonna have a drink of wine, and rest.—The Gilroy Subdivision this is.

The first run I ever made on the Gilroy Subdivision, that night dark and clean, standing by the engine with my lamp and lootbag waiting for the big men to make up their minds here comes this young kid out of the dark, no railroad man but obviously a bummer but on the bum from college or good family or if not with cleanteeth smile and no broken down datebag river Jack from the bottoms of the world night—said, "This thing going to L.A.?"—"Well it's going about part of the way to there, about 50 miles to Watsonville then if you stick on it they might route you down to San Luis Obispo too and that's about halfway to L.A."—"Ba what d'I care about halfway to L.A. I want to go all the way to L.A.—what are you a railroad brakebanana?" "Yeah, I'm a student"—"What's a student"—"Well it's a guy learning and getting, well I aint getting paid" (this being my student chain gang run all the way down)—"Ah well I dont like going up and down the same rail, if you ask me goin to sea is the real life, now that's where I'm headed or hitch hike to New York, either way, I wouldnt want to be a railroad man."—"What you talkin about man it's great and you're moving all the time and you make a lot of money and no body bothers you out there."—"Neverthefuckingless you keep going up and down the same rail dont you for krissakes?" so I told him what how and where boxcar to get on, "Krissakes dont hurt yourself always remember when you try to go around proving you're a big adventurer of the American night and wanta you hop freights like Joel McCrea heroes of old movies Jesus you dumb son a bitch hang on angel with your tightest hand and dont let your feet drag under that iron roundwheel it'll have less regard for the bone of your leg than it has for this toothpick in my mouty" "Ah you shitt you shit you think I'm afraid of a goddamn railroad train I'm going off to join the goddam navy and be on carriers and there's your iron for you I'll land my airplane half on iron half on water and crashbang and jet to the moon too." "Good luck to you guy, dont fall off hang tight grip wrists dont fuck up and tout and when you gets to L.A. give my regards to Lana Turner."—The train was starting to leave and the kid had disappeared up the long black bed and snakeline redcars—I jumped up on the engine with the regular head man who was going to show me how the run runs, and the fireman, and hoghead.—Off we chugged, over the crossing, over to the Del Monte curve and where the head man showed me how you hang on with one hand and lean out and crook your arm and grab the train orders off the string—then out to Lick, the night, the stars.— Never will forget, the fireman wore a black leather jacket and a white skidrow San Frisco seaman Embarcadero cap, with visor, in the ink of this night he looked exactly like a revolutionary Bridges Curran Bryson hero of old waterfront smosh flops, I could see him with meaty hand waving a club in forgotten union publications rotting in gutters of backalley bars, I could see him with hands deep in pocket going angrily thru the uneccentric unworkingbums of 3rd Street to his rendezvous with the fate of the fish at the waterfront gold blue pier edge where boys sit of afternoons dreaming under clouds on bits of piers with the slap of skeely love waters at their feet, white masts of ships, orange masts of ships with black hulls and all your orient trade pouring in under the Golden Gate, this guy I tell you was like a sea dog not a railroad firemen yet there he sat with his snow white cap in the grimeblack night and rode that fireman's seat like a jockey, chug and we were really racing, they were opening her up wanted to make good time to get past Gilroy before any orders would fuck them up, so across the onlitt tintight and with our big pot 3500 style engine headlights throwing its feverish big lick tongue over the wurrling and incurling and outflying track we go swinging and roaring and flying down that line like fucking madmen and the fireman doesnt exactly hold on to his white hat but he has hand on fire throttle and keeps close eye on valves and tags and steam bubblers and outside looks on the rail and the wind blows his nose back but ee god he bouncing on that seat exactly like a jocket

riding a wild horse, why we had a hoghead that night which
was my first night so wild he had the throttle opened fullblack
and kept yanking at it with one heel against the iron scum of
the floor trying to open her up further and if possible tear the
locomotive apart to get more out of her and leave the track
and fly up in the night over the prune fields, what a magnificent opening night it was for me to ride a fast run like that
with a bunch of speed demons and that magnificent fireman
with his unpredestined impossible unprecedentable hat white
in the black black railroad.—And all the time and the conversations they have, and the visions in his hat I saw of the public
hair restaurant on Howard, how I saw that Frisco California
white and gray of rain fogs and the back alleys of bottles, breens,
derbies, mustachios of beer, oysters, flying seals, crossing hills,
bleak bay windows, eye diddle for old churches with handouts
for seadogs barkling and snurling in avenues of lost opportunity time, ah—loved it all, and the first night the finest night,
the blood, "railroading gets in yr blood" the old hoghead is
yelling at me as he bounces up and down in his seat and the
wind blows his striped cap visor back and the engine like a
huge beast is lurching side to side 70 miles per hour breaking
all rulebook rules, zomm, zomm, were crashing through the
night and out there Carmelity is coming, Jose is making her
electricities mix and interrun with his and the whole earth
charged with juices turns up the organo to the flower, the un-
foldment, the stars bend to it, the whole world's coming as the
big engine booms and balls by with the madmen of the white
cap California in there flossing and wow there's just no end to
all this wine—

4

Slobs of the Kitchen Sea

Have you seen a great freighter slide by in the bay on a dreamy afternoon and as you stretch your eyes along the iron serpentine length in search of people, seamen, ghosts who must be operating this dreaming vessel so softly parting harbor waters off its steel-shin bow with snout pointed to the Four Winds of the World you see nothing, no one, not a soul?

And there it goes in broad daylight, dismal sad hulk faintly throbbing, incomprehensibly jingling and jangling in the engine room, chuffing, gently churning at the rear the buried giant waterscrew onward working out to sea, eternity, stars of the mad mate's sexton at rosy Manzanillan night fall offcoast of the sad surf world—to skeels of other fisher's bays, mysteries, opium nights in the porthole kingdoms, narrow main drags of the Kurd.—Suddenly my God you realize you've been looking at some motionless white specks on the deck, between decks in the house section, and there they are . . . the motley messmen in white jackets, they've been leaning all the time motionless like fixed parts of the ship at the galley alleyway hatch.—It's after dinner, the rest of the crew's well fed and fast asleep in fitful bunks of nap—themselves such still watchers of the world as they slide out to Time no watcher of the ship can avoid being fooled and scrutinized long before he sees they're human, they're the only living thing in sight.—Mohammedan Chicos, hideous little Slavs of the sea peering out from witless messcoats—Negroes with cook hats to crown the shiny tortured forehead black—by garbage cans of eternity the Latin fellaheen repose and drowse of lullish noon.—And O the lost insane gulls yowking, falling around in a gray and restless shroud at the moving poop—O the wake slowly roiling in the churn of the wild propeller that from the engine room on a shaft is being wound and wound by combustions and pressures and irritable labors of Germanic Chief Engineers and Greek Wipers with sweat bandanas and only the Bridge can point this restless energy to some Port of Reason across vast lonesome incredible seas of madness.—Who's on the forepeak? Who's on the afterdeck? Who's on the flying bridge, mate?—not a loving soul.—Old bateau negotiates our sleepy retired bay and heads for the Narrows the mouths of Neptune Osh thinning smalling as we watch—past beacon—past point of land—bleak, grimy, gray thin veil of drowsiness flups from the stack, sends heat waves to heaven—flags on shrouds wake up to the first sea wind. We can hardly make out the name of the ship painted mournfully on the bow and on a board along the topdeck bulwark.

Soon the first long waves'll make this ship a swelling sea snake, foam will be pressed unfurling at the solemn mouth.— Where the messboys we saw leaning on that homey afterdishes rail, in sun? They'll have gone in by now, closed the shutters on the long jail time of sail at sea time, iron'll be clamped bong and flat dull as wood on the drunken hopes of Port, the fevered raving gladnesses of the Embarcadero night first ten drinks white hats bobbing in a brown pocked bar all blue Frisco wild with seamen people trolleys restaurants hills night is now just the sloping whitehill town behind your Golden Gate bridge, out we go.—

One o'clock. The S.S. *William Carothers* is sailing to the Panama Canal and Gulf of Mexico.—

One snowy flag of wash flutters from the poop an emblem of the gone-in messmen's silence.—Have you seen them floating out to sea past your commuter's ferry, your drawbridge driving-to-work Ford, scullionish, greasy aproned, depraved, evil, seedy as coffee grounds in a barrel, unimportant as orange peels on an oily deck, white as seagull dung—pale as feathers— birdy—demented raunchy slop boys and Sicilian adventurers of the mustachio Sea? And wondered about their lives? Georgie Varewsky when I first saw him that morning in the Union Hall looked so much the part of the spectral scullion sailing to his obscurity Singapores that I knew I had seen him a hundred times before—somewhere—and I knew I was going to see him a hundred times again.

He had that wonderfully depraved look not only of the dedicated feverish European Waiter alcoholic but something ratty and sly—wild, he peered at no one, was aloof in the hall like an aristocrat of some own interior silence and reason to say nothing, as, you will find, all true drinkers in their drinking sickness which is the reprieve from excitement will have a thin, loose smile vague at the corners of their mouths and be communicant with something deep inside themselves be it revulsion or shuddering hangoveral joy and wont communicate with others for the nonce (thats the business of the screaming-drinking night), will instead stand alone, suffer, smile, inwardly laugh alone, kings of pain.—His pants were baggy, his tortured jacket must have been crumpled under his head all night. —Low at the end of one long arm and finger hung a lowly smoking lost butt lit a few hours before and alternately lit and forgotten and crushed and carried blocks across shuddering gray necessary activity.—You could see by looking at him that he had spent all his money and had to get another ship.— He stood, slightly bent forward at the waist, ready for any charmingly humorous and otherwise thing to happen.—Short, blond, Slavic—he had serpentine cheekbones pearshaped which in drink of nightbefore'd been greased and fevered and now were pale worm skin—over this his crafty luminous blue eyes slanted looking.—His hair was thin, baldish, also tortured as if some great God Hand of Drunken Night had given it a grip and a yank—skewish, thin, ash color, Baltic. —He had a fuzz of beard—shoes scuffledown.—You'd picture him in an immaculate white jacket hair slicked at the sides in Parisian and Transatlantic saloons but even that could never remove that Slavic secret wickedness in his stealthy looks and's only looking at his own shoe tops.—Lips full, red, rich, pressed and murmured together and as if to mumble "Senevabitch . . ."

The job call came up, I got the bedroom steward job, Georgie Varewski the furtive shivering guilty sicklooking blond got the messman job smiling his wan aristocratic pale faroff smile.—The name of the ship was S.S. *William Carothers.* We were all supposed to report at a place called the Army Base at 6 A.M. I went right up to my new shipmate and asked him: "Where *is* this Army Base?"

He looked me over with a sly smile—"I show you. Meet me in bar on 210 Market Street—Jamy's—10 o'clock tonight—we go in, sleep on the ship, take the A train across the bridge—"

"Okay, it's a deal."

"Senevabitch I feel much better now."

"What happened." I thought he was relieved he had just gotten a job he thought he wouldnt get.

"I was seek. All last night I drink every goddam thing I see—"

"What?"

"Mix it."

"Beer? Whiskey?"

"Beer, whiskey, wine—goddam green dr-r-ink—" We were standing outside on the great steps of the hall high above the blue waters of San Francisco Bay, and they were there, the white ships on the tide, and all my love rose to sing my new-found seaman's life.—The Sea! Real ships! My sweet ship had come in, no dream but true with tangled rigging and actual shipmates and the job slip secure in my wallet and only the night before I'd been kicking cockroaches in my tiny dark room in Third Street slums.—I felt like hugging my friend.— "What's your name? This is great!"

"George—Georg-ee—I'm a Polock, they call it me, Crazy Polock. Everybody knows it me. I drrreenk and drreenk and vugup all the time and lose my job, miss my ship—they give it me one more chance—I was so seek I couldnt see—now I feel it a little better—"

"Have a beer, that'll straighten you out—"

"*No!* I start all over again, I go cr-razy, two, three beers, *boom!* I'm gone, I take it off, you not see me any more." Forlorn smile, shrug. "Is the way it is. Crazy Polock."

"They gave me B.R.—they gave you Mess."

"They give it me one more chance then is 'Geor-gie, boom, go away, drop dead, you fired, you no seaman, funny senevabitch, vugup too mach'—I *know,*" he grins.—"They see my eyes, all shining, they say 'Georgie iss drunk again'—no—one more beer I cant,—I not vugup now till we sail—"

"Where we goin?"

"Mobile load up—Far East—probably Japann, Yokohama— Sasebo—Kobe—I don know—Probably Korrea—Probably Saigon—Indo China—nobody knows—I show you how to do your work if you are a new man—I'm Georgie Varewski Crazy Polock—I dont give it fuk,—"

"Okay Pal. We'll meet 10 o'clock tonight.—"

"210 Market—and dont get drrunk and dont show up!"

"And you too! if you miss I'll go alone."

"Dont worry—I have it no money not a senevabitch cent.—No money to eat it—"

"Dont you need a couple bucks to eat?" I took out my wallet.

He looked at me slyly. "You got it?"

"Two bucks sure."

"Okay."

He went off, hands in pants pockets humbly, defeatedly, but on swift determined feet hustling in a straight line to his goal and as I looked I saw he really was walking extremely fast—head down, bemused upon the world and all the ports of the world he'd go cut in with rapid steps.—

I turned to breathe the great fresh air of harbors, exulting on my good luck—I pictured myself with grave face pointed seaward through the final Gate of Golden America never to return, I saw shrouds of gray sea dripping from my prow—

I never dwelt on the dark farcical furious real life of this roaring working world, wow.

In roaring bloodshot of my own I showed up at 10 o'clock that night without my gear just my seaman buddy Al Sublette who was celebrating my "last night ashore" with me.—Varewski was sitting deep in the profound bar drinkless, with two drunken drinking seamen.—He hadnt touched a drop since I'd seen him and with what forlorn discipline eyeing cups proffered and otherwise and all the explanations.—The swirl of the world was upon this bar as I came reeling in on a slant, the Van Gogh boards flowing to brown slatwall johns, spittoons, scrapetables of the back—like eternity saloons of Moody Lowell and with the same.—It's been so, in bars of Tenth Avenue New York I —and Georgie too—the first three beers on an October dusk, the glee of scream of children in the iron streets, the wind, the ships in the band of the river—the way the sparkle glow spreads in the belly giving strength and turning the world from a place of gnash-serious absorption in the details of struggle and complaint, into a gigantic gut joy capable of swelling like a distended shadow by distance hugened and with the same concomitant loss of density and strength so that in the morning after the 30th beer and 10 whiskies and early morning goof vermouths on rooftops, in topcoats, cellars, places of energy subtracted, not added, the more you drink the more there is false strength, false strength is subtractable.—Flup, the man's dead in the morning, the brown drear happiness of bars and saloons is the whole world's shuddering void and the nerve-ends being slowly living deathly cut in the center of the gut, the slow paralysis of fingers, hands—the spectre and horror of a man once rosy babe now a shivering ghost in cracking surrealist night of cities, forgotten faces, money hurled, food hurled, drinks, drinks, drinks, the thousand chewed talks in dimnesses. —O the joy of the whitecap seaman or ex seaman wino howling in a Third Street alley in San Francisco beneath the cat's moon and even as the solemn ship the Golden Gate waters shoves aside, bow-watch lonely whiteshirt ablebodied seaman Japan-pointed on the forepeak with his sobering cup of coffee, the pocknosed bum of bottles is ready to crash against narrow walls, invoke his death in nerveless degrees, find his feeble tape of love in the winding stool of lonely gloom saloons—all illusion.

"You senevabitch you d-r-r-onk," laughed Georgie seeing me roll in eyes wild money dripping from my pants—pounding on the bar—"Beer! beer!"—And still he wouldnt drink—"I no vugup till I get it ship—this time I lose for good the union good get pissyass at me, it's goombye Georgie boom."—And his face full of sweat, his sticky eyes avoiding cold foams at tops of beerglasses, his fingers still clutching a low smoking butt all begrimed with nicotine and gnarled from the work of the world.

"Hey man where is your mother?" I yelled seeing him so alone littleboyish and forsaken in all the brown complicated millionmoth stress and screaming strain of drink, work, sweat—

"She iss in East Poland with my sister.—She will not come to West Germany because she iss religious and stay hum and is proud—she go to church—I send her nothing—Wat's the use?"

His amigo wanted a dollar out of me.—"Who is this?"

"Come on, give it him dollar, you got ship now,—he iss seaman—" I didnt want to but I did give him the dollar and as Georgie and I and friend Al left he called me a c-sucker for having been so reluctant.—So I went back to belt him or at least swim around the sea of his insolence a minute and lead him to apologies but all was a blur and I sensed crashing fists and cracking wood and skulls and police wagons in the brown crazy air.—It staggered somewhere, Georgie left, it was night —Al left—I staggered in the lonely night streets of Frisco dimly realizing I must make the ship at six or miss it.

I woke up at 5 in the morning in my old railroad room with the torn carpet and shade that was drawn over a few feet of soot roof to the endless tragedy of a Chinese family the boy child of which as I say was in continual torment of tears, his pappy slapping him to silence every night, the mother screaming.—Now at dawn a gray silence in which the fact exploded, "I've missed my ship"—I still had an hour to make it.—Picked up my already packed seabag and rushed out—tottering bagashoulder, in the gray mist of fateful Frisco to go catch my racy A Train for over-the-bay-bridge ride to the Army Base.—A taxi from the A Train and I was at the ship's slapping hem, her stack with a "T" for Transfuel on it showed over the gray Navy dumpshed.—I hurried deeper in.—It was a Liberty ship black with orange booms and blue and orange stack—WILLIAM H. CAROTHERS—not a soul in sight—I ran up the weaving gangplank with my burden bag, tossed it to the deck, looked around.—Steaming clatters from the galley straight ahead.— Instantly I knew there'd be trouble when a little ratty German with red eyes began yipping at me about how late I was, I had my railroad watch to prove I was only 12 minutes late but he was raining red sweats of hatred—later we called him Hitler.— A cook with cool little mustache stepped in:

"He's only 12 minutes late.—C'mon let's get breakfast going and talk about it later."—

"Goddam guys tink dey can come on late and I wont say nottin.—You gonna be pantryman," he said suddenly smiling to ingratiate this nice idea of his.

Pantry *shit* I was about to say but the cook took me by the arm: "You were sent out as bedroom steward, you'll be bedroom steward.—Just for this morning do what he says.—You want him to wash the dishes this morning?"

"Yeh—We shorthanded."

And already I could feel the steam of a hot Oakland day pressing down on my hangover brow.—There was Georgie Varewski smiling at me—"I get it out jacket—we co workers this morning—I sha you."—He took me down the steel horror alleys to the linen locker, unbearable heat and sorrow that stretched ahead of my bones only lately I'd at least in bum's freedom stretched at will anytime in hobo exile hotel.—I was in the Army now—I gulped down a quick benny to face the music—I saved my job.—From horror groanings and sleepy nausea at the sink with allnight's watch and longshore dishes piled I whammed inside 20 minutes into active keen energetic benevolence asking everyone including the ferret steward questions, gripping people by the arm, leaning, listening to troubles, being kind, working like a dog, doing extras, absorbing every word instruction Georgie said from benzedrine despair to love, work, learn.—sweating buckets to the steel—

Suddenly I saw myself in the foc'sle mirror, slickhaired, ring eyed, whitejacketed sudden-waiter-slave of scows where a week before I'd walked erect longwaist on the Plomteau Local, railroad afternoons in drowsy gravel spurs giving the pot the come ahead with no lapse in dignity when stooping swift to throw a sweet switch.—Here I was a goddam scullion and it was writ on my greasy brow, and at less pay too.—All for China, all for the opium dens of Yokohama.—

Breakfast swam by in a dream, I raced through everything benny wild,—it took 24 hours before I even paused to unpack my bag or look out at the waters and call them Oakland's.—

I was taken to my bedroom steward's quarters by the retiring B.R. who was an old pale skinned man from Richmond Hill Long Island (that is, had taken sun baths belowdecks in the glare of dry linens just laundered and stashed).— Two bunks in one room but horribly placed next to the upsurging fires from the engine room, for a headrest one had the smokestack, it was so hot.—I looked around in despair.—The old man was confidential, poked me:—"Now if you havent been a B.R. before you might have trouble."—This meant I must look seriously at his white countenance and nod, peer deeply into it, become buried in the vast cosmos of him, learn all—B.R. all.— "If you want I'll show you where everything is but I aint s'posed to cause I'm gettin off—however."—He did get off, it took him two days to pack, a full hour alone to pull on horribly diseased sad convalescent socks the color was white over his white little thin ankles—to tie his shoelaces—to run his finger through the back of his locker, floors, bulkheads for any speck he might've forgotten to pack—a little sickly belly protruding from the shapelessness of his stick.—Was this B.R. Jack Kerouac in 1983?

"Well come on, show me what's what! I gotta get goin—"

"Take it easy, hold your water—only the captain's up and he aint been down to breakfast.—I'll show you—now look— that's if you wanta—now I'm getting off and I don't have to" and he forgot what he was gonna say and returned to his white socks.—There was something of the hospital in him.— I rushed to find Georgie.—The ship was one vast new iron nightmare—no sweet salt sea.

And there I am staggering around the tragic darkness of the slavish alleyway with brooms, mops, handles, sticks, rags sticking out of me like a sad porcupine—my face downcast, worried, intent—aloft in the aerial world from that sweet previous Skid Row bed of underground comfort.—I have a huge carton (empty) for the dumpings of officers' ashtrays and waste-baskets—I have two mops, one for toilet floors, one for decks —a wet rag and dry rag—emergency shifts and ideas of my own. —I go frantically searching for my work—incomprehensible people are trying to get around me in the alleyways to get the work of the ship done.—After a few desultory hair drooping lugubrious licks at the Chief Mate's floor he comes in from breakfast, chats affably with me, he's going off to be captain on a ship, feels good.—I comment on the interesting notes in the discarded notebooks in his wastebasket, concerning stars. —"Go up in the chartroom," he says, "and you'll find a lot of interesting notebooks in the basket up there."—Later I do and it's locked.—The captain appears—I stare at him befuddled, sweaty, waiting.—He sees at once the idiot with the pail, his crafty brain begins working at once.—

He was a short distinguished looking grayhaired man with hornrim glasses, good sporty clothes, sea green eyes, quiet unassuming look.—Beneath this lurked an insane mischievous perverted spirit that even at that first moment began to manifest itself when he said "Yes Jack all you have to do is learn to do your job right and everything will be alright—now as for instance in cleaning—now look come in here"—he insisted I go in deep in his quarters, where he could speak low—"When you—now look—you dont—" (I began to see his mad way in the stutterings, changings of mind, hiccupings of meaning)—"you dont use the same mop for deck *and* toilet" he said nastily, in a nasty tone, almost snarling and where a minute ago I'd marveled at the dignity of his calling, the great charts on his workdesk, now I wrinkled my nose to realize this idiotic man was all hung up on mops.—"There's such things as germs, you know," he said, as if I didn't know although little he knew how little I cared about his germs.—There we were in the California harbor morning consulting on these matters in his immaculate cabin, that thing was like a Kingdom to my skidrow closet and would it make any difference to him anyway not on your life—

"Yes I'll do it that way, dont worry—er—man—captain—sir—" (no idea yet how to sound natural in new sea militarisms). —His eyes twinkled, he leaned forward, there was something unwholesome and something, some hole card not shown.—I covered all the officers' rooms doing desultory work not really knowing how and waiting for when Georgie or somebody would show me.—No time for naps, hungover in the afternoon I had to do the 3rd Cook's scullion work in the galley sink with huge pots and pans till the man came from the union hall.—He was a big Armenian with close set eyes, fat, weight about 260: he took bites day in day out at his work—sweet potatoes, pieces of cheese, fruit, he tasted it all and had big meals in between.

His room (and mine) was the first in the port alleyway facing forward.—Next door was the deck engineer, Ted Joyner, alone; oft and many a night at sea he invited me in there for a snort and always with confidential deepsouth florid faced friendly and—"Now I'm goan tell you the truth, *I* dont really like so-and-so and that's the way I feel, but I'm goan tell you the truth, now, lissen, this is no shit and I'm gonna tell you the truth, it's just a matter of—well I really dont like it and I'm goan tell you the truth, ah dont mince words—now do I Jack?"—nevertheless the prime gentleman of the ship, he was from deep in Florida and weighed also 250 question being who ate most he or Gavril my big 3rd cook roommate, I would say Ted did.

Now I'm going to tell you the truth.

Next door were the two Greek wipers, George one, the other never spoke and hardly told his name.—George from Greece, this being in fact a Greek owned Liberty operating under the American flag which many a time thereafter fluttered over my sleep in afternoon cots on the poop deck.—When I looked at George I thought of the brown leaves of the Mediterranean, old tawny ports, ouzos and figs of the Isle of Crete or Cyprus, he was that color and had a little mustache and olive green eyes and a sunny disposition.—Amazing how he took all the kidding from the rest of the crew concerning that Greek predilection to love it up the rear—"Yey, yey!" he'd laugh scatteringly—"Up de ass, yey yey."—His non-committal roommate was a young man before our very eyes in the process of growing old—still youthful of face and with little lover mustache and still youthful of figure in arms and legs he was growing a pot that looked all out of proportion and seemed bigger every time I watched him after supper.—Some lost love affair had just made him give up attempts to look young and loverlike I presumed.—

The mess hall was next to their foc'sle—then Georgie's room, the pantryman's and saloon messman who didnt arrive till the second day—then at the forward end facing the bow, the Chief Cook and the 2nd Cook and Baker. Chief Cook was Chauncey Preston a Negro also from Florida but way down in the Keys and in fact he had a West Indian look besides regular American Southern Negro of hot fields especially when in there sweating at the range or hammering at beef sections with a cleaver, an excellent cook and sweet person, said to me as I passed with dishes "What you got there love?" and hard and wiry as a boxer, his black figure perfect, you wondered he never got fat on those amazing yams and yam sauces and pigs knuckle stews and Southern Fried Chicken he made.—But the first wonderful meal he made you heard the deep quiet menacing voice of the blond curlylocks Swedish bosun: "If we dont want our food salted on this ship, we dont want it salted" and Prez answered from the galley in just as deep and quiet a menacing voice "If you dont like it dont eat it." You could see it coming, the trip . . .

The 2nd Cook and Baker was a hipster, a union man, that is a unionist—a jazz devotee—a sharp dresser—a soft, mustached, elegant, pale gold colored cook of the blue seas who said to me "Man, pay no attention to the beefs and the performances on this or any other ship you might hang up on in the future, just do your work the best way you know, and" (wink) "you'll make it—dad, I'm hep, you understand, right?"

"You got it."

"So just be cool and we'll all be one happy family, you'll see. What I mean, man, it's people—that's all—it's people.—Chief Cook Prez, is people—real people—the captain, the Chief Steward, okay, no.—We know that—we stand together—"

"I'm hip—"

He was over 6 feet, wore snazzy white and blue canvas shoes, a fantastic rich Japanese silk sports shirt bought coolly in Sasebo—Beside his bunk a great longdistance Shortwave Zenith portable radio to pick up the bops and shmops of the world from here to hottest Madras—but let nobody play it unless he was there—

My big room mate Gavril the 3rd Cook was also hip, also unionist, but a lonely big fat furtive unloving and unloved slob of the sea—"Man, I have every record Frank Sinatra ever made including *I Cant Get Started* made in New Jersey in 1938"—

"Dont tell me things are going to look up?" I thought. And there was Georgie, wonderful Georgie and the promise of a thousand drunken nights in the mysterious odorous real ocean-girdled Orient World.—I was ready.—

After washing galley pots and pans all afternoon, a chore I'd tasted before in 1942 in the gray cold seas of Greenland and now found less demeaning, more like one's proper dive in hell and guilt-earned labor of the steams, punishment in hot water and scald for all the bluesky puffs I'd leaned on lately—(and a nap at four just before supper dishes)—I took off for my first night ashore in the company of Georgie and Gavril. We put on clean shirts, combed, went down the gangplank in the cool of evening: this is sea men.

But oh so typical of seamen, that they never do anything—just go ashore with money in their pockets and amble around dully and even with a kind of uninterested sorrow, visitors from another world, a floating prison, in civilian clothes most uninteresting looking anyway.—We walked across the Navy's vast supply dumps—huge graypainted warehouses, sprinklers watering lost lawns that no one wanted or ever used and which ran between tracks of the Navy Yard railroad.—Immense distances at dusk with no one in sight in the redness.—Sad groups of sailors swimming their way out of the Giant Macrocosmos to find a Microcosmic bug and go to pleasures of downtown Oakland which are really nil, just streets, bars, jukeboxes with Hawaiian hula girls painted on—barbershops, desultory liquor stores, the characters of life hanging around. —I knew the only place to get kicks, to get women, way in the Mexican or Negro streets which were on the outskirts but I followed Georgie and "Heavy" as we later called the 3rd Cook to a bar in Oakland downtown where we just sat in the brown gloom, Georgie not drinking, Heavy fidgeting.—I drank wine, I didnt know where to go, what do.—

I found a few good Gerry Mulligan records on the box and played them.

But the next day we sailed out the Golden Gate in a gray foggy suppertime dusk, before you knew it we had turned the headlands of San Francisco and lost them beneath the gray waves.—

The trip down the West Coast of America and Mexico, again, only this time at sea within full sight of the vague brown coastline where sometimes on clear days I could definitely see the arroyos and canyons of the Southern Pacific rail where it lined along the surf—like looking at an old dream.

Some nights I slept on deck in a cot and Georgie Varewski said "You senevabitch one morning I wake up you wont be here—goddam Pacific, you teenk goddam Pacific is quiet ocean? big tidal wave come some night when you dreaming of girls and pof, no more you—you be washed away."

Holy sunrises and holy sunsets in the Pacific with everybody on board quietly working or reading in their bunks, the booze all gone.—Calm days, which I'd open at dawn with a grapefruit cut in halves at the rail of the ship, and below me there they were, the smiling porpoise leaping and curlicueing in the wet gray air, sometimes in the powerful driving rains that made sea and rain the same. I wrote a haiku about it:

> *Useless, useless!*
> *—Heavy rain driving*
> *Into the sea!*

Calm days that I went and fouled up, because I foolishly traded my bedroom job for the dishwasher job, which is the best job on the ship because of sudsy privacy, but then I foolishly transferred to the officers' waiter (saloon messman) and that was the worst shot on the ship. "Why dont you smile nice and say good morning?" said the captain as I laid down his eggs before him.

"I'm not the smiling type."

"Is that the way to present breakfast to an officer? Lay it down gently with both hands."

"Okay."

Meanwhile the Chief Engineer is yelling: "Where's the goddam pineapple juice, I dont want no goddam orange juice!" and I have to run below to the bottom stores so when I get back the Chief Mate is burning because his breakfast's late. The Chief Mate has a full mustache and thinks he's a hero in a Hemingway novel who has to be served punctiliously.

And when we sail through the Panama Canal I cant keep my eyes off the exotic green trees and leaves, palms, huts, guys in straw hats, the deep brown warm tropical mud out there along the banks of the canal (with South America just over the swamp in Colombia) but the officers are yelling: "Come on, goddamit, didnt you ever see the Panama Canal before, where the hell is lunch?"

We sailed up the Caribbean (blue sparkler) to Mobile Bay and into Mobile where I went ashore, got drunk with the boys and later went to a hotel room with the pretty young Rose of Dauphine Street and missed a morning's work.—When Rosy and I were walking hand in hand down Main Street at 10 A.M. (a terrible sight both of us without underwear or socks, just my pants, her dress, T-shirts, shoes, walking along drunk, and she's a cutie too) it was the captain, lurking around with his tourist camera, who saw it all.—Back on the ship they give me hell and I say I'm going to quit in New Orleans.

So the ship sails from Mobile Alabama westward to the mouths of the Mississippi in a lightning storm at midnight which lights up the salt marshes and vastnesses of that great hole where all America pours out her heart, her mud and hopes in one grand falling slam of water into the doom of the Gulf, the rebirth of the Void, into the Night.—There I am drunk on the cot on deck looking at it all with hungover eyes.

And the ship goes chugging right up the Mississippi River right back into the heart of the American land where I'd just been hitch hiking, damnit, there wasnt about to be no Exotic Sasebo for me. Georgie Varewski looked at me and grinned:— "Senevabitch Jackcrack, vugup huh?" The ship goes and docks at some calm green shore like the shores of Tom Sawyer, somewhere upriver from La Place, to load on barrels of oil for Japan.

I collect my pay of about $300, wad it up together with my $300 left from the railroad, heave the dufflebag on back again, and there I go again.

I look into the mess hall where all the boys are sitting around and not one of them is looking at me.—I feel eerie—I say "Well when'd they say you're sailing?"

They looked at me blankly, with eyes that didnt see me, as though I was a ghost.—When Georgie looked at me it was also there in his eyes, a thing that said: "Now that you are no longer a member of the crew, on this ghostly vehicle, you are dead to us." "We cant possibly get any more out of you," I could have added, remembering all the times they insisted on my company for dull smoky bull sessions in bunks with great fat bellies spilling out like blob in the horrible tropical heat, not even one porthole open.—Or the greasy confidences about malefactions that had no charm.

Prez the Negro chief cook had been fired and was going into town with me and say goodbye on the sidewalks of old

New Orleans.—It was an anti-Negro management—the captain was worse than anyone else.—

Prez said "I'd sure like to go to New York with ya and go down to Birdland but I gotta get a ship."

We walked off the gangplank in the silence of the afternoon.

The second cook's car en route to New Orleans zoomed by us on the highway.

5

New York Scenes

A T this time my mother was living alone in a little apartment in Jamaica Long Island, working in the shoe factory, waiting for me to come home so I could keep her company and escort her to Radio City once a month. She had a tiny bedroom waiting for me, clean linen in the dresser, clean sheets in the bed. It was a relief after all the sleepingbags and bunks and railroad earth. It was another of the many opportunities she's given me all her life to just stay home and write.

I always give her all my leftover pay. I settled down to long sweet sleeps, day-long meditations in the house, writing, and long walks around beloved old Manhattan a half hour subway ride away. I roamed the streets, the bridges, Times Square, cafeterias, the waterfront, I looked up all my poet beatnik friends and roamed with them, I had love affairs with girls in the Village, I did everything with that great mad joy you get when you return to New York City.

I've heard great singing Negroes call it "The Apple!"

"There now is your insular city of the Manhattoes, belted round by wharves," sang Herman Melville.

"Bound round by flashing tides," sang Thomas Wolfe.

Whole panoramas of New York everywhere, from New Jersey, from skyscrapers.—

Even from bars, like a Third Avenue bar—4 P.M. the men are all roaring in clink bonk glass brassfoot barrail "where ya goin" excitement—October's in the air, in the Indian Summer sun of door.—Two Madison Avenue salesmen who been working all day long come in young, well dressed, justsuits, puffing cigars, glad to have the day done and the drink comin in, side by side march in smiling but there's no room at the roaring (Shit!) crowded bar so they stand two deep from it waiting and smiling and talking.—Men do love bars and good bars should be loved.—It's full of businessmen, workmen, Finn MacCools of Time.—Be-overalled oldgray topers dirty and beerswiggin glad.—Nameless truck busdrivers with flashlites slung from hips—old beatfaced beerswallowers sadly upraising purple lips to happy drinking ceilings.—Bartenders are fast, courteous, interested in their work as well as clientele.—Like Dublin at 4:30 P.M. when the work is done, but this is great New York Third Avenue, free lunch, smells of Moody street exhaust river lunch in road of grime bysmashing the door, guitarplaying long sideburned heroes smell out there on wood doorsteps of afternoon drowse.—But it's New York towers rise beyond, voices crash mangle to talk and chew the gossip till Earwicker drops his load—Ah Jack Fitzgerald Mighty Murphy where are you? —Semi bald blue shirt tattered shovellers in broken end dungarees fisting glasses of glistenglass foam top brown afternoon beer.—The subway rumbles underneath as man in homburg in vest but coatless executive changes from right to left foot on ye brass rail.—Colored man in hat, dignified, young, paper underarm, says goodbye at bar warm and paternal leaning over men —elevator operator around the corner.—And wasnt this where they say Novak the real estator who used to stay up late a-nights linefaced to become right and rich in his little white worm cellule of the night typing up reports and letters wife and kids go mad at home at eleven P.M.—ambitious, worried, in a little office of the Island, right on the street undignified but open to all business and in infancy any business can be small as ambition's big—pushing how many daisies now? and never made his million, never had a drink with So Long Gee Gee and I Love You Too in this late afternoon beer room of men excited shifting stools and footbottom rail scuffle heel soles in New York?—Never called Old Glasses over and offered his rim red nose a drink—never laughed and let the fly his nose use as a landingmark—but ulcerated in the middle of the night to be rich and get his family the best.—So the best American sod's his blanket now, made in upper mills of Hudson Bay Moonface Sassenach and carted down by housepainter in white coveralls (silent) to rim the roam of his once formed flesh, and let worms ram—Rim! So have another beer, topers—Bloody mugglers! Lovers!

Simpler things in life

My friends and I in New York city have our own special way of having fun without having to spend much money and most important of all without having to be importuned by formalistic bores, such as, say, a swell evening at the mayor's ball.—We dont have to shake hands and we dont have to make appointments and we feel all right.—We sorta wander around like children.—We walk into parties and tell everybody what we've been doing and people think we're showing off.—They say: "Oh look at the beatniks!"

Take, for example, this typical evening you can have:— *we're*

Emerging from the Seventh Avenue subway on 42nd Street, *a product of our environment* you pass the john, which is the beatest john in New York—you never can tell if it's open or not, usually there's a big chain in front of it saying it's out of order, or else it's got some white-haired decaying monster slinking outside, a john which all seven million people in New York City have at one time passed and taken strange notice of—past the new charcoal-fried-hamburger stand, Bible booths, operatic jukeboxes, and a seedy underground used-magazine store next to a peanut-brittle store smelling of subway arcades—here and there a used copy of that old bard Plotinus sneaked in with the remainders of collections of German high-school textbooks—where they sell long ratty-looking hotdogs (no, actually they're quite beautiful, particularly if you havent got 15 cents and are looking for someone in Bickford's Cafeteria who can lay some smash on you) (lend you some change).—

Coming up that stairway, people stand there for hours and hours drooling in the rain, with soaking wet umbrellas—lots of boys in dungarees scared to go into the Army standing halfway up the stairway on the iron steps waiting for God Who knows what, certainly among them some romantic heroes just in from Oklahoma with ambitions to end up yearning in the arms of some unpredictable sexy young blonde in a penthouse on the Empire State Building—some of them probably stand there dreaming of owning the Empire State Building by virtue of a magic spell which they've dreamed up by a creek in the backwoods of a ratty old house on the outskirts of Texarkana.— Ashamed of being seen going into the dirty movie (what's its

America built by hobos-
Holy is everyone ' world is beautiful - this land made for you ; me

name?) across the street from the New York *Times*—The lion
and the tiger passing, as Tom Wolfe used to say about certain
types passing that corner.—

Leaning against that cigar store with a lot of telephone
booths on the corner of 42nd and Seventh where you make
beautiful telephone calls looking out into the street and it gets
real cozy in there when it's raining outside and you like to pro-
long the conversation, who do you find? Basketball teams?
Basketball coaches? All those guys from the rollerskating rink
go there? Cats from the Bronx again, looking for some action,
really looking for romance? Strange duos of girls coming out
of dirty movies? Did you ever see them? Or bemused drunken
businessmen with their hats tipped awry on their graying
heads staring catatonically upward at the signs floating by on
the Times Building, huge sentences about Khrushchev reeling
by, the populations of Asia enumerated in flashing lightbulbs,
always five hundred periods after each sentence.—Suddenly a
psychopathically worried policeman appears on the corner and
tells everybody to go away.—This is the center of the greatest
city the world has ever known and this is what beatniks do
here.—"Standing on the street corner waiting for no one is
Power," sayeth poet Gregory Corso.

Instead of going to night clubs—if you're in a position to
make the nightclub scene (most beatniks rattle empty pockets
passing Birdland)—how strange to stand on the sidewalk and
just watch that weird eccentric from Second Avenue looking
like Napoleon going by feeling cooky crumbs in his pocket, or
a young 15-year-old kid with a bratty face, or suddenly somebody swishing by in a baseball hat (because that's what you
see), and finally an old lady dressed in seven hats and a long
ratty fur coat in the middle of the July night carrying a huge
Russian woolen purse filled with scribbled bits of paper which
say "Festival Foundation Inc., 70,000 Germs" and moths flying
out of her sleeve—she rushes up and importunes Shriners. And
dufflebag soliders without a war—harmonica players off freight
trains.—Of course there are the normal New Yorkers, looking
ridiculously out of place and as odd as their own neat oddity,
carrying pizzas and *Daily Newses* and headed for brown base-
ments or Pennsylvania trains—W. H. Auden himself may be
seen fumbling by in the rain—Paul Bowles, natty in a Dacron

suit, passing through on a trip from Morocco, the ghost of Herman Melville himself followed by Bartleby the Wall Street Scrivener and Pierre the ambiguous hipster of 1848 out on a walk—to see what's up in the news flashes of the *Times*—Let's go back to the corner newsstand.—SPACE BLAST . . . POPE WASHES FEET OF POOR . . .

Let's go across the street to Grant's, our favored dining place. For 65 cents you get a huge plate of fried clams, a lot of French fried potatoes, a little portion of cole slaw, some tartar sauce, a little cup of red sauce for fish, a slice of lemon, two slices of fresh rye bread, a pat of butter, another ten cents brings a glass of rare birch beer.—What a ball it is to eat here! Migrations of Spaniards chewing on hotdogs, standing up, leaning against big pots of mustard.—Ten different counters with different specialties.—Ten-cent cheese sandwiches, two liquor bars for the Apocalypse, oh yeah and great indifferent bartenders.—And cops that stand in the back getting free meals —drunken saxophone players on the nod—lonely dignified ragpickers from Hudson Street supping soup without a word to anybody, with black fingers, woe.—Twenty thousand customers a day—fifty thousand on rainy days—one hundred thousand on snowy days.—Operation twenty-four hours a night. Privacy—supreme under a glary red light full of conversation.—Toulouse-Lautrec, with his deformity and cane, sketching in the corner.—You can stay there for five minutes and gobble up your food, or else stay there for hours having insane philosophical conversation with your buddy and wondering about the people.—"Let's have a hotdog before we go to the movie!" and you get so high in there you never get to the movies because it's better than a show about Doris Day on a holiday in the Caribbean.

"But what are we gonna do tonight? Marty would go to a movie but we're going to connect for some junk.—Let's go down to the Automat."

"Just a minute, I've got to shine my shoes on top of a fire hydrant."

"You wanta see yourself in the fun mirror?"

"Wanta take four pictures for a quarter? Because we're on the eternal scene. We can look at the picture and remember it when we're wise old white-haired Thoreaus in cabins."

"Ah, the fun mirrors are gone, they used to have fun mirrors here."

"How about the Laff Movie?"

"That's gone too."

"They got the flea circus."

"They still got donzinggerls?"

"The burlesque is gone millions and millions of years ago."

"Shall we go down by the Automat and watch the old ladies eating beans, or the deaf-mutes that stand in front of the window there and you watch 'em and try to figure the invisible language as it flees across the window from face to face and finger to finger . . . ? Why does Times Square feel like a big room?"

Across the street is Bickford's, right in the middle of the block under the Apollo Theater marquee and right next door to a little bookshop that specializes in Havelock Ellis and Rabelais with thousands of sex fiends leafing at the bins.— Bickford's is the greatest stage on Times Square—many people have hung around there for years man and boy searching God alone knows for what, maybe some angel of Times Square who would make the whole big room home, the old homestead— civilization needs it.—What's Times Square doing there any- way? Might as well enjoy it.—Greatest city the world has ever seen.—Have they got a Times Square on Mars? What would the Blob do on Times Square? Or St. Francis?

A girl gets off a bus in the Port Authority Terminal and goes into Bickford's, Chinese girl, red shoes, sits down with coffee, looking for daddy.

There's a whole floating population around Times Square that has always made Bickford's their headquarters day and night. In the old days of the beat generation some poets used to go in there to meet the famous character "Hunkey" who used to come in and out in an oversized black raincoat and a cigarette holder looking for sombody to lay a pawnticket on— Remington typewriter, portable radio, black raincoat—to score for some toast, (get some money) so he can go uptown and get in trouble with the cops or any of his boys. Also a lot of stupid gangsters from 8th Avenue used to cut in—maybe they still do—the ones from the early days are all in jail or dead. Now the poets just go there and smoke a peace pipe, looking for the ghost of Hunkey or his boys, and dream over the fading cups of tea.

The beatniks make the point that if you went there every night and stayed there you could start a whole Dostoevski season on Times Square by yourself and meet all the midnight newspaper peddlers and their involvements and families and woes—religious fanatics who would take you home and give you long sermons over the kitchen table about the "new apocalypse" and similar ideas:—"My Baptist minister back in Winston-Salem told me the reason that God invented television was that when Christ comes back to earth again they shall crucify Him right on the streets of this here Babylon and they gonna have television cameras pointin' down on that spot and the streets shall run with blood and every eye shall see."

Still hungry, go out down to the Oriental Cafeteria— "favored dining spot" also—some night life—cheap—down in the basement across the street from the Port Authority monolith bus terminal on 40th Street and eat big oily lambs' heads with Greek rice for 90¢.—Oriental zig-zag tunes on the jukebox.

Depends how high you are by now—assuming you've picked up on one of the corners—say 42nd Street and 8th Avenue, near the great Whelan's drug store, another lonely haunt spot where you can meet people—Negro whores, ladies limping in a Benzedrine psychosis.—Across the street you can see the ruins of New York already started—the Globe Hotel being torn down there, an empty tooth hole right on 44th Street—and the green McGraw-Hill building gaping up in the sky, higher than you'd believe—lonely all by itself down towards the Hudson River where freighters wait in the rain for their Montevideo limestone.—

Might as well go on home. It's getting old.—Or: "Let's make the Village or go to the Lower East Side and play Symphony Sid on the radio—or play our Indian records—and eat big dead Puerto Rican steaks—or lung stew—see if Bruno has slashed any more car roofs in Brooklyn—though Bruno's gentled now, maybe he's written a new poem."

Or look at Television. Night life—Oscar Levant talking about his melancholia on the Jack Paar show.

The Five Spot on 5th Street and Bowery sometimes features

Thelonious Monk on the piano and you go on there. If you know the proprietor you sit down at the table free with a beer, but if you dont know him you can sneak in and stand by the ventilator and listen. Always crowded weekends. Monk cogitates with deadly abstraction, clonk, and makes a statement, huge foot beating delicately on the floor, head turned to one side listening, entering the piano.

Lester Young played there just before he died and used to sit in the back kitchen between sets. My buddy poet Allen Ginsberg went back and got on his knees and asked him what he would do if an atom bomb fell on New York. Lester said he would break the window in Tiffany's and get some jewels anyway. He also said, "What you doin' on your knees?" not realizing he is a great hero of the beat generation and now enshrined. The Five Spot is darkly lit, has weird waiters, good music always, sometimes John "Train" Coltrane showers his rough notes from his big tenor horn all over the place. On weekends parties of well-dressed uptowners jam-pack the place talking continuously—nobody minds.

O for a couple of hours, though, in the Egyptian Gardens in the lower West Side Chelsea district of Greek restaurants.— Glasses of ouzo, Greek liqueur, and beautiful girls dancing the belly dance in spangles and beaded bras, the incomparable Zara on the floor and weaving like mystery to the flutes and tingtang beats of Greece—when she's not dancing she sits in the orchestra with the men plapping a drum against her belly, dreams in her eyes.—Huge crowds of what appear to be Suburbia couples sit at the tables clapping to the swaying Oriental idea.—If you're late you have to stand along the wall.

Wanta dance? The Garden Bar on Third Avenue where you can do fantastic sprawling dances in the dim back room to a jukebox, cheap, the waiter doesnt care.

Wanta just talk? The Cedar Bar on University Place where all the painters hang out and a 16-year-old kid who was there one afternoon squirting red wine out of a Spanish wine skin into his friends' mouths and kept missing. . . .

The night clubs of Greenwich Village known as the Half Note, the Village Vanguard, the Café Bohemia, the Village Gate also feature jazz (Lee Konitz, J. J. Johnson, Miles Davis), but you've got to have mucho money and it's not so much that you've got to have mucho money but the sad commercial atmosphere is killing jazz and jazz *is* killing itself there, because jazz belongs to open joyful ten-cent beer joints, as in the beginning.

There's a big party at some painter's loft, wild loud flamenco on the phonograph, the girls suddenly become all hips and heels and people try to dance between their flying hair.— Men go mad and start tackling people, flying wedges hurtle across the room, men grab men around the knees and lift them nine feet from the floor and lose their balance and nobody gets hurt, blonk.—Girls are balanced hands on men's knees, their skirts falling and revealing frills on their thighs.— Finally everybody dresses to go home and the host says dazedly. —"You all look so *respectable.*"

Or somebody just had an opening, or there's a poetry reading at the Living Theater, or at the Gaslight Café, or at the Seven Arts Coffee Gallery, up around Times Square (9th Avenue and 43rd Street, amazing spot) (begins at midnight Fridays), where afterward everybody rushes out to the old wild bar.—Or else a huge party at Leroi Jones's—he's got a new issue of Yugen Magazine which he printed himself on a little cranky machine and everybody's poems are in it, from San Francisco to Gloucester Mass., and costs only 50 cents.—Historic publisher, secret hipster of the trade.—Leroi's getting sick of parties, everyone's always taking off his shirt and dancing, three sentimental girls are crooning over poet Raymond Bremser, my buddy Gregory Corso is arguing with a New York *Post* reporter saying, "But you dont understand Kangaroonian weep! Forsake thy trade! Flee to the Enchenedian Islands!"

Let's get out of here, it's too literary.—Let's go get drunk on the Bowery or eat those long noodles and tea in glasses at Hong Fat's in Chinatown.—What are we always eating for? Let's walk over the Brooklyn Bridge and build up another appetite.—How about some okra on Sands Street?

Shades of Hart Crane!

"Let's go see if we can find Don Joseph!"

"Who's Don Joseph?"

Don Joseph is a terrific cornet player who wanders around the Village with his little mustache and his arms hangin at the sides with the cornet, which creaks when he plays softly, nay whispers, the greatest sweetest cornet since Bix and more.— He stands at the jukebox in the bar and plays with the music for a beer.—He looks like a handsome movie actor.—He's the great super glamorous secret Bobby Hackett of the jazz world.

What about that guy Tony Fruscella who sits crosslegged on the rug and plays Bach on his trumpet, by ear, and later on at night there he is blowing with the guys at a session, modern jazz—

Or George Jones the secret Bowery shroud who plays great tenor in parks at dawn with Charley Mariano, for kicks, because they love jazz, and that time on the waterfront at dawn they played a whole session as the guy beat on the dock with a stick for the beat.

Talkin of Bowery shrouds, what about Charley Mills walkin down the street with bums drinkin his bottle of wine singing in twelve tone scale.

"Let's go see the strange great secret painters of America and discuss their paintings and their visions with them—Iris Brodie with her delicate fawn Byzantine filigree of Virgins—"

"Or Miles Forst and his black bull in the orange cave."

"Or Franz Kline and his spiderwebs."

"His bloody spiderwebs!"

"Or Willem de Kooning and his White."

"Or Robert De Niro."

"Or Dody Muller and her Annunciations in seven feet tall flowers."

"Or Al Leslie and his giant feet canvases."

"Al Leslie's giant is sleeping in the Paramount building."

There's another great painter, his name is Bill Heine, he's a really secret subterranean painter who sits with all those weird new cats in the East Tenth street coffeeshops that dont look coffeeshops at all but like sorta Henry Street basement secondhand clothes stores except you see an African sculpture or maybe a Mary Frank sculpture over the door and inside they play Frescobaldi on the hi fi.

Ah, let's go back to the Village and stand on the corner of Eighth Street and Sixth Avenue and watch the intellectuals go by.—AP reporters lurching home to their basement apartments on Washington Square, lady editorialists with huge German police dogs breaking their chains, lonely dikes melting by, unknown experts on Sherlock Holmes with blue fingernails going up to their rooms to take scopolamine, a muscle-bound young man in a cheap gray German suit explaining something weird to his fat girl friend, great editors leaning politely at the newsstand buying the early edition of the *Times*, great fat furniture movers out of 1910 Charlie Chaplin films coming home with great bags full of chop suey (feeding everybody), Picasso's melancholy harlequin now owner of a print and frame shop musing on his wife and newborn child lifting up his finger for a taxi, rolypoly recording engineers rush in fur hats, girl artists down from Columbia with D. H. Lawrence problems picking up 50-year-old men, old men in the Kettle of Fish, and the melancholy spectre of New York Women's prison that looms high and is folded in silence as the night itself—at sunset their windows look like oranges—poet e. e. cummings buying a package of cough drops in the shade of that monstrosity.—If it's raining you can stand under the awning in front of Howard Johnson's and watch the street from the other side.

Beatnik Angel Peter Orlovsky in the supermarket five doors away buying Uneeda Biscuits (late Friday night), ice cream, caviar, bacon, pretzels, sodapop, *TV Guide*, Vaseline, three toothbrushes, chocolate milk (dreaming of roast suckling pig), buying whole Idaho potatoes, raisin bread, wormy cabbage by mistake, and fresh-felt tomatoes and collecting purple stamps. —Then he goes home broke and dumps it all on the table, takes out a big book of Mayakovsky poems, turns on the 1949 television set to the horror movie, and goes to sleep.

And this is the beat night life of New York.

6.

Alone on a Mountaintop

A FTER all this kind of fanfare, and even more, I came to a point where I needed solitude and just stop the machine of "thinking" and "enjoying" what they call "living," I just wanted to lie in the grass and look at the clouds—

They say, too, in ancient scripture:—"Wisdom can only be obtained from the viewpoint of solitude."

And anyway I was sick and tired of all the ships and railroads and Times Squares of all time—

I applied with the U.S. Agriculture Department for a job as a fire lookout in the Mount Baker National Forest in the High Cascades of the Great Northwest.

Just to look at these words made me shiver to think of cool pine trees by a morning lake.

I beat my way out to Seattle three thousand miles from the heat and dust of eastern cities in June.

Anybody who's been to Seattle and missed Alaskan Way, the old water front, has missed the point—here the totem-pole stores, the waters of Puget Sound washing under old piers, the dark gloomy look of ancient warehouses and pier sheds, and the most antique locomotives in America switching boxcars up and down the water front, give a hint, under the pure cloud-mopped sparkling skies of the Northwest, of great country to come. Driving north from Seattle on Highway 99 is an exciting experience because suddenly you see the Cascade Mountains rising on the northeast horizon, truly *Komo Kulshan* under their uncountable snows.—The great peaks covered with trackless white, worlds of huge rock twisted and heaped and sometimes almost spiraled into fanstastic unbelievable shapes.

All this is seen far above the dreaming fields of the Stilaquamish and Skagit valleys, agricultural flats of peaceful green, the soil so rich and dark it is proudly referred to by inhabitants as second only to the Nile in fertility. At Milltown Washington your car rolls over the bridge across the Skagit River.—To the left—seaward, westward—the Skagit flows into Skagit Bay and the Pacific Ocean.—At Burlington you turn right and head for the heart of the mountains along a rural valley road through sleepy little towns and one bustling agricultural market center known as Sedro-Woolley with hundreds of cars parked aslant on a typical countrytown Main Street of hardware stores, grain-and-feed stores and five-and-tens.—On deeper into the deepening valley, cliffs rich with timber appearing by the side of the road, the narrowing river rushing more swiftly now, a pure translucent green like the green of the ocean on a cloudy day but a saltless rush of melted snow from the High Cascades —almost good enough to drink north of Marblemount.—The road curves more and more till you reach Concrete, the last town in Skagit Valley with a bank and a five-and-ten—after that the mountains rising secretly behind foothills are so close that now you don't see them but begin to feel them more and more.

At Marblemount the river is a swift torrent, the work of the quiet mountains.—Fallen logs beside the water provide good seats to enjoy a river wonderland, leaves jiggling in the good clean northwest wind seem to rejoice, the topmost trees on nearby timbered peaks swept and dimmed by low-flying clouds seem contented.—The clouds assume the faces of hermits or of nuns, or sometimes look like sad dog acts hurrying off into the wings over the horizon.—Snags struggle and gurgle in the heaving bulk of the river.—Logs rush by at twenty miles an hour. The air smells of pine and sawdust and bark and mud and twigs—birds flash over the water looking for secret fish.

As you drive north across the bridge at Marblemount and on to Newhalem the road narrows and twists until finally the Skagit is seen pouring over rocks, frothing, and small creeks come tumbling from steep hillsides and pile right in—The mountains rise on all sides, only their shoulders and ribs visible, their heads out of sight and now snowcapped.

At Newhalem extensive road construction raises a cloud of

dust over shacks and cats and rigs, the dam there is the first in a series that create the Skagit watershed which provides all the power for Seattle.

The road ends at Diablo, a peaceful company settlement of neat cottages and green lawns surrounded by close packed peaks named Pyramid and Colonial and Davis.—Here a huge lift takes you one thousand feet up to the level of Diablo Lake and Diablo Dam.—Over the dam pours a jet roar of water through which a stray log could go shooting out like a toothpick in a one-thousand-foot arc.—Here for the first time you're high enough really to begin to see the Cascades. Dazzles of light to the north show where Ross Lake sweeps back all the way to Canada, opening a view of the Mt. Baker National Forest as spectacular as any vista in the Colorado Rockies.

The Seattle City Light and Power boat leaves on regular schedule from a little pier near Diablo Dam and heads north between steep timbered rocky cliffs toward Ross Dam, about half an hour's ride. The passengers are power employees, hunters and fishermen and forestry workers. Below Ross Dam the footwork begins—you must climb a rocky trail one thousand feet to the level of the dam. Here the vast lake opens out, disclosing small resort floats offering rooms and boats for vacationists, and just beyond, the floats of the U.S. Forestry Service. From this point on, if you're lucky enough to be a rich man or a forest-fire lookout, you can get packed into the North Cascade Primitive Area by horse and mule and spend a summer of complete solitude.

I was a fire lookout and after two nights of trying to sleep in the boom and slap of the Forest Service floats, they came for me one rainy morning—a powerful tugboat lashed to a large corral float bearing four mules and three horses, my own groceries, feed, batteries and equipment.—The muleskinner's name was Andy and he wore the same old floppy cowboy hat he'd worn in Wyoming twenty years ago. "Well, boy, now we're gonna put you away where we cant reach ya—you better get ready."

"It's just what I want, Andy, be alone for three solid months nobody to bother me."

"It's what you're sayin now but you'll change your tune after a week."

I didnt believe him.—I was looking forward to an experience men seldom earn in this modern world: complete and comfortable solitude in the wilderness, day and night, sixty-three days and nights to be exact. We had no idea how much snow had fallen on my mountain during the winter and Andy said: "If there didnt it means you gotta hike two miles down that hard trail every day or every other day with two buckets, boy. I aint envyin' you—I been back there. And one day it's gonna be hot and you're about ready to broil, and bugs you cant even count 'em, and next day a li'l' ole summer blizzard come hit you around the corner of Hozomeen which sits right there near Canada in your back yard and you wont be able to stick logs fast enough in that potbelly stove of yours."—But I had a full rucksack loaded with turtleneck sweaters and warm shirts and pants and long wool socks bought on the Seattle water front, and gloves and an earmuff cap, and lots of instant soup and coffee in my grub list.

"Shoulda brought yourself a quart of brandy, boy," says Andy shaking his head as the tug pushed our corral float up Ross Lake through the log gate and around to the left dead north underneath the immense rain shroud of Sourdough Mountain and Ruby Mountain.

"Where's Desolation Peak?" I asked, meaning my own mountain (*A mountain to be kept forever*, I'd dreamed all that spring) (O lonesome traveler!)

"You aint gonna see it today till we're practically on top it and by that time you'll be so soakin' wet you wont care."

Assistant Ranger Marty Gohlke of Marblemount Ranger Station was with us too, also giving me tips and instructions. Nobody seemed to envy Desolation Peak except me. After two hours pushing through the storming waves of the long rainy lake with dreary misty timber rising steeply on both sides and the mules and horses chomping on their feedbags patient in the downpour, we arrived at the foot of Desolation Trail and the tugman (who'd been providing us with good hot coffee in the pilot cabin) eased her over and settled the float against a steep muddy slope full of bushes and fallen trees.—The muleskinner whacked the first mule and she lurched ahead with her double-sided pack of batteries and canned goods, hit the mud with forehoofs, scrambled, slipped, almost fell back in the lake and finally gave one mighty heave and went skittering out of sight in the fog to wait on the trail for the other mules and her master.—We all got off, cut the barge loose, waved to the tug man, mounted our horses and started up a sad and dripping party in heavy rain.

At first the trail, always steeply rising, was so dense with shrubbery we kept getting shower after shower from overhead and against our out-saddled knees.—The trail was deep with round rocks that kept causing the animals to slip.—At one point a great fallen tree made it impossible to go on until Old Andy and Marty went ahead with axes and cleared a short cut around the tree, sweating and cursing and hacking as I watched the animals.—By-and-by they were ready but the mules were afraid of the rough steepness of the short cut and had to be prodded through with sticks.—Soon the trail reached alpine meadows powdered with blue lupine everywhere in the drenching mists, and with little red poppies, tiny-budded flowers as delicate as designs on a small Japanese teacup.—Now the trail zigzagged widely back and forth up the high meadow.—Soon we saw the vast foggy heap of a rock-cliff face above and Andy yelled "Soon's we get up high as that we're almost there but that's another two thousand feet though you think you could reach up and touch it!"

I unfolded my nylon poncho and draped it over my head, and, drying a little, or, rather, ceasing to drip, I walked alongside the horse to warm my blood and began to feel better. But the other boys just rode along with their heads bowed in the rain. As for altitude all I could tell was from some occasional frightening spots on the trail where we could look down on distant treetops.

The alpine meadow reached to timber line and suddenly a great wind blew shafts of sleet on us.—"Gettin' near the top now!" yelled Andy—and suddenly there was snow on the trail, the horses were chumping through a foot of slush and mud, and to the left and right everything was blinding white in the gray fog.—"About five and a half thousand feet right now" said Andy rolling a cigarette as he rode in the rain.—

We went down, then up another spell, down again, a slow gradual climb, and then Andy yelled "There she is!" and up ahead in the mountaintop gloom I saw a little shadowy peaked shack standing alone on the top of the world and gulped with fear:

"This my home all summer? And *this* is summer?"

The inside of the shack was even more miserable, damp and dirty, leftover groceries and magazines torn to shreds by rats and mice, the floor muddy, the windows impenetrable.—But hardy Old Andy who'd been through this kind of thing all his life got a roaring fire crackling in the potbelly stove and had me lay out a pot of water with almost half a can of coffee in it saying "Coffee aint no good 'less it's *strong!*" and pretty soon the coffee was boiling a nice brown aromatic foam and we got our cups out and drank deep.—

Meanwhile I'd gone out on the roof with Marty and removed the bucket from the chimney and put up the weather pole with the anemometer and done a few other chores—when we came back in Andy was frying Spam and eggs in a huge pan and it was almost like a party.—Outside, the patient animals chomped on their supper bags and were glad to rest by the old corral fence built of logs by some Desolation lookout of the Thirties.

Darkness came, incomprehensible.

In the gray morning after they'd slept in sleeping bags on the floor and I on the only bunk in my mummy bag, Andy and Marty left, laughing, saying, "Well, whatayou think now hey? We been here twelve hours and you still aint been able to see more than twelve feet!"

"By gosh that's right, what am I going to do for watching fires?"

"Dont worry boy, these clouds'll roll away and you'll be able to see a hunnerd miles in every direction."

I didn't believe it and I felt miserable and spent the day trying to clean up the shack or pacing twenty careful feet each way in my "yard" (the ends of which appeared to be sheer drops into silent gorges), and I went to bed early.—About bedtime I saw my first star, briefly, then giant phantom clouds billowed all around me and the star was gone.—But in that instant I thought I'd seen a mile-down maw of grayblack lake where Andy and Marty were back in the Forest Service boat which had met them at noon.

In the middle of the night I woke up suddenly and my hair was standing on end—I saw a huge black shadow in my window.—Then I saw that it had a star above it, and realized that this was Mt. Hozomeen (8080 feet) looking in my window from miles away near Canada.—I got up from the forlorn bunk with the mice scattering underneath and went outside and gasped to see black mountain shapes gianting all around, and not only that but the billowing curtains of the northern lights shifting behind the clouds.—It was a little too much for a city boy—the fear that the Abominable Snowman might be breathing behind me in the dark sent me back to bed where I buried my head inside my sleeping bag.—

But in the morning—Sunday, July sixth—I was amazed and overjoyed to see a clear blue sunny sky and down below, like a radiant pure snow sea, the clouds making a marshmallow cover for all the world and all the lake while I abided in warm sunshine among hundreds of miles of snow-white peaks.—I brewed coffee and sang and drank a cup on my drowsy warm doorstep.

At noon the clouds vanished and the lake appeared below, beautiful beyond belief, a perfect blue pool twenty five miles long and more, and the creeks like toy creeks and the timber green and fresh everywhere below and even the joyous little unfolding liquid tracks of vacationists' fishingboats on the lake and in the lagoons.—A perfect afternoon of sun, and behind the shack I discovered a snowfield big enough to provide me with buckets of cold water till late September.

My job was to watch for fires. One night a terrific lightning storm made a dry run across the Mt. Baker National Forest without any rainfall.—When I saw that ominous black cloud flashing wrathfully toward me I shut off the radio and laid the aerial on the ground and waited for the worst.—Hiss! hiss! said the wind, bringing dust and lightning nearer.—Tick! said the lightning rod, receiving a strand of electricity from a strike on nearby Skagit Peak.—Hiss! tick! and in my bed I felt the earth move.—Fifteen miles to the south, just east of Ruby Peak and somewhere near Panther Creek, a large fire raged, a huge orange spot.—At ten o'clock lightning hit it again and it flared up dangerously.—

I was supposed to note the general area of lightning strikes. —By midnight I'd been staring so intently out the dark window I got hallucinations of fires everywhere, three of them right in Lightning Creek, phosphorescent orange verticals of ghost fire that seemed to come and go.

In the morning, there at 177° 16′ where I'd seen the big fire was a strange brown patch in the snowy rock showing where the fire had raged and sputtered out in the all-night rain that followed the lightning. But the result of this storm was disastrous fifteen miles away at McAllister Creek where a great blaze had outlasted the rain and exploded the following afternoon in a cloud that could be seen from Seattle. I felt sorry for the fellows who had to fight these fires, the smoke-jumpers who parachuted down on them out of planes and the trail crews who hiked to them, climbing and scrambling over slippery rocks and scree slopes, arriving sweaty and exhausted only to face the wall of heat when they got there. As a lookout I had it pretty easy and only had to concentrate on reporting the exact location (by instrument findings) of every blaze I detected.

Most days, though, it was the routine that occupied me.— Up at seven or so every day, a pot of coffee brought to a boil over a handful of burning twigs, I'd go out in the alpine yard with a cup of coffee hooked in my thumb and leisurely make my wind speed and wind direction and temperature and moisture readings—then, after chopping wood, I'd use the two-way radio and report to the relay station on Sourdough.—At 10 A.M. I usually got hungry for breakfast, and I'd make delicious pancakes, eating them at my little table that was decorated with bouquets of mountain lupine and sprigs of fir.

Early in the afternoon was the usual time for my kick of the day, instant chocolate pudding with hot coffee.—Around two or three I'd lie on my back on the meadowside and watch the clouds float by, or pick blueberries and eat them right there. The radio was on loud enough to hear any calls for Desolation.

Then at sunset I'd roust up my supper out of cans of yams and Spam and peas, or sometimes just pea soup with corn muffins baked on top of the wood stove in aluminum

foil.—Then I'd go out to that precipitous snow slope and
shovel my two pails of snow for the water tub and gather an
armful of fallen firewood from the hillside like the proverbial
Old Woman of Japan.—For the chipmunks and conies I put
pans of leftovers under the shack, in the middle of the night I
could hear them clanking around. The rat would scramble
down from the attic and eat some too.

Sometimes I'd yell questions at the rocks and trees, and
across gorges, or yodel—"What is the meaning of the void?"
The answer was perfect silence, so I knew.—

Before bedtime I'd read by kerosene lamp whatever books
were in the shack.—It's amazing how people in solitary
hunger after books.—After poring over every word of a medical tome, and the synopsized versions of Shakespeare's plays
by Charles and Mary Lamb, I climbed up in the little attic and
put together torn cowboy pocket books and magazines the
mice had ravaged—also played stud poker with three imaginary players.

Around bedtime I'd bring a cup of milk almost to a boil
with a tablespoon of honey in it, and drink that for my lamby
nightcap, then I'd curl up in my sleeping bag.

No man should go through life without once experiencing
healthy, even bored solitude in the wilderness, finding himself
depending solely on himself and thereby learning his true and
hidden strength.—Learning, for instance, to eat when he's
hungry and sleep when he's sleepy.

Also around bedtime was my singing time. I'd pace up and
down the well-worn path in the dust of my rock singing all the
show tunes I could remember, at the top of my voice too, with
nobody to hear except the deer and the bear.

In the red dusk, the mountains were symphonies in pink
snow—Jack Mountain, Three Fools Peak, Freezeout Peak,
Golden Horn, Mt. Terror, Mt. Fury, Mt. Despair, Crooked
Thumb Peak, Mt. Challenger and the incomparable Mt. Baker
bigger than the world in the distance—and my own little Jackass Ridge that completed the Ridge of Desolation.—Pink snow
and the clouds all distant and frilly like ancient remote cities of
Buddhaland splendor, and the wind working incessantly—
whish, whish—booming, at times rattling my shack.

For supper I made chop suey and baked some biscuits and

put the leftovers in a pan for deer that came in the moonlit night and nibbled like big strange cows of peace—long-antlered buck and does and babies too—as I meditated in the alpine grass facing the magic moon-laned lake.—And I could see firs reflected in the moonlit lake five thousand feet below, upside down, pointing to infinity.—

And all the insects ceased in honor of the moon.

Sixty-three sunsets I saw revolve on that perpendicular hill—mad raging sunsets pouring in sea foams of cloud through unimaginable crags like the crags you grayly drew in pencil as a child, with every rose-tint of hope beyond, making you feel just like them, brilliant and bleak beyond words.—

Cold mornings with clouds billowing out of Lightning Gorge like smoke from a giant fire but the lake cerulean as ever.

August comes in with a blast that shakes your house and augurs little Augusticity—then that snowy-air and woodsmoke feeling—then the snow comes sweeping your way from Canada, and the wind rises and dark low clouds rush up as out of a forge. Suddenly a green-rose rainbow appears right on your ridge with steamy clouds all around and an orange sun turmoiling . . .

> What is a rainbow,
> Lord?—a hoop
> For the lowly

. . . and you go out and suddenly your shadow is ringed by the rainbow as you walk on the hilltop, a lovely-haloed mystery making you want to pray.—

A blade of grass jiggling in the winds of infinity, anchored to a rock, and for your own poor gentle flesh no answer.

Your oil lamp burning in infinity.

One morning I found bear stool and signs of where the monster had taken a can of frozen milk and squeezed it in his paws and bit into it with one sharp tooth trying to suck out the paste.—In the foggy dawn I looked down the mysterious Ridge of Starvation with its fog-lost firs and its hills humping into invisibility, and the wind blowing the fog by like a faint blizzard and I realized that somewhere in the fog stalked the bear.

And it seemed as I sat there that this was the Primordial Bear, and that he owned all the Northwest and all the snow and commanded all the mountains.—He was King Bear, who could crush my head in his paws and crack my spine like a stick and this was his house, his yard, his domain.—Though I looked all day, he would not show himself in the mystery of those silent foggy slopes—he prowled at night among unknown lakes, and in the early morning the pearl-pure light that shadowed mountainsides of fir made him blink with respect.— He had millenniums of prowling here behind him, he had seen the Indians and Redcoats come and go, and would see much more.—He continuously heard the reassuring rapturous rush of silence, except when near creeks, he was aware of the light material the world is made of, yet he never discoursed, nor communicated by signs, nor wasted a breath complaining—he just nibbled and pawed and lumbered along snags paying no attention to things inanimate or animate.—His big mouth chew-chewed in the night, I could hear it across the mountain in the starlight.—Soon he would come out of the fog, huge, and come and stare in my window with big burning eyes.—He was Avalokitesvara the Bear, and his sign was the gray wind of autumn.—

I was waiting for him. He never came.

Finally the autumn rains, all-night gales of soaking rain as I lie warm as toast in my sleeping bag and the mornings open cold wild fall days with high wind, racing fogs, racing clouds, sudden bright sun, pristine light on hill patches and my fire crackling as I exult and sing at the top of my voice.—Outside my window a wind-swept chipmunk sits up straight on a rock, hands clasped he nibbles an oat between his paws—the little nutty lord of all he surveys.

Thinking of the stars night after night I begin to realize "The stars are words" and all the innumerable worlds in the Milky Way are words, and so is this world too. And I realize that no matter where I am, whether in a little room full of thought, or in this endless universe of stars and mountains, it's all in my mind. There's no need for solitude. So love life for what it is, and form no preconceptions whatever in your mind.

What strange sweet thoughts come to you in the mountain solitudes!—One night I realized that when you give people understanding and encouragement a funny little meek childish look abashes their eyes, no matter what they've been doing they weren't sure it was right—lambies all over the world.

For when you realize that God is Everything you know that you've got to love everything no matter how bad it is, in the ultimate sense it was neither good nor bad (consider the dust), it was just *what was*, that is, what was made to appear.—Some kind of drama to teach something to something, some "despiséd substance of divinest show."

And I realized I didnt have to hide myself in desolation but could accept society for better or for worse, like a wife—I saw that if it wasnt for the six senses, of seeing, hearing, smelling, touching, tasting and thinking, the self of that, which is nonexistent, there would be no phenomena to perceive at all, in fact no six senses or self.—The fear of extinction is much worse than extinction (death) itself.—To chase after extinction in the old Nirvanic sense of Buddhism is ultimately silly, as the dead indicate in the silence of their blissful sleep in Mother Earth which is an Angel hanging in orbit in Heaven anyway.—

I just lay on the mountain meadowside in the moonlight, head to grass, and heard the silent recognition of my temporary woes.— Yes, so to try to *attain* to Nirvana when you're already there, to attain to the top of a mountain when you're already there and only have to stay—thus, to *stay* in the Nirvana Bliss, is all I have to do, you have to do, no effort, no path really, no discipline but just to know that all is empty and awake, a Vision and a Movie in God's Universal Mind (*Alaya-Vijnana*) and to stay more or less wisely in that.—Because silence itself is the sound of diamonds which can cut through anything, the sound of Holy Emptiness, the sound of extinction and bliss, that graveyard silence which is like the silence of an infant's smile, the sound of eternity, of the blessedness surely to be believed, the sound of nothing-ever-happened-except-God (which I'd soon hear in a noisy Atlantic tempest). —What exists is God in His Emanation, what does not exist is God in His peaceful Neutrality, what neither exists nor does not exist is God's immortal primordial dawn of Father Sky (this world this very minute).—So I said:—"Stay in that, no dimensions here to any of the mountains or mosquitos and whole milky ways of worlds—" Because sensation is emptiness, old age is emptiness.—'T's only the Golden Eternity of God's Mind so practise kindness and sympathy, remember that men are *not responsible in themselves as men* for their ignorance and unkindness, they should be pitied, God does pity it, because who says anything about anything since everything is just what it is, free of interpretations.—God is not the "attainer," he is the "farer" in that which everything is, the "abider"—one caterpillar, a thousand hairs of God.—So know constantly that this is only you, God, empty and awake and eternally free as the unnumerable atoms of emptiness everywhere.—

I decided that when I would go back to the world down there I'd try to keep my mind clear in the midst of murky human ideas smoking like factories on the horizon through which I would walk, forward . . .

When I came down in September a cool old golden look had come into the forest, auguring cold snaps and frost and the eventual howling blizzard that would cover my shack completely, unless those winds at the top of the world would keep her bald. As I reached the bend in the trail where the shack would disappear and I would plunge down to the lake to meet the boat that would take me out and home, I turned and blessed Desolation Peak and the little pagoda on top and thanked them for the shelter and the lesson I'd been taught.

7.

Big Trip to Europe

I SAVED every cent and then suddenly I blew it all on a big glorious trip to Europe or anyplace, and I felt light and gay, too.

It took a few months but I finally bought a ticket on a Yugoslavian freighter bound from Brooklyn Busch Terminal for Tangier, Morocco.

A February morning in 1957 we sailed. I had a whole double stateroom to myself, all my books, peace, quiet and study. For once I was going to be a writer who didnt have to do other people's work.

Gastank cities of America fading beyond the waves here we go across the Atlantic now on a run that takes twelve days to Tangier that sleepy Arabic port on the other side—and after the west waved land had receded beneath the cap lick, bang, we hit a bit of a tempest that builds up till Wednesday morning the waves are two stories high coming in over our bow and crashing over and frothing in my cabin window enough to make any old seadog duck and those poor Yugoslavian buggers out there sent to lash loose trucks and fiddle with halyards and punchy whistling lines in that salt boorapoosh gale, blam, and twasnt until later I learned these hardy Slavs had two little kittykats stashed away belowdecks and after the storm had abated (and I had seen the glowing white vision of God in my tremors of thought to think we'd might have to lower the boats away in the hopeless mess of mountainous seas—pow pow pow the waves coming in harder and harder, higher and higher, till Wednesday morning when I looked out of my porthole from a restless try-sleep on my belly with pillows on each side of me to prevent me from pitching, I look and see a wave so immense and Jonah-like coming at me from starboard I just cant believe it, just cant believe I got on that Yugoslav freighter for my big trip to Europe at just the wrong time, just the boat that would carry me indeed to the other shore, to go join coral

Hart Crane in those undersea gardens)—the poor little kitty
cats tho when the storm's abated and moon come out and
looked like a dark olive prophesying Africa (O the history of
the world is full of olives) here are the two little swickle jaws
sitting facing each other on a calm eight o'clock hatch in the
calm Popeye moonlight of the Sea Hag and finally I got them
to come in my stateroom and purr on my lap as we thereafter
gently swayed to the other shore, the Afric shore and not the
one death'll take us to.—But in the moment of the storm I
wasnt so cocky as I am now writing about it, I was certain it
was the end and I did see that everything is God, that nothing
ever happened except God, the raging sea, the poor groomus
lonesome boat sailing beyond every horizon with big long tortured body and with no arbitrary conception of any awakened
worlds or any myriads of angel flower bearing Devas honoring
the place where the Diamond was studied, pitching like a bottle
in that howling void, but soon enough the fairy hills and honey
thighs of the sweethearts of Africa, the dogs, cats, chickens,
Berbers, fish heads and curlylock singing keeners of the sea
with its Mary star and the white house lighthouse mysterioso
supine—"What was that storm anyway?" I manage to ask by
means of signs and pig English of my blond cabinboy (go
up on mast be blond Pip) and he says to me only "BOORA-
POOSH! BOORAPOOSHE!" with pig poosh of his lips,
which later from English-speaking passenger I learn means
only "North Wind," the name given for North Wind in the
Adriatic.—

Only passenger on the ship beside myself is a middleaged
ugly woman with glasses a Yugoslavian iron curtain Russian spy
for sure sailed with me so she could study my passport in secret
in the captain's cabin at night and then forge it and then finally
I never gets to Tangier but am hid belowsides and taken to
Yugoslavia forever nobody hears from me ever again and the
only thing I dont suspect the crew of the Red ship (with her
Red Star of the blood of the Russias on the stack) is of starting
the tempest that almost done us in and folded us over the olive
of the sea, that was how bad it was in fact then I began to have
reverse paranoiac reveries that they themselves were holding
conclaves in the sea sway lantern foc'sle saying "That capitalist
scum American on board is a Jonah, the storm has come

because of him, throw him over" so I lie there on my bunk
rolling violently from side to side dreaming of how it will be
with me thrun in that ocean out there (with her 80 mile an
hour sprays coming off the top of waves high enough to
swamp the Bank of America) how the whale if it can get to me
before I drown upsidedown will indeed swallow me and leave
me in its groomus dick interior to go salt me off its tip tongue
on some (O God amighty) on some cross shore in the last
curlylock forbidden unknown sea shore, I'll be laying on the
beach Jonah with my vision of the ribs—in real life tho all it is,
the sailors werent particularly worried by the immense seas, to
them just another boorapoosh, to them just only what they
call "Veoory bod weather" and in the diningroom there I am
every evening alone at a long white table cloth with the Russian spy woman, facing her dead center, a Continental seating
arrangement that prevents me from relaxing in my chair and
staring into space as I eat or wait for the next course, it's tuna
fish and olive oil and olives for breakfast, it's salted fish for
breakfast, what I wouldnt have given for some peanut butter
and milkshakes I cant say.—I canna say the Scotch neer invented seas like that to put the mouse scare in the hem haw
roll plan—but the pearl of the water, the swiggin whirl, the
very glisten-remembered white cap flick in high winds, the Vision of God I had as being all and the same myself, the ship,
the others, the dreary kitchen, the dreary slob kitchen of the
sea with her swaying pots in the gray gloom as tho the pots
know they're about to contain fish stew in the serious kitchen
below the kitchen of the serious sea, the swaying and clank
clank, O that old ship tho with all her long hull which at first
in Brooklyn dock I'd secretly thought "My God it is too
long," now is not long enough to stay still in the immense
playfulnesses of God, plowing on, plowing on and shuddering
all iron—and too after I'd thought "Why do they have to
spend a whole day here in gastank majoun town" (in New Jersey, what's the name, Perth Amboy) with a big black sinister I
must say hose bent in over from the gas dock pumping in and
pumping in quietly all that whole Sunday, with lowering winter skies all orange flare crazy and nobody on the long empty
pier when I go out to walk after the olive oil supper but one
guy, my last American, walking by looking at me a little fishy

thinking I'm a member of the Red crew, pumping in all day filling those immense fuel tanks of the old *Slovenia* but once we're at sea in that God storm I'm so glad and groan to think we did spend all day loading fuel, how awful it would have been to run out of fuel in the middle of that storm and just bob there helpless turning this way and that.—To escape the storm on that Wednesday morning for instance the captain simply turned his back to it, he could never take it from the side, only front or back, the roll-in biggies, and when he did make his turn about 8 A.M. I thought we were going to founder for sure, the whole ship with that unmistakable wrack snap went swiftly to the one side, with elastic bounce you could feel she was coming back the other way all the way, the waves from boorapoosh helped, hanging on to my porthole and looking out (not cold but spray in my face) here we go pitching over again into an upcoming sea rise and I'm looking face to face with a vertical wall of sea, the ship jerks, the keel holds, the long keel underneath that's now a little fish flapper after in the dock I'd thought "How deep these pier slips have to be hold in those long keels so they wont scrape bottom."—Over we go, the waves wash onto the deck, my porthole and face is splashed completely, the water spills into my bed, (O my bed the sea) and over again the other way, then a steady as she goes as the captain gets the *Slovenia* around with her back to the storm and we flee south.—Soon enough I thought we'd be deep with inward stare in an endless womb bliss, drowned —in the grinning sea that restores impossibly.—O snowy arms of God, I saw His arms there on the side of the Jacob's Ladder place where, if we had to disembark and go over (as tho life-boats would do anything but crash like splinter against the shipside in that madness) the white personal Face of God telling me "Ti Jean, dont worry, if I take you today, and all the other poor devils on this tub, it's because nothing ever happened except Me, everything is Me—" or as Lankavatara Scripture says, "There's nothing in the world but Mind itself" ("There's nothing in the world but the Golden Eternity of God's mind," I say)—I saw the words EVERYTHING IS GOD, NOTHING EVER HAPPENED EXCEPT GOD writ in milk on that sea dip—bless you, an endless train into an endless graveyard is all this life is, but it was never anything but

God, nothing else but that—so the higher the monstrous sinker comes fooling and calling me down names the more I shall joy old Rembrandt with my bear cup and wrassle all the Tolstoy kidders in this side of fingertwick, pluck as you will, and Afric we'll reach, and did reach anyway, and if I learned a lesson it was lesson in WHITE—radiate all you will sweet darkness and bring ghosts and angels and so we'll put-put right along to the tree shore, the rocky shore, the final swan salt, O Ezekiel for came that afternoon so sweet and calm and Mediterranean-like when we began to see land, twasnt till I saw the keen little grin on the captain's face as he gazed through his binoculars I really believed it, but finally I could see it myself, Africa, I could see the cuts in the mountains, the dry arroyo rills before I could see the mountains themselves and finally did see them, pale green gold, not knowing till about 5 they were really the mountains of Spain, old Hercules was somewhere up there ahead holding up the world on his shoulders thus the hush and glassy silence of these entry waters to Hesperid.—Sweet Mary star ahead, and all the rest, and further on too I could see Paris, my big kleig light vision Paris where I'd go get off a train at outside town Peuples du Pais, and walk 5 miles deeper and deeper as in a dream into the city of Paris itself arriving finally at some golden center of it I envisioned then, which was silly, as it turned out, as tho Paris had a center.—Faint little white dots at the foot of the long green Africa mountain and yessiree that was the sleepy little Arab city of Tangier waiting for me to explore it that night so I go down into my stateroom and keep checking my rucksack to see it's well packed and ready for me to swing down the gangplank with and get my passport stamped with Arabic figures "Oieieh eiieh ekkei."—Meanwhile a lot of trade going by, boats, several beat Spanish freighters you couldnt believe so beat, bleak, small, that have to face boorapooshes with nothing but half our length and half our girth and over there the long stretches of sand on the shore of Spain indicative of dryer Cadizes that I had dreamed yet I still insisted on dreaming of the Spanish cape, the Spanish star, the Spanish gutter song.—And finally one amazing little Moroccan fishingboat putting out to sea with a small crew of about five, in sloppy Catch-Mohammed pants some of them (balloony pantaloons they wear in case they give birth to Mohammed) and some with red fezzes but red fezzes like you never thought they'd be real fezzes with wow grease and creases and dust on them, real red fezzes of real life in real Africa the wind blowing and the little fishing sloop with its incredible high poop made of Lebanon wood—putting out to the curlylock song of the sea, the stars all night, the nets, the twang of Ramadan . . .

Of course world travel isn't as good as it seems, it's only after you've come back from all the heat and horror that you forget to get bugged and remember the weird scenes you saw.—In Morocco I went for a walk one beautiful cool sunny afternoon (with breeze from Gibraltar) and my friend and I walked to the outskirts of the weird Arab town commenting on the architecture, the furniture, the people, the sky which he said would look green at nightfall and the quality of the food in the various restaurants around town, adding, he did, "Besides I'm just a hidden agent from another planet and the trouble is I dont know why they sent me, I've forgotten the goddam message dearies" so I says "I'm a messenger from heaven too" and suddenly we saw a herd of goats coming down the road and behind it an Arab shepherd boy of ten who held a little baby lamb in his arms and behind him came the mother lamb bleating and baa haa ing for him to take real good extryspecial care of the babe, which the boy said "Egraya fa y kapata kata-patafataya" and spat it out of his throat in the way Semites speak.—I said "Look, a real shepherd boy carrying a baby lamb!" and Bill said "O well, the little prigs are always rushing around carrying lambs." Then we walked down the hill to a place where a holy man or that is, a devout Mohammedan, kneeled praying to the setting sun towards Mecca and Bill turned to me and said: "Wouldnt it be wonderful if we were real American tourists and I suddenly rushed up with a camera to snap his picture?" . . . then added: "By the way, how do we walk around him?"

"Around his right," I said anyway.

We wended our way homeward to the chatty outdoor cafe where all the people gathered at nightfall beneath screaming trees of birds, near the Zoco Grande, and decided to follow the railroad track. It was hot but the breeze was cool from the

Mediterranean. We came to an old Arab hobo sitting on the rail of the track recounting the Koran to a bunch of raggedy children listening attentively or at least obediently. Behind them was their mother's house, a tin hut, there she was in white hanging white and blue and pink wash in front of a pale blue tin hovel in the bright African sun.—I didnt know what the holy man was doing, I said "He's an idiot of some kind?"— "No," says Bill, "he's a wandering Sherifian pilgrim preaching the gospel of Allah to the children—he's a *hombre que rison*, a man who prays, they got some *hombres que rison* in town that wear white robes and go around barefoot in the alleys and dont let no bluejeaned hoodlums start a fight on the street, he just walks up and stares at them and they scat. Besides, the people of Tangiers aint like the people of West Side New York, when there's a fight starts in the street among the Arab hoods all the men rush up out of mint tea shops and beat the shit out of them. They aint got men in America any more, they just sit there and eat pizzas before the late show, my dear." This man was William Seward Burroughs, the writer, and we were heading now down the narrow alleys of the Medina (the "Casbah" is only the Fort part of town) to a little bar and restaurant where all the Americans and exiles went. I wanted to tell somebody about the shepherd boy, the holy man and the man on the tracks but no one was interested. The big fat Dutch owner of the bar said "I cant find a good poy in this town" (saying "poy," not boy, but meaning boy).—Burroughs doubled up in laughter.

We went from there to the late afternoon cafe where sat all the decayed aristocrats of America and Europe and a few eager enlightened healthy Arabs or near-Arabs or diplomats or whatever they were.—I said to Bill: "Where do I get a woman in this town?"

He said: "There's a few whores that hang around, you have to know a cabdriver or something, or better than that there's a cat here in town, from Frisco, Jim, he'll show you what corner and what to do" so that night me and Jim the painter go out and stand on the corner and sure enough here come two veiled women, with delicate cotton veil over their mouths and half-way up their noses, just their dark eyes you see, and wearing long flowing robes and you see their shoes cuttin through the robes and Jim hailed a cab which was waiting there and off we went to the pad which was a patio affair (mine) with tile patio overlooking the sea and a Sherifian beacon that turned on and turned on, around and around, flashing in my window every now and again, as, alone with one of the mysterious shrouds, I watched her flip off the shroud and veil and saw standing there a perfect little Mexican (or that is to say Arab) beauty perfect and brown as ye old October grapes and maybe like the wood of Ebon and turned to me with her lips parted in curious "Well what are you doing standing there?" so I lighted a candle on my desk. When she left she went downstairs with me where some of my connections from England and Morocco and U.S.A. were all blasting home made pipes of Opium and singing Cab Calloway's old tune, "I'm gonna kick the gong around."—On the street she was very polite when she got into the cab.

From there I went to Paris later, where nothing much happened except the most beautiful girl in the world who didnt like my rucksack on my back and had a date anyway with a guy with a small mustache who stands hand in sidepocket with a sneer in the nightclub movies of Paris.

Wow—and in London what do I see but a beautiful, a heavenly beautiful blonde standing against a wall in Soho calling out to welldressed men. Lots of makeup, with blue eye shadow, the most beautiful women in the world are definitely English . . . unless like me you like em dark.

But there was more to Morocco than walks with Burroughs and whores in my room, I took long hikes by myself, sipped Cinzano at sidewalk cafes *solitaire*, sat on the beach . . .

There was a railroad track on the beach that brought the train from Casablanca—I used to sit in the sand watching the weird Arab brakemen and their funny little CFM Railroad (Central Ferrocarril Morocco).—The cars had thin spoked wheels, just bumpers instead of couplings, double cylindrical bumpers each side, and the cars were tied on by means of a simple chain.—The tagman signalled with ordinary stophand and go-ahead goose and had a thin piercing whistle and screamed in Arabic spitting-from-the-throat to the rear man. —The cars had no handbrakes and no rung ladders.—Weird

Arab bums sat in coal hoppers being switched up and down the sandy seashore, expecting to go to Tetuan . . .

One brakeman wore a fez and balloon pantaloons—I could just picture the dispatcher in a full Jalaba robe sitting with his pipe of hasheesh by the phone.—But they had a good Diesel switch engine with a fezzed hoghead inside at the throttle and a sign on the side of the engine that said DANGER A MORT (danger unto death).—Instead of handbrakes they ran rushing in flowing robes and released a horizontal bar that braked the wheels with brake shoes—it was insane—they were miraculous railroad men.—The tagman ran yelling "Thea! Thea! Mohammed! Thea!"—Mohammed was the head man, he stood up at the far end of the sand gazing sadly.—Meanwhile veiled Arab women in long Jesus robes walked around picking up bits of coal by the tracks—for the night's fish, the night's heat.—But the sand, the rails, the grass, was as universal as old Southern Pacific. . . . White robes by the blue sea railroad bird sand . . .

I had a very nice room as I say on the roof, with a patio, the stars at night, the sea, the silence, the French landlady, the Chinese housekeeper—the six foot seven Hollander pederast who lived next door and brought Arab boys up every night.— Nobody bothered me.

The ferry boat from Tangier to Algeciras was very sad because it was all lit up so gayly for the terrible business of going to the other shore.—

In the Medina I found a hidden Spanish restaurant serving the following menu for 35 cents: one glass red wine, shrimp soup with little noodles, pork with red tomato sauce, bread, one egg fried, one orange on a saucer and one black espresso coffee: I swear on my arm.—

For the business of writing and sleeping and thinking I went to the local cool drugstore and bought Sympatina for excitement, Diosan for the codeine dream, and Soneryl for sleep.— Meanwhile Burroughs and I also got some opium from a guy in a red fez in the Zoco Chico and made some home made pipes with old olive oil cans and smoked singing "Willie the Moocher" and the next day mixed hash and kif with honey and spices and made big "Majoun" cakes and ate them, chewing, with hot tea, and went on long prophetic walks to the fields of little white flowers.—One afternoon high on hasheesh I meditated on my sun roof thinking "All things that move are God, and all things that dont move are God" and at this re-utterance of the ancient secret all things that moved and made noise in the Tangier afternoon seemed to suddenly rejoice, and all things that didnt move seemed pleased . . .

Tangier is a charming, cool, nice city, full of marvelous Continental restaurants like *El Paname* and *L'Escargo* with mouth-watering cuisine, sweet sleeps, sunshine, and galleries of holy Catholic priests near where I lived who prayed to the seaward every evening.—Let there be orisons everywhere!—

Meanwhile mad genius Burroughs sat typing wildhaired in his garden apartment the following words:—"Motel Motel Motel loneliness moans across the continent like fog over still oily water tidal rivers . . ." (meaning America.) (America's always rememberable in exile.)

On Moroccan Independence Day my big 50-year-old sexy Arab Negress maid cleaned my room and folded my filthy un-washed T-shirt neatly on a chair . . .

And yet sometimes Tangier was unutterably dull, no vibrations, so I'd walk two miles along the beach among the ancient rhythmic fishermen who hauled nets in singing gangs with some ancient song along the surf, leaving the fish slopping in sea-eye sand, and sometimes I'd watch the terrific soccer games being played by mad Arab boys in the sand some of them throwing in scores with backward tosses of their heads to applause of galleries of children.—

And I'd walk the Maghreb Land of huts which is as lovely as the land of old Mexico with all those green hills, burros, old trees, gardens.—

One afternoon I sat in a riverbottom that fed into the sea and watched the high tide swelling in higher than my head and a sudden rainstorm got me to running back along the beach to town like a trotting track star, soaked, then suddenly on the boulevard of cafes and hotels the sun came out and illuminated the wet palm trees and it gave me an old feeling—I had that old feeling—I thought of everybody.

Weird town. I sat in the Zoco Chico at a cafe table watching the types go by: A weird Sunday in Fellaheen Arabland with you'd expect mystery white windows and ladies throwing daggers and do see but by God the woman up there I saw in a white veil sitting and peering by a Red Cross above a little sign that said:—"Practicantes, Sanio Permanente, TF No. ⚎ 9766" the cross being red—right over a tobacco shop with luggage and pictures, where a little barelegged boy leaned on a counter with a family of wristwatched Spaniards.—Meanwhile English sailors from the submarines passed trying to get drunker and drunker on Malaga yet quiet and lost in home regret.—Two little Arab hepcats had a brief musical confab (boys of ten) and then parted with a push of arms and wheeling of arms, one boy had a yellow skullcap and a blue zoot suit.—The black and white tiles of the outdoor cafe where I sat were soiled by lonely Tangier time—a little baldcropped boy walked by, went to a man at a table near me, said "Yo" and the waiter rushed up and scatted him off shouting "Yig."—A brown ragged robe priest sat with me at a table (an *hombre que rison*) but looked off with hands on lap at brilliant red fez and red girl sweater and red boy shirt green scene . . . Dreaming of Sufi . . .

Oh the poems that a Catholic will get in an Islam Land:— "Holy Sherifian Mother blinking by the black sea . . . did you save the Phoenecians drowning three thousand years ago? . . . O soft queen of the midnight horses. . . . bless the Marocaine rough lands!" . . .

For they were suren hell rough lands and I found out one day by climbing way up into the back hills.—First I went down the coast, in the sand, where the seagulls all together in a group by the sea were like having a refection at table, a shiny table—at first I thought they were praying—the head gull said grace.—Sitting in the sea side sand I wondered if the microscopic red bugs in it ever met and mated.—I tried to count a pinch of sand knowing there are as many worlds as the sands in all the oceans.—O honored of the worlds! for just then an old robed Bodhisattva, an old robed bearded realizer of the greatness of wisdom came walking by with a staff and a shapeless skin bag and a cotton pack and a basket on his back, with white cloth around his hoary brown brow.—I saw him coming from miles away down the beach—the shrouded Arab by the sea.—We didnt even nod to each other—it was too much, we'd known each other too long ago—

After that I climbed inland and reached a mountain over-

looking all Tangier Bay and came to a quiet shepherd slope, ah
the honk of asses and maaaa of sheep up there rejoicing in
Vales, and the silly happy trills of crazybirds goofing in the solitude of rocks and brush swept by sun heat swept by sea wind,
and all the warm ululations shimmering.—Quiet brush-and-
twig huts looking like Upper Nepal.—Fierce looking Arab
shepherds went by scowling at me, dark, bearded, robed, bare
knee'd.—To the South were the distant African mountains.—
Below me on the steep slope where I sat were quiet powder
blue villages.—Crickets, sea roar.—Peaceful mountain Berber
Villages or farm settlements, women with huge bundles of
twigs on their backs going down the hill—little girls among
browsing bulls.—Dry arroyos in the fat green meadowland.—
And the Carthaginians have disappeared?

When I went down back to the beach in front of Tangier
White City it was night and I looked at the hill where I lived all
besparkled, and thought, "And I live up there full of imaginary
conceptions?"

The Arabs were having their Saturday night parade with
bagpipes, drums and trumpets: it put me in the mind of a
Haiku:—

> Walking along the night beach
> —Military music
> On the boulevard.

Suddenly one night in Tangier where as I say I'd been somewhat bored, a lovely flute began to blow around three o'clock
in the morning, and muffled drums beat somewhere in the
depths of the Medina.—I could hear the sounds from my sea-
facing room in the Spanish quarter, but when I went out on
my tiled terrace there was nothing there but a sleeping Spanish
dog.—The sounds came from blocks away, toward the markets,
under the Mohammedan stars.—It was the beginning of Ramadan, the month-long fast. How sad: because Mohammed
had fasted from sunrise to sundown, a whole world would too
because of belief under these stars.—Out on the other crook
of the bay the beacon turned and sent its shaft into my terrace
(twenty dollars a month), swung around and swept the Berber
hills where weirder flutes and stranger deeper drums were

blowing, and out into the mouth of the Hesperides in the soft-ing dark that leads to the dawn off the coast of Africa.—I sud-denly felt sorry that I had already bought my boat ticket to Marseille and was leaving Tangier.

If you ever take the packet from Tangier to Marseille never go fourth-class.—I thought I was such a clever world-weary traveler and saving five dollars, but when I got on the packet the following morning at 7 A.M. (a great blue shapeless hulk that had looked so romantic to me steaming around the little Tangier jetty from down-the-coast Casablanca) I was instantly told to wait with a gang of Arabs and then after a half hour herded down into the fo'c'sle—a French Army barracks. All the bunks were occupied so I had to sit on the deck and wait another hour. After a few desultory explorations among the stewards I was told that I had not been assigned a bunk and that no arrangements had been made to feed me or anything. I was practically a stowaway. Finally I saw a bunk no one seemed to be using and appropriated it, angrily asking the sol-dier nearby, "*Ill y a quelqu'un ici?*" He didn't even bother to answer, just gave me a shrug, not necessarily a Gallic shrug but a great world-weary life-weary shrug of Europe in general. I was suddenly sorry I was leaving the rather listless but earnest sincerity of the Arab world.

The silly tub took off across the Strait of Gibraltar and im-mediately began to pitch furiously in the long ground swells, probably the worst in the world, that take place off the rock bottom of Spain.—It was almost noon by now.—After a short meditation on the burlap-covered bunk I went out to the deck where the soldiers were scheduled to line up with their ration plates, and already half the French Army had regurgitated on the deck and it was impossible to walk across it without slipping.—Meanwhile I noticed that even the third-class pas-sengers had dinner set out for them in their dining room and that they had rooms and service.—I went back to my bunk and pulled out my old camp pack equipment, and aluminum pot and cup and spoon from my rucksack, and waited.—The Arabs were still sitting on the floor.—The big fat German chief steward, looking like a Prussian bodyguard, came in and an-nounced to the French troops fresh from duty on the hot bor-ders of Algeria to snap to it and do a cleaning job.—They stared at him silently and he went away with his retinue of ratty stewards.

At noon everybody began to stir about and even sing.—I saw the soldiers straggling forward with their pans and spoons and followed them, then advanced with the line to a dirty kitchen pot full of plain boiled beans which were slopped into my pot after a desultory glance from the scullion who wandered why my pot looked a little different.—But to make the meal a success I went to the bakery in the bow and gave the fat baker, a Frenchman with a mustache, a tip, and he gave me a beautiful oven-fresh little loaf of bread and with this I sat on a coil of rope on the bow hatch and ate in the clean winds and actually enjoyed the meal.—Off to the portside Gibraltar rock was already receding, the waters were getting calmer, and soon it would be lazy afternoon with the ship well into the route toward Sardinia and southern France.—And suddenly (as I had had such long daydreams about this trip, all ruined now, of a beautiful glittering voyage on a magnificent "packet" with red wine in thin-stemmed glasses and jolly Frenchmen and blondes) a little hint of what I was looking for in France (to which I'd never been) came over the public-address system: a song called *Mademoiselle de Paris* and all the French soldiers on the bow with me sitting protected against the wind behind bulkheads and housings suddenly got romantic-looking and began to talk heatedly about their girls at home and everything suddenly seemed to point to Paris at last.

I resolved to walk from Marseille up on Route N8 toward Aix-en-Provence and then start hitchhiking. I never dreamed that Marseille was such a big town. After getting my passport stamped I strode across the rail yards, pack on back. The first European I greeted on his home soil was an old handlebar-mustached Frenchman who crossed the tracks with me, but he did not return my happy greeting, "*Allo l'Père!*"—But that was all right, the very cobbles and trolley tracks were paradise for me, the ungraspable springtime France at last. I walked along, among those 18th Century smokepot tenements spouting coal smoke, passing a huge garbage wagon with a great work horse and the driver in a beret and striped polo shirt.—An old 1929 Ford suddenly rattled by toward the water front containing four bereted toughs with butts in mouth like characters in some forgotten French movie of my mind.—I went to a kind of bar that was open early Sunday morning where I sat at a table and drank hot coffee served by a dame in her bathrobe, though no pastries—but I got them across the street in the *boulangerie* smelling of crisp fresh Napoleons and *croissants*, and ate heartily while reading *Paris Soir* and with the music on the radio already announcing news of my eagered-for Paris— sitting there with inexplicable tugging memories as though I'd been born before and lived before in this town, been brothers with someone, and bare trees fuzzing green for spring as I looked out of the window.—How old my old life in France, my long old Frenchness, seemed—all those names of the shops, *épicerie*, *boucherie*, the early-morning little stores like those of my French-Canadian home, like Lowell Massachusetts on a Sunday.—*Quel différence?* I was very happy suddenly.

My plan, seeing the largeness of the city, was to take a bus to Aix and the road north to Avignon and Lyon and Dijon and Sens and Paris, and I figured that tonight I would sleep in the grass of Provence in my sleeping bag, but it turned out different. —The bus was marvelous, it was just a local bus and went climbing out of Marseille through tiny communities where you'd see little French fathers puttering in neat gardens as their children came in the front door with long loaves of bread for breakfast, and the characters that got on and off the bus were so familiar I wished my folks had been there to see them, hear them say, "*Bonjour, Madame Dubois. Vous avez été à la Messe?*" It didnt take long to get to Aix-en-Provence where I sat at a sidewalk café over a couple of vermouths and watched Cézanne's trees and the gay French Sunday: a man going by with pastries and two-yard-long breads and sprinkled around the horizon the dull-red rooftops and distant blue-haze hills attesting to Cézanne's perfect reproduction of the Provençal color, a red he used even in still-life apples, a brown red, and backgrounds of dark smokeblue.—I thought "The gaiety, the sensibleness of France is so good after the moroseness of the Arabs."

After the vermouths I went to the Cathedral of St. Sauveur, which was just a shortcut to the highway, and there passing an old man with white hair and beret (and all around on the horizon Cezanne's springtime "green" which I had forgotten went with his smokyblue hills and rust-red roof) I cried.—I cried in the Cathedral of the Savior to hear the choir boys sing a gorgeous old thing, while angels seemed to be hovering around— I couldn't help myself—I hid behind a pillar from the occasional inquiring eyes of French families on my huge rucksack (eighty pounds) and wiped my eyes, crying even at the sight of the 6th Century Baptistery—all old Romanesque stones with the hole in the ground still, where so many other infants had been baptized all with eyes of lucid liquid diamond understanding.

I left the church and headed for the road, walked about a mile, disdaining to hitchhike at first, and finally sat by the side of the road on a grassy hill overlooking a pure Cézanne landscape— little farm roofs and trees and distant blue hills with the suggestions of the type of cliff that is more predominant northward toward Van Gogh's country at Arles.—The highway was full of small cars with no room or cyclists with their hair blowing.—I trudged and thumbed hopelessly for five miles, then gave it up at Eguilles, the first bus stop on the highway, there was no hitchhiking in France I could see.—At a rather expensive café in Eguilles, with French families dining in the open patio, I had coffee and then knowing the bus would come in about an hour, went strolling down a country dirt road to examine the inner view of Cézanne's country and found a mauve-tan farmhouse in a quiet fertile rich valley—rustic, with weathered pink-powder roof tiles, a gray-green mild warmness, voices of girls, gray stacks of baled hay, a fertilized chalky garden, a cherry tree in white bloom, a rooster crowing at midday mildly, tall "Cézanne" trees in back, apple trees, pussywillows in the meadow in the clover, an orchard, an old blue wagon under the barn port, a pile of wood, a dry white-twig fence near the kitchen.

Then the bus came and we went through the Arles country and now I saw the restless afternoon trees of Van Gogh in the high mistral wind, the cypress rows tossing, yellow tulips in window boxes, a vast outdoor café with huge awning, and the gold sunlight.—I saw, understood, Van Gogh, the bleak cliffs beyond. . . . At Avignon I got off to transfer to the Paris Express. I bought my ticket to Paris but had hours to wait and wandered down in late afternoon along the main drag— thousands of people in Sunday best on their dreary interminable provincial stroll.

I strolled into a museum full of stone carvings from the days of Pope Benedict XIII, including one splendid woodcarving showing the Last Supper with bunched Apostles grieving head-to-head, Christ in the middle, hand up, and suddenly one of the bunched heads in deeper-in relief is staring right at you and it is Judas!—Farther down the aisle one pre-Roman, apparently Celtic monster, all old carved stone.—And then out in the cobblestoned back-alley of Avignon (city of dust), alleys dirtier than Mexico slums (like New England streets near the dump in the Thirties), with women's shoes in gutters running with medieval slop water, and all along the stone wall raggedy children playing in forlorn swirls of mistral dust, enough to make Van Gogh weep.—

And the famous much-sung bridge of Avignon, stone, half-gone now in the spring-rushing Rhône, with medieval-walled castles on the horizon hills (for tourists now, once the baronial castle-supporter of the town).—Sort of juvenile delinquents lurking in the Sunday afternoon dust by the Avignon wall smoking forbidden butts, girls of thirteen smirking in high heels, and down the street a little child playing in the watery gutter with the skeleton of a doll, bonging on his upturned tub for a beat.—And old cathedrals in the alleys of town, old churches now just crumbling relics.

Nowhere in the world is as dismal as Sunday afternoon with the mistral wind blowing in the cobbled back streets of poor old Avignon. When I sat in a café in the main street reading the papers, I understood the complaint of French poets about provincialism, the dreary provincialism that drove Flaubert and Rimbaud mad and made Balzac muse.

Not one beautiful girl to be seen in Avignon except in that café, and she a sensational slender rose in dark glasses confiding love affairs to her girl friend at the table next to mine, and outside the multitudes roamed up and down, up and down, back and forth, nowhere to go, nothing to do—Madame Bovary is wringing her hands in despair behind lace curtains,

Genêt's heroes are waiting for the night, the De Musset youth is buying a ticket for the train to Paris.—What can you do in Avignon on a Sunday afternoon? Sit in a café and read about the comeback of a local clown, sip your vermouth, and meditate the carved stone in the museum.

But I did have one of the best five-course meals in all Europe in what appeared to be a "cheap" sidestreet restaurant: good vegetable soup, an exquisite omelet, broiled hare, wonderful mashed potatoes (mashed through a strainer with lots of butter), a half bottle of red wine and bread and then a delicious flan with syrup, all for supposedly ninety-five cents, but the waitress raised the price from 380 francs to 575 as I ate and I didn't bother to contest the bill.

In the railroad station I stuck fifty francs into the gum machine, which didnt give, and all the officials most flagrantly passed the buck (*"Demandez au contrôleur!"*) and (*"Le contrôleur ne s'occupe pas de ça!"*) and I became somewhat discouraged by the dishonesty of France, which I'd noticed at once on that hellship packet especially after the honest religiousness of the Moslems.—Now a train stopped, southbound to Marseille, and an old woman in black lace stepped out and walked along and soon dropped one of her black leather gloves and a well-dressed Frenchman rushed up and picked up the glove and dutifully laid it on a post so that I had to grab the glove and run after her and give it to her.—I knew then why it is the French who perfected the guillotine—not the English, not the Germans, not the Danes, not the Italians and not the Indians, but the French my own people.

To cap it all, when the train came there were absolutely no seats and I had to ride all night in the cold vestibule.—When I got sleepy I had to flatten my rucksack on the cold-iron vestibule doors and I lay there curled, legs up, as we rushed through the unseen Provences and Burgundys of the gnashing French map.—Six thousand francs for this great privilege.

Ah but in the morning, the suburbs of Paris, the dawn spreading over the moody Seine (like a little canal), the boats on the river, the outer industrial smokes of the city, then the Gare de Lyon and when I stepped out on Boulevard Diderot I thought seeing one glimpse of long boulevards leading every direction with great eight-story ornate apartments with monarchial façades, "Yes, they made themselves a *city*!"—Then crossing Boulevard Diderot to have coffee, good *expresso* coffee and *croissants* in a big city place full of workingmen, and through the glass I could see women in full long dresses rushing to work on motorbikes, and men with silly crash helmets (*La Sporting France*), taxis, broad old cobblestoned streets, and that nameless city smell of coffee, antiseptics and wine.

Walking, thence, in a cold brisk-red morning, over the Austerlitz Bridge, past the Zoo on the Quai St.-Bernard where one little old deer stood in the morning dew, then past the Sorbonne, and my first sight of Notre Dame strange as a lost dream.—And when I saw a big rimed woman statue on Boulevard St.-Germain I remembered my dream that I was once a French schoolboy in Paris.—I stopped at a café, ordered Cinzano, and realized the racket of going-to-work was the same here as in Houston or in Boston and no better—but I felt a vast promise, endless streets, streets, girls, places, meanings, and I could understand why Americans stayed here, some for lifetimes.—And the first man in Paris I had looked at in the Gare de Lyon was a dignified Negro in a Homburg.

What endless human types passed my café table: old French ladies, Malay girls, schoolboys, blond boys going to college, tall young brunettes headed for the law classes, hippy pimply secretaries, bereted goggled clerks, bereted scarved carriers of milk bottles, dikes in long blue laboratory coats, frowning older students striding in trench coats like in Boston, seedy little cops (in blue caps) fishing through their pockets, cute ponytailed blondes in high heels with zip notebooks, goggled bicyclists with motors attached to the rear of their cycles, bespectacled Homburgs walking around reading *Le Parisien* and breathing mist, bushyheaded mulattoes with long cigarettes in their mouths, old ladies carrying milk cans and shopping bags, rummy W. C. Fieldses spitting in the gutter and with hands-a-pockets going to their shops for another day, a young Chinese-looking French girl of twelve with separated teeth almost in tears (frowning, and with a bruise on her shin, schoolbooks in hand, cute and serious like Negro girls in Greenwich Village), porkpie executive running and catching his bus sensationally and vanishing with it, mustachioed longhaired Italian youths coming in the bar for their morning shot of wine, huge bumbling bankers of the Bourse in expensive suits fishing for newspaper pennies in their palms (bumping into women at the bus stop), serious thinkers with pipes and packages, a lovely redhead with dark glasses trotting pip pip on her heels to the bus, and a waitress slopping mop water in the gutter.—

Ravishing brunettes with tight-fitting skirts. Schoolgirlies with long boyish bobs plirping lips over book and memorizing lessons fidgetly (waiting to meet young Marcel Proust in the park after school), lovely young girls of seventeen walking with low-heeled sure strides in long red coats to downtown Paris.— An apparent East Indian, whistling, leading a dog on a leash. —Serious young lovers, boy arming girl's shoulders.—Statue of Danton pointing nowhere, Paris hepcat in dark glasses faintly mustached waiting there.—Little suited boy in black beret, with well-off father going to morning joys.

The next day I strolled down Boulevard St.-Germain in a spring wind, turned in at the church of St.-Thomas-d'Aquin and saw a huge gloomy painting on the wall showing a warrior, fallen off his horse, being stabbed in the heart by an enemy, at whom he looked directly with sad understanding Gallic eyes and one hand outheld as if to say, "It's my life" (it had that Delacroix horror). I meditated on this painting in the bright colorful Champs-Élysées and watched the multitudes go by. Glum I walked past a movie house advertising *War and Peace*, where two Russian-sabered sablecaped grenadiers chatted amiably and in French come-on with two American women tourists.

Long walks down the boulevards with a flask of cognac.— Each night a different room, each day four hours to find a room, on foot with full pack.—In the skid-row sections of Paris numerous frowsy dames said "*complet*" coldly when I asked for unheated cockroach rooms in the gray Paris gloom. —I walked and hurried angrily bumping people along the Seine.—In little cafés I had compensatory steaks and wine, chewing slowly.

Noon, a café near Les Halles, onion soup, *pâté de maison* and bread, for a quarter.—Afternoon, the girls in fur coats along Boulevard St.-Denis, perfumed.—"*Monsieur?*"

"Sure. . . ."

Finally I found a room I could keep for all of three days, a dismal dirty cold hovel hotel run by two Turkish pimps but the kindest fellows I'd met yet in Paris. Here, window open to dreary rains of April, I slept my best sleeps and gathered strength for daily twenty-mile hikes around the Queen of Cities.

But the next day I was suddenly unaccountably happy as I sat in the park in front of Trinité Church near Gare St.-Lazare among children and then went inside and saw a mother praying with a devotion that startled her son.—A moment later I saw a tiny mother with a barelegged little son already as tall as she.

I walked around, it started to sleet on Pigalle, suddenly the sun broke out on Rochechouart and I discovered Montmartre. —Now I knew where I would live if I ever came back to Paris.—Carousels for children, marvelous markets, *hors d'oeuvres* stalls, wine barrel stores, cafés at the foot of the magnificent white Sacré-Coeur basilica, lines of women and children waiting for hot German crullers, new Norman cider inside.—Beautiful girls coming home from parochial school.— A place to get married and raise a family, narrow happy streets full of children carrying long loaves of bread.—For a quarter I bought a huge chunk of Gruyère cheese from a stall, then a huge chunk of jellied meat delicious as crime, then in a bar a quiet glass of port, and then I went to see the church high on the cliff looking down on the rain-wet roofs of Paris.

La Basilique du Sacré-Coeur de Jésus is beauteous, maybe in its way one of the most beautiful of all churches (if you have a rococo soul as I have): blood-red crosses in the stainedglass windows with a westerly sun sending golden shafts against opposite bizarre Byzantine blues representing other sacristies— regular blood baths in the blue sea—and all the poor sad plaques commemorating the building of the church after the sack by Bismarck.

Down the hill in the rain, I went to a magnificent restaurant on Rue de Clignancourt and had that unbeatable French puréed soup and a whole meal with a basket of French bread and my wine and the thin-stemmed glasses I had dreamed about.—Looking across the restaurant at the shy thighs of a newlywed girl having her big honeymoon supper with her

young farmer husband, neither of them saying anything.—
Fifty years of this they'd do now in some provincial kitchen or
dining room.—The sun breaking through again, and with full
belly I wandered among the shooting galleries and carousels of
Montmartre and I saw a young mother hugging her little girlie
with a doll, bouncing her and laughing and hugging her
because they had had so much fun on the hobbyhorse and I
saw Dostoevski's divine love in her eyes (and above on the hill
over Montmartre, He held out His arms).

Feeling wonderful now, I strolled about and cashed a traveler's check at the Gare du Nord and walked all the way, gay
and fine, down Boulevard de Magenta to the huge Place de la
République and on down, cutting sometimes into side streets.
—Night now, down Boulevard du Temple and Avenue Voltaire
(peeking into windows of obscure Breton restaurants) to
Boulevard Beaumarchais where I thought I'd see the gloomy
Bastille prison but I didn't even know it was torn down in 1789
and asked a guy, "*Où est la vieille prison de la Révolution?*" and
he laughed and told me there were a few remnant stones in the
subway station.—Then down in the subway: amazing clean
artistic ads, imagine an ad for wine in America showing a naked
ten-year-old girl with a party hat coiled around a bottle of
wine.—And the amazing map that lights up and shows your
route in colored buttons when you press the destination
button.—Imagine the New York I.R.T. And the clean trains, a
bum on a bench in a clean surrealistic atmosphere (not to be
compared with the 14th Street stop on the Canarsie line).

Paris paddywagons flew by singing *dee* da, *dee* da.—

The next day I strolled examining bookstores and went into
the Benjamin Franklin Library, the site of the old Café Voltaire
(facing the Comédie Française) where everybody from Voltaire to Gauguin to Scott Fitzgerald drank and now the scene
of prim American librarians with no expression.—Then I
strolled to the Pantheon and had delicious pea soup and a
small steak in a fine crowded restaurant full of students and
vegetarian law professors.—Then I sat in a little park in Place
Paul-Painlevé and dreamily watched a curving row of beautiful
rosy tulips rigid and swaying fat shaggy sparrows, beautiful
short-haired *mademoiselles* strolling by. It's not that French
girls are beautiful, it's their cute mouths and the sweet way

they talk French (their mouths pout rosily), the way they've perfected the short haircut and the way they amble slowly when they walk, with great sophistication, and of course their chic way of dressing and undressing.

Paris, a stab in the heart finally.

The Louvre—miles and miles of hiking before great canvases.

In David's immense canvas of Napoleon I and Pius VII I could see little altar boys far in the back fondling a *maréchal*'s sword hilt (the scene is Nôtre-Dame-de-Paris, with the Empress Josephine kneeling pretty as a boulevard girl). Fragonard, so delicate next to Van Dyck, and a big smoky Rubens (*La Mort de Dido*).—But the Rubens got better as I looked, the muscle tones in cream and pink, the rimshot luminous eyes, the dull purple velvet robe on the bed. Rubens was happy because nobody was posing for him for a fee and his gay *Kermesse* showed an old drunk about to be sick.—Goya's *Marquesa do la Solana* could hardly have been more modern, her silver fat shoes pointed like fish crisscrossed, the immense diaphanous pink ribbons over a sisterly pink face.—A typical French woman (not educated) suddenly said, "*Ah, c'est trop beau!*" "It's too beautiful!"

But Brueghel, wow! His *Battle of Arbelles* had at least 600 faces clearly defined in an impossibly confused mad battle leading nowhere.—No wonder Céline loved him.—A complete understanding of world madness, thousands of clearly defined figures with swords and above them the calm mountains, trees on a hill, clouds, and everyone laughed when they saw that insane masterpiece that afternoon, they knew what it meant.

And Rembrandt.—The dim trees in the darkness of crépuscule château with its hints of a Transylvanian vampire castle.— Set side by side with this his *Hanging Beef* was completely modern with its splash of blood paint. Rembrandt's brushstroke swirled in the face of the *Christ at Emmaus*, and the floor in *Sainte Famille* was completely detailed in the color of planks and nails.—Why should anyone paint after Rembrandt, unless Van Gogh? The *Philosopher in Meditation* was my favorite for its Beethoven shadows and light, I liked also *Hermit Reading* with his soft old brow, and *St. Matthew Being*

Inspired by the Angel was a miracle—the rough strokes, and the drip of red paint in the angel's lower lip and the saint's own rough hands ready to write the Gospel . . . ah miraculous too the veil of mistaken angel smoke on Tobias' departing angel's left arm.—What can you do?

Suddenly I walked into the 19th Century room and there was an explosion of light—of bright gold and daylight. Van Gogh, his crazy blue Chinese church with the hurrying woman, the secret of it the Japanese spontaneous brushstroke that, for instance, made the woman's back show, her back all white unpainted canvas except for a few black thick script strokes.— Then the madness of blue running in the roof where Van Gogh had a ball—I could see the joy red mad gladness he rioted in in that church heart.—His maddest picture was gardens with insane trees whirling in the blue swirl sky, one tree finally exploding into just black lines, almost silly but divine— the thick curls and butter burls of color, beautiful oil rusts, glubs, creams, greens.

I studied Degas' ballet pictures—how serious the perfect faces in the orchestra, then suddenly the explosion on the stage—the pink film rose of the ballerina gowns, the puffs of color.—And Cézanne, who painted exactly as he saw, more accurate and less divine than holy Van Gogh—his green apples, his crazy blue lake with acrostics in it, his trick of hiding perspective (one jetty in the lake can do it, and one mountain line). Gauguin—seeing him beside these masters, he seemed to me almost like a clever cartoonist.—Compared to Renoir, too, whose painting of a French afternoon was so gorgeously colored with the Sunday afternoon of all our childhood dreams —pinks, purples, reds, swings, dancers, tables, rosy cheeks and bubble laughter.

On the way out of the bright room, Frans Hals, the gayest of all painters who ever lived. Then one last look at Rembrandt's St. Matthew's angel—its smeared red mouth *moved* when I looked.

April in Paris, sleet in Pigalle, and last moments.—In my skid-row hotel it was cold and still sleeting so I put on my old blue jeans, old muffcap, railroad gloves and zip-up rain jacket, the same clothes I'd worn as a brakeman in the mountains of California and as a forester in the Northwest, and hurried across the Seine to Les Halles for a last supper of fresh bread and onion soup and *pâté*.—Now for delights, walking in the cold dusk of Paris amid vast flower markets, then succumbing to thin crisp *frites* with rich sausage hot dog from a stall on the windswept corner, then into a mobbed mad restaurant full of gay workers and bourgeois where I was temporarily peeved because they forgot to bring me wine too, so gay and red in a clean stemmed glass.—After eating, sauntering on home to pack for London tomorrow, then deciding to buy one final Parisian pastry, intending a Napoleon as usual, but because the girl thought I'd said "Milanais" I accepted her offer and took a bite of my Milanais as I crossed the bridge and bang! the absolutely final greatest of all pastries in the world, for the first time in my life I felt overpowered by a taste sensation, a rich brown mocha cream covered with slivered almonds and just a touch of cake but so pungent that it stole through my nose and taste buds like bourbon or rum with coffee and cream.—I hurried back, bought another and had the second one with a little hot *espresso* in a café across the street from the Sarah Bernhardt Theater—my last delight in Paris savoring the taste and watching Proustian showgoers coming out of the theater to hail cabs.

In the morning, at six, I rose and washed at the sink and the water running in my faucet talked in a kind of Cockney accent.—I hurried out with full pack on back, and in the park a bird I never heard, a Paris warbler by the smoky morning Seine.

I took the train to Dieppe and off we went, through smoky suburbs, through Normandy, through gloomy fields of pure green, little stone cottages, some red brick, some half-timbered, some stone, in a drizzle along the canal-like Seine, colder and colder, through Vernon and little places with names like Vauvay and Something-sur-Cie, to gloomy Rouen, which is a horrible rainy dreary place to have been burned at the stake.—All the time my mind excited with the thought of England by nightfall, London, the fog of real old London.—As usual I was standing in the cold vestibule, no room inside the train, sitting occasionally on my pack crowded in with a gang of shouting Welsh schoolboys and their quiet coach who loaned me the *Daily Mail* to read.—After Rouen the ever-more-gloomy Normandy hedgerows and meadows, then Dieppe with its red rooftops and old quais and cobblestoned streets with bicyclists, the chimney pots smoking, gloom rain, bitter cold in April and I sick of France at last.

The channel boat crowded to the hilt, hundreds of students and scores of beautiful French and English girls with pony tails and short haircuts.—Swiftly we left the French shore and after a spate of blank water we began to see green carpets and meadows stopped abruptly as with a pencil line at chalk cliffs, and it was that sceptered isle, England, springtime in England.

All the students sang in gay gangs and went through to their chartered London coach car but I was made to sit (I was a take-a-seater) because I had been silly enough to admit that I had only fifteen shillings equivalent in my pocket.—I sat next to a West Indies Negro who had no passport at all and was carrying piles of strange old coats and pants—he answered strangely the questions of the officers, looked extremely vague and in fact I remembered he had bumped into me absent-mindedly in the boat on the way over.—Two tall English bobbies in blue were watching him (and myself) suspiciously, with sinister Scotland Yard smiles and strange long-nosed brooding attentiveness like in old Sherlock Holmes movies.—The Negro looked at them terrified. One of his coats dropped on the floor but he didn't bother to pick it up.—A mad gleam had come into the eyes of the immigration officer (young intellectual fop) and now another mad gleam in some detective's eye and suddenly I realized the Negro and I were surrounded.—Out came a huge jolly redheaded customs man to interrogate us.

I told them my story—I was going to London to pick up a royalty check from an English publisher and then on to New York on the *Île de France*.—They didn't believe my story—I wasn't shaved, I had a pack on my back, I looked like a bum.

"What do you *think* I am!" I said and the redheaded man said "That's just it, we don't quite know in the least what you were doing in Morocco, or in France, or arriving in England with fifteen bob." I told them to call my publishers or my agent in London. They called and got no answer—it was Saturday. The bobbies were watching me, stroking their chins.—

The Negro had been taken into the back by now—suddenly I heard a horrible moaning, as of a psychopath in a mental hospital, and I said "What's that?"

"That's your Negro friend."

"What's the matter with him?"

"He has no passport, no money, and is apparently escaped from a mental institution in France. Now do you have any way to verify this story of yours, otherwise we s'll have to detain you."

"In custody?"

"Quite. My dear fellow, you can't come into England with fifteen bob."

"My dear fellow, you can't put an American in jail."

"Oh yes we can, if we have grounds for suspicion."

"Dont you believe I'm a writer?"

"We have no way of knowing this."

"But I'm going to miss my train. It's due to leave any minute."

"My dear fellow . . ." I rifled through my bag and suddenly found a note in a magazine about me and Henry Miller as writers and showed it to the customs man. He beamed:

"Henry Miller? That's most unusual. We stopped *him* several years ago, he wrote quite a bit about Newhaven." (This was a grimmer New Haven than the one in Connecticut with its dawn coalsmokes.) But the customs man was immensely pleased, checked my name again, in the article and on my papers, and said, "Well, I'm afraid it's going to be all smiles and handshakes now. I'm awfully sorry. I think we can let you through—with the provision that you leave England inside a month."

"Don't worry." As the Negro screamed and banged somewhere inside and I felt a horrible sorrow because he had not made it to the other shore, I ran to the train and made it barely in time.—The gay students were all in the front somewhere and I had a whole car to myself, and off we went silently and fast in a fine English train across the countryside of olden Blake lambs.—And I was safe.

English countryside—quiet farms, cows, meads, moors, narrow roads and bicycling farmers waiting at crossings, and ahead, Saturday night in London.

Outskirts of the city in late afternoon like the old dream of sun rays through afternoon trees.—Out at Victoria Station, where some of the students were met by limousines.—Pack on back, excited, I started walking in the gathering dusk down Buckingham Palace Road seeing for the first time long deserted streets. (Paris is a woman but London is an independent man puffing his pipe in a pub.)—Past the Palace, down the Mall through St. James's Park, to the Strand, traffic and fumes and shabby English crowds going out to movies, Trafalgar Square, on to Fleet Street where there was less traffic and dimmer pubs and sad side alleys, almost clear to St. Paul's Cathedral where it got too Johnsonianly sad.—So I turned back, tired, and went into the King Lud pub for a sixpenny Welsh rarebit and a stout.

I called my London agent on the phone, telling him my plight. "My dear fellow it's awfully unfortunate I wasnt in this afternoon. We were visiting mother in Yorkshire. Would a fiver help you?"

"Yes!" So I took a bus to his smart flat at Buckingham Gate (I had walked right past it after getting off the train) and went up to meet the dignified old couple.—He with goatee and fireplace and Scotch to offer me, telling me about his one-hundred-year-old mother reading all of Trevelyan's *English Social History*.—Homburg, gloves, umbrella, all on the table, attesting to his way of living, and myself feeling like an American hero in an old movie.—Far cry from the little kid under a river bridge dreaming of England.—They fed me sandwiches, gave me money, and then I walked around London savoring the fog in Chelsea, the bobbies wandering in the milky mist, thinking, "Who will strangle the bobby in the fog?" The dim lights, the English soldier strolling with one arm around his girl and with the other hand eating fish and chips, the honk of cabs and buses, Piccadilly at midnight and a bunch of Teddy Boys asking me if I knew Gerry Mulligan.—Finally I got a fifteen-bob room in the Mapleton Hotel (in the attic) and had a long divine sleep with the window open, in the morning the carillons blowing all of an hour round eleven and the maid bringing in a tray of toast, butter, marmalade, hot milk and a pot of coffee as I lay there amazed.

And on Good Friday afternoon a heavenly performance of

the *St. Matthew Passion* by the St. Paul's choir, with full orchestra and a special service choir.—I cried most of the time
and saw a vision of an angel in my mother's kitchen and
longed to go home to sweet America again.—And realized
that it didn't matter that we sin, that my father died only of
impatience, that all my own petty gripes didnt matter either.—
Holy Bach spoke to me and in front of me was a magnificent
marble bas-relief showing Christ and three Roman soldiers listening: "And he spake unto them do violence to no man, nor
accuse any falsely, and be content with thy wages." Outside as
I walked in the dusk around Christopher Wren's great masterpiece and saw the gloomy overgrown ruins of Hitler's blitz
around the cathedral, I saw my own mission.

In the British Museum I looked up my family in *Rivista
Araldica*, IV, Page 240, "Lebris de Keroack. Canada, originally from Brittany. Blue on a stripe of gold with three silver
nails. Motto: Love, work and suffer."

I could have known.

At the last moment I discovered the Old Vic while waiting
for my boat train to Southampton,—The performance was
Antony and Cleopatra.—It was a marvelously smooth and
beautiful performance, Cleopatra's words and sobbings more
beautiful than music, Enobarbus noble and strong, Lepidus
wry and funny at the drunken rout on Pompey's boat,
Pompey warlike and harsh, Antony virile, Caesar sinister, and
though the cultured voices criticized the Cleopatra in the
lobby at intermission, I knew that I had seen Shakespeare as it
should be played.

On the train en route to Southampton, brain trees growing
out of Shakespeare's fields, and the dreaming meadows full of
lamb dots.

8.

The Vanishing American Hobo

THE American hobo has a hard time hoboing nowadays
due to the increase in police surveillance of highways, railroad yards, sea shores, river bottoms, embankments and the
thousand-and-one hiding holes of industrial night.—In California, the pack rat, the original old type who goes walking
from town to town with supplies and bedding on his back, the
"Homeless Brother," has practically vanished, along with the
ancient gold-panning desert rat who used to walk with hope in
his heart through struggling Western towns that are now so
prosperous they dont want old bums any more.—"Man dont
want no pack rats here even though they founded California"
said an old man hiding with a can of beans and an Indian fire
in a river bottom outside Riverside California in 1955.—Great
sinister tax-paid police cars (1960 models with humorless
searchlights) are likely to bear down at any moment on the
hobo in his idealistic lope to freedom and the hills of holy silence and holy privacy.—There's nothing nobler than to put up
with a few inconveniences like snakes and dust for the sake of
absolute freedom.

I myself was a hobo but only of sorts, as you see, because I
knew someday my literary efforts would be rewarded by social
protection—I was not a real hobo with no hope ever except
that secret eternal hope you get sleeping in empty boxcars flying up the Salinas Valley in hot January sunshine full of
Golden Eternity toward San Jose where mean-looking old
bo's 'll look at you from surly lips and offer you something to
eat and a drink too—down by the tracks or in the Guadaloupe
Creekbottom.

The original hobo dream was best expressed in a lovely little
poem mentioned by Dwight Goddard in his *Buddhist Bible*:

> *Oh for this one rare occurrence*
> *Gladly would I give ten thousand pieces of gold!*

A hat is on my head, a bundle on my back,
And my staff, the refreshing breeze and the full moon.

In America there has always been (you will notice the peculiarly Whitmanesque tone of this poem, probably written by old Goddard) a definite special idea of footwalking freedom going back to the days of Jim Bridger and Johnny Appleseed and carried on today by a vanishing group of hardy old timers still seen sometimes waiting in a desert highway for a short bus ride into town for panhandling (or work) and grub, or wandering the Eastern part of the country hitting Salvation Armies and moving on from town to town and state to state toward the eventual doom of big-city skid rows when their feet give out.—Nevertheless not long ago in California I did see (deep in the gorge by a railroad track outside San Jose buried in eucalyptus leaves and the blessed oblivion of vines) a bunch of cardboard and jerrybuilt huts at evening in front of one of which sat an aged man puffing his 15¢ Granger tobacco in his corncob pipe. (Japan's mountains are full of free huts and old men who cackle over root brews waiting for Supreme Enlightenment which is only obtainable through occasional complete solitude.)

In America camping is considered a healthy sport for Boy Scouts but a crime for mature men who have made it their vocation.—Poverty is considered a virtue among the monks of civilized nations—in America you spend a night in the calaboose if you're caught short without your vagrancy change (it was fifty cents last I heard of, Pard—what now?)

In Brueghel's time children danced around the hobo, he wore huge and raggy clothes and always looked straight ahead indifferent to the children, and the families didnt mind the children playing with the hobo, it was a natural thing. But today mothers hold tight their children when the hobo passes through town because of what newspapers made the hobo to be—the rapist, the strangler, child-eater.—Stay away from strangers, they'll give you poison candy. Though the Brueghel hobo and the hobo today are the same, the children are different.—Where is even the Chaplinesque hobo? The old Divine Comedy hobo? The hobo is Virgil, he leadeth.—The hobo enters the child's world (like in the famous painting by

Brueghel of a huge hobo solemnly passing through the washtub village being barked at and laughed at by children, St. Pied Piper) but today it's an adult world, it's not a child's world.— Today the hobo's made to slink—everybody's watching the cop heroes on TV.

Benjamin Franklin was like a hobo in Pennsylvania; he walked through Philly with three big rolls under his arms and a Massachussetts halfpenny on his hat.—John Muir was a hobo who went off into the mountains with a pocketful of dried bread, which he soaked in creeks.

Did Whitman terrify the children of Louisiana when he walked the open road?

What about the Black Hobo? Moonshiner? Chicken snatcher? Remus? The black hobo in the South is the last of the Brueghel bums, children pay tribute and stand in awe making no comment. You see him coming out of the piney barren with an old unspeakable sack. Is he carrying coons? Is he carrying Br'er Rabbit? Nobody knows what he's carrying.

The Forty Niner, the ghost of the plains, Old Zacatecan Jack the Walking Saint, the prospector, the spirits and ghosts of hoboism are gone—but they (the prospectors) wanted to fill their unspeakable sacks with gold.—Teddy Roosevelt, political hobo—Vachel Lindsay, troubadour hobo, seedy hobo —how many pies for one of *his* poems? The hobo lives in a Disneyland, Pete-the-Tramp land, where everything is human lions, tin men, moondogs with rubber teeth, orange-and-purple paths, emerald castles in the distance looming, kind philosophers of witches.—No witch ever cooked a hobo.— The hobo has two watches you can't buy in Tiffany's, on one wrist the sun, on the other wrist the moon, both bands are made of sky.

> *Hark! Hark! The dogs do bark,*
> *The beggars are coming to town;*
> *Some in rags, some in tags,*
> *And some in velvet gowns.*

The Jet Age is crucifying the hobo because how can he hop a freight jet? Does Louella Parsons look kindly upon hobos, I wonder? Henry Miller would allow the hobos to swim in his swimming pool.—What about Shirley Temple, to whom the hobo gave the Bluebird? Are the young Temples bluebirdless?

Today the hobo has to hide, he has fewer places to hide, the cops are looking for him, *calling all cars, calling all cars, hobos seen in the vicinity of Bird-in-Hand*—Jean Valjean weighed with his sack of candelabra, screaming to youth, "There's your *sou*, your *sou*!" Beethoven was a hobo who knelt and listened to the light, a deaf hobo who could not hear other hobo complaints.—Einstein the hobo with his ratty turtleneck sweater made of lamb, Bernard Baruch the disillusioned hobo sitting on a park bench with voice-catcher plastic in his ear waiting for John Henry, waiting for somebody very mad, waiting for the Persian epic.—

Sergei Esenin was a great hobo who took advantage of the Russian Revolution to rush around drinking potato juice in the backward villages of Russia (his most famous poem is called *Confessions of a Bum*) who said at the moment they were storming the Czar "Right now I feel like pissing through the window at the moon." It is the egoless hobo that will give birth to a child someday—Li Po was a mighty hobo.—ego is the greatest hobo—Hail Hobo Ego! Whose monument someday will be a golden tin coffee can.

Jesus was a strange hobo who walked on water.—

Buddha was also a hobo who paid no attention to the other hobo.—

Chief Rain-In-The-Face, weirder even.—

W. C. Fields—his red nose explained the meaning of the triple world, Great Vehicle, Lesser Vehicle, Diamond Vehicle.

The hobo is born of pride, having nothing to do with a community but with himself and other hobos and maybe a dog.— Hobos by the railroad embankments cook at night huge tin cans of coffee.—Proud was the way the hobo walked through a town by the back doors where pies were cooling on window sills, the hobo was a mental leper, he didnt need to beg to eat, strong Western bony mothers knew his tinkling beard and tattered toga, *come and get it!* But proud be proud, still there was some annoyance because sometimes when she called *come and get it*, hordes of hobos came, ten or twenty at time, and it was

kind of hard to feed that many, sometimes hobos were incon-
siderate, but not always, but when they were, they no longer
held their pride, they became bums—they migrated to the
Bowery in New York, to Scollay Square in Boston, to Pratt
Street in Baltimore, to Madison Street in Chicago, to 12th
Street in Kansas City, to Larimer Street in Denver, to South
Main Street in Los Angeles, to downtown Third Street in San
Francisco, to Skid Road in Seattle ("blighted areas" all)—

The Bowery is the haven for hobos who came to the big city
to make the big time by getting pushcarts and collecting cardboard.—Lots of Bowery bums are Scandinavian, lots of them
bleed easily because they drink too much.—When winter comes
bums drink a drink called smoke, it consists of wood alcohol
and a drop of iodine and a scab of lemon, this they gulp down
and wham! they hibernate all winter so as not to catch cold,
because they dont live anywhere, and it gets very cold outside
in the city in winter.—Sometimes hobos sleep arm-in-arm to
keep warm, right on the sidewalk. Bowery Mission veterans say
that the beer-drinking bums are the most belligerent of the lot.

Fred Bunz is the great Howard Johnson's of the bums—it is
located on 277 Bowery in New York. They write the menu in
soap on the windows.—You see the bums reluctantly paying
fifteen cents for pig brains, twenty-five cents for goulash, and
shuffling out in thin cotton shirts in the cold November night
to go and make the lunar Bowery with a smash of broken bottle
in an alley where they stand against a wall like naughty boys.—
Some of them wear adventurous rainy hats picked up by the
track in Hugo Colorado or blasted shoes kicked off by Indians
in the dumps of Juarez, or coats from the lugubrious salon of
the seal and fish.—Bum hotels are white and tiled and seem
as though they were upright johns.—Used to be bums told
tourists that they once were successful doctors, now they tell
tourists they were once guides for movie stars or directors in
Africa and that when TV came into being they lost their safari
rights.

In Holland they dont allow bums, the same maybe in Copen-
hagen. But in Paris you can be a bum—in Paris bums are
treated with great respect and are rarely refused a few francs.—
There are various kinds of classes of bums in Paris, the highclass bum has a dog and a baby carriage in which he keeps all

his belongings, and that usually consists of old *France Soirs*, rags, tin cans, empty bottles, broken dolls.—This bum sometimes has a mistress who follows him and his dog and carriage around.—The lower bums dont own a thing, they just sit on the banks of the Seine picking their nose at the Eiffel Tower.—

The bums in England have English accents, and it makes them seem strange—they don't understand bums in Germany. —America is the motherland of bumdom.—

American hobo Lou Jenkins from Allentown Pennsylvania was interviewed at Fred Bunz's on The Bowery.—"What you wanta know all this info for, what you want?"

"I understand that you've been a hobo travelin' around the country."

"How about givin' a fella few bits for some wine before we talk."

"Al, go get the wine."

"Where's this gonna be in, the *DailyNews*?"

"No, in a book."

"What are you young kids doing here, I mean where's the drink?"

"Al's gone to the liquor store—You wanted Thunderbird, wasnt it?"

"Yair."

Lou Jenkins then grew worse—"How about a few bits for a flop tonight?"

"Okay, we just wanta ask you a few questions like why did you leave Allentown?"

"My wife.—My wife,—Never get married. You'll never live it down. You mean to say it's gonna be in a book hey what I'm sayin'?"

"Come on say something about bums or something."

"Well whattaya wanta know about bums? Lot of 'em around, kinda tough these days, no money—lissen, how about a good meal?"

"See you in the Sagamore." (Respectable bums' cafeteria at Third and Cooper Union.)

"Okay kid, thanks a lot."—He opens the Thunderbird bottle with one expert flip of the plastic seal.—Glub, as the moon rises resplendent as a rose he swallows with big ugly lips thirsty to gulp the throat down, Sclup! and down goes the drink and his eyes be-pop themselves and he licks tongue on top lip and says "H-a-h!" And he shouts "Dont forget my name is spelled Jenkins, J-e-n-k-y-n-s.—"

Another character—"You say that your name is Ephram Freece of Pawling New York?"

"Well, no, my name is James Russell Hubbard."

"You look pretty respectable for a bum."

"My grandfather was a Kentucky colonel."

"Oh?"

"Yes."

"Whatever made you come here to Third Avenue?"

"I really cant do it, I dont care, I cant be bothered, I feel nothing, I dont care any more. I'm sorry but—somebody stole my razor blade last night, if you can lay some money on me I'll buy myself a Schick razor."

"Where will you plug it in? Do you have such facilities?"

"A Schick injector."

"Oh."

"And I always carry this book with me—*The Rules of St. Benedict*. A dreary book, but well I got another book in my pack. A dreary book too I guess."

"Why do you read it then?"

"Because I found it—I found it in Bristol last year."

"What are you interested in? You like interested in something?"

"Well, this other book I got there is er, yee, er, a big strange book—you shouldnt be interviewing me. Talk to that old nigra fella over there with the harmonica—I'm no good for nothing, all I want is to be left alone—"

"I see you smoke a pipe."

"Yeah—Granger tobacco. Want some?"

"Will you show me the book?"

"No I aint got it with me, I only got this with me."—He points to his pipe and tobacco.

"Can you say something?"

"Lightin flash."

The American Hobo is on the way out as long as sheriffs operate with as Louis-Ferdinand Céline said, "One line of crime and nine of boredom," because having nothing to do in the middle of the night with everybody gone to sleep they pick on the first human being they see walking.—They pick on lovers on the beach even. They just dont know what to do with themselves in those five-thousand-dollar police cars with the two-way Dick Tracy radios except pick on anything that moves in the night and in the daytime on anything that seems to be moving independently of gasoline, power, Army or police.— I myself was a hobo but I had to give it up around 1956 because of increasing television stories about the abominableness of strangers with packs passing through by themselves independently—I was surrounded by three squad cars in Tucson Arizona at 2 A.M. as I was walking pack-on-back for a night's sweet sleep in the red moon desert:

"Where you goin'?"

"Sleep."

"Sleep where?"

"On the sand."

"Why?"

"Got my sleeping bag."

"Why?"

"Studyin' the great outdoors."

"Who are you? Let's see your identification."

"I just spent a summer with the Forest Service."

"Did you get paid?"

"Yeah."

"Then why dont you go to a hotel?"

"I like it better outdoors and it's free."

"Why?"

"Because I'm studying hobo."

"What's so good about that?"

They wanted an *explanation* for my hoboing and came close to hauling me in but I was sincere with them and they ended up scratching their heads and saying "Go ahead if that's what you want."—They didnt offer me a ride four miles out to the desert.

And the sheriff of Cochise allowed me to sleep on the cold clay outside Bowie Arizona only because he didnt know about it.—

There's something strange going on, you cant even be alone any more in the primitive wilderness ("primitive areas" so-called), there's always a helicopter comes and snoops around, you need camouflage.—Then they begin to demand that you observe strange aircraft for Civil Defense as though you knew the difference between regular strange aircraft and any kind of strange aircraft.—As far as I'm concerned the only thing to do is sit in a room and get drunk and give up your hoboing and your camping ambitions because there aint a sheriff or fire warden in any of the new fifty states who will let you cook a little meal over some burning sticks in the tule brake or the hidden valley or anyplace any more because he has nothing to do but pick on what he sees out there on the landscape moving independently of the gasoline power army police station.—I have no ax to grind: I'm simply going to another world.

Ray Rademacher, a fellow staying at the Mission in the Bowery, said recently, "I wish things was like they was when my father was known as Johnny the Walker of the White Mountains.—He once straightened out a young boy's bones after an accident, for a meal, and left. The French people around there called him '*Le Passant*.'" (He who passes through.)

The hobos of America who can still travel in a healthy way are still in good shape, they can go hide in cemeteries and drink wine under cemetery groves of trees and micturate and sleep on cardboards and smash bottles on the tombstones and not care and not be scared of the dead but serious and humorous in the cop-avoiding night and even amused and leave litters of their picnic between the grizzled slabs of Imagined Death, cussing what they think are real days, but Oh the poor bum of the skid row! There he sleeps in the doorway, back to wall, head down, with his right hand palm-up as if to receive from the night, the other hand hanging, strong, firm, like Joe Louis hands, pathetic, made tragic by unavoidable circumstance— the hand like a beggar's upheld with the fingers forming a suggestion of what he deserves and desires to receive, shaping the alms, thumb almost touching finger tips, as though on the tip of the tongue he's about to say in sleep and with that gesture what he couldnt say awake: "Why have you taken this away from me, that I cant draw my breath in the peace and sweetness of my own bed but here in these dull and nameless rags on this humbling stoop I have to sit waiting for the wheels of the city to roll," and further, "I dont want to show my hand but in sleep I'm helpless to straighten it, yet take this opportunity to see my plea, I'm alone, I'm sick, I'm dying—see my hand up-tipped, learn the secret of my human heart, give me the thing, give me your hand, take me to the emerald mountains beyond the city, take me to the safe place, be kind, be nice, smile—I'm too tired now of everything else, I've had enough, I give up, I quit, I want to go home, take me home O brother in the night—take me home, lock me in safe, take me to where all is peace and amity, to the family of life, my mother, my father, my sister, my wife and you my brother and you my friend—but no hope, no hope, no hope, I wake up and I'd give a million dollars to be in my own bed—O Lord save me—" In evil roads behind gas tanks where murderous dogs snarl from behind wire fences cruisers suddenly leap out like getaway cars but from a crime more secret, more baneful than words can tell.

The woods are full of wardens.

FROM THE JOURNALS
1949–1954

The Saga of the Mist—

Trip from New York to San Francisco, 1949. N.Y. across the tunnel to New Jersey—the "Jersey night" of Allen Ginsberg. We in the car jubilant, beating on the dashboard of the '49 Hudson coupe . . . headed West. And I haunted by something I have yet to remember. And a rainy, road-glistening, misty night again. Big white sign saying "West" → "South" ←——— our gleeful choices. Neal and I and Louanne talking of the value of life as we speed along, in such thoughts as "Whither goest thou America in thy shiny car at night?" and in the mere fact that we're together under such rainy circumstances talking heart to heart. Seldom had I been so glad of life. We stopped for gas at the very spot where Neal and I had stopped on the No. Carolina trip 3 weeks before, near Otto's lunch diner. And remembered the funny strange events there. Then we drove on playing bebop music on the radio. But what was I haunted by? It was sweet to sit near Louanne. In the backseat Al and Rhoda made love. And Neal drove with the music, huzzaing.

We talked like this through Philadelphia and beyond. And occasionally some of us dozed. Neal got lost outside of Baltimore and wound up in

MARYLAND — WASHINGTON

ridiculously narrow little tar road in the woods (he was trying to find a shortcut.) "Doesn't look like Route One," he said ruefully, and as it was so obvious to everyone it seemed a very funny remark (I forget why now, in its totality.) We arrived in Washington at dawn and passed a great display of war machines that were set out for Truman's inauguration day—jet planes, tanks, catapults, submarines, and finally a rowboat which touched Neal's rueful attention. He is sometimes fascinatingly "great" in this manner. Then, in search of coffee in Arlington Va. We got routed onto a traffic circle rotary-drive that took us whether we like it or not to a coffee shop that was not open. (The greatness of Neal is that he will always

777

remember everything that happened, including this, with significant personal connotation.) We wound out, and back on the highway found a diner; where we had breakfast as the sun came out. (I remember the young proprietor's face when Big Al stole a coffee cake. Rhoda went back to Washington in a local bus; and Al drove, Neal sleeping, till he was stopped for speeding outside of Richmond. We almost all wound up in jail on vag charges with undertones of the Mann act—but paid a $15 fine and went free. A hitchhiker was with us. Neal raged about the arresting officer whom he would have loved to kill. Near Emporia Va. we picked up a mad hitchhiker who said he was Jewish (Herb-

N.Y. TO N.O   VIRGINIA — NO. CAROLINA

ert Diamond) and made his living knocking at the doors of Jewish homes all over the country demanding money. "I am a Jew!—give the money." "What kicks!" cried Neal (why does the world have to otherwise deprive Neal of his kicks—and I too?) The Jewish pilgrim sat in back with Al and the other hitchhiker reading a muddy paperbacked book he had found in some culvert of the wilderness—a detective story, which he read as if the Torah. In Rocky Mount N.C. we dispatched him to a Jewish home I know of, the Temkos, jewellers. (uncle of Alan Temko), but he never returned. Meanwhile we jubilantly bought bread & cheese, and ate on Main Street in the car. Had I ever been so in Rocky Mt.?—and was it not the place from which I had written a strange melancholy letter to Neal, and where Ann had hath her way, and where the sad fair was? and where my sister almost died? and where I had seen the Forest of Arden in a tobacco warehouse? Therefore, it is these mysteries in the homely commonplace earth that convince me of the real existence of God (no words.) For what is Rocky Mount after all? *Why* Rock Mt . . . ?

In Fayetteville our hitch-hiker failed to produce desired money (in Dunn actually) so we moved on without him, I sleeping. Then I drove in So. Carolina, which again was flat and dark in the night (with star-shiny roads, and southern dullness somewhere around.) I drove to beyond Macon Georgia where one could begin to smell the earth and see greeneries in the dark. Woke up just outside Mobile Ala., and soft airs of summer (in January.) We played jubilantly as we had done and did do clear across the continent (Neal & Louanne piggybacking, etc.) In Gulfport Miss. We ate royally with our last monies prior to New Orleans, in a seaside restaurant. (It was Neal's theft of a tankful of gas that saved us; a divine theft as far as I'm concerned, Promethean at least.) We began to hear rumors of New Orleans and "chicken, jazz n' gumbo" bebop shows on the radio, with much wild backalley jazz of the "drive" variety; so we yelled happily in the car. I lay in the back looking at the gray Gulf sky as we rolled—how happy we were! as we'd been through trials and hunger. (Travel is travail.)

"Smell the people!" said Neal of New Orleans; and the smell of the big river (which Lucien has recently characterized as 'female,' because its mud comes from the male Missouri.) The smell of people, of the river, and summer—"the summer's south America," as I had predicted—and the smell of loam, petals, and molasses, in Algiers, where we waited at a filling station before going to Bill's. I'll never forget the wild expectancy of that moment—the rickety street, the palms, the great late-afternoon clouds over the Mississippi, the girls going by, the children, the soft bandanas of air coming like odor instead of air, the smell of people and rivers.

And then Burroughs' tragic old house in the field, and Joan Adams in the back kitchen door "looking for a fire." God is what I love.

Also, the ferry, of course—

NEW ORLEANS

Crossing the Algiers Ferry—

What is the Mississippi River? Near Idaho, near West Yellowstone, near the furthest, darkest corner of Wyoming, the headwaters of the Missouri, modest as a dell of brooks, begin—A log is cracked by elemental lightnings there in the wild corners of wild states . . . and meanders restlessly floating down-stream. Timbers and hairy abutments (shaggier than those on the Avon-like Hudson) stand in the northern light as the log proceeds. Lost moose from dignified heights stare (pouting) with dignified eyes. ("If I had an eye the trees would have eyes"—Allen Ginsberg.)

Bozeman . . . Three   Forks . . . Helena . . . Cascade . . . (I've never been there; and now they have power plants and chemical factories along these shores where Jim Bridger was wild, poetic, and rugged with freedom, saintly with hard-ships) . . . Wolf Point . . . Williston North Dakota, and Mandon . . . The winter snows . . . Pierre . . . Sioux City . . . Council Bluffs (there I've been in a gray dawn, and saw no council of the wagon chiefs, no bluffs but suburban cot-tages) . . . Kansas City.

The Missouri rushes hugely into the floods of the Missis-sippi at St. Louis, bearing the Odyssiac log from lonely Mon-tana down to the

ALGIERS, LOUISIANA

wide night shores by Hannibal, Cairo, Greenville, and Natchez . . . and by old Algiers of Louisiana (where Bill Burroughs sits now.) "Unions! That's what it is!—unions!"

My ferry plows the brown water to New Orleans; I look over the rail; and there is that Montana log passing by . . . Like me a wanderer in burrowed water-beds moving slowly with satisfaction and eternity. In the night, in the rainy night . . .

But the Mississippi—and my log—journeys by Baton Rouge, where, miles to the west, some underground, supernatural phe-nomena of the flood has created bayoux (who knows?)—west of Opelousas, southeast of Ogallala, southwest of Ashtabula—and there in the bayoux, too, (and therefore), across my pa-tient soul's-eye floats the wraith of mist, the ghost, the swamp-gyre, the light in the night, the fog-shroud of the Mississippi and Montana and of all the haunted earth: to bring me the message of the log. Ghost by ghost these bayoux-shapes swim by in the hanging night, from mossy palaces, from the mansion of the snake; and I have read the big elaborate manuscript of the night.

And what is the Mississippi River? It is the movement of the night; and the secret of sleep; and the emptier of American streams which bear, (as the log is borne,) the story of our truer fury:—

THE GULF OF MEXICO

the fury of the deadly and damaging soul which never sleeps. . . . And says in the night, "It's what I always feel, you know?" I know? You know? Who know? But this is vague . . . untrue. (Rock-in-the-belly.)

The Mississippi River ends in the Gulf—called Mexico— likelier Night: and my riven, wandering log, all water-heavy and sunken and turning over, floats out to the sea . . . around the keys . . . where the ocean-going ship (like an eternal ferry) passes again its strange destiny like a wraith. And Old Bill sits under the lamp (reading Kafka's diaries), while I, a careless poet, I, an eye, a man, a wraith, a watcher of rivers, night; panorama and continents (and of men and women); in San Francisco scribble.

For the rain is the sea coming back, and the river—no lake— is the rain become night, and the night is water and earth, and there are no stars that show to the shrouded earth their infolded loopings in other worlds no longer we need: I know (and do scribble.)

And the rainy night, a river, is God, as the sea the rivers and rains conceals. All is safe. Secure.

—   —

Will I ever see my sea around the riverbend? or merely roll to it at night in silence: some eternity is the Gulf of Mexico.

RICHMOND, CALIF. — 'FRISCO

TEA—DISCOVERIES (riding back to Frisco from Richmond Calif. on rainy night, in Hudson; sulking in back seat.)

Don't get hung up on difficult, miserable discoveries of your "true self"—rather, enjoy and goof off (and thereby avoid these self-knowledges.) Neal's lack. But Oh the pangs of travel! the spirituality of hashish!

And what a revelation to know that I was born sad—that it was no trauma that made me so sad—but God:—who made me that way.

I saw also that Neal—well, I saw Neal at the wheel of the car Allen Anson-ish and more, a wild machinery of kicks and sniffs and gulps and maniacal laughter, a kind of human dog; and then I saw Allen Ginsberg—17th century poet in dark vestments standing in a sky of Rembrandt darkness, one thin leg before the other in meditation; then I myself, like Slim Gailland, stuck my head out of the window with Billy Holliday eyes and offered my soul to the whole world, big sad eyes . . . (like the whores in the Richmond mud-shack saloon.) Saw how much genius I had, too (inasmuch as I could knock myself *out* so?) Knowing the genius, therefore, preferred *solitude* & *decencies.* Saw how sullen, blank Louanne hated me (without fearing me as she fears & wants to subdue Neal.) Saw how unimportant I was to them; and the stupidity of my designs on her, and my betrayal of male friends concerning their women (Neal, Hal, G. J., even Ed's Beverly, & of course Cru, and unknown unnumbered others in other lives.)

OLD 'FRISCO

The Strange Dickensian Vision on Market Street
I was just walking home from Larkin & Geary where Louanne had betrayed me so dumbly (details elsewhere), in the spring-like night of Market St.—filled again, strangely, as always in San Francisco, with moral pangs and dark moral worries & decisions; and walking a mile and a half to Guerrero and thence to Liberty St. (Carolyn's apartment)—when I passed a strange little hash-house near, or beyond, Van Ness, on right side of Market—arrested by the sign "Fish & Chips." I looked in hungrily (though I had just eaten steamed clams and hot broth in Geary St. bar while waiting for Louanne)—Place filled with hungry eaters who haven't too much money to spend. The proprietor was a hairy-armed, grave, strong little Greek of sorts;

and his wife a pink-faced, anxious English-woman (as English-womany as any in a film.) I had just come from the dawdling company of whores & pimps & some thieves, perhaps even footpads, and was roaming the street hungry, penniless, watchful. This poor woman glanced at me standing there in the outside shadows, with a kind of terrified anxiety. Something went through me, a definite feeling that in another life this poor, dear woman had been my mother, and that I, like a Dickens footpad, was returning after many years in the shadow of the gallows, in English 19th century gaols, her wandering 'blackguardly' son . . .

MARKET ST., 'FRISCO

hungry to cheat her once more (though not at once.) "No," she seemed to say as she shot that terrified glance at me (was I then leering in?), "don't come back and plague your honest hardworking mother. You are no longer like a son to me—and like your father, my first husband 'ere this kindly Greek took pity on me, you are no good, inclined to drunkenness and routs and final disgraceful robbery of the fruits of my 'umble labours in the hashery. Oh son! did you not ever go on your knees and pray for deliverance for all your sins and scoundrel's acts! Lost boy!—depart! do not haunt my soul, I have done well forgetting you. Re-open no auld wounds: Be as if you had never returned and looked in to me—to see my labouring humilities, my few scrubb'd pennies—hungry to grab, quick to deprive, sullen, unloving, mean-minded son of my flesh— Please go! Please do not return! And see my sweet Greek, he is just, he is humble . . . Son! son!"—

I walked by filled with a whole night-world of memories, all of them so distinctly & miraculously *English* somehow, as if I had actually lived all this—(I was struck dumb, stopped in ec-stasy on Market St., trying to re-construct the events that must have transpired between my former sonhood to this poor woman in England up until this one

LOWELL-LIKE FRISCO

haunted moment in San Francisco California in 1949.) I don't

jest. But there is no more to it than this. Now refer to the incident of "Big Pop" with Burroughs in Louisiana (in the bookie
joint) and to his belief in other lives. On page 79 (ref.)

Incidentally I walked on from the fish 'n chips place to Carolyn Robinson Cassady's apartment on Liberty St. and noticed
as I climbed the steep steps in the yard that only in San Francisco and Lowell Mass. can there be such steep, star-pack't
nights—so dark and Goudt-rich as in "Farewell Song, Sweet
From my Trees"—tree-swishing, cool nights—so spiritual, so
reminiscent for me, of me; and suggestive of "the future."

San Francisco is so homelike to me; and I would live there
someday.

NEW ORLEANS—THE GIRL'S SUICIDE
That night we crossed the ferry, high, little did we know, &
sympathize with soul-thoughts, of a girl who perhaps just then
was planning to jump in the water. Perhaps when Neal & I
commented eagerly about the old Vulcan's forge of the ship,
the boiler furnace—which glowed so dull red in the brown fog
of the river night;—or perhaps when Louanne & I leaned on
the rail watching the somber, swelling brown flood; or when,
gleefully, we laughed; and watched the freighters docked in
New Orleans across the water, the ghostly Cereno ships with
Spanish balconies & moss, wreath'd in fog; the mysterious
mist on the water itself; the intimation and revelation of the
whole Mississippi River winding north into the mid-American
night (with hints of Arkansas, Missouri, Iowa); and orange
New Orleans itself in the night. What was the girl thinking?
where was she from? Did her brothers in Ohio scowl fiercely
when she was spoken of by men at the taxi stand? Did she walk
home nights in the icy streets of winter, huddled in the little
coat she had bought from her work savings? Did she sweetly
fall in love with some tall, brown, never-available construction-
worker who came for her occasionally in his well-pressed topcoat, in his Ford coupe? Did she dance with him at the sad,
roseate ballrooms? And make jokes about the moon? And sigh
& groan & cry in her pillow? What horror was there in mossy

New Orleans, what real final sadness did she see? (In the Latin Quarter streets at night.)

Next day in the paper we read about her suicide, and remembered it; and thought of it.

NEW ORLEANS THINGS

NEW ORLEANS—Algiers Ferry, Canal St., Mickey in the grocery store ("Do you cats blow bop?"); Newton St., Wagner St., the levee down the road; the nightfalls; Basin St., Rampart St., the Bourbon; Dauphine St.; Latin Quarter; hopping the freights with Neal & Al; high on the grass; Andrew Jackson park;—Joan, Julie, Willie; Helen; playing ball, making shelves; "Big Pop" in the Gretna bookie joint; groceries and Joan's benny; throwing knives; air pistol practice in the living room; crepes; weed;—the radio's Chicken Jazz n' Gumbo show; the "man" with the ice cream wagon—the front room with cot and pad; Louanne the Miss Lou on the trellised porch . . . the great Mississippi Valley clouds in the afternoon; the sultry nights; Sunday in the breezy yard, Bill sits all day under his lamp (with shades drawn); and morphine-heavy he drowses or speaks, all's the same. Helen's "plantation" room & bed; the jam and coffee on the front-room floor; shattered benzedrine tubes; the rickety backyard, and the unkempt grass; the smell of piss and rivers; the Gulf rain; Canal street like Market street like any street, Immortal Street leading to the ambiguity of Universal Water whether Mississippi or Pacific.

NEW HAMPSHIRE SOURCES

ROUTE OF MY MERRIMACK RIVER (in New England)
The Pemigewasset is its main branch and begins at Newfound Lake northwest of Laconia, at Hebron N.H., only 85 miles from Lowell Mass. But below Hookset N.H. this Merrimac River begins to assume the depth, rush, personality & loneliness of a great American river, till, by the time it roars humpbacked over the Pawtucket rocks it has accumulated a water-power that is truly awful to hear. (This has been confirmed by Hal, a Coloradoan, who was amazed.)

Here is the route, and some of the feeding sources apparent on the map:

Newfound Lake fed by streams from Mt. Crosby and possibly by the Baker River of the White Mountains. Winnipesaukee is to the east. Pemigewasset flows down through Bristol; Hill; (WEST OF LACONIA) down to Franklin. Meanwhile there are the Franklin Falls and the Eastman Falls Dams—flowing thereby through Webster Place, near the birthplace of Daniel Webster—to Gerrish, and Boscawen: here there are feedings from Blackwater Reservoir and from Rocky Pond, Sanborn Pond, and many nameless creeks. Now from some Pittsfield Creek, the river is further fed, and named Merrimack. To Penacook, Concord (and Lake Penacook)—to Bow (Turkey Pond), Pembroke; Hookset (SHINGLE PONDS, AND BEAR BROCK)—Manchester and the Massabesic Lake, and a stream from Weare thence Goffs Falls, and by a rock cavern, to Reeds Ferry; Merrimack; Thorntons Ferry—to Nashua and Hudson (fed from Hollis, and Canobie Lake.) and by the Nashua River. To Tyngsboro (Tyngsboro LAKEVIEW pond and creek from Pepperell.) Then *Lowell*—fed by Long Pond (Pine Brook) and Thoreau's Concord River—on to the Atlantic at Newburyport & Plum Island.

109 Liberty St. 'Frisco   *SECRET, UNCOMMUNICATIVE*
The secret of time is the moment, when ripples of high expectation run—or the actual moment of "highness" itself when all is solved. We know time. Slim Gaillard's knowledge of time.

Danny Kaye's "Dinah" is of course reminiscent of Sebastian . . . "Played that record over and over again in the North Pole in 1942." (I said.)

The ripples engendered by many subsidiary events connected with my memory of Sebastian (and his world of "gargeous womans") finally broke into a rushing stream when I heard and thought of it. This explains my lifelong search for moments of vision when all is cleared . . . the big trees in the white desert appearing, and the soft footfall of my approach to them. "We know time." And we anticipate the future when we pigeonhole our ripples as we go along, knowing the joyous solution to come at its given moment. Is this not too unclear though?

"NEAL'S CALIFORNIA"

It is a whole new concept, & world, in itself. He explained all about the various divisions of the S.P. railroad the moment we arrived in the state: at the edges of the Mojave outside of L.A., at Tehatchepi, and Bakersfield later. He also showed me (all the way up the San Joaquin Valley) the rooming houses where he stayed, the diners where he ate; even the water stops where he jumped off the train to pick grapes for himself & the other brakemen. In Bakersfield, just across the tracks where I had drunk wine with Bea in 1947 at night, he showed me where a woman lived whom he had entertained—places where he had done nothing more spectacular than sit and wait. He remembers *all*. His California was a long sunny place of railroads, grapes, pinochle games in cabooses, women in towns like Tracy or Watsonville, Chinese & Mexican restaurants behind the tracks, great stretches of land—hot, sweaty, important— And moreover, he is a true Californian, in the sense that everybody in California is like a broken-down movie actor, i.e., handsome, decadent, Casanova-ish, where all the women really love to try various beds. In Frisco, particularly, Neal fits in with the special California type . . . where perfect strangers talk to you most intimately on the street. California is as if a land of lonely & exiled & eccentric *lovers* come to foregather, like birds. Everyone is debauched, completely (somehow.) And there is that old-fashioned look of the land, & the towns, (*not* in L.A., but on up) still reminiscent of the Golden American West we think of. The nights are "unbearably romantic" . . . & sadder than the East's. [MORE ANON]

San Francisco to Portland (698 miles) *Feb 4 & 5th '49*
Dumb sullen goodbye with Neal and Louanne after night in Richmond Calif. at wild jazz & whore joint with Ed Saucier & Jan Carter (drummer.)—(the tea; the Pip pulling out her chair; the Billy Holliday gals; and "Shut up!"). Goodbye at the 3rd St. bus station—Greyhound. Oakland. Sleep through

Sacramento Valley up through Red Bluff, etc. (Same as San Joaquin?) Woke up at 7 A.M. in Redding. Cold—white bunch-grass hills all around, empty streets . . . Up through Shasta Lake by Buckhorn & Hatchet Mts.—spectacular Northwest timber & snow scenery . . . (Hal once said it was like Colorado.) Ghostly Mt. Shasta in distance . . . Mountain lakes; high blue sky of mountain airs. Lamoine . . . railroad shacks; flats. Across spectacular mountains and timbered ridges to Dunsmuir—little railroad & lumber town in the mountains (Mt. Shasta and the walking snows.) Cloud-flirt'd Shasta—Narrow ridge-town, & snow. Vision of little boy: basketball yard at school, father railroader below in hollow; Xmas night; the Shasta snow-wraiths walking; the ghost of the Great Shaman Fool leading him on to white-woman-shrouded sloper. (How the ghost-wraiths disport shamelessly in the blue high day up there, not waiting for night even—but N I G H T *does* come too . . .) On to Mt. Shasta (silly ski-girl.) And then grim weed . . . "What'd he do up in Weed? The big Inn facing empty spaces north and the coal shuttles; snow & cold—Men in the hotel. Mountain pines. Grim, desolate town.

NORTHERN CALIFORNIA

After weed (big lonely Black-Butte in snow) the great clouds far off over the Cascade Ranges and Siskyous of Oregon (clouds of Oregon Trail.) Then Dorris, Calif., and the intimation of ice caves far to the east down spatial corridors of snow . . . Then Klamath Falls in the flats of the Klamath River: snowy, joyous American town in the morning; "affairs in the sunny town; winter; Geo. Martin; redbrick alleys like Lowell of Duluoz." A walk in the winey air. Little kids lean over bridge-rail, steaming Klamath River, distant Sierra Nevadas of California (No.). Three towns: *Dunsmuir*, Lowell-like, medieval, Alpine, Dr. Saxish—and *Weed*:—grim, western, Oxbow-like (Nevada), rough marshalls and ranchmen—and *Klamath Falls*: joyous, bell-ringing, snowy, sunny, homelike.

Up by great Klamath Lake, on west ridge of timber hills leading to East Oregon craters, wastes, rangelands and that mysteriously unknown junction of Oregon, Idaho and Nevada (east of McDermitt.) Land of Shastas past—land of Modocs now, of lake Indians. Modoc Point. Agency Lake. Long leisurely Sun Pass. Lake in volcanic crater; and prick-point summit that God wouldn't dare sit on (Diamond Lake summit?) Great snowy rocks in the Northwest air, and timber, timber . . . .

(Mt. Shasta haunts poor Dunsmuir, poor Weed, and even me now: a ghostly, shrouded, sneering mount.)

Great Pengra Pass . . . four feet of snow. Big glorious redwoods cloth'd in snow, drooping, nodding, standing, serried, gaunt, trimm'd, orchestral in snow, whole arpeggios of snowy redwood, & vaults of blue sky in between.

PENGRA & WILLAMETTE IN OREGON

(Trees grow straight on crooked cliffsides.) The hairy forecliffs leaning over us.) Down Pengra Pass (asleep mostly) to Oakridge . . .

The little Willamette Valley, a thin strip of poor farms haunted by distant volcanic craters in the dusk. Pleasant Hill? founded 1848?—how Bourgeois the pioneers were! (The cemetery there full of Oregon pioneers.) Underdeveloped region. Oregon is a wilderness where people have to live in poor little valleys like the Willamette and still be haunted (as they milk sweet cows) by the Encantadas of the blasted West . . . Then the snows melt in Pengra and little Willamette floods Eugene, Albany, Junction City, Oregon City, Salem (shows them who's little, and shows up the sterile impotent volcanoes paralyzed in rage out there.)

Ah!—and there's the Columbia for floods, joined by the Willamette (and the big Snake), for the flooding of other cities. Eugene a dull Durham-like college town . . . so Corvallis? And Albany & Salem Oregon. But Oregon City, town of Big Watery Willamette now, Holyoke-town of paper mills & gastanks, and ridges with houses above, and whore in the redbrick alley: a definite town.

Portland, like filling stations and hipsters and Portland-sized cities, is the same as any other same-sized city in U.S.A. or like any other gas stations & hipsters all over. Rainy snow here.

THE PORTLAND THOUGHTS

We crossed great dark Columbia over bridge. River once adventurous & commercial pulse of Portland, now barred off from "public" by tugworks, naval bases, etc., etc., as Mississippi River is barred off in Algiers La., with wire fences. Many chop suey joints in Portland, like in Salt Lake City (!!). I anticipated rainy snow in "drenched with suffering" story of 1945, about rooming house in Portland. The mysteries of naturalism & supernaturalism meet.

Many thoughts tonight . . . eating chili in Broadway (Portland) restaurant . . . O'Flannery's. Saturday night in Portland, Oregon . . . girl-and-boy dates.

Pathos of distance softens my anger at Neal & Louanne now. We all are as we are—(and I saw what I was a few times in 'Frisco with horror.) Ah well . . . Neal's new morality still stands, but not as an end in itself. More on this in proper pages.

Tonight I sleep across Columbia Valley. Next writing-stop is Butte, Montana. God bless us all. For the wages of sin *is* death . . . and eternal life is still ours somehow. This is Neal & Louanne. As for me, I shall be myself as made (no psychology remains, and no philosophy.) There is no beyond behind my beyond, and no behind beyond my behind . . . all us say that don't we?

HOBOES IN PORTLAND

Portland to Butte (Written in Spokane Feb. 6)
Now I will get to the source of the rainy night: The Snow—North, the West that makes Mississippis—that makes the rainy night we cross on tidal highways . . . Now I'll come close and touch the source of it all—and thereby, perhaps, what Wolfe meant by "undiscovered Montanas."

Two hobo-panhandlers in back of bus on way out at midnight (2 "scufflers"); said they were bound for The Dalles to beat a dollar or two. Drunk—"Goddamit don't get us thrown off at Hood River!" "Beat the busdriver for a couple!" We rolled in the big darkness of the Columbia River valley, in a blizzard. I could see little but big trees, bluffs, terrifying darknesses

—and the lights across the big river (big enough to have its Cape Horn to Mississippi's Cape Girardeau.) Vancouver Wash. across the snowy darkness, on the shore . . .

Thought of Hood River and how dismal it would be to get thrown off there:—in the hooded night, on wild watery shores, among logs, crags . . . I woke up after a nap and a chat with the hobo ("My originator is Kansas City, Jackson County" and "my place of origination is Texas"—or Bakersfield, or Modesto, or Delano—couldn't make up his mind which lie was most suitable. Said he would be an oldtime outlaw if J. Edgar Hoover had not made it against the law to steal. Said he was going to the Dalles to steal—a small farming & lumber town, he said—

THE GREAT COLUMBIA VALLEY

WASHINGTON

Up ahead there in the frightful night's valley of the Columbia. I lied and said I had driven a stolen car from N.Y. to Frisco. He said he believed me implicitly.—so after this chat, I slept and woke up at Tonompah (?) Falls—

A hooded white phantom dropped water from his huge icy forehead (which I could not altogether see in the eerie light.) So Dr. Sax had been here too . . . in this hooded night of the Columbia. Hundreds of feet high, from the rock-bluff worn shelfwise by the patient frightful Columbia, from icy brows, this water dropped (from its mouthlike hole) and evaporated midways to mist. We were apparently on the floor of the valley now, looking up at ancient shores of rock. I was scared because I could not see what was in the darkness up-&-beyond the hood of ice, the Falls—what hairy horrors? what craggy night (no stars.)

The busdriver plunged along then over mad ridges . . . I slept through Hood River, the Dalles.

Woke up briefly, glanced at Wallula, site of the old 1818 Fort (Walla Wall Fort—IN A MESA CUT)—in a Mesa-like country of sagebrush and plains where the Columbia swung around to meet the Snake (in the brown plains of Pasco) and the Yakima a little beyond. On the horizon, the misty long hills called

Horse Heaven; and southward (O Oregon!) the Whitman Nat'l Park.

Then northeast through Connell, Lind, Sprague, Cheney (wheat and cattlelands like East Wyoming)

EASTERN WASHINGTON — IDAHO

In a gale of blizzards to Spokane—snowy big town on Sunday afternoon. (Walked in snow to recover my hoary old black jacket.) Sprague a redbrick, wheat-silo, Nebraska-like town.

From Spokane (perhaps really a meditative place after all for my nun-aunt Caroline) to Idaho—Coeur d'Alene—

(But Oh that dark Columbia land!) (I see, tho, how close the Snake River came to be an eastern slope river for the maws of the Mississippi—how it originates a mile from the Continental Divide in Jackson Hole Wyoming; but the Columbia won it, at Pasco; and the Oregon Territory was saved much more—tho the Columbia can handle it, winding all the way from Canada to Astoria's mouth.) (Therefore the Northwest has its rainy night, as Lowell has the Merrimac, and Asheville its Broad, and Harrisburg its Susquehanna.) Is there any connection between the "ghost of the Susquehanna" and the "Hood River hoboes"? Of course. But to Idaho . . .

FEB. 7—Slept through Coeur d'Alene (Ah well-)—but no mind, I saw the lakes and mountains no less, and could not help it: they came eastward, and Coeur d'Alene like Spokane was in the flatland. But immediately we climbed a great ridge along the frozen snowy lake and mounted to great heights. Fourth of July pass; and the great piney snows, over Coeur d'Alene Lake. The drops were sheer. I thought of the Coeur d'Alene Indians and all this they had.

We came along and down to the waterbed of the

THE BITTERROOT NIGHT

Coeur d'Alene river, to Cataldo. There I saw the clusters of houses homesteading in the wild mountain holes. A car was stuck; a big jovial young man was running out to help; dogs barking, chimneys smoking, children, women.—all the joyous northern life I think of occasionally, like in Maine, with frozen red sunsets, snow, smoke, kitchens of Idaho, home. Then to Wallace . . . some big mines . . . Then Mullan, in the heart of great sheer slopes rising near. Here I thought of Jim Bridger, and how, when waking in the morning in the valley-hole where Mullan now is, he looked ahead where the riverbed indisputably led him—on across the vast craglands he himself owned, then. I did not see him scrambling slopes, as many of us literally do in civilization, but following the eternity of waterbeds: under those piney heights, under the snow stars. The man who had written a poem:

"I saw a petrified bird in a petrified tree,
Singing his petrified song." (In Petrified Forest.)

Unknown Jim Bridger, one of the true poets of America; grinding his coffee and slicing his bacon and frying the deer meat in the winter's shadow of the unknown Bitterroot Mountains. What must he have thought? and the men of him, a squawman and solitary?

It got dark and we went over Lookout Pass in the Bitterroots at night. We rose to the great heights in the snowy gray; and way below in the gulch burned one single shack-light—almost a mile below. Two boys in a car

MONTANA ENTRY

almost went off the ridge avoiding our bus. In the silence while we waited for the busdriver to help them shovelling the drifts, I saw and heard the secret of the Bitterroots . . . (I've known these things before.) From down the pass to Deborgia, Montana, and on to Frenchtown and Missoula. We followed the Bitterroot River bed (it starts near Butte and winds along these loneliest of mountains to Flathead Lake, north). In Deborgia I began to see what Montana was like: and I shall never forget it. It is something that would please the soul of any man (who is serious, somehow.) Ranchers, lumberjacks & miners in a small bar, talking, playing cards & slot machines, while all around outside is the Montana night of bear & moose & wolf, of pines, & snow, and secret rivers, and the Bitterroots, the Bitterroots . . . One small light where they are, & the immensest dark, starpack't. The knowledge of what young men have thought of their Montana (and in 1870?)—and of what old men feel in it. The lovely women hidden. But that was only the beginning.

Missoula I did not like—a college town of skiiers, (at least what I saw around the bus station.)

I slept enroute to great Butte.

And why is Butte—over the Divide, near Anaconda, and Pipestone Pass—greater? Well, look at the names that surround it. Before I arrived in Montana I thought of stopping at Missoula, to rest, & to see; because I had heard it mentioned so much by hoboes (in 1947 in Wyoming, for instance.) But it is only a

THE BUTTE NIGHT

great rail-junction . . . In any case, just to look at the map, and to see Butte in the rough geographies of the divide, is to think of Twain's Nevada, (for me.) And it is so—In Butte I stored my bag in a locker. A drunken Indian wanted me to go drinking with him, but I cautiously declined. Yet a short walk around the sloping streets (in below zero weather at night) showed that everybody in Butte was drunk. This was a Sunday night—I hoped the saloons would stay open till I had at least seen my fill. *They closed at dawn*, if at all. I walked into one great oldtime saloon and had a giant beer. On the wall in back they had a big electric signboard flashing gambling-numbers. The bartender told me about it, and since I was a beginner allowed me to select his numbers in the hope that I would have beginner's luck. No soap . . . but he told me of Butte. Arrived there 22 years ago, and stayed. "Montanans drink too much, fight too much, and love too much." I watched the wonderful characters in there . . . old prospectors, gamblers, whores, miners, Indians, cowboys; & tourists who seemed different. Another gambling-saloon was indescribable with riches: groups of sullen Indians (Blackfeet) drinking red whisky in the john; hundreds of men of all kinds playing cards; and one old professional house-gambler who tore my heart out he reminded me so much my father (big; green eyeshade; handkerchief protruding from back pocket; great rugged, pock-marked, angelic face (unlike Pop's) and the

FROM BUTTE TO THREE FORKS, MONT.

big asthmatic, laborious sadness of such men. I could not take my eyes off him. My whole concept of "On the Road" changed & matured as I watched him. (Explained properly elsewhere.) The whole meaning was there for me, and specifically, it was as tho I were descending from metaphysical "rainy" preoccupations to dear man again . . . in all ways, writing & otherwise . . . (having now escaped Neal's compulsive *mystique de haschisch.*) Another old man, in his eighties, or nineties, called "John" by respectful men, coolly played cards till dawn, with slitted eyes; and it amazed me no end that he has been playing cards in the Montana saloon-night of spittoons, smoke & whisky since 1880, (days of the winter cattle drive to Texas, and of Sitting Bull.) Another old man with an old, loving sheepdog (all the dogs, as in Colorado, are shaggy sheepdogs) packed off in the cold mountain night after satisfying his soul at cards. It was like my father's old world of gambling again, but in the Montana night, & *moreso* somehow. Ah, dear father. And the young cowhands; and miners; and wild women. Even the Greeks, who are like Lowell Greeks . . . only *moreso* in Montana. How explain? Why bother. Even *Chinamen!*

At dawn I caught the bus. Soon we were going down the slope; and looking back, I saw Butte, still lit like jewelry, sparkling on the mountainside . . . 'Gold Hill'—and the blue northern dawn. Again the wild rocks & snows & valleys & rangelands & timber, & sagebrush. In a short while we were at Three Forks . . . where the Madison & the Missouri, in strange confluence, act; where the Missouri in

YELLOWSTONE VALLEY

Midwinter lay flooded & frozen covered with snow, over vast acres of ranch land:—hint of floods in the Natchez cobblestones a thousand miles away, hint of loamy plantations crumbling far around, over, & down the trail of the Missouri (north-wing'd) and the Mississippi (river of southern urge) in distant Louisiana. In Three Forks, in a nippy dawn, I saw the old street, the boardwalks, the old stores, the horses, the old cars—and the distant Bitterroots & Rocky Mountains snow-covered: and the young men who all looked like football play-ers or cowhands; the secret, delicious, unknown women.—At Bozeman I saw the ends of the world again: the Wyoming Tetons, & Granite Peak; & the Rockies & Bitterroots; & something like a distant *glacier* to the Canadian north some-how, all around, all over. This is like looking down the end of the world in Wyoming, in Arizona, in Texas (before El Paso), in Oregon at Mevrill, and many other places in the West. We mounted the Rockies—among mountain ranches & sheep—and descended to Livingston in the Yellowstone valley. The Yellowstone, like the Nebraska Platte, like the Nile, is one of the great valleys of the world: in the snowy waste the trees of the valley endlessly wind away, protecting ranches & farms. Always, in Montana, the great sense of northern distances, in Canada, or southerly to Wyoming—and east to . . . *Dakota*. It is one of the most isolated places in the world. Bigtimber, Mont., which I loved, is fine, but it is a world of wildlands from either Denver or . . . Bismarck? Boise? Where? Mon-tana is concealed in just this way, and this explains why it is the only state in the union which has its own personality, & the only truly Western state in the West.

BIGTIMBER, MONT.

Butte to Minneapolis
Montana is "protected" by Dakota, Wyoming, Idaho, and strange Saskatchewan from this silly world!—all power to it!—(and at the same time, recall, it is the *actual* source of the rainy night.) Big Muddy's muddy cradle.

Bigtimber. There I saw such a scene, such a thing: all these oldtimers sitting around in an old ramshackle inn, at noon, (in the middle of the snowy prairie)—playing cards by old stoves: *even at noon*. Montana is the land of manly life, manly absorp-tions, and manly laziness! And a boy of twenty, with one arm missing, lost either at war or at work, gazing sadly at me, won-dering who I was and what I did in the world. He sat in the middle of the old men, his tribal elders, gazing on the stranger, the alien, the secret Poe or Lafcadio Hearn that I felt like then. How sad!—and how beautiful he was because he was unable to work forever, and must sit forever with the oldtimers, and worry about how his buddies are punching cows and roistering outside. How protected he is by the old men, by Montana. *Nowhere else in the world would I say it were at all beautiful for a young man to have but one arm.* See? I shall never forget also the huge cup of coffee I drank in this inn, for a nickel; nor that poor, beautiful boy, who, though sad, seemed to realize that he was *home*, more than I can say with all my arms.—The bus then rolled on, by buttes, ranchlands, by the Yellowstone trees, by distant canyons & cuts, by Montana . . .

In Billings, at about 2 in the afternoon, it was at least 10 degrees below zero. I saw three of the most beautiful young girls I've ever seen in all my life, all within minutes, eating in a sort of high school lunchroom with

"YELLOWSTONE RED"

their grave boyfriends. Ame Montana . . . We drove on. And got to the other great Montana town that I'll never forget, & will re-visit . . . *Miles City.* Here, at dusk, it was about 20 below. I walked around. There had been many splendid ranches in the Yellowstone bed all the way, and now here were the ranchers themselves, with their families, in town for provisions. The women were shopping, the men were in the magnificent gambling saloons. In a drugstore window I saw a book on sale—so beautiful!—"Yellowstone Red," a story of a man in the early days of the valley, & his tribulations & triumphs. Is this not better reading in Miles City than the Iliad?—their *own* epic? There were many excellent saddle stores; there being an old saddle firm in town, and a leather factory at the east end. The gambling saloons were of course reminiscent of Butte and Bigtimber, though the people looked more prosperous, and it was afternoon, almost suppertime. A man in an old vest, tired of cards, rises from a table (underneath a wall covered with old photos of ranchers, and elk antlers), sits down nearer the bar, and eats a thick, juicy steak. Meanwhile his wife and pretty daughter come back for him, and eat with him. The sons, all decked in new boots, come in from the cold in those Montana sheepskin coats, and they eat. Then, after a few more hours in town, they pack things in the car and drive back to the ranch on the Yellowstone, where the cattle stand in winter pasture, safe from the West's worst winter. It is exceedingly cold in Montana but no—

MILES CITY, MONTANA

where else do people dress so well against it—so that the bitterness of the climate is nullified by good horse sense. Most men wear earmuffs—that is, caps with visors & earmuffs, like hunting caps. I saw many a cowboy in the high Texas plateau near Sonora, on horseback, wearing these caps, last month. The final thing I loved so much about Miles City is the perfect unity and meaning of its existence. It is a town (in the original sense of that word's meaning) intended for the preservation, enhancement, & continuation of human life. There is no "decadence," not even so innocent a decadence as hoboes represent. People are lucky in Miles City, they live well, they respect each other, they stick together, & their lives there are a rich chronicle of absorptions, interesting considerations, & solemn joy—no hysteria, nothing "forced"—a mild foregathering of mild birds. They winter and they summer with equal mild strength. Life is joyous . . . and yet life is also dangerous there: wherever men are, there's danger; but I consider the danger from mild men the only human danger I should not want to welcome. In Miles City I believe I would mind my own business. And I believe others would do so, too. You can have your Utopian orgies: at least, if it comes down to an orgy, I should prefer an orgy with the Montanans, for just such reasons.

Now an even more *moving* part of the trip was yet to come . . . a discovery of the astonishing spirit of the modern West, in "darkest" North Dakota. Yes, in North Dakota there are people I would value more than all the people, taken generally, in New York and all Europe to boot—and I would take these North Dakotans specifically. If I wanted to depend on the blood of men & women, I would go to this No. Dakota and nowhere else.

NORTH DAKOTA—THE NIGHT IN THE BADLANDS
In the bitter winter night of snow-plains we rolled to Terry
and then Glendive, Mont. I had been dozing. Certain passengers got on at this last Montana way-station, and soon we were
in Beach, No. Dakota. What a dismal, bitter night—with a cold
moon. To my surprise, at Medora, the Incalculable Missouri
had worn a rock canyon and this was the Heart of the Badlands. What is it the Missouri does not do?—what lands?—
rock? alluvial? will you have frozen rangelands, or black
canyons, or Iowa vales, or *deltas*? By January moonlight, in
this northernmost part of America, the ghostly snow-rocks
and buttes stood in bulging, haunted shapes . . . ambiguous
heaths for bearded badmen in flight from the law of raw
towns. Such a town was Medora; and Belfield . . . the great
American West that stretches so far from Pasco Washington to
places north of Oshkosh, Nebraska. No more "badmen"—not
on horseback—but the same rugged, undeniable world for
rugged necessary soulfulness. Thus stood my thoughts (which
were also haunted by the moony rocks & snows of the Badlands Canyon) when, outside of Dickinson, the mad busdriver
almost went off the road on a sudden low snowdrift. It didn't
phase him the least, till, a mile out of Dickinson, we came
upon impassable drifts, and a traffic jam in the black Dakota
midnight blasted by heathwinds from the Saskatchewan Plain.
—There were lights, and many sheep-skinned men toiling with
shovels, and confusion—and the bitterest cold out there, some
25 below, I judge conservatively. Another bus

DICKINSON, NORTH DAKOTA

Eastbound was stuck; a truck; and many cars. Major cause of
the congestion was a small panel truck carrying slot-machines
to Montana—so that these great commerces were held up by
slot-machines so needless in the Dakota steppes. From the little
Western town of Dickinson nearby came crews of eager young
men with shovels, most of them wearing red baseball caps (or
airforce caps, like the caps worn by 2 So. Dakota boys I met on
the road in 1947.) And heavy jackets, boots, earmuffs—led by

the sheriff, a strong joyous boy of 25 or so himself. They pitched in—it was an attritive, swirling, arctic-like night: I thought of their mothers and wives waiting at home with hot coffee, as though the traffic jam in the snow was an emergency touching Dickinson itself. Is this the "isolationist" middle-west? Where in the effete-thinking East would men work for others, for nothing, at midnight in howling freezing gales? The scene out beyond the men and the lights was as the plain of Desolation itself . . . the Greenland ice cap in darkness. We in the bus watched. Once in a while the boys came in to warm up . . . some said it was 40 below, I don't know. Some of the boys were fourteen, even twelve years old. Finally the busdriver, a maniacal and good man, decided to pile on through. He gunned the Diesel motor and the big bus that said "Chicago" on it went sloughing through drifts. We swerved into the panel truck: I believe we might have hit the jackpot. Then we swerved into a

THE DAKOTANS

brand new 1949 Ford. Wham! wham! Finally we were back on dry ground after an hour of travails. For me it was just a good show, I had no boots to go out in. In Dickinson the café was crowded and full of late Friday night excitement—about the snow-jam mainly. All around, on the walls, were photos of old ranchers and even some of fabled out-laws and characters. The Dickinson boys of a less robust breed shot a homey pool in the back. The pretty girls sat with husbands and families. Hot coffee was the big order. Men came in and out from the howling badlands midnight with news of further travails. We heard that the rotary plow had swerved into the new Ford and the mighty rotaries had disposed of the back end in a manner reminiscent of shrapnel bursts—that parts of the new car were so sent to graze in various parts of the snowy range. Or the rotary plow just went sowing? In any case, I hated to leave this marvelous atmosphere, this *real* town, where Nature & Custom found a grand way of meeting and joining forces. Men work against each other only when it is safe to abandon men—only when and where. The Dakotans paid little attention to us now that we were safe; we needed them, they came; but they had no need of us, "Chicago" slickers that we really were. I took one last look at the place, and the pictures on the wall, and the people, and wished that I had been born & raised & died in Dickinson, North Dakota.

NO MORE DAKOTA

We got stuck again outside town but the boys were there again with the rotary plow. A big truck-trailer was stuck deep; the driver was lost in the wastes without them. They hauled chains and chipped ice and shouted, all as if they enjoyed saving the situation. In the East we would despair. We got out and zoomed on across Dakota. I slept in the back, after one interruption when the motor caught on fire. While I slept the bus stalled in Bismarck, in a solid-frozen dawn; all the passengers got out because the heater failed and the inside of the bus was below zero temperature. They huddled in a diner. The bus was driven to a garage and repaired. Through all this I slept calm and wonderful, and had pleasant dreams, of Dakota in June, or of enchanted summers somewhere. I woke up refreshed in Fargo (isn't it a cold-sounding name?) It was −30 below.

And then the trip across the flat, snowy, sunny Minnesota of farms and church steeples was of course uneventful, except for a road outside Moorhead that was obviously designed by a really malignant architect to jiggle one's stomach out in regular, mathematically computed intervals. No mind.

And how dull it was to be in the East again . . . no more raw hopes: all was decided and satisfied here. I talked to a fine old man going into St. Cloud, however, who remembered 19th century Minnesota "when the Indians were out at Alexandria" (few miles

MINNEAPOLIS — ST. PAUL

west of Osakis Lake.) Nothing wrong with Minnesota except the middleclass . . . which is ruining the entire nation anyway. At St. Cloud great Father Mississippi flowed in a deep rocky bed beneath Lowell-like bridges; and great clouds, as at the destination in New Orleans, hovered over this northern valley. I have only one objection to make to Minnesota, namely, it is not Montana. This is the objection of a man in love—with the western America. We drove to Anoka and then St. Paul.

This famous river port still has the old 1870 brick along the waterfront . . . now the scene of great fruit and wholesale markets, just as in Kansas City near the downhill Missouri shore. St. Paul is smaller and older and more rickety than Minneapolis, but there is a depressing Pittsburgh-like sootiness about it . . . even in joyous snowy winter. Minneapolis is a sprawling dark city shooting off *white communities* across the montonous flats. The only soulful beauty here is rendered by the Mississippi and also by a hopeless hint of Mille Lacs and the Rainy River country to the North. The people are eastern (of course it's called 'middlewestern') city people; and their corresponding *look, talk, & absorptions.* Blame it on me; I hate almost everything. I would have liked to see Duluth merely because of Sinclair Lewis and Lake Superior.

These are my melancholy opinions.

Then, after a meal in a Minneapolis lunch-house and a freezing walk in the black streets, and

WISCONSIN — CHICAGO — MICHIGAN

a short talk with a young man in the bus station who had a Fire of Phenomenality in his eyes and ended up giving me religious tracts (one more involved & free-thinking than the other, designed for blokes), the bus rolled into Wisconsin and to the charming river-darknesses of Eau Claire.

Eau Claire belongs to a type of American town I always like: it is on a river and it is dark and the stars shine stark-bright, and there is something *steep* about the night. Such towns are Lowell, Oregon City, Holyoke Mass., Asheville N.C., Gardiner Maine, St. Cloud, Stuebenville O., Lexington Mo., Klamath Falls Ore., and so on—even Frisco of course.

After Eau Claire and a glimpse of the flat Wisconsin night of pines & marshes, I slept and was borne down to Chicago at dawn.

The same scraggly streets in dirty dawns . . . the eastern metropolis again . . . Negro workingmen waiting for work-buses and coughing; the early traffic in cars; the great Rubble of City stretching in all directions like a puzzle and a damnation and an enigma. It was the same Chicago as in '47 . . . but this time I did not stop to examine the "riotous, tinkling night" of Bop at the Loop; and beans in hungry diners.

I hated Gary, I even hated South Bend (land of car-dealers and gravelly desolation): what are we going to do?

Then the lovely Indiana and Ohio farmlands I had seen many times before; finally Toledo (Holy Toledo!)—where I got off to hitch-hike to Detroit and walked 3 miles to get out on the highway.

BEAT IN DETROIT
(Sitting on my bag on the floor of the men's room.)

DETROIT Feb. 9, 1949
I got off the bus at Toledo on a wild desire to see ex-wife, ex-love, ex-joy Edie . . . I hitched to Detroit in the sunny afternoon. I made it in three rides from three fine men (a young law student from Monroe Mich.; a machinist from Flat Rock Mich.; and another guy who told little of himself.) But I called Edie's mother and Edie wasn't there. I wandered the streets (with my last 85 cents) more beat than ever—(except 1947 in Harrisburg and 2 weeks ago on Ellis & O'Farrell Streets with Louanne.) And I had rages, awful rages. I still have them tonight (but a little less since I learned I can go back to Toledo and on to N.Y. on my ticket.) But I only have 25 cents now, and the Parker family spoke to me over the phone as tho I were a bum and Parker's wife flatly declined to lend me 3 bucks to eat on. Goddamn the whole crummy world. I rested up in the library reading up on Jim Bridger, Montana, and the Oregon Trail . . . for my own purposes. Tired and hungry as I am, I worry less about food and sleep than these people who won't lend me $3—and who were once my relatives. I wish Edie was here. I talked wistfully to her mother for an hour on the phone. And coincident with this feeling is a growing chagrin about my lost anger at Neal in Frisco five days ago. Life is so short!—we part, we wander; we *never* return. I die here.

THE OLD MAN OF RIVERS

NEW ORLEANS TO TUCSON—JAN. 1949

We left at dusk—waving goodbye to Bill and Joan and children Julie and Willie; and to tall, sad Al Hinkle and his wife Helen. Just Neal, Louanne and I in the big Hudson; bound for California 2,000 miles away. Wheeled through Algiers in the sultry old light—once more crossed on the dolorous ferry to New Orleans, by crabb'd ships at muddy-splashed river piers, by the bulging flood of the Brown Old Man of Rivers, and into the ancient slip at the foot of Canal Street.

Neal and I were still dreamily uncertain of whether it was Market St. in Frisco or not—at dreamy moments. This is when the mind surpasses life itself. More will be said and must be said about the sweet, small lake of the mind which ignores Time & Space in a Preternatural Metaphysical Dream of Life . . . On we went into the violet darkness up to Baton Rouge on a double highway. Neal drove grimly as the little blonde dozed, I dreamed.

At Baton Rouge we looked for the river bridge.

And lo! my friends, finally we crossed the River of the Myth of the Rainy Night at a place magically known as Port Allen, Louisiana. O Port Allen! Port Allen!—my heart on your tidal highway doth spread and fall like rain, with love and an intelligence like unto softest raindrops. O lights!—lights at the river cape and at the port; warm, sweet, mys-

POEM OF RAIN & RIVERS

terious tapers burning here at the place of places where is the fruition of the fleshly rain. For rain is alive and rivers cry too, cry too—Port Allen like Allen poor Allen, ah me.

No, no—to cross the Mississippi River at night, at night in violet Louisiana, Oh Inviolate Louisiana, is to bridge the Bridge of Bridges—to assume for once the dark, dear knowledge of a heritage which has yet no name and of which, poor heritage, we have never spoken aloud, and need not speak.

For what is the Mississippi River?

It begins in Montana snows and flows to the Mouths of the

South . . . to the Gulf that is Night . . . and outward to return in Rain, Rain, Rain that sleeps.

O what is the Mississippi River?

It is the Water of Life, the Water of Night, the Water of
Sleep—and the Water, the soft brown Water of Earth. It is that
which has and does receive all—our Rain, our Rivers, our Sleep,
our Earth, and the White Night of our Souls . . . the Lamb
that White Tears weeps.

And what is the Mississippi River?

It is the River we all know and see. It is where Rain tends,
and Rain softly connects us all together, as we together tend as
Rain to the All-River of Togetherness to the Sea.

For this is mortal earth we live on, and the River of Rains is
what our lives are like—a washed clod in the rainy night, a soft
plopping from drooping Missouri banks, a dissolving (Ah!—a
learning), a spreading, a riding of

"LITTLE RAINDROP THAT IN DAKOTA FELL"

the tide down the eternal waterbed, a contributing to brown,
dark, watery foams; a voyaging past endless lands & trees &
Immortal Levees (for the Cities refuse the Flood, the Cities
build Walls against Muddy Reality, the Cities where men play
golf on cultivated swards which once were watery-weedy
beneath our Flood)—down we go between shores Real and
Artificial—down a long by Memphis, Greenville, Eudora,
Vicksburg, Natchez, Port Allen, and Port Orleans, and Port of
the Deltas (by Potash, Venice, and the Night's Gulf of Gulfs)
—down along, down along, as the earth turns and day follows
night again and again, in Venice of the Deltas and in Powder
River of the Big Horn Mountains (name your humble source)
—down along, down along—and out lost to the Gulf of Mortality in Blue Eternities.

So the stars shine warm in the Gulf of Mexico at night.

Then from soft and thunderous Carib comes tidings, rum-
blings, electricities, furies and wraths of Life-Giving Rainy God
—and from the Continental Divide come Swirls of Atmosphere and Snow-Fire and winds of the Eagle Rainbow and
Shrieking Midwife wraiths—then there are Labourings over
the Toiling Waves—and Little Raindrop that in Dakota fell

and in Missouri gathered Earth and Mortal Mud, selfsame
Little Raindrop Indestructible—rise! be Resurrected in the
Gulfs of Night, and Fly! Fly! Fly on back over the Down-Alongs
whence previous you came—and live again! live again!—go

MISSISSIPPI RIVER NIGHT

gather muddy roses again, and bloom in the Waving Mells of
the Waterbed, and sleep, sleep, sleep . . .

God bless Life, oh God bless Life.

Then, with the radio on to a mysterious mystery program
(and as I looked out the window and saw a sign saying "USE
COOPER'S PAINT" and answered: "Allright, I will.")—then
we rolled across the Hoodwink Night of the Louisiana Plains
to Opelousas—and towards the Bayous at DeQuincy and
Starks; where we were to read the Chinese Manuscript of the
American Night.

But first we stopped for gas in Opelousas.

In the rickety streets of the soft & flowery night of January's
Louisiana, I wandered into a grocery store and came out with
a bread and a jar of cheese. Every *cent* counted if we were to
reach Frisco. There was no one in the haunted store. We rolled
on across the dark pasture-plains of the delta south; playing
more mystery programs on the radio.

We passed through Lawtell, Eunice, Kinder, Ragley and
DeQuincy . . . western rickety Louisiana towns becoming
more and more a Sabine-like bayou country; till finally
between Starks and Deweyville we passed over a dirt road
through the bayou wilds. An elevated road, with mossy trees
on each side, and hints of darkest swamp-water, and no road-
lamps . . . sheer snaky dark. The mansion of the copperhead,
the moccasin, & the mottled adder; drooping vines, silence;
star sheen on dark ferns, and the reeds of the mires. Neal
stopped the car and turned out the lights.

We were in the silence of this mireful, drooping dark.

LOUISIANA BAYOUX

The red "ampere" Lutlon glowed on the dashboard . . . the
one red eye in the swamp of the dark. Louanne shuddered and

squealed. Neal turned the headlamps on again; they but illuminated a wall of living vines.

Then we crossed the Sabine River on a new bridge and
zoomed on over the Neches (these secret swamprivers of the
Deep South night) into oily-fragrant, dark, pinpoint-sparkling,
misty, vast, mysterious Beaumont Texas. (NOTE: North of
Eunice is *Ruston*, Big Slim's rickety hometown, his home in
Louisiana; I thought of it at Eunice. "Maw, I wanta be a hobo
someday," Wm. Holmes Big Slim Hubbard said to his mother
as a child in Ruston.)

But now Texas, the East Texas oilfields; and Neal saying:
"We'll *drive* and *drive* and we'll still be in Texas at this time
tomorrow night." Across the beginning of the Big Texas Night,
across the Trinity River at Liberty, and on into Houston and
more hints of Bayou Dark.

Evocations of Bill's old house here in 1947 . . . of Hunkey,
Joan, Julie, Allen & Neal; and the Armadillos. And Neal driving the car through haunted night-streets of Houston at 3 A.M.
reminiscing of former beat adventures with Hunkey, on this
corner, in that amusement center, in that bar, down that street.
The rickety niggertown. The downtown commercial streets. A
Houston wrangler suddenly roaring by on a motorcycle with
his girl . . . a poet of the Texas night, singing: "Houston,
Austin, Dallas, Fort Worth . . . and sometimes Kansas City,
sometimes old San Antone." Neal singing: "Oh look at that
gone cunt with him! Wow!"

We get gas and proceed, now, towards the range-West I so
dearly want to see again . . . to Austin . . . through Gid-
dings and Bastrop. I sleep thru Johnson City and wake up at
Fredericksburg. Louanne is

TEXAS RAINY NIGHT

driving, Neal is sleeping. Louanne and I talk. It is cold; there is
snow in the bunchgrass hills. It is the worst winter in western
history. I take over the wheel at Fredericksburg and drive carefully over snowy roads through Harper, Segovia, Sonora,
about 200 miles, while they sleep.

IMPORTANT NOTE: I just said I slept from Houston to
Austin. I had forgotten that I drove that night in a lashing rain

while they slept. At Hempstead, near the Brazos River, in a haunted rain-lashed rickety cow-town, a raincoated cowboy-hatted sheriff on horseback (the only human abroad in the abysmal muddy night) directed me to Austin. Outside of this little town, in the rain-mad night, a car came in my direction, headlights flaring. Rain was so heavy the road was but a blur. The headlights were coming right at me, either on my side of the road or I was on their side. At the last impossible moment of this blurry head-on collision, I swung the car off the road into the flat shoulder of deep mud. The car backed up. It had forced me off my own side. In the car were four sinister men, drunk, but grave.

"Which way is it to Houston?" I was too stunned and dismayed to demand that they help me out of the mud. Also I didn't want to get mixed up with them in this rainy wilderness. The rainy night in Texas, and in the American wilderness past, is not at all protective, but the greatest of menaces.

They went off towards Houston at my mute direction.

Then I woke up Neal and for half an hour, while Louanne was at the wheel, we kneeled in the mud in torrents of rain, and pushed . . . pushed the very night.

TEXAS THOUGHTS

We finally got the tormented Hudson out, and got all wet and muddy, and cold and miserable; and it was then I slept, to wake up to the snows of Fredericksburg. Neal lets Louanne and I drive because he knows that each one at the wheel knows precisely what to do, though we might deny it, and "everything takes care of itself, everything is all right." (NOTE WITHIN A NOTE: When I went to Frisco again in August of same year, Neal's shoes in the closet had not been cleaned yet of their cake of Texas mud from that night.)

In Sonora, to return to the next day, we repasted on bread and spread-cheese, and Neal drove then clear across the rest of Texas. I slept some and woke up in the orange-rocked, sage-brushed Pecos Canyon country, in golden afternoon light. We delightedly talked of many things, blasted, and finally all three of us took our clothes off and enjoyed the sun in our bellies as we drove westward into it at 70 miles per hour.

Ozone . . . Sheffield . . . Fort Stockton. I told them of my idea for a western movie using all of us in an epical cowtown and our likely transformations in such an atmosphere: Neal a wildbuck outlaw; Louanne a dancer in the saloon; I the son of the newspaper publisher and occasional wild rider on the plains; Allen Ginsberg the scissor-sharpener prophet from the mountains; Burroughs the town recluse, retired Confederate colonel, family tyrant, opium-eater and friend of the Chinese; Hunkey the town bum living in Chinese Alley; Al Hinkle the haunter of gambling tables . . . and so on. (Good idea for movie story someday.) We visited an old stoneheap monument Spanish church-ruins in the sagebrush, naked under coats.

Then on towards El Paso and Tucson.

"REDDISH MOUNTS OF MEXICO"

NEW ORLEANS TO FRISCO VIA TUCSON—JAN. 1949
I slept through Ft. Stockton and Van Horn and woke up at Ft. Hancock near the Rio Grande River. Another river! It was late afternoon. We descended, as I say on p. 44, from the plateau of Texas into the great world-valley that separates Texas from Mexico. Rolled under valley trees through Fabens, Clint, Ysleta, with the river and the reddish mounts of Mexico on our left. Neal told me a long story about the unbelievably repetitious radio station at Clint, whose program he used to listen to in a Colorado reformatory. Just records, Mexican and Cowboy, with repetitions of advertisement for a "high school correspondence course" which all the young wranglers in the West at one time or another think of writing in for . . . because, uneducated, they feel they should have a diploma of some kind.

We came into El Paso at dusk. It was to be a year and a half later the same Neal and I would make the amazing jump from Texas into the Indian land of Mexico. But now our eyes were bent on Frisco and the Coast. However we were so broke it was decided something should be done in El Paso. To be honest, we thought of hustling, in some innocenter way, with the attractive blonde, but nothing ever came of it. It was cold as fall in El Paso, and grew dark. We buzzed the Travel Bureau

but no one was going West. We lingered around the bus station to persuade would-be customers of the Greyhound Bus
Lines to switch to our Slow Boat to China. Actually, we were
too bashful to approach any one,

THE KID ON HIS WAY TO OREGON

even the college boy who watched Louanne so flusterdly (she
was giving him the works for exercise.) Neal finally ran into a
'buddy'—some dumb kid from reform school who said 'Let's
go mash somebody on the head and get his money.' Neal made
him talk, and laughed, and enjoyed, and ran off for five minutes with him, while L. and I had ourselves a ball of sorts in the
car. So it went, in the dark sidestreets of El Paso and all that
desert in front of us and no gas-money. Finally Neal returned
and we decided to chance it to Tucson, Arizona, anyway, where
my friend Harrington could feed us a meal and lend me gas
money. 'On the way,' Neal said, 'we will pick up hitch-hikers
and get a half-buck from each one; that's 2 gallons and forty
miles.' Well, right outside El Paso, after we skirted the Rio
Grande in its Juarez night all a-glitter over yonder, and reached
a main highway, there stood our first (and last) hitch-hiker.
Forget his name, but he had one embryonic, useless hand, was
about eighteen, quiet and sweet natured, and said he was going
from Alabama to Oregon without a cent . . . home was Oregon, poor kid. Neal liked his sweetness so, and him too, that he
took him on anyway "for kicks," and that is the goodness of
Neal. Off we went towards Las Cruces, which Neal had negotiated earlier on his way to our meet in North Carolina, and
now we actually had "another mouth to feed." I slept through
Las Cruces, in the back seat, and woke up at dawn to find the
car stopped on a mesquite mountainside, everybody sleeping,
Neal at the wheel, the Kid beside him Louanne in the back,
and a cold fog at the car-windows. I got out to

REFERENCE MADE TO TRIPS WRITTEN

stretch my legs and look at the West. It was very cold indeed.
But what a scene met my eyes when the dawn-fog dispersed
and the sun appeared all of a sudden over the mountains. I

didn't know where we were, but it was in the vicinity of Benson. Dewy cactus, red gold sunrises, giant mists, a purity so intense it takes a city man a double take to understand what he's
seeing & smelling—and hearing from the birds. Trucks far
down the mountain growling on the dew road.

(The rest of this trip is carefully and completely recorded in
the 1950 "On the Road" of Dean Moriarty and Sal Paradise—
the trooper in Benson, the stay in Tucson, the Okie hitchhiker
outside El Paso, the drive thru Techatchapi Pass & Bakersfield
& Tulare & on into Frisco where I had the Market Street
Vision)

-----------------------*-----------------------

LIFE, LIFE

T-NOTES—Here is how I think we look at each other & get
to know each other in this strange existence of ours. (Isn't it
strange?) We all know what a certain someone is when he is
alone, we have our private portrait of him, sometimes even a
set, loving image. (How this "loving image" can be shaken
when we see someone who has changed over the years.) The
private portrait of someone is so funny, so awful, so very beautiful: especially someone we love,—that is, dote upon?—IN just
this way, when I saw Joan's rocky, gaunt, red face after a year
—and she was so pretty, so plumpishly German once—my
"loving image" of her underwent a kind of defamation. It is
that serious.

But the main point here: when someone we dote upon turns
to us from his immortal solitary posture and seeks to speak to
us, to communicate, to cadge, cavil, enjoin, persuade, anoint,
or impress, with appropriate expressions and exertions, we see,
instead of the loving image, a kind of horrible new revelation
of reality, so suddenly existent, and forever, so ineradicable
too, and fear for ourselves and our poor private portraits and
notions; we quake; yet at the same time, in a kind of sweet si-
multaneity that *redeems*, (and life is so full of redemptions we
never acknowledge!) we also see the dear 'routine' of this person, his manner of 'coming out' to us, that pitiful admixture of
pride, deceit, shyness & underlying real regard, tender hope,

and all, which is seen to have existed before anyway, and is compared and noted with regard to other revelations, & related to the loving image again—again—and again.

JUST ON THE ROAD SOMEWHERE

I have had the pleasure of noting this in the way that Louanne watched Neal over many days & nights of driving. First she sullenly, ruefully observed his set, rigid posture at the wheel while he drove; his little demonstrations of will & vigour in the way he flicked the car around curves; and most of all, his hang-jawed wonderment as he suddenly fairly forgot he was not alone and dwelt in his "eternity," with sad silence. She would sit there doting over his sullen air of male self-containment, his absentminded rumination, his very *bulgant* face; then a small smile would come across her face, because she was just so amazed he existed, and that he knew her, and was so amazingly himself all raging & sniffy & crazy-wayed. Ah, that smile of hers, that which all men want from their women, the smile of tender dotage & sinister envy. And she *loved* him so much—so much so that she would want to keep his head in some secret place, there to go and gaze at it every day; or one of his hands; or feet . . . the bony manliness of him.

But, lo! there was Neal suddenly turning to her, seeing her (with absorbed afterthought), realizing she was watching him *that way*, & realizing she was there, and smiling the false, flirtatious smile of his. I, in the back seat watching, and Louanne in front, would burst out in simultaneous glee. Moreover, Neal, far from being "found out," or disturbed or anything, would merely grin the way men grin when they know people are laughing at them because they love them and see them: a grin of knowing consistency lightened by a mixture of watery, good-natured buffoonery, & self-acceptance. This is by the way one of the few human gestures without words, a wordless realization that one is after all funny.

ARIZONA THINGS

ARIZONA

Some notions: in Wickenburg, in 1947, tho it was a hot

desert day, dry & sunny, I saw a man and his wife and kids in a small buckboard dragging trees from their yard, in the shade of many trees: it was a kind of joyous Arizona suddenly. This was all later confirmed when I travelled up through Prescott, Oak Creek canyon, and timbered Flagstaff, where, in high woodsy airs viewing distant desert-horizons far off, one feels the peculiar joy of canyon country, high country, timber country: a kind of mountain gladness (is it not logical that the yodel originated in the mountains?) When crossing the Colorado river near Indio, you see an Arizona of desolations . . . especially near Salome . . . a desert, with a shack a mile off the road every 30 miles or so, and crossroad towns—and far off, the Mexican mountains where the gila monster sung himself; and mesquite, gopher holes, cactus, buttes, lonely mesas way away.

In the mountains near Benson it is a kind of heaven at sunrise—cool, purple airs; reddish mountainsides; emerald pastures in valleys; the dew; the transmuting clouds of gold.

Tucson is situated in beautiful flat mesquite and river-bed country overlooked by snowy ranges like the Catalina. The people are transient, wild, ambitious, busy, gay; downtown bustles & promises to bustle much more; it is "Californian."

Fort Lowell Road, following riverbed trees, is a long green garden in the mesquite plain.

EL PASO & TEHATCHAPI, CALIF.

TWO VIEWS—EL PASO & MOJAVE
There are two interesting vantages in the West I can think of where you can see unbelievably vast valleys—valleys so all-inclusive that they floor three or four rail roads, and you can see locomotive smoke miles apart simultaneously puffing.

There is the valley of the Rio Grande as seen from east of El Paso. Here, at reddening sundown, we drove over a long straight road under trees (a riverbed road again.) To our left, across the river, across the green farmlands, were the jagged mountains of Mexico—a reddish wall, a monastery wall too, behind which the sun seemed to be setting, sadly, to the accompaniment of some brooding Mexican guitars we heard on the car radio. I am sure there were no better way for me to see

Mexico for the first time. And to think of night settling down behind those mountains,—! in secret, soft Mexico, a purple shawl over their vineyards and dobe-towns, with stars coming on so red, so dark; and perhaps that Moorish moon.

Straight ahead the valley seemed to drop us off some topmost level of the world, down to territorial slopes where the separate locomotives toiled in various directions . . . as tho the valley were the *world*.

Same thing just before the town of Mojave in California, in the kind of valley formed by high Mojave's plateau descending to the west, with the high Sierras of Tehatchapi Pass straight ahead north: again, a bewildering view of the ends of the world, & the rail roads in the various distances, like smoke-signals going from nation to nation. And *after* Tehatchapi?

A view of the whole floor of California!! (Bakersfield.)

COLORADO

THE DIVIDE   May, 1949
The Continental Divide is where rain and rivers are decided . . . and in the shadow of this central event in the myth of the rainy night, dwell now I. Westwood Colo. might have, should have been called Foothill Colo. This is where I live. I am watching the wrath of sources here . . . and the Lamb is in my bed.

And here too, the melodious airs and rumorous murmurs of summer afternoon,—in Colorado fields—vast afternoon excitements blowing in from the Plains—and to our west the severe yet smiling mountains of day.

I am Rubens . . . and this is my Netherlands beneath the church-steps. Here I will learn the Day.

NEW YORK — NEW JERSEY

NEW YORK TO DENVER; MAY, 1949
The trip on which I spent 90 cents for food, in order to save money in my search, in Denver, for a house in which I dwelled when I wrote words on opposite page 70. Took a bus all the way. As we rolled out of New York at midnight, and as I fondly remembered A.'s love-bed of an hour before (Spanish girl),

and as I contemplated this important move in my life which would consume my first $1000 advance from the publishers but would settle the family once and for all, as we rolled on into the red, red night of America, towards that home-town Denver, I sang the following song:-

"Been to Butte Montana
Been to Portland Maine
And been in all the rain—
But tell my pretty baby,
I ain't goin' back to New Orleans;
Tell my pretty baby
I'm goin' on home to Denver-town."

I had intense visions of the sheer joy of life . . . which occurs for me so often in travel, coupled with a grand appreciation of its mystery, & personal wonder.

After the usual run to Pittsburgh over the uninteresting garden-like drives of the East, in this case the Pennsylvania Turnpike, in a hot noon I got off the bus to wait for the Chicago coach. Walked in downtown Pittsburgh to find a cheap lunchroom.

Was already weary from the night's traveling.

PENNSYLVANIA—OHIO RIVER

I found a lunchroom and had two 5 cent cups of coffee with some of my sandwiches. (Let me repeat that I was practicing an ascetism necessary to my soul & my plan for the folks, even though Paul the night before, after driving me to the bus station in N.Y., had spent almost $5 on a movie & parking lot. Possibly I spent only 90 cents on this trip to Denver *because* of that. I should have *foreseen* enough at that moment.)

The trip to Chicago was more interesting. In the lullal afternoon we rolled into the Pennsylvania hills with their mounds of dug-out sand, and scarred mine-sides, and general doleful industrial ruination—although green else about. At Weirton, West Virginia, it was pretty much a town risen from these things—a mining town, haunted by scarred mountain-sides beyond each sooty backstreet. Main Street was a beehive of shopping activity in the Friday afternoon, the excitement

of a work-week ended . . . men in shirt-sleeves, women, &
children.

Yet the moment we crossed the ever-so majestic Ohio River
on the other side of town, and rolled across the bridge, to
Steubenville, Ohio, it changed—from mining-country bleakness to a Wabash-like shore of soft trees; even though it's a
kind of factory town, Steubenville.

In the late afternoon we rolled across a hillier Ohio than
that I had known before northwards around Ashtabula &
Cleveland, (Joe Martin itinerary.)

At dusk, into the spacious avenues of Columbus.

Then on to Indianapolis, Indiana, across the moonlit night.
I watched the moony fields

INDIANA—ST. LOUIS

which in the Fall, as I had seen them Fall of '47, are shrouded
in a moon-mist & haunted by the frowsy shapes of harvest
stacks . . . Indiana corn. But in May-night, Indiana is precisely that which you feel when you sing "Oh the moon is
bright tonight along the Wabash!"—so I sang it. Later, I conversed with a fellow-passenger, a young actor named Howard
Miller, from Muncie, Indiana, who had lain in the night long
ago dreaming of Broadway, and was coming home to work in
his father's grocery store awhile. He reminded me of Hal
Chase.

After Indianapolis I fell asleep, in spite of the beauty of the
night and its moon, and woke up just as we rolled into East St.
Louis, Illinois, about nine in the morning. I had known all
about this wild old town from Burroughs before . . . a redbrick river-town. Was not chagrined for sleeping, as I knew the
land between Indianapolis & St. Louis from previously.

Across the bridge!—across the Mississippi River!—under
morning sun-clouds!—in cool May air!—into St. Louis.
Again I crossed the River.

I shaved in the men's room of the bus station, using a young
fellow-passenger's razor—a psychiatrist, of all things; then
took a walk to the riverfront, where I'd been before, and
loafed on a corner, like a veritable young Wade Moultrie.

Back to the bus—and across the beautiful afternoon of Missouri, with its balsamic odours of clover, fresh-cut hay, & sun-warmed, rich earth. Whole vistas of this.

MISSOURI AFTERNOON

No land could be more fertile than Missouri land. It is still odorous from the relatively recent presence of the River—rank with greeneries. There must be more beautiful trees in lush Missouri than anywhere in the world. And such fields, such ripeness, such summerlands! No wonder Missourians are vain of their home. No wonder Mark Twain's "Campaign That Failed" was such a pleasant failure. In this world of fields, knolls, and hazy green distances, I almost regretted we would start climbing the gradual climb to the Higher Plains, to the Kansas prairies, & Colorado rangelands, for say what I will about the West—Missouri, and Illinois with its enchanted rivers, Indiana and Ohio, and New York State & New England, & all the South . . . represent the soft, sweet East of this world, as distinguished from the wild and arid west—and to make a choice between the two is like tearing out & examining the foundations of one's heart, where all ideas about life are stored. Shall it be the soft, sweet life of the Idyl? . . . or the wild & thirsty life? The life of enclosed horizons, the life of the sweet trees—or the life of vast, yearning plains. What does it do to any town, That at the end of its street at night, one either sees the *groves* of night—or the *desert* of night? Citizens take deeper note of this than they know.

MISSOURI

Somewhere in Callaway county I got off the bus and took a walk from the way-station into the heart of these lovely drowsing greeneries. It was dry & hot; there were cows; I sat in the grass. I wished I lived in Missouri—especially in afternoons.

We had passed through St. Charles & Warrenton: we now proceeded to Columbia, and at Boonville cross't the mighty Big Muddy. Pathetic that I should dwell so much on earth & rivers . . . for Boonville is one of the most ironic & ugly-souled towns in this world, and I do Love-of God no honor in avoiding issues of men. Boonville (a beautiful town outwardly, with ancient trees, shady streets, old houses) is remarkable for its preponderance of old men, octogenarians who look like Civil War vets and crawl along the sidewalks. Nothing wrong in the freedom of many old men, except that there is a large boy's reformatory in Boonville—those who can walk, may not; those who cannot, may.

I slept some on the way to Marshall. It rained. Somewhere along the line we picked up a poor slatternly woman and two children. I sat one of them on my lap; and he never budged an inch, or said a word, and ended up taking my hand in perfect understanding that I was his good friend & father-like fellow traveller. No "rich kid" would behave like that, but in little Missouri Ozarkie it is natural. Part Indian.

At Lexington, in the gray rain, the magnificent Missouri River showed its big face to me just as rainbows bloomed. A huge island split it into two wide, muddy channels.

MISSOURI—KANSAS CITY

This is a great river of rivers. I think the Mississippi is less patriarchal. The Missouri is wild & beautiful. It comes from stranger sources than Minnesota—nameless sources at Three Forks (the Gallatin, the Madison, the Jefferson) which are not *names* for what is up there, and will never do for me.—I opened the window to smell Big Muddy. A man from Kansas City conversed with me.

We entered Independence, or that is, bypassed it, and I saw no signs of what it used to be in the days of Parkman not Truman.

We entered Kansas City. I checked my bag and took a 5-mile walk down to the railroad yards overlooking the confluence of the Missouri and Kansas Rivers, an airport, and amazingly high levees. You can see the flood danger. The Missouri has a mean flow at this fork.

I walked back uphill through the old K.C. riverfront warehouses & meat packing plants; past fruit markets where extremely strange old men sat with extremely strange old dogs—in a long sunset. I noticed old K.C. and the new high-suburban one uphill—just as St. Paul; a city moves away from its original source, with all the brash forgetfulness of an ungrateful child grown fat & silly. But I cannot judge this century; besides I love this century; only, I love the last much more . . . or, in a different and personal-interesting way.

I walked up Broadway far as W. 12th St. It was Saturday night, all humming with excitement in the heat. The buffet bars are marvelous places.

NEW YORK TO DENVER, MAY 1949, (CONTINUED)

I walked in the downtown section; entered a tough poolhall-bar; had a beer in a buffet, & went back to the bus. I kept thinking how hot it was in Kansas City and dearly, eagerly, joyously looked forward to climbing out of the low Missouri Valley, to that place of my hopes—

High on the hill of the Western night
Denver, where the stars are wild . . .

I even sang this, tho I forget the exact words. I invented this song for motorcycle wanderers of the midwest night. He is in hot K.C., he wants to zoom down to Tulsa and Fort Worth, or out to Denver, Pueblo, Albuquerque—anyplace but here, in the hot Missouri night. He wants to go *up the hill*—and what a hill!—to where it's cool and clear and starry. At nine o'clock our bus rolled in that direction. Across the river, and zooming to Topeka.

In Topeka, I had a terrific frosted strawberry malt in a wild bus station on Saturday night. A crazy motorcycle kid, without any preamble, all decked in boots & studded cap, told me he had just wrecked his new motorcycle. He was proud as hell, and mad-eyed.

The bus zoomed on along the Kansas River to Manhattan. The prairie grew more desolated—it was dark out there. I kept my window part opened; the ladies in back of me complained. I slept a little. That psychiatrist who had traveled to St. Louis—what in the hell for was he coming out here to

psychoanalyze such wonderful people like that motorcycle kid? Which is best—wreck a motorcycle on a Saturday night, or stay home reading Freud? What is the earth for—what is the night for—what is food & strength for—what is man for? For joy, for joy.

In Manhattan, about one o'clock in the morning, it was wild and crazy. At the end of the streets you could see & mostly sense that great, wide, impenetrable prairie darkness, the likes of which exists nowhere else in the world. Though you cannot *see* the plane, you can *feel* that all this is in flat, black endlessness—that it is all around, and once blew tumbleweed, and still does. I once saw a cheap movie about Kansas with Randolph Scott and Robert Ryan, and though it was probably just filmed in a California backlot, somehow—by some accident and some love of my attention—it seemed just as I saw Manhattan, Kansas, that night . . . it was a ghost town . . . at each end-of-street nothing but the wall of dark, and hugest humming silence of an entire territory of grass rustling in the wind, and little feelings of blown dust quietly in the darkness, dust from hundreds of wide miles away. The feeling that there are no hills, no roads—just grass, just flat.

Though Manhattan, Kansas, in 1949 was not surrounded so wildly, so desolatedly any more, it was still *true* to its past— almost truer.

From out of this incomprehensible desert of

MANHATTAN, KANSAS

night came wild careening jaloppies driven by drunken boys. They roared into town at the other end, abruptly from the plains, and were suddenly zooming around where I stood in crazy U-turns. Above, the sky was black; as black as the walls at street's-end. They paid no attention to this. They wanted to go in the wild dance-bar which adjoined our bus-stop lunchroom. They piled out of the cars. A fight was developing among the revolving doors; sides were lining up; girls were peeking from the bar windows. Time and again I looked around us all at that incredible plane of darkness; never have I been so aware of the existence of man on his dark plain, in his pit of impenetrable night; his furies within it; his comings & goings, carelessly, on the *plane* of his haunt, his earth, his cruel

& sightless, huge universe. I was also awed, on another level, by the great wild joy which existed here, *further in* on the plains from K.C. and Topeka; as though, isolated and doomed off from the life of cosmopolitan cities, they here took on the craziness of the native coyote instead. I never saw such crazy kids . . . the way they drove, the way they wanted to fight, the way they ate and drank. No old folks were in sight, just kids in a haunted town in the plains. The smell of the night was sweet . . . a prairie May-night—the smell of the Kansas River, of hamburgers, of cigarettes . . . and that strangely haunting smell of gasoline in the air.

KANSAS-NIGHT COW

On our way in, just outside Manhattan, near the bend of the Big Blue River, our busdriver had rammed into a cow on the highway. Everybody made jokes about steak. It was a terrific bony concussion. In Manhattan we all signed as witnesses to the event—an event which struck me as being sad. An old white-faced cow, in its world of darkness, its rummaging, foraging, joyous, peaceful existence, doth cross the hot pavement of man from clover to sweetest clover—musing perhaps—and out of the dark comes the monster with the blazing eyes and the sign says 'Denver'—and WHAM! Dead cow; cloven brainpan; blood on the hot road, on the hot radiator. To this—from the incredibly sweet moment-before. For a cow in the night, with all the sweetgrass in the prairie to loll over, has thoughts of its own in the secret wides out there . . . thoughts which are not far from mine when I ride by.

This is my elegy to the *Kansas-Night Cow*

KANSAS-NIGHT COW
Bovine skull, so lately stored
With cuds of grassy thought,
And eyes a moment before
Which kenned dark plains
And airy deeps—stairy-secret,
Ghostly, white-faced, silent cow—
Thou nun of night in prairies—

I sympathize with thy bones
All broken on this hot highway.
   The fool eats hamburger of thy doom
   Yet learneth nothing of thee so shy.

WEST KANSAS WILDS

—Finally I slept, and as the bus made its slow upward mount
to the High Plains, dreamed—but what it ever was who will
ever know or understand? Someday we'll all have died and
nothing settled . . . just the forlorn rags of growing old, and
nearer, to the bleak affinities of grave & history. Woke up,
having slept through Abilene, Salina, *Ogallah*,—in Oakley,
where we all had breakfast in a ramshackle inn in the cold gray
morning.

At Cheyenne Wells in sunny Sunday morning a blue eyed
cowboy got on the bus & smiled at everyone as he hustled his
bag to the rear, his clothes smelling of the clean Plains—his
smile so sincere & open everyone was embarrassed & looked
away—and I knew we'd reached the True West. This same
cowboy told me where to go in Denver for fieldhand work.

Afternoon thundershowers partially hid the wall of the Divide as we rolled down East Colfax into Denver.

That night I'd finally contacted Brierly and he flashed his
spotlight on me on the corner of Colfax & Broadway, our
meet.

Inside 3 days I has the cottage out Alameda Avenue & was
cooking up steaks in the backyard & reading cowboy stories in
the furnitureless house at night, HAPPY!

WILD NIGHT IN BROWNSVILLE

BROWNSVILLE TEXAS TO ROCKY MOUNT,—JULY 1952
Hitchhiking all the way, with a 5-dollar bill and a big packbag
—No time to stop cause I wanta be home for 4th July—Start
off walking from Mexican bus across Matamoros, out dusty
streets, to border, American guards, & into Brownsville—out

to connecting highway, where I'm picked up by Hotrod
Johnny Bowen of Brownsville who wants me to have a beer with
him—A few beers in roadhouse—Now he wants me to drink
with him all night—wants me to get a job in Brownsville—He
is a crazy lonely kid—wants me to go see his pregnant wife—
we drink and do, she throws him out (they're separated)—
Wants me to meet his Drive-In sister, she says "I don't wanta
be told who to go out with"—he's crazy

—He plays pinball machine all up & down the highway, we
get drunk, drive 100 mph thru intersections, play pool with a
buncha Mexicans downtown Brownsville one of whom
"borrows" $1 from me & I so drunk I give it, out of my 5—

At dawn I'm broke—we sleep in his house, Texas cottage—
Next day I'm sick & also dysentery fever

—Have soda, he gives me back my $5—I go out on road &
am sick in gas station toilet—sit a long while resting—Then I
hitch—Got 3000 miles to go—Immediate ride to Harlingen
along endless fence of King Ranch, with old hillbilly who
hearing of Mexican whores thinks it wd. be a good idea to
bring a truckload to Chicago—Long wait in hot sun at Harlingen, I drink cokes,—Get ride to Rosenberg Texas from young
Mexican medical student—Then spot ride into Houston
where drunken construction worker invites me into his motel
room for shower & when I come out he on his belly naked
begging me to screw him—I leave, wont do it—he's crying—I
get ride from little faggot who owns Dandy Courts, says
"Hitch out here in front of my court (motel), if

ALL THOSE BLACKEYED PEAS

you don't get a ride come in & sleep" but I do get ride from
oil truck driven by wild talking rhythmic Cherokee Indian
mentioned on p. 74 of DHARMA BUMS, to Liberty Texas
at dawn, where I sleep on railroad loading platform—There
ride with flat truck carrying pile of black-eyed peas in bags,
we stop to fix load under "tarpolian" he called it, thru Beaumont to Baton Rouge—Hot sunny highway I suck on flavored
ice in a cup, get a ride up to Mississippi from some pleasant
Mississippian—Many spot rides thru the night, little towns, to
Jackson Miss.—One guy picks up another hitchhiker a strange

pale blond kid coming back from a Billy Graham revival meeting!—I wind up in mid of night in sleepy village of Newton Miss., no rides whatever, in fact no traffic, I just sit on curb in hot summernight sad, try to sleep a little in tiny bus station, sitting up head on war bag—In the morning a fine breakfast strengthens me (I ate so heartily tourists stared at me, pancakes & eggs & toast!)—Bam, a sudden ride from a fine gentlemen, kinda hip, in a new car, takes me up through Montgomery & Tuscaloosa Alabama & on up thru Georgia where he buys me great meal of Southern cornbread, blackeyed peas et etc (great restaurant on curvy country road) & up through stopping in Tobacco Road crossroads for a beer among the strange Georgia Crackers, funny!—then up to Florence S.C. at dusk, end of ride, long ride, where I call Ma long distance & then hitch, getting final ride from big fat Walter Brown of Baltimore chugging 30 miles an hour up swamps of S.C. & southern N.C. (stopping midnight in diner with 10-year-old girl plays "Rocket 69" on jukebox) & Rocky Mount at dawn—Hungry! Exhausted! Grateful! Broke! Gaunt! Home!

DOWN TO CAROLINA

NEW YORK TO SAN JOSE—FEB. 1954
Wearing silly new tan Dragnet raincoat & carrying 'essential pack' for Baja California hermit life but inside temporary expedient American suitcase, walked home & Ma's love in cold night to Sutphin (wearing railroad gloves, earflap hat, 2 jackets under coat, 2 shirts) (& two pair jeans!)—E train to Port Authority, & thus began a voyage I shouldn't have taken—Bus to Washington at 10 P.M.—Sitting relaxed in front-up seat, practising rest & meditation, avoiding looking, thinking—bus takes NJ turnpike and rolls uninterrupted to Delaware, the Howard Johnson's only flashing by—At H.J.'s I get out and stand in cold deep-breathing—At Washington it's a little warmer, dawn, sun, I get off bus and hurry to Virginia bridge, stopping first for free breakfast of Farina, toast & eggs in Cafeteria—walk over bridge & realize awfulness—all these details—my hand hurts—thousands of cars raging around in a gasoline stink, haggard faces don't care, I abandoned bleakly in evil blank universe—Why didnt I go back home then?

Would have saved $250—But it was an 'instructive' trip. At the rotary drives with (earlier) Neal & Louanne & Hinkle I'd driven around in snow, now I stood, on cold brown grass, cant get a ride—Walk further. Finally near Pentagon a businessman picks me up—we talk of mushrooming population of Washington & Alexandria (when I get there I realize I know & remember & can talk about everything).—He drives me to outside Fredericksburg where I have quick snack in ice cream stand & cut out, thumb, for ride from Negro truckdriver ambitious, married, smart, quiet, like Willie Mays—Ride to Richmond, bleak, in cold gray I walk stretching truck-tucked legs, to junction, where ulcer-suffering carpenter rides me—I advise him to rest & think nothin,—All this time I've been radiating mental peace in silence to my benefactors & now I speak a little wisdom—He is surprised and interested—Drops me at James River bridge where I buy $60 of Traveller's Cheques foolishly, in bank, thinking I'll hitch all the way to San Josay——

Ride from guy who sells used cars, his brother behind him somewhere on road in their own car—Driving he is to Sanford, N.C.(!)—Good

SAD ROCKINGHAM

ride—I relax—We go thru Petersburg, South Hill, Novlina, Henderson, (all fated places. In So. Hill a dozen times I've passed, The Universal Ghost in All of US)—thru Raleigh, Sanford. There I tried to get a good night's sleep in a railroad hotel by the seaboard tracks, & did—Fine bed, old hotel, brakemen & conductors in the old lobby playing cards—I drank my brandy a bit—Practiced dhyana at dawn, resting mind from dreams of sex with "Eddie Fisher's Jewish girl"—Great freight trains balling by all night, B W A M !—Sad mist nightlamps of Carolina-like Obispo but another, sadder railroad) Dogs & cocks at dawn . . .

Morning, big sausage & eggs & pancakes breakfast; bought nose inhalors, cough drops, gum; stood on road (Hiway No. 1) at 9 A.M. fresh & ready for California.

Sinister bad luck—the foolish look of my raincoat shoulderstraps & hat with earmuffs, like eccentric killer on road—No rider—Walked 3 miles up a hill, out to country, angry—Finally, ride at afternoon, late, from big Armand, Okie, to Southern Pines—beautiful burnt gold warm afternoon with sough of pines & fragrance—Wanted to sit down there, why go 3000 miles to sit down & be Buddha?

Ride from non-committal soldier swiftly to Rockingham— Where, night falling, I buy ticket to Los Angeles at little Greyhound station, giving girl my precious $60 Travellers Checks —Waiting for bus I wander Saturday Afternoon streets among farmers & feed stores & conversations of sidewalks—Buy a bag of peanuts but clerk didn't tell me they were unroasted but eat them anyway in empty car fender lot, for proteins—amen, Negro children—One peanut has worm in it I can tell, as I swallow soft salty rot of something sad soup & crackers in North Carolina beer lunchroom with fat funny jokesters— Crazy conversation in street with Negro bus porter who tells all local histories, I radiate him mental peace—He tells of local Negro family had just slaughtered all its hogs & smoked them for the year & fire burns down house & hogs & feed & furniture, all—(just the other night)—Sun sets on sad little countrytown—Bus comes, crowded, I give my seat to old man to all as far as Charlotte.

Then in the night to Spartanburg, and Atlanta at dawn. I see the Southern Railroad tracks—

To Birmingham Alabama and Bessemer, vast mournful city with Negro shack slums & Sunday morning bicycles—

At Columbus Mississippi at noon I go up little hill to Faulknerian Sunday mainstreet and eat Duncan Hines lunch of soup

SWEET ESCAPEE IN JUAREZ

& exquisite croquettes & Caesar salad & homemade invisible lemon meringue pie that melted away—among Southern aristocrats in suits talking of huntin & fishin.

Across Mississippi all Sunday afternoon with hills suddenly dropping into flat Delta and passenger tells me local news & says lots of snaky at last delta hills—insisted on sitting with me to talk—We cross spectral Faulkner countries & I hear his dialect—till Greenville Mississippi at Sunday Night silence at

last Mississippi Gene's hometown) and I take quick walk to
levee and see great silent river moveless, in the peace & old
Showboats now Nightclubs tied at shore—and haunted trees
of Arkansas Huck Finn 'cross the way—crossing the Mississippi once more—

Across the night to El Dorado Arkansas where suddenly I
look up & see the stars & feel great joy and say:

> Release yourself sweet escapee,
> Death owns bones;
> But Infinite Emptiness
> Of pure perfect Mind
> Who how much owns?
> All, all of it

Dallas at dawn and take quick brisk walk around streets, after
shave & puttin on jeans, and buy bag of fresh donuts & eat
them with coffee in bus station—All day across Texas in the
crowded bus—stop at Boomtown Odessa where I walk & get
soup in lunchroom—whole town brand new, long on the highway, rich, useless, lonely in the vast plain with its oil towers
mistlike on endless horizons—On to El Paso, arriving 8 P.M.—
I walk quick to railroad hotel and get stuffy inside windowless
room but sleep—

In morning I get out for day of exploration of El Paso &
Juarez—Clear blue sky, warm sun, redbrick sorrow & fences
this side, dusty gray dobes and sad dry earth of Tarahumare
other side of Rio Grande—Get big pancake breakfast in American Mexican restaurant—whole town Indian, rickety, second-
hand clothing stores with ancient sheeplined cowboy coats—I
go across sad railroad plazas of dust to Juarez Bridge & cross
for 2 cents—into the blissful peace of the Fellaheen village at
hotsun noon—smells of tortilla, drowse of children & dogs,
heat, little long streets—I go

A TARAHUMARE AFTERNOON

clear out of town to river levee and squat on ground & see
America across the way and on this side an Indian mother
kneeling at the river washing clothes with little baby son
clinging lovingly to her back as he stands there—Thought, "If

my mother was only simple as to do her wash at the river"—
Felt happiness. But no-good drunken kid insisted on talking to
me, bumming Bull Durham, offering tea, etc.—But I get him
to talk Tarahumare dialect for me—We stroll—He explain-it
Mexico—he's a good kid actually but stoned—We met two
hipsters in a field who look like gangsters, which they are—
they beat my Indian for his money sometimes—I avoid them
and they cut, zoot-suited thru the bushes—In the field the ancient farmer and his wooden plow and his peace—Across the
river the SP yards, spuff up smoky heights head West for
Lordsburg & Yuma—It never occurs to me to continue the
journey by SP freight—Ole 373! The Zipper!—(next time)

I give kid 99 cents for tea & he never returns, going up into
bare sand humps where Indians forage in junk up to their
knees—Family are building new adobes—I meditate in sun on
levee, cruiser goes by & vanishes—I put on shoes & roam the
junk hills of the Tarahumare of El Paso—I circle way around—
find tattered Mexican comic books—pass Indians taking shits in
plain sight of women—examine how dobes are made—Watch
Tarahumare dobe-makers knead manure and mud with shovels
then dump it in frames and smooth and remove frames & leave
block to harden in sun—Indian seeing me watch says, smiling
"No sabe?"—I go back to downtown Juarez, roam in markets
selling desert cactus and herbs & mysterious seeds & roots,
wow—dig girls, cant stop looking at brunette lovelies—Have
beer & raw oysters in cool bar—Beers & write in guitar-singer
bar—Visit railroad station & dig funny yardgoats & boxcars &

BOOMIN TO YUMA

big fiesta crowds milling round station platform in hot sun—I
eat coconut delicacies & sit on rail—sit in sun listening to guitar
singers near bridge, on sidewalk with back to wall—Next time I
get straw hat and practice "siesta" meditation in streets of sweet
Mexico—Return to El Paso, buy for $2 an Army field coat with
huge pockets, go to dusty hike & dance alley & sit while little
Negro girl plays around me—Give her Mexican gumballs—Go
to El Paso station & roam around in hot red sun—rest feet in
park—Get on bus at sundown, roll across redness—

Lordsburg at night, big freight pulling in from West as we

stop rest stop—I rush out and buy bread & butter from almost-closed Chinese grocer and rush back to bus and three hoboes off eastbound freight panhandle me but I got nothin —They say they coming from California—Young Big Slim hobo says, "We been over that San-Luis-Obispo-*Bump!*"— hump!—

Bus rolls in night, I eat bread & butter humbly as two soldiers goof in backseat loud—Tucson in midnight, nice & warm, dark desert invisible but downtown lonely bright like Denver—On to Yuma, at dawn, where I sit on Yuma Yard-office bench up a flight of wooden stairs from the bus station, watching SP freights coming east & west, & spread butter on my bread & eat like student just in—In empty lot below I see mesquite bushes with still pieces of the yellow alogoraba pod hanging, one of Indian desert mysterious delicacies—(ripe in August)—Bus rolls on in opening dawn into Imperial Valley, to El Centro where cars parked diagonal on broad lonely Main Street—Beyond strip of irrigated agriculture the Imperial Valley is a desert—Orange groves, cotton—new houses—On into San Diego desert of rocks and cactus and lone sand hills—I see the Little Agave out there, with cabbage below and 12 foot stalk reaching up, the

STORMY MASON

great desert delicacy of the Cornhusk Indians—not a sign of em—nothing—a great lone desert for the hermitage, full of hidden food & water (kopash cactus has water inside)—But grim—On into San Diego, warm, sunny, down off the desert mountain pass—(Forget to mention Jacumba, stop between Yuma & El Centro, on the border, thus, birds at misty dawn & a man walking out of the trees of Mexico into the American sleepy border street of shacks & trees & backyard dumps)— (Future place for me)—

San Diego rich, dull, full of old men, traffic, the sea-smell— Up the bus goes thru gorgeous sea-side wealthy homes of all colors of the rainbow on the blue sea—cream clouds—red flowers—dry sweet atmosphere—very rich, new cars, 50 miles of it incredibly, an American Monte Carlo—Up to LA where I dig city again, to Woody Herman's band on marquee—Get off bus & walk down South Main St burdened with all pack and have jumbo beers for hot sun thirst—Go on down to SP rail-yards, singin, "An oldtime non-lovin hard-livin brakeman," buy wieners and wine in Italian store, go to yards, inquire about Zipper. At redsun five all clerks go home, yard quiet—I light wood fire behind section shanty and cook dogs and eat oranges & cupcakes, smoke Bull Durham & rest—Chinese New Year plap-plaps nearby—At 7 I get foolishly on Zipper caboose and talk to rear brakeman as train is made up—BRAM! SLAM! brakeman struggles to fix mantle and lamp and start coal fire—Conductor is Stormy Mason—Doesn't bide by my papers, order me out of the caboose—train is underway to Santa Barbara

—"Then get on out there, you cant ride in here or I pull the air!"—I curse and go out crummy door and light lamp (leaving gear in crummy) and tender brakeman tells me "Be careful" and I climb up ladder at last boxcar's side and run over walk-ramps keeping lamp unlit until watching switchman finished thinking I'm a hobo and yelling "There's a flatcar

"HE DONE MADE A BUM OUTA ME"

up ahead!" because if lamp lit they be confused—That's me!—all over!—and as train rolls & clacks I run & jump & come to flatcar, which has big machiners lashed on (SP trucks) and I get under & sit & sing "He done made a bum outa me!" and for first time in months, in cold rushing night air of California Golden Coast, uncork wine & drink up—raw, bad, rotgut—but I warm and sing all the way—

It gets cold in constant nightwind so I wrap up in my coat & huddle & freeze & sing—

At Santa Barbara I've had enuf but I see there's nothin but cold misty swamps beyond the tracks, & the cold seashore, so I wait till Stormy Mason is gone from crummy at his run's end & sneak back 12 cars to empty caboose, remove suitcase & bring it back to the flatcar, where I unpack blanket & wrap up & drink wine—Soon new crew gets Zipper underway for San Luis Obispo.

Now comes colder bleaker grimmer coast of after Gaviota, up by Surf, Tansair; Antonio

—I don't dare even look but over wild clack of wheels huddle & meditate, shivering—under stars—At San Luis Obispo, straightshot run, I get off shakey, no more wine, I get off before train stops, at roadhouse, & walk down to old Colonies Hotel of my brakeman days

—Closed, asleep—So I go downtown among familiar bleak palms & cottages to hotel & pay $1.50 for room & sleep, tearing up SP timetable & throwing it away "No more SP for me!" Blue morning I eat donuts & go out on 100 and hitch—Bah! I see a freight is leaving over overpass & I could have hopped it! But a ride comes just then from a crazy guy ex-infantry in new car, and up the San-Luis-Obispo-Bump we fly, to Santa Margarita, arriving one hour or 40 min. before the freight—So I have soup in ole familiar sweet Margarita where I'd made my first student-run breakfast & seen the

THE GOLDEN AGE IN A BOXCAR

Pome sectionhands at dewy morning—Bar that sells little bags of beef jerky & pinon nuts is closed, so I buy candy & sit in siding grass near my old hillswinger's shanty (to which I no longer have the key), in hot sun on moist ground wait—

Here comes the train, because an Eastbound is a-comin he'll stop—I get on engineer's side of tracks, right where I'd dreamed of the murderous hoboes chasing me (!), and calmly get in a boxcar, not a soul in sight—

Soon we start & on we go to Templeton, Hanery, Paso Robles, Wunpost, and on up the Salinas Valley

—The great riverbottom at Wunpost, another place for a bhikku hermitage!

—Hot sun pours into wide open door, I drowse—Train heads in at Templeton, I get out and lay in green bankside, still & happy, bliss, ignoring calls of hoboes 10 cars down—This where we'd had our break-in-2, conductor MacKinnon, & I'd talked to some bo's in my brakie past—Toot toot, I get back on as slack echoes up and on,

—We fly to Salinas and Watsonville in the hot delight of California in the afternoon—And I think "Death is the Golden Age."

At one point I force myself to throw up all that bad candy—

At Watsonville, familiar sad Watsonville, now only 50 miles from my goal, I get off, walk to west end of yard, sit in grass by the piles, & wait for next train—A little sick

—Meditate—Passing hobo sees me & lets drop one of his free cabbages—Later I pick it up & munch on it—My nausea disappears!

Red sun is like liquid in the rails—Night, purple, Watson-ville across the lettuce fields & my old Pajaro river-bottom lights up sad—I ask harder about next train

—Soon I see its number

—I make sure, asking car-knockers, & get on in dark

—At 8:30 we thus

THE MOON OF SARIPUTRA

roll right on out to Aromas and Chittenden, to sleepy Gilroy again, & sweet Madrone, & Morgan Hill, and ole Coyote, & into San Jose—by this time I'm dancing and singing at top of my lungs in the whole big rattling black boxcar, glad, healthy, full of raw cabbage & guts—Arrive S.J. yards where I drop off my boxcar east of the yard-office so none of the familiar brake-men see me—As I wait at crossing for crummy to pass, so I can get out on Neal's avenue bus line, a switchman, seeing me, with pack, thinking I'm trying to get on eastbound rail, says, "Get on the Zipper, she's leaving in a minute for LA!" Ho!—I go to gas station & call Neal—He comes to get me in his jalopy that makes our voices hum & throb as in a dream—I buy beer & we talk all night. I tell Carolyn "Do you realize that you're God!" I run the parking lot for a few weeks, get-ting kicks, playing chess in the shanty with Neal getting high in the afternoon of old—Every night after supper I go & sit under a Western Pacific railyard tree in a field, a great unfold-ing infolding bodhi tree, & meditate under the stars an hour—sometimes in the cactus grove I sit, & hear the fieldmice snore—The moon of Sariputra shines down on me and the long night of life is almost over.

—Adoration to the Buddhas!

CHRONOLOGY

NOTE ON THE TEXTS

NOTES

Chronology

1922   Born Jean-Louis Kerouac on March 12 at the family home at 9 Lupine Road in Lowell, Massachusetts, the third child of Joseph Alcide Leon (Leo) Kerouac and Gabrielle Lévesque Kerouac, and is baptized at St. Louis-de-France Church on March 19. (Father, born 1889 in St. Hubert, Quebec, immigrated with his family to Nashua, New Hampshire, where he learned printing. He later moved to Lowell, where he became the manager and printer of *L'Etoile*, a weekly French newspaper, and sold insurance. Mother, born 1895 in St. Pacome, Quebec, also immigrated as a child to Nashua. Orphaned at age 16, she was working in a shoe factory when she married Leo Kerouac on October 25, 1915. Their first son, Gerard, was born on August 23, 1916, and their daughter Caroline was born on October 25, 1918.) Family speaks French-Canadian dialect at home.

1923   Father opens his own print shop in Lowell.

1925   Family moves to 35 Burnaby Street. Gerard becomes seriously ill with rheumatic fever.

1926   Family moves to 34 Beaulieu Street. Gerard dies on June 2.

1927   Family moves to 320 Hildreth Street.

1928   Kerouac enters St. Louis-de-France parochial school, where classes are taught in both English and French. Family moves to 240 Hildreth Street.

1930   Family moves to 66 West Street.

1932   Family leaves Centralville section of Lowell and moves to Phebe Avenue in the Pawtucketville section, where father becomes the manager of a social club. Kerouac attends St. Joseph's parochial school.

1933–35   Enters Bartlett Junior High School in 1933, where all classes are conducted in English. Begins keeping his first journals and records his achievements in sports. Develops a baseball game played with cards, marbles, and dice, and invents an imaginary league and fictitious players. Writes short stories, draws cartoons, and invents mysterious character "Dr. Sax." Reads extensively in school and at the public library.

1936   Merrimack River floods in March, causing extensive damage to father's print shop. Family moves to 35 Sarah Avenue. Kerouac enters Lowell High School in the tenth grade.

1937–39   Excels in sports, especially as a sprinter in track and a running back in football. Reads Thomas Wolfe, William Saroyan, Henry David Thoreau, Mark Twain, and others. Father sells his shop in 1937 and becomes a printer for hire while mother begins working in a shoe factory; financial strain is increased by father's gambling and drinking. Family moves to tenement at 736 Moody Street. Kerouac becomes close friends with Sebastian Sampas and discusses literature, philosophy, and politics with him and a small group of friends.

1939–40   Graduates from Lowell High School on June 28, 1939. Receives football scholarship from Columbia University on condition that he attend Horace Mann, a preparatory school in the Bronx, for a year. Lives with his mother's stepmother in Brooklyn and commutes to school by subway. Publishes his first fiction in the *Horace Mann Quarterly* and is introduced to live jazz in Harlem by classmate Seymour Wyse. Writes about jazz and sports for the school newspaper.

1940   Enters Columbia in September. Fractures tibia in his right leg during his second game with the freshman squad and spends months recuperating.

1941   Receives high grades in French and literature courses but fails chemistry. Spends summer in Lowell and in New Haven, where his parents move in August. Returns to Columbia in September. Quarrels with the coaching staff, quits the football team, and leaves school. Moves to Hartford, Connecticut, where he works as a gas station attendant and writes a short story collection, "Atop an Underwood" (some of the stories are posthumously published in *Atop an Underwood: Early Stories and Other Writing* in 1999). Returns to Lowell when his parents move back to the city. Registers for naval aviation training after the Japanese bomb Pearl Harbor. Becomes a sports reporter for the *Lowell Sun* while waiting to be called up.

1942   Quits the *Sun* in March and goes to Washington, D.C., where he works on the construction of the Pentagon and as a short-order cook. Returns to Lowell, then joins the Merchant Marine and sails from Boston in July as a scullion on the army transport ship *Dorchester*. Sails along the Greenland coast before returning to Boston in October. (The *Dorchester* is sunk by a German submarine on February 3, 1943, with the loss of 675 lives.) Accepts invitation to rejoin the Columbia football squad, but quits after he is benched during the Army game. Stays in New York during the fall and begins affair with Edie Parker (b. 1922), an art student from Grosse Pointe, Michigan. Works on novel *The Sea Is My Brother* (published in 2011). Returns to Lowell in December.

1943   Fails examination for flight training and is sent in March to naval boot camp in Newport, Rhode Island, where he is committed to the base hospital for psychiatric observation after repeated acts of insubordination. Transferred to Bethesda, Maryland, where he is diagnosed as having "schizoid tendencies" and given a psychiatric discharge from military service. Joins his parents, who are now living at 94-10 Cross Bay Boulevard in Ozone Park, Queens, New York. Rejoins the Merchant Marine and sails from New York in September on the *George Weems*, a Liberty ship carrying bombs to Liverpool. Returns to New York in October. Divides his time between Ozone Park and apartment on West 118th Street that Edie Parker shares with Joan Vollmer Adams. Meets Columbia undergraduate Lucien Carr (b. 1925).

1944   Introduced by Carr to William S. Burroughs (b. 1917), Columbia undergraduate Allen Ginsberg (b. 1926), and David Kammerer (b. 1911), Carr's former scoutmaster who had followed him to New York from St. Louis. Sebastian Sampas dies on March 2 after being wounded while serving as an army medic on the Anzio beachhead in Italy. Works on *Galloway*, novel that eventually becomes *The Town and the City*. Carr fatally stabs Kammerer in Riverside Park on August 14, then visits Kerouac, who helps Carr dispose of his knife and Kammerer's glasses.

Kerouac is arrested as a material witness after Carr turns himself in and is jailed when his father refuses to post bail. Marries Edie Parker in a civil ceremony on August 22 and is released after she obtains bail money from her family. They move to Grosse Pointe, Michigan, where Kerouac works in a ball-bearing factory. (Carr pleads guilty to manslaughter and serves two years in prison.) Sails from New York in October on the Liberty ship *Robert Treat Paine*, but jumps ship in Norfolk, Virginia, and returns to New York. On November 16 Kerouac estimates that he has written 500,000 words since 1939, including "nine unfinished novels." Edie returns to New York at Christmas and they move in with Joan Vollmer Adams in apartment on West 115th Street.

1945   Kerouac and Burroughs collaborate on *And the Hippos Were Boiled in Their Tanks*, a novel based on the Kammerer-Carr case (published in 2008). Explores the Times Square underworld with Burroughs and Herbert Huncke, a drug addict, petty thief, and street hustler. Separates from Edie during the summer. Helps care for his father, who has stomach cancer. Hospitalized in December with thrombo-phlebitis, a debilitating circulatory condition in the legs possibly related to his 1940 football injury; Kerouac also attributes his illness to his heavy use of Benzedrine and marijuana.

1946   Kerouac, Burroughs, and Ginsberg are interviewed for the Alfred Kinsey study *Sexual Behavior in the Human Male* (published in 1948). Father dies on May 17 and is buried with Gerard in Nashua. Kerouac continues work on *The Town and the City*. Agrees to Edie Parker's request that their marriage be annulled. In December Kerouac is introduced by his friend Hal Chase to Neal Cassady (b. 1926), a self-educated car thief and hustler from Denver who is visiting New York with his wife, Luanne.

1947   Travels to North Carolina in June to visit his sister, Caroline, and her second husband, Paul Blake. Leaves New York in July to visit Cassady and Ginsberg in Denver, traveling by bus to Chicago and then hitchhiking the rest of the way. Meets Carolyn Robinson, a graduate student at the University of Denver (she and Cassady marry in April 1948). Travels by bus in August to San Francisco, where Henri Cru (a friend from Horace Mann) gets him a job as a security guard in Marin City. Travels through California before returning to New York in October.

1948   Completes first draft of *The Town and the City* in May. Begins writing an early version of *On the Road*. Visits sister in Rocky Mount, North Carolina, in June after the birth of his nephew Paul Blake Jr. Meets writer John Clellon Holmes in July. Takes literature courses taught by Elbert Lenrow and Alfred Kazin at the New School for Social Research in New York. Cassady arrives in Rocky Mount while Kerouac is visiting his sister at Christmas and drives with him back to New York.

1949   Leaves New York in January with Cassady, Luanne, and Al Hinkle and drives to Algiers, Louisiana, where they visit Burroughs and Joan Vollmer Adams, who have been living together for several years. Continues on to San Francisco with Cassady and Luanne, then returns to New York by bus in February. Columbia professor Mark Van Doren recommends *The Town and the City* to Robert Giroux at Harcourt, Brace, who offers Kerouac a $1,000 advance in late March. Kerouac and Giroux work on cutting and revising the manuscript. Moves to Denver in May and rents house at 61 West Center Street in Westwood. Continues working on *On the Road*. Travels to San Francisco in August, then drives back to New York with Cassady, visiting Edie in Grosse Pointe along the way. Moves in with his mother at 94-21 134th Street in Richmond Hill, Queens.

1950   *The Town and the City* is published on March 2; it receives mixed reviews and sells poorly. Travels to Denver in May, then drives with Cassady to Mexico City, where he visits Burroughs. Returns to New York in August. Meets Joan Haverty (b. 1931) on November 3 and marries her in a civil ceremony on November 17. They live in a loft on West 21st Street, then move in with Kerouac's mother in Queens. Receives a long letter from Neal Cassady in December. (Kerouac will later say that Cassady's "fast, mad, confessional" letters inspired "the spontaneous style of *On the Road*.")

1951   Moves to a studio apartment at 454 West 20th Street in Manhattan with Joan, who is working in a department store. Begins new version of *On the Road* on April 2 and types it in three weeks on a 120-foot-long paper scroll.

Separates from Joan and moves in with Lucien Carr and
Allen Ginsberg. Denies paternity when Joan tells him she
is pregnant with his child. Robert Giroux rejects the scroll
version of *On the Road*. Hires Rae Everitt of MCA as his
literary agent. Suffers severe attack of thrombophlebitis
while visiting his sister in North Carolina. Enters Kings-
bridge VA Hospital in the Bronx in August. Burroughs
accidentally kills Joan Vollmer Adams in Mexico City on
September 7 after she drunkenly challenges him to shoot
a glass off her head. Kerouac leaves the hospital in September and returns to Richmond Hill. Begins rewriting
On the Road in an even more spontaneous form (re-
worked version is posthumously published as *Visions of
Cody* in 1972). Moves to San Francisco in December to
live with Neal and Carolyn Cassady and their children at
29 Russell Street.

1952   Works as baggage handler for the Southern Pacific Railroad. Receives $250 advance for *On the Road* from Ace
Books. Daughter Janet Michelle Kerouac is born in Albany
on February 16. Kerouac begins affair with Carolyn Cassady. Drives with the Cassadys to the Arizona-Mexico
border, then takes bus to Mexico City, where he stays
with Burroughs. Writes *Doctor Sax*, May–June. Joins his
mother and sister in North Carolina in July, then moves
in with the Cassadys in San Jose in September. Works as a
brakeman for the Southern Pacific. Lives in a skid row
hotel in San Francisco for a month because of the tension
caused by his affair with Carolyn Cassady, then returns to
San Jose in November. John Clellon Holmes publishes
novel *Go*, in which Kerouac is fictionalized as Gene Paster-
nak, and "This Is the Beat Generation," an essay in the
November 16 *New York Times Magazine*. Kerouac travels
to Mexico City with Neal Cassady, then returns to his
mother in Queens.

1953   Writes *Maggie Cassidy*. Meets with Malcolm Cowley of
Viking Press to discuss the possible publication of his work.
Travels in April to San Luis Obispo, California, where he
again works for the Southern Pacific. Leaves job in May
and sails from San Francisco to New Orleans as a kitchen
worker on the S.S. *William Carruthers*. Returns to Queens
in June. Writes *The Subterraneans*, October 21–24. In
response to questions about his composition methods

from Ginsberg and Burroughs, writes "Essentials of Spontaneous Prose."

1954   Leaves New York in late January to live with the Cassadys in San Jose. Works as a parking-lot attendant and studies Buddhist texts. Returns to his mother in Queens in April. Hires Sterling Lord as his literary agent (Lord will represent him for the rest of Kerouac's life). Works on *Some of the Dharma* (posthumously published in 1997). Malcolm Cowley publishes essay in *The Saturday Review* in August in which he credits Kerouac with inventing the phrase "beat generation" and writes: "his long unpublished narrative, *On the Road*, is the best record of their lives." Kerouac visits Lowell in October.

1955   In January Alfred A. Knopf becomes the sixth publisher to reject *On the Road*. Joan Haverty takes Kerouac to court seeking child support, but his lawyer, Eugene Brooks (Allen Ginsberg's brother), succeeds in having the case postponed because of Kerouac's recurring phlebitis. Kerouac and his mother move to North Carolina. "Jazz of the Beat Generation," excerpted from *On the Road* and *Visions of Cody*, appears in *New World Writing* in April. Travels to Mexico City in July. Begins *Tristessa* and *Mexico City Blues* before going to San Francisco in September. Meets the poets Kenneth Rexroth, Lawrence Ferlinghetti, Michael McClure, Philip Lamantia, Philip Whalen, and Gary Snyder. Attends poetry reading at the Six Gallery in San Francisco on October 7 where Allen Ginsberg reads from *Howl* for the first time. Visits the Sawtooth Mountains of Idaho with Gary Snyder in October. Rides freight cars through California. *The Paris Review* publishes "The Mexican Girl," another excerpt from *On the Road*. Kerouac returns to North Carolina and begins *Visions of Gerard* on December 27.

1956   Completes *Visions of Gerard* on January 16. Hitchhikes to California in March. Lives with Gary Snyder in a cabin in Mill Valley, where he writes *Old Angel Midnight* (posthumously published in 1993) and *The Scripture of the Golden Eternity*. Hitchhikes in June to Mount Baker National Forest in northern Washington. Works for two months as a firewatcher in the Cascade Mountains, staying in a lookout cabin on Desolation Peak. Returns to San Francisco in September before going to Mexico City, where he begins *Desolation Angels.* Ginsberg's *Howl and Other Poems* is published by City Light Books. Kerouac returns to New York in November. Viking Press accepts *On the Road* for publication.

1957   Makes his final revisions to *On the Road* in January. (Viking had insisted that names and locations in the book be changed to avoid possible libel suits.) Begins affair with writer Joyce Glassman (b. 1935, later Joyce Johnson). Sails in February for Tangier, where he visits Burroughs and helps type his novel *Naked Lunch* (a title originally suggested by Kerouac for a different manuscript). Visits Paris and London in April before returning to New York. Moves with his mother to Berkeley, California, in May, but in July they move to Orlando, Florida, where his sister is now living. Visits Mexico City, then goes back to New York. *On the Road* is published on September 5, becomes a bestseller, and makes Kerouac a national celebrity. (In *The New York Times*, critic Gilbert Millstein calls it "the most beautifully executed, the clearest, and the most important utterance yet made by the generation Kerouac himself named years ago as 'beat,' and whose principal avatar he is.") Despite the success of *On the Road*, Viking rejects all of Kerouac's unpublished manuscripts, including *Doctor Sax, Tristessa,* and *Desolation Angels.* Writes play *Beat Generation* (published in 2005) and novel *The Dharma Bums* in Orlando during the fall. Returns to New York in late December to give a series of readings with live jazz backing.

1958   Gives series of interviews, including one with Mike Wallace for the *New York Post. The Subterraneans* is published by Grove Press in February and receives almost entirely bad reviews. Buys house at 34 Gilbert Avenue in Northport, Long Island. Suffers broken arm, broken nose, and possible concussion when he is beaten outside a bar in Greenwich Village. *San Francisco Chronicle* columnist Herb Caen uses the term "beatnik" in print for the first time on April 2. Kerouac drives from New York to Florida and back with photographer Robert Frank. Moves into Northport home with his mother in April. Neal Cassady begins serving sentence for marijuana trafficking in July (he is released from San Quentin in the summer of 1960). *The Dharma Bums* is published by Viking on October 2.

Affair with Joyce Glassman ends. Kerouac's health worsens as the result of years of heavy drinking and Benzedrine use.

1959   Records narration for improvised Beat film *Pull My Daisy*, directed by Robert Frank and painter Alfred Leslie. Writes introduction for the U.S. edition of Frank's photographic collection *The Americans*. Grove Press publishes *Doctor Sax* as a trade paperback in April, and *Maggie Cassidy* is published as a mass-market paperback by Avon in July. Kerouac begins writing column for *Escapade* magazine. Moves to 49 Earl Avenue in Northport with his mother. Travels to Los Angeles in November and reads from *Visions of Cody* on the Steve Allen television show. *Mexico City Blues* is published by Grove Press. On November 30 *Life* magazine publishes "Beats: Sad But Noisy Rebels," article by staff writer Paul O'Neil attacking Kerouac and Neal Cassady.

1960   Works on *Lonesome Traveler* and *Book of Dreams*. Totem Press publishes *The Scripture of the Golden Eternity*. Avon publishes *Tristessa* as a mass-market paperback in June. Film version of *The Subterraneans*, directed by Ranald MacDougall, is a critical and commercial failure (Kerouac received $15,000 for the film rights). Spends summer at Lawrence Ferlinghetti's cabin in Bixby Canyon in Big Sur, where he suffers mental breakdown while trying to deal with his worsening alcoholism. Sees Carolyn Cassady for the last time before returning to Long Island in September. *Lonesome Traveler*, a collection of travel pieces, is published by McGraw-Hill on September 27.

1961   Meets Timothy Leary in January with Ginsberg and takes LSD. *Book of Dreams* is published by City Lights Books. Leaves Northport and moves with his mother in April to 1309 Alfred Drive in Orlando. Spends a month in Mexico City during the summer and completes the second part of *Desolation Angels*. In August *Confidential* magazine publishes "My Ex-Husband Jack Kerouac Is an Ingrate," article detailing Joan Haverty Aly's ongoing attempts to collect child support from Kerouac. Writes *Big Sur* in Orlando, September 30–October 9. Goes on an extended drinking spree in New York in the fall.

1962   Meets his daughter Jan, now 10, for the first time when they undergo blood tests in February, and is ordered to

pay $12 a week in child support. Grove Press publishes the
first American edition of Burroughs' *Naked Lunch* in
March. *Big Sur* is published by Farrar, Straus, and Cudahy
on September 11. Buys house at 7 Judy Ann Court in
Northport and moves there with his mother in December.

1963   Works on *Vanity of Duluoz*, a novel he first began in 1942.
Visions of Gerard is published by Farrar, Straus and Cudahy in September and receives poor reviews.

1964   Gives drunken reading at Harvard University in March.
Sees Neal Cassady for the last time when he comes to
New York City with Ken Kesey and the Merry Pranksters
during the summer. Sells Northport house and moves
with his mother to 5155 Tenth Avenue North in St. Petersburg, Florida. Caroline Kerouac Blake dies of a heart
attack in Orlando on September 19; she is buried in an
unmarked grave because Kerouac is unable to pay for a
headstone.

1965   Suffers two broken ribs when he is attacked in a St. Petersburg bar in March. *Desolation Angels* is published by
Coward-McCann on May 3. Visits Paris and Brittany in
June in an attempt to research his ancestry. Writes *Satori
in Paris* soon after his return to Florida.

1966   Moves with his mother in the spring to 20 Bristol Avenue
in the Cape Cod town of Hyannis, Massachusetts. *Satori
in Paris* is published by Grove Press. Visited in August by
Ann Charters, who is compiling his bibliography. (Charters will publish the first biography of Kerouac in 1973.)
Mother suffers massive stroke on September 9 that leaves
her paralyzed. Kerouac briefly visits Milan and Rome to
promote the Italian publication of *Big Sur*. Marries Stella
Sampas (b. 1918), the sister of his Lowell friend Sebastian
Sampas, in Hyannis on November 18.

1967   Moves in January with Stella and his mother to house at
271 Sanders Avenue in Lowell. Completes *Vanity of Duluoz*. Gives lengthy interview to the poets Ted Berrigan,
Aram Saroyan, and Duncan McNaughton for publication
in *The Paris Review*. Sees his daughter Jan for the second
and last time in November.

1968   Neal Cassady collapses and dies on February 4 in San
Miguel de Allende, Mexico. *Vanity of Duluoz* is published
by Coward-McCann on February 6. Visits Portugal,

Spain, Switzerland, and Germany in March. Sees Burroughs and Ginsberg for the last time in early September when he goes to New York for the taping of William F. Buckley's television program *Firing Line*. Returns to St. Petersburg, moving to 5169 Tenth Avenue North with Stella and his mother.

1969   Completes *Pic* (published in 1971). Suffers cracked ribs when he is beaten outside a bar in early September. "After Me, the Deluge," article in which Kerouac disassociates himself from the New Left, appears in the *Chicago Tribune* on September 28. Collapses at home on the morning of October 20 and dies at St. Anthony's Hospital in St. Petersburg on October 21 from massive internal bleeding caused by cirrhosis of the liver. A Requiem Mass is held at St. Jean Baptiste Church in Lowell on October 24, after which Kerouac is buried in Edson Catholic Cemetery.

Note on the Texts

This volume contains five books published by Jack Kerouac between 1957 and 1960: *On the Road* (1957), *The Dharma Bums* (1958), *The Subterraneans* (1958), *Tristessa* (1960), and *Lonesome Traveler* (1960). It also contains selections from the journals related to *On the Road* that Kerouac kept in the late 1940s and early 1950s.

Kerouac began writing a series of notes, outlines, and incomplete drafts for *On the Road* in 1948. He wrote the first complete draft of the novel in three weeks in April 1951. This version was typed on a continuous roll of paper, the text of which Kerouac soon retyped to produce a typescript of more than 400 pages. The draft was circulated among his friends and literary associates, and eventually reached Malcolm Cowley, an editor at Viking Press. Cowley responded favorably and advised Viking in 1953 to publish the novel, but the firm hesitated. Kerouac tried unsuccessfully to interest other publishers in the novel, which he sometimes circulated under the title *The Beat Generation*, and submitted excerpts from the manuscript for publication in periodicals and anthologies. "Jazz of the Beat Generation," taken from chapters 10 and 14 of Book Three, appeared in *New World Writing* 7 (1955); "The Mexican Girl," taken from chapters 12 and 13 of Book One, was published in *The Paris Review* (Winter 1955) and selected for *The Best Short Stories of 1956*, edited by Martha Foley; "A Billowy Trip in the World," an excerpt from chapter 5 of Book Four, appeared in *New Directions* 16 (1957). In December 1956 Viking decided to accept the novel. Cowley suggested cuts and revisions, some of which Kerouac accepted as he prepared *On the Road* for publication; some of these changes were made to disguise the persons and places Kerouac had written about. Cowley did not, however, send Kerouac galleys of the final version, which contained changes that Kerouac was not shown before the book was printed. (In a letter dated July 21, 1957, Kerouac protested that Cowley had "yanked much out of *On the Road* . . . without my permission or even sight of galley proofs!") *On the Road* was published by the Viking Press on September 5, 1957, and soon became a best seller. An English edition was brought out the following year by Andre Deutsch. The text printed here is taken from the 1957 Viking edition of *On the Road*.

The success of *On the Road* led Viking to approach Kerouac for a follow-up book. He responded to their offer by writing the novel *The Dharma Bums* in the fall of 1957, while he was living in Orlando,

Florida. When Kerouac received proofs from Viking in June 1958, he was dismayed at a copyeditor's emendations and asked for new proofs to be set based exactly on the typescript as he had submitted it. Helen Taylor, his editor at Viking, refused this request but did allow him to make changes to the copyedited set of proofs. An excerpt from the novel appeared as "Meditation in the Woods" in the *Chicago Review* (Summer 1958). *The Dharma Bums* was published by the Viking Press on October 2, 1958; an English edition was published by Andre Deutsch two years later. The text printed here is taken from the 1958 Viking edition.

The Subterraneans was written in three nights in October 1953. Kerouac later wrote in a prefatory note to a Norwegian translation of the novel that "*The Subterraneans* is a true story about a love affair I had with a Negro girl in America. Only the names and identifying circumstances are changed." After receiving several rejections from publishers, it was submitted by his agent, Sterling Lord, to *Evergreen Review*, a magazine published by Grove Press. Donald Allen, an editor at Grove, expressed interest in publishing a version of the novel in *Evergreen Review* while having Grove Press issue *The Subterraneans* in book form. When concerns about libel were raised, Kerouac wrote to Lord in October 1956, asking him to "tell Don Allen that *Subterraneans is* already libel-safe & fixed,—The real-life story took place in N.Y. not Frisco, the girl was Negro not Indian, and the 'villain' who laid my love is now my best friend," referring to Gregory Corso. The excerpt intended for publication in *Evergreen Review* was withdrawn after Kerouac saw proofs and was angered at editorial changes made by Allen, which he called a "horrible castration job." Because of his complaints about the editing done for *Evergreen Review*, the novel was published by Grove in February 1958 largely as Kerouac had submitted it. An English edition was brought out by Andre Deutsch in 1960. The text printed here is taken from the 1958 Grove Press edition of *The Subterraneans*.

Kerouac wrote "Trembling and Chaste," the first section of *Tristessa*, while living in Mexico City during the summer of 1955, then set the novel aside until the fall of 1956, when he wrote "Later." The manuscript was rejected by Viking Press. (Malcolm Cowley remarked in October 1957 that *Tristessa* "raises the question whether Jack has been completely ruined as a publishable writer by Allan Ginsburg [*sic*] and his exercises in automatic or self-abusive writing.") Kerouac considered adding a third part but eventually decided against doing so, writing to Ginsberg in December 1959 after the novel was accepted by Avon Books that he had "just concluded an amiable wrangle over TRISTESSA to have it published just as it is (no additions)." Avon published *Tristessa* as a 35-cent paperback original in June 1960. World Distributors in London brought out the first English edition of the novel in 1963. The text printed here is taken from the 1960 Avon Books edition of *Tristessa*.

Several of the essays collected in *Lonesome Traveler* were published in magazines between 1957 and 1960: a version of "The Railroad Earth" appeared as "October in the Railroad Earth," *Evergreen Review*, Summer 1958, and as "Conclusion of the Railroad Earth," *Evergreen Review*, January–February 1960, while another excerpt was published in *Black Mountain Review*, Autumn 1957. Excerpts from "Mexico Fellaheen" were published in *Escapade*, October 1959, and, as "The Statue of Christ," in *Jubilee*, June 1958. "Alone on a Mountaintop," "New York Scenes" (as "The Roaming Beatniks"), "Big Trip to Europe" (as "Tangier to London: A Beatnik Pilgrimage"), and "The Vanishing American Hobo" were published in *Holiday* in October 1958, October 1959, February 1960, and March 1960, respectively. *Lonesome Traveler* was published by McGraw-Hill Book Company on September 27, 1960. Andre Deutsch brought out the collection (using the British spelling "Traveller" in the title) two years later. The 1960 McGraw-Hill edition contains the text printed here.

The selections from Kerouac's journals published in this volume are taken from the notebook Kerouac labeled "Journals 1949–50" on its cover. An edition of this notebook was published in *Windblown World* (New York: Penguin, 2004), edited by Douglas Brinkley. Its first page reads "RAIN AND RIVERS / The marvelous notebook presented / to me by Neal Cassady / in San Francisco / :—Which I have Crowded in Words—:" As explained by Brinkley in *Windblown World*, the journal "depicts trips through every region of the country as early as 1949 and one as late as 1954, from New York, through the South and Mexico, into California and the Northwest, and back to New York and Massachusetts through the Midwest. Kerouac has added a heading to each of his pages, to indicate the region he is writing in or about." The text printed here is taken from *Windblown World*, and follows its practice of rendering these headings in capital letters. Bracketed insertions used in *Windblown World* to fully identify persons that Kerouac referred to only by their first or last name have been deleted in this volume.

This volume presents the texts of the original printings chosen for inclusion here, but it does not attempt to reproduce nontextual features of their typographic design. The texts are presented without change, except for the correction of typographical errors. Spelling, punctuation, and capitalization are not altered, even when inconsistent or irregular. The following is a list of typographical errors corrected, cited by page and line number: 185.25, tourist; 208.5, classic hitch, hiking; 330.29, him an; 337.9, learn appreciate; 398.1, Gary; 502.8, —Yeah; 505.8, —Well; 518.35, ballon; 520.5, of of; 531.5, *out*; 570.3, fells; 581.7, encephilitises; 583.14, walks; 583.39, putts; 613.7, shawls; 618.5, hassel; 626.35, descendents; 641.1, he all; 662.7, that; 670.5, you; 685.10, 'cause; 691.16, rallroad; 698.26, *No!*; 698.32, mach—; 709.20, ships; 719.32, Pat's; 720.22, Klein; 762.7, pub).; 765.18, pipe; 791.18, implicitly.); 795.6. him.) 808.30, some.

Notes

In the notes below, the reference numbers denote page and line of this volume (the line count includes headings). No note is made for material included in standard desk-reference books. Biblical quotations are keyed to the King James Version. Quotations from Shakespeare are keyed to *The Riverside Shakespeare*, ed. G. Blakemore Evans (Boston: Houghton Mifflin, 1974). For further biographical background than is contained in the Chronology, see Ann Charters, *Kerouac* (San Francisco: Straight Arrow Books, 1973); Barry Gifford and Lawrence Lee, *Jack's Book: An Oral Biography of Jack Kerouac* (New York: St. Martin's, 1978); Dennis McNally, *Desolate Angel* (New York: Random House, 1979); Gerald Nicosia, *Memory Babe: A Critical Biography of Jack Kerouac* (New York: Grove Press, 1983); Tom Clark, *Jack Kerouac: A Biography* (San Diego: Harcourt Brace Jovanich, 1984); John Suiter, *Poets on the Peaks: Gary Snyder, Philip Whalen & Jack Kerouac in the North Cascades* (New York: Counterpoint, 2002); Paul Maher Jr., *Kerouac: His Life and Work* (Lanham, Maryland: Taylor Trade Publishing, 2004).

ON THE ROAD

3.3   Dean] Based on Neal Cassady (1926–1968), whom Kerouac met in New York City in 1946. Marylou at 3.24 is Cassady's first wife, Luanne Henderson. Their brief marriage began in 1946; Cassady's second wife, Carolyn Robinson, appears in *On the Road* as Camille. Chad King (3.13) is based on Kerouac's friend Hal Chase, an anthropology student at Columbia who was a roommate of Ed White, the basis for Tim Gray (3.26). Carlo Marx (3.18) is based on poet Allen Ginsberg.

4.27–28   longbodied . . . woman] The portraits of women by the Italian artist Amedeo Modigliani (1884–1920) are conspicuous for being elongated and highly stylized.

7.13   Old Bull . . . Jane] Old Bull Lee is based on American novelist William S. Burroughs (1914–1997), whose works include *Naked Lunch* (1959) and *The Soft Machine* (1961). Jane is based on his companion Joan Vollmer Adams, whom Burroughs accidentally killed in 1951 after she drunkenly challenged him to shoot a glass off her head. Elmer Hassel is based on Herbert "Hunckey" Huncke, a friend of Burroughs. Roy Johnson and Big Ed Dunkel are based on Cassady's friends Bill Tomson and Al Hinkle, respectively.

10.16   Remi Boncœur] Based on Henri Cru, Kerouac's friend since their time together at the Horace Mann school in the Bronx.

13.3–4   Charlie Parker Ornithology period] Parker's "Ornithology" was recorded in 1946.

35.9   Roland Major] Based on Allan Temko (1924–2006), architecture critic, author of *Notre Dame of Paris* (1955). Kerouac knew him at Horace Mann and Columbia. The Rawlinses (35.13) are based on the literary magazine editor Bob Burford and his sister Beverly, with whom Kerouac was briefly romantically involved in 1950.

44.18–19 Wolfean romantic posh!] Novelist Thomas Wolfe (1900–1938), author of *Look Homeward, Angel* (1929) and *Of Time and the River* (1935), has been criticized for being pretentious, verbose, and overly sentimental. Wolfe's novels exerted a major influence on Kerouac early in his career.

45.33   Berthoud Pass] Mountain pass in Colorado.

46.13   Lillian Russell] Popular American operetta actress and singer (1860–1922).

47.8   *Fidelio*] Beethoven's only opera (1814).

47.15   Denver D. Doll] Based on the Denver lawyer and teacher Justin Brierly.

57.31   *The Mark of Zorro*] Adventure film (1940) directed by Rouben Mamoulian and starring Tyrone Power and Linda Darnell.

58.20   *Blue Book*] Popular magazine featuring genre stories and serialized novels by writers including Edgar Rice Burroughs, Conrad Richter, and Philip Wylie.

73.18   cutest little Mexican girl] Based on Bea Franco, with whom Kerouac was romantically involved in 1947.

74.37–39 Joel McCrea . . . *Travels*,] In the film *Sullivan's Travels* (1941), directed by Preston Sturges, a movie director, played by Joel McCrea, impersonates a hobo in order to experience poverty; Veronica Lake played his love interest.

78.15–16 Don Ameche! . . . George Murphy!] Actor Don Ameche (1908–1993), who played leading-man roles in films of the 1940s such as *Girl Trouble* (1942) and *Heaven Can Wait* (1943); dancer and actor George Murphy (1902–1992).

78.31   Jerry Colonna] Comedian, singer, and songwriter (1904–1986), best known for his role on Bob Hope's radio show in the 1940s.

79.26–27 Hamp's "Central Avenue Breakdown"] A 1940 composition by jazz bandleader and vibraphone player Lionel Hampton (1908–2002).

82.15–16   *Of Mice . . .* Meredith]   The 1939 film adaptation of John Steinbeck's novel *Of Mice and Men* starred Burgess Meredith, playing the guardian of Lennie, a mentally retarded man.

86.39   Simon Legree]   Wicked overseer in Harriet Beecher Stowe's novel *Uncle Tom's Cabin* (1852).

89.27   "Lover Man" . . . Holiday]   Billie Holiday's hit recording of the song "Lover Man," written by James Edward Davis, Roger J. Ramirez, and James Sherman, was released in 1944.

90.34   "Blue Skies."]   Irving Berlin's 1926 song, recorded by Bing Crosby, the Count Basie Orchestra, Frank Sinatra, and many other performers.

93.6–7   "*Le Grand Meaulnes*" by Alain-Fournier]   Novel (1913) translated into English as *The Wanderer* and *The Lost Domain*.

95.19   the Gap]   Cumberland Gap, a mountain pass in the Appalachians.

101.17–19   "The Hunt," . . . audience]   One of the live recordings featuring tenor saxophonists Dexter Gordon and Wardell Gray "battling" each other during extended jams.

106.29   like Hart Crane on the way back.]   Poet Hart Crane (1899–1932) committed suicide by jumping off the deck of the S.S. *Orizaba* while sailing from Mexico to the United States.

111.37   Tom Saybrook's]   Based on the novelist, critic, and poet John Clellon Holmes (1926–1988), author of the novel *Go* (1952) and two books of memoirs about Kerouac.

113.7   Damion]   Based on Lucien Carr (1925–2005), whom Kerouac met in 1943. In August 1944 Carr fatally stabbed David Kammerer (1911–1944), and served two years in prison after pleading guilty to manslaughter; Kerouac was detained as a material witness in the case.

113.34   Rollo Greb]   Based on the poet Alan Ansen (1922–2006).

121.30   Mann Act]   Passed in 1910, the act made it a federal felony to aid or participate in the transportation of women or girls in interstate or foreign commerce for immoral purposes.

122.23   said Louis-Ferdinand Céline]   In the essay "Homage to Émile Zola," published in translation in *New Directions in Prose & Poetry* 13 (1951).

129.8–9   Spengler]   German historian (1880–1936), author of *The Decline of the West* (1918–23).

129.35   Mayan Codices]   Hieroglyphic records of Mayan civilization, most of which were destroyed by the Spanish. Three codices and a fragment of a fourth survive.

132.38   fogbound Cereno ships]   A reference to Melville's story "Benito

Cereno" (from *The Piazza Tales*, 1856), which tells of a revolt on a slave ship; the ship is described as having "shreds of fog here and there raggedly furring her."

137.1   Reich]   Austrian-born psychoanalyst Wilhelm Reich (1897–1957), who developed the orgone accumulator as part of his unorthodox form of therapy.

148.27   Hal Hingham]   Based on novelist Alan Harrington (1918–1997), author of *The Secret Swinger* (1966) and *The Immortalist* (1969).

158.12   Slim Gaillard]   Jazz guitarist, scat-singer, and comedian (1916–1991). He was half of the duo Slim & Slam, which had a major hit in the 1930s with their recording of "Flat Foot Floogie."

158.39   "C-Jam Blues"]   A 1942 composition by Duke Ellington.

169.24–25   Eugene Sue's *Mysteries of Paris*]   Ten-volume novel (1842–43).

178.23   "Close Your Eyes."]   Song (1933) by Bernice Petkere.

179.8–9   all the messages to Garcia]   American writer Elbert Hubbard (1856–1915) wrote the inspirational tract *A Message to Garcia* (1899), based on an incident in the Spanish-American War.

186.31–32   'Hallelujah, I'm a bum]   Folk ballad celebrating the hobo life; its authorship is often attributed to songwriter Harry McClintock.

210.22–24   Mickey Cohen's men . . . California]   An enforcer for Benjamin "Bugsy" Siegel, gangster Mickey Cohen (1913–1976) became a leading figure in the Los Angeles underworld after Siegel's murder.

213.14–15   famous bop clarinetist . . . recently]   Swedish-born clarinetist Stan Hasselgard (1922–1948).

220.12–13   Singing Cowboy Eddie Dean]   Eddie Dean (1907–1999) starred as a singing cowboy in many B-movies of the 1940s, including *Colorado Serenade* (1946) and *West to Glory* (1947).

220.14–16   George Raft . . . picture about Istanbul]   *Background to Danger* (1943), directed by Raoul Walsh and based on Eric Ambler's novel (1937).

222.25   Inez]   Based on Diana Hansen, Neal Cassady's third wife. Cassady divorced Carolyn after Hansen became pregnant with his child.

225.3–4   Willie Jackson record, "Gator Tail."]   Saxophonist Willis Jackson (1928–1987) was a member of the Cootie Williams Orchestra, which recorded "Gator Tail" in 1948. "Gator" became Jackson's nickname.

225.19–20   Lester Young]   Saxophonist (1909–1959) whose career as a jazz musician began with the Count Basie Orchestra.

227.25   Stan Getz] Saxophonist (1927–1991) known for his mellow, lyrical
sound.

245.14–15   Wynonie Blues Harris and Lionel Hampton and Lucky
Millinder] Singer Wynonie "Mr. Blues" Harris (1915–1969) had several hits
with Lucky Millinder's band and on his own, including "Who Threw the
Whiskey in the Well" and "Good Rockin' Tonight"; Lionel Hampton, see
note 79.26–27; bandleader Lucky Millinder (1900–1966).

250.39   ALEMAN] Miguel Alemán Valdés (1900–1983), president of Mexico from 1948 to 1952.

258.16   Pérez Prado] Cuban bandleader and composer (1916–1989), who
as "King of the Mambo" popularized the mambo sound. He moved to Mexico in 1948.

267.13   Mission Orange] A brand of soda pop.

269.38–39   *rebozos*] Traditional Mexican woven shawls.

275.20   Laura] Based on Joan Haverty, Kerouac's second wife; they married in November 1950 and separated the following spring.

THE DHARMA BUMS

279.1   THE DHARMA BUMS] *The Dharma Bums* is a *roman à clef* that
Kerouac wrote in November 1957, shortly after the publication of *On the
Road*. The following is a partial list of characters matched with the people on
whom they are based: Rheinhold Cacoethes: poet Kenneth Rexroth; Warren
Coughlin: poet Philip Whalen; Francis DaPavia: poet Philip Lamantia; Alvah
Goldbook: poet Allen Ginsberg; Ike O'Shay: poet Michael McClure; Henry
Morley: poet John Montgomery; Cody Pomeray: Neal Cassady; Japhy Ryder:
poet Gary Snyder; Rol Sturlason: artist and printmaker Will Petersen; Arthur
Whane: Zen scholar and popularizer Alan Watts.

279.2   *Han Shan*] Literally "cold mountain," the name given to the author of a group of ascetic Buddhist poems composed during the T'ang Dynasty (618–907 CE) in China.

281.9–10   Camarillo . . . mad] In 1946, after being charged with inde-
cent exposure, resisting arrest, and suspected arson, Parker was ordered to
spend several months at Camarillo State Hospital, a psychiatric facility in California. His 1947 composition "Relaxin' at Camarillo" was named for his time
at the hospital.

282.5–6   Diamond Sutra] In Mahayana Buddhism, one of the *Prajna-
paramita* ("perfection of wisdom") sutras, attributed to Nagarjuna (second
century CE).

282.14   bhikku] Buddhist monk.

282.25–26   a prayer by Saint Teresa . . . roses] Popularly known as "the little flower," Saint Teresa of Lisieux (1873–1897), a French Carmelite nun, promised that after her death she would "let fall a shower of roses."

283.40   Avalokitesvara's]   In Buddhist cosmology, "the Lord Who Looks Down": the bodhisattva (enlightened one) who gazes with compassion upon the sorrows of the world. As noted at 287.23, in Japan the deity is known in its female form as the goddess Kannon (sometimes spelled "Kwannon").

285.31   I.W.W.]   The International Workers of the World, popularly known as the Wobblies.

290.6   chum Altman]   Philip Lamantia's friend John Hoffman, who had died in Mexico in 1954 at the age of 25.

291.20   Blyth]   English translator and critic Reginald Horace Blyth (1898–1964),who spent the latter half of his life in Korea and Japan. He published several volumes of haiku translations, helping to popularize the form in the West.

292.8   the complete works of D. T. Suzuki]   The writings of essayist and translator Daisetz Teitaro Suzuki (1870–1966), who was probably most responsible for raising awareness in the West of Zen Buddhism and other forms of Eastern philosophy; his works include the multi-volume *Essays in Zen Buddhism* (1927–34), *Manual of Zen Buddhism* (1934), *The Zen Doctrine of No-Mind* (1949), and *Living by Zen* (1949).

292.23   Han Shan]   See note 279.2.

297.39–40   flubbed up the name of Li Po]   Following the usage of the translator and scholar of East Asian culture Ernest Fenollosa (1853–1908), Pound called Li Po "Rihaku" in the adaptations of Li Po's poems he included in *Cathay* (1915), which were based on Fenollosa's translations.

298.10–11   new book . . . in Mexico]   Kerouac's *Mexico City Blues.*

298.11–13   "the wheel . . . nonsense . . ."]   Cf. the 211th Chorus of "Mexico City Blues": "The wheel of the quivering meat conception / Turns in the void expelling human beings, / Pigs, turtles, frogs, insects, nits / Mice, lice, lizards, rats, roan / Racinghorses, poxy bucolic pigtics, / Horrible unnameable lice of vultures / Murderous attacking dog-armies / Of Africa, Rhinos roaming in the jungle, / Vast boars and huge gigantic bull / Elephants, rams, eagles, condors, / Pones and Porcupines and Pills—."

301.29   viharas]   Monasteries.

302.4   Everett Massacre]   On November 5, 1916, more than 200 members of the I.W.W. sailed by ferry from Seattle to Everett, Washington, to support striking shingle mill workers there. They were met at the dock by the sheriff and scores of special deputies recruited by the local lumber companies. Shooting broke out, and five Wobblies and two deputies were killed or fatally wounded.

303.2 Samadhi] In yogic practice, the highest state of consciousness achieved through meditation.

303.40 "I know my redeemer liveth."] From Job's speech at Job 19:25.

304.6 samsara] The material world.

304.20 Tathagata] Here, an epithet for Buddha.

312.20 Kwannon] See note 283.40.

313.3 Ciardi and Bread Loaf writers] The poet John Ciardi (1916–1986) had served since 1947 on the staff of the Bread Loaf Writers' Conference in Vermont, an annual summer program sponsored by Middlebury College; he was named the program's director in 1956.

314.35–36 Aurora . . . Amida] Aurora, Roman goddess of the dawn; Amida, Japanese form of Amitabha, a celestial buddha.

319.3 John Burroughs] American naturalist and essayist (1837–1921).

319.17–18 "Comparisons are . . . Cervantes] See *Don Quixote*, part 2, chapter 23.

321.16 Chuangtse"] Fourth-century BCE Chinese philosopher. The writings attributed to him are some of the foundational texts of Taoism.

324.25 gazotsky] A Russian dance.

331.8–9 Nirmanakaya, Sambhogakaya, and Dharmakaya] Function, nature, and essence: the three aspects of enlightened being in Buddhism.

333.21 Surangamy sutries] I.e., the Surangama Sutra, Buddhist text emphasizing the importance of meditation.

335.36–37 like in the Bible . . . spirit] See Ecclesiastes 3:21: "Who knoweth the spirit of man that goeth upward, and the spirit of the beast that goeth downward to the earth?"

341.30 *plage*] French: beach.

350.20–21 Où sont les neiges d'antan?] "Where are the snows of yesteryear?": from François Villon's poem "Ballade des Dames du Temps Jadis."

351.3 *Cheer up . . . despots*] See Whitman's preface to the 1855 edition of *Leaves of Grass*: "The attitude of great poets is to cheer up slaves and horrify despots."

355.27–28 Inky Dinky Parly Voo!] Popular song during World War I.

355.31–32 mauvais sujet] French: bad person.

360.6 'even unto the least of these] Cf. the words of Jesus at Matthew 25:40: "Verily I say unto you, Inasmuch as ye have done unto one of the least of these my brethren, ye have done unto me."

379.17–18 "Already . . . world."] A conflation of 1 Corinthians 4:8 and 1 Corinthians 6:2.

379.20–22 "Meats . . . them."] 1 Corinthians 6:13.

380.12 "Ay, by . . . sound."] *I Henry IV*, IV.i.128.

382.34 "Tathata,"] Sanskrit: "such-ness" or "that-ness."

383.28 practicing Dhyana] Meditating.

385.15 Ananda's] Ananda was one of the Buddha's chief disciples.

387.36 John L. Lewis] American labor leader (1880–1969), president of the United Mine Workers (1920–60).

389.18–19 "Don't let . . . sings Frank Sinatra] From "We'll Be Together Again," by Carl Fischer and Frankie Laine; Sinatra's version of the song is included on the album *Songs for Swingin' Lovers!* (1956).

394.8–9 "Todos las granas . . . vacuidad!"] All the grains of sand in the Chihuahua desert are emptiness!

396.31 Coxie's army] Ohio populist politician Jacob Coxey (1854–1951) led a march of unemployed men to Washington, D.C., in 1894; the phrase "Coxey's army" became a byword for a disorganized group temporarily brought together for a single purpose.

397.5–6 like on TV . . . Wyatt Earp.] The television series *The Life and Legend of Wyatt Earp*, starring Hugh O'Brien, ran from 1955 to 1961.

400.21 Mara] Demon who tempted Buddha to try to prevent him from attaining enlightenment.

408.14 Nat Wills tramp] Born in England as Edward McGregor (1873–1917), Nat Wills was a vaudeville comedian and actor known as the "Happy Tramp."

408.31 drunk . . . like Li Po] Li Po's drunkenness was legendary: according to one popular story, he drowned while drunkenly trying to embrace the moon's reflection in the Yellow River.

420.6 Bodhisattva Mahasattva] Name applied to someone committed to the path of buddhahood.

421.26 prajna!] Sanskrit: wisdom.

422.5 Cal Tjader] Vibraphonist (1925–1982) who played Latin jazz and bebop. He performed and recorded as leader of the Cal Tjader Modern Mambo Quintet in the 1950s.

422.26 Ronald Firbank] English novelist (1886–1926), author of *The Flower Beneath the Foot* (1923) and *Concerning the Eccentricities of Cardinal Pirelli* (1926).

426.15 Mount Sumeru] In Buddhist cosmology, a holy mountain believed to stand at the center of the world.

429.24 Dwight Goddard] Trained as an engineer, Dwight Goddard (1861–1939) traveled to China in 1894 as a Baptist missionary. Drawn to Buddhism, he eventually studied at a Zen monastery in Japan and published the book *Was Jesus Influenced by Buddhism?* in 1927. When Goddard returned to the United States, he founded a Buddhist temple in Vermont, the organization Fellowship Following Buddha, and the magazine *Zen*. His anthology of Buddhist texts, *A Buddhist Bible*, was self-published in 1932 and brought out in a trade edition six years later.

438.24 Ashvhaghosha] First-century CE Indian religious teacher, poet, and dramatist, attributed author of *Awakening of Faith*.

445.5 Min 'n' Bill couple] In the 1930 film *Min and Bill* (1930), Marie Dressler starred as Min, a woman running a waterfront inn and raising an adopted teenage daughter; Bill, a veteran fishing-boat captain played by Wallace Beery, is her companion. The two characters have a volatile relationship.

457.11 "Wee Small Hours,"] "In the Wee Small Hours of the Morning," written by David Mann and Bob Hilliard, is the first song on Frank Sinatra's 1955 album *Wee Small Hours*.

THE SUBTERRANEANS

463.3 THE SUBTERRANEANS] "*The Subterraneans*," wrote Kerouac in a prefatory note to the Norwegian edition of the novel, "is a true story about a love affair I had with a Negro girl in America. Only the names and identifying circumstances are changed." The following is a list of some of the characters matched with the people who inspired them: Julien Alexander: Kerouac's friend Anton Rosenberg; Roger Beloit: saxophonist Allen Eager; Frank Carmody: novelist William S. Burroughs; Jane Carmody: Burroughs' companion Joan Vollmer Adams; Bennet Fitzpatrick: poet and editor Whit Burnett; Mardou Fox: Alene Lee, a woman with whom Kerouac had an affair in 1953; Yuri Gligoric: poet Gregory Corso; Arial Lavalina: novelist Gore Vidal; Leroy: Neal Cassady; Adam Moorad: poet Allen Ginsberg; Harold Sand: novelist William Gaddis; Sylvester Strauss: composer David Diamond; Sam Vedder: Lucien Carr.

465.30 the great Chu Berry] Leon "Chu" Berry (1908–1941) was one of the leading tenor saxophonists of the 1930s and early 1940s before his death in a car accident.

466.2 Sarah Vaughan Gerry Mulligan] Singer Sarah Vaughan (1924–1990); Gerry Mulligan (1927–1996), saxophonist, arranger, and composer at the center of West Coast jazz.

469.12 Stan Kenton] Bandleader, pianist, and arranger (1911–1979) who led an orchestra associated with "progressive jazz."

470.26   Jeri Southern] Jazz singer (1926–1991) who had her biggest hit in 1957 with the song "Fire Down Below."

477.9–10   Alfred Kazin . . . East] Critic and literary historian Alfred Kazin (1915–1998), author of *On Native Grounds* (1942), lectured frequently at the New School for Social Research in the 1940s and 1950s.

477.17–18   Rouault-like saintly obscurities] The French painter (1871–1958) often painted Christian subjects in a stylized, abstract idiom.

479.10   "*casus in eventu est*"] "The result is doubtful": Ovid, *Art of Love*, I. 379–80.

484.3   George Sanders in *The Moon and Sixpence*] The 1942 film adaptation of Somerset Maugham's novel *The Moon and Sixpence* (1919) starred George Sanders as Charles Strickland, a stockbroker who abandons his comfortable life and becomes a painter, ultimately settling in Tahiti.

484.12–13   *maquereaux*] French slang: pimps.

500.35   "Smart went Crazy," wrote Allen Ginsberg.] In "Bop Lyrics" (1949).

506.5–6   Tennessee Williams story . . . fag] "Desire and the Black Masseur," written in 1946 and included in Williams' story collection *One Arm* (1948).

510.6   Crazy Jane] Irish hag at the center of a series of poems by W. B. Yeats.

515.34   Crabbe Robinson] Henry Crabb Robinson (1775–1867), a journalist, lawyer, and diarist, was a friend of Blake's.

517.16   Shatov stairs] The dark and steep stairway outside the rooms of Ivan Shatov, an idealist intellectual in Dostoevsky's *The Devils* (1871–72; also known as *The Possessed* and *Demons*).

522.4   Billy Eckstine's] Singer and bandleader (1914–1993).

522.13–18   *Spotted Horses* . . . Faulkner   portable] Faulkner's story "Spotted Horses" was first published in 1931, then revised and incorporated into *The Hamlet* (1940); a version of the story was included in *The Portable Faulkner* (1946), an anthology edited by Malcolm Cowley that revived interest in Faulkner's work.

522.20   *The Lower Depths*] Jean Renoir's 1936 film of Maxim Gorky's play.

529.21–22   orgone accumulator] As Kerouac described it in *On the Road* (see 136.37–137.2), the orgone accumulator invented by Wilhelm Reich "is an ordinary box big enough for a man to sit inside on a chair: a layer of wood, a layer of metal, and another layer of wood gather in orgones from the atmosphere and hold them captive long enough for the human body to absorb more than a usual share. According to Reich, orgones are vibratory atmospheric atoms of the life-principle."

531.5   the tune *Are the Stars Out Tonight*]   "I Only Have Eyes for You," song (1934) written by Harry Warren and Al Rubin.

532.9   *yage*]   Ayahuasca, a hallucinogenic plant.

534.35–36   like a seer in Eliot, TIME TO CLOSE UP]   Cf. the recurring line in the pub scene in T. S. Eliot's *The Waste Land* (1922): "HURRY UP PLEASE IT'S TIME."

539.14   Gascoyne]   English surrealist poet and translator David Gascoyne (1916–2002).

540.10–11   *The Explanation of the Apocalypse*]   Commentary by the Anglo-Saxon monk the Venerable Bede (672–735).

540.20   *The Rake's Progress*]   Stravinsky's 1951 opera, with a libretto by W. H. Auden.

542.18–19   "God . . . dreams,"]   Cf. Proust's description of Marcel's Aunt Léonie in *Swann's Way*: ". . . a smile of joy, a pious act of thanksgiving to God, who is pleased to grant that life shall be less cruel than our dreams, feebly illumined her face. . . ."

552.37   Arthur Godfrey]   Radio and television personality (1903–1983), hosted several popular programs, including the variety show *Arthur Godfrey's Talent Scouts* and *Arthur Godfrey and Friends.*

557.17   *Brave Bulls*]   Film (1951) starring Mel Ferrer and Anthony Quinn, directed by Robert Rossen.

TRISTESSA

561.1   TRISTESSA]   The character Tristessa is based on Esperanza Villanueva, a drug addict and prostitute Kerouac knew in Mexico City.

565.26   New Look with Dior]   In 1947 the French fashion designer Christian Dior introduced the popular "New Look," which featured long, full skirts and cinched waists.

565.39   Damema]   "The selfless one," the name of the wife of the Tibetan Buddhist Marpa, a disciple of Naropa. The yogi and poet Milarepa was taught by Marpa. In a translation of Milarepa's hymns in Dwight Goddard's *A Buddhist Bible* (see note 429.24), which Kerouac read, Damema is called "Mother Divine of Buddhas." See the 237th chorus of Kerouac's *Mexico City Blues*: "Damema was the mother of Buddhas, / In Ancient India and Modern Asia / you put up a Virgin Mary very weird / in your altars and ikons, Damema / with crowns of light coming out of her head / and lotuses and incense sticks / and big sad blue eyes inside Flowers."

566.5   Amida]   See note 314.35–36.

566.23–24   *tapete*-straws]   Mat-straws.

567.36–39   Adoration . . . mystery."]   Cf. the conclusion of the Great
Dharani in the Surangama Sutra as it appears in Goddard, *A Buddhist Bible*.

569.4   "chinga"]   Spanish: fuck.

570.1   Virya]   Sanskrit: vital energy.

570.8   Number One of the Four Great Truths]   Life is suffering.

570.13–14   in the hellbottoms Kshitigarbha never dreamed to redeem]
The compassionate Boddhisattva Kshitigarbha descends into hell to help and
to rescue the souls imprisoned there.

570.15   Indian Joe of Huckleberry Finn]   The grave robber and murderer
Injun Joe is a villain in Mark Twain's *The Adventures of Tom Sawyer* (1876).

572.34   Bhiksunis]   Buddhist nuns.

572.34   Yasodhara's]   Buddha's wife.

584.5   comic Gordos]   Gordo ("Fatso") was the title character of a comic
strip written and illustrated by Gus Arriola (b. 1917).

584.16   zoot . . . haircuts]   Mexican-American youths calling themselves *pachucos* wore zoot suits and styled their hair in pompadours swept
back on the sides.

584.22   Genet]   French novelist, playwright, and activist Jean Genet
(1910–1986), whose early career as a petty criminal and prostitute was the
basis for books such as *The Miracle of the Rose* (1946) and *The Thief's Journal*
(1949).

585.13   Diamond Sutra]   See note 282.5–6.

585.22   Mara the Tempter]   See note 400.21.

586.18–20   like Omar Khayyam . . . sell."]   Cf. *The Rubáiyát of Omar
Khayyám*, in Edward FitzGerald's adaptation, stanza 95: "I wonder often
what the Vintners buy / One half so precious as the stuff they sell."

586.20   Al Damlette]   Kerouac's friend Al Sublette.

587.3   *Mira*]   Spanish: look.

587.6   dismal General Obregon]   Álvaro Obregón (1880–1928), who
fought the forces of Pancho Villa during the Mexican revolution. He served
as president of Mexico, 1920–24.

595.10   Marlon Brando Zapata]   Marlon Brando portrayed Mexican revolutionary Emiliano Zapata in the 1952 film *Viva Zapata!*, directed by Elia
Kazan.

598.19   "Junkey"]   William S. Burroughs's novel *Junkie* (1953), first published under the pseudonym William Lee.

607.34   Orozco]   Mexican artist José Clemente Orozco (1883–1949).

615.33   Min n Bill]   See note 445.5.

615.34   Mamie n Ike]   First Lady Mamie Eisenhower and President
Dwight Eisenhower.

615.36–37   Amos n Andy]   Popular radio and television comedy featuring
the African-American characters Amos and Andy, which ran from the 1920s
through the 1950s.

615.40   Fibber M'Gee . . . Molly]   The long-running radio program
Fibber McGee and Molly.

LONESOME TRAVELER

626.39   explorer Bernier]   Canadian Arctic explorer Joseph-Elzéar
Bernier (1852–1934).

627.24   Dave Garroways]   Dave Garroway (1913–1982), the first host of
NBC's *Today* show.

638.4   Pachucos]   See note 584.16.

640.5–6   Franchot Tone movies]   Actor Franchot Tone (1905–1968)
starred in *Five Graves to Cairo* (1943), *Phantom Lady* (1944), and many other
films.

643.24   Gandharva]   A supernatural being.

652.37   "Blood & Sand"]   Film (1941) about a bullfighter, directed by
Rouben Mamoulian and starring Tyrone Power, Linda Darnell, Rita Hay-
worth, Alla Nazimova, and Anthony Quinn.

653.12–13   streaming . . . heavens]   See Christopher Marlowe, *The
Tragical History of Doctor Faustus* (1604), V.ii: "See, see where Christ's blood
streams in the firmament!"

659.38   Jumpin' George]   Bay Area disc jockey George Oxford, who
played rhythm-and-blues.

659.40   "Mama, he treats your daughter mean,"]   A 1953 rhythm-and-
blues hit for singer Ruth Brown (1928–2006).

674.6   Sutter's Mill]   The site where gold was discovered in California in
January 1848.

692.35–36   Joel McCrea heroes of old movies]   See note 74.37–39.

693.18   Bridges Curran Bryson]   Harry Bridges, leader of the International Longshoremen's and Warehousemen's Union; Joseph Curran, head of

the National Maritime Union; Hugh Bryson, head of the Marine Cooks and Stewards Union.

711.20–21   "There . . . Melville.]   In *Moby-Dick*, "Loomings."

711.22   "Bound . . . Wolfe.]   Cf. Wolfe's *The Web and the Rock* (1939): "a unity of hope and joy, a music of triumph and enchantment . . . gleamed and sparkled in the flashing tides that girdled round the city."

715.2–3   Bartleby . . . Pierre]   Eponymous protagonists of Melville's story "Bartleby, the Scrivener" (1853) and of his novel *Pierre; or, The Ambiguities* (1852).

715.30–31   show . . . Caribbean]   *Romance on the High Seas* (1948).

720.36   Frescobaldi]   Italian Baroque composer and organist Girolamo Frescobaldi (1583–1643).

722.27–28   *Komo Kulshan* . . . snows]   Mount Baker in the Cascade Mountains was called *Komo Kulshan* ("white and shining") by the Native Americans of the region.

733.10–11   "despiséd divinest show."]   *Romeo and Juliet*, III.ii.77.

735.35–736.1   to go . . . gardens]   See note 106.29.

736.15   Devas]   Celestial beings akin to angels.

738.34–35   Lankavatara Scripture]   One of the fundamental texts of Mahayana Buddhism.

742.14–15   Cab Calloway's . . . around."]   "Kicking the gong around" is slang for smoking opium.

759.34–36   Rouen . . . stake.]   Rouen was where Joan of Arc was put to death.

762.33–34   Teddy Boys]   Young English street toughs of the 1950s and early 1960s who wore clothes inspired by the Edwardian era.

764.32   Dwight Goddard . . . *Buddhist Bible*]   See note 429.24.

766.37   Louella Parsons]   Popular gossip columnist.

767.10–11   Bernard Baruch . . . park bench]   Financier and philanthropist Bernard Baruch (1879–1965) advised several presidents and was often seen discussing affairs of state while sitting on a park bench in Washington's Lafayette Square.

767.26   Chief Rain-In-The-Face]   Hunkpapa Lakota (Sioux) chief (c. 1835–1905), one of the Indian leaders who fought at the battle of Little Big Horn.

770.38–39   Céline . . . boredom,"]   See note 122.23.

FROM THE JOURNALS 1949–1954

777.9   Neal and I and Louanne]   See note 3.3.

778.8   Mann act]   See note 121.30.

778.23   Alan Temko]   See note 35.9.

779.2   ECKSTINE'S "BEWILDERED."]   Billy Eckstine had a hit in 1948 with his version of "Bewildered," written by Leonard Whitcup and Teddy Powell.

779.28–29   Burroughs' . . . Joan Adams]   See note 7.13.

782.9   Allen Anson-ish]   I.e., Alan Ansen (see note 113.34).

782.13–14   Slim Gailland]   Slim Gaillard; see note 158.12.

782.23   Hal . . . Cru]   Hal Chase (see note 3.3); G. J. Apostolos, Kerouac's boyhood friend from Lowell; Beverly Burford (see note 35.9); Henri Cru (see note 10.16).

784.8–9   "Farewell . . . Trees"]   A 1941 story by Kerouac.

784.23   ghostly Cereno ships]   See note 132.38.

786.27   Danny Kaye's]   Comedian and entertainer Danny Kaye (1913–1987).

786.27–28   Sebastian]   Kerouac's best friend from high school, Sebastian Sampas. He was fatally wounded in 1944 while serving as an army medic in Italy.

797.27   "Yellowstone Red"]   Sentimental biography (1948) by Tom Ray.

820.10–11   a cheap movie . . . Ryan]   *Trail Street* (1947), directed by Ray Enright.

822.22   Brierly]   See note 47.15.

823.30–31   Cherokee Indian . . . BUMS]   See p. 333.

825.30   "Eddie Fisher's Jewish girl"]   Elizabeth Taylor, who converted to Judaism when she married Fisher.

832.13   SARIPUTRA]   One of Buddha's chief disciples.

THE LIBRARY OF AMERICA SERIES

Library of America fosters appreciation of America's literary heritage by publishing, and keeping permanently in print, authoritative editions of America's best and most significant writing. An independent nonprofit organization, it was founded in 1979 with seed funding from the National Endowment for the Humanities and the Ford Foundation.